THREE
TIMES
THREE

MYSTERY OMNIBUS

THREE
TIMES
THREE

MYSTERY OMNIBUS

Edited by
HOWARD HAYCRAFT
and
JOHN BEECROFT

DOUBLEDAY & COMPANY, INC.
GARDEN CITY, NEW YORK, 1964

All of the characters in this book are fictitious, and any resemblance to actual persons, living or dead, is purely coincidental.

Library of Congress Catalog Card Number 64-16225
Copyright © 1964 by Howard Haycraft and John Beecroft
All Rights Reserved
Printed in the United States of America

We are grateful to the following for permission to use the copyrighted material appearing in this omnibus:

James Brown Associates—"Pattern for Murder" by Frances and Richard Lockridge. Copyright 1955 by United Newspapers Magazine Corporation. Reprinted by permission of Richard Lockridge and his agents, James Brown Associates, Inc.
Robert Bloch—"Is Betsey Blake Still Alive?" by Robert Bloch, from *Ellery Queen's Mystery Magazine.* Copyright © 1958 by Davis Publications, Inc.
Collins Publishers—*Night at the Vulcan* by Ngaio Marsh. Published in the United Kingdom and Canada under the title *Opening Night.*
Dodd, Mead & Company—"Dead Man's Mirror" from *Dead Man's Mirror* by Agatha Christie. Copyright 1931, 1932 by Agatha Christie Mallowan.
David Higham Associates Ltd.—"Death by Invisible Hands" by John Dickson Carr, from *Ellery Queen's Mystery Magazine,* April 1958.
Alfred A. Knopf, Inc.—*The Lady in the Lake* by Raymond Chandler. Copyright 1943 by Raymond Chandler.
J. B. Lippincott Company—"After-Dinner Story" from *After-Dinner Story* by William Irish. Copyright 1936, 1937, 1938, 1941, 1944 by William Irish.
Little, Brown and Company—*Rogue Male* by Geoffrey Household. Copyright 1939 by Geoffrey Household. *Night at the Vulcan.* Copyright 1951 by Ngaio Marsh, from *Three-Act Special.* "The Adventure of the Gettysburg Bugle" by Ellery Queen, from Calendar of Crime. Copyright 1951 by Little, Brown and Company.
Pocket Books, Inc.—"The Empty Hours: An 87th Precinct Mystery" by Ed McBain, from *The Empty Hours.* Copyright © 1962 by Ed McBain.
Paul R. Reynolds & Son—"Silent Night" by Baynard Kendrick, from *Sleuth Mystery Magazine.* Copyright © 1958 by Fosdeck Publications, Inc.
Simon and Schuster, Inc.—"The Orderly World of Mr. Appleby" from *Mystery Stories* by Stanley Ellin. Copyright 1950 by Stanley Ellin. (Originally appeared in *Ellery Queen's Mystery Magazine.*)
The Viking Press, Inc.—"Murder Is No Joke" from *And Four to Go* by Rex Stout. Copyright © 1958 by Rex Stout.
A. Watkins, Inc.—"In the Teeth of the Evidence" by Dorothy L. Sayers, from *In the Teeth of the Evidence & Other Stories.* Copyright 1939 by Dorothy L. Sayers.
Willis Kingsley Wing—"The Case of the Irate Witness" by Erle Stanley Gardner, from *Collier's.* Copyright 1953 by Erle Stanley Gardner.

CONTENTS

Volume I

NOVEL
THE LADY IN THE LAKE *by Raymond Chandler*   11

> Hardboiled but literate, this modern mystery classic gives Private Eye *Philip Marlowe* his toughest test

STORY
IN THE TEETH OF THE EVIDENCE *by Dorothy L. Sayers*   189

> In which *Lord Peter Wimsey* looks down in the mouth and finds murder

STORY
THE CASE OF THE IRATE WITNESS
by Erle Stanley Gardner   203

> The only *Perry Mason* short story, complete with courtroom fireworks

STORY
PATTERN FOR MURDER
by Frances and Richard Lockridge   219

> The only *Mr. and Mrs. North* short story, with *Pam North* spotting an elusive clue

NOVELETTE
THE EMPTY HOURS: AN 87TH PRECINCT MYSTERY
by Ed McBain   233

> Another lady, another lake, and the boys of the *87th Precinct* on hand to solve double death

Volume II

NOVEL
ROGUE MALE *by Geoffrey Household*   295

> The hunter becomes the hunted in one of the greatest suspense novels ever written

STORY
SILENT NIGHT *by Baynard Kendrick*   421

> No one but blind *Captain Duncan Maclain* could have spotted the hidden clue that saved a child's life

STORY
DEATH BY INVISIBLE HANDS *by John Dickson Carr*   441

> On the face of it, an impossible crime—but *Dr. Gideon Fell* traps a ruthless killer

STORY
AFTER-DINNER STORY
by William Irish (Cornell Woolrich)   457

> Once begun, we dare you to put down this double-barreled suspense classic

NOVELETTE
DEAD MAN'S MIRROR *by Agatha Christie*   479

> *Hercule Poirot* solves the death of the last of the bad barons in this flawless puzzle by the High Priestess of the English detective story

Volume III

NOVELETTE
MURDER IS NO JOKE *by Rex Stout*   551

> *Nero Wolfe* and *Archie Goodwin* hear murder committed on the telephone, solve same

Contents

STORY
IS BETSEY BLAKE STILL ALIVE? *by Robert Bloch*   587

> Only in the fabulous world of Hollywood could this fantastic story, by the author of *Psycho,* have occurred

STORY
THE ADVENTURE OF THE GETTYSBURG BUGLE
by Ellery Queen   603

> *Ellery Queen* and *Nikki Porter* relive American history and find murder in the quiet Pennsylvania hills

STORY
THE ORDERLY WORLD OF MR. APPLEBY
by Stanley Ellin   621

> He thought he'd found the formula for the perfect crime—but had he?

NOVEL
NIGHT AT THE VULCAN *by Ngaio Marsh*   639

> Seldom has the excitement of the London theatre been so well captured as in this mystery, which is also a fine novel. Scotland Yard's *Roderick Alleyn* does the sleuthing

VOLUME I

THE LADY IN THE LAKE

by Raymond Chandler

1

The Treloar Building was, and is, on Olive Street, near Sixth, on the west side. The sidewalk in front of it had been built of black and white rubber blocks. They were taking them up now to give to the government, and a hatless pale man with a face like a building superintendent was watching the work and looking as if it was breaking his heart.

I went past him through an arcade of specialty shops into a vast black and gold lobby. The Gillerlain Company was on the seventh floor, in front, behind swinging double plate glass doors bound in platinum. Their reception room had Chinese rugs, dull silver walls, angular but elaborate furniture, sharp shiny bits of abstract sculpture on pedestals and a tall display in a triangular showcase in the corner. On tiers and steps and islands and promontories of shining mirror-glass it seemed to contain every fancy bottle and box that had ever been designed. There were creams and powders and soaps and toilet waters for every season and every occasion. There were perfumes in tall thin bottles that looked as if a breath would blow them over and perfumes in little pastel phials tied with ducky satin bows, like little girls at a dancing class. The cream of the crop seemed to be something very small and simple in a squat amber bottle. It was in the middle at eye height, had a lot of space to itself, and was labelled *Gillerlain Regal, The Champagne of Perfumes*. It was definitely the stuff to get. One drop of that in the hollow of your throat and the matched pink pearls started falling on you like summer rain.

A neat little blonde sat off in a far corner at a small PBX, behind a railing and well out of harm's way. At a flat desk in line with the doors was a tall, lean, dark-haired lovely whose name, according to the tilted embossed plaque on her desk, was Miss Adrienne Fromsett.

She wore a steel gray business suit and under the jacket a dark blue shirt and a man's tie of lighter shade. The edges of the folded handkerchief in the breast pocket looked sharp enough to slice bread. She wore a linked bracelet and no other jewelry. Her dark hair was parted and fell in loose but not unstudied waves. She had a smooth ivory skin and rather severe eyebrows and large dark eyes that looked as if they might warm up at the right time and in the right place.

I put my plain card, the one without the tommy gun in the corner, on her desk and asked to see Mr. Derace Kingsley.

She looked at the card and said: "Have you an appointment?"

"No appointment."

"It is very difficult to see Mr. Kingsley without an appointment."

That wasn't anything I could argue about.

"What is the nature of your business, Mr. Marlowe?"

"Personal."

"I see. Does Mr. Kingsley know you, Mr. Marlowe?"

"I don't think so. He may have heard my name. You might say I'm from Lieutenant M'Gee."

"And does Mr. Kingsley know Lieutenant M'Gee?"

She put my card beside a pile of freshly typed letterheads. She leaned back and put one arm on the desk and tapped lightly with a small gold pencil.

I grinned at her. The little blonde at the PBX cocked a shell-like ear and smiled a small fluffy smile. She looked playful and eager, but not quite sure of herself, like a new kitten in a house where they don't care much about kittens.

"I'm hoping he does," I said. "But maybe the best way to find out is to ask him."

She initialed three letters rapidly, to keep from throwing her pen set at me. She spoke again without looking up.

"Mr. Kingsley is in conference. I'll send your card in when I have an opportunity."

I thanked her and went and sat in a chromium and leather chair that was a lot more comfortable than it looked. Time passed and silence descended on the scene. Nobody came in or went out. Miss Fromsett's elegant hand moved over her papers and the muted peep of the kitten at the PBX was audible at moments, and the little click of the plugs going in and out.

I lit a cigarette and dragged a smoking stand beside the chair. The minutes went by on tiptoe, with their fingers to their lips. I looked the place over. You can't tell anything about an outfit like that. They might be making millions, and they might have the sheriff in the back room, with his chair tilted against the safe.

Half an hour and three or four cigarettes later a door opened behind Miss Fromsett's desk and two men came out backwards laughing. A third man held the door for them and helped them laugh. They all shook hands heartily and the two men went across the office and out. The third man dropped the grin off his face and looked as if he had never grinned in his life. He was a tall bird in a gray suit and he didn't want any nonsense.

"Any calls?" he asked in a sharp bossy voice.

Miss Fromsett said softly: "A Mr. Marlowe to see you. From Lieutenant M'Gee. His business is personal."

"Never heard of him," the tall man barked. He took my card, didn't even glance at me, and went back into his office. His door closed on the pneumatic closer and made a sound like 'phooey.' Miss Fromsett gave me a sweet sad smile and I gave it back to her in the form of an obscene leer. I ate another cigarette and more time staggered by. I was getting to be very fond of The Gillerlain Company.

Ten minutes later the same door opened again and the big shot came out with his hat on and sneered that he was going to get a haircut. He started off across the Chinese rug in a swinging athletic stride, made about half the distance to the door and then did a sharp cutback and came over to where I was sitting.

"You want to see me?" he barked.

He was about six feet two and not much of it soft. His eyes were stone gray with flecks of cold light in them. He filled a large size in smooth gray flannel with a narrow chalk stripe, and filled it elegantly. His manner said he was very tough to get along with.

I stood up. "If you're Mr. Derace Kingsley."

"Who the hell did you think I was?"

I let him have that trick and gave him my other card, the one with the business on it. He clamped it in his paw and scowled down at it.

"Who's M'Gee?" he snapped.

"He's just a fellow I know."

"I'm fascinated," he said, glancing back at Miss Fromsett. She liked it. She liked it very much. "Anything else you would care to let drop about him?"

"Well, they call him Violets M'Gee," I said. "On account of he chews little throat pastilles that smell of violets. He's a big man with soft silvery hair and a cute little mouth made to kiss babies with. When last seen he was wearing a neat blue suit, wide-toed brown shoes, gray homburg hat, and he was smoking opium in a short briar pipe."

"I don't like your manner," Kingsley said in a voice you could have cracked a Brazil nut on.

"That's all right," I said. "I'm not selling it."

He reared back as if I had hung a week-old mackerel under his nose. After a moment he turned his back on me and said over his shoulder:

"I'll give you exactly three minutes. God knows why."

He burned the carpet back past Miss Fromsett's desk to his door, yanked it open and let it swing to in my face. Miss Fromsett liked that too, but I thought there was a little sly laughter behind her eyes now.

2

The private office was everything a private office should be. It was long and dim and quiet and air-conditioned and its windows were shut and its gray venetian blinds half-closed to keep out the July glare. Gray drapes matched the gray carpeting. There was a large black and silver safe in the corner and a low row of low filing cases that exactly matched it. On the wall there was a huge tinted photograph of an elderly party with a chiselled beak and whiskers and a wing collar. The Adam's apple that edged through his wing collar looked harder than most people's chins. The plate underneath the photograph read: *Mr. Matthew Gillerlain 1860–1934.*

Derace Kingsley marched briskly behind about eight hundred dollars' worth of executive desk and planted his backside in a tall leather chair. He reached himself a panatela out of a copper and mahogany box and trimmed it and lit it with a fat copper desk lighter. He took his time about it. It didn't matter about my time. When he had finished this, he leaned back and blew a little smoke and said:

"I'm a business man. I don't fool around. You're a licensed detective your card says. Show me something to prove it."

I got my wallet out and handed him things to prove it. He looked at them and threw them back across the desk. The celluloid holder with the photostat of my license in it fell to the floor. He didn't bother to apologize.

"I don't know M'Gee," he said. "I know Sheriff Petersen. I asked for the name of a reliable man to do a job. I suppose you are the man."

"M'Gee is in the Hollywood sub-station of the sheriff's office," I said. "You can check on that."

"Not necessary. I guess you might do, but don't get flip with me. And remember when I hire a man he's my man. He does exactly what I tell him and he keeps his mouth shut. Or he goes out fast. Is that clear? I hope I'm not too tough for you."

"Why not leave that an open question?" I said.

He frowned. He said sharply: "What do you charge?"

"Twenty-five a day and expenses. Eight cents a mile for my car."

"Absurd," he said. "Far too much. Fifteen a day flat. That's plenty. I'll pay the mileage, within reason, the way things are now. But no joyriding."

I blew a little gray cloud of cigarette smoke and fanned it with my hand. I said nothing. He seemed a little surprised that I said nothing.

He leaned over the desk and pointed with his cigar. "I haven't hired you yet," he said, "but if I do, the job is absolutely confidential. No talking it over with your cop friends. Is that understood?"

"Just what do you want done, Mr. Kingsley?"

"What do you care? You do all kinds of detective work, don't you?"

"Not all kinds. Only the fairly honest kinds."

He stared at me level-eyed, his jaw tight. His gray eyes had an opaque look.

"For one thing I don't do divorce business," I said. "And I get a hundred down as a retainer—from strangers."

"Well, well," he said, in a voice suddenly soft. "Well, well."

"And as for your being too tough for me," I said, "most of the clients start out either by weeping down my shirt or bawling me out to show who's boss. But usually they end up very reasonable—if they're still alive."

"Well, well," he said again, in the same soft voice, and went on staring at me. "Do you lose very many of them?" he asked.

"Not if they treat me right," I said.

"Have a cigar," he said.

I took a cigar and put it in my pocket.

"I want you to find my wife," he said. "She's been missing for a month."

"Okay," I said. "I'll find your wife."

He patted his desk with both hands. He stared at me solidly. "I think you will at that," he said. Then he grinned. "I haven't been called down like that in four years," he said.

I didn't say anything.

"Damn it all," he said, "I liked it. I liked it fine." He ran a hand through his thick dark hair. "She's been gone a whole month," he said. "From a cabin we have in the mountains. Near Puma Point. Do you know Puma Point?"

I said I knew Puma Point.

"Our place is three miles from the village," he said, "partly over a private road. It's on a private lake. Little Fawn Lake. There's a dam three of us put up to improve the property. I own the tract with two other men. It's quite large, but undeveloped and won't be developed now for some time, of course. My friends have cabins, I have a cabin and a man named Bill Chess lives with his wife in another cabin rent free and looks after the place. He's a disabled veteran with a pension. That's all there is up there. My wife went up the middle of May, came down twice for week-ends, was due down the 12th of June for a party and never showed up. I haven't seen her since."

"What have you done about it?" I asked.

"Nothing. Not a thing. I haven't even been up there." He waited, wanting me to ask why.

I said: "Why?"

He pushed his chair back to get a locked drawer open. He took out a folded paper and passed it over. I unfolded it and saw it was a Postal Telegraph form. The wire had been filed at El Paso on June 14th at 9.19 A.M. It was addressed to Derace Kingsley, 965 Carson Drive, Beverly Hills, and read:

> "AM CROSSING TO GET MEXICAN DIVORCE STOP WILL MARRY CHRIS STOP GOOD LUCK AND GOODBY CRYSTAL."

I put this down on my side of the desk and he was handing me a large and very clear snapshot on glazed paper which showed a man and a woman sitting on the sand under a beach umbrella. The man wore trunks and the woman what looked like a very daring white sharkskin bathing suit. She was a slim blonde, young and shapely and smiling. The man was a hefty dark handsome lad with fine shoulders and legs, sleek dark hair and white teeth. Six feet of a standard type of homewrecker. Arms to hold you close and all his brains in his face. He was holding a pair of dark glasses in his hand and smiling at the camera with a practised and easy smile.

"That's Crystal," Kingsley said, "and that's Chris Lavery. She can have him and he can have her and to hell with them both."

I put the photo down on the telegram. "All right, what's the catch?" I asked him.

"There's no telephone up there," he said, "and there was nothing important about the affair she was coming down for. So I got the wire before I gave much thought to it. The wire surprised me only mildly. Crystal and I have been washed up for years. She lives her life and I live mine. She has her own money and plenty of it. About twenty thousand a year from a family holding corporation that owns valuable oil leases in Texas. She plays around and I knew Lavery was one of her playmates. I might have been a little surprised that she would actually marry him, because the man is nothing but a professional chaser. But the picture looked all right so far, you understand?"

"And then?"

"Nothing for two weeks. Then the Prescott Hotel in San Bernardino got in touch with me and said a Packard Clipper registered to Crystal Grace Kingsley at my address was unclaimed in their garage and what about it. I told them to keep it and I sent them a check. There was nothing much in that either. I figured she was still out of the state and that if they had gone in a car at all, they had gone in Lavery's car. The day before yesterday, however, I met Lavery in front of the Athletic Club down on the corner here. He said he didn't know where Crystal was."

Kingsley gave me a quick look and reached a bottle and two tinted glasses up on the desk. He poured a couple of drinks and pushed one over. He held his against the light and said slowly:

"Lavery said he hadn't gone away with her, hadn't seen her in two months, hadn't had any communication with her of any kind."

I said, "You believed him?"

He nodded, frowning, and drank his drink and pushed the glass to one side. I tasted mine. It was Scotch. Not very good Scotch.

"If I believed him," Kingsley said, "—and I was probably wrong to do it—it wasn't because he's a fellow you have to believe. Far from it. It's because he's a no good son of a bitch who thinks it is smart to lay his friends' wives and brag about it. I feel he would have been tickled pink to stick it into me and break it off that he had got my wife to run away with him and leave me flat. I know these tomcats and I know this one too well. He rode a route for us for a while and he was in trouble all the time. He couldn't keep his hands off the office help. And apart from all that there was this wire from El Paso and I told him about it and why would he think it worth while to lie about it?"

"She might have tossed him out on his can," I said. "That would have hurt him in his deep place—his Casanova complex."

Kingsley brightened up a little, but not very much. He shook his head. "I still more than halfway believe him," he said. "You'll have to prove me wrong. That's part of why I wanted you. But there's another and very worrying angle. I have a good job here, but a job is all it is. I can't stand scandal. I'd be out of here in a hurry if my wife got mixed up with the police."

"Police?"

"Among her other activities," Kingsley said grimly, "my wife occasionally finds time to lift things in department stores. I think it's just a sort of delusion of grandeur she gets when she has been hitting the bottle too hard, but it happens, and we have had some pretty nasty scenes in managers' offices. So far I've been able to keep them from filing charges, but if something like that happened in a strange city where nobody knew her—" He lifted his hands and let them fall with a smack on the desk— "well, it might be a prison matter, mightn't it?"

"Has she ever been fingerprinted?"

"She has never been arrested," he said.

"That's not what I mean. Sometimes in large department stores they make it a condition of dropping shoplifting charges that you give them your prints. It scares the amateurs and builds up a file of kleptomaniacs in their protective association. When the prints come in a certain number of times they call time on you."

"Nothing like that has happened to my knowledge," he said.

"Well, I think we might almost throw the shoplifting angle out of this for the time being," I said. "If she got arrested, she would get searched. Even if the cops let her use a Jane Doe name on the police blotter, they would be likely to get in touch with you. Also she would start yelling for help when she found herself in a jam." I tapped the blue and white telegraph form. "And this is a month old. If what you are thinking about happened around that time, the case would have been settled by now. If it was a first offense, she would get off with a scolding and a suspended sentence."

He poured himself another drink to help him with his worrying. "You're making me feel better," he said.

"There are too many other things that could have happened," I said. "That she did go away with Lavery and they split up. That she went away with some other man and the wire is a gag. That she went away alone or with a woman. That she drank herself over the edge and is holed up in some private sanatorium taking a cure. That she got into some jam we have no idea of. That she met with foul play."

"Good God, don't say that," Kingsley exclaimed.

"Why not? You've got to consider it. I get a very vague idea of Mrs. Kingsley—that she is young, pretty, reckless, and wild. That she drinks and does dangerous things when she drinks. That she is a sucker for the men and might take up with a stranger who might turn out to be a crook. Does that fit?"

He nodded. "Every word of it."

"How much money would she have with her?"

"She liked to carry enough. She has her own bank and her own bank account. She could have any amount of money."

"Any children?"

"No children."

"Do you have the management of her affairs?"

He shook his head. "She hasn't any—excepting depositing checks and drawing out money and spending it. She never invests a nickel. And her money certainly never does me any good, if that's what you are thinking." He paused and then said: "Don't think I haven't tried. I'm human and it's not fun to watch twenty thousand a year go down the drain and nothing to show for it but hangovers and boy friends of the class of Chris Lavery."

"How are you with her bank? Could you get a detail of the checks she has drawn for the past couple of months?"

"They wouldn't tell me. I tried to get some information of the sort once, when I had an idea she was being blackmailed. All I got was ice."

"We can get it," I said, "and we may have to. It will mean going to the Missing Persons Bureau. You wouldn't like that?"

"If I had liked that, I wouldn't have called you," he said.

I nodded, gathered my exhibits together and put them away in my pockets. "There are more angles to this than I can even see now," I said, "but I'll start by talking to Lavery and then taking a run up to Little Fawn Lake and asking questions there. I'll need Lavery's address and a note to your man in charge at the mountain place."

He got a letterhead out of his desk and wrote and passed it over. I read: "Dear Bill: This will introduce Mr. Philip Marlowe who wishes to look over the property. Please show him my cabin and assist him in every way. Yrs. Derace Kingsley."

I folded this up and put it in the envelope he had addressed while I was reading it. "How about the other cabins up there?" I asked.

"Nobody up this year so far. One man's in government service in Washington and the other is at Fort Leavenworth. Their wives are with them."

"Now Lavery's address," I said.

He looked at a point well above the top of my head. "In Bay City. I could find the house but I forget the address. Miss Fromsett can give it to you, I think. She needn't know why you want it. She probably will. And you want a hundred dollars, you said."

"That's all right," I said. "That's just something I said when you were tramping on me."

He grinned. I stood up and hesitated by the desk looking at him. After a moment I said: "You're not holding anything back, are you—anything important?"

He looked at his thumb. "No. I'm not holding anything back. I'm worried and I want to know where she is. I'm damn worried. If you get anything at all, call me any time, day or night."

I said I would do that, and we shook hands and I went back down the long cool office and out to where Miss Fromsett sat elegantly at her desk.

"Mr. Kingsley thinks you can give me Chris Lavery's address," I told her and watched her face.

She reached very slowly for a brown leather address book and turned the leaves. Her voice was tight and cold when she spoke.

"The address we have is 623 Altair Street, in Bay City. Telephone Bay City 12523. Mr. Lavery has not been with us for more than a year. He may have moved."

I thanked her and went on to the door. From there I glanced back at her. She was sitting very still, with her hands clasped on her desk, staring into space. A couple of red spots burned in her cheeks. Her eyes were remote and bitter.

I got the impression that Mr. Chris Lavery was not a pleasant thought to her.

3

Altair Street lay on the edge of the V forming the inner end of a deep canyon. To the north was the cool blue sweep of the bay out to the point above Malibu. To the south the beach town of Bay City was spread out on a bluff above the coast highway.

It was a short street, not more than three or four blocks, and ended in a tall iron fence enclosing a large estate. Beyond the gilded spikes of the fence I could see trees and shrubs and a glimpse of lawn and part of a curving driveway, but the house was out of sight. On the inland side of Altair Street the houses were well kept and fairly large, but the few scattered bungalows on the edge of the canyon were nothing much. In the short half block ended by the iron fence were only two houses, on opposite sides of the street and almost directly across from each other. The smaller was number 623.

I drove past it, turned the car in the paved half circle at the end of the street and came back to park in front of the lot next to Lavery's place. His house was built downwards, one of those clinging vine effects, with the front door a little below street level, the patio on the roof, the bedrooms in the basement, and a garage like the corner pocket on a pool table. A crimson bougainvillea was rustling against the front wall and the flat stones of the front walk were edged with Korean moss. The door was narrow, grilled and topped by a lancet arch. Below the grill there was an iron knocker. I hammered on it.

Nothing happened. I pushed the bell at the side of the door and heard it ring inside not very far off and waited and nothing happened. I worked on the knocker again. Still nothing. I went back up the walk and along to the garage and lifted the door far enough to see that a car with white side-walled tires was inside. I went back to the front door.

A neat black Cadillac coupe came out of the garage across the way, backed, turned and came along past Lavery's house, slowed, and a thin man in dark glasses looked at me sharply, as if I hadn't any business to be there. I gave him my steely glare and he went on his way.

I went down Lavery's walk again and did some more hammering on his knocker. This time I got results. The Judas window opened and I was looking at a handsome bright-eyed number through the bars of the grill.

"You make a hell of a lot of noise," a voice said.

"Mr. Lavery?"

He said he was Mr. Lavery and what about it. I poked a card through the grill. A large brown hand took the card. The bright brown eyes came back and the voice said: "So sorry. Not needing any detectives today please."

"I'm working for Derace Kingsley."

"The hell with both of you," he said, and banged the Judas window.

I leaned on the bell beside the door and got a cigarette out with my free hand and had just struck the match on the woodwork beside the door when it was yanked open and a big guy in bathing trunks, beach sandals, and a white terry cloth bathrobe started to come out at me.

I took my thumb off the bell and grinned at him. "What's the matter?" I asked him. "Scared?"

"Ring that bell again," he said, "and I'll throw you clear across the street."

"Don't be childish," I told him. "You know perfectly well I'm going to talk to you and you're going to talk to me."

I got the blue and white telegram out of my pocket and held it in front of his bright brown eyes. He read it morosely, chewed his lip and growled:

"Oh for Chrissake, come on in then."

He held the door wide and I went in past him, into a dim pleasant room with an apricot Chinese rug that looked expensive, deepsided chairs, a number of white drum lamps, a big Capehart in the corner, a long and very wide davenport in pale tan mohair shot with dark brown, and a fireplace with a copper screen and an overmantel in white wood. A fire was laid behind the screen and partly masked by a large spray of manzanita bloom. The bloom was turning yellow in places, but was still pretty. There was a bottle of Vat 69 and glasses on a tray and a copper icebucket on a low round burl walnut table with a glass top. The room went clear to the back of the house and ended in a flat arch through which showed three narrow windows and the top few feet of the white iron railing of the staircase going down.

Lavery swung the door shut and sat on the davenport. He grabbed a cigarette out of a hammered silver box and lit it and looked at me irritably. I sat down opposite him and looked him over. He had everything in the way of good looks the snapshot had indicated. He had a terrific torso and magnificent thighs. His eyes were chestnut brown and the whites of them slightly gray-white. His hair was rather long and curled a little over his temples. His brown skin showed no signs of dissipation. He was a nice piece of beef, but to me that was all he was. I could understand that women would think he was something to yell for.

"Why not tell us where she is?" I said. "We'll find out eventually anyway and if you tell us now, we won't be bothering you."

"It would take more than a private dick to bother me," he said.

"No, it wouldn't. A private dick can bother anybody. He's persistent and used to snubs. He's paid for his time and he would just as soon use it to bother you as any other way."

"Look," he said, leaning forward and pointing his cigarette at me. "I know what that wire says, but it's the bunk. I didn't go to El Paso with Crystal Kingsley. I haven't seen her in a long time—long before the date of that wire. I haven't had any contact with her. I told Kingsley that."

"He didn't have to believe you."

"Why would I lie to him?" He looked surprised.

"Why wouldn't you?"

"Look," he said earnestly, "it might seem so to you, but you don't know her. Kingsley has no strings on her. If he doesn't like the way she behaves he has a remedy. These proprietary husbands make me sick."

"If you didn't go to El Paso with her," I said, "why did she send this telegram?"

"I haven't the faintest idea."

"You can do better than that," I said. I pointed to the spray of manzanita in the fireplace. "You pick that up at Little Fawn Lake?"

"The hills around here are full of manzanita," he said contemptuously.

"It doesn't bloom like that down here."

He laughed. "I was up there the third week in May. If you have to know. I suppose you can find out. That's the last time I saw her."

"You didn't have any idea of marrying her?"

He blew smoke and said through it: "I've thought of it, yes. She has money. Money is always useful. But it would be too tough a way to make it."

I nodded, but didn't say anything. He looked at the manzanita spray in the fireplace and leaned back to blow smoke in the air and show me the strong brown line of his throat. After a moment, when I still didn't say anything, he began to get restless. He glanced down at the card I had given him and said:

"So you hire yourself out to dig up dirt? Doing well at it?"

"Nothing to brag about. A dollar here, a dollar there."

"And all of them pretty slimy," he said.

"Look, Mr. Lavery, we don't have to get into a fight. Kingsley thinks you know where his wife is, but won't tell him. Either out of meanness or motives of delicacy."

"Which way would he like it?" the handsome brown-faced man sneered.

"He doesn't care, as long as he gets the information. He doesn't care a great deal what you and she do together or where you go or whether she divorces him or not. He just wants to feel sure that everything is all right and that she isn't in trouble of any kind."

Lavery looked interested. "Trouble? What kind of trouble?" He licked the word around on his brown lips, tasting it.

"Maybe you won't know the kind of trouble he is thinking of."

"Tell me," he pleaded sarcastically. "I'd just love to hear about some kind of trouble I didn't know about."

"You're doing fine," I told him. "No time to talk business, but always time for a wisecrack. If you think we might try to get a hook into you because you crossed a state line with her, forget it."

"Go climb up your thumb, wise guy. You'd have to prove I paid the freight, or it wouldn't mean anything."

"This wire has to mean something," I said stubbornly. It seemed to me that I had said it before, several times.

"It's probably just a gag. She's full of little tricks like that. All of them silly, and some of them vicious."

"I don't see any point in this one."

He flicked cigarette ash carelessly at the glass top table. He gave me a quick up from under look and immediately looked away.

"I stood her up," he said slowly. "It might be her idea of a way to get back at me. I was supposed to run up there one week-end. I didn't go. I was—sick of her."

I said: "Uh-huh," and gave him a long steady stare. "I don't like that so well. I'd like it better if you did go to El Paso with her and had a fight and split up. Could you tell it that way?"

He flashed solidly behind the sunburn.

"God damn it," he said, "I told you I didn't go anywhere with her. Not anywhere. Can't you remember that?"

"I'll remember it when I believe it."

He leaned over to snub out his cigarette. He stood up with an easy movement, not hurried at all, pulled the belt of his robe tight, and moved out to the end of the davenport.

"All right," he said in a clear tight voice. "Out you go. Take the air. I've had enough of your third-degree tripe. You're wasting my time and your own—if it's worth anything."

I stood up and grinned at him. "Not a lot, but for what it's worth I'm being paid for it. It couldn't be, for instance, that you ran into a little unpleasantness in some department store—say at the stocking or jewelry counter."

He looked at me very carefully, drawing his eyebrows down at the corners and making his mouth small.

"I don't get it," he said, but there was thought behind his voice.

"That's all I wanted to know," I said. "And thanks for listening. By the way, what line of business are you in—since you left Kingsley?"

"What the hell business is it of yours?"

"None. But of course I can always find out," I said, and moved a little way towards the door, not very far.

"At the moment I'm not doing anything," he said coldly. "I expect a commission in the navy almost any day."

"You ought to do well at that," I said.

"Yeah. So long, snooper. And don't bother to come back. I won't be at home."

I went over to the door and pulled it open. It stuck on the lower sill, from the beach moisture. When I had it open, I looked back at him. He was standing there narrow-eyed, full of muted thunder.

"I may have to come back," I said. "But it won't be just to swop gags. It will be because I find something out that needs talking over."

"So you still think I'm lying," he said savagely.

"I think you have something on your mind. I've looked at too many faces not to know. It may not be any of my business. If it is, you're likely to have to throw me out again."

"A pleasure," he said. "And next time bring somebody to drive you home. In case you land on your fanny and knock your brains out."

Then without any rhyme or reason that I could see, he spat on the rug in front of his feet.

It jarred me. It was like watching the veneer peel off and leave a tough kid in an alley. Or like hearing an apparently refined woman start expressing herself in four-letter words.

"So long, beautiful hunk," I said, and left him standing there. I closed the door, had to jerk it to get it shut, and went up the path to the street. I stood on the sidewalk looking at the house across the way.

4

It was a wide shallow house with rose stucco walls faded out to a pleasant pastel shade and trimmed with dull green at the window frames. The roof was of green tiles, round rough ones. There was a deeply inset front door framed in a mosaic of multi-colored pieces of tiling and a small flower garden in front, behind a low stucco wall topped by an iron railing which the beach moisture had begun to corrode. Outside the wall to the left was the three-car garage, with a door opening inside the yard and a concrete path going from there to a side door of the house.

Set into the gate post was a bronze tablet which read: "Albert S. Almore, M.D."

While I was standing there staring across the street, the black Cadillac I had already seen came purring around the corner and then down the block. It slowed and started to sweep outwards to get turning space to go into the garage, decided my car was in the way of that, and went on to the end of the road and turned in the widened-out space in front of the ornamental iron railing. It came back slowly and went into the empty third of the garage across the way.

The thin man in sun glasses went along the sidewalk to the house, carrying a double-handled doctor's bag. Halfway along he slowed down to stare across at me. I went along towards my car. At the house he used a key and as he opened the door he looked across at me again.

I got into the Chrysler and sat there smoking and trying to make up my mind whether it was worth while hiring somebody to pull a tail on Lavery. I decided it wasn't, not the way things looked so far.

Curtains moved at a lower window close to the side door Dr. Almore had gone in at. A thin hand held them aside and I caught the glint of light on glasses. They were held aside for quite some time, before they fell together again.

I looked along the street at Lavery's house. From this angle I could see that his service porch gave on a flight of painted wooden steps to a sloping concrete walk and a flight of concrete steps ending in the paved alley below.

I looked across at Dr. Almore's house again, wondering idly if he knew Lavery and how well. He probably knew him, since theirs were the only two houses in the block. But being a doctor, he wouldn't tell me anything about him. As I looked, the curtains which had been lifted apart were now completely drawn aside.

The middle segment of the triple window they had masked had no screen. Behind it, Dr. Almore stood staring across my way, with a sharp frown on his thin face. I shook cigarette ash out of the window and he turned abruptly and sat down at a desk. His double-handled bag was on the desk in front of him. He sat rigidly, drumming on the desk beside the bag. His hand reached for the telephone, touched it and came away again. He lit a cigarette and shook the match violently, then strode to the window and stared out at me some more.

This was interesting, if at all, only because he was a doctor. Doctors, as a rule, are the least curious of men. While they are still internes they hear enough secrets to last them a lifetime. Dr. Almore seemed interested in me. More than interested, bothered.

I reached down to turn the ignition key, then Lavery's front door opened and I took my hand away and leaned back again. Lavery came briskly up the walk of his house, shot a glance down the street and turned to go into his garage. He was dressed as I had seen him. He had a rough towel and a steamer rug over his arm. I heard the garage door lift up, then the car door open and shut, then the grind and cough of the starting car. It backed up the steep incline to the street, white steamy exhaust pouring from its rear end. It was a cute little blue convertible, with the top folded down and Lavery's sleek dark head just rising above it. He was now wearing a natty pair of sun-goggles with very wide white sidebows. The convertible swooped off down the block and danced around the corner.

There was nothing in that for me. Mr. Christopher Lavery was bound for the edge of the broad Pacific, to lie in the sun and let the girls see what they didn't necessarily have to go on missing.

I gave my attention back to Dr. Almore. He was on the telephone now, not talking, holding it to his ear, smoking and waiting. Then he leaned forward as you do when the voice comes back, listened, hung up and wrote something on a pad in front of him. Then a heavy book with yellow sides appeared on his desk and he opened it just about in the middle. While he was doing this he gave one quick look out of the window, straight at the Chrysler.

He found his place in the book, leaned down over it and quick puffs of smoke appeared in the air over the pages. He wrote something else, put the book away, and grabbed for the telephone again. He dialed, waited, began to speak quickly, pushing his head down and making gestures in the air with his cigarette.

He finished his call and hung up. He leaned back and sat there brooding, staring down at his desk, but not forgetting to look out of the window every half minute. He was waiting, and I waited with him, for no reason at all. Doctors make many phone calls, talk to many people. Doctors look out of their front windows, doctors frown, doctors show nervousness, doctors have things on their mind and show the strain. Doctors are just people, born to sorrow, fighting the long grim fight like the rest of us.

But there was something about the way this one behaved that intrigued me. I looked at my watch, decided it was time to get something to eat, lit another cigarette and didn't move.

It took about five minutes. Then a green sedan whisked around the corner and bore down the block. It coasted to a stop in front of Dr. Almore's house and its tall buggywhip aerial quivered. A big man with dusty blond hair got out and went up to Dr. Almore's front door. He rang the bell and leaned down to strike a match on the step. His head came around and he stared across the street exactly at where I was sitting.

The door opened and he went into the house. An invisible hand gathered the curtains at Dr. Almore's study window and blanked the room. I sat there and stared at the sun-darkened lining of the curtains. More time trickled by.

The front door opened again and the big man loafed casually down the steps and through the gate. He snapped his cigarette end off into the distance and rumpled his hair. He shrugged once, pinched the end of his chin, and walked diagonally across the street. His steps in the quiet were leisurely and distinct. Dr. Almore's curtains moved apart again behind him. Dr. Almore stood in his window and watched.

A large freckled hand appeared on the sill of the car door at my elbow. A large face, deeply-lined hung above it. The man had eyes of metallic blue. He looked at me solidly and spoke in a deep harsh voice.

"Waiting for somebody?" he asked.

"I don't know," I said. "Am I?"

"I'll ask the questions."

"Well, I'll be damned," I said. "So that's the answer to the pantomime."

"What pantomime?" He gave me a hard level unfriendly stare from his very blue eyes.

I pointed across the street with my cigarette. "Nervous Nellie and the telephone. Calling the cops, after first getting my name from the Auto Club, probably, then looking it up in the city directory. What goes on?"

"Let me see your driver's license."

I gave him back his stare. "You fellows ever flash a buzzer—or is acting tough all the identification you need?"

"If I have to get tough, fellow, you'll know it."

I leaned down and turned my ignition key and pressed the starter. The motor caught and idled down.

"Cut that motor," he said savagely, and put his foot on the running-board.

I cut the motor again and leaned back and looked at him.

"God damn it," he said, "do you want me to drag you out of there and bounce you on the pavement?"

I got my wallet out and handed it to him. He drew the celluloid pocket out and looked at my driver's license, then turned the pocket over and looked at the photostat of my other license on the back. He rammed it contemptuously back into the wallet and handed me the wallet. I put it away. His hand dipped and came up with a blue and gold police badge.

"Degarmo, detective-lieutenant," he said in his heavy brutal voice.

"Pleased to meet you, lieutenant."

"Skip it. Now tell why you're down here casing Almore's place."

"I'm not casing Almore's place, as you put it, lieutenant. I never heard of Dr. Almore and I don't know of any reason why I should want to case his house."

He turned his head to spit. I was meeting the spitting boys today.

"What's your grift then? We don't like peepers down here. We don't have one in town."

"Is that so?"

"Yeah, that's so. So come on, talk it up. Unless you want to ride down to the clubhouse and sweat it out under the bright lights."

I didn't answer him.

"Her folks hire you?" he asked suddenly.

I shook my head.

"The last boy that tried it ended up on the road gang, sweetheart."

"I bet it's good," I said, "if only I could guess. Tried what?"

"Tried to put the bite on him," he said thinly.

"Too bad I don't know how," I said. "He looks like an easy man to bite."

"That line of talk don't buy you anything," he said.

"All right," I said. "Let's put it this way. I don't know Dr. Almore, never heard of him, and I'm not interested in him. I'm down here visiting a friend and looking at the view. If I'm doing anything else, it doesn't happen to be any of your business. If you don't like that, the best thing to do is to take it down to headquarters and see the day captain."

He moved a foot heavily on the running board and looked doubtful. "Straight goods?" he asked slowly.

"Straight goods."

"Aw hell, the guy's screwy," he said suddenly and looked back over his shoulder at the house. "He ought to see a doctor." He laughed, without any amusement in the laugh. He took his foot off my running board and rumpled his wiry hair.

"Go on—beat it," he said. "Stay off our reservation, and you won't make any enemies."

I pressed the starter again. When the motor was idling gently I said: "How's Al Norgaard these days?"

He stared at me. "You knew Al?"

"Yeah. He and I worked on a case down here a couple of years ago—when Wax was chief of police."

"Al's in the military police. Wish I was," he said bitterly. He started to walk away and then swung sharply on his heel. "Go on, beat it before I change my mind," he snapped.

He walked heavily across the street and through Dr. Almore's front gate again.

I let the clutch in and drove away. On the way back to the city, I listened to my thoughts. They moved fitfully in and out, like Dr. Almore's thin nervous hands pulling at the edges of his curtains.

Back in Los Angeles I ate lunch and went up to my office in the Cahuenga Building to see what mail there was. I called Kingsley from there.

"I saw Lavery," I told him. "He told me just enough dirt to sound frank. I tried to needle him a little, but nothing came of it. I still like the idea that they quarreled and split up and that he hopes to fix it up with her yet."

"Then he must know where she is," Kingsley said.

"He might, but it doesn't follow. By the way a rather curious thing happened to me on Lavery's street. There are only two houses. The other belongs to a Dr. Almore." I told him briefly about the rather curious thing.

He was silent for a moment at the end and then he said: "Is this Dr. Albert Almore?"

"Yes."

"He was Crystal's doctor for a time. He came to the house several times when she was—well, when she had been overdrinking. I thought him a little too quick with a hypodermic needle. His wife—let me see, there was something about his wife. Oh yes, she committed suicide."

I said, "When?"

"I don't remember. Quite a long time ago. I never knew them socially. What are you going to do now?"

I told him I was going up to Puma Lake, although it was a little late in the day to start.

He said I would have plenty of time and that they had an hour more of daylight in the mountains.

I said that was fine and we hung up.

5

San Bernardino baked and shimmered in the afternoon heat. The air was hot enough to blister my tongue. I drove through it gasping, stopped long enough to buy a pint of liquor in case I fainted before I got to the mountains, and started up the long grade to Crestline. In fifteen miles the road climbed five thousand feet, but even then it was far from cool. Thirty miles of mountain driving brought me to the tall pines and a place called Bubbling Springs. It had a clapboard store and a gas pump, but it felt like paradise. From there on it was cool all the way.

The Puma Lake dam had an armed sentry at each end and one in the middle. The first one I came to had me close all the windows of the car before crossing over the dam. About a hundred yards from the dam a rope with cork floats barred the pleasure boats from coming any closer. Beyond these details the war did not seem to have done anything much to Puma Lake.

Canoes paddled about on the blue water and rowboats with outboard motors put-putted and speedboats showing off like fresh kids made wide swathes of foam and turned on a dime and girls in them shrieked and dragged their hands in the water. Jounced around in the wake of the speedboats people who had paid two dollars for a fishing license were trying to get a dime of it back in tired-tasting fish.

The road skimmed along a high granite outcrop and dropped to meadows of coarse grass in which grew what was left of the wild irises and white and purple lupine and bugle flowers and columbine and penny-royal and desert paint brush. Tall yellow pines probed at the clear blue sky. The road dropped again to lake level and the landscape began to be full of girls in gaudy slacks and snoods and peasant handkerchiefs and rat rolls and fatsoled sandals and fat white thighs. People on bicycles wobbled cautiously over the highway and now and then an anxious-looking bird thumped past on a power-scooter.

A mile from the village the highway was joined by another lesser road which curved back into the mountains. A rough wooden sign under the highway sign said: *Little Fawn Lake 1¾ miles.* I took it. Scattered cabins were perched along the slopes for the first mile and then nothing. Presently another very narrow road debouched from this one and another rough wooden sign said: *Little Fawn Lake. Private Road. No Trespassing.*

I turned the Chrysler into this and crawled carefully around huge bare granite rocks and past a little waterfall and through a maze of black oak trees and ironwood and manzanita and silence. A blue jay squawked on a branch and a squirrel scolded at me and beat one paw angrily on the pine cone it was holding. A scarlet-topped woodpecker stopped probing in the bark long enough to look at me with one beady eye and then dodge behind the tree trunk to look at me with the other one. I came to a five-barred gate and another sign.

Beyond the gate the road wound for a couple of hundred yards through trees and then suddenly below me was a small oval lake deep in trees and rocks and wild grass, like a drop of dew caught in a curled leaf. At the near end of it was a rough concrete dam with a rope handrail across the top and an old millwheel at the side. Near that stood a small cabin of native pine with the bark on it.

Across the lake the long way by the road and the short way by the top of the dam a large redwood cabin overhung the water and farther along, each well separated from the others, were two other cabins. All three were shut up and quiet, with drawn curtains. The big one had orange-yellow venetian blinds and a twelve-paned window facing on the lake.

At the far end of the lake from the dam was what looked like a small pier and band pavilion. A warped wooden sign on it was painted in large white letters: *Camp Kilkare*. I couldn't see any sense in that in these surroundings, so I got out of the car and started down towards the nearest cabin. Somewhere behind it an axe thudded.

I pounded on the cabin door. The axe stopped. A man's voice yelled from somewhere. I sat down on a rock and lit a cigarette. Steps came around the corner of the cabin, uneven steps. A man with a harsh face and a swarthy skin came into view carrying a double-bitted axe.

He was heavily-built and not very tall and he limped as he walked, giving his right leg a little kick out with each step and swinging the foot in a shallow arc. He had a dark unshaven chin and steady blue eyes and grizzled hair that curled over his ears and needed cutting badly. He wore blue denim pants and a blue shirt open on a brown muscular neck. A cigarette hung from the corner of his mouth. He spoke in a tight tough city voice.

"Yeah?"

"Mr. Bill Chess?"

"That's me."

I stood up and got Kingsley's note of introduction out of my pocket and handed it to him. He squinted at the note, then clumped into the cabin and came back with glasses perched on his nose. He read the note carefully and then again. He put it in his shirt pocket, buttoned the flap of the pocket, and put his hand out.

"Pleased to meet you, Mr. Marlowe."

We shook hands. He had a hand like a wood rasp.

"You want to see Kingsley's cabin, huh? Glad to show you. He ain't selling for Chrissake?" He eyed me steadily and jerked a thumb across the lake.

"He might," I said. "Everything's for sale in California."

"Ain't that the truth? That's his—the redwood job. Lined with knotty pine, composition roof, stone foundations and porches, full bath and shower, venetian blinds all around, big fireplace, oil stove in the big bedroom—and brother, you need it in the spring and fall—Pilgrim combination gas and wood range, everything first class. Cost about eight thousand and that's money for a mountain cabin. And private reservoir in the hills for water."

"How about electric light and telephone?" I asked, just to be friendly.

"Electric light, sure. No phone. You couldn't get one now. If you could, it would cost plenty to string the lines out here."

He looked at me with steady blue eyes and I looked at him. In spite of his weathered appearance he looked like a drinker. He had the thickened and glossy skin, the too noticeable veins, the bright glitter in the eyes.

I said: "Anybody living there now?"

"Nope. Mrs. Kingsley was here a few weeks back. She went down the hill. Back any day, I guess. Didn't he say?"

I looked surprised. "Why? Does she go with the cabin?"

He scowled and then put his head back and burst out laughing. The roar of his laughter was like a tractor backfiring. It blasted the woodland silence to shreds.

"Jesus, if that ain't a kick in the pants!" he gasped. "Does she go with the—" He put out another bellow and then his mouth shut tight as a trap.

"Yeah, it's a swell cabin," he said, eyeing me carefully.

"The beds comfortable?" I asked.

He leaned forward and smiled. "Maybe you'd like a face full of knuckles," he said.

I stared at him with my mouth open. "That one went by me too fast," I said, "I never laid an eye on it."

"How would I know if the beds are comfortable?" he snarled, bending down a little so that he could reach me with a hard right, if it worked out that way.

"I don't know why you wouldn't know," I said. "I won't press the point. I can find out for myself."

"Yeah," he said bitterly, "think I can't smell a dick when I meet one? I played hit and run with them in every state in the Union. Nuts to you, pal. And nuts to Kingsley. So he hires himself a dick to come up here and see am I wearing his pajamas, huh? Listen, Jack, I might have a stiff leg and all, but the women I could get—"

I put a hand out, hoping he wouldn't pull it off and throw it in the lake.

"You're slipping your clutch," I told him. "I didn't come up here to enquire into your love life. I never saw Mrs. Kingsley. I never saw Mr. Kingsley until this morning. What the hell's the matter with you?"

He dropped his eyes and rubbed the back of his hand viciously across his mouth, as if he wanted to hurt himself. Then he held the hand in front of his eyes and squeezed it into a hard fist and opened it again and stared at the fingers. They were shaking a little.

"Sorry, Mr. Marlowe," he said slowly. "I was out on the roof last night and I've got a hangover like seven Swedes. I've been up here alone for a month and it's got me talking to myself. A thing happened to me."

"Anything a drink would help?"

His eyes focussed sharply on me and glinted. "You got one?"

I pulled the pint of rye out of my pocket and held it so that he could see the green label over the cap.

"I don't deserve it," he said. "God damn it, I don't. Wait till I get a couple of glasses or would you come into the cabin?"

"I like it out here. I'm enjoying the view."

He swung his stiff leg and went into his cabin and came back carrying a couple of small cheese glasses. He sat down on the rock beside me smelling of dried perspiration.

I tore the metal cap off the bottle and poured him a stiff drink and a light one for myself. We touched glasses and drank. He rolled the liquor on his tongue and a bleak smile put a little sunshine into his face.

"Man that's from the right bottle," he said. "I wonder what made me sound off like that. I guess a guy gets the blues up here all alone. No company, no real friends, no wife." He paused and added with a sidewise look. "Especially no wife."

I kept my eyes on the blue water of the tiny lake. Under an overhanging rock a fish surfaced in a lance of light and a circle of widening ripples. A light breeze moved the tops of the pines with a noise like a gentle surf.

"She left me," he said slowly. "She left me a month ago. Friday the 12th of June. A day I'll remember."

I stiffened, but not too much to pour more whiskey into his empty glass. Friday the 12th of June was the day Mrs. Crystal Kingsley was supposed to have come into town for a party.

"But you don't want to hear about that," he said. And in his faded blue eyes was the deep yearning to talk about it, as plain as anything could possibly be.

"It's none of my business," I said. "But if it would make you feel any better—"

He nodded sharply. "Two guys will meet on a park bench," he said, "and start talking about God. Did you ever notice that? Guys that wouldn't talk about God to their best friend."

"I know that," I said.

He drank and looked across the lake. "She was one swell kid," he said softly. "A little sharp in the tongue sometimes, but one swell kid. It was love at first sight with me and Muriel. I met her in a joint in Riverside, a year and three months ago. Not the kind of joint where a guy would expect to meet a girl like Muriel, but that's how it happened. We got married. I loved her. I knew I was well off. And I was too much of a skunk to play ball with her."

I moved a little to show him I was still there, but I didn't say anything for fear of breaking the spell. I sat with my drink untouched in my hand. I like to drink, but not when people are using me for a diary.

He went on sadly: "But you know how it is with marriage—any marriage. After a while a guy like me, a common no good guy like me, he wants to feel a leg. Some other leg. Maybe it's lousy, but that's the way it is."

He looked at me and I said I had heard the idea expressed.

He tossed his second drink off. I passed him the bottle. A blue jay went up a pine tree hopping from branch to branch without moving his wings or even pausing to balance.

"Yeah," Bill Chess said. "All these hillbillies are half crazy and I'm getting that way too. Here I am sitting pretty, no rent to pay, a good pension check every month, half my bonus money in war bonds, I'm married to as neat a little blonde as ever you clapped an eye on and all the time I'm nuts and I don't know it. I go for *that*." He pointed hard at the redwood cabin across the lake. It was turning the color of oxblood in the late afternoon light. "Right in the front yard," he said, "right under the windows, and a showy little tart that means no more to me than a blade of grass. Jesus, what a sap a guy can be."

He drank his third drink and steadied the bottle on a rock. He fished a cigarette out of his shirt, fired a match on his thumbnail and puffed rapidly. I breathed with my mouth open, as silent as a burglar behind a curtain.

"Hell," he said at last, "you'd think if I had to jump off the dock, I'd go a little ways from home and pick me a change in types at least. But little roundheels over there ain't even that. She's a blonde like Muriel, same size and weight, same type, almost the same color eyes. But, brother, how different from then on in. Pretty, sure, but no prettier to anybody and not half so pretty to me. Well, I'm over there burning trash that morning and minding my own business, as much as I ever mind it. And she comes to the back door of the cabin in peekaboo pajamas so thin you can see the pink of her nipples against the cloth. And she says in her lazy, no-good voice: 'Have a drink, Bill. Don't work so hard on such a beautiful morning.' And me, I like a drink too well and I go to the kitchen door and take it. And then I take another and then I take another and then I'm in the house. And the closer I get to her the more bedroom her eyes are."

He paused and swept me with a hard level look.

"You asked me if the beds over there were comfortable and I got sore. You didn't mean a thing. I was just too full of remembering. Yeah—the bed I was in was comfortable."

He stopped talking and I let his words hang in the air. They fell slowly and after them was silence. He leaned to pick the bottle off the rock and stare at it. He seemed to fight with it in his mind. The whiskey won the fight, as it always does. He took a long savage drink out of the bottle and then screwed the cap on tightly, as if that meant something. He picked up a stone and flicked it into the water.

"I came back across the dam," he said slowly, in a voice already thick with alcohol. "I'm as smooth as a new piston head. I'm getting away with something. Us boys can be so wrong about those little things, can't we? I'm not getting away with anything at all. Not anything at all. I listen to Muriel telling me and she don't even raise her voice. But she tells me things about myself I didn't even imagine. Oh yeah, I'm getting away with it lovely."

"So she left you," I said, when he fell silent.

"That night. I wasn't even here. I felt too mean to stay even half sober. I hopped into my Ford and went over to the north side of the lake and holed up with a couple of no-goods like myself and got good and stinking. Not that it did me any good. Along about 4 A.M. I got back home and Muriel is gone, packed up and gone, nothing left but a note on the bureau and some cold cream on the pillow."

He pulled a dog-eared piece of paper out of a shabby old wallet and passed it over. It was written in pencil on blue-lined paper from a notebook. It read:

"I'm sorry, Bill, but I'd rather be dead than live with you any longer. Muriel."

I handed it back. "What about over there?" I asked, pointing across the lake with a glance.

Bill Chess picked up a flat stone and tried to skip it across the water, but it refused to skip.

"Nothing over there," he said. "She packed up and went down the same night. I didn't see her again. I don't want to see her again. I haven't heard a word from Muriel in the whole month, not a single word. I don't have any idea at all where she's at. With some other guy, maybe. I hope he treats her better than I did."

He stood up and took keys out of his pocket and shook them. "So if you want to go across and look at Kingsley's cabin, there isn't a thing to stop you. And thanks for listening to the soap opera. And thanks for the liquor. Here." He picked the bottle up and handed me what was left of the pint.

6

We went down the slope to the bank of the lake and the narrow top of the dam. Bill Chess swung his stiff leg in front of me, holding on to the rope handrail set in iron stanchions. At one point water washed over the concrete in a lazy swirl.

"I'll let some out through the wheel in the morning," he said over his shoulder. "That's all the darn thing is good for. Some movie outfit put it up three years ago. They made a picture up here. That little pier down at the other end is some more of their work. Most of what they built is torn down and hauled away, but Kingsley had them leave the pier and the millwheel. Kind of gives the place a touch of color."

I followed him up a flight of heavy wooden steps to the porch of the Kingsley cabin. He unlocked the door and we went into hushed warmth. The closed up room was almost hot. The light filtering through the slatted blinds made narrow bars across the floor. The living room was long and cheerful and had Indian rugs, padded mountain furniture with metal-strapped joints, chintz curtains, a plain hardwood floor, plenty of lamps and a little built-in bar with round stools in one corner. The room was neat and clean and had no look of having been left at short notice.

We went into the bedrooms. Two of them had twin beds and one a large double bed with a cream-colored spread having a design in plum-colored wool stitched over it. This was the master bedroom, Bill Chess said. On a dresser of varnished wood there were toilet articles and accessories in jade green enamel and stainless steel, and an assortment of cosmetic oddments. A couple of cold cream jars had the wavy gold brand of the Gillerlain Company on them. One whole side of the room consisted of closets with sliding doors. I slid one open and peeked inside. It seemed to be full of women's clothes of the sort they wear at resorts. Bill Chess watched me sourly while I pawed them over. I slid the door shut and pulled open a deep shoe drawer underneath. It contained at least half a dozen pairs of new-looking shoes. I heaved the drawer shut and straightened up.

Bill Chess was planted squarely in front of me, with his chin pushed out and his hard hands in knots on his hips.

"So what did you want to look at the lady's clothes for?" he asked in an angry voice.

"Reasons," I said. "For instance Mrs. Kingsley didn't go home when she left here. Her husband hasn't seen her since. He doesn't know where she is."

He dropped his fists and twisted them slowly at his sides. "Dick it is," he snarled. "The first guess is always right. I had myself about talked out of it. Boy, did I open up to you. Nellie with her hair in her lap. Boy, am I a smart little egg!"

"I can respect a confidence as well as the next fellow," I said, and walked around him into the kitchen.

There was a big green and white combination range, a sink of lacquered yellow pine, an automatic water heater in the service porch, and opening off the other side of the kitchen a cheerful breakfast room with many windows and an expansive plastic breakfast set. The shelves were gay with colored dishes and glasses and a set of pewter serving dishes.

Everything was in apple-pie order. There were no dirty cups or plates on the drain board, no smeared glasses or empty liquor bottles hanging around. There were no ants and no flies. Whatever loose living Mrs. Derace Kingsley indulged in she managed without leaving the usual Greenwich Village slop behind her.

I went back to the living room and out on the front porch again and waited for Bill Chess to lock up. When he had done that and turned to me with his scowl well in place I said:

"I didn't ask you to take your heart out and squeeze it for me, but I didn't try to stop you either. Kingsley doesn't have to know his wife made a pass at you, unless there's a lot more behind all this than I can see now."

"The hell with you," he said, and the scowl stayed right where it was.

"All right, the hell with me. Would there be any chance your wife and Kingsley's wife went away together?"

"I don't get it," he said.

"After you went to drown your troubles they could have had a fight and made up and cried down each other's necks. Then Mrs. Kingsley might have taken your wife down the hill. She had to have something to ride in, didn't she?"

It sounded silly, but he took it seriously enough.

"Nope. Muriel didn't cry down anybody's neck. They left the weeps out of Muriel. And if she did want to cry on a shoulder, she wouldn't have picked little roundheels. And as for transportation she has a Ford of her own. She couldn't drive mine easily on account of the way the controls are switched over for my stiff leg."

"It was just a passing thought," I said.

"If any more like it pass you, let them go right on," he said.

"For a guy that takes his long wavy hair down in front of complete strangers, you're pretty damn touchy," I said.

He took a step towards me. "Want to make something of it?"

"Look, pal," I said, "I'm working hard to think you are a fundamentally good egg. Help me out a little, can't you?"

He breathed hard for a moment and then dropped his hands and spread them helplessly.

"Boy, can I brighten up anybody's afternoon," he sighed. "Want to walk back around the lake?"

"Sure, if your leg will stand it."

"Stood it plenty of times before."

We started off side by side, as friendly as puppies again. It would probably last all of fifty yards. The roadway, barely wide enough to pass a car, hung above the level of the lake and dodged between high rocks. About halfway to the far end another smaller cabin was built on a rock foundation. The third was well beyond the end of the lake, on a patch of almost level ground. Both were closed up and had that long-empty look.

Bill Chess said after a minute or two: "That straight goods little roundheels lammed off?"

"So it seems."

"You a real dick or just a shamus?"

"Just a shamus."

"She go with some guy?"

"I should think it likely."

"Sure she did. It's a cinch. Kingsley ought to be able to guess that. She had plenty of friends."

"Up here?"

He didn't answer me.

"Was one of them named Lavery?"

"I wouldn't know," he said.

"There's no secret about this one," I said. "She sent a wire from El Paso saying she and Lavery were going to Mexico." I dug the wire out of my pocket and held it out. He fumbled his glasses loose from his shirt and stopped to read it. He handed the paper back and put his glasses away again and stared out over the blue water.

"That's a little confidence for you to hold against some of what you gave me," I said.

"Lavery was up here once," he said slowly.

"He admits he saw her a couple of months ago, probably up here. He claims he hasn't seen her since. We don't know whether to believe him. There's no reason why we should and no reason why we shouldn't."

"She isn't with him now, then?"

"He says not."

"I wouldn't think she would fuss with little details like getting married," he said soberly. "A Florida honeymoon would be more in her line."

"But you can't give me any positive information? You didn't see her go or hear anything that sounded authentic?"

"Nope," he said. "And if I did, I doubt if I would tell. I'm dirty, but not that kind of dirty."

"Well, thanks for trying," I said.

"I don't owe you any favors," he said. "The hell with you and every other God damn snooper."

"Here we go again," I said.

We had come to the end of the lake now. I left him standing there and walked out on the little pier. I leaned on the wooden railing at the end of it and saw that what had looked like a band pavilion was nothing but two pieces of propped up wall meeting at a flat angle towards the dam. About two feet deep of overhanging roof was stuck on the wall, like a coping. Bill Chess came up behind me and leaned on the railing at my side.

"Not that I don't thank you for the liquor," he said.

"Yeah. Any fish in the lake?"

"Some smart old bastards of trout. No fresh stock. I don't go for fish much myself. I don't bother with them. Sorry I got tough again."

I grinned and leaned on the railing and stared down into the deep still water. It was green when you looked down into it. There was a swirl of movement down there and a swift greenish form moved in the water.

"There's Granpa," Bill Chess said. "Look at the size of that old bastard. He ought to be ashamed of himself getting so fat."

Down below the water there was what looked like an underwater flooring. I couldn't see the sense of that. I asked him.

"Used to be a boat landing before the dam was raised. That lifted the water level so far the old landing was six feet under."

A flat-bottomed boat dangled on a frayed rope tied to a post of the pier. It lay in the water almost without motion, but not quite. The air was peaceful and calm and sunny and held a quiet you don't get in cities. I could have stayed there for hours doing nothing but forgetting all about Derace Kingsley and his wife and her boy friends.

There was a hard movement at my side and Bill Chess said, "Look there!" in a voice that growled like mountain thunder.

His hard fingers dug into the flesh of my arm until I started to get mad. He was bending far out over the railing, staring down like a loon, his face as white as the weather tan would let it get. I looked down with him into the water at the edge of the submerged staging.

Languidly at the edge of this green and sunken shelf of wood something waved out from the darkness, hesitated, waved back again out of sight under the flooring.

The something had looked far too much like a human arm.

Bill Chess straightened his body rigidly. He turned without a sound and clumped back along the pier. He bent to a loose pile of stones and heaved. His panting breath reached me. He got a big one free and lifted it breast high and started back out on the pier with it. It must have weighed a hundred pounds. His neck muscles stood out likes ropes under canvas under his taut brown skin. His teeth were clamped tight and his breath hissed between them.

He reached the end of the pier and steadied himself and lifted the rock high. He held it a moment poised, his eyes staring down now, measuring. His mouth made a vague distressful sound and his body lurched forward hard against the quivering rail and the heavy stone smashed down into the water.

The splash it made went over both of us. The rock fell straight and true and struck on the edge of the submerged planking, almost exactly where we had seen the thing wave in and out.

For a moment the water was a confused boiling, then the ripples widened off into the distance, coming smaller and smaller with a trace of froth at the middle, and there was a dim sound as of wood breaking under water, a sound that seemed to come to us a long time after it should have been audible. An ancient rotted plank popped suddenly through the surface, stuck out a full foot of its jagged end, and fell back with a flat slap and floated off.

The depths cleared again. Something moved in them that was not a board. It rose slowly, with an infinitely careless languor, a long dark twisted something that rolled lazily in the water as it rose. It broke surface casually, lightly, without haste. I saw wool, sodden and black, a leather jerkin blacker than ink, a pair of slacks. I saw shoes and something that bulged nastily between the shoes and the cuffs of the slacks. I saw a wave of dark blond hair straighten out in the water and hold still for a brief instant as if with a calculated effect, and then swirl into a tangle again.

The thing rolled over once more and an arm flapped up barely above the skin of the water and the arm ended in a bloated hand that was the hand of a freak. Then the face came. A swollen pulpy gray white mass without features, without eyes, without mouth. A blotch of gray dough, a nightmare with human hair on it.

A heavy necklace of green stones showed on what had been a neck, half imbedded, large rough green stones with something that glittered joining them together.

Bill Chess held the handrail and his knuckles were polished bones.

"Muriel!" his voice said croakingly. "Sweet Christ, it's Muriel!"

His voice seemed to come to me from a long way off, over a hill, through a thick silent growth of trees.

7

Behind the window of the board shack one end of a counter was piled with dusty folders. The glass upper half of the door was lettered in flaked black paint. *Chief of Police. Fire Chief. Town Constable. Chamber of Commerce.* In the lower corners a USO card and a Red Cross emblem were fastened to the glass.

I went in. There was a pot-bellied stove in the corner and a rolltop desk in the other corner behind the counter. There was a large blue print map of the district on the wall and beside that a board with four hooks on it, one of which supported a frayed and much mended mackinaw. On the counter beside the dusty folders lay the usual sprung pen, exhausted blotter and smeared bottle of gummy ink. The end wall beside the desk was covered with telephone numbers written in hardbitten figures that would last as long as the wood and looked as if they had been written by a child.

A man sat at the desk in a wooden armchair whose legs were anchored to flat boards, fore and aft, like skis. A spittoon big enough to coil a hose in was leaning against the man's right leg. He had a sweat-stained Stetson on the back of his head and his large hairless hands were clasped comfortably over his stomach, above the waistband of a pair of khaki pants that had been scrubbed thin years ago. His shirt matched the pants except that it was even more faded. It was buttoned tight to the man's thick neck and undecorated by a tie. His hair was mousy brown except at the temples, where it was the color of old snow. He sat more on his left hip than his right, because there was a hip holster down inside his right hip pocket, and a half foot of forty-five gun reared up and bored into his solid back. The star on his left breast had a bent point.

He had large ears and friendly eyes and his jaws munched slowly and he looked as dangerous as a squirrel and much less nervous. I liked everything about him. I leaned on the counter and looked at him and he looked at me and nodded and loosed half a pint of tobacco juice down his right leg into the spittoon. It made a nasty sound of something falling into water.

I lit a cigarette and looked around for an ashtray.

"Try the floor, son," the large friendly man said.

"Are you Sheriff Patton?"

"Constable and deputy sheriff. What law we got to have around here I'm it. Come election anyways. There's a couple of good boys running against me this time and I might get whupped. Job pays eighty a month, cabin, firewood and electricity. That ain't hay in these little old mountains."

"Nobody's going to whip you," I said. "You're going to get a lot of publicity."

"That so?" he asked indifferently and ruined the spittoon again.

"That is, if your jurisdiction extends over to Little Fawn Lake."

"Kingsley's place. Sure. Something bothering over there, son?"

"There's a dead woman in the lake."

That shook him to the core. He unclasped his hands and scratched one ear. He got to his feet by grasping the arms of his chair and deftly kicking it back from under him. Standing up he was a big man and hard. The fat was just cheerfulness.

"Anybody I know?" he enquired uneasily.

"Muriel Chess. I guess you know her. Bill Chess's wife."

"Yep, I know Bill Chess." His voice hardened a little.

"Looks like suicide. She left a note which sounded as if she was just going away. But it could be a suicide note just as well. She's not nice to look at. Been in the water a long time, about a month, judging by the circumstances."

He scratched his other ear. "What circumstances would that be?" His eyes were searching my face now, slowly and calmly, but searching. He didn't seem in any hurry to blow his whistle.

"They had a fight a month ago. Bill went over to the north shore of the lake and was gone some hours. When he got home she was gone. He never saw her again."

"I see. Who are you, son?"

"My name is Marlowe. I'm up from L.A. to look at the property. I had a note from Kingsley to Bill Chess. He took me around the lake and we went out on that little pier the movie people built. We were leaning on the rail and looking down into the water and something that looked like an arm waved out under the submerged flooring, the old boat landing. Bill dropped a heavy rock in and the body popped up."

Patton looked at me without moving a muscle.

"Look, sheriff, hadn't we better run over there? The man's half crazy with shock and he's there all alone."

"How much liquor has he got?"

"Very little when I left. I had a pint but we drank most of it talking."

He moved over to the rolltop desk and unlocked a drawer. He brought up three or four bottles and held them against the light.

"This baby's near full," he said, patting one of them. "Mount Vernon. That ought to hold him. County don't allow me no money for emergency liquor, so I just have to seize a little here and there. Don't use it myself. Never could understand folks letting theirselves get gummed up with it."

He put the bottle on his left hip and locked the desk up and lifted the flap in the counter. He fixed a card against the inside of the glass door panel. I looked at the card as we went out. It read: *Back in Twenty Minutes—Maybe.*

"I'll run down and get Doc Hollis," he said. "Be right back and pick you up. That your car?"

"Yes."

"You can follow along then, as I come back by."

He got into a car which had a siren on it, two red spotlights, two foglights, a red and white fire plate, a new air raid horn on top, three axes, two heavy coils of rope and a fire extinguisher in the back seat, extra gas and oil and water cans in a frame on the running board, an extra spare tire roped to the one on the rack, the stuffing coming out of the upholstery in dingy wads, and half an inch of dust over what was left of the paint.

Behind the right hand lower corner of the windshield there was a white card printed in block capitals. It read:

"VOTERS, ATTENTION! KEEP JIM PATTON CONSTABLE. HE IS TOO OLD TO GO TO WORK."

He turned the car and went off down the street in a swirl of white dust.

8

He stopped in front of a white frame building across the road from the stage depot. He went into the white building and presently came out with a man who got into the back seat with the axes and the rope.

The official car came back up the street and I fell in behind it. We sifted along the main stem through the slacks and shorts and French sailor jerseys and knotted bandannas and knobby knees and scarlet lips. Beyond the village we went up a dusty hill and stopped at a cabin. Patton touched the siren gently and a man in faded blue overalls opened the cabin door.

"Get in, Andy. Business."

The man in blue overalls nodded morosely and ducked back into the cabin. He came back out wearing an oyster-gray lion hunter's hat and got in under the wheel of Patton's car while Patton slid over. He was about thirty, dark, lithe, and had the slightly dirty and slightly underfed look of the native.

We drove out to Little Fawn Lake with me eating enough dust to make a batch of mud pies. At the five-barred gate Patton got out and let us through and we went on down to the lake. Patton got out again and went to the edge of the water and looked along towards the little pier. Bill Chess was sitting naked on the floor of the pier, with his head in his hands. There was something stretched out on the wet planks beside him.

"We can ride a ways more," Patton said.

The two cars went on to the end of the lake and all four of us trouped down to the pier from behind Bill Chess's back. The doctor stopped to cough rackingly into a handkerchief and then looked thoughtfully at the handkerchief. He was an angular bug-eyed man with a sad sick face.

The thing that had been a woman lay face down on the boards with a rope under the arms. Bill Chess's clothes lay to one side. His stiff leg, flat and scarred at the knee, was stretched out in front of him, the other leg bent up and his forehead resting against it. He didn't move or look up as we came down behind him.

Patton took the pint bottle of Mount Vernon off his hip and unscrewed the top and handed it.

"Drink hearty, Bill."

There was a horrible, sickening smell in the air. Bill Chess didn't seem to notice it, nor Patton nor the doctor. The man called Andy got a dusty brown blanket out of the car and threw it over the body. Then without a word he went and vomited under a pine tree.

Bill Chess drank a long drink and sat holding the bottle against his bare bent knee. He began to talk in a stiff wooden voice, not looking at anybody, not talking to anybody in particular. He told about the quarrel and what happened after it, but not why it had happened. He didn't mention Mrs. Kingsley even in the most casual way. He said that after I left him he had got a rope and stripped and gone down into the water and got the thing out. He had dragged it ashore and then got it up on his back and carried it out on the pier. He didn't know why. He had gone back into the water again then. He didn't have to tell us why.

Patton put a cut of tobacco into his mouth and chewed on it silently, his calm eyes full of nothing. Then he shut his teeth tight and leaned down to pull the blanket off the body. He turned the body over carefully, as if it might come to pieces. The late afternoon sun winked on the necklace of large green stones that were partly imbedded in the swollen neck. They were roughly carved and lustreless, like soapstone or false jade. A gilt chain with an eagle clasp set with small brilliants joined the ends. Patton straightened his broad back and blew his nose on a tan handkerchief.

"What you say, Doc?"

"About what?" the bug-eyed man snarled.

"Cause and time of death."

"Don't be a damn fool, Jim Patton."

"Can't tell nothing, huh?"

"By looking at that? Good God!"

Patton sighed. "Looks drowned all right," he admitted. "But you can't always tell. There's been cases where a victim would be knifed or poisoned or something, and they would soak him in the water to make things look different."

"You get many like that up here?" the doctor enquired nastily.

"Only honest to God murder I ever had up here," Patton said, watching Bill Chess out of the corner of his eye, "was old Dad Meacham over on the north shore. He had a shack in Sheedy Canyon, did a little panning in summer on an old placer claim he had back in the valley near Belltop. Folks didn't see him around for a while in late fall, then come a heavy snow and his roof caved in to one side. So we was over there trying to prop her up a bit, figuring Dad had gone down the hill for the winter without telling anybody, the way them old prospectors do things. Well by gum, old Dad never went down the hill at all. There he was in bed with most of a kindling axe in the back of his head. We never did find out who done it. Somebody figured he had a little bag of gold hid away from the summer's panning."

He looked thoughtfully at Andy. The man in the lion hunter's hat was feeling a tooth in his mouth. He said:

"'Course we know who done it. Guy Pope done it. Only Guy was dead nine days of pneumonia before we found Dad Meacham."

"Eleven days," Patton said.

"Nine," the man in the lion hunter's hat said.

"Was all of six years ago, Andy. Have it your own way, son. How you figure Guy Pope done it?"

"We found about three ounces of small nuggets in Guy's cabin along with some dust. Never was anything bigger'n sand on Guy's claim. Dad had nuggets all of a pennyweight, plenty of times."

"Well, that's the ways it goes," Patton said, and smiled at me in a vague manner. "Fellow always forgets something, don't he? No matter how careful he is."

"Cop stuff," Bill Chess said disgustedly and put his pants on and sat down again to put on his shoes and shirt. When he had them on he stood up and reached down for the bottle and took a good drink and laid the bottle carefully on the planks. He thrust his hairy wrists out towards Patton.

"That's the way you guys feel about it, put the cuffs on and get it over," he said in a savage voice.

Patton ignored him and went over to the railing and looked down. "Funny place for a body to be," he said. "No current here to mention, but what there is would be towards the dam."

Bill Chess lowered his wrists and said quietly: "She did it herself, you darn fool. Muriel was a fine swimmer. She dived down in and swum under the boards there and just breathed water in. Had to. No other way."

"I wouldn't quite say that, Bill," Patton answered him mildly. His eyes were as blank as new plates.

Andy shook his head. Patton looked at him with a sly grin. "Crabbin' again, Andy?"

"Was nine days, I tell you. I just counted back," the man in the lion hunter's hat said morosely.

The doctor threw his arms up and walked away, with one hand to his head. He coughed into his handkerchief again and again looked into the handkerchief with passionate attention.

Patton winked at me and spat over the railing. "Let's get on to this one, Andy."

"You ever try to drag a body six feet under water?"

"Nope, can't say I ever did, Andy. Any reason it couldn't be done with a rope?"

Andy shrugged. "If a rope was used, it will show on the corpse. If you got to give yourself away like that, why bother to cover up at all?"

"Question of time," Patton said. "Fellow has his arrangements to make."

Bill Chess snarled at them and reached down for the whiskey. Looking at their solemn mountain faces I couldn't tell what they were really thinking.

Patton said absently: "Something was said about a note."

Bill Chess rummaged in his wallet and drew the folded piece of ruled paper loose. Patton took it and read it slowly.

"Don't seem to have any date," he observed.

Bill Chess shook his head sombrely. "No. She left a month ago. June 12th."

"Left you once before, didn't she?"

"Yeah." Bill Chess stared at him fixedly. "I got drunk and stayed with a chippy. Just before the first snow last December. She was gone a week and came back all prettied up. Said she just had to get away for a while and had been staying with a girl she used to work with in L.A."

"What was the name of this party?" Patton asked.

"Never told me and I never asked her. What Muriel did was all silk with me."

"Sure. Note left that time, Bill?" Patton asked smoothly.

"No."

"This note here looks middling old," Patton said, holding it up.

"I carried it a month," Bill Chess growled. "Who told you she left me before?"

"I forget," Patton said. "You know how it is in a place like this. Not much folks don't notice. Except maybe in summer time where there's a lot of strangers about."

Nobody said anything for a while and then Patton said absently: "June 12th you say she left? Or you thought she left? Did you say the folks across the lake were up here then?"

Bill Chess looked at me and his face darkened again. "Ask this snoopy guy—if he didn't already spill his guts to you."

Patton didn't look at me at all. He looked at the line of mountains far beyond the lake. He said gently: "Mr. Marlowe here didn't tell me anything at all, Bill, except how the body come up out of the water and who it was. And that Muriel went away, as you thought, and left a note you showed him. I don't guess there's anything wrong in that, is there?"

There was another silence and Bill Chess stared down at the blanket-covered corpse a few feet away from him. He clenched his hands and a thick tear ran down his cheek.

"Mrs. Kingsley was here," he said. "She went down the hill that same day. Nobody was in the other cabins. Perrys and Farquars ain't been up at all this year."

Patton nodded and was silent. A kind of charged emptiness hung in the air, as if something that had not been said was plain to all of them and didn't need saying.

Then Bill Chess said wildly: "Take me in, you sons of bitches! Sure I did it! I drowned her. She was my girl and I loved her. I'm a heel, always was a heel, always will be a heel, but just the same I loved her. Maybe you guys wouldn't understand that. Just don't bother to try. Take me in, damn you!"

Nobody said anything at all.

Bill Chess looked down at his hard brown fist. He swung it up viciously and hit himself in the face with all his strength.

"You rotten son of a bitch," he breathed in a harsh whisper.

His nose began to bleed slowly. He stood and the blood ran down his lip, down the side of his mouth, to the point of his chin. A drop fell sluggishly to his shirt.

Patton said quietly: "Got to take you down the hill for questioning, Bill. You know that. We ain't accusing you of anything, but the folks down there have got to talk to you."

Bill Chess said heavily: "Can I change my clothes?"

"Sure. You go with him, Andy. And see what you can find to kind of wrap up what he got here."

They went off along the path at the edge of the lake. The doctor cleared his throat and looked out over the water and sighed.

"You'll want to send the corpse down in my ambulance, Jim, won't you?"

Patton shook his head. "Nope. This is a poor county, Doc. I figure the lady can ride cheaper than what you get for that ambulance."

The doctor walked away from him angrily, saying over his shoulder: "Let me know if you want me to pay for the funeral."

"That ain't no way to talk," Patton sighed.

The Indian Head Hotel was a brown building on a corner across from the new dance hall. I parked in front of it and used its rest room to wash my face and hands and comb the pine needles out of my hair, before I went into the dining-drinking parlor that adjoined the lobby. The whole place was full to overflowing with males in leisure jackets and liquor breaths and females in highpitched laughs, oxblood fingernails and dirty knuckles. The manager of the joint, a low budget tough guy in shirt sleeves and a mangled cigar, was prowling the room with watchful eyes. At the cash desk a pale-haired man was fighting to get the war news on a small radio that was as full of static as the mashed potatoes were full of water. In the deep back corner of the room, a hillbilly orchestra of five pieces, dressed in ill-fitting white jackets and purple shirts, was trying to make itself heard above the brawl at the bar and smiling glassily into the fog of cigarette smoke and the blur of alcoholic voices. At Puma Point summer, that lovely season, was in full swing.

I gobbled what they called the regular dinner, drank a brandy to sit on its chest and hold it down, and went out on to the main street. It was still broad daylight but some of the neon signs had been turned on, and the evening reeled with the cheerful din of auto horns, children screaming, bowls rattling, skeeballs clunking, .22's snapping merrily in shooting galleries, juke boxes playing like crazy, and behind all this out on the lake the hard barking roar of the speedboats going nowhere at all and acting as though they were racing with death.

In my Chrysler a thin, serious-looking, brown-haired girl in dark slacks was sitting smoking a cigarette and talking to a dude ranch cowboy who sat on my running board. I walked around the car and got into it. The cowboy strolled away hitching his jeans up. The girl didn't move.

"I'm Birdie Keppel," she said cheerfully, "I'm the beautician here daytimes and evenings I work on the Puma Point Banner. Excuse me sitting in your car."

"That's all right," I said. "You want to just sit or you want me to drive you somewhere?"

"You can drive down the road a piece where it's quieter, Mr. Marlowe. If you're obliging enough to talk to me."

"Pretty good grapevine you've got up here," I said and started the car.

I drove down past the post office to a corner where a blue and white arrow marked *Telephone* pointed down a narrow road towards the lake. I turned down that, drove down past the telephone office, which was a log cabin with a tiny railed lawn in front of it, passed another small cabin and pulled up in front of a huge oak tree that flung its branches all the way across the road and a good fifty feet beyond it.

"This do, Miss Keppel?"

"Mrs. But just call me Birdie. Everybody does. This is fine. Pleased to meet you, Mr. Marlowe. I see you come from Hollywood, that sinful city."

She put a firm brown hand out and I shook it. Clamping bobbie pins into fat blondes had given her a grip like a pair of iceman's tongs.

"I was talking to Doc Hollis," she said, "about poor Muriel Chess. I thought you could give me some details. I understand you found the body."

"Bill Chess found it really. I was just with him. You talk to Jim Patton?"

"Not yet. He went down the hill. Anyway I don't think Jim would tell me much."

"He's up for re-election," I said. "And you're a newspaper woman."

"Jim's no politician, Mr. Marlowe, and I could hardly call myself a newspaper woman. This little paper we get out up here is a pretty amateurish proposition."

"Well, what do you want to know?" I offered her a cigarette and lit it for her.

"You might just tell me the story."

"I came up here with a letter from Derace Kingsley to look at his property. Bill Chess showed me around, got talking to me, told me his wife had moved out on him and showed me the note she left. I had a bottle along and he punished it. He was feeling pretty blue. The liquor loosened him up, but he was lonely and aching to talk anyway. That's how it happened. I didn't know him. Coming back around the end of the lake we went out on the pier and Bill spotted an arm waving out from under the planking down in the water. It turned out to belong to what was left of Muriel Chess. I guess that's all."

"I understand from Doc Hollis she had been in the water a long time. Pretty badly decomposed and all that."

"Yes. Probably the whole month he thought she had been gone. There's no reason to think otherwise. The note's a suicide note."

"Any doubt about that, Mr. Marlowe?"

I looked at her sideways. Thoughtful dark eyes looked out at me under fluffed out brown hair. The dusk had begun to fall now, very slowly. It was no more than a slight change in the quality of the light.

"I guess the police always have doubts in these cases," I said.

"How about you?"

"My opinion doesn't go for anything."

"But for what it's worth?"

"I only met Bill Chess this afternoon," I said. "He struck me as a quick-tempered lad and from his own account he's no saint. But he seems to have been in love with his wife. And I can't see him hanging around there for a month knowing she was rotting down in the water under that pier. Coming out of his cabin in the sunlight and looking along that soft blue water and seeing in his mind what was under it and what was happening to it. And knowing he put it there."

"No more can I," Birdie Keppel said softly. "No more could anybody. And yet we know in our minds that such things have happened and will happen again. Are you in the real estate business, Mr. Marlowe?"

"No."

"What line of business are you in, if I may ask?"

"I'd rather not say."

"That's almost as good as saying," she said. "Besides Doc Hollis heard you tell Jim Patton your full name. And we have an L.A. city directory in our office. I haven't mentioned it to anyone."

"That's nice of you," I said.

"And what's more, I won't," she said. "If you don't want me to."

"What does it cost me?"

"Nothing," she said. "Nothing at all. I don't claim to be a very good newspaper man. And we wouldn't print anything that would embarrass Jim Patton. Jim's the salt of the earth. But it does open up, doesn't it?"

"Don't draw any wrong conclusions," I said. "I had no interest in Bill Chess whatever."

"No interest in Muriel Chess?"

"Why would I have any interest in Muriel Chess?"

She snuffed her cigarette out carefully into the ashtray under the dashboard. "Have it your own way," she said. "But here's a little item you might like to think about, if you don't know it already. There was a Los Angeles copper named De Soto up here about six weeks back, a big roughneck with damn poor manners. We didn't like him and we didn't open up to him much. I mean the three of us in the Banner office didn't. He had a photograph with him and he was looking for a woman called Mildred Haviland, he said. On police business. It was an ordinary photograph, an enlarged snapshot, not a police photo. He said he had information the woman was staying up here. The photo looked a good deal like Muriel Chess. The hair seemed to be reddish and in a very different style than she has worn it here, and the eyebrows were all plucked to narrow arches, and that changes a woman a good deal. But it did look a good deal like Bill Chess's wife."

I drummed on the door of the car and after a moment I said, "What did you tell him?"

"We didn't tell him anything. First off, we couldn't be sure. Second, we didn't like his manner. Third, even if we had been sure and had liked his manner, we likely would not have sicced him on to her. Why would we? Everybody's done something to be sorry for. Take me. I was married once—to a professor of classical languages at Redlands University." She laughed lightly.

"You might have got yourself a story," I said.

"Sure. But up here we're just people."

"Did this man De Soto see Jim Patton?"

"Sure, he must have. Jim didn't mention it."

"Did he show you his badge?"

She thought and then shook her head. "I don't recall that he did. We just took him for granted, from what he said. He certainly acted like a tough city cop."

"To me that's a little against his being one. Did anybody tell Muriel about this guy?"

She hesitated, looking quietly out through the windshield for a long moment before she turned her head and nodded.

"I did. Wasn't any of my damn business, was it?"

"What did she say?"

"She didn't say anything. She gave a funny little embarrassed laugh, as if I had been making a bad joke. Then she walked away. But I did get the impression that there was a queer look in her eyes, just for an instant. You still not interested in Muriel Chess, Mr. Marlowe?"

"Why should I be? I never heard of her until I came up here this afternoon. Honest. And I never heard of anybody named Mildred Haviland either. Drive you back to town?"

"Oh no, thanks. I'll walk. It's only a few steps. Much obliged to you. I kind of hope Bill doesn't get into a jam. Especially a nasty jam like this."

She got out of the car and hung on one foot, then tossed her head and laughed. "They say I'm a pretty good beauty operator," she said. "I hope I am. As an interviewer I'm terrible. Goodnight."

I said goodnight and she walked off into the evening. I sat there watching her until she reached the main street and turned out of sight. Then I got out of the Chrysler and went over towards the telephone company's little rustic building.

10

A tame doe deer with a leather dog collar on wandered across the road in front of me. I patted her rough hairy neck and went into the telephone office. A small girl in slacks sat at a small desk working on the books. She got me the rate to Beverly Hills and the change for the coin box. The booth was outside, against the front wall of the building.

"I hope you like it up here," she said. "It's very quiet, very restful."

I shut myself into the booth. For ninety cents I could talk to Derace Kingsley for five minutes. He was at home and the call came through quickly but the connection was full of mountain static.

"Find anything up there?" he asked me in a three highball voice. He sounded tough and confident again.

"I've found too much," I said. "And not at all what we want. Are you alone?"

"What does that matter?"

"It doesn't matter to me. But I know what I'm going to say. You don't."

"Well, get on with it, whatever it is," he said.

"I had a long talk with Bill Chess. He was lonely. His wife had left him—a month ago. They had a fight and he went out and got drunk and when he came back she was gone. She left a note saying she would rather be dead than live with him any more."

"I guess Bill drinks too much," Kingsley's voice said from very far off.

"When he got back, both the women had gone. He has no idea where Mrs. Kingsley went. Lavery was up here in May, but not since. Lavery admitted that much himself. Lavery could, of course, have come up again while Bill was out getting drunk, but there wouldn't be a lot of point to that and there would be two cars to drive down the hill. And I thought that possibly Mrs. K. and Muriel Chess might have gone away together, only Muriel also had a car of her own. But that idea, little as it was worth, has been thrown out by another development. Muriel Chess didn't go away at all. She went down into your little private lake. She came back up today. I was there."

"Good God!" Kingsley sounded properly horrified. "You mean she drowned herself?"

"Perhaps. The note she left could be a suicide note. It would read as well that way as the other. The body was stuck down under that old submerged landing below the pier. Bill was the one who spotted an arm moving down there while we were standing on the pier looking down into the water. He got her out. They've arrested him. The poor guy's pretty badly broken up."

"Good God!" Kingsley said again. "I should think he would be. Does it look as if he—" He paused as the operator came in on the line and demanded another forty-five cents. I put in two quarters and the line cleared.

"Look as if he what?"

Suddenly very clear, Kingsley's voice said: "Look as if he murdered her?"

I said: "Very much. Jim Patton, the constable up here, doesn't like the note not being dated. It seems she left him once before over some woman. Patton sort of suspects Bill might have saved up an old note. Anyhow they've taken Bill down to San Bernardino for questioning and they've taken the body down to be post-mortemed."

"And what do you think?" he asked slowly.

"Well, Bill found the body himself. He didn't have to take me around by that pier. She might have stayed down in the water very much longer, or forever. The note could be old because Bill had carried it in his wallet and handled it from time to time, brooding over it. It could just as easily be undated this time as another time. I'd say notes like that are undated more often than not. The people who write them are apt to be in a hurry and not concerned with dates."

"The body must be pretty far gone. What can they find out now?"

"I don't know how well equipped they are. They can find out if she died by drowning, I guess. And whether there are any marks of violence that wouldn't be erased by water and decomposition. They could tell if she had been shot or stabbed. If the hyoid bone in the throat was broken, they could assume she was throttled. The main thing for us is that I'll have to tell why I came up here. I'll have to testify at an inquest."

"That's bad," Kingsley growled. "Very bad. What do you plan to do now?"

"On my way home I'll stop at the Prescott Hotel and see if I can pick up anything there. Were your wife and Muriel Chess friendly?"

"I guess so. Crystal's easy enough to get along with most of the time. I hardly knew Muriel Chess."

"Did you ever know anybody named Mildred Haviland?"

"What?"

I repeated the name.

"No," he said. "Is there any reason why I should?"

"Every question I ask you ask another right back," I said. "No, there isn't any reason why you should know Mildred Haviland. Especially if you hardly knew Muriel Chess. I'll call you in the morning."

"Do that," he said, and hesitated. "I'm sorry you had to walk into such a mess," he added, and then hesitated again and said goodnight and hung up.

The bell rang again immediately and the long distance operator told me sharply I had put in five cents too much money. I said the sort of thing I would be likely to put into an opening like that. She didn't like it.

I stepped out of the booth and gathered some air into my lungs. The tame doe with the leather collar was standing in the gap in the fence at the end of the walk. I tried to push her out of the way, but she just leaned against me and wouldn't push. So I stepped over the fence and went back to the Chrysler and drove back to the village.

There was a hanging light in Patton's headquarters but the shack was empty and his "Back in Twenty Minutes" sign was still against the inside of the glass part of the door. I kept on going down to the boat landing and beyond to the edge of a deserted swimming beach.

A few put-puts and speedboats were still fooling around on the silky water. Across the lake tiny yellow lights began to show in toy cabins perched on miniature slopes. A single bright star glowed low in the northeast above the ridge of the mountains. A robin sat on the spike top of a hundred foot pine and waited for it to be dark enough for him to sing his goodnight song.

In a little while it was dark enough and he sang and went away into the invisible depths of sky. I snapped my cigarette into the motionless water a few feet away and climbed back into the car and started back in the direction of Little Fawn Lake.

11

The gate across the private road was padlocked. I put the Chrysler between two pine trees and climbed the gate and pussy-footed along the side of the road until the glimmer of the little lake bloomed suddenly at my feet. Bill Chess's cabin was dark. The three cabins on the other side were abrupt shadows against the pale granite outcrop. Water gleamed white where it trickled across the top of the dam, and fell almost soundlessly along the sloping outer face to the brook below. I listened, and heard no other sound at all.

The front door of the Chess cabin was locked. I padded along to the back and found a brute of a padlock hanging at that. I went along the walls feeling window screens. They were all fastened. One window higher up was screenless, a small double cottage window halfway down the north wall. This was locked too. I stood still and did some more listening. There was no breeze and the trees were as quiet as their shadows.

I tried a knife blade between the two halves of the small window. No soap. The catch refused to budge. I leaned against the wall and thought and then suddenly I picked up a large stone and smacked it against the place where the two frames met in the middle. The catch pulled out of dry wood with a tearing noise. The window swung back into darkness. I heaved up on the sill and wangled a cramped leg over and edged through the opening. I rolled and let myself down into the room. I turned, grunting a little from the exertion at that altitude, and listened again.

A blazing flash beam hit me square in the eyes.

A very calm voice said: "I'd rest right there, son. You must be all tuckered out."

The flash pinned me against the wall like a squashed fly. Then a light switch clicked and a table lamp glowed. The flash went out. Jim Patton was sitting in an old brown Morris chair beside the table. A fringed brown scarf hung over the end of the table and touched his thick knee. He wore the same clothes he had worn that afternoon, with the addition of a leather jerkin which must have been new once, say about the time of Grover Cleveland's first term. His hands were empty except for the flash. His eyes were empty. His jaws moved in gentle rhythm.

"What's on your mind, son—besides breaking and entering?"

I poked a chair out and straddled it and leaned my arms on the back and looked around the cabin.

"I had an idea," I said. "It looked pretty good for a while, but I guess I can learn to forget it."

The cabin was larger than it had seemed from outside. The part I was in was the living room. It contained a few articles of modest furniture, a rag rug on the pineboard floor, a round table against the end wall and two chairs set against it. Through an open door the corner of a big black cookstove showed.

Patton nodded and his eyes studied me without rancor. "I heard a car coming," he said. "I knew it had to be coming here. You walk right nice though. I didn't hear you walk worth a darn. I've been a mite curious about you, son."

I said nothing.

"I hope you don't mind me callin' you 'son,'" he said. "I hadn't ought to be so familiar, but I got myself into the habit and I can't seem to shake it. Anybody that don't have a long white beard and arthritis is 'son' to me."

I said he could call me anything that came to mind. I wasn't sensitive.

He grinned. "There's a mess of detectives in the L.A. phone book," he said. "But only one of them is called Marlowe."

"What made you look?"

"I guess you might call it lowdown curiosity. Added to which Bill Chess told me you was some sort of dick. You didn't bother to tell me yourself."

"I'd have got around to it," I said. "I'm sorry it bothered you."

"It didn't bother me none. I don't bother at all easy. You got any identification with you?"

I got my wallet out and showed him this and that.

"Well, you got a good build on you for the work," he said satisfied. "And your face don't tell a lot of stories. I guess you was aiming to search the cabin."

"Yeah."

"I already pawed around considerable myself. Just got back and come straight here. That is, I stopped by my shack a minute and then come. I don't figure I could let you search the place, though." He scratched his ear. "That is, dum if I know whether I could or not. You telling who hired you?"

"Derace Kingsley. To trace his wife. She skipped out on him a month ago. She started from here. So I started from here. She's supposed to have gone away with a man. The man denies it. I thought maybe something up here might give me a lead."

"And did anything?"

"No. She's traced pretty definitely as far as San Bernardino and then El Paso. There the trail ends. But I've only just started."

Patton stood up and unlocked the cabin door. The spicy smell of the pines surged in. He spat outdoors and sat down again and rumpled the mousy brown hair under his Stetson. His head with the hat off had the indecent look of heads that are seldom without hats.

"You didn't have no interest in Bill Chess at all?"

"None whatever."

"I guess you fellows do a lot of divorce business," he said. "Kind of smelly work, to my notion."

I let that ride.

"Kingsley wouldn't have asked help from the police to find his wife, would he?"

"Hardly," I said. "He knows her too well."

"None of what you've been saying don't hardly explain your wanting to search Bill's cabin," he said judiciously.

"I'm just a great guy to poke around."

"Hell," he said, "you can do better than that."

"Say I am interested in Bill Chess then. But only because he's in trouble and rather a pathetic case—in spite of being a good deal of a heel. If he murdered his wife, there's something here to point that way. If he didn't, there's something to point that way too."

He held his head sideways, like a watchful bird. "As for instance what kind of thing?"

"Clothes, personal jewelry, toilet articles, whatever a woman takes with her when she goes away, not intending to come back."

He leaned back slowly. "But she didn't go away, son."

"Then the stuff should be still here. But if it was still here, Bill would have noticed she hadn't taken it. He would know she hadn't gone away."

"By gum, I don't like it either way," he said.

"But if he murdered her," I said, "then he would have to get rid of the things she ought to have taken with her, if she had gone away."

"And how do you figure he would do that, son?" The yellow lamplight made bronze of one side of his face.

"I understand she had a Ford car of her own. Except for that I'd expect him to burn what he could burn and bury what he could not burn out in the woods. Sinking it in the lake might be dangerous. But he couldn't burn or bury her car. Could he drive it?"

Patton looked surprised. "Sure. He can't bend his right leg at the knee, so he couldn't use the footbrake very handy. But he could get by with the handbrake. All that's different on Bill's own Ford is the brake pedal is set over on the left side of the post, close to the clutch, so he can shove them both down with one foot."

I shook ash from my cigarette into a small blue jar that had once contained a pound of orange honey, according to the small gilt label on it.

"Getting rid of the car would be his big problem," I said. "Wherever he took it he would have to get back, and he would rather not be seen coming back. And if he simply abandoned it on a street, say, down in San Bernardino, it would be found and identified very quickly. He wouldn't want that either. The best stunt would be to unload it on a hot car dealer, but he probably doesn't know one. So the chances are he hid it in the woods within walking distance of here. And walking distance for him would not be very far."

"For a fellow that claims not to be interested, you're doing some pretty close figuring on all this," Patton said dryly. "So now you've got the car hid out in the woods. What then?"

"He has to consider the possibility of its being found. The woods are lonely, but rangers and woodcutters get around in them from time to time. If the car is found, it would be better for Muriel's stuff to be found in it. That would give him a couple of outs—neither one very brilliant but both at least possible. One, that she was murdered by some unknown party who fixed things to implicate Bill when and if the murder was discovered. Two, that Muriel did actually commit suicide, but fixed things so that he would be blamed. A revenge suicide."

Patton thought all this over with calm and care. He went to the door to unload again. He sat down and rumpled his hair again. He looked at me with solid scepticism.

"The first one's possible like you say," he admitted. "But only just, and I don't have anybody in mind for the job. There's that little matter of the note to be got over."

I shook my head. "Say Bill already had the note from another time. Say she went away, as he thought, without leaving a note. After a month had gone by without any word from her he might be just worried and uncertain enough to show the note, feeling it might be some protection to him in case anything had happened to her. He didn't say any of this, but he could have had it in his mind."

Patton shook his head. He didn't like it. Neither did I. He said slowly: "As to your other notion, it's just plain crazy. Killing yourself and fixing things so as somebody else would get accused of murdering you don't fit in with my simple ideas of human nature at all."

"Then your ideas of human nature are too simple," I said. "Because it has been done, and when it has been done, it has nearly always been done by a woman."

"Nope," he said, "I'm a man fifty-seven years old and I've seen a lot of crazy people, but I don't go for that worth a peanut shell. What I like is that she did plan to go away and did write the note, but he caught her before she got clear and saw red and finished her off. Then he would have to do all them things we been talking about."

"I never met her," I said. "So I wouldn't have any idea what she would be likely to do. Bill said he met her in a place in Riverside something over a year ago. She may have had a long and complicated history before that. What kind of girl was she?"

"A mighty cute little blonde when she fixed herself up. She kind of let herself go with Bill. A quiet girl, with a face that kept its secrets. Bill says she had a temper, but I never seen any of it. I seen plenty of nasty temper in him."

"And did you think she looked like the photo of somebody called Mildred Haviland?"

His jaws stopped munching and his mouth became almost primly tight. Very slowly he started chewing again.

"By gum," he said, "I'll be mighty careful to look under the bed before I crawl in tonight. To make sure you ain't there. Where did you get that information?"

"A nice little girl called Birdie Keppel told me. She was interviewing me in the course of her spare time newspaper job. She happened to mention that an L.A. cop named De Soto was showing the photo around."

Patton smacked his thick knee and hunched his shoulders forward.

"I done wrong there," he said soberly, "I made one of my mistakes. This big bruiser showed his picture to darn near everybody in town before he showed it to me. That made me kind of sore. It looked some like Muriel, but not enough to be sure by any manner of means. I asked him what she was wanted for. He said it was police business. I said I was in that way of business myself, in an ignorant countrified kind of way. He said his instructions were to locate the lady and that was all he knew. Maybe he did wrong to take me up short like that. So I guess I done wrong to tell him I didn't know anybody that looked like his little picture."

The big calm man smiled vaguely at the corner of the ceiling, then brought his eyes down and looked at me steadily.

"I'll thank you to respect this confidence, Mr. Marlowe. You done right nicely in your figuring too. You ever happen to go over to Coon Lake?"

"Never heard of it."

"Back about a mile," he said, pointing over his shoulder with a thumb, "there's a little narrow wood road turns over west. You can just drive it and miss the trees. It climbs about five hundred feet in another mile and comes out by Coon Lake. Pretty little place. Folks go up there to picnic once in a while, but not often. It's hard on tires. There's two three small shallow lakes full of reeds. There's snow up there even now in the shady places. There's a bunch of old handhewn log cabins that's been falling down ever since I recall, and there's a big broken down frame building that Montclair University used to use for a summer camp maybe ten years back. They ain't used it in a very long time. This building sits back from the lakes in heavy timber. Round at the back of it there's a wash house with an old rusty boiler and along of that there's a big woodshed with a sliding door hung on rollers. It was built for a garage but they kept their wood in it and they locked it up out of season. Wood's one of the few things people will steal up here, but folks who might steal it off a pile wouldn't break a lock to get it. I guess you know what I found in that woodshed."

"I thought you went down to San Bernardino."

"Changed my mind. Didn't seem right to let Bill ride down there with his wife's body in the back of the car. So I sent it down in Doc's ambulance and I sent Andy down with Bill. I figured I kind of ought to look around a little more before I put things up to the sheriff and the coroner."

"Muriel's car was in the woodshed?"

"Yep. And two unlocked suitcases in the car. Packed with clothes and packed kind of hasty, I thought. Women's clothes. The point is, son, no stranger would have known about that place."

I agreed with him. He put his hand into the slanting side pocket of his jerkin and brought out a small twist of tissue paper. He opened it up on his palm and held the hand out flat.

"Take a look at this."

I went over and looked. What lay on the tissue was a thin gold chain with a tiny lock hardly larger than a link of the chain. The gold had been snipped through, leaving the lock intact. The chain seemed to be about seven inches long. There was white powder sticking to both chain and paper.

"Where would you guess I found that?" Patton asked.

I picked the chain up and tried to fit the cut ends together. They didn't fit. I made no comment on that, but moistened a finger and touched the powder and tasted it.

"In a can or box of confectioner's sugar," I said. "The chain is an anklet. Some women never take them off, like wedding rings. Whoever took this one off didn't have the key."

"What do you make of it?"

"Nothing much," I said. "There wouldn't be any point in Bill cutting it off Muriel's ankle and leaving that green necklace on her neck. There wouldn't be any point in Muriel cutting it off herself—assuming she had lost the key—and hiding it to be found. A search thorough enough to find it wouldn't be made unless her body was found first. If Bill cut it off, he would have thrown it into the lake. But if Muriel wanted to keep it and yet hide it from Bill, there's some sense in the place where it was hidden."

Patton looked puzzled this time. "Why is that?"

"Because it's a woman's hiding place. Confectioner's sugar is used to make cake icing. A man would never look there. Pretty clever of you to find it, sheriff."

He grinned a little sheepishly. "Hell, I knocked the box over and some of the sugar spilled," he said. "Without that I don't guess I ever would have found it." He rolled the paper up again and slipped it back into his pocket. He stood up with an air of finality.

"You staying up here or going back to town, Mr. Marlowe?"

"Back to town. Until you want me for the inquest. I suppose you will."

"That's up to the coroner, of course. If you'll kind of shut that window you bust in, I'll put this lamp out and lock up."

I did what he said and he snapped his flash on and put out the lamp. We went out and he felt the cabin door to make sure the lock had caught. He closed the screen softly and stood looking across the moonlit lake.

"I don't figure Bill meant to kill her," he said sadly. "He could choke a girl to death without meaning to at all. He has mighty strong hands. Once done he has to use what brains God gave him to cover up what he done. I feel real bad about it, but that don't alter the facts and the probabilities. It's simple and natural and the simple and natural things usually turn out to be right."

I said: "I should think he would have run away. I don't see how he could stand it to stay here."

Patton spat into the black velvet shadow of a manzanita bush. He said slowly: "He had a government pension and he would have to run away from that too. And most men can stand what they've got to stand, when it steps up and looks them straight in the eye. Like they're doing all over the world right now. Well, goodnight to you. I'm going to walk down to that little pier again and stand there awhile in the moonlight and feel bad. A night like this, and we got to think about murders."

He moved quietly off into the shadows and became one of them himself. I stood there until he was out of sight and then went back to the locked gate and climbed over it. I got into the car and drove back down the road looking for a place to hide.

12

Three hundred yards from the gate a narrow track, sifted over with brown oak leaves from last fall, curved around a granite boulder and disappeared. I followed it around and bumped along the stones of the outcrop for fifty or sixty feet, then swung the car around a tree and set it pointing back the way it had come. I cut the lights and switched off the motor and sat there waiting.

Half an hour passed. Without tobacco it seemed a long time. Then far off I heard a car motor start up and grow louder and the white beam of headlights passed below me on the road. The sound faded into the distance and a faint dry tang of dust hung in the air for a while after it was gone.

I got out of my car and walked back to the gate and to the Chess cabin. A hard push opened the sprung window this time. I climbed in again and let myself down to the floor and poked the flash I had brought across the room to the table lamp. I switched the lamp on and listened a moment, heard nothing, and went out to the kitchen. I switched on a hanging bulb over the sink.

The woodbox beside the stove was neatly piled with split wood. There were no dirty dishes in the sink, no foul-smelling pots on the stove. Bill Chess, lonely or not, kept his house in good order. A door opened from the kitchen into the bedroom, and from that a very narrow door led into a tiny bathroom which had evidently been built on to the cabin fairly recently. The clean celotex lining showed that. The bathroom told me nothing.

The bedroom contained a double bed, a pinewood dresser with a round mirror on the wall above it, a bureau, two straight chairs, and a tin waste basket. There were two oval rag rugs on the floor, one on each side of the bed. On the walls Bill Chess had tacked up a set of war maps from the National Geographic. There was a silly-looking red and white flounce on the dressing table.

I poked around in the drawers. An imitation leather trinket box with an assortment of gaudy costume jewelry had not been taken away. There was the usual stuff women use on their faces and fingernails and eyebrows, and it seemed to me that there was too much of it. But that was just guessing. The bureau contained both man's and woman's clothes, not a great deal of either. Bill Chess had a very noisy check shirt with starched matching collar, among other things.

Underneath a sheet of blue tissue paper in one corner I found something I didn't like. A seemingly brand new peach-colored silk slip trimmed with lace. Silk slips were not being left behind that year, not by any woman in her senses.

This looked bad for Bill Chess. I wondered what Patton had thought of it.

I went back to the kitchen and prowled the open shelves above and beside the sink. They were thick with cans and jars of household staples. The confectioner's sugar was in a square brown box with a torn corner. Patton had made an attempt to clean up what was spilled. Near the sugar were salt, borax, baking soda, cornstarch, brown sugar and so on. Something might be hidden in any of them.

Something that had been clipped from a chain anklet whose cut ends did not fit together.

I shut my eyes and poked a finger out at random and it came to rest on the baking soda. I got a newspaper from the back of the woodbox and spread it out and dumped the soda out of the box. I stirred it around with a spoon. There seemed to be an indecent lot of baking soda, but that was all there was. I funnelled it back into the box and tried the borax. Nothing but borax. Third time lucky. I tried the cornstarch. It made too much fine dust, and there was nothing but cornstarch.

The sound of distant steps froze me to the ankles. I reached up and yanked the light out and dodged back into the living room and reached for the lamp switch. Much too late to be of any use, of course. The steps sounded again, soft and cautious. The hackles rose on my neck.

I waited in the dark, with the flash in my left hand. A deadly long two minutes crept by. I spent some of the time breathing, but not all.

It wouldn't be Patton. He would walk up to the door and open it and tell me off. The careful quiet steps seemed to move this way and that, a movement, a long pause, another movement, another long pause. I sneaked across to the door and twisted the knob silently. I yanked the door wide and stabbed out with the flash.

It made golden lamps of a pair of eyes. There was a leaping movement and a quick thudding of hoofs back among the trees. It was only an inquisitive deer.

I closed the door again and followed my flashlight beam back into the kitchen. The small round glow rested squarely on the box of confectioner's sugar.

I put the light on again, lifted the box down and emptied it on the newspaper.

Patton hadn't gone deep enough. Having found one thing by accident he had assumed that was all there was. He hadn't seemed to notice that there ought to be something else.

Another twist of white tissue showed in the fine white powdered sugar. I shook it clean and unwound it. It contained a tiny gold heart, no larger than a woman's little fingernail.

I spooned the sugar back into the box and put the box back on the shelf and crumpled the piece of newspaper into the stove. I went back to the living room and turned the table lamp on. Under that brighter light the tiny engraving on the back of the little gold heart could just be read without a magnifying glass.

It was in script. It read: *Al to Mildred. June* 28*th* 1938. *With all my love.*

Al to Mildred. Al somebody to Mildred Haviland. Mildred Haviland was Muriel Chess. Muriel Chess was dead—two weeks after a cop named De Soto had been looking for her.

I stood there, holding it, wondering what it had to do with me. Wondering, and not having the faintest glimmer of an idea.

I wrapped it up again and left the cabin and drove back to the village.

Patton was in his office telephoning when I got around there. The door was locked. I had to wait while he talked. After a while he hung up and came to unlock the door.

I walked in past him and put the twist of tissue paper on his counter and opened it up.

"You didn't go deep enough into the powdered sugar," I said.

He looked at the little gold heart, looked at me, went around behind the counter and got a cheap magnifying glass off his desk. He studied the back of the heart. He put the glass down and frowned at me.

"Might have known if you wanted to search that cabin, you was going to do it," he said gruffly. "I ain't going to have trouble with you, am I, son?"

"You ought to have noticed that the cut ends of the chain didn't fit," I told him.

He looked at me sadly. "Son, I don't have your eyes." He pushed the little heart around with his square blunt finger. He stared at me and said nothing.

I said: "If you were thinking that anklet meant something Bill could have been jealous about, so was I—provided he ever saw it. But strictly on the cuff I'm willing to bet he never did see it and that he never heard of Mildred Haviland."

Patton said slowly: "Looks like maybe I owe this De Soto party an apology, don't it?"

"If you ever see him," I said.

He gave me another long empty stare and I gave it right back to him. "Don't tell me, son," he said. "Let me guess all for myself that you got a brand new idea about it."

"Yeah. Bill didn't murder his wife."

"No?"

"No. She was murdered by somebody out of her past. Somebody who had lost track of her and then found it again and found her married to another man and didn't like it. Somebody who knew the country up here—as hundreds of people do who don't live here—and knew a good place to hide the car and the clothes. Somebody who hated and could dissimulate. Who persuaded her to go away with him and when everything was ready and the note was written, took her around the throat and gave her what he thought was coming to her and put her in the lake and went his way. Like it?"

"Well," he said judiciously, "it does make things kind of complicated, don't you think? But there ain't anything impossible about it. Not one bit impossible."

"When you get tired of it, let me know. I'll have something else," I said.

"I'll just be doggone sure you will," he said, and for the first time since I had met him he laughed.

I said goodnight again and went out, leaving him there moving his mind around with the ponderous energy of a homesteader digging up a stump.

13

At somewhere around eleven I got down to the bottom of the grade and parked in one of the diagonal slots at the side of the Prescott Hotel in San Bernardino. I pulled an overnight bag out of the boot and had taken three steps with it when a bellhop in braided pants and a white shirt and black bow tie yanked it out of my hand.

The clerk on duty was an eggheaded man with no interest in me or in anything else. He wore parts of a white linen suit and he yawned as he handed me the desk pen and looked off into the distance as if remembering his childhood.

The hop and I rode a four by four elevator to the second floor and walked a couple of blocks around corners. As we walked it got hotter and hotter. The hop unlocked a door into a boy's size room with one window on an air shaft. The air-conditioner inlet up in the corner of the ceiling was about the size of a woman's handkerchief. The bit of ribbon tied to it fluttered weakly, just to show that something was moving.

The hop was tall and thin and yellow and not young and as cool as a slice of chicken in aspic. He moved his gum around in his face, put my bag on a chair, looked up at the grating and then stood looking at me. He had eyes the color of a drink of water.

"Maybe I ought to have asked for one of the dollar rooms," I said. "This one seems a mite close-fitting."

"I reckon you're lucky to get one at all. This town's fair bulgin' at the seams."

"Bring us up some ginger ale and glasses and ice," I said.

"Us?"

"That is, if you happen to be a drinking man."

"I reckon I might take a chance this late."

He went out. I took off my coat, tie, shirt and undershirt and walked around in the warm draft from the open door. The draft smelled of hot iron. I went into the bathroom sideways—it was that kind of bathroom—and doused myself with tepid cold water. I was breathing a little more freely when the tall languid hop returned with a tray. He shut the door and I brought out a bottle of rye. He mixed a couple of drinks and we made the usual insincere smiles over them and drank. The perspiration started from the back of my neck down my spine and was halfway to my socks before I put the glass down. But I felt better all the same. I sat on the bed and looked at the hop.

"How long can you stay?"

"Doin' what?"

"Remembering."

"I ain't a damn bit of use at it," he said.

"I have money to spend," I said, "in my own peculiar way." I got my wallet unstuck from the lower part of my back and spread tired-looking dollar bills along the bed.

"I beg yore pardon," the hop said. "I reckon you might be a dick."

"Don't be silly," I said. "You never saw a dick playing solitaire with his own money. You might call me an investigator."

"I'm interested," he said. "The likker makes my mind work."

I gave him a dollar bill. "Try that on your mind. And can I call you Big Tex from Houston?"

"Amarillo," he said. "Not that it matters. And how do you like my Texas drawl? It makes me sick, but I find people go for it."

"Stay with it," I said. "It never lost anybody a dollar yet."

He grinned and tucked the folded dollar neatly into the watch pocket of his pants.

"What were you doing on Friday, June 12th?" I asked him. "Late afternoon or evening. It was a Friday."

He sipped his drink and thought, shaking the ice around gently and drinking past his gum. "I was right here, six to twelve shift," he said.

"A woman, slim, pretty blonde, checked in here and stayed until time for the night train to El Paso. I think she must have taken that because she was in El Paso Sunday morning. She came here driving a Packard Clipper registered to Crystal Grace Kingsley, 965 Carson Drive, Beverly Hills. She may have registered as that, or under some other name, and she may not have registered at all. Her car is still in the hotel garage. I'd like to talk to the boys that checked her in and out. That wins another dollar—just thinking about it."

I separated another dollar from my exhibit and it went into his pocket with a sound like caterpillars fighting.

"Can do," he said calmly.

He put his glass down and left the room, closing the door. I finished my drink and made another. I went into the bathroom and used some more warm water on my torso. While I was doing this the telephone on the wall tinkled and I wedged myself into the minute space between the bathroom door and the bed to answer it.

The Texas voice said: "That was Sonny. He was inducted last week. Another boy we call Les checked her out. He's here."

"Okay. Shoot him up, will you?"

I was playing with my second drink and thinking about the third when a knock came and I opened the door to a small, green-eyed rat with a tight, girlish mouth.

He came in almost dancing and stood looking at me with a faint sneer.

"Drink?"

"Sure," he said coldly. He poured himself a large one and added a whisper of ginger ale, put the mixture down in one long swallow, tucked a cigarette between his smooth little lips and snapped a match alight while it was coming up from his pocket. He blew smoke and went on staring at me. The corner of his eye caught the money on the bed, without looking directly at it. Over the pocket of his shirt, instead of a number, the word *Captain* was stitched.

"You Les?" I asked him.

"No." He paused. "We don't like dicks here," he added. "We don't have one of our own and we don't care to bother with dicks that are working for other people."

"Thanks," I said. "That will be all."

"Huh?" The small mouth twisted unpleasantly.

"Beat it," I said.

"I thought you wanted to see me," he sneered.

"You're the bell captain?"

"Check."

"I wanted to buy you a drink. I wanted to give you a buck. Here." I held it out to him. "Thanks for coming up."

He took the dollar and pocketed it, without a word of thanks. He hung there, smoke trailing from his nose, his eyes tight and mean.

"What I say here goes," he said.

"It goes as far as you can push it," I said. "And that couldn't be very far. You had your drink and you had your graft. Now you can scram out."

He turned with a swift tight shrug and slipped out of the room noiselessly.

Four minutes passed, then another knock, very light. The tall boy came in grinning. I walked away from him and sat on the bed again.

"You didn't take to Les, I reckon?"

"Not a great deal. Is he satisfied?"

"I reckon so. You know what captains are. They have to have their cut. Maybe you better call me Les, Mr. Marlowe."

"So you checked her out."

"No, that was all a stall. She never checked in at the desk. But I remember the Packard. She gave me a dollar to put it away for her and to look after her stuff until train time. She ate dinner here. A dollar gets you remembered in this town. And there's been talk about the car bein' left so long."

"What was she like to look at?"

"She wore a black and white outfit, mostly white, and a panama hat with a black and white band. She was a neat blonde lady like you said. Later on she took a hack to the station. I put her bags into it for her. They had initials on them but I'm sorry I can't remember the initials."

"I'm glad you can't," I said. "It would be too good. Have a drink. How old would she be?"

He rinsed the other glass and mixed a civilized drink for himself.

"It's mighty hard to tell a woman's age these days," he said. "I reckon she was about thirty, or a little more or a little less."

I dug in my coat for the snapshot of Crystal and Lavery on the beach and handed it to him.

He looked at it steadily and held it away from his eyes, then close.

"You won't have to swear to it in court," I said.

He nodded. "I wouldn't want to. These small blondes are so much of a pattern that a change of clothes or light or makeup makes them all alike or all different." He hesitated, staring at the snapshot.

"What's worrying you?" I asked.

"I'm thinking about the gent in this snap. He enter into it at all?"

"Go on with that," I said.

"I think this fellow spoke to her in the lobby, and had dinner with her. A tall good-lookin' jasper, built like a fast light-heavy. He went in the hack with her too."

"Quite sure about that?"

He looked at the money on the bed.

"Okay, how much does it cost?" I asked wearily.

He stiffened, laid the snapshot down and drew the two folded bills from his pocket and tossed them on the bed.

"I thank you for the drink," he said, "and to hell with you." He started for the door.

"Oh sit down and don't be so touchy," I growled.

He sat down and looked at me stiff-eyed.

"And don't be so damn southern," I said. "I've been knee deep in hotel hops for a lot of years. If I've met one who wouldn't pull a gag, that's fine. But you can't expect me to expect to meet one that wouldn't pull a gag."

He grinned slowly and nodded quickly. He picked the snapshot up again and looked at me over it.

"This gent takes a solid photo," he said. "Much more so than the lady. But there was another little item that made me remember him. I got the impression the lady didn't quite like him walking up to her so openly in the lobby."

I thought that over and decided it didn't mean anything much. He might have been late or have missed some earlier appointment. I said:

"There's a reason for that. Did you notice what jewelry the lady was wearing? Rings, ear-pendants, anything that looked conspicuous or valuable?"

He hadn't noticed, he said.

"Was her hair long or short, straight or waved or curly, natural blonde or bleached?"

He laughed. "Hell, you can't tell that last point, Mr. Marlowe. Even when it's natural they want it lighter. As to the rest, my recollection is it was rather long, like they're wearing it now and turned in a little at the bottom and rather straight. But I could be wrong." He looked at the snapshot again. "She has it bound back here. You can't tell a thing."

"That's right," I said. "And the only reason I asked you was to make sure you didn't over-observe. The guy that sees too much detail is just as unreliable a witness as the guy that doesn't see any. He's nearly always making half of it up. You check just about right, considering the circumstances. Thanks very much."

I gave him back his two dollars and a five to keep them company. He thanked me, finished his drink and left softly. I finished mine and washed off again and decided I would rather drive home than sleep in that hole. I put my shirt and coat on again and went downstairs with my bag.

The redheaded rat of a captain was the only hop in the lobby. I carried my bag over to the desk and he didn't move to take it off my hands. The eggheaded clerk separated me from two dollars without even looking at me.

"Two bucks to spend the night in this manhole," I said, "when for free I could have a nice airy ashcan."

The clerk yawned, got a delayed reaction, and said brightly: "It gets quite cool here about three in the morning. From then on until eight, or even nine, it's quite pleasant."

I wiped the back of my neck and staggered out to the car. Even the seat of the car was hot, at midnight.

I got home about two-forty-five and Hollywood was an icebox. Even Pasadena had felt cool.

14

I dreamed I was far down in the depths of icy green water with a corpse under my arm. The corpse had long blond hair that kept floating around in front of my face. An enormous fish with bulging eyes and a bloated body and scales shining with putrescence swam around leering like an elderly roué. Just as I was about to burst from lack of the air, the corpse came alive under my arm and got away from me and then I was fighting with the fish and the corpse was rolling over and over in the water, spinning its long hair.

I woke up with a mouth full of sheet and both hands hooked on the head-frame of the bed and pulling hard. The muscles ached when I let go and lowered them. I got up and walked the room and lit a cigarette, feeling the carpet with bare toes. When I had finished the cigarette, I went back to bed.

It was nine o'clock when I woke up again. The sun was on my face. The room was hot. I showered and shaved and partly dressed and made the morning toast and eggs and coffee in the dinette. While I was finishing up there was a knock at the apartment door.

I went to open it with my mouth full of toast. It was a lean, serious-looking man in a severe gray suit.

"Floyd Greer, lieutenant, Central Detective Bureau," he said and walked into the room.

He put out a dry hand and I shook it. He sat down on the edge of a chair, the way they do, and turned his hat in his hands and looked at me with the quiet stare they have.

"We got a call from San Bernardino about that business up at Puma Lake. Drowned woman. Seems you were on hand when the body was discovered."

I nodded and said, "Have some coffee?"

"No thanks. I had breakfast two hours ago."

I got my coffee and sat down across the room from him.

"They asked us to look you up," he said. "Give them a line on you."

"Sure."

"So we did that. Seems like you have a clean bill of health so far as we are concerned. Kind of coincidence a man in your line would be around when the body was found."

"I'm like that," I said. "Lucky."

"So I just thought I'd drop around and say howdy."

"That's fine. Glad to know you, lieutenant."

"Kind of a coincidence," he said again, nodding. "You up there on business, so to speak?"

"If I was," I said, "my business had nothing to do with the girl who was drowned, so far as I know."

"But you couldn't be sure?"

"Until you've finished with a case, you can't ever be quite sure what its ramifications are, can you?"

"That's right." He circled his hat brim through his fingers again, like a bashful cowboy. There was nothing bashful about his eyes. "I'd like to feel sure that if these ramifications you speak of happened to take in this drowned woman's affairs, you would put us wise."

"I hope you can rely on that," I said.

He bulged his lower lip with his tongue. "We'd like a little more than a hope. At the present time you don't care to say?"

"At the present time I don't know anything that Patton doesn't know."

"Who's he?"

"The constable up at Puma Point."

The lean serious man smiled tolerantly. He cracked a knuckle and after a pause said: "The San Berdoo D. A. will likely want to talk to you—before the inquest. But that won't be very soon. Right now they're trying to get a set of prints. We lent them a technical man."

"That will be tough. The body's pretty far gone."

"It's done all the time," he said. "They worked out the system back in New York where they're all the time pulling in floaters. They cut patches of skin off the fingers and harden them in a tanning solution and make stamps. It works well enough as a rule."

"You think this woman had a record of some kind?"

"Why, we always take prints of a corpse," he said. "You ought to know that."

I said: "I didn't know the lady. If you thought I did and that was why I was up there, there's nothing in it."

"But you wouldn't care to say just why you *were* up there," he persisted.

"So you think I'm lying to you," I said.

He spun his hat on a bony forefinger. "You got me wrong, Mr. Marlowe. We don't think anything at all. What we do is investigate and find out. This stuff is just routine. You ought to know that. You been around long enough." He stood up and put his hat on. "You might let me know if you have to leave town. I'd be obliged."

I said I would and went to the door with him. He went out with a duck of his head and a sad half-smile. I watched him drift languidly down the hall and punch the elevator button.

I went back out to the dinette to see if there was any more coffee. There was about two-thirds of a cup. I added cream and sugar and carried my cup over to the telephone. I dialed Police Headquarters downtown and asked for the Detective Bureau and then for Lieutenant Floyd Greer.

The voice said: "Lieutenant Greer is not in the office. Anybody else do?"

"De Soto in?"

"Who?"

I repeated the name.

"What's his rank and department?"

"Plain clothes something or other."

"Hold the line."

I waited. The burring male voice came back after a while and said: "What's the gag? We don't have a De Soto on the roster. Who's this talking?"

I hung up, finished my coffee and dialed the number of Derace Kingsley's office. The smooth and cool Miss Fromsett said he had just come in and put me through without a murmur.

"Well," he said, loud and forceful at the beginning of a fresh day, "what did you find out at the hotel?"

"She was there all right. And Lavery met her there. The hop who gave me the dope brought Lavery into it himself, without any prompting from me. He had dinner with her and went with her in a cab to the railroad station."

"Well, I ought to have known he was lying," Kingsley said slowly. "I got the impression he was surprised when I told him about the telegram from El Paso. I was just letting my impressions get too sharp. Anything else?"

"Not there. I had a cop calling on me this morning, giving me the usual looking over and warning not to leave town without letting him know. Trying to find out why I went to Puma Point. I didn't tell him and as he wasn't even aware of Jim Patton's existence, it's evident that Patton didn't tell anybody."

"Jim would do his best to be decent about it," Kingsley said. "Why were you asking me last night about some name—Mildred something or other?"

I told him, making it brief. I told him about Muriel Chess's car and clothes being found and where.

"That looks bad for Bill," he said. "I know Coon Lake myself, but it would never have occurred to me to use that old woodshed—or even that there was an old woodshed. It not only looks bad, it looks premeditated."

"I disagree with that. Assuming he knew the country well enough it wouldn't take him any time to search his mind for a likely hiding place. He was very restricted as to distance."

"Maybe. What do you plan to do now?" he asked.

"Go up against Lavery again, of course."

He agreed that that was the thing to do. He added: "This other, tragic as it is, is really no business of ours, is it?"

"Not unless your wife knew something about it."

His voice sounded sharply, saying: "Look here, Marlowe, I think I can understand your detective instinct to tie everything that happens into one compact knot, but don't let it run away with you. Life isn't like that at all—not life as I have known it. Better leave the affairs of the Chess family to the police and keep your brains working on the Kingsley family."

"Okay," I said.

"I don't mean to be domineering," he said.

I laughed heartily, said goodby, and hung up. I finished dressing and went down to the basement for the Chrysler. I started for Bay City again.

15

I drove past the intersection of Altair Street to where the cross street continued to the edge of the canyon and ended in a semi-circular parking place with a sidewalk and a white wooden guard fence around it. I sat there in the car a little while, thinking, looking out to sea and admiring the blue gray fall of the foothills towards the ocean. I was trying to make up my mind whether to try handling Lavery with a feather or go on using the back of my hand and the edge of my tongue. I decided I could lose nothing by the soft approach. If that didn't produce for me—and I didn't think it would—nature could take its course and we could bust up the furniture.

The paved alley that ran along halfway down the hill below the houses on the outer edge was empty. Below that, on the next hillside street, a couple of kids were throwing a boomerang up the slope and chasing it with the usual amount of elbowing and mutual insult. Farther down still a house was enclosed in trees and a red brick wall. There was a glimpse of washing on the line in the backyard and two pigeons strutted along the slope of the roof bobbing their heads. A blue and tan bus trundled along the street in front of the brick house and stopped and a very old man got off with slow care and settled himself firmly on the ground and tapped with a heavy cane before he started to crawl back up the slope.

The air was clearer than yesterday. The morning was full of peace. I left the car where it was and walked along Altair Street to No. 623.

The venetian blinds were down across the front windows and the place had a sleepy look. I stepped down over the Korean moss and punched the bell and saw that the door was not quite shut. It had dropped in its frame, as most of our doors do, and the spring bolt hung a little on the lower edge of the lock plate. I remembered that it had wanted to stick the day before, when I was leaving.

I gave the door a little push and it moved inward with a light click. The room beyond was dim, but there was some light from west windows. Nobody answered my ring. I didn't ring again. I pushed the door a little wider and stepped inside.

The room had a hushed warm smell, the smell of late morning in a house not yet opened up. The bottle of Vat 69 on the round table by the davenport was almost empty and another full bottle waited beside it. The copper ice bucket had a little water in the bottom. Two glasses had been used, and half a siphon of carbonated water.

I fixed the door about as I had found it and stood there and listened. If Lavery was away I thought I would take a chance and frisk the joint. I didn't have anything much on him, but it was probably enough to keep him from calling the cops.

In the silence time passed. It passed in the dry whirr of the electric clock on the mantel, in the far-off toot of an auto horn on Aster Drive, in the hornet drone of a plane over the foothills across the canyon, in the sudden lurch and growl of the electric refrigerator in the kitchen.

I went farther into the room and stood peering around and listening and hearing nothing except those fixed sounds belonging to the house and having nothing to do with the humans in it. I started along the rug towards the archway at the back.

A hand in a glove appeared on the slope of the white metal railing, at the edge of the archway, where the stairs went down. It appeared and stopped.

It moved and a woman's hat showed, then her head. The woman came quietly up the stairs. She came all the way up, turned through the arch and still didn't seem to see me. She was a slender woman of uncertain age, with untidy brown hair, a scarlet mess of a mouth, too much rouge on her cheekbones, shadowed eyes. She wore a blue tweed suit that looked like the dickens with the purple hat that was doing its best to hang on to the side of her head.

She saw me and didn't stop or change expression in the slightest degree. She came slowly on into the room, holding her right hand away from her body. Her left hand wore the brown glove I had seen on the railing. The right hand glove that matched it was wrapped around the butt of a small automatic.

She stopped then and her body arched back and a quick distressful sound came out of her mouth. Then she giggled, a high nervous giggle. She pointed the gun at me, and came steadily on.

I kept on looking at the gun and not screaming.

The woman came close. When she was close enough to be confidential she pointed the gun at my stomach and said:

"All I wanted was my rent. The place seems well taken care of. Nothing broken. He has always been a good tidy careful tenant. I just didn't want him to get too far behind in the rent."

A fellow with a kind of strained and unhappy voice said politely: "How far behind is he?"

"Three months," she said. "Two hundred and forty dollars. Eighty dollars is very reasonable for a place as well furnished as this. I've had a little trouble collecting before, but it always came out very well. He promised me a check this morning. Over the telephone. I mean he promised to give it to me this morning."

"Over the telephone," I said. "This morning."

I shuffled around a bit in an inconspicuous sort of way. The idea was to get close enough to make a side swipe at the gun, knock it outwards, and then jump in fast before she could bring it back in line. I've never had a lot of luck with the technique, but you have to try it once in a while. This looked like the time to try it.

I made about six inches, but not nearly enough for a first down. I said: "And you're the owner?" I didn't look at the gun directly. I had a faint, a very faint hope that she didn't know she was pointing it at me.

"Why, certainly. I'm Mrs. Fallbrook. Who did you think I was?"

"Well, I thought you might be the owner," I said. "You talking about the rent and all. But I didn't know your name." Another eight inches. Nice smooth work. It would be a shame to have it wasted.

"And who are you, if I may enquire?"

"I just came about the car payment," I said. "The door was open just a teensy weensy bit and I kind of shoved in. I don't know why."

I made a face like a man from the finance company coming about the car payment. Kind of tough, but ready to break into a sunny smile.

"You mean Mr. Lavery is behind in his car payments?" she asked, looking worried.

"A little. Not a great deal," I said soothingly.

I was all set now. I had the reach and I ought to have the speed. All it needed was a clean sharp sweep inside the gun and outward. I started to take my left foot out of the rug.

"You know," she said, "it's funny about this gun. I found it on the stairs. Nasty oily things, aren't they? And the stair carpet is a very nice gray chenille. Quite expensive."

And she handed me the gun.

My hand went out for it, as stiff as an eggshell, almost as brittle. I took the gun. She sniffed with distaste at the glove which had been wrapped around the butt. She went on talking in exactly the same tone of cockeyed reasonableness. My knees cracked, relaxing.

"Well of course it's much easier for you," she said. "About the car, I mean. You can just take it away, if you have to. But taking a house with nice furniture in it isn't so easy. It takes time and money to evict a tenant. There is apt to be bitterness and things get damaged, sometimes on purpose. The rug on this floor cost over two hundred dollars, secondhand. It's only a jute rug, but it has a lovely coloring, don't you think? You'd never know it was only jute, secondhand. But that's silly too because they're always secondhand after you've used them. And I walked over here too, to save my tires for the government. I could have taken a bus part way, but the darn things never come along except going in the wrong direction."

I hardly heard what she said. It was like surf breaking beyond a point, out of sight. The gun had my interest.

I broke the magazine out. It was empty. I turned the gun and looked into the breech. That was empty too. I sniffed the muzzle. It reeked.

I dropped the gun into my pocket. A six-shot .25 caliber automatic. Emptied out. Shot empty, and not too long ago. But not in the last half hour either.

"Has it been fired?" Mrs. Fallbrook enquired pleasantly. "I certainly hope not."

"Any reason why it should have been fired?" I asked her. The voice was steady, but the brain was still bouncing.

"Well, it was lying on the stairs," she said. "After all, people do fire them."

"How true that is," I said. "But Mr. Lavery probably had a hole in his pocket. He isn't home, is he?"

"Oh no." She shook her head and looked disappointed. "And I don't think it's very nice of him. He promised me the check and I walked over—"

"When was it you phoned him?" I asked.

"Why, yesterday evening." She frowned, not liking so many questions.

"He must have been called away," I said.

She stared at a spot between my big brown eyes.

"Look, Mrs. Fallbrook," I said. "Let's not kid around any more, Mrs. Fallbrook. Not that I don't love it. And not that I like to say this. But you didn't shoot him, did you—on account of he owed you three months' rent?"

She sat down very slowly on the edge of a chair and worked the tip of her tongue along the scarlet slash of her mouth.

"Why, what a perfectly horrid suggestion," she said angrily. "I don't think you are nice at all. Didn't you say the gun had not been fired?"

"All guns have been fired sometime. All guns have been loaded sometime. This one is not loaded now."

"Well, then—" she made an impatient gesture and sniffed at her oily glove.

"Okay, my idea was wrong. Just a gag anyway. Mr. Lavery was out and you went through the house. Being the owner, you have a key. Is that correct?"

"I didn't mean to be interfering," she said, biting a finger. "Perhaps I ought not to have done it. But I have a right to see how things are kept."

"Well, you looked. And you're sure he's not here?"

"I didn't look under the beds or in the icebox," she said coldly. "I called out from the top of the stairs when he didn't answer my ring. Then I went down to the lower hall and called out again. I even peeped into the bedroom." She lowered her eyes as if bashfully and twisted a hand on her knee.

"Well, that's that," I said.

She nodded brightly. "Yes, that's that. And what did you say your name was?"

"Vance," I said. "Philo Vance."

"And what company are you employed with, Mr. Vance?"

"I'm out of work right now," I said. "Until the police commissioner gets in a jam again."

She looked startled. "But you said you came about a car payment."

"That's just part-time work," I said. "A fill-in job."

She rose to her feet and looked at me steadily. Her voice was cold saying: "Then in that case I think you had better leave now."

I said: "I thought I might take a look around first, if you don't mind. There might be something you missed."

"I don't think that is necessary," she said. "This is my house. I'll thank you to leave now, Mr. Vance."

I said: "And if I don't leave, you'll get somebody who will. Take a chair again, Mrs. Fallbrook. I'll just glance through. This gun, you know, is kind of queer."

"But I told you I found it lying on the stairs," she said angrily. "I don't know anything else about it. I don't know anything about guns at all. I—I never shot one in my life." She opened a large blue bag and pulled a handkerchief out of it and sniffled.

"That's your story," I said. "I don't have to get stuck with it."

She put her left hand out to me with a pathetic gesture, like the erring wife in East Lynne.

"Oh, I shouldn't have come in!" she cried. "It was horrid of me. I know it was. Mr. Lavery will be furious."

"What you shouldn't have done," I said, "was let me find out the gun was empty. Up to then you were holding everything in the deck."

She stamped her foot. That was all the scene lacked. That made it perfect.

"Why, you perfectly loathsome man," she squawked. "Don't you dare touch me! Don't you take a single step towards me! I won't stay in this house another minute with you. How *dare* you be so insulting—"

She caught her voice and snapped it in mid-air like a rubber band. Then she put her head down, purple hat and all, and ran for the door. As she passed me she put a hand out as if to stiff arm me, but she wasn't near enough and I didn't move. She jerked the door wide and charged out through it and up the walk to the street. The door came slowly shut and I heard her rapid steps above the sound of its closing.

I ran a fingernail along my teeth and punched the point of my jaw with a knuckle, listening. I didn't hear anything anywhere to listen to. A six-shot automatic, fired empty.

"Something," I said out loud, "is all wrong with this scene."

The house seemed now to be abnormally still. I went along the apricot rug and through the archway to the head of the stairs. I stood there for another moment and listened again.

I shrugged and went quietly down the stairs.

16

The lower hall had a door at each end and two in the middle side by side. One of these was a linen closet and the other was locked. I went along to the end and looked in at a spare bedroom with drawn blinds and no sign of being used. I went back to the other end of the hall and stepped into a second bedroom with a wide bed, a cafe-au-lait rug, angular furniture in light wood, a box mirror over the dressing table and a long fluorescent lamp over the mirror. In the corner a crystal greyhound stood on a mirror-top table and beside him a crystal box with cigarettes in it.

Face powder was spilled around on the dressing table. There was a smear of dark lipstick on a towel hanging over the waste basket. On the bed were pillows side by side, with depressions in them that could have been made by heads. A woman's handkerchief peeped from under one pillow. A pair of sheer black pajamas lay across the foot of the bed. A rather too emphatic trace of chypre hung in the air.

I wondered what Mrs. Fallbrook had thought of all this.

I turned around and looked at myself in the long mirror of a closet door. The door was painted white and had a crystal knob. I turned the knob in my handkerchief and looked inside. The cedar-lined closet was fairly full of man's clothes. There was a nice friendly smell of tweed. The closet was not entirely full of man's clothes.

There was also a woman's black and white tailored suit, mostly white, black and white shoes under it, a panama with a black and white rolled band on a shelf above it. There were other woman's clothes, but I didn't examine them.

I shut the closet door and went out of the bedroom, holding my handkerchief ready for more doorknobs.

The door next the linen closet, the locked door, had to be the bathroom. I shook it, but it went on being locked. I bent down and saw there was a short, slit-shaped opening in the middle of the knob. I knew then that the door was fastened by pushing a button in the middle of the knob inside, and that the slit-like opening was for a metal key without wards that would spring the lock open in case somebody fainted in the bathroom, or the kids locked themselves in and got sassy.

The key for this ought to be kept on the top shelf of the linen closet, but it wasn't. I tried my knife blade, but that was too thin. I went back to the bedroom and got a flat nail file off the dresser. That worked. I opened the bathroom door.

A man's sand-colored pajamas were tossed over a painted hamper. A pair of heelless green slippers lay on the floor. There was a safety razor on the edge of the washbowl and a tube of cream with the cap off. The bathroom window was shut, and there was a pungent smell in the air that was not quite like any other smell.

Three empty shells lay bright and coppery on the nile green tiles of the bathroom floor, and there was a nice clean hole in the frosted pane of the window. To the left and a little above the window were two scarred places in the plaster where the white showed behind the paint and where something, such as a bullet, had gone in.

The shower curtain was green and white oiled silk and it hung on shiny chromium rings and it was drawn across the shower opening. I slid it aside, the rings making a thin scraping noise, which for some reason sounded indecently loud.

I felt my neck creak a little as I bent down. He was there all right —there wasn't anywhere else for him to be. He was huddled in the corner under the two shining faucets, and water dripped slowly on his chest, from the chromium showerhead.

His knees were drawn up but slack. The two holes in his naked chest were dark blue and both of them were close enough to his heart to have killed him. The blood seemed to have been washed away.

His eyes had a curiously bright and expectant look, as if he smelled the morning coffee and would be coming right out.

Nice efficient work. You have just finished shaving and stripped for the shower and you are leaning in against the shower curtain and adjusting the temperature of the water. The door opens behind you and somebody comes in. The somebody appears to have been a woman. She has a gun. You look at the gun and she shoots it.

She misses with three shots. It seems impossible, at such short range, but there it is. Maybe it happens all the time. I've been around so little.

You haven't anywhere to go. You could lunge at her and take a chance, if you were that kind of fellow, and if you were braced for it. But leaning in over the shower faucets, holding the curtains closed, you are off balance. Also you are apt to be somewhat petrified with panic, if you are at all like other people. So there isn't anywhere to go, except into the shower.

That is where you go. You go into it as far as you can, but a shower stall is a small place and the tiled wall stops you. You are backed up against the last wall there is now. You are all out of space, and you are all out of living. And then there are two more shots, possibly three, and you slide down the wall, and your eyes are not even frightened any more now. They are just the empty eyes of the dead.

She reaches in and turns the shower off. She sets the lock of the bathroom door. On her way out of the house she throws the empty gun on the stair carpet. She should worry. It is probably your gun.

Is that right? It had better be right.

I bent and pulled at his arm. Ice couldn't have been any colder or any stiffer. I went out of the bathroom, leaving it unlocked. No need to lock it now. It only makes work for the cops.

I went into the bedroom and pulled the handkerchief out from under the pillow. It was a minute piece of linen rag with a scalloped edge embroidered in red. Two small initials were stitched in the corner, in red. *A.F.*

"Adrienne Fromsett," I said. I laughed. It was a rather ghoulish laugh.

I shook the handkerchief to get some of the chypre out of it and folded it up in a tissue and put it in a pocket. I went back upstairs to the living room and poked around in the desk against the wall. The desk contained no interesting letters, phone numbers or provocative match folders. Or if it did, I didn't find them.

I looked at the phone. It was on a small table against the wall beside the fireplace. It had a long cord so that Mr. Lavery could be lying on his back on the davenport, a cigarette between his smooth brown lips, a tall cool one at the table at his side, and plenty of time for a nice long cosy conversation with a lady friend. An easy, languid, flirtatious, kidding, not too subtle and not too blunt conversation, of the sort he would be apt to enjoy.

All that wasted too. I went away from the telephone to the door and set the lock so I could come in again and shut the door tight, pulling it hard over the sill until the lock clicked. I went up the walk and stood in the sunlight looking across the street at Dr. Almore's house.

Nobody yelled or ran out of the door. Nobody blew a police whistle. Everything was quiet and sunny and calm. No cause for excitement whatever. It's only Marlowe, finding another body. He does it rather well by now. Murder-a-day Marlowe, they call him. They have the meat wagon following him around to follow up on the business he finds.

A nice enough fellow, in an ingenuous sort of way.

I walked back to the intersection and got into my car and started it and backed it and drove away from there.

17

The bellhop at the Athletic Club was back in three minutes with a nod for me to come with him. We rode up to the fourth floor and went around a corner and he showed me a half open door.

"Around to the left, sir. As quietly as you can. A few of the members are sleeping."

I went into the club library. It contained books behind glass doors and magazines on a long central table and a lighted portrait of the club's founder. But its real business seemed to be sleeping. Outward-jutting bookcases cut the room into a number of small alcoves and in the alcoves were high backed leather chairs of an incredible size and softness. In a number of the chairs old boys were snoozing peacefully, their faces violet with high blood pressure, thin racking snores coming out of their pinched noses.

I climbed over a few feet and stole around to the left. Derace Kingsley was in the very last alcove in the far end of the room. He had two chairs arranged side by side, facing into the corner. His big dark head just showed over the top of one of them. I slipped into the empty one and gave him a quick nod.

"Keep your voice down," he said. "This room is for after-luncheon naps. Now what is it? When I employed you it was to save me trouble, not to add trouble to what I already had. You made me break an important engagement."

"I know," I said, and put my face close to his. He smelled of highballs, in a nice way. "She shot him."

His eyebrows jumped and his face got that stony look. His teeth clamped tight. He breathed softly and twisted a large hand on his kneecap.

"Go on," he said, in a voice the size of a marble.

I looked back over the top of my chair. The nearest old geezer was sound asleep and blowing the dusty fuzz in his nostrils back and forth as he breathed.

"No answer at Lavery's place," I said. "Door slightly open. But I noticed yesterday it sticks on the sill. Pushed it open. Room dark, two glasses with drinks having been in them. House very still. In a moment a slim dark woman calling herself Mrs. Fallbrook, landlady, came up the stairs with her glove wrapped around a gun. Said she had found it on the stairs. Said she came to collect her three months' back rent. Used her key to get in. Inference is she took the chance to snoop around and look the house over. Took the gun from her and found it had been fired recently, but didn't tell her so. She said Lavery was not home. Got rid of her by making her mad and she departed in high dudgeon. She may call the police, but it's much more likely she will just go out and hunt butterflies and forget the whole thing—except the rent."

I paused. Kingsley's head was turned towards me and his jaw muscles bulged with the way his teeth were clamped. His eyes looked sick.

"I went downstairs. Signs of a woman having spent the night. Pajamas, face powder, perfume, and so on. Bathroom locked, but got it open. Three empty shells on the floor, two shots in the wall, one in the window. Lavery in the shower stall, naked and dead."

"My God!" Kingsley whispered. "Do you mean to say he had a woman with him last night and she shot him this morning in the bathroom?"

"Just what did you think I was trying to say?" I asked.

"Keep your voice down," he groaned. "It's a shock, naturally. Why in the bathroom?"

"Keep your own voice down," I said. "Why not in the bathroom? Could you think of a place where a man would be more completely off guard?"

He said: "You don't know that a woman shot him. I mean, you're not sure, are you?"

"No," I said. "That's true. It might have been somebody who used a small gun and emptied it carelessly to look like a woman's work. The bathroom is downhill, facing outwards on space and I don't think shots down there would be easily heard by anyone not in the house. The woman who spent the night might have left—or there need not have been any woman at all. The appearances could have been faked. *You* might have shot him."

"What would I want to shoot him for?" he almost bleated, squeezing both kneecaps hard. "I'm a civilized man."

That didn't seem to be worth an argument either. I said: "Does your wife own a gun?"

He turned a drawn miserable face to me and said hollowly: "Good God, man, you can't really think that!"

"Well does she?"

He got the words out in small gritty pieces. "Yes—she does. A small automatic."

"You buy it locally?"

"I—I didn't buy it at all. I took it away from a drunk at a party in San Francisco a couple of years ago. He was waving it around, with an idea that that was very funny. I never gave it back to him." He pinched his jaw hard until his knuckles whitened. "He probably doesn't even remember how or when he lost it. He was that kind of a drunk."

"This is working out almost too neatly," I said. "Could you recognize this gun?"

He thought hard, pushing his jaw out and half closing his eyes. I looked back over the chairs again. One of the elderly snoozers had waked himself up with a snort that almost blew him out of his chair. He coughed, scratched his nose with a thin dried-up hand, and fumbled a gold watch out of his vest. He peered at it bleakly, put it away, and went to sleep again.

I reached in my pocket and put the gun on Kingsley's hand. He stared down at it miserably.

"I don't know," he said slowly. "It's like it, but I can't tell."

"There's a serial number on the side," I said.

"Nobody remembers the serial numbers of guns."

"I was hoping you wouldn't," I said. "It would have worried me very much."

His hand closed around the gun and he put it down beside him in the chair.

"The dirty rat," he said softly. "I suppose he ditched her."

"I don't get it," I said. "The motive was inadequate for you, on account of you're a civilized man. But it was adequate for her."

"It's not the same motive," he snapped. "And women are more impetuous than men."

"Like cats are more impetuous than dogs."

"How?"

"Some women are more impetuous than some men. That's all that means. We'll have to have a better motive, if you want your wife to have done it."

He turned his head enough to give me a level stare in which there was no amusement. White crescents were bitten into the corners of his mouth.

"This doesn't seem to me a very good spot for the light touch," he said. "We can't let the police have this gun. Crystal had a permit and the gun was registered. So they will know the number, even if I don't. We can't let them have it."

"But Mrs. Fallbrook knows I had the gun."

He shook his head stubbornly. "We'll have to chance that. Yes, I know you're taking a risk. I intend to make it worth your while. If the set-up were possible for suicide, I'd say put the gun back. But the way you tell it, it isn't."

"No. He'd have to have missed himself with the first three shots. But I can't cover up a murder, even for a ten-dollar bonus. The gun will have to go back."

"I was thinking of more money than that," he said quietly. "I was thinking of five hundred dollars."

"Just what did you expect to buy with it?"

He leaned close to me. His eyes were serious and bleak, but

not hard. "Is there anything in Lavery's place, apart from the gun, that might indicate Crystal has been there lately?"

"A black and white dress and a hat like the bellhop in Bernardino described on her. There may be a dozen things I don't know about. There almost certainly will be fingerprints. You say she was never printed, but that doesn't mean they won't get her prints to check. Her bedroom at home will be full of them. So will the cabin at Little Fawn Lake. And her car."

"We ought to get the car—" he started to say. I stopped him.

"No use. Too many other places. What kind of perfume does she use?"

He looked blank for an instant. "Oh—Gillerlain Regal, the Champagne of Perfumes," he said woodenly. "A Chanel number once in a while."

"What's this stuff of yours like?"

"A kind of chypre. Sandalwood chypre."

"The bedroom reeks with it," I said. "It smelled like cheap stuff to me. But I'm no judge."

"Cheap?" he said, stung to the quick. "My God, cheap? We get thirty dollars an ounce for it."

"Well, this stuff smelled more like three dollars a gallon."

He put his hands down hard on his knees and shook his head. "I'm talking about money," he said. "Five hundred dollars. A check for it right now."

I let the remark fall to the ground, eddying like a soiled feather. One of the old boys behind us stumbled to his feet and groped his way wearily out of the room.

Kingsley said gravely: "I hired you to protect me from scandal, and of course to protect my wife, if she needed it. Through no fault of yours the chance to avoid scandal is pretty well shot. It's a question of my wife's neck now. I don't believe she shot Lavery. I have no reason for that belief. None at all. I just feel the conviction. She may even have been there last night, this gun may even be her gun. It doesn't prove she killed him. She would be as careless with the gun as with anything else. Anybody could have got hold of it."

"The cops down there won't work very hard to believe that," I said. "If the one I met is a fair specimen, they'll just pick the first head they see and start swinging with their blackjacks. And hers will certainly be the first head they see when they look the situation over."

He ground the heels of his hands together. His misery had a theatrical flavor, as real misery so often has.

"I'll go along with you up to a point," I said. "The set-up down there is almost too good, at first sight. She leaves clothes there she has been seen wearing and which can probably be traced. She leaves the gun on the stairs. It's hard to think she would be as dumb as that."

"You give me a little heart," Kingsley said wearily.

"But none of that means anything," I said. "Because we are looking at it from the angle of calculation, and people who commit crimes of passion or hatred, just commit them and walk out. Everything I have heard indicates that she is a reckless foolish woman. There's no sign of planning in any of the scene down there. There's every sign of a complete lack of planning. But even if there wasn't a thing down there to point to your wife, the cops would tie her up to Lavery. They will investigate his background, his friends, his women. Her name is bound to crop up somewhere along the line, and when it does, the fact that she has been out of sight for a month will make them sit up and rub their horny palms with glee. And of course they'll trace the gun, and if it's her gun—"

His hand dived for the gun in the chair beside him.

"Nope," I said. "They'll have to have the gun. Marlowe may be a very smart guy and very fond of you personally, but he can't risk the suppression of such vital evidence as the gun that killed a man. Whatever I do has to be on the basis that your wife is an obvious suspect, but that the obviousness can be wrong."

He groaned and put his big hand out with the gun on it. I took it and put it away. Then I took it out again and said: "Lend me your handkerchief. I don't want to use mine. I might be searched."

He handed me a stiff white handkerchief and I whiped the gun off carefully all over and dropped it into my pocket. I handed him back the handkerchief.

"My prints are all right," I said. "But I don't want yours on it. Here's the only thing I can do. Go back down there and replace the gun and call the law. Ride it out with them and let the chips fall where they have to. The story will have to come out. What I was doing down there and why. At the worst they'll find her and prove she killed him. At the best they'll find her a lot quicker than I can and let me use my energies proving that she didn't kill him, which means, in effect, proving that somebody else did. Are you game for that?"

He nodded slowly. He said: "Yes—and the five hundred stands. For showing Crystal didn't kill him."

"I don't expect to earn it," I said. "You may as well understand that now. How well did Miss Fromsett know Lavery? Out of office hours?"

His face tightened up like a charleyhorse. His fists went into hard lumps on his thighs. He said nothing.

"She looked kind of queer when I asked her for his address yesterday morning," I said.

He let a breath out slowly.

"Like a bad taste in the mouth," I said. "Like a romance that fouled out. Am I too blunt?"

His nostrils quivered a little and his breath made noise in them for a moment. Then he relaxed and said quietly:

"She—she knew him rather well—at one time. She's a girl who would do about what she pleased in that way. Lavery was, I guess, a fascinating bird—to women."

"I'll have to talk to her," I said.

"Why?" he asked shortly. Red patches showed in his cheeks.

"Never mind why. It's my business to ask all sorts of questions of all sorts of people."

"Talk to her then," he said tightly. "As a matter of fact she knew the Almores. She knew Almore's wife, the one who killed herself. Lavery knew her too. Could that have any possible connection with this business?"

"I don't know. You're in love with her, aren't you?"

"I'd marry her tomorrow, if I could," he said stiffly.

I nodded and stood up. I looked back along the room. It was almost empty now. At the far end a couple of elderly relics were still blowing bubbles. The rest of the soft chair boys had staggered back to whatever it was they did when they were conscious.

"There's just one thing," I said, looking down at Kingsley. "Cops get very hostile when there is a delay in calling them after a murder. There's been delay this time and there will be more. I'd like to go down there as if it was the first visit today. I think I can make it that way, if I leave the Fallbrook woman out."

"Fallbrook?" He hardly knew what I was talking about. "Who the hell—oh yes, I remember."

"Well, don't remember. I'm almost certain they'll never hear a peep from her. She's not the kind to have anything to do with the police of her own free will."

"I understand," he said.

"Be sure you handle it right then. Questions will be asked you *before* you are told Lavery is dead, before I'm allowed to get in touch with you—so far as they know. Don't fall into any traps. If you do, I won't be able to find anything out. I'll be in the clink."

"You could call me from the house down there—before you call the police," he said reasonably.

"I know. But the fact that I don't will be in my favor. And they'll check the phone calls one of the first things they do. And if I call you from anywhere else, I might just as well admit that I came up here to see you."

"I understand," he said again. "You can trust me to handle it."

We shook hands and I left him standing there.

18

The Athletic Club was on a corner across the street and half a block down from the Treloar Building. I crossed and walked north to the entrance. They had finished laying rose-colored concrete where the rubber sidewalk had been. It was fenced around, leaving a narrow gangway in and out of the building. The space was clotted with office help going in from lunch.

The Gillerlain Company's reception room looked even emptier than the day before. The same fluffy little blonde was tucked in behind the PBX in the corner. She gave me a quick smile and I gave her the gunman's salute, a stiff forefinger pointing at her, the three lower fingers tucked back under it, and the thumb wiggling up and down like a western gunfighter fanning his hammer. She laughed heartily, without making a sound. This was more fun than she had had in a week.

I pointed to Miss Fromsett's empty desk and the little blonde nodded and pushed a plug in and spoke. A door opened and Miss Fromsett swayed elegantly out to her desk and sat down and gave me her cool expectant eyes.

"Yes, Mr. Marlowe? Mr. Kingsley is not in, I'm afraid."

"I just came from him. Where do we talk?"

"Talk?"

"I have something to show you."

"Oh, yes?" She looked me over thoughtfully. A lot of guys had probably tried to show her things, including etchings. At another time I wouldn't have been above taking a flutter at it myself.

"Business," I said. "Mr. Kingsley's business."

She stood up and opened the gate in the railing. "We may as well go into his office then."

We went in. She held the door for me. As I passed her I sniffed. Sandalwood. I said:

"Gillerlain Regal, the Champagne of Perfumes?"

She smiled faintly, holding the door. "On my salary?"

"I didn't say anything about your salary. You don't look like a girl who has to buy her own perfume."

"Yes, that's what it is," she said. "And if you want to know, I detest wearing perfume in the office. He makes me."

We went down the long dim office and she took a chair at the end of the desk. I sat where I had sat the day before. We looked at each other. She was wearing tan today, with a ruffled jabot at her throat. She looked a little warmer, but still no prairie fire.

I offered her one of Kingsley's cigarettes. She took it, took a light from his lighter, and leaned back.

"We needn't waste time being cagey," I said. "You know by now who I am and what I am doing. If you didn't know yesterday morning, it's only because he loves to play big shot."

She looked down at the hand that lay on her knee, then lifted her eyes and smiled almost shyly.

"He's a great guy," she said. "In spite of the heavy executive act he likes to put on. He's the only guy that gets fooled by it after all. And if you only knew what he has stood from that little tramp—" She waved her cigarette—"well, perhaps I'd better leave that out. What was it you wanted to see me about?"

"Kingsley said you knew the Almores."

"I knew Mrs. Almore. That is, I met her a couple of times."

"Where?"

"At a friend's house. Why?"

"At Lavery's house?"

"You're not going to be insolent, are you, Mr. Marlowe?"

"I don't know what your definition of that would be. I'm going to talk business as if it was business, not international diplomacy."

"Very well." She nodded slightly. "At Chris Lavery's house, yes. I used to go there—once in a while. He had cocktail parties."

"Then Lavery knew the Almores—or Mrs. Almore."

She flushed very slightly. "Yes. Quite well."

"And a lot of other women—quite well, too. I don't doubt that. Did Mrs. Kingsley know her too?"

"Yes, better than I did. They called each other by their first names. Mrs. Almore is dead, you know. She committed suicide, about a year and a half ago."

"Any doubt about that?"

She raised her eyebrows, but the expression looked artificial to me, as if it just went with the question I asked, as a matter of form.

She said: "Have you any particular reason for asking that question in that particular way? I mean, has it anything to do with—with what you are doing?"

"I didn't think so. I still don't know that it has. But yesterday Dr. Almore called a cop just because I looked at his house. After he had found out from my car license who I was. The cop got pretty tough with me, just for being there. He didn't know what I was doing and I didn't tell him I had been calling on Lavery. But Dr. Almore must have known that. He had seen me in front of Lavery's house. Now why would he think it necessary to call a cop? And why would the cop think it smart to say that the last fellow who tried to put the bite on Almore ended up on the road gang? And why would the cop ask me if her folks—meaning Mrs. Almore's folks, I suppose—had hired me? If you can answer any of those questions, I might know whether it's any of my business."

She thought about it for a moment, giving me one quick glance while she was thinking, and then looking away again.

"I only met Mrs. Almore twice," she said slowly. "But I think I can answer your questions—all of them. The last time I met her was at Lavery's place, as I said, and there were quite a lot of people there. There was a lot of drinking and loud talk. The women were not with their husbands and the men were not with their wives, if any. There was a man there named Brownwell who was very tight. He's in the navy now, I heard. He was ribbing Mrs. Almore about her husband's practice. The idea seemed to be that he was one of those doctors who run around all night with a case of loaded hypodermic needles, keeping the local fast set from having pink elephants for breakfast. Florence Almore said she didn't care how her husband got his money as long as he got plenty of it and she had the spending of it. She was tight too and not a very nice person sober, I should imagine. One of these slinky glittering females who laugh too much and sprawl all over their chairs, showing a great deal of leg. A very light blonde with a high color and indecently large baby-blue eyes. Well, Brownwell told her not to worry, it would always be a good racket. In and out of the patient's house in fifteen minutes and anywhere from ten to fifty bucks a trip. But one thing bothered him, he said, how ever a doctor could get hold of so much dope without underworld contacts. He asked Mrs. Almore if they had many nice gangsters to dinner at their house. She threw a glass of liquor in his face."

I grinned, but Miss Fromsett didn't. She crushed her cigarette out in Kingsley's big copper and glass tray and looked at me soberly.

"Fair enough," I said. "Who wouldn't, unless he had a large hard fist to throw?"

"Yes. A few weeks later Florence Almore was found dead in the garage late at night. The door of the garage was shut and the car motor was running." She stopped and moistened her lips slightly. "It was Chris Lavery who found her. Coming home at God knows what o'clock in the morning. She was lying on the concrete floor in pajamas, with her head under a blanket which was also over the exhaust pipe of the car. Dr. Almore was out. There was nothing about the affair in the papers, except that she had died suddenly. It was well hushed up."

She lifted her clasped hands a little and then let them fall slowly into her lap again. I said:

"Was something wrong with it, then?"

"People thought so, but they always do. Some time later I heard what purported to be the lowdown. I met this man Brownwell on Vine Street and he asked me to have a drink with him. I didn't like him, but I had half an hour to kill. We sat at the back of Levy's bar and he asked me if I remembered the babe who threw the drink in his face. I said I did. The conversation then went something very like this. I remember it very well.

"Brownwell said: 'Our pal Chris Lavery is sitting pretty, if he ever runs out of girl friends he can touch for dough.'

"I said: 'I don't think I understand.'

"He said: 'Hell, maybe you don't want to. The night the Almore woman died she was over at Lou Condy's place losing her shirt at roulette. She got into a tantrum and said the wheels were crooked and made a scene. Condy practically had to drag her into his office.

He got hold of Dr. Almore through the Physicians' Exchange and after a while the doc came over. He shot her with one of his busy little needles. Then he went away, leaving Condy to get her home. It seems he had a very urgent case. So Condy took her home and the doc's office nurse showed up, having been called by the doc, and Condy carried her upstairs and the nurse put her to bed. Condy went back to his chips. So she had to be carried to bed and yet the same night she got up and walked down to the family garage and finished herself off with monoxide. What do you think of that?' Brownwell was asking me.

"I said: 'I don't know anything about it. How do you?'

"He said: 'I know a reporter on the rag they call a newspaper down there. There was no inquest and no autopsy. If any tests were made, nothing was told about them. They don't have a regular coroner down there. The undertakers take turns at being acting coroner, a week at a time. They're pretty well subservient to the political gang naturally. It's easy to fix a thing like that in a small town, if anybody with any pull wants it fixed. And Condy had plenty at that time. He didn't want the publicity of an investigation and neither did the doctor.' "

Miss Fromsett stopped talking and waited for me to say something. When I didn't, she went on: "I suppose you know what all this meant to Brownwell."

"Sure. Almore finished her off and then he and Condy between them bought a fix. It has been done in cleaner little cities than Bay City ever tried to be. But that isn't all the story, is it?"

"No. It seems Mrs. Almore's parents hired a private detective. He was a man who ran a night watchman service down there and he was actually the second man on the scene that night, after Chris. Brownwell said he must have had something in the way of information but he never got a chance to use it. They arrested him for drunk driving and he got a jail sentence."

I said: "Is that all?"

She nodded. "And if you think I remember it too well, it's part of my job to remember conversations."

"What I was thinking was that it doesn't have to add up to very much. I don't see where it has to touch Lavery, even if he was the one who found her. Your gossipy friend Brownwell seems to think what happened gave somebody a chance to blackmail the doctor. But there would have to be some evidence, especially when you're trying to put the bite on a man who has already cleared himself with the law."

Miss Fromsett said: "I think so too. And I'd like to think blackmail was one of the nasty little tricks Chris Lavery didn't quite run to. I think that's all I can tell you, Mr. Marlowe. And I ought to be outside."

She started to get up. I said: "It's not quite all. I have something to show you."

I got the little perfumed rag that had been under Lavery's pillow out of my pocket and leaned over to drop it on the desk in front of her.

19

She looked at the handkerchief, looked at me, picked up a pencil and pushed the little piece of linen around with the eraser end.

"What's on it?" she asked. "Flyspray?"

"Some kind of sandalwood, I thought."

"A cheap synthetic. Repulsive is a mild word for it. And why did you want me to look at this handkerchief, Mr. Marlowe?" She leaned back again and stared at me with level cool eyes.

"I found it in Chris Lavery's house, under the pillow on his bed. It has initials on it."

She unfolded the handkerchief without touching it by using the rubber tip of the pencil. Her face got a little grim and taut.

"It has two letters embroidered on it," she said in a cold angry voice. "They happen to be the same letters as my initials. Is that what you mean?"

"Right," I said. "He probably knows half a dozen women with the same initials."

"So you're going to be nasty after all," she said quietly.

"Is it your handkerchief—or isn't it?"

She hesitated. She reached out to the desk and very quietly got herself another cigarette and lit it with a match. She shook the match slowly, watching the small flame creep along the wood.

"Yes, it's mine," she said, "I must have dropped it there. It's a long time ago. And I assure you I didn't put it under a pillow on his bed. Is that what you wanted to know?"

I didn't say anything, and she added: "He must have lent it to some woman who—who would like this kind of perfume."

"I get a mental picture of the woman," I said. "And she doesn't quite go with Lavery."

Her upper lip curled a little. It was a long upper lip. I like long upper lips.

"I think," she said, "you ought to do a little more work on your mental picture of Chris Lavery. Any touch of refinement you may have noticed is purely coincidental."

"That's not a nice thing to say about a dead man," I said.

For a moment she just sat there and looked at me as if I hadn't said anything and she was waiting for me to say something. Then a slow shudder started at her throat and passed over her whole body. Her hands clenched and the cigarette bent into a crook. She looked down at it and threw it into the ashtray with a quick jerk of her arm.

"He was shot in his shower," I said. "And it looks as if it was done by some woman who spent the night there. He had just been shaving. The woman left a gun on the stairs and this handkerchief on the bed."

She moved very slightly in her chair. Her eyes were perfectly empty now. Her face was as cold as a carving.

"And did you expect me to be able to give you information about that?" she asked me bitterly.

"Look, Miss Fromsett, I'd like to be smooth and distant and subtle about all this too. I'd like to play this sort of game just once the way somebody like you would like it to be played. But nobody will let me—not the clients, nor the cops, nor the people I play against. However hard I try to be nice I always end up with my nose in the dirt and my thumb feeling for somebody's eye."

She nodded as if she had only just barely heard me. "When was he shot?" she asked, and then shuddered slightly again.

"This morning, I suppose. Not long after he got up. I said he had just shaved and was going to take a shower."

"That," she said, "would probably have been quite late. I've been here since eight-thirty."

"I didn't think you shot him."

"Awfully kind of you," she said. "But it is my handkerchief, isn't it? Although not my perfume. But I don't suppose policemen are very sensitive to quality in perfume—or in anything else."

"No—and that goes for private detectives too," I said. "Are you enjoying this a lot?"

"God," she said, and put the back of her hand hard against her mouth.

"He was shot at five or six times," I said. "And missed all but twice. He was cornered in the shower stall. It was a pretty grim scene, I should think. There was a lot of hate on one side of it. Or a pretty cold-blooded mind."

"He was quite easy to hate," she said emptily. "And poisonously easy to love. Women—even decent women—make such ghastly mistakes about men."

"All you're telling me is that you once thought you loved him, but not any more, and that you didn't shoot him."

"Yes?" Her voice was light and dry now, like the perfume she didn't like to wear at the office. "I'm sure you'll respect the confidence." She laughed shortly and bitterly. "Dead," she said. "The poor, egotistical, cheap, nasty, handsome, treacherous guy. Dead and cold and done with. No, Mr. Marlowe, I didn't shoot him."

I waited, letting her work it out of her. After a moment she said quietly: "Does Mr. Kingsley know?"

I nodded.

"And the police, of course."

"Not yet. At least not from me. I found him. The house door wasn't quite shut. I went in. I found him."

She picked the pencil up and poked at the handkerchief again. "Does Mr. Kingsley know about this scented rag?"

"Nobody knows about that, except you and I, and whoever put it there."

"Nice of you," she said dryly. "And nice of you to think what you thought."

"You have a certain quality of aloofness and dignity that I like," I said. "But don't run it into the ground. What would you expect me to think? Do I pull the hankie out from under the pillow and sniff it and hold it out and say, 'Well, well, Miss Adrienne Fromsett's initials and all. Miss Fromsett must have known Lavery, perhaps very intimately. Let's say, just for the book, as intimately as my nasty little mind can conceive. And that would be pretty damn intimately. But this is cheap synthetic sandalwood and Miss Fromsett wouldn't use cheap scent. And this was under Lavery's pillow and Miss Fromsett just never keeps her hankies under a man's pillow. Therefore this has absolutely nothing to do with Miss Fromsett. It's just an optical delusion.' "

"Oh shut up," she said.

I grinned.

"What kind of girl do you think I am?" she snapped.

"I came in too late to tell you."

She flushed, but delicately and all over her face this time. Then, "Have you any idea who did it?"

"Ideas, but that's all they are. I'm afraid the police are going to find it simple. Some of Mrs. Kingsley's clothes are hanging in Lavery's closet. And when they know the whole story—including what happened at Little Fawn Lake yesterday—I'm afraid they'll just reach for the handcuffs. They have to find her first. But that won't be so hard for them."

"Crystal Kingsley," she said emptily. "So he couldn't be spared even that."

I said: "It doesn't have to be. It could be an entirely different motivation, something we know nothing about. It could have been somebody like Dr. Almore."

She looked up quickly, then shook her head. "It could be," I insisted. "We don't know anything against it. He was pretty nervous yesterday, for a man who has nothing to be afraid of. But, of course, it isn't only the guilty who are afraid."

I stood up and tapped on the edge of the desk looking down at her. She had a lovely neck. She pointed to the handkerchief.

"What about that?" she asked dully.

"If it was mine, I'd wash that cheap scent out of it."

"It has to mean something, doesn't it? It might mean a lot."

I laughed. "I don't think it means anything at all. Women are always leaving their handkerchiefs around. A fellow like Lavery would collect them and keep them in a drawer with a sandalwood sachet. Somebody would find the stock and take one out to use. Or he would lend them, enjoying the reactions to the other girls' initials. I'd say he was that kind of a heel. Goodby, Miss Fromsett, and thanks for talking to me."

I started to go, then I stopped and asked her: "Did you hear the name of the reporter down there who gave Brownwell all his information?"

She shook her head.

"Or the name of Mrs. Almore's parents?"

"Not that either. But I could probably find that out for you. I'd be glad to try."

"How?"

"Those things are usually printed in death notices, aren't they? There is pretty sure to have been a death notice in the Los Angeles papers."

"That would be very nice of you," I said. I ran a finger along the edge of the desk and looked at her sideways. Pale ivory skin, dark and lovely eyes, hair as light as hair can be and as dark as night can be.

I walked back down the room and out. The little blonde at the PBX looked at me expectantly, her small red lips parted, waiting for more fun.

I didn't have any more. I went on out.

20

No police cars stood in front of Lavery's house, nobody hung around on the sidewalk and when I pushed the front door open there was no smell of cigar or cigarette smoke inside. The sun had gone away from the windows and a fly buzzed softly over one of the liquor glasses. I went down to the end and hung over the railing that led downstairs. Nothing moved in Mr. Lavery's house. Nothing made sound except very faintly down below in the bathroom the quiet trickle of water dripping on a dead man's shoulder.

I went to the telephone and looked up the number of the police department in the directory. I dialed and while I was waiting for an answer, I took the little automatic out of my pocket and laid it on the table beside the telephone.

When the male voice said: "Bay City police—Smoot talking," I said: "There's been a shooting at 623 Altair Street. Man named Lavery lives there. He's dead."

"Six-two-three Altair. Who are you?"

"The name is Marlowe."

"You there in the house?"

"Right."

"Don't touch anything at all."

I hung up, sat down on the davenport and waited.

Not very long. A siren whined far off, growing louder with great surges of sound. Tires screamed at a corner, and the siren wail died to a metallic growl, then to silence, and the tires screamed again in front of the house. The Bay City police conserving rubber. Steps hit the sidewalk and I went over to the front door and opened it.

Two uniformed cops barged into the room. They were the usual large size and they had the usual weathered faces and suspicious eyes. One of them had a carnation tucked under his cap, behind his right ear. The other one was older, a little gray and grim. They stood and looked at me warily, then the older one said briefly:

"All right, where is it?"

"Downstairs in the bathroom, behind the shower curtain."

"You stay here with him, Eddie."

He went rapidly along the room and disappeared. The other one looked at me steadily and said out of the corner of his mouth:

"Don't make any false moves, buddy."

I sat down on the davenport again. The cop ranged the room with his eyes. There were sounds below stairs, feet walking. The cop with me suddenly spotted the gun lying on the telephone table. He charged at it violently, like a downfield blocker.

"This the death gun?" he almost shouted.

"I should imagine so. It's been fired."

"Ha!" He leaned over the gun, baring his teeth at me, and put his hand to his holster. His finger tickled the flap off the stud and he grasped the butt of the black revolver.

"You should what?" he barked.

"I should imagine so."

"That's very good," he sneered. "That's very good indeed."

"It's not that good," I said.

He reeled back a little. His eyes were being careful of me. "What you shoot him for?" he growled.

"I've wondered and wondered."

"Oh, a wisenheimer."

"Let's just sit down and wait for the homicide boys," I said. "I'm reserving my defense."

"Don't give me none of that," he said.

"I'm not giving you any of anything. If I had shot him, I wouldn't be here. I wouldn't have called up. You wouldn't have found the gun. Don't work so hard on the case. You won't be on it more than ten minutes."

His eyes looked hurt. He took his cap off and the carnation dropped to the floor. He bent and picked it up and twirled it between his fingers, then dropped it behind the fire screen.

"Better not do that," I told him. "They might think it's a clue and waste a lot of time on it."

"Aw hell." He bent over the screen and retrieved the carnation and put it in his pocket. "You know all the answers, don't you, buddy?"

The other cop came back up the stairs, looking grave. He stood in the middle of the floor and looked at his wrist watch and made a note in a notebook and then looked out of the front windows, holding the venetian blinds to one side to do it.

The one who had stayed with me said: "Can I look now?"

"Let it lie, Eddie. Nothing in it for us. You call the coroner?"

"I thought homicide would do that."

"Yeah, that's right. Captain Webber will be on it and he likes to do everything himself." He looked at me and said: "You're a man named Marlowe?"

I said I was a man named Marlowe.

"He's a wise guy, knows all the answers," Eddie said.

The older one looked at me absently, looked at Eddie absently, spotted the gun lying on the telephone table and looked at that not at all absently.

"Yeah, that's the death gun," Eddie said. "I ain't touched it."

The other nodded. "The boys are not so fast today. What's your line, mister? Friend of his?" He made a thumb towards the floor.

"Saw him yesterday for the first time. I'm a private operative from L.A."

"Oh." He looked at me very sharply. The other cop looked at me with deep suspicion.

"Cripes, that means everything will be all balled up," he said.

That was the first sensible remark he had made. I grinned at him affectionately.

The older cop looked out of the front window again. "That's the Almore place across the street, Eddie," he said.

Eddie went and looked with him. "Sure is," he said. "You can read the plate. Say, this guy downstairs might be the guy—"

"Shut up," the other one said and dropped the venetian blind. They both turned around and stared at me woodenly.

A car came down the block and stopped and a door slammed and more steps came down the walk. The older of the prowl car boys opened the door to two men in plain clothes, one of whom I already knew.

21

The one who came first was a small man for a cop, middle-aged, thin-faced, with a permanently tired expression. His nose was sharp and bent a little to one side, as if somebody had given it the elbow one time when it was into something. His blue pork pie hat was set very square on his head and chalk-white hair showed under it. He wore a dull brown suit and his hands were in the side pockets of the jacket, with the thumbs outside the seam.

The man behind him was Degarmo, the big cop with the dusty blond hair and the metallic blue eyes and the savage, lined face who had not liked my being in front of Dr. Almore's house.

The two uniformed men looked at the small man and touched their caps.

"The body's in the basement, Captain Webber. Been shot twice after a couple of misses, looks like. Dead quite some time. This party's name is Marlowe. He's a private eye from Los Angeles. I didn't question him beyond that."

"Quite right," Webber said sharply. He had a suspicious voice. He passed a suspicious eye over my face and nodded briefly. "I'm Captain Webber," he said. "This is Lieutenant Degarmo. We'll look at the body first."

He went along the room. Degarmo looked at me as if he had never seen me before and followed him. They went downstairs, the older of the two prowl car men with them. The cop called Eddie and I stared each other down for a while.

I said: "This is right across the street from Dr. Almore's place, isn't it?"

All the expression went out of his face. There hadn't been much to go. "Yeah. So what?"

"So nothing," I said.

He was silent. The voices came up from below, blurred and indistinct. The cop cocked his ear and said in a more friendly tone: "You remember that one?"

"A little."

He laughed. "They killed that one pretty," he said. "They wrapped it up and hid it in back of the shelf. The top shelf in the bathroom closet. The one you can't reach without standing on a chair."

"So they did," I said. "I wonder why."

The cop looked at me sternly. "There was good reasons, pal. Don't think there wasn't. You know this Lavery well?"

"Not well."

"On to him for something?"

"Working on him a little," I said. "You knew him?"

The cop called Eddie shook his head. "Nope. I just remembered it was a guy from this house found Almore's wife in the garage that night."

"Lavery may not have been here then," I said.

"How long's he been here?"

"I don't know," I said.

"Would be about a year and a half," the cop said, musingly. "The L.A. papers give it any play?"

"Paragraph on the Home Counties page," I said, just to be moving my mouth.

He scratched his ear and listened. Steps were coming back up the stairs. The cop's face went blank and he moved away from me and straightened up.

Captain Webber hurried over to the telephone and dialed the number and spoke, then held the phone away from his ear and looked back over his shoulder.

"Who's deputy coroner this week, Al?"

"Ed Garland," the big lieutenant said woodenly.

"Call Ed Garland," Webber said into the phone. "Have him come over right away. And tell the flash squad to step on it."

He put the phone down and barked sharply: "Who handled this gun?"

I said: "I did."

He came over and teetered on his heels in front of me and pushed his small sharp chin up at me. He held the gun delicately on a handkerchief in his hand.

"Don't you know enough not to handle a weapon found at the scene of a crime?"

"Certainly," I said. "But when I handled it I didn't know there had been a crime. I didn't know the gun had been fired. It was lying on the stairs and I thought it had been dropped."

"A likely story," Webber said bitterly. "You get a lot of that sort of thing in your business?"

"A lot of what sort of thing?"

He kept his hard stare on me and didn't answer.

I said: "How would it be for me to tell you my story as it happened?"

He bridled at me like a cockerel. "Suppose you answer my questions exactly as I choose to put them."

I didn't say anything to that. Webber swivelled sharply and said to the two uniformed men: "You boys can get back to your car and check in with the despatcher."

They saluted and went out, closing the door softly until it stuck, then getting as mad at it as anybody else. Webber listened until their car went away. Then he put the bleak and callous eye on me once more.

"Let me see your identification."

I handed him my wallet and he rooted in it. Degarmo sat in a chair and crossed his legs and stared up blankly at the ceiling. He got a match out of his pocket and chewed the end of it. Webber gave me back my wallet. I put it away.

"People in your line make a lot of trouble," he said.

"Not necessarily," I said.

He raised his voice. It had been sharp enough before. "I said they made a lot of trouble, and a lot of trouble is what I meant. But get this straight. You're not going to make any in Bay City."

I didn't answer him. He jabbed a forefinger at me.

"You're from the big town," he said. "You think you're tough and you think you're wise. Don't worry. We can handle you. We're a small place, but we're very compact. We don't have any political tug-of-war down here. We work on the straight line and we work fast. Don't worry about us, mister."

"I'm not worrying," I said. "I don't have anything to worry about. I'm just trying to make a nice clean dollar."

"And don't give me any of the flip talk," Webber said. "I don't like it."

Degarmo brought his eyes down from the ceiling and curled a forefinger to stare at the nail. He spoke in a heavy bored voice.

"Look, chief, the fellow downstairs is called Lavery. He's dead. I knew him a little. He was a chaser."

"What of it?" Webber snapped, not looking away from me.

"The whole set-up indicates a dame," Degarmo said. "You know what these private eyes work at. Divorce stuff. Suppose we'd let him tie into it, instead of just trying to scare him dumb."

"If I'm scaring him," Webber said, "I'd like to know it. I don't see any signs of it."

He walked over to the front window and yanked the venetian blind up. Light poured into the room almost dazzlingly, after the long dimness. He came back bouncing on his heels and poked a thin hard finger at me and said:

"Talk."

I said, "I'm working for a Los Angeles business man who can't take a lot of loud publicity. That's why he hired me. A month ago his wife ran off and later a telegram came which indicated she had gone with Lavery. But my client met Lavery in town a couple of days ago and he denied it. The client believed him enough to get worried. It seems the lady is pretty reckless. She might have taken up with some bad company and got into a jam. I came down to see Lavery and he denied to me that he had gone with her. I half believed him but later I got reasonable proof that he had been with her in a San Bernardino hotel the night she was believed to have left the mountain cabin where she had been staying. With that in my pocket I came down to tackle Lavery again. No answer to the bell, the door was slightly open. I came inside, looked around, found the gun and searched the house. I found him. Just the way he is now."

"You had no right to search the house," Webber said coldly.

"Of course not," I agreed. "But I wouldn't be likely to pass up the chance either."

"The name of this man you're working for?"

"Kingsley." I gave him the Beverly Hills address. "He manages a cosmetic company in the Treloar Building on Olive. The Gillerlain Company."

Webber looked at Degarmo. Degarmo wrote lazily on an envelope. Webber looked back at me and said: "What else?"

"I went up to this mountain cabin where the lady had been staying. It's at a place called Little Fawn Lake, near Puma Point, forty-six miles into the mountains from San Bernardino."

I looked at Degarmo. He was writing slowly. His hand stopped a moment and seemed to hang in the air stiffly, then it dropped to the envelope and wrote again. I went on:

"About a month ago the wife of the caretaker at Kingsley's place up there had a fight with him and left, as everybody thought. Yesterday she was found drowned in the lake."

Webber almost closed his eyes and rocked on his heels. Almost softly he asked: "Why are you telling me this? Are you implying a connection?"

"There's a connection in time. Lavery had been up there. I don't know of any other connection, but I thought I'd better mention it."

Degarmo was sitting very still, looking at the floor in front of him. His face was tight and he looked even more savage than usual. Webber said:

"This woman that was drowned? Suicide?"

"Suicide or murder. She left a goodby note. But her husband has been arrested on suspicion. The name is Chess. Bill and Muriel Chess, his wife."

"I don't want any part of that," Webber said sharply. "Let's confine ourselves to what went on here."

"Nothing went on here," I said, looking at Degarmo. "I've been down here twice. The first time I talked to Lavery and didn't get anywhere. The second time I didn't talk to him and didn't get anywhere."

Webber said slowly: "I'm going to ask you a question and I want an honest answer. You won't want to give it, but now will be as good a time as later. You know I'll get it eventually. The question is this. You have looked through the house and I imagine pretty thoroughly. Have you seen anything that suggests to you that this Kingsley woman has been here?"

"That's not a fair question," I said. "It calls for a conclusion of the witness."

"I want an answer to it," he said grimly. "This isn't a court of law."

"The answer is yes," I said. "There are women's clothes hanging in a closet downstairs that have been described to me as being worn by Mrs. Kingsley at San Bernardino the night she met Lavery there. The description was not exact though. A black and white suit, mostly white, and a panama hat with a rolled black and white band."

Degarmo snapped a finger against the envelope he was holding. "You must be a great guy for a client to have working for him," he said. "That puts the woman right in this house where a murder has been committed and she is the woman he's supposed to have gone away with. I don't think we'll have to look far for the killer, chief."

Webber was staring at me fixedly, with little or no expression on his face but a kind of tight watchfulness. He nodded absently to what Degarmo had said.

I said: "I'm assuming you fellows are not a pack of damn fools. The clothes are tailored and easy to trace. I've saved you an hour by telling you, perhaps even no more than a phone call."

"Anything else?" Webber asked quietly.

Before I could answer, a car stopped outside the house, and then another. Webber skipped over to open the door. Three men came in, a short, curly-haired man and a large ox-like man, both carrying heavy black leather cases. Behind them a tall thin man in a dark gray suit and black tie. He had very bright eyes and a poker face.

Webber pointed a finger at the curly-haired man and said: "Downstairs in the bathroom, Busoni. I want a lot of prints from all over the house, particularly any that seem to be made by a woman. It will be a long job."

"I do all the work," Busoni grunted. He and the ox-like man went along the room and down the stairs.

"We have a corpse for you, Garland," Webber said to the third man. "Let's go down and look at him. You've ordered the wagon?"

The bright-eyed man nodded briefly and he and Webber went downstairs after the other two.

Degarmo put the envelope and pencil away. He stared at me woodenly.

I said: "Am I supposed to talk about our conversation yesterday —or is that a private transaction?"

"Talk about it all you like," he said. "It's our job to protect the citizen."

"You talk about it," I said. "I'd like to know more about the Almore case."

He flushed slowly and his eyes got mean. "You said you didn't know Almore."

"I didn't yesterday, or know anything about him. Since then I've learned that Lavery knew Mrs. Almore, that she committed suicide, that Lavery found her dead, and that Lavery has at least been suspected of blackmailing him—or of being in a position to blackmail him. Also both your prowl-car boys seemed interested in the fact that Almore's house was across the street from here. And one of them remarked that the case had been killed pretty, or words to that effect."

Degarmo said in a slow deadly tone: "I'll have the badge off the son of a bitch. All they do is flap their mouths. God damn empty-headed bastards."

"Then there's nothing in it," I said.

He looked at his cigarette. "Nothing in what?"

"Nothing in the idea that Almore murdered his wife, and had enough pull to get it fixed."

Degarmo came to his feet and walked over to lean down at me. "Say that again," he said softly.

I said it again.

He hit me across the face with his open hand. It jerked my head around hard. My face felt hot and large.

"Say it again," he said softly.

I said it again. His hand swept and knocked my head to one side again.

"Say it again."

"Nope. Third time lucky. You might miss." I put a hand up and rubbed my cheek.

He stood leaning down, his lips drawn back over his teeth, a hard animal glare in his very blue eyes.

"Any time you talk like that to a cop," he said, "you know what you got coming. Try it on again and it won't be the flat of a hand I'll use on you."

I bit hard on my lips and rubbed my cheek.

"Poke your big nose into our business and you'll wake up in an alley with the cats looking at you," he said.

I didn't say anything. He went and sat down again, breathing hard. I stopped rubbing my face and held my hand out and worked the fingers slowly, to get the hard clench out of them.

"I'll remember that," I said. "Both ways."

22

It was early evening when I got back to Hollywood and up to the office. The building had emptied out and the corridors were silent. Doors were open and the cleaning women were inside with their vacuum cleaners and their dry mops and dusters.

I unlocked the door to mine and picked up an envelope that lay in front of the mail slot and dropped it on the desk without looking at it. I ran the windows up and leaned out, looking at the early neon lights glowing, smelling the warm, foody air that drifted up from the alley ventilator of the coffee shop next door.

I peeled off my coat and tie and sat down at the desk and got the office bottle out of the deep drawer and bought myself a drink. It didn't do any good. I had another, with the same result.

By now Webber would have seen Kingsley. There would be a general alarm out for his wife, already, or very soon. The thing looked cut and dried to them. A nasty affair between two rather nasty people, too much loving, too much drinking, too much proximity ending in a savage hatred and a murderous impulse and death.

I thought this was all a little too simple.

I reached for the envelope and tore it open. It had no stamp. It read: "Mr. Marlowe: Florence Almore's parents are a Mr. and Mrs. Eustace Grayson, presently residing at the Rossmore Arms, 640 South Oxford Avenue. I checked this by calling the listed phone number. Yrs. Adrienne Fromsett."

An elegant handwriting, like the elegant hand that wrote it. I pushed it to one side and had another drink. I began to feel a little less savage. I pushed things around on the desk. My hands felt thick and hot and awkward. I ran a finger across the corner of the desk and looked at the streak made by the wiping off of the dust. I looked at the dust on my finger and wiped that off. I looked at my watch. I looked at the wall. I looked at nothing.

I put the liquor bottle away and went over to the washbowl to rinse the glass out. When I had done that I washed my hands and bathed my face in cold water and looked at it. The flush was gone from the left cheek, but it looked a little swollen. Not very much, but enough to make me tighten up again. I brushed my hair and looked at the gray in it. There was getting to be plenty of gray in it. The face under the hair had a sick look. I didn't like the face at all.

I went back to the desk and read Miss Fromsett's note again. I smoothed it out on the glass and sniffed it and smoothed it out some more and folded it and put it in my coat pocket.

I sat very still and listened to the evening grow quiet outside the open windows. And very slowly I grew quiet with it.

The Rossmore Arms was a gloomy pile of dark red brick built around a huge forecourt. It had a plush-lined lobby containing silence, tubbed plants, a bored canary in a cage as big as a dog-house, a smell of old carpet dust and the cloying fragrance of gardenias long ago.

The Graysons were on the fifth floor in front, in the north wing. They were sitting together in a room which seemed to be deliberately twenty years out of date. It had fat overstuffed furniture and brass doorknobs, shaped like eggs, a huge wall mirror in a gilt frame, a marble-topped table in the window and dark red plush side drapes by the windows. It smelled of tobacco smoke and behind that the air was telling me they had had lamb chops and broccoli for dinner.

Grayson's wife was a plump woman who might once have had big baby-blue eyes. They were faded out now and dimmed by glasses and slightly protuberant. She had kinky white hair. She sat darning socks with her thick ankles crossed, her feet just reaching the floor, and a big wicker sewing basket in her lap.

Grayson was a long stooped yellow-faced man with high shoulders, bristly eyebrows and almost no chin. The upper part of his face meant business. The lower part was just saying goodby. He wore bifocals and he had been gnawing fretfully at the evening paper. I had looked him up in the city directory. He was a C.P.A. and looked it every inch. He even had ink on his fingers and there were four pencils in the pocket of his open vest.

He read my card carefully for the seventh time and looked me up and down and said slowly:

"What is it you want to see us about, Mr. Marlowe?"

"I'm interested in a man named Lavery. He lives across the street from Dr. Almore. Your daughter was the wife of Dr. Almore. Lavery is the man who found your daughter the night she—died."

They both pointed like bird dogs when I deliberately hesitated on the last word. Grayson looked at his wife and she shook her head.

"We don't care to talk about that," Grayson said promptly. "It is much too painful to us."

I waited a moment and looked gloomy with them. Then I said: "I don't blame you. I don't want to make you. I'd like to get in touch with the man you hired to look into it, though."

They looked at each other again. Mrs. Grayson didn't shake her head this time.

Grayson asked: "Why?"

"I'd better tell you a little of my story." I told them what I had been hired to do, not mentioning Kingsley by name. I told them the incident with Degarmo outside Almore's house the day before. They pointed again on that.

Grayson said sharply: "Am I to understand that you were unknown to Dr. Almore, had not approached him in any way, and that he nevertheless called a police officer because you were outside his house?"

I said: "That's right. Had been outside for at least an hour though. That is, my car had."

"That's very queer," Grayson said.

"I'd say that was one very nervous man," I said. "And Degarmo asked me if her folks—meaning your daughter's folks—had hired me. Looks as if he didn't feel safe yet, wouldn't you say?"

"Safe about what?" He didn't look at me saying this. He re-lit his pipe, slowly, then tamped the tobacco down with the end of a big metal pencil and lit it again.

I shrugged and didn't answer. He looked at me quickly and looked away. Mrs. Grayson didn't look at me, but her nostrils quivered.

"How did he know who you were?" Grayson asked suddenly.

"Made a note of the car license, called the Auto Club, looked up the name in the directory. At least that's what I'd have done and I saw him through his window making some of the motions."

"So he has the police working for him," Grayson said.

"Not necessarily. If they made a mistake that time, they wouldn't want it found out now."

"Mistake!" He laughed almost shrilly.

"Okay," I said. "The subject is painful but a little fresh air won't hurt it. You've always thought he murdered her, haven't you? That's why you hired this dick—detective."

Mrs. Grayson looked up with quick eyes and ducked her head down and rolled up another pair of mended socks.

Grayson said nothing.

I said: "Was there any evidence, or was it just that you didn't like him?"

"There was evidence," Grayson said bitterly, and with a sudden clearness of voice, as if he had decided to talk about it after all.

"There must have been. We were told there was. But we never got it. The police took care of that."

"I heard they had this fellow arrested and sent up for drunk driving."

"You heard right."

"But he never told you what he had to go on?"

"No."

"I don't like that," I said. "That sounds a little as if this fellow hadn't made up his mind whether to use his information for your benefit or keep it and put a squeeze on the doctor."

Grayson looked at his wife again. She said quietly: "Mr. Talley didn't impress me that way. He was a quiet unassuming little man. But you can't always judge, I know."

I said: "So Talley was his name. That was one of the things I hoped you would tell me."

"And what were the others?" Grayson asked.

"How can I find Talley—and what it was that laid the groundwork of suspicion in your minds. It must have been there, or you wouldn't have hired Talley without a better showing from him that *he* had grounds."

Grayson smiled very thinly and primly. He reached for his little chin and rubbed it with one long yellow finger.

Mrs. Grayson said: "Dope."

"She means that literally," Grayson said at once, as if the single word had been a green light. "Almore was, and no doubt is, a dope doctor. Our daughter made that clear to us. In his hearing too. He didn't like it."

"Just what do you mean by a dope doctor, Mr. Grayson?"

"I mean a doctor whose practice is largely with people who are living on the raw edge of nervous collapse, from drink and dissipation. People who have to be given sedatives and narcotics all the time. The stage comes when an ethical physician refuses to treat them any more, outside a sanatorium. But not the Dr. Almores. *They* will keep on as long as the money comes in, as long as the patient remains alive and reasonably sane, even if he or she becomes a hopeless addict in the process. A lucrative practice," he said primly, "and I imagine a dangerous one to the doctor."

"No doubt of that," I said. "But there's a lot of money in it. Did you know a man named Condy?"

"No. We know who he was. Florence suspected he was a source of Almore's narcotic supply."

I said: "Could be. He probably wouldn't want to write himself too many prescriptions. Did you know Lavery?"

"We never saw him. We knew who he was."

"Ever occur to you that Lavery might have been blackmailing Almore?"

It was a new idea to him. He ran his hand over the top of his head and brought it down over his face and dropped it to his bony knee. He shook his head.

"No. Why should it?"

"He was first to the body," I said. "Whatever looked wrong to Talley must have been equally visible to Lavery."

"Is Lavery that kind of man?"

"I don't know. He has no visible means of support, no job. He gets around a lot, especially with women."

"It's an idea," Grayson said. "And those things can be handled very discreetly." He smiled wryly. "I have come across traces of them in my work. Unsecured loans, long outstanding. Investments on the face of them worthless made by men who would not be likely to make worthless investments. Bad debts that should obviously be charged off and have not been, for fear of inviting scrutiny from the income tax people. Oh yes, those things can easily be arranged."

I looked at Mrs. Grayson. Her hands had never stopped working. She had a dozen pairs of darned socks finished. Grayson's long bony feet would be hard on socks.

"What's happened to Talley? Was he framed?"

"I don't think there's any doubt about it. His wife was very bitter. She said he had been given a doped drink in a bar and he had been drinking with a policeman. She said a police car was waiting across the street for him to start driving and that he was picked up at once. Also that he was given only the most perfunctory examination at the jail."

"That doesn't mean too much. That's what he told her after he was arrested. He'd tell her something like that automatically."

"Well, I hate to think the police are not honest," Grayson said. "But these things are done, and everybody knows it."

I said: "If they made an honest mistake about your daughter's death, they would hate to have Talley show them up. It might mean several lost jobs. If they thought what he was really after was blackmail, they wouldn't be too fussy about how they took care of him. Where is Talley now? What it all boils down to is that if there was any solid clue, he either had it or was on the track of it and knew what he was looking for."

Grayson said: "We don't know where he is. He got six months, but that expired long ago."

"How about his wife?"

He looked at his own wife. She said briefly: "1618½ Westmore Street, Bay City. Eustace and I sent her a little money. She was left bad off."

I made a note of the address and leaned back in my chair and said: "Somebody shot Lavery this morning in his bathroom."

Mrs. Grayson's pudgy hands became still on the edges of the basket. Grayson sat with his mouth open, holding his pipe in front of it. He made a noise of clearing his throat softly, as if in the presence of the dead. Nothing ever moved slower than his old black pipe going back between his teeth.

"Of course it would be too much to expect," he said and let it hang in the air and blew a little pale smoke at it, and then added, "that Dr. Almore had any connection with that."

"I'd like to think he had," I said. "He certainly lives at a handy distance. The police think my client's wife shot him. They have a good case too, when they find her. But if Almore had anything to do with it, it must surely arise out of your daughter's death. That's why I'm trying to find out something about that."

Grayson said: "A man who has done one murder wouldn't have more than twenty-five per cent of the hesitation in doing another." He spoke as if he had given the matter considerable study.

I said: "Yeah, maybe. What was supposed to be the motive for the first one?"

"Florence was wild," he said sadly. "A wild and difficult girl. She was wasteful and extravagant, always picking up new and rather doubtful friends, talking too much and too loudly, and generally acting the fool. A wife like that can be very dangerous to a man like Albert S. Almore. But I don't believe that was the prime motive, was it, Lettie?"

He looked at his wife, but she didn't look at him. She jabbed a darning needle into a round ball of wool and said nothing.

Grayson sighed and went on: "We had reason to believe he was carrying on with his office nurse and that Florence had threatened him with a public scandal. He couldn't have anything like that, could he? One kind of scandal might too easily lead to another."

I said: "How did he do the murder?"

"With morphine, of course. He always had it, he always used it. He was an expert in the use of it. Then when she was in a deep coma he would have placed her in the garage and started the car motor. There was no autopsy, you know. But if there had been, it was known that she had been given a hypodermic injection that night."

I nodded and he leaned back satisfied and ran his hand over his head and down his face and let it fall slowly to his bony knee. He seemed to have given a lot of study to this angle too.

I looked at them. A couple of elderly people sitting there quietly, poisoning their minds with hate, a year and a half after it had happened. They would like it if Almore had shot Lavery. They would love it. It would warm them clear down to their ankles.

After a pause I said: "You're believing a lot of this because you want to. It's always possible that she committed suicide, and that the cover-up was partly to protect Condy's gambling club and partly to prevent Almore having to be questioned at a public hearing."

"Rubbish," Grayson said sharply. "He murdered her all right. She was in bed, asleep."

"You don't know that. She might have been taking dope herself. She might have established a tolerance for it. The effect wouldn't last long in that case. She might have got up in the middle of the night and looked at herself in the glass and seen devils pointing at her. These things happen."

"I think you have taken up enough of our time," Grayson said.

I stood up. I thanked them both and made a yard towards the door and said: "You didn't do anything more about it after Talley was arrested?"

"Saw an assistant district attorney named Leach," Grayson grunted. "Got exactly nowhere. He saw nothing to justify his office in interfering. Wasn't even interested in the narcotic angle. But Condy's place was closed up about a month later. That might have come out of it somehow."

"That was probably the Bay City cops throwing a little smoke. You'd find Condy somewhere else, if you knew where to look. With all his original equipment intact."

I started for the door again and Grayson hoisted himself out of his chair and dragged across the room after me. There was a flush on his yellow face.

"I didn't mean to be rude," he said. "I guess Lettie and I oughtn't to brood about this business the way we do."

"I think you've both been very patient," I said. "Was there anybody else involved in all this that we haven't mentioned by name?"

He shook his head, then looked back at his wife. Her hands were motionless holding the current sock on the darning egg. Her head was tilted a little to one side. Her attitude was of listening, but not to us.

I said: "The way I got the story, Dr. Almore's office nurse put Mrs. Almore to bed that night. Would that be the one he was supposed to be playing around with?"

Mrs. Grayson said sharply: "Wait a minute. We never saw the girl. But she had a pretty name. Just give me a minute."

We gave her a minute. "Mildred something," she said, and snapped her teeth.

I took a deep breath. "Would it be Mildred Haviland, Mrs. Grayson?"

She smiled brightly and nodded. "Of course, Mildred Haviland. Don't you remember, Eustace?"

He didn't remember. He looked at us like a horse that has got into the wrong stable. He opened the door and said: "What does it matter?"

"And you said Talley was a small man," I bored on. "He wouldn't for instance be a big loud bruiser with an overbearing manner?"

"Oh no," Mrs. Grayson said. "Mr. Talley is a man of not more than medium height, middle-aged, with brownish hair and a very quiet voice. He had a sort of worried expression. I mean, he looked as if he always had it."

"Looks as if he needed it," I said.

Grayson put his bony hand out and I shook it. It felt like shaking hands with a towel rack.

"If you get him," he said and clamped his mouth hard on his pipe stem, "call back with a bill. If you get Almore, I mean, of course."

I said I knew he meant Almore, but that there wouldn't be any bill.

I went back along the silent hallway. The self-operating elevator was carpeted in red plush. It had an elderly perfume in it, like three widows drinking tea.

The house on Westmore Street was a small frame bungalow behind a larger house. There was no number visible on the smaller house, but the one in front showed a stencilled *1618* beside the door, with a dim light behind the stencil. A narrow concrete path led along under windows to the house at the back. It had a tiny porch with a single chair on it. I stepped up on the porch and rang the bell.

It buzzed not very far off. The front door was open behind the screen but there was no light. From the darkness a querulous voice said:

"What is it?"

I spoke into the darkness. "Mr. Talley in?"

The voice became flat and without tone. "Who wants him?"

"A friend."

The woman sitting inside in the darkness made a vague sound in her throat which might have been amusement. Or she might just have been clearing her throat.

"All right," she said. "How much is this one?"

"It's not a bill, Mrs. Talley. I suppose you are Mrs. Talley?"

"Oh, go away and let me alone," the voice said. "Mr. Talley isn't here. He hasn't been here. He won't be here."

I put my nose against the screen and tried to peer into the room. I could see the vague outlines of its furniture. From where the voice came from also showed the shape of a couch. A woman was lying on it. She seemed to be lying on her back and looking up at the ceiling. She was quite motionless.

"I'm sick," the voice said. "I've had enough trouble. Go away and leave me be."

I said: "I've just come from talking to the Graysons."

There was a little silence, but no movement, then a sigh. "I never heard of them."

I leaned against the frame of the screen door and looked back along the narrow walk to the street. There was a car across the way with parking lights burning. There were other cars along the block.

I said: "Yes, you have, Mrs. Talley. I'm working for them. They're still in there pitching. How about you? Don't you want something back?"

The voice said: "I want to be let alone."

"I want information," I said. "I'm going to get it. Quietly if I can. Loud, if it can't be quiet."

The voice said: "Another copper, eh?"

"You know I'm not a copper, Mrs. Talley. The Graysons wouldn't talk to a copper. Call them up and ask them."

"I never heard of them," the voice said. "I don't have a phone, if I knew them. Go away, copper. I'm sick. I've been sick for a month."

"My name is Marlowe," I said. "Philip Marlowe. I'm a private eye in Los Angeles, I've been talking to the Graysons. I've got something, but I want to talk to your husband."

The woman on the couch let out a dim laugh which barely reached across the room. "You've got something," she said. "That sounds familiar. My God it does! You've got something. George Talley had something too—once."

"He can have it again," I said, "if he plays his cards right."

"If that's what it takes," she said, "you can scratch him off right now."

I leaned against the doorframe and scratched my chin instead. Somebody back on the street had clicked a flashlight on. I didn't know why. It went off again. It seemed to be near my car.

The pale blur of face on the couch moved and disappeared. Hair took its place. The woman had turned her face to the wall.

"I'm tired," she said, her voice now muffled by talking at the wall. "I'm so damn tired. Beat it, mister. Be nice and go away."

"Would a little money help any?"

"Can't you smell the cigar smoke?"

I sniffed. I didn't smell any cigar smoke. I said, "No."

"They've been here. They were here two hours. God, I'm tired of it all. Go away."

"Look, Mrs. Talley—"

She rolled on the couch and the blur of her face showed again. I could almost see her eyes, not quite.

"Look yourself," she said. "I don't know you. I don't want to know you. I have nothing to tell you. I wouldn't tell it, if I had. I live here, mister, if you call it living. Anyway it's the nearest I can get to living. I want a little peace and quiet. Now you get out and leave me alone."

"Let me in the house," I said. "We can talk this over. I think I can show you—"

She rolled suddenly on the couch again and feet struck the floor. A tight anger came into her voice.

"If you don't get out," she said, "I'm going to start yelling my head off. Right now. Now!"

"Okay," I said quickly. "I'll stick my card in the door. So you won't forget my name. You might change your mind."

I got the card out and wedged it into the crack of the screen door. I said: "Well goodnight, Mrs. Talley."

No answer. Her eyes were looking across the room at me, faintly luminous in the dark. I went down off the porch and back along the narrow walk to the street.

Across the way a motor purled gently in the car with the parking lights on it. Motors purl gently in thousands of cars on thousands of streets, everywhere.

I got into the Chrysler and started it up.

25

Westmore was a north and south street on the wrong side of town. I drove north. At the next corner I bumped over disused interurban tracks and on into a block of junk yards. Behind wooden fences the decomposing carcasses of old automobiles lay in grotesque designs, like a modern battlefield. Piles of rusted parts looked lumpy under the moon. Roof high piles, with alleys between them.

Headlights glowed in my rear view mirror. They got larger. I stepped on the gas and reached keys out of my pocket and unlocked the glove compartment. I took a .38 out and laid it on the car seat close to my leg.

Beyond the junk yards there was a brick field. The tall chimney of the kiln was smokeless, far off over waste land. Piles of dark bricks, a low wooden building with a sign on it, emptiness, no one moving, no light.

The car behind me gained. The low whine of a lightly touched siren growled through the night. The sound loafed over the fringes of a neglected golf course to the east, across the brickyard to the west. I speeded up a bit more, but it wasn't any use. The car behind me came up fast and a huge red spotlight suddenly glared all over the road.

The car came up level and started to cut in. I stood the Chrysler on its nose, swung out behind the police car, and made a U turn with half an inch to spare. I gunned the motor the other way. Behind me sounded the rough clashing of gears, the howl of an infuriated motor, and the red spotlight swept for what seemed miles over the brickyard.

It wasn't any use. They were behind me and coming fast again. I didn't have any idea of getting away. I wanted to get back where there were houses and people to come out and watch and perhaps to remember.

I didn't make it. The police car heaved up alongside again and a hard voice yelled:

"Pull over, or we'll blast a hole in you!"

I pulled over to the curb and set the brake. I put the gun back in the glove compartment and snapped it shut. The police car jumped on its springs just in front of my left front fender. A fat man slammed out of it roaring.

"Don't you know a police siren when you hear one? Get out of that car!"

I got out of the car and stood beside it in the moonlight. The fat man had a gun in his hand.

"Gimme your license!" he barked in a voice as hard as the blade of a shovel.

I took it out and held it out. The other cop in the car slid out from under the wheel and came around beside me and took what I was holding out. He put a flash on it and read.

"Name of Marlowe," he said. "Hell, the guy's a shamus. Just think of that, Cooney."

Cooney said: "Is that all? Guess I won't need this." He tucked the gun back in his holster and buttoned the leather flap down over it. "Guess I can handle this with my little flippers," he said. "Guess I can at that."

The other one said: "Doing fifty-five. Been drinking, I wouldn't wonder."

"Smell the bastard's breath," Cooney said.

The other one leaned forward with a polite leer. "Could I smell the breath, shamus?"

I let him smell the breath.

"Well," he said judiciously, "he ain't staggering. I got to admit that."

"'S a cold night for summer. Buy the boy a drink, Officer Dobbs."

"Now that's a sweet idea," Dobbs said. He went to the car and got a half pint bottle out of it. He held it up. It was a third full. "No really solid drinking here," he said. He held the bottle out. "With our compliments, pal."

"Suppose I don't want a drink," I said.

"Don't say that," Cooney whined. "We might get the idea you wanted footprints on your stomach."

I took the bottle and unscrewed the cap and sniffed. The liquor in the bottle smelled like whiskey. Just whiskey.

"You can't work the same gag all the time," I said.

Cooney said: "Time is eight twenty-seven. Write it down, Officer Dobbs."

Dobbs went to the car and leaned in to make a note on his report. I held the bottle up and said to Cooney: "You insist that I drink this?"

"Naw. You could have me jump on your belly instead."

I tilted the bottle, locked my throat, and filled my mouth with whiskey. Cooney lunged forward and sank a fist in my stomach. I sprayed the whiskey and bent over choking. I dropped the bottle.

I bent to get it and saw Cooney's fat knee rising at my face. I stepped to one side and straightened and slammed him on the nose with everything I had. His left hand went to his face and his voice howled and his right hand jumped to his gun holster. Dobbs ran at me from the side and his arm swung low. The blackjack hit me behind the left knee, the leg went dead and I sat down hard on the ground, gritting my teeth and spitting whiskey.

Cooney took his hand away from his face full of blood.

"Jesus," he cracked in a thick horrible voice. "This is blood. My blood." He let out a wild roar and swung his foot at my face.

I rolled far enough to catch it on my shoulder. It was bad enough taking it there.

Dobbs pushed between us and said: "We got enough, Charlie. Better not get it all gummed up."

Cooney stepped backwards three shuffling steps and sat down on the running board of the police car and held his face. He groped for a handkerchief and used it gently on his nose.

"Just gimme a minute," he said through the handkerchief. "Just a minute, pal. Just one little minute."

Dobbs said, "Pipe down. We got enough. That's the way it's going to be." He swung the blackjack slowly beside his leg. Cooney got up off the running board and staggered forward. Dobbs put a hand against his chest and pushed him gently. Cooney tried to knock the hand out of his way.

"I gotta see blood," he croaked. "I gotta see more blood."

Dobbs said sharply, "Nothing doing. Pipe down. We got all we wanted."

Cooney turned and moved heavily away to the other side of the police car. He leaned against it muttering through his handkerchief. Dobbs said to me:

"Up on the feet, boy friend."

I got up and rubbed behind my knee. The nerve of the leg was jumping like an angry monkey.

"Get in the car," Dobbs said. "Our car."

I went over and climbed into the police car.

Dobbs said: "You drive the other heap, Charlie."

"I'll tear every god damn fender off'n it," Cooney roared.

Dobbs picked the whiskey bottle off the ground, threw it over the fence, and slid into the car beside me. He pressed the starter.

"This is going to cost you," he said. "You hadn't ought to have socked him."

I said: "Just why not?"

"He's a good guy," Dobbs said. "A little loud."

"But not funny," I said. "Not at all funny."

"Don't tell him," Dobbs said. The police car began to move. "You'd hurt his feelings."

Cooney slammed into the Chrysler and started it and clashed the gears as if he was trying to strip them. Dobbs tooled the police car smoothly around and started north again along the brickyard.

"You'll like our new jail," he said.

"What will the charge be?"

He thought a moment, guiding the car with a gentle hand and watching in the mirror to see that Cooney followed along behind.

"Speeding," he said. "Resisting arrest. H.B.D." H.B.D. is police slang for "had been drinking."

"How about being slammed in the belly, kicked in the shoulder, forced to drink liquor under threat of bodily harm, threatened with a gun and struck with a blackjack while unarmed? Couldn't you make a little something more out of that?"

"Aw forget it," he said wearily. "You think this sort of thing is my idea of a good time?"

"I thought they cleaned this town up," I said. "I thought they had it so that a decent man could walk the streets at night without wearing a bullet proof vest."

"They cleaned it up some," he said. "They wouldn't want it too clean. They might scare away a dirty dollar."

"Better not talk like that," I said. "You'll lose your union card."

He laughed. "The hell with them," he said. "I'll be in the army in two weeks."

The incident was over for him. It meant nothing. He took it as a matter of course. He wasn't even bitter about it.

26

The cell block was almost brand new. The battleship gray paint on the steel walls and door still had the fresh gloss of newness disfigured in two or three places by squirted tobacco juice. The overhead light was sunk in the ceiling behind a heavy frosted panel. There were two bunks on one side of the cell and a man snored in the top bunk, with a dark gray blanket wrapped around him. Since he was asleep that early and didn't smell of whiskey or gin and had chosen the top berth where he would be out of the way, I judged he was an old lodger.

I sat on the lower bunk. They had tapped me for a gun but they hadn't stripped my pockets. I got out a cigarette and rubbed the hot swelling behind my knee. The pain radiated all the way to the ankle. The whiskey I had coughed on my coat front had a rank smell. I held the cloth up and breathed smoke into it. The smoke floated up around the flat square of lighted glass in the ceiling. The jail seemed very quiet. A woman was making a shrill racket somewhere very far off, in another part of the jail. My part was as peaceful as a church.

The woman was screaming, wherever she was. The screaming had a thin sharp unreal sound, something like the screaming of coyotes in the moonlight, but it didn't have the rising keening note of the coyote. After a while the sound stopped.

I smoked two cigarettes through and dropped the butts into the small toilet in the corner. The man in the upper berth still snored. All I could see of him was damp greasy hair sticking out over the edge of the blanket. He slept on his stomach. He slept well. He was one of the best.

I sat down on the bunk again. It was made of flat steel slats with a thin hard mattress over them. Two dark gray blankets were folded on it quite neatly. It was a very nice jail. It was on the twelfth floor of the new city hall. It was a very nice city hall. Bay City was a very nice place. People lived there and thought so. If I lived there, I would probably think so. I would see the nice blue bay and the cliffs and the yacht harbor and the quiet streets of houses, old houses brooding under old trees and new houses with sharp green lawns and wire fences and staked saplings set into the parkway in front of them. I knew a girl who lived on Twenty-fifth Street. It was a nice street. She was a nice girl. She liked Bay City.

She wouldn't think about the Mexican and Negro slums stretched out on the dismal flats south of the old interurban tracks. Nor of the waterfront dives along the flat shore south of the cliffs, the sweaty little dance halls on the pike, the marihuana joints, the narrow fox faces watching over the tops of newspapers in far too quiet hotel lobbies, nor the pickpockets and grifters and con men and drunk rollers and pimps and queens on the board walk.

I went over to stand by the door. There was nobody stirring across the way. The lights in the cell block were bleak and silent. Business in the jail was rotten.

I looked at my watch. Nine fifty-four. Time to go home and get your slippers on and play over a game of chess. Time for a tall cool drink and a long quiet pipe. Time to sit with your feet up and think of nothing. Time to start yawning over your magazine. Time to be a human being, a householder, a man with nothing to do but rest and suck in the night air and rebuild the brain for tomorrow.

A man in the blue-gray jail uniform came along between the cells reading numbers. He stopped in front of mine and unlocked the door and gave me the hard stare they think they have to wear on their pans forever and forever and forever. I'm a cop, brother, I'm tough, watch your step, brother, or we'll fix you up so you'll crawl on your hands and knees, brother, snap out of it, brother, let's get a load of the truth, brother, let's go, and let's not forget we're tough guys, we're cops, and we do what we like with punks like you.

"Out," he said.

I stepped out of the cell and he relocked the door and jerked his thumb and we went along to a wide steel gate and he unlocked that and we went through and he relocked it and the keys tinkled pleasantly on the big steel ring and after a while we went through a steel door that was painted like wood on the outside and battleship gray on the inside.

Degarmo was standing there by the counter talking to the desk sergeant.

He turned his metallic blue eyes on me and said: "How you doing?"

"Fine."

"Like our jail?"

"I like your jail fine."

"Captain Webber wants to talk to you."

"That's fine," I said.

"Don't you know any words but fine?"

"Not right now," I said. "Not in here."

"You're limping a little," he said. "You trip over something?"

"Yeah," I said. "I tripped over a blackjack. It jumped up and bit me behind the left knee."

"That's too bad," Degarmo said, blank-eyed. "Get your stuff from the property clerk."

"I've got it," I said. "It wasn't taken away from me."

"Well, that's fine," he said.

"It sure is," I said. "It's fine."

The desk sergeant lifted his shaggy head and gave us both a long stare. "You ought to see Cooney's little Irish nose," he said. "If you want to see something fine. It's spread over his face like syrup on a waffle."

Degarmo said absently: "What's the matter? He get in a fight?"

"I wouldn't know," the desk sergeant said. "Maybe it was the same blackjack that jumped up and bit him."

"For a desk sergeant you talk too damn much," Degarmo said.

"A desk sergeant always talks too God damn much," the desk sergeant said. "Maybe that's why he isn't a lieutenant on homicide."

"You see how we are here," Degarmo said. "Just one great big happy family."

"With beaming smiles on our faces," the desk sergeant said, "and our arms spread wide and welcome, and a rock in each hand."

Degarmo jerked his head at me and we went out.

Captain Webber pushed his sharp bent nose across the desk at me and said: "Sit down."

I sat down in a round-backed wooden armchair and eased my left leg away from the sharp edge of the seat. It was a large neat corner office. Degarmo sat at the end of the desk and crossed his legs and rubbed his ankle thoughtfully, looked out of a window.

Webber went on: "You asked for trouble, and you got it. You were doing fifty-five miles an hour in a residential zone and you attempted to get away from a police car that signaled you to stop with its siren and red spotlight. You were abusive when stopped and you struck an officer in the face."

I said nothing. Webber picked a match off his desk and broke it in half and threw the pieces over his shoulder.

"Or are they lying—as usual?" he asked.

"I didn't see their report," I said. "I was probably doing fifty-five in a residential district, or anyhow within city limits. The police car was parked outside a house I visited. It followed me when I drove away and I didn't at that time know it was a police car. It had no good reason to follow me and I didn't like the look of it. I went a little fast, but all I was trying to do was get to a better lighted part of town."

Degarmo moved his eyes to give me a bleak meaningless stare. Webber snapped his teeth impatiently.

He said: "After you knew it was a police car you made a half turn in the middle of the block and still tried to get away. Is that right?"

I said: "Yes. It's going to take a little frank talk to explain that."

"I'm not afraid of a little frank talk," Webber said. "I tend to kind of specialize in frank talk."

I said: "These cops that picked me up were parked in front of the house where George Talley's wife lives. They were there before I got there. George Talley is the man who used to be a private detective down here. I wanted to see him. Degarmo knows why I wanted to see him."

Degarmo picked a match out of his pocket and chewed on the soft end of it quietly. He nodded, without expression. Webber didn't look at him.

I said: "You are a stupid man, Degarmo. Everything you do is stupid, and done in a stupid way. When you went up against me yesterday in front of Almore's house you had to get tough when there was nothing to get tough about. You had to make me curious when I had nothing to be curious about. You even had to drop hints which showed me how I could satisfy that curiosity, if it became important. All you had to do to protect your friends was keep your mouth shut until I made a move. I never would have made one, and you would have saved all this."

Webber said: "What the devil has all this got to do with your being arrested in the twelve hundred block on Westmore Street?"

"It has to do with the Almore case," I said. "George Talley worked on the Almore case—until he was pinched for drunk driving."

"Well, I never worked on the Almore case," Webber snapped. "I don't know who stuck the first knife into Julius Caesar either. Stick to the point, can't you?"

"I am sticking to the point. Degarmo knows about the Almore case and he doesn't like it talked about. Even your prowl car boys know about it. Cooney and Dobbs had no reason to follow me unless it was because I visited the wife of a man who had worked on the Almore case. I wasn't doing fifty-five miles an hour when they started to follow me. I tried to get away from them because I had a good idea I might get beaten up for going there. Degarmo had given me that idea."

Webber looked quickly at Degarmo. Degarmo's hard blue eyes looked across the room at the wall in front of him.

I said: "And I didn't bust Cooney in the nose until after he had forced me to drink whiskey and then hit me in the stomach when I drank it, so that I would spill it down my coat front and smell of it. This can't be the first time you have heard of that trick, captain."

Webber broke another match. He leaned back and looked at his small tight knuckles. He looked again at Degarmo and said: "If you got made chief of police today, you might let me in on it."

Degarmo said: "Hell, the shamus just got a couple of playful taps. Kind of kidding. If a guy can't take a joke—"

Webber said: "You put Cooney and Dobbs over there?"

"Well—yes, I did," Degarmo said. "I don't see where we have to put up with these snoopers coming into our town and stirring up a lot of dead leaves just to promote themselves a job and work a couple of old suckers for a big fee. Guys like that need a good sharp lesson."

"Is that how it looks to you?" Webber asked.

"That's exactly how it looks to me," Degarmo said.

"I wonder what fellows like you need," Webber said. "Right now I think you need a little air. Would you please take it, lieutenant?"

Degarmo opened his mouth slowly. "You mean you want me to breeze on out?"

Webber leaned forward suddenly and his sharp little chin seemed to cut the air like the forefoot of a cruiser. "Would you be so kind?"

Degarmo stood up slowly, a dark flush staining his cheekbones. He leaned a hard hand flat on the desk and looked at Webber. There was a little charged silence. He said:

"Okay, captain. But you're playing this wrong."

Webber didn't answer him. Degarmo walked to the door and out. Webber waited for the door to close before he spoke.

"Is it your line that you can tie this Almore business a year and a half ago to the shooting in Lavery's place today? Or is it just a smoke screen you're laying down because you know damn well Kingsley's wife shot Lavery?"

I said: "It was tied to Lavery before he was shot. In a rough sort of way, perhaps only with a granny knot. But enough to make a man think."

"I've been into this matter a little more thoroughly than you might think," Webber said coldly. "Although I never had anything personally to do with the death of Almore's wife and I wasn't chief of detectives at that time. If you didn't even know Almore yesterday morning, you must have heard a lot about him since."

I told him exactly what I had heard, both from Miss Fromsett and from the Graysons.

"Then it's your theory that Lavery may have blackmailed Dr. Almore?" he asked at the end. "And that that may have something to do with the murder?"

"It's not a theory. It's no more than a possibility. I wouldn't be doing a job if I ignored it. The relations, if any, between Lavery and Almore might have been deep and dangerous or just the merest acquaintance, or not even that. For all I positively know they may never even have spoken to each other. But if there was nothing funny about the Almore case, why get so tough with anybody who shows an interest in it? It could be coincidence that George Talley was hooked for drunk driving just when he was working on it. It could be coincidence that Almore called a cop because I stared at his house, and that Lavery was shot before I could talk to him a second time. But it's no coincidence that two of your men were watching Talley's home tonight, ready, willing and able to make trouble for me, if I went there."

"I grant you that," Webber said. "And I'm not done with that incident. Do you want to file charges?"

"Life's too short for me to be filing charges of assault against police officers," I said.

He winced a little. "Then we'll wash all that out and charge it to experience," he said. "And as I understand you were not even booked, you're free to go home any time you want to. And if I were you, I'd leave Captain Webber to deal with the Lavery case and with any remote connection it might turn out to have with the Almore case."

I said: "And with any remote connection it might have with a woman named Muriel Chess being found drowned in a mountain lake near Puma Point yesterday?"

He raised his little eyebrows. "You think that?"

"Only you might not know her as Muriel Chess. Supposing that you knew her at all you might have known her as Mildred Haviland, who used to be Dr. Almore's office nurse. Who put Mrs. Almore to bed the night she was found dead in the garage, and who, if there was any hanky-panky about that, might know who it was, and be bribed or scared into leaving town shortly thereafter."

Webber picked up two matches and broke them. His small bleak eyes were fixed on my face. He said nothing.

"And at that point," I said, "you run into a real basic coincidence, the only one I'm willing to admit in the whole picture. For this Mildred Haviland met a man named Bill Chess in a Riverside beer parlor and for reasons of her own married him and went to live with him at Little Fawn Lake. And Little Fawn Lake was the property of a man whose wife was intimate with Lavery, who had found Mrs. Almore's body. That's what I call a real coincidence. It can't be anything else, but it's basic, fundamental. Everything else flows from it."

Webber got up from his desk and went over to the water cooler and drank two paper cups of water. He crushed the cups slowly in his hand and twisted them into a ball and dropped the ball into a brown metal basket under the cooler. He walked to the windows and stood looking out over the bay. This was before the dim-out went into effect, and there were many lights in the yacht harbor.

He came slowly back to the desk and sat down. He reached up and pinched his nose. He was making up his mind about something.

He said slowly: "I can't see what the hell sense there is in trying to mix that up with something that happened a year and a half later."

"Okay," I said, "and thanks for giving me so much of your time." I got up to go.

"Your leg feel pretty bad?" he asked, as I leaned down to rub it.

"Bad enough, but it's getting better."

"Police business," he said almost gently, "is a hell of a problem. It's a good deal like politics. It asks for the highest type of men, and there's nothing in it to attract the highest type of men. So we have to work with what we get—and we get things like this."

"I know," I said. "I've always known that. I'm not bitter about it. Goodnight, Captain Webber."

"Wait a minute," he said. "Sit down a minute. If we've got to have the Almore case in this, let's drag it out into the open and look at it."

"It's about time somebody did that," I said. I sat down again.

28

Webber said quietly: "I suppose some people think we're just a bunch of crooks down here. I suppose they think a fellow kills his wife and then calls me up on the phone and says: 'Hi, Cap, I got a little murder down here cluttering up the front room. And I've got five hundred iron men that are not working.' And then I say: 'Fine. Hold everything and I'll be right down with a blanket.'"

"Not quite that bad," I said.

"What did you want to see Talley about when you went to his house tonight?"

"He had some line on Florence Almore's death. Her parents hired him to follow it up, but he never told them what it was."

"And you thought he would tell you?" Webber asked sarcastically.

"All I could do was try."

"Or was it just that Degarmo getting tough with you made you feel like getting tough right back at him?"

"There might be a little of that in it too," I said.

"Talley was a petty blackmailer," Webber said contemptuously.

"On more than one occasion. Any way to get rid of him was good enough. So I'll tell you what it was he had. He had a slipper he had stolen from Florence Almore's foot."

"A slipper?"

He smiled faintly. "Just a slipper. It was later found hidden in his house. It was a green velvet dancing pump with some little stones set into the heel. It was custom made, by a man in Hollywood who makes theatrical footwear and such. Now ask me what was important about this slipper?"

"What was important about it, captain?"

"She had two pair of them, exactly alike, made on the same order. It seems that is not unusual. In case one of them gets scuffed or some drunken ox tries to walk up a lady's leg." He paused and smiled thinly. "It seems that one pair had never been worn."

"I think I'm beginning to get it," I said.

He leaned back and tapped the arms of his chair. He waited.

"The walk from the side door of the house to the garage is rough concrete," I said. "Fairly rough. Suppose she didn't walk it, but was carried. And suppose whoever carried her put her slippers on—and got one that had not been worn."

"Yes?"

"And suppose Talley noticed this while Lavery was telephoning to the doctor, who was out on his rounds. So he took the unworn slipper, regarding it as evidence that Florence Almore had been murdered."

Webber nodded his head. "It was evidence if he left it where it was, for the police to find it. After he took it, it was just evidence that he was a rat."

"Was a monoxide test made of her blood?"

He put his hands flat on his desk and looked down at them. "Yes," he said. "And there was monoxide all right. Also the investigating officers were satisfied with appearances. There was no sign of violence. They were satisfied that Dr. Almore had not murdered his wife. Perhaps they were wrong. I think the investigation was a little superficial."

"And who was in charge of it?" I asked.

"I think you know the answer to that."

"When the police came, didn't they notice that a slipper was missing?"

"When the police came there was no slipper missing. You must remember that Dr. Almore was back at his home, in response to Lavery's call, before the police were called. All we know about the missing shoe is from Talley himself. He might have taken the unworn shoe from the house. The side door was unlocked. The maids were asleep. The objection to that is that he wouldn't have been likely to know there was an unworn slipper to take. I wouldn't put it past him to think of it. He's a sharp sneaky little devil. But I can't fix the necessary knowledge on him."

We sat there and looked at each other, thinking about it.

"Unless," Webber said slowly, "we can suppose that this nurse of Almore's was involved with Talley in a scheme to put the bite on Almore. It's possible. There are things in favor of it. There are more things against it. What reason have you for claiming that the girl drowned up in the mountains was this nurse?"

"Two reasons, neither one conclusive separately, but pretty powerful taken together. A tough guy who looked and acted like Degarmo was up there a few weeks ago showing a photograph of Mildred Haviland that looked something like Muriel Chess. Different hair and eyebrows and so on, but a fair resemblance. Nobody helped him much. He called himself De Soto and said he was a Los Angeles cop. There isn't any Los Angeles cop named De Soto. When Muriel Chess heard about it, she looked scared. If it was Degarmo, that's easily established. The other reason is that a golden anklet with a heart on it was hidden in a box of powdered sugar in the Chess cabin. It was found after her death, after her husband had been arrested. On the back of the heart was engraved: *Al to Mildred. June 28th 1938. With all my love.*"

"It could have been some other Al and some other Mildred," Webber said.

"You don't really believe that, captain."

He leaned forward and made a hole in the air with his forefinger. "What do you want to make of all this exactly?"

"I want to make it that Kingsley's wife didn't shoot Lavery. That his death had something to do with the Almore business. And with Mildred Haviland. And possibly with Dr. Almore. I want to make it that Kingsley's wife disappeared because something happened that gave her a bad fright, that she may or may not have guilty knowledge, but that she hasn't murdered anybody. There's five hundred dollars in it for me, if I can determine that. It's legitimate to try."

He nodded. "Certainly it is. And I'm the man that would help you, if I could see any grounds for it. We haven't found the woman, but the time has been very short. But I can't help you put something on one of my boys."

I said: "I heard you call Degarmo Al. But I was thinking of Almore. His name's Albert."

Webber looked at his thumb. "But he was never married to the girl," he said quietly. "Degarmo was. I can tell you she led him a pretty dance. A lot of what seems bad in him is the result of it."

I sat very still. After a moment I said: "I'm beginning to see things I didn't know existed. What kind of a girl was she?"

"Smart, smooth and no good. She had a way with men. She could make them crawl over her shoes. The big boob would tear your head off right now, if you said anything against her. She divorced him, but that didn't end it for him."

"Does he know she is dead?"

Webber sat quiet for a long moment before he said: "Not from anything he has said. But how could he help it, if it's the same girl?"

"He never found her in the mountains—so far as we know."

I stood up and leaned down on the desk. "Look, captain, you're not kidding me, are you?"

"No. Not one damn bit. Some men are like that and some women can make them like it. If you think Degarmo went up there looking for her because he wanted to hurt her, you're as wet as a bar towel."

"I never quite thought that," I said. "It would be possible, provided Degarmo knew the country up there pretty well. Whoever murdered the girl did."

"This is all between us," he said. "I'd like you to keep it that way."

I nodded, but I didn't promise him. I said goodnight again and left. He looked after me as I went down the room. He looked hurt and sad.

The Chrysler was in the police lot at the side of the building with the keys in the ignition and none of the fenders smashed. Cooney hadn't made good on his threat. I drove back to Hollywood and went up to my apartment in the Bristol. It was late, almost midnight.

The green and ivory hallway was empty of all sound except that a telephone bell was ringing in one of the apartments. It rang insistently and got louder as I came near to my door. I unlocked the door. It was my telephone.

I walked across the room in darkness to where the phone stood on the ledge of an oak desk against the side wall. It must have rung at least ten times before I got to it.

I lifted it out of the cradle and answered, and it was Derace Kingsley on the line.

His voice sounded tight and brittle and strained. "Good Lord, where in hell have you been?" he snapped. "I've been trying to reach you for hours."

"All right. I'm here now," I said. "What is it?"

"I've heard from her."

I held the telephone very tight and drew my breath in slowly and let it out slowly. "Go ahead," I said.

"I'm not far away. I'll be over there in five or six minutes. Be prepared to move."

He hung up.

I stood there holding the telephone halfway between my ear and the cradle. Then I put it down very slowly and looked at the hand that had held it. It was half open and clenched stiff, as if it was still holding the instrument.

29

The discreet midnight tapping sounded on the door and I went over and opened it. Kingsley looked as big as a horse in a creamy shetland sports coat with a green and yellow scarf around the neck inside the loosely turned up collar. A dark reddish brown snapbrim hat was pulled low on his forehead and under its brim, his eyes looked like the eyes of a sick animal.

Miss Fromsett was with him. She was wearing slacks and sandals and a dark green coat and no hat and her hair had a wicked lustre. In her ears hung ear drops made of a pair of tiny artificial gardenia blooms, hanging one above the other, two on each ear. Gillerlain Regal, the Champagne of Perfumes, came in at the door with her.

I shut the door and indicated the furniture and said: "A drink will probably help."

Miss Fromsett sat in an armchair and crossed her legs and looked around for cigarettes. She found one and lit it with a long casual flourish and smiled bleakly at a corner of the ceiling.

Kingsley stood in the middle of the floor trying to bite his chin. I went out to the dinette and mixed three drinks and brought them in and handed them. I went over to the chair by the chess table with mine.

Kingsley said: "What have you been doing and what's the matter with the leg?"

I said: "A cop kicked me. A present from the Bay City police department. It's a regular service they give down there. As to where I've been—in jail for drunk driving. And from the expression on your face, I think I may be right back there soon."

"I don't know what you're talking about," he said shortly. "I haven't the foggiest idea. This is no time to kid around."

"All right, don't," I said. "What did you hear and where is she?"

He sat down with his drink and flexed the fingers of his right hand and put it inside his coat. It came out with an envelope, a long one.

"You have to take this to her," he said. "Five hundred dollars. She wanted more, but this is all I could raise. I cashed a check at a night club. It wasn't easy. She has to get out of town."

I said: "Out of what town?"

"Bay City somewhere. I don't know where. She'll meet you at a place called the Peacock Lounge, on Arguello Boulevard, at Eighth Street, or near it."

I looked at Miss Fromsett. She was still looking at the corner of the ceiling as if she had just come along for the ride.

Kingsley tossed the envelope across and it fell on the chess table. I looked inside it. It was money all right. That much of his story made sense. I let it lie on the small polished table with its inlaid squares of brown and pale gold.

I said: "What's the matter with her drawing her own money? Any hotel would clear a check for her. Most of them would cash one. Has her bank account got lockjaw or something?"

"That's no way to talk," Kingsley said heavily. "She's in trouble. I don't know how she knows she's in trouble. Unless a pickup order has been broadcast. Has it?"

I said I didn't know. I hadn't had much time to listen to police calls. I had been too busy listening to live policemen.

Kingsley said: "Well, she won't risk cashing a check now. It was all right before. But not now." He lifted his eyes slowly and gave me one of the emptiest stares I had ever seen.

"All right, we can't make sense where there isn't any," I said. "So she's in Bay City. Did you talk to her?"

"No. Miss Fromsett talked to her. She called the office. It was just after hours but that cop from the beach, Captain Webber, was with me. Miss Fromsett naturally didn't want her to talk at all then. She told her to call back. She wouldn't give any number we could call."

I looked at Miss Fromsett. She brought her glance down from the ceiling and pointed it at the top of my head. There was nothing in her eyes at all. They were like drawn curtains.

Kingsley went on: "I didn't want to talk to her. She didn't want to talk to me. I don't want to see her. I guess there's no doubt she shot Lavery. Webber seemed quite sure of it."

"That doesn't mean anything," I said. "What he says and what he thinks don't even have to be on the same map. I don't like her knowing the cops were after her. It's a long time since anybody listened to the police short wave for amusement. So she called back later. And then?"

"It was almost half-past six," Kingsley said. "We had to sit there in the office and wait for her to call. You tell him." He turned his head to the girl.

Miss Fromsett said: "I took the call in Mr. Kingsley's office. He was sitting right beside me, but he didn't speak. She said to send the money down to the Peacock place and asked who would bring it."

"Did she sound scared?"

"Not in the least. Completely calm. I might say, icily calm. She had it all worked out. She realized somebody would have to bring the money she might not know. She seemed to know Derry—Mr. Kingsley wouldn't bring it."

"Call him Derry," I said. "I'll be able to guess who you mean."

She smiled faintly. "She will go into this Peacock Lounge every hour about fifteen minutes past the hour. I—I guess I assumed you would be the one to go. I described you to her. And you're to wear Derry's scarf. I described that. He keeps some clothes at the office and this was among them. It's distinctive enough."

It was all of that. It was an affair of fat green kidneys laid down on an egg yolk background. It would be almost as distinctive as if I went in there wheeling a red, white and blue wheelbarrow.

"For a blimp brain she's doing all right," I said.

"This is no time to fool around," Kingsley put in sharply.

"You said that before," I told him. "You've got a hell of a crust assuming I'll go down there and take a getaway stake to somebody I know the police are looking for."

He twisted a hand on his knee and his face twisted into a crooked grin.

"I admit it's a bit thick," he said. "Well, how about it?"

"It makes accessories after the fact out of all three of us. That might not be too tough for her husband and his confidential secretary to talk out of, but what they would do to me would be nobody's dream of a vacation."

"I'm going to make it worth your while," he said. "And we wouldn't be accessories, if she hasn't done anything."

"I'm willing to suppose it," I said. "Otherwise I wouldn't be talking to you. And in addition to that, if I decide she did do any murder, I'm going to turn her over to the police."

"She won't talk to you," he said.

I reached for the envelope and put it in my pocket. "She will, if she wants this." I looked at my strap watch. "If I start right away, I might make the one-fifteen deadline. They must know her by heart in that bar after all these hours. That makes it nice too."

"She's dyed her hair dark brown," Miss Fromsett said. "That ought to help a little."

I said: "It doesn't help me to think she is just an innocent wayfarer." I finished my drink and stood up. Kingsley swallowed his at a gulp and stood up and got the scarf off his neck and handed it to me.

"What did you do to get the police on your neck down there?" he asked.

"I was using some information Miss Fromsett very kindly got for me. And that led to my looking for a man named Talley who worked on the Almore case. And that led to the clink. They had the house staked. Talley was the dick the Graysons hired," I added, looking at the tall dark girl. "You'll probably be able to explain to him what it's all about. It doesn't matter anyway. I haven't time to go into it now. You two want to wait here?"

Kingsley shook his head. "We'll go to my place and wait for a call from you."

Miss Fromsett stood up and yawned. "No. I'm tired, Derry. I'm going home and going to bed."

"You'll come with me," he said sharply. "You've got to keep me from going nuts."

"Where do you live, Miss Fromsett?" I asked.

"Bryson Tower on Sunset Place. Apartment 716. Why?" She gave me a speculative look.

"I might want to reach you some time."

Kingsley's face looked bleakly irritated, but his eyes still were the eyes of a sick animal. I wound his scarf around my neck and went out to the dinette to switch off the light. When I came back they were both standing by the door. Kingsley had his arm around her shoulders. She looked very tired and rather bored.

"Well, I certainly hope—" he started to say, then took a quick step and put his hand out. "You're a pretty level guy, Marlowe."

"Go on, beat it," I said. "Go away. Go far away."

He gave a queer look and they went out.

I waited until I heard the elevator come up and stop, and the doors open and close again, and the elevator start down. Then I went out myself and took the stairs down to the basement garage and got the Chrysler awake again.

30

The Peacock Lounge was a narrow front next to a gift shop in whose window a tray of small crystal animals shimmered in the street light. The Peacock had a glass brick front and soft light glowed out around the stained glass peacock that was set into the brick. I went in around a Chinese screen and looked along the bar and then sat at the outer edge of a small booth. The light was amber, the leather was Chinese red and the booths had polished plastic tables. In one booth four soldiers were drinking beer moodily, a little glassy in the eyes and obviously bored even with drinking beer. Across from them a party of two girls and two flashy-looking men were making the only noise in the place. I saw nobody that looked like my idea of Crystal Kingsley.

A wizened waiter with evil eyes and a face like a gnawed bone put a napkin with a printed peacock on it down on the table in front of me and gave me a bacardi cocktail. I sipped it and looked at the amber face of the bar clock. It was just past one-fifteen.

One of the men with the two girls got up suddenly and stalked along to the door and went on. The voice of the other man said:

"What did you have to insult the guy for?"

A girl's tinny voice said: "Insult him? I like that. He propositioned me."

The man's voice said complainingly: "Well, you didn't have to insult him, did you?"

One of the soldiers suddenly laughed deep in his chest and then wiped the laugh off his face with a brown hand and drank a little more beer. I rubbed the back of my knee. It was hot and swollen still but the paralyzed feeling had gone away.

A tiny, white-faced Mexican boy with enormous black eyes came in with morning papers and scuttled along the booths trying to make a few sales before the barman threw him out. I bought a paper and looked through it to see if there were any interesting murders. There were not.

I folded it and looked up as a slim, brown-haired girl in coal black slacks and a yellow shirt and a long gray coat came out of somewhere and passed the booth without looking at me. I tried to make up my mind whether her face was familiar or just such a standard type of lean, rather hard, prettiness that I must have seen it ten thousand times. She went out of the street door around the screen. Two minutes later the little Mexican boy came back in, shot a quick look at the barman, and scuttled over to stand in front of me.

"Mister," he said, his great big eyes shining with mischief. Then he made a beckoning sign and scuttled out again.

I finished my drink and went after him. The girl in the gray coat and yellow shirt and black slacks was standing in front of the gift shop, looking in at the window. Her eyes moved as I went out. I went and stood beside her.

She looked at me again. Her face was white and tired. Her hair looked darker than dark brown. She looked away and spoke to the window.

"Give me the money, please." A little mist formed on the plate glass from her breath.

I said: "I'd have to know who you are."

"You know who I am," she said softly. "How much did you bring?"

"Five hundred."

"It's not enough," she said. "Not nearly enough. Give it to me quickly. I've been waiting half of eternity for somebody to get here."

"Where can we talk?"

"We don't have to talk. Just give me the money and go the other way."

"It's not that simple. I'm doing this at quite a risk. I'm at least going to have the satisfaction of knowing what goes on and where I stand."

"Damn you," she said acidly, "why couldn't he come himself? I don't want to talk. I want to get away as soon as I can."

"You didn't want him to come himself. He understood that you didn't even want to talk to him on the phone."

"That's right," she said quickly and tossed her head.

"But you've got to talk to me," I said. "I'm not as easy as he is. Either to me or to the law. There's no way out of it. I'm a private detective and I have to have some protection too."

"Well, isn't he charming," she said. "Private detective and all." Her voice held a low sneer.

"He did the best he knew how. It wasn't easy for him to know what to do."

"What do you want to talk about?"

"You, and what you've been doing and where you've been and what you expect to do. Things like that. Little things, but important."

She breathed on the glass of the shop window and waited while the mist of her breath disappeared.

"I think it would be much better," she said in the same cool empty voice, "for you to give me the money and let me work things out for myself."

"No."

She gave me another sharp sideways glance. She shrugged the shoulders of the gray coat impatiently.

"Very well, if it has to be that way. I'm at the Granada, two blocks north on Eighth. Apartment 618. Give me ten minutes. I'd rather go in alone."

"I have a car."

"I'd rather go alone." She turned quickly and walked away.

She walked back to the corner and crossed the boulevard and disappeared along the block under a line of pepper trees. I went and sat in the Chrysler and gave her her ten minutes before I started it.

The Granada was an ugly gray building on a corner. The plate glass entrance door was level with the street. I drove around the corner and saw a milky globe with *Garage* painted on it. The entrance to the garage was down a ramp into the hard rubber-smelling silence of parked cars in rows. A lanky Negro came out of a glassed-in office and looked the Chrysler over.

"How much to leave this here a short time? I'm going upstairs."

He gave me a shady leer. "Kinda late, boss. She needs a good dustin' too. Be a dollar."

"What goes on here?"

"Be a dollar," he said woodenly.

I got out. He gave me a ticket. I gave him the dollar. Without my asking him he said the elevator was in back of the office, by the Men's Room.

I rode up to the sixth floor and looked at numbers on doors and listened to stillness and smelled beach air coming in at the ends of corridors. The place seemed decent enough. There would be a few happy ladies in any apartment house. That would explain the lanky Negro's dollar. A great judge of character, that boy.

I came to the door of Apartment 618 and stood outside it a moment and then knocked softly.

31

She still had the gray coat on. She stood back from the door and I went past her into a square room with twin wall beds and a minimum of uninteresting furniture. A small lamp on a window table made a dim yellowish light. The window behind it was open.

The girl said: "Sit down and talk then."

She closed the door and went to sit in a gloomy Boston rocker across the room. I sat down on a thick davenport. There was a dull green curtain hanging across an open door space, at one end of the davenport. That would lead to dressing room and bathroom. There was a closed door at the other end. That would be the kitchenette. That would be all there was.

The girl crossed her ankles and leaned her head back against the chair and looked at me under long beaded lashes. Her eyebrows were thin and arched and as brown as her hair. It was a quiet, secret face. It didn't look like the face of a woman who would waste a lot of motion.

"I got a rather different idea of you," I said, "from Kingsley."

Her lips twisted a little. She said nothing.

"From Lavery too," I said. "It just goes to show that we talk different languages to different people."

"I haven't time for this sort of talk," she said. "What is it you have to know?"

"He hired me to find you. I've been working on it. I supposed you would know that."

"Yes. His office sweetie told me that over the phone. She told me you would be a man named Marlowe. She told me about the scarf."

I took the scarf off my neck and folded it up and slipped it into a pocket. I said:

"So I know a little about your movements. Not very much. I know you left your car at the Prescott Hotel in San Bernardino and that you met Lavery there. I know you sent a wire from El Paso. What did you do then?"

"All I want from you is the money he sent. I don't see that my movements are any of your business."

"I don't have to argue about that," I said. "It's a question of whether you want the money."

"Well, we went to El Paso," she said, in a tired voice. "I thought of marrying him then. So I sent that wire. You saw the wire?"

"Yes."

"Well, I changed my mind. I asked him to go home and leave me. He made a scene."

"Did he go home and leave you?"

"Yes. Why not?"

"What did you do then?"

"I went to Santa Barbara and stayed there a few days. Over a week, in fact. Then to Pasadena. Same thing. Then to Hollywood. Then I came down here. That's all."

"You were alone all this time?"

She hesitated a little and then said: "Yes."

"Not with Lavery—any part of it?"

"Not after he went home."

"What was the idea?"

"Idea of what?" Her voice was a little sharp.

"Idea of going these places and not sending any word. Didn't you know he would be very anxious?"

"Oh, you mean my husband," she said coolly. "I don't think I worried much about him. He'd think I was in Mexico, wouldn't he? As for the idea of it all—well, I just had to think things out. My life had got to be a hopeless tangle. I had to be somewhere quite alone and try to straighten myself out."

"Before that," I said, "you spent a month at Little Fawn Lake trying to straighten it out and not getting anywhere. Is that it?"

She looked down at her shoes and then up at me and nodded earnestly. The wavy brown hair surged forward along her cheeks. She put her left hand up and pushed it back and then rubbed her temple with one finger.

"I seemed to need a new place," she said. "Not necessarily an interesting place. Just a strange place. Without associations. A place where I would be very much alone. Like a hotel."

"How are you getting on with it?"

"Not very well. But I'm not going back to Derace Kingsley. Does he want me to?"

"I don't know. Why did you come down here, to the town where Lavery was?"

She bit a knuckle and looked at me over her hand.

"I wanted to see him again. He's all mixed up in my mind. I'm not in love with him, and yet—well, I suppose in a way I am. But I don't think I want to marry him. Does that make sense?"

"That part of it makes sense. But staying away from home in a lot of crummy hotels doesn't. You've lived your own life for years, as I understand it."

"I had to be alone, to—to think things out," she said a little desperately and bit the knuckle again, hard. "Won't you please give me the money and go away?"

"Sure. Right away. But wasn't there any other reason for your going away from Little Fawn Lake just then? Anything connected with Muriel Chess, for instance?"

She looked surprised. But anyone can look surprised. "Good heavens, what would there be? That frozen-faced little drip—what is she to me?"

"I thought you might have had a fight with her—about Bill."

"Bill? Bill Chess?" She seemed even more surprised. Almost too surprised.

"Bill claims you made a pass at him."

She put her head back and let out a tinny and unreal laugh. "Good heavens, that muddy-faced boozer?" Her face sobered suddenly. "What's happened? Why all the mystery?"

"He might be a muddy-faced boozer," I said. "The police think he's a murderer too. Of his wife. She's been found drowned in the lake. After a month."

She moistened her lips and held her head on one side, staring at me fixedly. There was a quiet little silence. The damp breath of the Pacific slid into the room around us.

"I'm not too surprised," she said slowly. "So it came to that in the end. They fought terribly at times. Did you think that had something to do with my leaving?"

I nodded. "There was a chance of it."

"It didn't have anything to do with it at all," she said seriously, and shook her head back and forth. "It was just the way I told you. Nothing else."

"Muriel's dead," I said. "Drowned in the lake. You don't get much of a boot out of that, do you?"

"I hardly knew the girl," she said. "Really. She kept to herself. After all—"

"I don't suppose you knew she had once worked in Dr. Almore's office?"

She looked completely puzzled now. "I was never in Dr. Almore's office," she said slowly. "He made a few house calls a long time ago. I—what are you talking about?"

"Muriel Chess was really a girl called Mildred Haviland, who had been Dr. Almore's office nurse."

"That's a queer coincidence," she said wonderingly. "I knew Bill met her in Riverside. I didn't know how or under what circumstances or where she came from. Dr. Almore's office, eh? It doesn't have to mean anything, does it?"

I said, "No. I guess it's a genuine coincidence. They do happen. But you see why I had to talk to you. Muriel being found drowned and you having gone away and Muriel being Mildred Haviland who was connected with Dr. Almore at one time—as Lavery was also, in a different way. And of course Lavery lives across the street from Dr. Almore. Did he, Lavery, seem to know Muriel from somewhere else?"

She thought about it, biting her lower lip gently. "He saw her up there," she said finally. "He didn't act as if he had ever seen her before."

"And he would have," I said. "Being the kind of guy he was."

"I don't think Chris had anything to do with Dr. Almore," she said. "He knew Dr. Almore's wife. I don't think he knew the doctor at all. So he probably wouldn't know Dr. Almore's office nurse."

"Well, I guess there's nothing in all this to help me," I said. "But you can see why I had to talk to you. I guess I can give you the money now."

I got the envelope out and stood up to drop it on her knee. She let it lie there. I sat down again.

"You do this character very well," I said. "This confused innocence with an undertone of hardness and bitterness. People have made a bad mistake about you. They have been thinking of you as a reckless little idiot with no brains and no control. They have been very wrong."

She stared at me, lifting her eyebrows. She said nothing. Then a small smile lifted the corners of her mouth. She reached for the envelope, tapped it on her knee, and laid it aside on the table. She stared at me all the time.

"You did the Fallbrook character very well too," I said. "Looking back on it, I think it was a shade overdone. But at the time it had me going all right. That purple hat that would have been all right on blonde hair but looked like hell on straggly brown, that messed-up makeup that looked as if it had been put on in the dark by somebody with a sprained wrist, the jittery screwball manner. All very good. And when you put the gun in my hand like that—I fell like a brick."

She snickered and put her hands in the deep pockets of her coat. Her heels tapped on the floor.

"But why did you go back at all?" I asked. "Why take such a risk in broad daylight, in the middle of the morning?"

"So you think I shot Chris Lavery?" she said quietly.

"I don't think it. I know it."

"Why did I go back? Is that what you want to know?"

"I don't really care," I said.

She laughed. A sharp cold laugh. "He had all my money," she said. "He had stripped my purse. He had it all, even silver. That's why I went back. There wasn't any risk at all. I know how he lived. It was really safer to go back. To take in the milk and the newspaper for instance. People lose their heads in these situations. I don't, I didn't see why I should. It's so very much safer not to."

"I see," I said. "Then of course you shot him the night before. I ought to have thought of that, not that it matters. He had been shaving. But guys with dark beards and lady friends sometimes shave the last thing at night, don't they?"

"It has been heard of," she said almost gaily. "And just what are you going to do about it?"

"You're a cold-blooded little bitch if ever I saw one," I said. "Do about it? Turn you over to the police naturally. It will be a pleasure."

"I don't think so." She threw the words out, almost with a lilt. "You wondered why I gave you the empty gun. Why not? I had another one in my bag. Like this."

Her right hand came up from her coat pocket and she pointed it at me.

I grinned. It may not have been the heartiest grin in the world, but it was a grin.

"I've never liked this scene," I said. "Detective confronts murderer. Murderer produces gun, points same at detective. Murderer tells detective the whole sad story, with the idea of shooting him at the end of it. Thus wasting a lot of valuable time, even if in the end murderer did shoot detective. Only murderer never does. Something always happens to prevent it. The gods don't like this scene either. They always manage to spoil it."

"But this time," she said softly and got up and moved towards me softly across the carpet, "suppose we make it a little different. Suppose I don't tell you anything and nothing happens and I do shoot you?"

"I still wouldn't like the scene," I said.

"You don't seem to be afraid," she said, and slowly licked her lips coming towards me very gently without any sound of footfalls on the carpet.

"I'm not afraid," I lied. "It's too late at night, too still, and the window is open and the gun would make too much noise. It's too long a journey down to the street and you're not good with guns. You would probably miss me. You missed Lavery three times."

"Stand up," she said.

I stood up.

"I'm going to be too close to miss," she said. She pushed the gun against my chest. "Like this. I really can't miss now, can I? Now be very still. Hold your hands up by your shoulders and then don't move at all. If you move at all, the gun will go off."

I put my hands up beside my shoulders. I looked down at the gun. My tongue felt a little thick, but I could still wave it.

Her probing left hand didn't find a gun on me. It dropped and she bit her lip, staring at me. The gun bored into my chest. "You'll have to turn around now," she said, polite as a tailor at a fitting.

"There's something a little off key about everything you do," I said. "You're definitely not good with guns. You're much too close to me, and I hate to bring this up—but there's that old business of the safety catch not being off. You've overlooked that too."

So she started to do two things at once. To take a long step backwards and to feel with her thumb for the safety catch, without taking her eyes off my face. Two very simple things, needing only a second to do. But she didn't like my telling her. She didn't like my thought riding over hers. The minute confusion of it jarred her.

She let out a small choked sound and I dropped my right hand and yanked her face hard against my chest. My left hand smashed down on her right wrist, the heel of my hand against the base of her thumb. The gun jerked out of her hand to the floor. Her face writhed against my chest and I think she was trying to scream.

Then she tried to kick me and lost what little balance she had left. Her hands came up to claw at me. I caught her wrist and began to twist it behind her back. She was very strong, but I was very much stronger. So she decided to go limp and let her whole weight sag against the hand that was holding her head. I couldn't hold her up with one hand. She started to go down and I had to bend down with her.

There were vague sounds of our scuffling on the floor by the davenport, and hard breathing, and if a floor board creaked I didn't hear it. I thought a curtain ring checked sharply on a rod. I wasn't sure and I had no time to consider the question. A figure loomed up suddenly on my left, just behind, and out of range of clear vision. I knew there was a man there and that he was a big man.

That was all I knew. The scene exploded into fire and darkness. I didn't even remember being slugged. Fire and darkness and just before the darkness a sharp flash of nausea.

32

I smelled of gin. Not just casually, as if I had taken four or five drinks of a winter morning to get out of bed on, but as if the Pacific Ocean was pure gin and I had nose-dived off the boat deck. The gin was in my hair and eyebrows, on my chin and under my chin. It was on my shirt. I smelled like dead toads.

My coat was off and I was lying flat on my back beside the davenport on somebody's carpet and I was looking at a framed picture. The frame was of cheap soft wood varnished and the picture showed part of an enormously high pale yellow viaduct across which a shiny black locomotive was dragging a Prussian blue train. Through one lofty arch of the viaduct a wide yellow beach showed and was dotted with sprawled bathers and striped beach umbrellas. Three girls walked close up, with paper parasols, one girl in cerise, one in pale blue, one in green. Beyond the beach a curving bay was bluer than any bay has any right to be. It was drenched with sunshine and flecked and dotted with aching white sails. Beyond the inland curve of the bay three ranges of hills rose in three precisely opposed colors, gold and terra cotta and lavender.

Across the bottom of the picture was printed in large capitals

SEE THE FRENCH RIVIERA BY THE BLUE TRAIN.

It was a fine time to bring that up.

I reached up wearily and felt the back of my head. It felt pulpy. A shoot of pain from the touch went clear to the soles of my feet. I groaned, and made a grunt out of the groan, from professional pride —what was left of it. I rolled over slowly and carefully and looked at the foot of a pulled down wall bed; one twin, the other being still up in the wall. The flourish of design on the painted wood was familiar. The picture had hung over the davenport and I hadn't even looked at it.

When I rolled a square gin bottle rolled off my chest and hit the floor. It was water white, and empty. It didn't seem possible there could be so much gin in just one bottle.

I got my knees under me and stayed on all fours for a while, sniffing like a dog who can't finish his dinner, but hates to leave it. I moved my head around on my neck. It hurt. I moved it around some more and it still hurt, so I climbed up on my feet and discovered I didn't have any shoes on.

The shoes were lying against the baseboard, looking as dissipated as shoes ever looked. I put them on wearily. I was an old man now. I was going down the last long hill. I still had a tooth left though. I felt it with my tongue. It didn't seem to taste of gin.

"It will all come back to you," I said. "Some day it will all come back to you. And you won't like it."

There was the lamp on the table by the open window. There was the fat green davenport. There was the doorway with the green curtain across it. Never sit with your back to a green curtain. It always turns out badly. Something always happens. Who had I said that to? A girl with a gun. A girl with a clear empty face and dark brown hair that had been blonde.

I looked around for her. She was still there. She was lying on the pulled-down twin bed.

She was wearing a pair of tan stockings and nothing else. Her hair was tumbled. There were dark bruises on her throat. Her mouth was open and a swollen tongue filled it to overflowing. Her eyes bulged and the whites of them were not white.

Across her naked belly four angry scratches leered crimson red against the whiteness of flesh. Deep angry scratches, gouged out by four bitter fingernails.

On the davenport there were tumbled clothes, mostly hers. My coat was there also. I disentangled it and put it on. Something crackled under my hand in the tumbled clothes. I drew out a long envelope with money still in it. I put it in my pocket. Marlowe, five hundred dollars. I hoped it was all there. There didn't seem much else to hope for.

I stepped on the balls of my feet softly, as if walking on very thin ice. I bent down to rub behind my knee and wondered which hurt most, my knee, or my head when I bent down to rub the knee.

Heavy feet came along the hallway and there was a hard mutter of voices. The feet stopped. A hard fist knocked on the door.

I stood there leering at the door, with my lips drawn back tight against my teeth. I waited for somebody to open the door and walk in. The knob was tried, but nobody walked in. The knocking began again, stopped, the voices muttered again. The steps went away. I wondered how long it would take to get the manager with a pass key. Not very long.

Not nearly long enough for Marlowe to get home from the French Riviera.

I went to the green curtain and brushed it aside and looked down a short dark hallway into a bathroom. I went in there and put the light on. Two wash rugs on the floor, a bath mat folded over the edge of the tub, a pebbled glass window at the corner of the tub. I shut the bathroom door and stood on the edge of the tub and eased the window up. This was the sixth floor. There was no screen. I put my head out and looked into darkness and a narrow glimpse of a street with trees. I looked sideways and saw that the bathroom window of the next apartment was not more than three feet away. A well-nourished mountain goat could make it without any trouble at all.

The question was whether a battered private detective could make it, and if so, what the harvest would be.

Behind me a rather remote and muffled voice seemed to be chanting the policeman's litany: "Open it up or we'll kick it in." I sneered back at the voice. They wouldn't kick it in because kicking in a door is hard on the feet. Policemen are kind to their feet. Their feet are about all they are kind to.

I grabbed a towel off the rack and pulled the two halves of the window down and eased out on the sill. I swung half of me over to the next sill, holding on to the frame of the open window. I could just reach to push the next window down, if it was unlocked. It wasn't unlocked. I got my foot over there and kicked the glass over the catch. It made a noise that ought to have been heard in Reno. I wrapped the towel around my left hand and reached in to turn the catch. Down on the street a car went by, but nobody yelled at me.

I pushed the broken window down and climbed across to the other sill. The towel fell out of my hand and fluttered down into the darkness to a strip of grass far below, between the two wings of the building.

I climbed in at the window of the other bathroom.

33

I climbed down into darkness and groped through darkness to a door and opened it and listened. Filtered moonlight coming through north windows showed a bedroom with twin beds, made up and empty. Not wall beds. This was a larger apartment. I moved past the beds to another door and into a living room. Both rooms were closed up and smelled musty. I felt my way to a lamp and switched it on. I ran a finger along the wood of a table edge. There was a light film of dust, such as accumulates in the cleanest room when it is left shut up.

The room contained a library dining table, an armchair radio, a book rack built like a hod, a big bookcase full of novels with their jackets still on them, a dark wood highboy with a siphon and a cut glass bottle of liquor and four striped glasses upside down on an Indian brass tray. Beside this paired photographs in a double silver frame, a youngish middle-aged man and woman, with round healthy faces and cheerful eyes. They looked out at me as if they didn't mind my being there at all.

I sniffed the liquor, which was Scotch, and used some of it. It made my head feel worse but it made the rest of me feel better. I put light on the bedroom and poked into closets. One of them had a man's clothes, tailor-made, plenty of them. The tailor's label inside a coat pocket declared the owner's name to be H. G. Talbot. I went to the bureau and poked around and found a soft blue shirt that looked a little small for me. I carried it into the bathroom and stripped mine off and washed my face and chest and wiped my hair off with a wet towel and put the blue shirt on. I used plenty of Mr. Talbot's rather insistent hair tonic on my hair and used his brush and comb to tidy it up. By that time I smelled of gin only remotely, if at all.

The top button of the shirt wouldn't meet its buttonhole so I poked into the bureau again and found a dark blue crepe tie and strung it around my neck. I got my coat back on and looked at myself in the mirror. I looked slightly too neat for that hour of the night, even for as careful a man as Mr. Talbot's clothes indicated him to be. Too neat and too sober.

I rumpled my hair a little and pulled the tie loose, and went back to the whiskey decanter and did what I could about being too sober. I lit one of Mr. Talbot's cigarettes and hoped that Mr. and Mrs. Talbot, wherever they were, were having a much better time than I was. I hoped I would live long enough to come and visit them.

I went to the living room door, the one giving on the hallway, and opened it and leaned in the opening smoking. I didn't think it was going to work. But I didn't think waiting there for them to follow my trail through the window was going to work any better.

A man coughed a little way down the hall and I poked my head out farther and he was looking at me. He came towards me briskly, a small sharp man in a neatly pressed police uniform. He had reddish hair and red-gold eyes.

I yawned and said languidly: "What goes on, officer?"

He stared at me thoughtfully. "Little trouble next door to you. Hear anything?"

"I thought I heard knocking. I just got home a little while ago."

"Little late," he said.
"That's a matter of opinion," I said. "Trouble next door, ah?"
"A dame," he said. "Know her?"
"I think I've seen her."
"Yeah," he said. "You ought to see her now . . ." He put his hands to his throat and bulged his eyes out and gurgled unpleasantly.
"Like that," he said. "You didn't hear nothing, huh?"
"Nothing I noticed—except the knocking."
"Yeah. What was the name?"
"Talbot."
"Just a minute, Mr. Talbot. Wait there just a minute."
He went along the hallway and leaned into an open doorway through which light streamed out. "Oh, lieutenant," he said. "The man next door is on deck."
A tall man came out of the doorway and stood looking along the hall straight at me. A tall man with rusty hair and very blue, blue eyes. Degarmo. That made it perfect.
"Here's the guy lives next door," the small neat cop said helpfully. "His name's Talbot."
Degarmo looked straight at me, but nothing in his acid blue eyes showed that he had ever seen me before. He came quietly along the hall and put a hard hand against my chest and pushed me back into the room. When he had me half a dozen feet from the door he said over his shoulder:
"Come in here and shut the door, Shorty."
The small cop came in and shut the door.
"Quite a gag," Degarmo said lazily. "Put a gun on him, Shorty."
Shorty flicked his black belt holster open and had his .38 in his hand like a flash. He licked his lips.
"Oh boy," he said softly, whistling a little. "Oh boy. How'd you know, lieutenant?"
"Know what?" Degarmo asked, keeping his eyes fixed on mine. "What were you thinking of doing, pal—going down to get a paper—to find out if she was dead?"
"Oh boy," Shorty said. "A sex-killer. He pulled the girl's clothes off and choked her with his hands, lieutenant. How'd you know?"
Degarmo didn't answer him. He just stood there, rocking a little on his heels, his face empty and granite-hard.
"Yah, he's the killer, sure," Shorty said suddenly. "Sniff the air in here, lieutenant. The place ain't been aired out for days. And look at

the dust on those bookshelves. And the clock on the mantel's stopped, lieutenant. He come in through the—lemme look a minute, can I, lieutenant?"

He ran out of the room into the bedroom. I heard him fumbling around. Degarmo stood woodenly.

Shorty came back. "Come in at the bathroom window. There's broken glass in the tub. And something stinks of gin in there something awful. You remember how that apartment smelled of gin when we went in? Here's a shirt, lieutenant. Smells like it was washed in gin."

He held the shirt up. It perfumed the air rapidly. Degarmo looked at it vaguely and then stepped forward and yanked my coat open and looked at the shirt I was wearing.

"I know what he done," Shorty said. "He stole one of the guy's shirts that lives here. You see what he done, lieutenant?"

"Yeah." Degarmo held his hand against my chest and let it fall slowly. They were talking about me as if I was a piece of wood.

"Frisk him, Shorty."

Shorty ran around me feeling here and there for a gun. "Nothing on him," he said.

"Let's get him out the back way," Degarmo said. "It's our pinch, if we make it before Webber gets here. That lug Reed couldn't find a moth in a shoe box."

"You ain't even detailed on the case," Shorty said doubtfully. "Didn't I hear you was suspended or something?"

"What can I lose?" Degarmo asked, "if I'm suspended?"

"I can lose this here uniform," Shorty said.

Degarmo looked at him wearily. The small cop blushed and his bright red-gold eyes were anxious.

"Okay, Shorty. Go and tell Reed."

The small cop licked his lip. "You say the word, lieutenant, and I'm with you. I don't have to know you got suspended."

"We'll take him down ourselves, just the two of us," Degarmo said. "Yeah, sure."

Degarmo put his finger against my chin. "A sex-killer," he said quietly. "Well, I'll be damned." He smiled at me thinly, moving only the extreme corners of his wide brutal mouth.

We went out of the apartment and along the hall the other way from Apartment 618. Light streamed from the still open door. Two men in plain clothes now stood outside it smoking cigarettes inside their cupped hands, as if a wind was blowing. There was a sound of wrangling voices from the apartment.

We went around the bend of the hall and came to the elevator. Degarmo opened the fire door beyond the elevator shaft and we went down echoing concrete steps, floor after floor. At the lobby floor Degarmo stopped and held his hand on the doorknob and listened. He looked back over his shoulder.

"You got a car?" he asked me.

"In the basement garage."

"That's an idea."

We went on down the steps and came out into the shadowy basement. The lanky Negro came out of the little office and I gave him my car check. He looked furtively at the police uniform on Shorty. He said nothing. He pointed to the Chrysler.

Degarmo climbed under the wheel of the Chrysler. I got in beside him and Shorty got into the back seat. We went up the ramp and out into the damp cool night air. A big car with twin red spotlights was charging towards us from a couple of blocks away.

Degarmo spat out of the car window and yanked the Chrysler the other way. "That will be Webber," he said. "Late for the funeral again. We sure skinned his nose on that one, Shorty."

"I don't like it too well, lieutenant. I don't, honest."

"Keep the chin up, kid. You might get back on homicide."

"I'd rather wear buttons and eat," Shorty said. The courage was oozing out of him fast.

Degarmo drove the car hard for ten blocks and then slowed a little. Shorty said uneasily:

"I guess you know what you're doing, lieutenant, but this ain't the way to the Hall."

"That's right," Degarmo said. "It never was, was it?"

He let the car slow down to a crawl and then turned into a residential street of small exact houses squatting behind small exact lawns. He braked the car gently and coasted over to the curb and stopped about the middle of the block. He threw an arm over the back of the seat and turned his head to look back at Shorty.

"You think this guy killed her, Shorty?"

"I'm listening," Shorty said in a tight voice.

"Got a flash?"

"No."

I said: "There's one in the car pocket on the left side."

Shorty fumbled around and metal clicked and the white beam of the flashlight came on. Degarmo said:

"Take a look at the back of this guy's head."

The beam moved and settled. I heard the small man's breathing behind me and felt it on my neck. Something felt for and touched the bump on my head. I grunted. The light went off and the darkness of the street rushed in again.

Shorty said: "I guess maybe he was sapped, lieutenant. I don't get it."

"So was the girl," Degarmo said. "It didn't show much but it's there. She was sapped so she could have her clothes pulled off and be clawed up before she was killed. So the scratches would bleed. Then she was throttled. And none of this made any noise. Why would it? And there's no telephone in that apartment. Who reported it, Shorty?"

"How the hell would I know? A guy called up and said a woman had been murdered in 618 Granada Apartments on Eighth. Reed was still looking for a cameraman when you come in. The desk said a guy with a thick voice, likely disguised. Didn't give any name at all."

"All right then," Degarmo said. "If you had murdered the girl, how would you get out of there?"

"I'd walk out," Shorty said. "Why not? Hey," he barked at me suddenly, "why didn't you?"

I didn't answer him. Degarmo said tonelessly: "You wouldn't climb out of a bathroom window six floors up and then bust in another bathroom window into a strange apartment where people would likely be sleeping, would you? You wouldn't pretend to be the guy that lived there and you wouldn't throw away a lot of your time by calling the police, would you? Hell, that girl could have laid there for a week. You wouldn't throw away the chance of a start like that, would you, Shorty?"

"I don't guess I would," Shorty said cautiously. "I don't guess I would call up at all. But you know these sex fiends do funny things, lieutenant. They ain't normal like us. And this guy could have had help and the other guy could have knocked him out to put him in the middle."

"Don't tell me you thought that last bit up all by yourself," Degarmo grunted. "So here we sit, and the fellow that knows all the answers is sitting here with us and not saying a word." He turned his big head and stared at me. "What were you doing there?"

"I can't remember," I said. "The crack on the head seems to have blanked me out."

"We'll help you to remember," Degarmo said. "We'll take you up back in the hills a few miles where you can be quiet and look at the stars and remember. You'll remember all right."

Shorty said: "That ain't no way to talk, lieutenant. Why don't we just go back to the Hall and play this the way it says in the rule book?"

"To hell with the rule book," Degarmo said. "I like this guy. I want to have one long sweet talk with him. He just needs a little coaxing, Shorty. He's just bashful."

"I don't want any part of it," Shorty said.

"What you want to do, Shorty?"

"I want to go back to the Hall."

"Nobody's stopping you, kid. You want to walk?"

Shorty was silent for a moment. "That's right," he said at last, quietly. "I want to walk." He opened the car door and stepped out on to the curbing. "And I guess you know I have to report all this, lieutenant?"

"Right," Degarmo said. "Tell Webber I was asking for him. Next time he buys a hamburger, tell him to turn down an empty plate for me."

"That don't make any sense to me," the small cop said. He slammed the car door shut. Degarmo let the clutch in and gunned the motor and hit forty in the first block and a half. In the third block he hit fifty. He slowed down at the boulevard and turned east and began to cruise along at a legal speed. A few late cars drifted by both ways, but for the most part the world lay in the cold silence of early morning.

After a little while we passed the city limits and Degarmo spoke. "Let's hear you talk," he said quietly. "Maybe we can work this out."

The car topped a long rise and dipped down to where the boulevard wound through the parklike grounds of the veteran's hospital. The tall triple electroliers had halos from the beach fog that had drifted in during the night. I began to talk.

"Kingsley came over to my apartment tonight and said he had heard from his wife over the phone. She wanted some money quick. The idea was I was to take it to her and get her out of whatever trouble she was in. My idea was a little different. She was told how to identify me and I was to be at the Peacock Lounge at Eighth and Arguello at fifteen minutes past the hour. Any hour."

Degarmo said slowly: "She had to breeze and that meant she had something to breeze from, such as murder." He lifted his hands lightly and let them fall on the wheel again.

"I went down there, hours after she had called. I had been told her hair was dyed brown. She passed me going out of the bar, but I didn't know her. I had never seen her in the flesh. All I had seen was what looked like a pretty good snapshot, but could be that and still not a very good likeness. She sent a Mexican kid in to call me out. She wanted the money and no conversation. I wanted her story. Finally she saw she would have to talk a little and told me she was at the Granada. She made me wait ten minutes before I followed her over."

Degarmo said: "Time to fix up a plant."

"There was a plant all right, but I'm not sure she was in on it. She didn't want me to come up there, didn't want to talk. Yet she ought to have known I would insist on some explanation before I gave up the money, so her reluctance could have been just an act, to make me feel that I was controlling the situation. She could act all right. I found that out. Anyhow I went and we talked. Nothing she said made very much sense until we talked about Lavery getting shot. Then she made too much sense too quick. I told her I was going to turn her over to the police."

Westwood Village, dark except for one all night service station and a few distant windows in apartment houses, slid away to the north of us.

"So she pulled a gun," I said. "I think she meant to use it, but she got too close to me and I got a headlock on her. While we were wrestling around, somebody came out from behind a green curtain and slugged me. When I came out of that the murder was done."

Degarmo said slowly: "You get any kind of a look at who slugged you?"

"No. I felt or half saw he was a man and a big one. And this lying on the davenport, mixed in with clothes." I reached Kingsley's yellow and green scarf out of my pocket and draped it over his knee. "I saw Kingsley wearing this earlier this evening," I said.

Degarmo looked down at the scarf. He lifted it under the dashlight. "You wouldn't forget that too quick," he said. "It steps right up and smacks you in the eye. Kingsley, huh? Well, I'm damned. What happened then?"

"Knocking on the door. Me still woozy in the head, not too bright and a bit panicked. I had been flooded with gin and my shoes and coat stripped off and maybe I looked and smelled a little like somebody who would yank a woman's clothes off and strangle her. So I got out through the bathroom window, cleaned myself up as well as I could, and the rest you know."

Degarmo said: "Why didn't you lie dormy in the place you climbed into?"

"What was the use? I guess even a Bay City cop would have found the way I had gone in a little while. If I had any chance at all, it was to walk out before that was discovered. If nobody was there who knew me, I had a fair chance of getting out of the building."

"I don't think so," Degarmo said. "But I can see where you didn't lose much trying. What's your idea of the motivation here?"

"Why did Kingsley kill her—if he did? That's not hard. She had been cheating on him, making him a lot of trouble, endangering his job and now she had killed a man. Also, she had money and Kingsley wanted to marry another woman. He might have been afraid that with money to spend she could beat the rap and be left laughing at him. If she didn't beat the rap, and got sent up, her money would be just as thoroughly beyond his reach. He'd have to divorce her to get rid of her. There's plenty of motive for murder in all that. Also he saw a chance to make me the goat. It wouldn't stick, but it would make confusion and delay. If murderers didn't think they could get away with their murders, very few would be committed."

Degarmo said: "All the same it could be somebody else, somebody who isn't in the picture at all. Even if he went down there to see her, it could still be somebody else. Somebody else could have killed Lavery too."

"If you like it that way."

He turned his head. "I don't like it any way at all. But if I crack the case, I'll get by with a reprimand from the police board. If I don't crack it, I'll be thumbing a ride out of town. You said I was dumb.

Okay, I'm dumb. Where does Kingsley live? One thing I know is how to make people talk."

"965 Carson Drive, Beverly Hills. About five blocks on you turn north to the foothills. It's on the left side, just below Sunset. I've never been there, but I know how the block numbers run."

He handed me the green and yellow scarf. "Tuck that back into your pocket until we want to spring it on him."

35

It was a two-storied white house with a dark roof. Bright moonlight lay against its wall like a fresh coat of paint. There were wrought iron grilles against the lower halves of the front windows. A level lawn swept up to the front door, which was set diagonally into the angle of a jutting wall. All the visible windows were dark.

Degarmo got out of the car and walked along the parkway and looked back along the drive to the garage. He moved down the driveway and the corner of the house hid him. I heard the sound of a garage door going up, then the thud as it was lowered again. He reappeared at the corner of the house, shook his head at me, and walked across the grass to the front door. He leaned his thumb on the bell and juggled a cigarette out of his pocket with one hand and put it between his lips.

He turned away from the door to light it and the flare of the match cut deep lines into his face. After a while there was light on the fan over the door. The peephole in the door swung back. I saw Degarmo holding up his shield. Slowly and as if unwillingly the door was opened. He went in.

He was gone four or five minutes. Light went on behind various windows, then off again. Then he came out of the house and while he was walking back to the car the light went off in the fan and the whole house was again as dark as we had found it.

He stood beside the car smoking and looking off down the curve of the street.

"One small car in the garage," he said. "The cook says it's hers. No sign of Kingsley. They say they haven't seen him since this morning. I looked in all the rooms. I guess they told the truth. Webber and a print man were there late this afternoon and the dusting powder is still all over the main bedroom. Webber would be getting prints to check against what we found in Lavery's house. He didn't tell me what he got. Where would he be—Kingsley?"

"Anywhere," I said. "On the road, in a hotel, in a Turkish bath getting the kinks out of his nerves. But we'll have to try his girl friend first. Her name is Fromsett and she lives at the Bryson Tower on Sunset Place. That's away downtown, near Bullock's Wilshire."

"She does what?" Degarmo asked, getting in under the wheel.

"She holds the fort in his office and holds his hand out of office hours. She's no office cutie, though. She has brains and style."

"This situation is going to use all she has," Degarmo said. He drove down to Wilshire and we turned east again.

Twenty-five minutes brought us to the Bryson Tower, a white stucco palace with fretted lanterns in the forecourt and tall date palms. The entrance was in an L, up marble steps, through a Moorish archway, and over a lobby that was too big and a carpet that was too blue. Blue Ali Baba oil jars were dotted around, big enough to keep tigers in. There was a desk and a night clerk with one of those mustaches that get stuck under your fingernail.

Degarmo lunged past the desk towards an open elevator beside which a tired old man sat on a stool waiting for a customer. The clerk snapped at Degarmo's back like a terrier.

"One moment, please. Whom did you wish to see?"

Degarmo spun on his heel and looked at me wonderingly. "Did he say 'whom'?"

"Yeah, but don't hit him," I said. "There is such a word."

Degarmo licked his lips. "I knew there was," he said. "I often wondered where they kept it. Look, buddy," he said to the clerk, "we want up to seven-sixteen. Any objection?"

"Certainly I have," the clerk said coldly. "We don't announce guests at—" he lifted his arm and turned it neatly to look at the narrow oblong watch on the inside of his wrist,—"at twenty-three minutes past four in the morning."

"That's what I thought," Degarmo said. "So I wasn't going to bother you. You get the idea?" He took his shield out of his pocket and held it so that the light glinted on the gold and the blue enamel. "I'm a police lieutenant."

The clerk shrugged. "Very well. I hope there isn't going to be any trouble. I'd better announce you then. What names?"

"Lieutenant Degarmo and Mr. Marlowe."

"Apartment 716. That will be Miss Fromsett. One moment."

He went behind a glass screen and we heard him talking on the phone after a longish pause. He came back and nodded.

"Miss Fromsett is in. She will receive you."

"That's certainly a load off my mind," Degarmo said. "And don't bother to call your house peeper and send him up to the scatter. I'm allergic to house peepers."

The clerk gave a small cold smile and we got into the elevator.

The seventh floor was cool and quiet. The corridor seemed a mile long. We came at last to a door with 716 on it in gilt numbers in a circle of gilt leaves. There was an ivory button beside the door. Degarmo pushed it and chimes rang inside the door and it was opened.

Miss Fromsett wore a quilted blue robe over her pajamas. On her feet were small tufted slippers with high heels. Her dark hair was fluffed out engagingly and the cold cream had been wiped from her face and just enough makeup applied.

We went past her into a rather narrow room with several handsome oval mirrors and gray period furniture upholstered in blue damask. It didn't look like apartment house furniture. She sat down on a slender love seat and leaned back and waited calmly for somebody to say something.

I said: "This is Lieutenant Degarmo of the Bay City police. We're looking for Kingsley. He's not at his house. We thought you might be able to give us an idea where to find him."

She spoke to me without looking at me. "Is it that urgent?"

"Yes. Something has happened."

"What has happened?"

Degarmo said bluntly: "We just want to know where Kingsley is, sister. We don't have time to build up a scene."

The girl looked at him with a complete absence of expression. She looked back at me and said:

"I think you had better tell me, Mr. Marlowe."

"I went down there with the money," I said. "I met her as arranged. I went to her apartment to talk to her. While there I was slugged by a man who was hidden behind a curtain. I didn't see the man. When I came out of it she had been murdered."

"Murdered?"

I said: "Murdered."

She closed her fine eyes and the corners of her lovely mouth drew in. Then she stood up with a quick shrug and went over to a small, marble-topped table with spindly legs. She took a cigarette out of a small embossed silver box and lit it, staring emptily down at the table. The match in her hand was waved more and more slowly until it stopped, still burning, and she dropped it into a tray. She turned and put her back to the table.

"I suppose I ought to scream or something," she said. "I don't seem to have any feeling about it at all."

Degarmo said: "We don't feel so interested in your feelings right now. What we want to know is where Kingsley is. You can tell us or not tell us. Either way you can skip the attitudes. Just make your mind up."

She said to me quietly: "The lieutenant here is a Bay City officer?"

I nodded. She turned at him slowly, with a lovely contemptuous dignity. "In that case," she said, "he has no more right in my apartment than any other loud-mouthed bum that might try to toss his weight around."

Degarmo looked at her bleakly. He grinned and walked across the room and stretched his long legs from a deep downy chair. He waved his hand at me.

"Okay, you work on her. I can get all the co-operation I need from the L.A. boys, but by the time I had things explained to them, it would be a week from next Tuesday."

I said: "Miss Fromsett, if you know where he is, or where he started to go, please tell us. You can understand that he has to be found."

She said calmly, "Why?"

Degarmo put his head back and laughed. "This babe is good," he said. "Maybe she thinks we should keep it a secret from him that his wife has been knocked off."

"She's better than you think," I told him. His face sobered and he bit his thumb. He looked her up and down insolently.

She said: "Is it just because he has to be told?"

I took the yellow and green scarf out of my pocket and shook it out loose and held it in front of her.

"This was found in the apartment where she was murdered. I think you have seen it."

She looked at the scarf and she looked at me, and in neither of the glances was there any meaning. She said: "You ask for a great deal of confidence, Mr. Marlowe. Considering that you haven't been such a very smart detective after all."

"I ask for it," I said, "and I expect to get it. And how smart I've been is something you don't really know anything about."

"This is cute," Degarmo put in. "You two make a nice team. All you need is acrobats to follow you. But right now—"

She cut through his voice as if he didn't exist. "How was she murdered?"

"She was strangled and stripped naked and scratched up."

"Derry wouldn't have done anything like that," she said quietly.

Degarmo made a noise with his lips. "Nobody ever knows what anybody else will do, sister. A cop knows that much."

She still didn't look at him. In the same level tone she asked: "Do you want to know where we went after we left your apartment and whether he brought me home—things like that?"

"Yes."

"Because if he did, he wouldn't have had time to go down to the beach and kill her? Is that it?"

I said, "That's a good part of it."

"He didn't bring me home," she said slowly. "I took a taxi on Hollywood Boulevard, not more than five minutes after we left your place. I didn't see him again. I supposed he went home."

Degarmo said: "Usually the bim tries to give her boy friend a bit more alibi than that. But it takes all kinds, don't it?"

Miss Fromsett said to me: "He wanted to bring me home, but it was a long way out of his way and we were both tired. The reason I was telling you this is because I know it doesn't matter in the least. If I thought it did, I wouldn't tell you."

"So he did have time," I said.

She shook her head. "I don't know. I don't know how much time was needed. I don't know how he could have known where to go. Not from me, not from her through me. She didn't tell me." Her dark eyes were on mine, searching, probing. "Is this the kind of confidence you ask for?"

I folded the scarf up and put it back in my pocket. "We want to know where he is now."

"I can't tell you because I have no idea." Her eyes had followed the scarf down to my pocket. They stayed there. "You say you were slugged. You mean knocked unconscious?"

"Yes. By somebody who was hidden out behind a curtain. We still fall for it. She pulled a gun on me and I was busy trying to take it away from her. There's no doubt she shot Lavery."

Degarmo stood up suddenly: "You're making yourself a nice smooth scene, fellow," he growled. "But you're not getting anywhere. Let's blow."

I said: "Wait a minute. I'm not finished. Suppose he had something on his mind, Miss Fromsett, something that was eating pretty deep into him. That was how he looked tonight. Suppose he knew more about all this than we realized—or than I realized—and knew things were coming to a head. He would want to go somewhere quietly and try to figure out what to do. Don't you think he might?"

I stopped and waited, looking sideways at Degarmo's impatience. After a moment the girl said tonelessly: "He wouldn't run away or hide, because it wasn't anything he could run away and hide from. But he might want a time to himself to think."

"In a strange place, in a hotel," I said, thinking of the story that had been told me in the Granada. "Or in a much quieter place than that."

I looked around for the telephone.

"It's in my bedroom," Miss Fromsett said, knowing at once what I was looking for.

I went down the room and through the door at the end. Degarmo was right behind me. The bedroom was ivory and ashes of roses. There was a big bed with no footboard and a pillow with the rounded hollow of a head. Toilet articles glistened on a built-in dresser with paneled mirrors on the wall above it. An open door showed mulberry bathroom tiles. The phone was on a night table by the bed.

I sat down on the edge of the bed and patted the place where Miss Fromsett's head had been and lifted the phone and dialed long distance. When the operator answered I asked for Constable Jim Patton at Puma Point, person to person, very urgent. I put the phone back in the cradle and lit a cigarette. Degarmo glowered down at me, standing with his legs apart, tough and tireless and ready to be nasty.

"What now?" he grunted.

"Wait and see."

"Who's running this show?"

"You're asking me shows that. I am—unless you want the Los Angeles police to run it."

He scratched a match on his thumbnail and watched it burn and tried to blow it out with a long steady breath that just bent the flame over. He got rid of that match and put another between his teeth and chewed on it. The phone rang in a moment.

"Ready with your Puma Point call."

Patton's sleepy voice came on the line. "Yes? This is Patton at Puma Point."

"This is Marlowe in Los Angeles," I said. "Remember me?"

"Sure I remember you, son. I ain't only half awake though."

"Do me a favor," I said. "Although I don't know why you should. Go or send over to Little Fawn Lake and see if Kingsley is there. Don't let him see you. You can spot his car outside the cabin or maybe see lights. And see that he stays put. Call me back as soon as you know. I'm coming up. Can you do that?"

Patton said: "I got no reason to stop him if he wants to leave."

"I'll have a Bay City police officer with me who wants to question him about a murder. Not your murder, another one."

There was a drumming silence along the wire. Patton said: "You ain't just bein' tricky, are you, son?"

"No. Call me back at Tunbridge 2722."

"Should likely take me half an hour," he said.

I hung up. Degarmo was grinning now. "This babe flash you a signal I couldn't read?"

I stood up off the bed. "No. I'm just trying to read his mind. He's no cold killer. Whatever fire there was is all burned out of him by now. I thought he might go to the quietest and most remote place he knows—just to get a grip of himself. In a few hours he'll probably turn himself in. It would look better for you if you got to him before he did that."

"Unless he puts a slug in his head," Degarmo said coldly. "Guys like him are very apt to do that."

"You can't stop him until you find him."

"That's right."

We went back into the living room. Miss Fromsett poked her head out of her kitchenette and said she was making coffee, and did we want any. We had some coffee and sat around looking like people seeing friends off at the railroad station.

The call from Patton came through in about twenty-five minutes. There was light in the Kingsley cabin and a car was parked beside it.

36

We ate some breakfast at Alhambra and I had the tank filled. We drove out Highway 70 and started moving past the trucks into the rolling ranch country. I was driving. Degarmo sat moodily in the corner, his hands deep in his pockets.

I watched the fat straight rows of orange trees spin by like the spokes of a wheel. I listened to the whine of the tires on the pavement and I felt tired and stale from lack of sleep and too much emotion.

We reached the long slope south of San Dimas that goes up to a ridge and drops down into Pomona. This is the ultimate end of the fog belt, and the beginning of that semi-desert region where the sun is as light and dry as old sherry in the morning, as hot as a blast furnace at noon, and drops like an angry brick at nightfall.

Degarmo stuck a match in the corner of his mouth and said almost sneeringly:

"Webber gave me hell last night. He said he was talking to you and what about."

I said nothing. He looked at me and looked away again. He waved a hand outwards. "I wouldn't live in this damn country if they gave it to me. The air's stale before it gets up in the morning."

"We'll be coming to Ontario in a minute. We'll switch over to Foothill Boulevard and you'll see five miles of the finest grevillea trees in the world."

"I wouldn't know one from a fireplug," Degarmo said.

We came to the center of town and turned north on Euclid, along the splendid parkway. Degarmo sneered at the grevillea trees.

After a while he said: "That was my girl that drowned in the lake up there. I haven't been right in the head since I heard about it. All I can see is red. If I could get my hands on that guy Chess—"

"You made enough trouble," I said, "letting her get away with murdering Almore's wife."

I stared straight ahead through the windshield. I knew his head moved and his eyes froze on me. I didn't know what his hands were doing. I didn't know what expression was on his face. After a long time his words came. They came through tight teeth and edgeways, and they scraped a little as they came out.

"You a little crazy or something?"

"No," I said. "Neither are you. You know as well as anybody could know anything that Florence Almore didn't get up out of bed and walk down to that garage. You know she was carried. You know that was why Talley stole her slipper, the slipper that had never walked on a concrete path. You knew that Almore gave his wife a shot in the arm at Condy's place and that it was just enough and not any too much. He knew his shots in the arm the way you know how to rough up a bum that hasn't any money or any place to sleep. You know that Almore didn't murder his wife with morphine and that if he wanted to murder her, morphine would be the last thing in the world he would use. But you know that somebody else did, and that Almore carried her down to the garage and put her there—technically still alive to breathe in some monoxide, but medically just as dead as though she had stopped breathing. You know all that."

Degarmo said softly: "Brother, how did you ever manage to live so long?"

I said: "By not falling for too many gags and not getting too much afraid of professional hard guys. Only a heel would have done what Almore did, only a heel and a badly scared man who had things on his soul that wouldn't stand daylight. Technically he may even have been guilty of murder. I don't think the point has ever been settled. Certainly he would have a hell of a time proving that she was in such a deep coma that she was beyond any possibility of help. But as a practical matter of who killed her, you know the girl killed her."

Degarmo laughed. It was a grating unpleasant laugh, not only mirthless, but meaningless.

We reached Foothill Boulevard and turned east again. I thought it was still cool, but Degarmo was sweating. He couldn't take his coat off because of the gun under his arm.

I said: "The girl, Mildred Haviland, was playing house with Almore and his wife knew it. She had threatened him. I got that from her parents. The girl, Mildred Haviland, knew all about morphine and where to get all of it she needed and how much to use. She was alone in the house with Florence Almore, after she put her to bed. She was in a perfect spot to load a needle with four or five grains and shoot it into an unconscious woman through the same puncture Almore had already made. She would die, perhaps while Almore was still out of the house, and he would come home and find her dead. The problem would be his. He would have to solve it. Nobody would believe anybody else had doped his wife to death. Nobody that didn't know all the circumstances. But you knew. I'd have to think you much more of a damn fool than I think you are to believe you didn't know. You covered the girl up. You were in love with her still. You scared her out of town, out of danger, out of reach, but you covered up for her. You let the murder ride. She had you that way. Why did you go up to the mountains looking for her?"

"And how did I know where to look?" he said harshly. "It wouldn't bother you to add an explanation of that, would it?"

"Not at all," I said. "She got sick of Bill Chess and his boozing and his tempers and his down-at-heels living. But she had to have money to make a break. She thought she was safe now, that she had something on Almore that was safe to use. So she wrote him for money. He sent you up to talk to her. She didn't tell Almore what her present name was or any details or where or how she was living. A letter addressed to Mildred Haviland at Puma Point would reach her. All she had to do was ask for it. But no letter came and nobody connected her with Mildred Haviland. All you had was an old photo and your usual bad manners, and they didn't get you anywhere with those people."

Degarmo said gratingly: "Who told you she tried to get money from Almore?"

"Nobody. I had to think of something to fit what happened. If Lavery or Mrs. Kingsley had known who Muriel Chess had been, and had tipped it off, you would have known where to find her and what name she was using. You didn't know those things. Therefore the lead had to come from the only person up there who knew who she was, and that was herself. So I assume she wrote to Almore."

"Okay," he said at last. "Let's forget it. It doesn't make any difference any more now. If I'm in a jam, that's my business. I'd do it again, in the same circumstances."

"That's all right," I said. "I'm not planning to put the bite on anybody myself. Not even on you. I'm telling you this mostly so you won't try to hang any murders on Kingsley that don't belong on him. If there is one that does, let it hang."

"Is that why you're telling me?" he asked.

"Yeah."

"I thought maybe it was because you hated my guts," he said.

"I'm all done with hating you," I said. "It's all washed out of me. I hate people hard, but I don't hate them very long."

We were going through the grape country now, the open sandy grape country along the scarred flanks of the foothills. We came in a little while to San Bernardino and I kept on through it without stopping.

37

At Crestline, elevation 5000 feet, it had not yet started to warm up. We stopped for a beer. When we got back into the car, Degarmo took the gun from his underarm holster and looked it over. It was a

.38 Smith and Wesson on a .44 frame, a wicked weapon with a kick like a .45 and a much greater effective range.

"You won't need that," I said. "He's big and strong, but he's not that kind of tough."

He put the gun back under his arm and grunted. We didn't talk any more now. We had no more to talk about. We rolled around the curves and along the sharp sheer edges walled with white guard rails and in some places with walls of field stone and heavy iron chains. We climbed through the tall oaks and on to the altitudes where the oaks are not so tall and the pines are taller and taller. We came at last to the dam at the end of Puma Lake.

I stopped the car and the sentry threw his piece across his body and stepped up to the window.

"Close all the windows of your car before proceeding across the dam, please."

I reached back to wind up the rear window on my side. Degarmo held his shield up. "Forget it, buddy. I'm a police officer," he said with his usual tact.

The sentry gave him a solid expressionless stare. "Close all windows, please," he said in the same tone he had used before.

"Nuts to you," Degarmo said. "Nuts to you, soldier boy."

"It's an order," the sentry said. His jaw muscles bulged very slightly. His dull grayish eyes stared at Degarmo. "And I didn't write the order, mister. Up with the windows."

"Suppose I told you to go jump in the lake," Degarmo sneered.

The sentry said: "I might do it. I scare easily." He patted the breech of his rifle with a leathery hand.

Degarmo turned and closed the windows on his side. We drove across the dam. There was a sentry in the middle and one at the far end. The first one must have flashed them some kind of signal. They looked at us with steady watchful eyes, without friendliness.

I drove on through the piled masses of granite and down through the meadows of coarse grass where cows grazed. The same gaudy slacks and short shorts and peasant handkerchiefs as yesterday, the same light breeze and golden sun and clear blue sky, the same smell of pine needles, the same cool softness of a mountain summer. But yesterday was a hundred years ago, something crystallized in time, like a fly in amber.

I turned off on the road to Little Fawn Lake and wound around the huge rocks and past the little gurgling waterfall. The gate into

Kingsley's property was open and Patton's car was standing in the road pointing towards the lake, which was invisible from that point. There was nobody in it. The card sign on the windshield still read "*Keep Jim Patton Constable. He Is Too Old To Go To Work.*"

Close to it and pointed the other way was a small battered coupe. Inside the coupe a lion hunter's hat. I stopped my car behind Patton's and locked it and got out. Andy got out of the coupe and stood staring at us woodenly.

I said: "This is Lieutenant Degarmo of the Bay City police."

Andy said: "Jim's just over the ridge. He's waiting for you. He ain't had any breakfast."

We walked up the road to the ridge as Andy got back into his coupe. Beyond it the road dropped to the tiny blue lake. Kingsley's cabin across the water seemed to be without life.

"That's the lake," I said.

Degarmo looked down at it silently. His shoulders moved in a heavy shrug. "Let's go get the bastard," was all he said.

We went on and Patton stood up from behind a rock. He was wearing the same old Stetson and khaki pants and shirt buttoned to his thick neck. The star on his left breast still had a bent point. His jaws moved slowly, munching.

"Nice to see you again," he said, not looking at me, but at Degarmo.

He put his hand out and shook Degarmo's hard paw. "Last time I seen you, lieutenant, you was wearing another name. Kind of undercover, I guess you'd call it. I guess I didn't treat you right neither. I apologize. Guess I know who that photo of yours was all the time."

Degarmo nodded and said nothing.

"Likely if I'd of been on my toes and played the game right, a lot of trouble would have been saved," Patton said. "Maybe a life would have been saved. I feel kind of bad about it, but then again I ain't a fellow that feels too bad about anything very long. Suppose we sit down here and you tell me what it is we're supposed to be doing now."

Degarmo said: "Kingsley's wife was murdered in Bay City last night. I have to talk to him about it."

"You mean you suspect him?" Patton asked.

"And how," Degarmo grunted.

Patton rubbed his neck and looked across the lake. "He ain't showed outside the cabin at all. Likely he's still asleep. Early this morning I snuck around the cabin. There was a radio goin' then and I heard sounds like a man would make playing with a bottle and a glass. I stayed away from him. Was that right?"

"We'll go over there now," Degarmo said.

"You got a gun, lieutenant?"

Degarmo patted under his left arm. Patton looked at me. I shook my head, no gun.

"Kingsley might have one too," Patton said. "I don't hanker after no fast shooting around here, lieutenant. It wouldn't do me no good to have a gunfight. We don't have that kind of community up here. You look to me like a fellow who would jack his gun out kind of fast."

"I've got plenty of swift, if that's what you mean," Degarmo said. "But I want this guy talking."

Patton looked at Degarmo, looked at me, looked back at Degarmo and spat tobacco juice in a long stream to one side.

"I ain't heard enough to even approach him," he said stubbornly.

So we sat down on the ground and told him the story. He listened silently, not blinking an eye. At the end he said to me: "You got a funny way of working for people, seems to me. Personally I think you boys are plumb misinformed. We'll go over and see. I'll go in first—in case you would know what you are talking about and Kingsley would have a gun and would be a little desperate. I got a big belly. Makes a nice target."

We stood up off the ground and started around the lake the long way. When we came to the little pier I said:

"Did they autopsy her yet, sheriff?"

Patton nodded. "She drowned all right. They say they're satisfied that's how she died. She wasn't knifed or shot or had her head cracked in or anything. There's marks on the body, but too many to mean anything. And it ain't a very nice body to work with."

Degarmo looked white and angry.

"I guess I oughtn't to have said that, lieutenant," Patton added mildly. "Kind of tough to take. Seeing you knew the lady pretty well."

Degarmo said: "Let's get it over and do what we have to do."

We went on along the shore of the lake and came to Kingsley's cabin. We went up the heavy steps. Patton went quietly across the porch to the door. He tried the screen. It was not hooked. He opened it and tried the door. That was unlocked also. He held the door shut, with the knob turned in his hand, and Degarmo took hold of the screen and pulled it wide. Patton opened the door and we walked into the room.

Derace Kingsley lay back in a deep chair by the cold fireplace with his eyes closed. There was an empty glass and an almost empty whiskey bottle on the table beside him. The room smelled of whiskey. A dish near the bottle was choked with cigarette stubs. Two crushed empty packs lay on top of the stubs.

All the windows in the room were shut. It was already close and hot in there. Kingsley was wearing a sweater and his face was flushed and heavy. He snored and his hands hung lax outside the arms of the chair, the fingertips touching the floor.

Patton moved to within a few feet of him and stood looking silently down at him for a long moment before he spoke.

"Mr. Kingsley," he said then, in a calm steady voice, "we got to talk to you a little."

38

Kingsley moved with a kind of jerk, and opened his eyes and moved them without moving his head. He looked at Patton, then at Degarmo, lastly at me. His eyes were heavy, but the light sharpened in them. He sat up slowly in the chair and rubbed his hands up and down the sides of his face.

"I was asleep," he said. "Fell asleep a couple of hours ago. I was as drunk as a skunk, I guess. Anyway, much drunker than I like to be." He dropped his hands and let them hang.

Patton said: "This is Lieutenant Degarmo of the Bay City police. He has to talk to you."

Kingsley looked briefly at Degarmo and his eyes came around to stare at me. His voice when he spoke again sounded sober and quiet and tired to death.

"So you let them get her?" he said.

I said: "I would have, but I didn't."

Kingsley thought about that, looking at Degarmo. Patton had left the front door open. He pulled the orange-yellow venetian blinds up at two front windows and pulled the windows up. He sat in a chair near one of them and clasped his hands over his stomach. Degarmo stood glowering down at Kingsley.

"Your wife is dead, Kingsley," he said brutally. "If it's any news to you."

Kingsley stared at him and moistened his lips.

"Takes it easy, don't he?" Degarmo said. "Show him the scarf."

I took the green and yellow scarf out and dangled it. Degarmo jerked a thumb. "Yours?"

Kingsley nodded. He moistened his lips again.

"Careless of you to leave it behind you," Degarmo said. He was breathing a little hard. His nose was pinched and deep lines ran from his nostrils to the corners of his mouth.

Kingsley said very quietly: "Leave it behind me where?" He had barely glanced at the scarf. He hadn't looked at all at me.

"In the Granada Apartments, on Eighth Street, in Bay City. Apartment 716. Am I telling you something?"

Kingsley now very slowly lifted his eyes to meet mine. "Is that where she was?" he breathed.

I nodded. "She didn't want me to go there. I wouldn't give her the money until she talked to me. She admitted she killed Lavery. She pulled a gun and planned to give me the same treatment. Somebody came from behind the curtain and knocked me out without letting me see him. When I came to she was dead." I told him how she was dead and how she looked. I told him what I had done and what had been done to me.

He listened without moving a muscle of his face. When I had done talking he made a vague gesture towards the scarf.

"What has that got to do with it?"

"The lieutenant regards it as evidence that you were the party hidden out in the apartment."

Kingsley thought that over. He didn't seem to get the implications of it very quickly. He leaned back in the chair and rested his head against the back. "Go on," he said at length. "I suppose you know what you're talking about. I'm quite sure I don't."

Degarmo said: "All right, play dumb. See what it gets you. You could begin by accounting for your time last night after you dropped your biddy at her apartment house."

Kingsley said evenly: "If you mean Miss Fromsett, I didn't. She went home in a taxi. I was going home myself, but I didn't. I came up here instead. I thought the trip and the night air and the quiet might help me to get straightened out."

"Just think of that," Degarmo jeered. "Straightened out from what, if I might ask?"

"Straightened out from all the worry I had been having."

"Hell," Degarmo said, "a little thing like strangling your wife and clawing her belly wouldn't worry you that much, would it?"

"Son, you hadn't ought to say things like that," Patton put in from the background. "That ain't no way to talk. You ain't produced anything yet that sounds like evidence."

"No?" Degarmo swung his hard head at him. "What about this scarf, fatty? Isn't that evidence?"

"You didn't fit it in to anything—not that I heard," Patton said peacefully. "And I ain't fat either, just well covered."

Degarmo swung away from him disgustedly. He jabbed his finger at Kingsley.

"I suppose you didn't go down to Bay City at all," he said harshly.

"No. Why should I? Marlowe was taking care of that. And I don't see why you are making a point of the scarf. Marlowe was wearing it."

Degarmo stood rooted and savage. He turned very slowly and gave me his bleak angry stare.

"I don't get this," he said. "Honest, I don't. It wouldn't be that somebody is kidding me, would it? Somebody like you?"

I said: "All I told about the scarf was that it was in the apartment and that I had seen Kingsley wearing it earlier this evening. That seemed to be all you wanted. I might have added that I had later worn the scarf myself, so the girl I was to meet could identify me that much easier."

Degarmo backed away from Kingsley and leaned against the wall at the end of the fireplace. He pulled his lower lip out with thumb and forefinger of his left hand. His right hand hung lax at his side, the fingers slightly curved.

I said: "I told you all I had ever seen of Mrs. Kingsley was a snapshot. One of us had to be sure of being able to identify the other. The scarf seemed obvious enough for identification. As a matter of fact I had seen her once before, although I didn't know it when I went to meet her. But I didn't recognize her at once," I turned to Kingsley. "Mrs. Fallbrook," I said.

"I thought you said Mrs. Fallbrook was the owner of the house," he answered slowly.

"That's what she said at the time. That's what I believed at the time. Why wouldn't I?"

Degarmo made a sound in his throat. His eyes were a little crazy, I told him about Mrs. Fallbrook and her purple hat and her fluttery manner and the empty gun she had been holding and how she gave it to me.

When I stopped, he said very carefully: "I didn't hear you tell Webber any of that."

"I didn't tell him. I didn't want to admit I had already been in the house three hours before. That I had gone to talk it over with Kingsley before I reported it to the police."

"That's something we're going to love you for," Degarmo said with a cold grin. "Jesus, what a sucker I've been. How much you paying this shamus to cover up your murders for you, Kingsley?"

"His usual rates," Kingsley told him emptily. "And a five hundred dollar bonus if he can prove my wife didn't murder Lavery."

"Too bad he can't earn that," Degarmo sneered.

"Don't be silly," I said. "I've already earned it."

There was a silence in the room. One of those charged silences which seem about to split apart with a peal of thunder. It didn't. It remained, hung heavy and solid, like a wall. Kingsley moved a little in his chair, and after a long moment, he nodded his head.

"Nobody could possibly know that better than you know it, Degarmo," I said.

Patton had as much expression on his face as a chunk of wood. He watched Degarmo quietly. He didn't look at Kingsley at all. Degarmo looked at a point between my eyes, but not as if that was anything in the room with him. Rather as if he was looking at something very far away, like a mountain across a valley.

After what seemed a very long time, Degarmo said quietly: "I don't see why. I don't know anything about Kingsley's wife. To the best of my knowledge I never laid eyes on her—until last night."

He lowered his eyelids a little and watched me broodingly. He knew perfectly well what I was going to say. I said it anyway.

"And you never saw her last night. Because she had already been dead for over a month. Because she had been drowned in Little Fawn Lake. Because the woman you saw dead in the Granada Apartments was Mildred Haviland, and Mildred Haviland was Muriel Chess. And since Mrs. Kingsley was dead long before Lavery was shot, it follows that Mrs. Kingsley did not shoot him."

Kingsley clenched his fists on the arms of his chair, but he made no sound, no sound at all.

There was another heavy silence. Patton broke it by saying in his careful slow voice: "That's kind of a wild statement, ain't it? Don't you kind of think Bill Chess would know his own wife?"

I said: "After a month in the water? With his wife's clothes on her and some of his wife's trinkets? With water-soaked blonde hair like his wife's hair and almost no recognizable face? Why would he even have a doubt about it? She left a note that might be a suicide note. She was gone away. They had quarreled. Her clothes and car had gone away. During the month she was gone, he had heard nothing from her. He had no idea where she had gone. And then this corpse comes up out of the water with Muriel's clothes on it. A blonde woman about his wife's size. Of course there would be differences and if any substitution had been suspected, they would have been found and checked. But there was no reason to suspect any such thing. Crystal Kingsley was still alive. She had gone off with Lavery. She had left her car in San Bernardino. She had sent a wire to her husband from El Paso. She was all taken care of, so far as Bill Chess was concerned. He had no thoughts about her at all. She didn't enter the picture anywhere for him. Why should she?"

Patton said: "I ought to of thought of it myself. But if I had, it would be one of those ideas a fellow would throw away almost as quick as he thought of it. It would look too kind of far-fetched."

"Superficially yes," I said. "But only superficially. Suppose the body had not come up out of the lake for a year, or not at all, unless the lake was dragged for it. Muriel Chess was gone and nobody was going to spend much time looking for her. We might never have heard of her again. Mrs. Kingsley was a different proposition. She had money and connections and an anxious husband. She would be searched for, as she was, eventually. But not very soon, unless something happened to start suspicion. It might have been a matter of months before anything was found out. The lake might have been dragged, but if a search along her trail seemed to indicate that she had actually left the lake and gone down the hill, even as far as San Bernardino, and the train from there east, then the lake might never have been dragged. And even if it was and the body was found, there was rather better than an even chance that the body would not be correctly identified. Bill Chess was arrested for his wife's murder. For all I know he might even have been convicted of it, and that would have been that, as far as the body in the lake was concerned. Crystal Kingsley would still be missing, and it would be an unsolved mystery. Eventually it would be assumed that something had happened to her and that she was no longer alive. But nobody would know where or when or how it had happened. If it hadn't been for Lavery, we might not be here talking about it now. Lavery is the key to the whole thing. He was in the Prescott Hotel in San Bernardino the night Crystal Kingsley was supposed to have left here. He saw a woman there who had Crystal Kingsley's car, who was wearing Crystal Kingsley's clothes, and of course he knew who she was. But he didn't have to know there was anything wrong. He didn't have to know they were Crystal Kingsley's clothes or that the woman had put Crystal Kingsley's car in the hotel garage. All he had to know was that he met Muriel Chess. Muriel took care of the rest."

I stopped and waited for somebody to say anything. Nobody did. Patton sat immovable in his chair, his plump, hairless hands clasped comfortably across his stomach. Kingsley leaned his head back and he had his eyes half closed and he was not moving. Degarmo leaned against the wall by the fireplace, taut and white-faced and cold, a big hard solemn man whose thoughts were deeply hidden.

I went on talking.

"If Muriel Chess impersonated Crystal Kingsley, she murdered her. That's elementary. All right, let's look at it. We know who she was and what kind of woman she was. She had already murdered before she met and married Bill Chess. She had been Dr. Almore's office nurse and his little pal and she had murdered Dr. Almore's wife in such a neat way that Almore had to cover up for her. And she had been married to a man in the Bay City police who also was sucker enough to cover up for her. She got the men that way, she could make them jump through hoops. I didn't know her long enough to see why, but her record proves it. What she was able to do with Lavery proves it. Very well, she killed people who got in her way, and Kingsley's wife got in her way too. I hadn't meant to talk about this, but it doesn't matter much now. Crystal Kingsley could make the men do a little jumping through hoops too. She made Bill Chess jump and Bill Chess's wife wasn't the girl to take that and smile. Also, she was sick to death of her life up here—she must have been—and she wanted to get away. But she needed money. She had tried to get it from Almore, and that sent Degarmo up here looking for her. That scared her a little. Degarmo is the sort of fellow you are never quite sure of. She was right not to be sure of him, wasn't she, Degarmo?"

Degarmo moved his foot on the ground. "The sands are running against you, fellow," he said grimly. "Speak your little piece while you can."

"Mildred didn't positively have to have Crystal Kingsley's car and clothes and credentials and what not, but they helped. What money she had must have helped a great deal, and Kingsley says she liked to have a good deal of money with her. Also she must have had jewelry which could eventually be turned into money. All this made killing her a rational as well as an agreeable thing to do. That disposes of motive, and we come to means and opportunity.

"The opportunity was made to order for her. She had quarreled with Bill and he had gone off to get drunk. She knew her Bill and how drunk he could get and how long he would stay away. She needed time. Time was of the essence. She had to assume that there was time. Otherwise the whole thing flopped. She had to pack her own clothes and take them in her car to Coon Lake and hide them there, because they had to be gone. She had to walk back. She had to murder Crystal Kingsley and dress her in Muriel's clothes and get her down in the lake. All that took time. As to the murder itself, I imagine she got her drunk or knocked her on the head and drowned her in the bathtub in this cabin. That would be logic and simple too. She was a nurse, she knew how to handle things like bodies. She knew how to swim—we have it from Bill that she was a fine swimmer. And a drowned body will sink. All she had to do was guide it down into the deep water where she wanted it. There is nothing in all this beyond the powers of one woman who could swim. She did it, she dressed in Crystal Kingsley's clothes, packed what else of hers she wanted, got into Crystal Kingsley's car and departed. And at San Bernardino she ran into her first snag, Lavery.

"Lavery knew her as Muriel Chess. We have no evidence and no reason whatever to assume that he knew her as anything else. He had seen her up here and he was probably on his way up here again when he met her. She wouldn't want that. All he would find would be a locked up cabin but he might get talking to Bill and it was part of her plan that Bill should not know positively that she had ever left Little Fawn Lake. So that when, and if, the body was found, he would identify it. So she put her hooks into Lavery at once, and that wouldn't be too hard. If there is one thing we know for certain about Lavery, it is that he couldn't keep his hands off the women. The more of them, the better. He would be easy for a smart girl like Mildred Haviland. So she played him and took him away with her. She took him to El Paso and there sent a wire he knew nothing about. Finally she played him back to Bay City. She probably couldn't help that. He wanted to go home and she couldn't let him get too far from her. Because Lavery was dangerous to her. Lavery alone could destroy all the indications that Crystal Kingsley had actually left Little Fawn Lake. When the search for Crystal Kingsley eventually began, it had to come to Lavery, and at that moment Lavery's life wasn't worth a plugged nickel. His first denials might not be believed, as they were not, but when he opened up with the whole story, that would be believed, because it could be checked. So the search began and immediately Lavery was shot dead in his bathroom, the very night after I went down to talk to him. That's about all there is to it, except why she went back to the house the next morning. That's just one of those things that murderers seem to do. She said he had taken her money, but I don't believe it. I think more likely she got to thinking he had some of his own hidden away, or that she had better edit the job with a cool head and make sure it was all in order and pointing the right way; or perhaps it was just what she said, and to take in the paper and the milk. Anything is possible. She went back and I found her there and she put on an act that left me with both feet in my mouth."

Patton said: "Who killed her, son? I gather you don't like Kingsley for that little job."

I looked at Kingsley and said: "You didn't talk to her on the phone, you said. What about Miss Fromsett? Did she think she was talking to your wife?"

Kingsley shook his head. "I doubt it. It would be pretty hard to fool her that way. All she said was that she seemed very changed and subdued. I had no suspicion then. I didn't have any until I got up here. When I walked into this cabin last night, I felt there was something wrong. It was too clean and neat and orderly. Crystal didn't leave things that way. There would have been clothes all over the bedroom, cigarette stubs all over the house, bottles and glasses all over the kitchen. There would have been unwashed dishes and ants and flies. I thought Bill's wife might have cleaned up, and then I remembered that Bill's wife wouldn't have, not on that particular day. She had been too busy quarreling with Bill and being murdered, or committing suicide, whichever it was. I thought about all this in a confused sort of way, but I don't claim I actually made anything of it."

Patton got up from his chair and went out on the porch. He came back wiping his lips with his tan handkerchief. He sat down again, and eased himself over on his left hip, on account of the hip holster on the other side. He looked thoughtfully at Degarmo. Degarmo stood against the wall, hard and rigid, a stone man. His right hand still hung down at his side, with the fingers curled.

Patton said: "I still ain't heard who killed Muriel. Is that part of the show or is that something that still has to be worked out?"

I said: "Somebody who thought she needed killing, somebody who had loved her and hated her, somebody who was too much of a cop to let her get away with any more murders, but not enough of a cop to pull her in and let the whole story come out. Somebody like Degarmo."

40

Degarmo straightened away from the wall and smiled bleakly. His right hand made a hard clean movement and was holding a gun. He held it with a lax wrist, so that it pointed down at the floor in front of him. He spoke to me without looking at me.

"I don't think you have a gun," he said. "Patton has a gun but I don't think he can get it out fast enough to do him any good. Maybe you have a little evidence to go with that last guess. Or wouldn't that be important enough for you to bother with?"

"A little evidence," I said. "Not very much. But it will grow. Somebody stood behind that green curtain in the Granada for more than half an hour and stood as silently as only a cop on a stake-out knows how to stand. Somebody who had a blackjack. Somebody who knew I had been hit with one without looking at the back of my head. You told Shorty, remember? Somebody who knew the dead girl had been hit with one too, although it wouldn't have showed and he wouldn't have been likely at that time to have handled the body enough to find out. Somebody who stripped her and raked her body with scratches in the kind of sadistic hate a man like you might feel for a woman who had made a small private hell for him. Somebody who has blood and cuticle under his fingernails right now, plenty enough for a chemist to work on. I bet you won't let Patton look at the fingernails of your right hand, Degarmo."

Degarmo lifted the gun a little and smiled. A wide white smile.

"And just how did I know where to find her?" he asked.

"Almore saw her—coming out of, or going into Lavery's house. That's what made him so nervous, that's why he called you when he saw me hanging around. As to how exactly you trailed her to the apartment, I don't know. I don't see anything difficult about it. You could have hid out in Almore's house and followed her, or followed Lavery. All that would be routine work for a copper."

Degarmo nodded and stood silent for a moment, thinking. His face was grim, but his metallic blue eyes held a light that was almost amusement. The room was hot and heavy with a disaster that could no longer be mended. He seemed to feel it less than any of us.

"I want to get out of here," he said at last. "Not very far maybe, but no hick cop is going to put the arm on me. Any objections?"

Patton said quietly: "Can't be done, son. You know I got to take you. None of this ain't proved, but I can't just let you walk out."

"You have a nice big belly, Patton. I'm a good shot. How do you figure to take me?"

"I been trying to figure," Patton said and rumpled his hair under his pushed back hat. "I ain't got very far with it. I don't want no holes in my belly. But I can't let you make a monkey of me in my own territory either."

"Let him go," I said. "He can't get out of these mountains. That's why I brought him up here."

Patton said soberly: "Somebody might get hurt taking him. That wouldn't be right. If it's anybody, it's got to be me."

Degarmo grinned. "You're a nice boy, Patton," he said. "Look, I'll put the gun back under my arm and we'll start from scratch. I'm good enough for that too."

He tucked the gun under his arm. He stood with his arms hanging, his chin pushed forward a little, watching. Patton chewed softly, with his pale eyes on Degarmo's vivid eyes.

"I'm sitting down," he complained. "I ain't as fast as you anyways. I just don't like to look yellow." He looked at me sadly. "Why the hell did you have to bring this up here? It ain't any part of my troubles. Now look at the jam I'm in." He sounded hurt and confused and rather feeble.

Degarmo put his head back a little and laughed. While he was still laughing, his right hand jumped for his gun again.

I didn't see Patton move at all. The room throbbed with the roar of his frontier Colt.

Degarmo's arm shot straight out to one side and the heavy Smith and Wesson was torn out of his hand and thudded against the knotty pine wall behind him. He shook his numbed right hand and looked down at it with wonder in his eyes.

Patton stood up slowly. He walked slowly across the room and kicked the revolver under a chair. He looked at Degarmo sadly. Degarmo was sucking a little blood off his knuckles.

"You give me a break," Patton said sadly. "You hadn't ought ever to give a man like me a break. I been a shooter more years than you been alive, son."

Degarmo nodded to him and straightened his back and started for the door.

"Don't do that," Patton told him calmly.

Degarmo kept on going. He reached the door and pushed on the screen. He looked back at Patton and his face was very white now.

"I'm going out of here," he said. "There's only one way you can stop me. So long, fatty."

Patton didn't move a muscle.

Degarmo went out through the door. His feet made heavy sounds on the porch and then on the steps. I went to the front window and looked out. Patton still hadn't moved. Degarmo came down off the steps and started across the top of the little dam.

"He's crossing the dam," I said. "Has Andy got a gun?"

"I don't figure he'd use one if he had," Patton said calmly. "He don't know any reason why he should."

"Well, I'll be damned," I said.

Patton sighed. "He hadn't ought to have given me a break like that," he said. "Had me cold. I got to give it back to him. Kind of puny too. Won't do him a lot of good."

"He's a killer," I said.

"He ain't that kind of killer," Patton said. "You lock your car?"

I nodded. "Andy's coming down to the other end of the dam," I said. "Degarmo has stopped him. He's speaking to him."

"He'll take Andy's car maybe," Patton said sadly.

"Well, I'll be damned," I said again. I looked back at Kingsley. He had his head in his hands and he was staring at the floor. I turned back to the window. Degarmo was out of sight beyond the rise. Andy was halfway across the dam, coming slowly, looking back over his shoulder now and then. The sound of a starting car came distantly. Andy looked up at the cabin, then turned back and started to run back along the dam.

The sound of the motor died away. When it was quite gone, Patton said: "Well, I guess we better go back to the office and do some telephoning."

Kingsley got up suddenly and went out to the kitchen and came back with a bottle of whiskey. He poured himself a stiff drink and drank it standing. He waved a hand at it and walked heavily out of the room. I heard bed springs creak.

Patton and I went quietly out of the cabin.

41

Patton had just finished putting his calls through to block the highways when a call came through from the sergeant in charge of the guard detail at Puma Lake dam. We went out and got into Patton's car and Andy drove very fast along the lake road through the village and along the lake shore back to the big dam at the end. We were waved across the dam to where the sergeant was waiting in a jeep beside the headquarters hut.

The sergeant waved his arm and started the jeep and we followed him a couple of hundred feet along the highway to where a few soldiers stood on the edge of the canyon looking down. Several cars had stopped there and a cluster of people was grouped near the soldiers. The sergeant got out of the jeep and Patton and Andy and I climbed out of the official car and went over by the sergeant.

"Guy didn't stop for the sentry," the sergeant said, and there was bitterness in his voice. "Damn near knocked him off the road. The sentry in the middle of the bridge had to jump fast to get missed. The one at this end had enough. He called the guy to halt. Guy kept going."

The sergeant chewed his gum and looked down into the canyon.

"Orders are to shoot in a case like that," he said. "The sentry shot." He pointed down to the grooves in the shoulder at the edge of the drop. "This is where he went off."

A hundred feet down in the canyon a small coupe was smashed against the side of a huge granite boulder. It was almost upside down, leaning a little. There were three men down there. They had moved the car enough to lift something out.

Something that had been a man.

IN THE TEETH OF THE EVIDENCE

by Dorothy L. Sayers

"Well, old son," said Mr. Lamplough, "and what can we do for you today?"

"Oh, some of your whizz-bang business, I suppose," said Lord Peter Wimsey, seating himself resentfully in the green velvet torture-chair and making a face in the direction of the drill. "Jolly old left-hand upper grinder come to bits on me. I was only eating an omelette, too. Can't understand why they always pick these moments. If I'd been cracking nuts or chewing peppermint jumbles I could understand it."

"Yes?" said Mr. Lamplough, soothingly. He drew an electric bulb, complete with mirror, as though by magic out of a kind of Maskelyne-and-Devant contraption on Lord Peter's left; a trail of flex followed it, issuing apparently from the bowels of the earth. "Any pain?"

"No *pain*," said Wimsey, irritably, "unless you count a sharp edge fit to saw your tongue off. Point is, why should it go pop like that? I wasn't doing anything to it."

"No?" said Mr. Lamplough, his manner hovering between the professional and the friendly, for he was an old Winchester man and a member of one of Wimsey's clubs, and had frequently met him on the cricket-field in the days of their youth. "Well, if you'll stop talking half a moment, we'll have a look at it. Ah!"

"Don't say, 'Ah!' like that, as if you'd found pyorrhoea and necrosis of the jaw and were gloating over it, you damned old ghoul. Just carve it out and stop it up and be hanged to you. And, by the way, what have you been up to? Why should I meet an inspector of police on your doorstep? You needn't pretend he came to have his bridgework attended to, because I saw his sergeant waiting for him outside."

"Well, it was rather curious," said Mr. Lamplough, dexterously gagging his friend with one hand and dabbing cotton-wool into the offending cavity with the other. "I suppose I oughtn't to tell you, but if I don't, you'll get it all out of your friends at Scotland Yard. They wanted to see my predecessor's books. Possibly you noticed that bit in the papers about a dental man being found dead in a blazing garage on Wimbledon Common?"

"Yonk—ugh?" said Lord Peter Wimsey.

"Last night," said Mr. Lamplough. "Pooped off about nine pipemma, and it took them three hours to put it out. One of those wooden garages—and the big job was to keep the blaze away from the house. Fortunately it's at the end of the row, with nobody at home. Apparently this man Prendergast was all alone there—just going off for a holiday or something—and he contrived to set himself and his car and his garage alight last night and was burnt to death. In fact, when they found him, he was so badly charred that they couldn't be sure it was he. So, being sticklers for routine, they had a look at his teeth."

"Oh, yes?" said Wimsey, watching Mr. Lamplough fitting a new drill into its socket. "Didn't anybody have a go at putting the fire out?"

"Oh, yes—but as it was a wooden shed, full of petrol, it simply went up like a bonfire. Just a little bit over this way, please. That's splendid." Gr-r-r, whizz, gr-r-r. "As a matter of fact, they seem to think it might just possibly be suicide. The man's married, with three children, and immured and all that sort of thing." Whizz, gr-r-r, buzz, gr-r-r, whizz. "His family's down at Worthing, staying with his mother-in-law or something. Tell me if I hurt you." Gr-r-r. "And I don't suppose he was doing any too well. Still, of course, he may easily have had an accident when filling up. I gather he was starting off that night to join them."

"A—ow—oo—oo—uh—ihi—ih?" inquired Wimsey naturally enough.

"How do I come into it?" said Mr. Lamplough, who, from long experience was expert in the interpretation of mumblings. "Well, only because the chap whose practice I took over here did this fellow Prendergast's dental work for him." Whizz. "He died, but left his books behind him for my guidance, in case any of his old patients should feel inclined to trust me." Gr-r-r, whizz. "I'm sorry. Did you feel that? As a matter of fact, some of them actually do. I suppose it's an instinct to trundle round to the same old place when you're in pain, like the dying elephants. Will you rinse, please?"

"I see," said Wimsey, when he had finished washing out chips of himself and exploring his ravaged molar with his tongue. "How odd it is that these cavities always seem so large. I feel as if I could put my head into this one. Still, I suppose you know what you're about. And are Prendergast's teeth all right?"

"Haven't had time to hunt through the ledger, yet, but I've said I'll go down to have a look at them as soon as I've finished with you. It's my lunch-time anyway, and my two o'clock patient isn't coming, thank goodness. She usually brings five spoilt children, and they all want to sit round and watch, and play with the apparatus. One of them got loose last time and tried to electrocute itself on the X-ray plant next door. And she thinks that children should be done at half-price. A little wider if you can manage it." Gr-r-r. "Yes, that's very nice. Now we can dress that and put in a temporary. Rinse, please."

"Yes," said Wimsey, "and for goodness' sake make it firm and not too much of your foul oil of cloves. I don't want bits to come out in the middle of dinner. You can't imagine the nastiness of caviar flavoured with cloves."

"No?" said Mr. Lamplough. "You may find this a little cold." Squirt, swish. "Rinse, please. You may notice it when the dressing goes in. Oh, you did notice it? Good. That shows that the nerve's all right. Only a little longer now. There! Yes, you may get down now. Another rinse? Certainly. When would you like to come in again?"

"Don't be silly, old horse," said Wimsey. "I am coming out to Wimbledon with you straight away. You'll get there twice as fast if I drive you. I've never had a corpse-in-blazing-garage before, and I want to learn."

There is nothing really attractive about corpses in blazing garages. Even Wimsey's war experience did not quite reconcile him to the object that lay on the mortuary slab in the police station. Charred out of all resemblance to humanity, it turned even the police surgeon pale, while Mr. Lamplough was so overcome that he had to lay down the books he had brought with him and retire into the open to recover himself. Meanwhile Wimsey, having put himself on terms of mutual confidence and esteem with the police officials, thoughtfully turned over the little pile of blackened odds and ends that represented the contents of Mr. Prendergast's pockets. There was nothing remarkable about them. The leather note-case still held the remains of a thickish wad of notes—doubtless cash in hand for the holiday at Worthing. The handsome gold watch (obviously a presentation) had stopped at seven minutes past nine. Wimsey remarked on its good state of preservation. Sheltered between the left arm and the body—that seemed to be the explanation.

"Looks as though the first sudden blaze had regularly overcome him," said the police inspector. "He evidently made no attempt to get out. He'd simply fallen forward over the wheel, with his head on the dashboard. That's why the face is so disfigured. I'll show you the remains of the car presently if you're interested, my lord. If the other gentleman's feeling better we may as well take the body first."

Taking the body was a long and unpleasant job. Mr. Lamplough, nerving himself with an effort and producing a pair of forceps and a probe, went gingerly over the jaws—reduced almost to their bony structure by the furnace heat to which they had been exposed—while the police surgeon checked entries in the ledger. Mr. Prendergast had a dental history extending back over ten years in the ledger, and had already had two or three fillings done before that time. These had been noted at the time when he first came to Mr. Lamplough's predecessor.

At the end of a long examination, the surgeon looked up from the notes he had been making.

"Well, now," he said, "let's check that again. Allowing for renewal of old work, I think we've got a pretty accurate picture of the present state of his mouth. There ought to be nine fillings in all. Small amalgam filling in right lower back wisdom tooth; big amalgam ditto in right lower back molar; amalgam fillings in right upper first and second bicuspids at point of contact; right upper incisor crowned—that all right?"

"I expect so," said Mr. Lamplough, "except that the right upper incisor seems to be missing altogether, but possibly the crown came loose and fell out." He probed delicately. "The jaw is very brittle—I can't make anything of the canal—but there's nothing against it."

"We may find the crown in the garage," suggested the Inspector.

"Fused porcelain filling in left upper canine," went on the surgeon; "amalgam fillings in left upper first bicuspid and lower second bicuspid and left lower thirteen-year-old molar. That seems to be all. No teeth missing and no artificials. How old was this man, Inspector?"

"About forty-five, Doc."

"My age. I only wish I had as good a set of teeth," said the surgeon. Mr. Lamplough agreed with him.

"Then I take it, this is Mr. Prendergast all right," said the Inspector.

"Not a doubt of it, I should say," replied Mr. Lamplough; "though I should like to find that missing crown."

"We'd better go round to the house, then," said the Inspector.

"Well, yes, thank you, my lord, I shouldn't mind a lift in that. Some car. Well, the only point now is, whether it was accident or suicide. Round to the right, my lord, and then second on the left—I'll tell you as we go."

"A bit out of the way for a dental man," observed Mr. Lamplough, as they emerged upon some scattered houses near the Common.

The Inspector made a grimace.

"I thought the same, sir, but it appears Mrs. Prendergast persuaded him to come here. So good for the children. Not so good for the practice, though. If you ask me, I should say Mrs. P. was the biggest argument we have for suicide. Here we are."

The last sentence was scarcely necessary. There was a little crowd about the gate of a small detached villa at the end of a row of similar houses. From a pile of dismal debris in the garden a smell of burning still rose, disgustingly. The Inspector pushed through the gate with his companions, pursued by the comments of the bystanders.

"That's the Inspector . . . that's Dr. Maggs . . . that'll be another doctor, him with the little bag . . . who's the bloke in the eye-glass? . . . Looks a proper nobleman, don't he, Florrie? . . . Why, he'll be the insurance bloke. . . . Coo! look at his grand car . . . that's where the money goes. . . . That's a Rolls, that is . . . no, silly, it's a Daimler. . . . Ow, well, it's all advertisement these days."

Wimsey giggled indecorously all the way up the garden path. The sight of the skeleton car amid the sodden and fire-blackened remains of the garage sobered him. Two police constables, crouched over the ruin with a sieve, stood up and saluted.

"How are you getting on, Jenkins?"

"Haven't got anything very much yet, sir, bar an ivory cigarette-holder. This gentleman"—indicating a stout, bald man in spectacles, who was squatting among the damaged coach-work, "is Mr. Tolley, from the motor-works, come with a note from the Superintendent, sir."

"Ah, yes. Can you give any opinion about this, Mr. Tolley? Dr. Maggs you know. Mr. Lamplough, Lord Peter Wimsey. By the way, Jenkins, Mr. Lamplough has been going into the corpse's dentistry, and he's looking for a lost tooth. You might see if you can find it. Now, Mr. Tolley?"

"Can't see much doubt about how it happened," said Mr. Tolley, picking his teeth thoughtfully. "Regular death-traps, these little saloons, when anything goes wrong unexpectedly. There's a front tank, you see, and it looks as though there might have been a bit of a leak behind the dash somewhere. Possibly the seam of the tank had got strained a bit, or the union had come loose. It's loose now, as a matter of fact, but that's not unusual after a fire, Rouse case or no Rouse case. You can get quite a lot of slow dripping from a damaged tank or pipe, and there seems to have been a coconut mat round the controls, which would prevent you from noticing. There'd be a smell, of course, but these little garages do often get to smell of petrol, and he kept several cans of the stuff here. More than the legal amount—but *that's* not unusual either. Looks to me as though he'd filled up his tank—there are two empty tins near the bonnet, with the caps loose—got in, shut the door, started up the car, perhaps, and then lit a cigarette. Then, if there were any petrol fumes about from a leak, the whole show would go up in his face—whoosh!"

"How was the ignition?"

"Off. He may never have switched it on, but it's quite likely he switched it off again when the flames went up. Silly thing to do, but lots of people *do* do it. The proper thing, of course, is to switch off the petrol and leave the engine running so as to empty the carburettor, but you don't always think straight when you're being burnt alive. Or he may have meant to turn off the petrol and been overcome before he could manage it. The tank's over here to the left, you see."

"On the other hand," said Wimsey, "he may have committed suicide and faked the accident."

"Nasty way of committing suicide."

"Suppose he'd taken poison first."

"He'd have had to stay alive long enough to fire the car."

"That's true. Suppose he'd shot himself—would the flash from the —no, that's silly—you'd have found the weapon in the case. Or a hypodermic? Same objection. Prussic acid might have done it—I mean, he might just have had time to take a tablet and then fire the car. Prussic acid's pretty quick, but it isn't absolutely instantaneous."

"I'll have a look for it, anyway," said Dr. Maggs.

They were interrupted by the constable.

"Excuse me, sir, but I think we've found the tooth. Mr. Lamplough says this is it."

Between his pudgy finger and thumb he held up a small, bony object, from which a small stalk of metal still protruded.

"That's a right upper incisor crown all right by the look if it," said Mr. Lamplough. "I suppose the cement gave way with the heat. Some cements are sensitive to heat, some, on the other hand, to damp. Well, that settles it, doesn't it?"

"Yes—well, we shall have to break it to the widow. Not that she can be in very much doubt, I imagine."

Mrs. Prendergast—a very much made-up lady with a face set in lines of habitual peevishness—received the news with a burst of loud sobs. She informed them, when she was sufficiently recovered, that Arthur had always been careless about petrol, that he smoked too much, that she had often warned him about the danger of small saloons, that she had told him he ought to get a bigger car, that the one he had was not really large enough for her and the whole family, that he *would* drive at night, though she had always said it was dangerous, and that if he'd listened to her, it would never have happened.

"Poor Arthur was not a good driver. Only last week, when he was taking us down to Worthing, he drove the car right up on a bank in trying to pass a lorry, and frightened us all dreadfully."

"Ah!" said the Inspector. "No doubt that's how the tank got strained." Very cautiously he inquired whether Mr. Prendergast could have had any reason for taking his own life. The widow was indignant. It was true that the practice had been declining of late, but Arthur would never have been so wicked as to do such a thing. Why, only three months ago, he had taken out a life-insurance for £500 and he'd never have invalidated it by committing suicide within the term stipulated by the policy. Inconsiderate of her as Arthur was, and whatever injuries he had done her as a wife, he wouldn't rob his innocent children.

The Inspector pricked up his ears at the word "injuries." What injuries?

Oh, well, of course, she'd known all the time that Arthur was carrying on with that Mrs. Fielding. You couldn't deceive her with all this stuff about teeth needing continual attention. And it was all very well to say that Mrs. Fielding's house was better run than her own. *That* wasn't surprising—a rich widow with no children and no responsibilities, of course she could afford to have everything nice. You couldn't expect a busy wife to do miracles on such a small housekeeping allowance. If Arthur had wanted things different, he should have been more generous, and it was easy enough for Mrs. Fielding to attract men, dressed up like a fashion-plate and no better than she should be. She'd told Arthur that if it didn't stop she'd divorce him. And since then he'd taken to spending all his evenings in Town, and what was he doing there—

The Inspector stemmed the torrent by asking for Mrs. Fielding's address.

"I'm sure I don't know," said Mrs. Prendergast. "She did live at Number 57, but she went abroad after I made it clear I wasn't going to stand any more of it. It's very nice to be some people, with plenty of money to spend. I've never been abroad since our honeymoon, and that was only to Boulogne."

At the end of this conversation, the Inspector sought Dr. Maggs and begged him to be thorough in his search for prussic acid.

The remaining testimony was that of Gladys, the general servant. She had left Mr. Prendergast's house the day before at 6 o'clock. She was to have taken a week's holiday while the Prendergasts were at Worthing. She had thought that Mr. Prendergast had seemed worried and nervous the last few days, but that had not surprised her, because she knew he disliked staying with his wife's people. She (Gladys) had finished her work and put out a cold supper and then gone home with her employer's permission. He had a patient—a gentleman from Australia, or some such a place, who wanted his teeth attended to in a hurry before going off on his travels again. Mr. Prendergast had explained that he would be working late, and would shut up the house himself, and she need not wait. Further inquiry showed that Mr. Prendergast had "scarcely touched" his supper, being, presumably, in a hurry to get off. Apparently, then, the patient had been the last person to see Mr. Prendergast alive.

The dentist's appointment-book was next examined. The patient figured there as "Mr. Williams 5.30," and the address-book placed Mr. Williams at a small hotel in Bloomsbury. The manager of the hotel said that Mr. Williams had stayed there for a week. He had given no address except "Adelaide," and had mentioned that he was revisiting the old country for the first time after twenty years and had no friends in London. Unfortunately, he could not be interviewed.

At about half-past ten the previous night, a messenger had called, bringing his card, to pay his bill and remove his luggage. No address had been left for forwarding letters. It was not a district messenger, but a man in a slouch hat and heavy dark overcoat. The night-porter had not seen his face very clearly, as only one light was on in the hall. He had told them to hurry up, as Mr. Williams wanted to catch the boat-train from Waterloo. Inquiry at the booking-office showed that a Mr. Williams had actually travelled on that train, being booked to Paris. The ticket had been taken that same night. So Mr. Williams had disappeared into the blue, and even if they could trace him, it seemed unlikely that he could throw much light on Mr. Prendergast's state of mind immediately previous to the disaster. It seemed a little odd, at first, that Mr. Williams, from Adelaide, staying in Bloomsbury, should have travelled to Wimbledon to get his teeth attended to, but the simple explanation was the likeliest: namely, that the friendless Williams had struck up an acquaintance with Prendergast in a café or some such place, and that a casual mention of his dental necessities had led to a project of mutual profit and assistance.

After which, nothing seemed to be left but for the coroner to bring in a verdict of Death by Misadventure and for the widow to send in her claim to the Insurance Company, when Dr. Maggs upset the whole scheme of things by announcing that he had discovered traces of a large injection of hyoscine in the body, and what about it? The Inspector, on hearing this, observed callously that he was not surprised. If ever a man had an excuse for suicide, he thought it was Mrs. Prendergast's husband. He thought that it would be desirable to make a careful search among the scorched laurels surrounding what had been Mr. Prendergast's garage. Lord Peter Wimsey agreed, but committed himself to the prophecy that the syringe would not be found.

Lord Peter Wimsey was entirely wrong. The syringe was found next day, in a position suggesting that it had been thrown out of the window of the garage after use. Traces of the poison were discovered to be present in it. "It's a slow-working drug," observed Dr. Maggs. "No doubt he jabbed himself, threw the syringe away, hoping it would never be looked for, and then, before he lost consciousness, climbed into the car and set light to it. A clumsy way of doing it."

"A damned ingenious way of doing it," said Wimsey. "I don't believe in that syringe, somehow." He rang up his dentist. "Lamplough, old horse," he said, "I wish you'd do something for me. I wish you'd go over those teeth again. No—not my teeth; Prendergast's."

"Oh, blow it!" said Mr. Lamplough, uneasily.

"No, but I wish you would," said his lordship.

The body was still unburied. Mr. Lamplough, grumbling very much, went down to Wimbledon with Wimsey, and again went through his distasteful task. This time he started on the left side.

"Lower thirteen-year-old molar and second bicuspid filled amalgam. The fire's got at those a bit, but they're all right. First upper bicuspid—bicuspids are stupid sort of teeth—always the first to go. That filling looks to have been rather carelessly put in—not what I should call good work; it seems to extend over the next tooth—possibly the fire did that. Left upper canine, cast porcelain filling on anterior face—"

"Half a jiff," said Wimsey, "Maggs' note says 'fused porcelain.' Is it the same thing?"

"No. Different process. Well, I suppose it's fused porcelain—difficult to see. I should have said it was cast, myself, but that's as may be."

"Let's verify it in the ledger. I wish Maggs had put the dates in—goodness knows how far I shall have to hunt back, and I don't understand this chap's writing or his dashed abbreviations."

"You won't have to go back very far if it's cast. The stuff only came in about 1928, from America. There was quite a rage for it then, but for some reason it didn't take on extraordinarily well over here. But some men use it."

"Oh, then it isn't cast," said Wimsey. "There's nothing here about canines, back to '28. Let's make sure; '27, '26, '25, '24, '23. Here you are. Canine, something or other."

"That's it," said Lamplough, coming to look over his shoulder. "Fused porcelain. I must be wrong, then. Easily see by taking it out. The grain's different, and so is the way it's put in."

"How, different?"

"Well," said Mr. Lamplough, "one's a cast, you see."

"And the other's fused. I did grasp that much. Well, go ahead and take it out."

"Can't very well; not here."

"Then take it home and do it there. Don't you see, Lamplough, how important it is? If it is cast porcelain, or whatever you call it, it *can't* have been done in '23. And if it was removed later, then another dentist must have done it. And he may have done other things—and in that case, those things ought to be there, and they're not. Don't you *see?*"

"I see you're getting rather agitato," said Mr. Lamplough; "all I can say is, I refuse to have this thing taken along to my surgery. Corpses aren't popular in Harley Street."

In the end, the body was removed, by permission, to the dental department of the local hospital. Here Mr. Lamplough, assisted by the staff dental expert, Dr. Maggs, and the police, delicately extracted the filling from the canine.

"If that," said he triumphantly, "is not cast porcelain I will extract all my own teeth without an anaesthetic and swallow them. What do you say, Benton?"

The hospital dentist agreed with him. Mr. Lamplough, who had suddenly developed an eager interest in the problem, nodded, and inserted a careful probe between the upper right bicuspids, with their adjacent fillings.

"Come and look at this, Benton. Allowing for the action of the fire and all this muck, wouldn't you have said this was a very recent filling? There, at the point of contact. Might have been done yesterday. And—here—wait a minute. Where's the lower jaw gone to? Get that fitted up. Give me a bit of carbon. Look at the tremendous bite there ought to be here, with that big molar coming down on to it. That filling's miles too high for the job. Wimsey—when was this bottom right-hand back molar filled?"

"Two years ago," said Wimsey.

"That's impossible," said the two dentists together, and Mr. Benton added:

"If you clean away the mess, you'll see it's a new filling. Never been bitten on, I should say. Look here, Mr. Lamplough, there's something odd here."

"Odd? I should say there was. I never thought about it when I was checking it up yesterday, but look at this old cavity in the lateral here. Why didn't he have that filled when all this other work was done? Now it's cleaned out you can see it plainly. Have you got a long probe? It's quite deep and must have given him jip. I say, Inspector, I want to have some of these fillings out. Do you mind?"

"Go ahead," said the Inspector, "we've got plenty of witnesses."

With Mr. Benton supporting the grisly patient and Mr. Lamplough manipulating the drill, the filling of one of the molars was speedily drilled out, and Mr. Lamplough said: "Oh, gosh!"—which, as Lord Peter remarked, just showed you what a dentist meant when he said "Ah!"

"Try the bicuspids," suggested Mr. Benton.

"Or this thirteen-year-old," chimed in his colleague.

"Hold hard, gentlemen," protested the Inspector, "don't spoil the specimen altogether."

Mr. Lamplough drilled away without heeding him. Another filling came out, and Mr. Lamplough said "Gosh!" again.

"It's all right," said Wimsey, grinning, "you can get out your warrant, Inspector."

"What's that, my lord?"

"Murder," said Wimsey.

"Why?" said the Inspector. "Do these gentlemen mean that Mr. Prendergast got a new dentist who poisoned his teeth for him?"

"No," said Mr. Lamplough; "at least, not what you mean by poisoning. But I've never seen such work in my life. Why, in two places the man hasn't even troubled to clear out the decay at all. He's just enlarged the cavity and stopped it up again anyhow. Why this chap didn't get thundering abscesses I don't know."

"Perhaps," said Wimsey, "the stoppings were put in too recently. Hullo! what now?"

"This one's all right. No decay here. Doesn't look as if there ever had been, either. But one can't tell about that."

"I dare say there never was. Get your warrant out, Inspector."

"For the murder of Mr. Prendergast? And against whom?"

"No. Against Arthur Prendergast for the murder of one, Mr. Williams, and, incidentally, for arson and attempted fraud. And against Mrs. Fielding too, if you like, for conspiracy. Though you mayn't be able to prove that part of it."

It turned out, when they found Mr. Prendergast in Rouen, that he had thought out the scheme well in advance. The one thing he had had to wait for had been to find a patient of his own height and build, with a good set of teeth and few home ties. When the unhappy Williams had fallen into his clutches, he had few preparations to make. Mrs. Prendergast had to be packed off to Worthing—a journey she was ready enough to take at any time—and the maid given a holiday. Then the necessary dental accessories had to be prepared and the victim invited out to tea at Wimbledon. Then the murder—a stunning blow from behind, followed by an injection. Then, the slow and horrid process of faking the teeth to correspond with Mr. Prendergast's own. Next, the exchange of clothes and the body carried down and placed in the car. The hypodermic put where it might be overlooked on a casual inspection and yet might plausibly be found if the presence of the drug should be discovered; ready, in the one case, to support a verdict of Accident and, in the second, of Suicide. Then the car soaked in petrol, the union loosened, the cans left about. The garage door and window left open, to lend colour to the story and provide a draught, and, finally, light set to the car by means of a train of petrol laid through the garage door. Then, flight to the station through the winter darkness and so by underground to London. The risk of being recognised on the underground was small, in Williams's hat and clothes and with a scarf wound about the lower part of the face. The next step was to pick up Williams's luggage and take the boat-train to join the wealthy and enamoured Mrs. Fielding in France. After which, Williams and Mrs. Williams could have returned to England, or not, as they pleased.

"Quite a student of criminology," remarked Wimsey, at the conclusion of this little adventure. "He'd studied Rouse and Furnace all right, and profited by their mistakes. Pity he overlooked that matter of the cast porcelain. Makes a quicker job, does it, Lamplough? Well, more haste, less speed. I do wonder, though, at what point of the proceedings Williams actually died."

"Shut up," said Mr. Lamplough, "and, by the way, I've still got to finish that filling for you."

THE CASE OF THE IRATE WITNESS

by Erle Stanley Gardner

The early-morning shadows cast by the mountains still lay heavily on the town's main street as the big siren on the roof of the Jebson Commercial Company began to scream shrilly.

The danger of fire was always present, and at the sound, men at breakfast rose and pushed their chairs back from the table. Men who were shaving barely paused to wipe lather from their faces; men who had been sleeping grabbed the first available garments. All of them ran to places where they could look for the first telltale wisps of smoke.

There was no smoke.

The big siren was still screaming urgently as the men formed into streaming lines, like ants whose hill has been attacked. The lines all moved toward the Jebson Commercial Company.

There the men were told that the doors of the big vault had been found wide open. A jagged hole had been cut into one door with an acetylene torch.

The men looked at one another silently. This was the fifteenth of the month. The big, twice-a-month payroll, which had been brought up from the Ivanhoe National Bank the day before, had been the prize.

Frank Bernal, manager of the company's mine, the man who ruled Jebson City with an iron hand, arrived and took charge. The responsibility was his, and what he found was alarming.

Tom Munson, the night watchman, was lying on the floor in a back room, snoring in drunken slumber. The burglar alarm, which had been installed within the last six months, had been bypassed by means of an electrical device. This device was so ingenious that it was apparent that, if the work were that of a gang, at least one of the burglars was an expert electrician.

Ralph Nesbitt, the company accountant, was significantly silent. When Frank Bernal had been appointed manager a year earlier, Nesbitt had pointed out that the big vault was obsolete.

Bernal, determined to prove himself in his new job, had avoided the expense of tearing out the old vault and installing a new one by investing in an up-to-date burglar alarm and putting a special night watchman on duty.

Now the safe had been looted of $100,000 and Frank Bernal had to make a report to the main office in Chicago, with the disquieting knowledge that Ralph Nesbitt's memo stating that the antiquated vault was a pushover was at this moment reposing in the company files.

Some distance out of Jebson City, Perry Mason, the famous trial lawyer, was driving fast along a mountain road. He had planned a weekend fishing trip for a long time, but a jury which had waited until midnight before reaching its verdict had delayed Mason's departure and it was now 8:30 in the morning.

His fishing clothes, rod, wading boots, and creel were all in the trunk. He was wearing the suit in which he had stepped from the courtroom, and having driven all night he was eager for the cool, piny mountains.

A blazing red light, shining directly at him as he rounded a turn in the canyon road, dazzled his road-weary eyes. A sign, *STOP—POLICE,* had been placed in the middle of the road. Two men, a grim-faced man with a .30–30 rifle in his hands and a silver badge on his shirt and a uniformed motorcycle officer, stood beside the sign.

Mason stopped his car.

The man with the badge, deputy sheriff, said, "We'd better take a look at your driving license. There's been a big robbery at Jebson City."

"That so?" Mason said. "I went through Jebson City an hour ago and everything seemed quiet."

"Where you been since then?"

"I stopped at a little service station and restaurant for breakfast."

"Let's take a look at your driving license."

Mason handed it to him.

The man started to return it, then looked at it again. "Say," he said, "you're Perry Mason, the big criminal lawyer!"

"Not a criminal lawyer," Mason said patiently, "a trial lawyer. I sometimes defend men who are accused of crime."

"What are you doing up in this country?"

"Going fishing."

The deputy looked at him suspiciously. "Why aren't you wearing your fishing clothes?"

"Because," Mason said, and smiled, "I'm not fishing."

"You said you were going fishing."

"I also intend," Mason said, "to go to bed tonight. According to you, I should be wearing my pajamas."

The deputy frowned. The traffic officer laughed and waved Mason on.

The deputy nodded at the departing car. "Looks like a live clue to me," he said, "but I can't find it in that conversation."

"There isn't any," the traffic officer said.

The deputy remained dubious, and later on, when a news-hungry reporter from the local paper asked the deputy if he knew of anything that would make a good story, the deputy said that he did.

And that was why Della Street, Perry Mason's confidential secretary, was surprised to read stories in the metropolitan papers stating that Perry Mason, the noted trial lawyer, was rumored to have been retained to represent the person or persons who had looted the vault of the Jebson Commercial Company. All this had been arranged, it would seem, before Mason's "client" had even been apprehended.

When Perry Mason called his office by long-distance the next afternoon, Della said, "I thought you were going to the mountains for a vacation."

"That's right. Why?"

"The papers claim you're representing whoever robbed the Jebson Commercial Company."

"First I've heard of it," Mason said. "I went through Jebson City before they discovered the robbery, stopped for breakfast a little farther on, and then got caught in a roadblock. In the eyes of some officious deputy, that seems to have made me an accessory after the fact."

"Well," Della Street said, "they've caught a man by the name of Harvey L. Corbin, and apparently have quite a case against him. They're hinting at mysterious evidence which won't be disclosed until the time of trial."

"Was he the one who committed the crime?" Mason asked.

"The police think so. He has a criminal record. When his employers at Jebson City found out about it, they told him to leave town. That was the evening before the robbery."

"Just like that, eh?" Mason asked.

"Well, you see, Jebson City is a one-industry town, and the company owns all the houses. They're leased to the employees. I understand Corbin's wife and daughter were told they could stay on until Corbin got located in a new place, but Corbin was told to leave town at once. You aren't interested, are you?"

"Not in the least," Mason said, "except that when I drive back I'll be going through Jebson City, and I'll probably stop to pick up the local gossip."

"Don't do it," she warned. "This man Corbin has all the earmarks of being an underdog, and you know how you feel about underdogs."

A quality in her voice made Perry suspicious. "You haven't been approached, have you, Della?"

"Well," she said, "in a way. Mrs. Corbin read in the papers that you were going to represent her husband, and she was overjoyed. It seems that she thinks her husband's implication in this is a raw deal. She hadn't known anything about his criminal record, but she loves him and is going to stand by him."

"You've talked with her?" Mason asked.

"Several times. I tried to break it to her gently. I told her it was probably nothing but a newspaper story. You see, Chief, they have Corbin dead to rights. They took some money from his wife as evidence. It was part of the loot."

"And she has nothing?"

"Nothing. Corbin left her forty dollars, and they took it all as evidence."

"I'll drive all night," he said. "Tell her I'll be back tomorrow."

"I was afraid of that," Della Street said. "Why did you have to call up? Why couldn't you have stayed up there fishing? Why did you have to get your name in the papers?"

Mason laughed and hung up.

Paul Drake, of the Drake Detective Agency, came in and sat in the big chair in Mason's office and said, "You have a bear by the tail, Perry."

"What's the matter, Paul? Didn't your detective work in Jebson City pan out?"

"It panned out all right, but the stuff in the pan isn't what you want, Perry," Drake explained.

"How come?"

"Your client's guilty."

"Go on," Mason said.

"The money he gave his wife was some of what was stolen from the vault."

"How do they know it was the stolen money?" Mason asked.

Drake pulled a notebook from his pocket. "Here's the whole picture. The plant manager runs Jebson City. There isn't any private property. The Jebson company controls everything."

"Not a single small business?"

Drake shook his head. "Not unless you want to consider garbage collecting as small business. An old coot by the name of George Addey lives five miles down the canyon; he has a hog ranch and collects the garbage. He's supposed to have the first nickel he ever earned. Buries his money in cans. There's no bank nearer than Ivanhoe City."

"What about the burglary? The men who did it must have moved in acetylene tanks and—"

"They took them right out of the company store," Drake said. And then he went on: "Munson, the watchman, likes to take a pull out of a flask of whiskey along about midnight. He says it keeps him awake. Of course, he's not supposed to do it, and no one was supposed to know about the whiskey, but someone did know about it. They doped the whiskey with a barbiturate. The watchman took his usual swig, went to sleep, and stayed asleep."

"What's the evidence against Corbin?" Mason asked.

"Corbin had a previous burglary record. It's a policy of the company not to hire anyone with a criminal record. Corbin lied about his past and got a job. Frank Bernal, the manager, found out about it, sent for Corbin about 8 o'clock the night the burglary took place, and ordered him out of town. Bernal agreed to let Corbin's wife and child stay on in the house until Corbin could get located in another city. Corbin pulled out in the morning, and gave his wife this money. It was part of the money from the burglary."

"How do they know?" Mason asked.

"Now there's something I don't know," Drake said. "This fellow

Bernal is pretty smart, and the story is that he can prove Corbin's money was from the vault."

Drake paused, then continued: "The nearest bank is at Ivanhoe City, and the mine pays off in cash twice a month. Ralph Nesbitt, the cashier, wanted to install a new vault. Bernal refused to okay the expense. So the company has ordered both Bernal and Nesbitt back to its main office at Chicago to report. The rumor is that they may fire Bernal as manager and give Nesbitt the job. A couple of the directors don't like Bernal, and this thing has given them their chance. They dug out a report Nesbitt had made showing the vault was a pushover. Bernal didn't act on that report." He sighed and then asked, "When's the trial, Perry?"

"The preliminary hearing is set for Friday morning. I'll see then what they've got against Corbin."

"They're laying for you up there," Paul Drake warned. "Better watch out, Perry. That district attorney has something up his sleeve, some sort of surprise that's going to knock you for a loop."

In spite of his long experience as a prosecutor, Vernon Flasher, the district attorney of Ivanhoe County, showed a certain nervousness at being called upon to oppose Perry Mason. There was, however, a secretive assurance underneath that nervousness.

Judge Haswell, realizing that the eyes of the community were upon him, adhered to legal technicalities to the point of being pompous both in rulings and mannerisms.

But what irritated Perry Mason was in the attitude of the spectators. He sensed that they did not regard him as an attorney trying to safeguard the interests of a client, but as a legal magician with a cloven hoof. The looting of the vault had shocked the community, and there was a tight-lipped determination that no legal tricks were going to do Mason any good *this* time.

Vernon Flasher didn't try to save his surprise evidence for a whirlwind finish. He used it right at the start of the case.

Frank Bernal, called as a witness, described the location of the vault, identified photographs, and then leaned back as the district attorney said abruptly, "You had reason to believe this vault was obsolete?"

"Yes, sir."

"It had been pointed out to you by one of your fellow employees, Mr. Ralph Nesbitt?"

"Yes, sir."

"And what did you do about it?"

"Are you," Mason asked in some surprise, "trying to cross-examine your own witness?"

"Just let him answer the question, and you'll see," Flasher replied grimly.

"Go right ahead and answer," Mason said to the witness.

Bernal assumed a more comfortable position. "I did three things," he said, "to safeguard the payrolls and to avoid the expense of tearing out the old vault and installing a new vault in its place."

"What were those three things?"

"I employed a special night watchman; I installed the best burglar alarm money could buy; and I made arrangements with the Ivanhoe National Bank, where we have our payrolls made up, to list the number of each twenty-dollar bill which was a part of each payroll."

Mason suddenly sat up straight.

Flasher gave him a glance of gloating triumph. "Do you wish the court to understand, Mr. Bernal," he said smugly, "that you have the numbers of the bills in the payroll which was made up for delivery on the fifteenth?"

"Yes, sir. Not *all* the bills, you understand. That would have taken too much time, but I have the numbers of all the twenty-dollar bills."

"And who recorded those numbers?" the prosecutor asked.

"The bank."

"And do you have that list of numbers with you?"

"I do. Yes, sir." Bernal produced a list. "I felt," he said, glancing coldly at Nesbitt, "that these precautions would be cheaper than a new vault."

"I move the list be introduced in evidence," Flasher said.

"Just a moment," Mason objected. "I have a couple of questions. You say this list is not in your handwriting, Mr. Bernal?"

"Yes, sir."

"Whose handwriting is it, do you know?" Mason asked.

"The assistant cashier of the Ivanhoe National Bank."

"Oh, all right," Flasher said. "We'll do it the hard way, if we have to. Stand down, Mr. Bernal, and I'll call the assistant cashier."

Harry Reedy, assistant cashier of the Ivanhoe Bank, had the mechanical assurance of an adding machine. He identified the list of numbers as being in his handwriting. He stated that he had listed the numbers of the twenty-dollar bills and put that list in an envelope which had been sealed and sent up with the money for the payroll.

"Cross-examine," Flasher said.

Mason studied the list. "These numbers are all in your handwriting?" he asked Reedy.

"Yes, sir."

"Did you yourself compare the numbers you wrote down with the numbers on the twenty-dollar bills?"

"No, sir. I didn't personally do that. Two assistants did that. One checked the numbers as they were read off, one as I wrote them down."

"The payrolls are for approximately a hundred thousand dollars, twice each month?"

"That's right. And ever since Mr. Bernal took charge, we have taken this means to identify payrolls. No attempt is made to list the bills in numerical order. The serial numbers are simply read off and written down. Unless a robbery occurs, there is no need to do anything further. In the event of a robbery, we can reclassify the numbers and list the bills in numerical order."

"These numbers are in your handwriting—every number?"

"Yes, sir. More than that, you will notice that at the bottom of each page I have signed my initials."

"That's all," Mason said.

"I now offer once more to introduce this list in evidence," Flasher said.

"So ordered," Judge Haswell ruled.

"My next witness is Charles J. Oswald, the sheriff," the district attorney announced.

The sheriff, a long, lanky man with a quiet manner, took the stand. "You're acquainted with Harvey L. Corbin, the defendant in this case?" the district attorney asked.

"I am."

"Are you acquainted with his wife?"

"Yes, sir."

"Now, on the morning of the fifteenth of this month, the morning of the robbery at the Jebson Commercial Company, did you have any conversation with Mrs. Corbin?"

"I did. Yes, sir."

"Did you ask her about her husband's activities the night before?"

"Just a moment," Mason said. "I object to this on the ground that any conversation the sheriff had with Mrs. Corbin is not admissible against the defendant, Corbin; furthermore, that in this state a wife cannot testify against her husband. Therefore, any statement she might make would be an indirect violation of that rule. Furthermore, I object on the ground that the question calls for hearsay."

Judge Haswell looked ponderously thoughtful, then said, "It seems to me Mr. Mason is correct."

"I'll put it this way, Mr. Sheriff," the district attorney said. "Did you, on the morning of the fifteenth, take any money from Mrs. Corbin?"

"Objected to as incompetent, irrelevant, and immaterial," Mason said.

"Your Honor," Flasher said irritably, "that's the very gist of our case. We propose to show that two of the stolen twenty-dollar bills were in the possession of Mrs. Corbin."

Mason said, "Unless the prosecution can prove the bills were given Mrs. Corbin by her husband, the evidence is inadmissible."

"That's just the point," Flasher said. "Those bills *were* given to her by the defendant."

"How do you know?" Mason asked.

"She told the sheriff so."

"That's hearsay," Mason snapped.

Judge Haswell fidgeted on the bench. "It seems to me we're getting into a peculiar situation here. You can't call the wife as a witness, and I don't think her statement to the sheriff is admissible."

"Well," Flasher said desperately, "in this state, Your Honor, we have a community-property law. Mrs. Corbin had this money. Since she is the wife of the defendant, it was community property. Therefore, it's partially his property."

"Well now, there," Judge Haswell said, "I think I can agree with you. You introduce the twenty-dollar bills. I'll overrule the objection made by the defense."

"Produce the twenty-dollar bills, Sheriff," Flasher said triumphantly.

The bills were produced and received in evidence.

"Cross-examine," Flasher said curtly.

"No questions of this witness," Mason said, "but I have a few questions to ask Mr. Bernal on cross-examination. You took him off the stand to lay the foundation for introducing the bank list, and I didn't have an opportunity to cross-examine him."

"I beg your pardon," Flasher said. "Resume the stand, Mr. Bernal."

His tone, now that he had the twenty-dollar bills safely introduced in evidence, had a gloating note to it.

Mason said, "This list which has been introduced in evidence is on the stationery of the Ivanhoe National Bank?"

"That's right. Yes, sir."

"It consists of several pages, and at the end there is the signature of the assistant cashier?"

"Yes, sir."

"And each page is initialed by the assistant cashier?"

"Yes, sir."

"This was the scheme which you thought of in order to safeguard the company against a payroll robbery?"

"Not to safeguard the company against a payroll robbery, Mr. Mason, but to assist us in recovering the money in the event there was a holdup."

"This was your plan to answer Mr. Nesbitt's objections that the vault was an outmoded model?"

"A part of my plan, yes. I may say that Mr. Nesbitt's objections had never been voiced until I took office. I felt he was trying to embarrass me by making my administration show less net returns than expected." Bernal tightened his lips and added, "Mr. Nesbitt had, I believe, been expecting to be appointed manager. He was disappointed. I believe he still expects to be manager."

In the spectators' section of the courtroom, Ralph Nesbitt glared at Bernal.

"You had a conversation with the defendant on the night of the fourteenth?" Mason asked Bernal.

"I did. Yes, sir."

"You told him that for reasons which you deemed sufficient you were discharging him immediately and wanted him to leave the premises at once?"

"Yes, sir. I did."

"And you paid him his wages in cash?"

"Mr. Nesbitt paid him in my presence, with money he took from the petty-cash drawer of the vault."

"Now, as part of the wages due him, wasn't Corbin given these two twenty-dollar bills which have been introduced in evidence?"

Bernal shook his head. "I had thought of that," he said, "but it would have been impossible. Those bills weren't available to us at that time. The payroll is received from the bank in a sealed package. Those two twenty-dollar bills were in that package."

"And the list of the numbers of the twenty-dollar bills?"

"That's in a sealed envelope. The money is placed in the vault. I lock the list of numbers in my desk."

"Are you prepared to swear that neither you nor Mr. Nesbitt had access to these two twenty-dollar bills on the night of the fourteenth?"

"That is correct."

"That's all," Mason said. "No further cross-examination."

"I now call Ralph Nesbitt to the stand," District Attorney Flasher said. "I want to fix the time of these events definitely, Your Honor."

"Very well," Judge Haswell said. "Mr. Nesbitt, come forward."

Ralph Nesbitt, after answering the usual preliminary questions, sat down in the witness chair.

"Were you present at a conversation which took place between the defendant, Harvey L. Corbin, and Frank Bernal on the fourteenth of this month?" the district attorney asked.

"I was. Yes, sir."

"What time did that conversation take place?"

"About 8 o'clock in the evening."

"And, without going into the details of that conversation, I will ask you if the general effect of it was that the defendant was discharged and ordered to leave the company's property?"

"Yes, sir."

"And he was paid the money that was due him?"

"In cash. Yes, sir. I took the cash from the safe myself."

"Where was the payroll then?"

"In the sealed package in a compartment in the safe. As cashier, I had the only key to that compartment. Earlier in the afternoon I had gone to Ivanhoe City and received the sealed package of money and the envelope containing the list of numbers. I personally locked the package of money in the vault."

"And the list of numbers?"

"Mr. Bernal locked that in his desk."

"Cross-examine," Flasher said.

"No questions," Mason said.

"That's our case, Your Honor," Flasher observed.

"May we have a few minutes indulgence?" Mason asked Judge Haswell.

"Very well. Make it brief," the judge agreed.

Mason turned to Paul Drake and Della Street. "Well, there you are," Drake said. "You're confronted with the proof, Perry."

"Are you going to put the defendant on the stand?" Della Street asked.

Mason shook his head. "It would be suicidal. He has a record of a prior criminal conviction. Also, it's a rule of law that if one asks about any part of a conversation on direct examination, the other side can bring out all the conversation. That conversation, when Corbin was discharged, was to the effect that he had lied about his past record. And I guess there's no question that he did."

"And he's lying now," Drake said. "This is one case where you're licked. I think you'd better cop a plea, and see what kind of a deal you can make with Flasher."

"Probably not any," Mason said. "Flasher wants to have the reputation of having given me a licking—wait a minute, Paul. I have an idea."

Mason turned abruptly, walked away to where he could stand by himself, his back to the crowded courtroom.

"Are you ready?" the judge asked.

Mason turned. "I am quite ready, Your Honor. I have one witness whom I wish to put on the stand. I wish a subpoena *duces tecum* issued for that witness. I want him to bring certain documents which are in his possession."

"Who is the witness, and what are the documents?" the judge asked.

Mason walked quickly over to Paul Drake. "What's the name of that character who has the garbage-collecting business," he said softly, "the one who has the first nickel he'd ever made?"

"George Addey."

The lawyer turned to the judge. "The witness that I want is George Addey, and the documents that I want him to bring to court with him are all the twenty-dollar bills that he has received during the past sixty days."

"Your Honor," Flasher protested, "this is an outrage. This is making a travesty out of justice. It is exposing the court to ridicule."

Mason said, "I give Your Honor my assurance that I think this witness is material, and that the documents are material. I will make an affidavit to that effect if necessary. As attorney for the defendant, may I point out that if the court refuses to grant this subpoena, it will be denying the defendant due process of law."

"I'm going to issue the subpoena," Judge Haswell said, testily, "and for your own good, Mr. Mason, the testimony had better be relevant."

George Addey, unshaven and bristling with indignation, held up his right hand to be sworn. He glared at Perry Mason.

"Mr. Addey," Mason said, "you have the contract to collect garbage from Jebson City?"

"I do."

"How long have you been collecting garbage there?"

"For over five years, and I want to tell you—"

Judge Haswell banged his gavel. "The witness will answer questions and not interpolate any comments."

"I'll interpolate anything I dang please," Addey said.

"That'll do," the judge said. "Do you wish to be jailed for contempt of court, Mr. Addey?"

"I don't want to go to jail, but I—"

"Then you'll remember the respect that is due the court," the judge said. "Now you sit there and answer questions. This is a court of law. You're in this court as a citizen, and I'm here as a judge, and I propose to see that the respect due to the court is enforced." There was a moment's silence while the judge glared angrily at the witness. "All right, go ahead, Mr. Mason," Judge Haswell said.

Mason said, "During the thirty days prior to the fifteenth of this month, did you deposit any money in any banking institution?"

"I did not."

"Do you have with you all the twenty-dollar bills that you received during the last sixty days?"

"I have, and I think making me bring them here is just like inviting some crook to come and rob me and—"

Judge Haswell banged with his gavel. "Any more comments of that sort from the witness and there will be a sentence imposed for contempt of court. Now you get out those twenty-dollar bills, Mr. Addey, and put them right up here on the clerk's desk."

Addey, mumbling under his breath, slammed a roll of twenty-dollar bills down on the desk in front of the clerk.

"Now," Mason said, "I'm going to need a little clerical assistance. I would like to have my secretary, Miss Street, and the clerk help me check through the numbers on these bills. I will select a few at random."

Mason picked up three of the twenty-dollar bills and said, "I am going to ask my assistants to check the list of numbers introduced in evidence. In my hand is a twenty-dollar bill that has the number L 07083274 A. Is that bill on the list? The next bill that I pick up is number L 07579190 A. Are any of those bills on the list?"

The courtroom was silent. Suddenly, Della Street said, "Yes, here's one that's on the list—bill number L 07579190 A. It's on the list, on page eight."

"What?" the prosecutor shouted.

"Exactly," Mason said, smiling. "So, if a case is to be made against a person merely because he has possession of the money that was stolen on the fifteenth of this month, then your office should prefer charges against this witness, George Addey, Mr. District Attorney."

Addey jumped from the witness stand and shook his fist in Mason's face. "You're a cockeyed liar!" he screamed. "There ain't a one of those bills but what I didn't have it before the fifteenth. The company cashier changes my money into twenties, because I like big bills. I bury 'em in cans, and I put the date on the side of the can."

"Here's the list," Mason said. "Check it for yourself."

A tense silence gripped the courtroom as the judge and the spectators waited.

"I'm afraid I don't understand this, Mr. Mason," Judge Haswell said, after a moment.

"I think it's quite simple," Mason said. "And I now suggest the court take a recess for an hour and check these other bills against this list. I think the district attorney may be surprised."

And Mason sat down and proceeded to put papers in his brief case.

Della Street, Paul Drake, and Perry Mason were sitting in the lobby of the Ivanhoe Hotel.

"When are you going to tell us?" Della Street asked fiercely. "Or do we tear you limb from limb? How could the garbage man have—?"

"Wait a minute," Mason said. "I think we're about to get results. Here comes the esteemed district attorney, Vernon Flasher, and he's accompanied by Judge Haswell."

The two strode over to Mason's group and bowed with cold formality.

Mason got up.

Judge Haswell began in his best courtroom voice. "A most deplorable situation has occurred. It seems that Mr. Frank Bernal has—well—"

"Been detained somewhere," Vernon Flasher said.

"Disappeared," Judge Haswell said. "He's gone."

"I expected as much," Mason said.

"Now will you kindly tell me just what sort of pressure you brought to bear on Mr. Bernal to—?"

"Just a moment, Judge," Mason said. "The only pressure I brought to bear on him was to cross-examine him."

"Did you know that there had been a mistake in the dates on those lists?"

"There was no mistake. When you find Bernal, I'm sure you will discover there was a deliberate falsification. He was short in his accounts, and he knew he was about to be demoted. He had a desperate need for a hundred thousand dollars in ready cash. He had evidently been planning this burglary, or, rather, this embezzlement, for some time. He learned that Corbin had a criminal record. He arranged to have these lists furnished by the bank. He installed a burglar alarm, and, naturally, knew how to circumvent it. He employed a watchman he knew was addicted to drink. He only needed to stage his coup at the right time. He fired Corbin and paid him off with bills that had been recorded by the bank on page eight of the list of bills *in the payroll on the first of the month.*

"Then he removed page eight from the list of bills contained in the payroll *of the fifteenth,* before he showed it to the police, and substituted page eight of the list for the *first of the month* payroll. It was that simple.

"Then he drugged the watchman's whiskey, took an acetylene torch, burned through the vault doors, and took all the money."

"May I ask how you knew all this?" Judge Haswell demanded.

"Certainly," Mason said. "My client told me he received those bills from Nesbitt, who took them from the petty-cash drawer in the safe. He also told the sheriff that. I happened to be the only one who believed him. It sometimes pays, Your Honor, to have faith in a man, even if he has made a previous mistake. Assuming my client was innocent, I knew either Bernal or Nesbitt must be guilty. I then realized that only Bernal had custody of the *previous* lists of numbers.

"As an employee, Bernal had been paid on the first of the month. He looked at the numbers on the twenty-dollar bills in his pay envelope and found that they had been listed on page eight of the payroll for the first.

"Bernal only needed to abstract all twenty-dollar bills from the petty-cash drawer, substitute twenty-dollar bills from his own pay envelope, call in Corbin, and fire him. His trap was set.

"I let him know I knew what had been done by bringing Addey into court and proving my point. Then I asked for a recess. That was so Bernal would have a chance to skip out. You see, flight may be received as evidence of guilt. It was a professional courtesy to the district attorney. It will help him when Bernal is arrested."

PATTERN FOR MURDER

by Frances and Richard Lockridge

Fern Hartley came to New York to die, although that was far from her intention. She came from Centertown, in the Middle West, and died during a dinner party—given in her honor, at a reunion of schoolmates. She died at the bottom of a steep flight of stairs in a house on West Twelfth Street. She was a little woman and she wore a fluffy white dress. She stared at unexpected death through strangely bright blue eyes. . . .

There had been nothing to foreshadow so tragic an ending to the party—nothing, at any rate, on which Pamela North, who was one of the schoolmates, could precisely put a finger. It was true that Pam, as the party progressed, had increasingly felt tenseness in herself; it was also true that, toward the end, Fern Hartley had seemed to behave somewhat oddly. But the tenseness, Pam told herself, was entirely her own fault, and as for Fern's behavior—well, Fern *was* a little odd. Nice, of course, but—trying. Pam had been tried.

She had sat for what seemed like hours with a responsive smile stiffening her lips and with no comparable response stirring in her mind. It was from that, surely, that the tenseness—the uneasiness—arose. Not from anything on which a finger could be put. It's my own fault, Pam North thought. This is a reunion, and I don't reunite. Not with Fern, anyway.

It had been Fern on whom Pam had responsively smiled. Memories of old days, of school days, had fluttered from Fern's mind like pressed flowers from the yellowed pages of a treasured book. They had showered about Pam North, who had been Fern's classmate at Southwest High School in Centertown. They had showered also about

Hortense Notson and about Phyllis Pitt. Classmates, too, they had been those years ago—they and, for example, a girl with red hair.

"—*red* hair," Fern Hartley had said, leaning forward, eyes bright with memory. "Across the aisle from you in Miss Burton's English class. Of *course* you remember, Pam. She went with the boy who stuttered."

I *am* Pamela North, who used to be Pamela Britton, Pam told herself, behind a fixed smile. I'm not an impostor; I did go to Southwest High. If only I could prove it by remembering something—anything. Any *little* thing.

"The teacher with green hair?" Pam North said, by way of experiment. "Streaks of, anyway? Because the dye—"

Consternation clouded Fern's bright eyes. *"Pam!"* she said. "That was another one entirely. Miss Burton was the one who—"

It had been like that from the start of the party—the party of three couples and Miss Fern Hartley, still of Centertown. They were gathered in the long living room of the Stanley Pitts' house—the gracious room which ran the depth of the small, perfect house—an old New York house, retaining the charm (if also something of the inconvenience) of the previous century.

As the party started that warm September evening, the charm was uppermost. From open casement windows at the end of the room there was a gentle breeze. In it, from the start, Fern's memories had fluttered.

And none of the memories had been Pam North's memories. Fern has total recall; I have total amnesia, Pam thought, while keeping the receptive smile in place, since one cannot let an old schoolmate down. Did the others try as hard? Pam wondered. Find themselves as inadequate to recapture the dear, dead days?

Both Hortense Notson and Phyllis Pitt had given every evidence of trying, Pam thought, letting her mind wander. Fern was now reliving a perfectly wonderful picnic, of their junior year. Pam was not.

Pam did not let the smile waver; from time to time she nodded her bright head and made appreciative sounds. Nobody had let Fern down; all had taken turns in listening—even the men. Jerry North was slacking now, but he had been valiant. His valor had been special, since he had never even been in Centertown. And Stanley Pitt had done his bit, too; of course, he was the host. Of course, Fern was the Pitts' house guest; what a lovely house to be a guest in, Pam thought, permitting her eyes briefly to accompany her mind in its wandering.

Stanley—what a distinguished-looking man he is, Pam thought—was with Jerry, near the portable bar. She watched Jerry raise his glass as he listened. Her own glass was empty, and nobody was doing anything about it. An empty glass to go with an empty mind, Pam thought, and watched Fern sip ginger ale. Fern never drank anything stronger. Not that she had anything against drinking. Of course not. But even one drink made her feel all funny.

"Well," Pam had said, when Fern had brought the subject up, earlier on. "Well, that's more or less the idea, I suppose. This side of hilarious, of course."

"You know," Fern said then, "you always did talk funny. Remember when we graduated and you—"

Pam didn't remember. Without looking away from Fern, or letting the smile diminish, Pam nevertheless continued to look around the room. How lovely Phyllis is, Pam thought—really is. Blonde Phyllis Pitt was talking to Clark Notson, blond also, and sturdy, and looking younger than he almost certainly was.

Clark had married Hortense in Centertown. He was older—Pam remembered that he had been in college when they were in high school. He had married her when she was a skinny, dark girl, who had had to be prouder than anyone else because her parents lived over a store and not, properly, in a house. And look at her now, Pam thought, doing so. Dark still—and slim and quickly confident, and most beautifully arrayed.

Well, Pam thought, we've all come a long way. (She nodded, very brightly, to another name from the past—a name signifying nothing.) Stanley Pitt and Jerry—neglecting his own wife, Jerry North was—had found something of fabulous interest to discuss, judging by their behavior. Stanley was making points, while Jerry listened and nodded. Stanley was making points one at a time, with the aid of the thumb and the fingers of his right hand. He touched thumb-tip to successive fingertips, as if to crimp each point in place. And Jerry—how selfish could a man get—ran a hand through his hair, as he did when he was interested.

"Oh," Pam said. "Of course I remember *him,* Fern."

A little lying is a gracious thing.

What a witness Fern would make, Pam thought. Everything that had happened—beginning, apparently, at the age of two—was brightly clear in her mind, not muddy as in the minds of so many. The kind of witness Bill Weigand, member in good standing of the New York

City Police Department, always hoped to find and almost never did—never had, that she could remember, in all the many investigations she and Jerry had shared since they first met Bill years ago.

Fern would be a witness who really remembered. If Fern, Pam thought, knew something about a murder, or where a body was buried, or any of the other important things which so often come up, she would remember it precisely and remember it whole. A good deal of sifting would have to be done, but Bill was good at that.

Idly, her mind still wandering, Pam hoped that Fern did not, in fact, know anything of buried bodies. It could, obviously, be dangerous to have so total a recall and to put no curb on it. She remembered, and this from association with Bill, how often somebody did make that one revealing remark too many. Pam sternly put a curb on her own mind and imagination. What could Fern—pleasant, bubbling Fern, who had not adventured out of Centertown, excepting for occasional trips like these—know of dangerous things?

Pam North, whose lips ached, in whose mind Fern's words rattled, looked hard at Jerry, down the room, at the bar. Get me out of this, Pam willed across the space between them. Get me out of this! It had been known to work or had sometimes seemed to work. It did not now. Jerry concentrated on what Stanley Pitt was saying. Jerry ran a hand through his hair.

"Oh, dear," Pam said, breaking into the flow of Fern's words, as gently as she could. "Jerry wants me for something. You know how husbands are."

She stopped abruptly, remembering that Fern didn't, never having had one. She got up—and was saved by Phyllis, who moved in. What a hostess, Pam thought, and moved toward Jerry and the bar. The idea of saying that to poor Fern, Pam thought. This is certainly one of my hopeless evenings. She went toward Jerry.

"I don't," she said when she reached him, "remember anything about anything. Except one teacher with green hair, and that was the wrong woman."

Jerry said it seemed very likely.

"There's something a little ghoulish about all this digging up of the past," Pam said. "Suppose some of it's still alive?" she added.

"Huh?" Jerry said.

He was told not to bother. And that Pam could do with a drink. Jerry poured, for them both, from a pitcher in which ice tinkled.

"Some time," Pam said, "she's going to remember that one thing too many. That's what I mean. You see?"

"No," Jerry said, simply.

"Not everybody," Pam said, a little darkly, "wants everything remembered about everything. Because—"

Stanley Pitt, who had turned away, turned quickly back. He informed Pam that she had something there.

"I heard her telling Hortense—" Stanley Pitt said, and stopped abruptly, since Hortense, slim and graceful (and *so* beautifully arrayed) was coming toward them.

"How Fern doesn't change," Hortense said. "Pam, do you remember the boy next door?"

"I don't seem to remember anything," Pam said. "Not anything at all."

"You don't remember," Hortense said. "I don't remember. Phyllis doesn't. And with it all, she's so—sweet." She paused. "Or is she?" she said. "Some of the things she brings up—always doing ohs, the boy next door was. How does one do an oh?"

"Oh," Jerry said, politely demonstrating, and then, "Was he the one with green hair?" The others looked blank at that, and Pam said it was just one of the things she'd got mixed up, and now Jerry was mixing it worse. And, Pam said, did Hortense ever feel she hadn't really gone to Southwest High School at all and was merely pretending she had? Was an impostor?

"Far as I can tell," Hortense said, "I never lived in Centertown. Just in a small, one-room vacuum. Woman without a past." She paused. "Except," she said, in another tone, "Fern remembers me in great detail."

Stanley Pitt had been looking over their heads—looking at his wife, now the one listening to Fern. In a moment of silence, Fern's voice fluted. "Really, a dreadful thing to happen," Fern said. There was no context.

"Perhaps," Stanley said, turning back to them, "it's better to have no past than to live in one. Better all around. And safer."

He seemed about to continue, but then Clark Notson joined them. Clark did not, Pam thought, look like a man who was having a particularly good time. "Supposed to get Miss Hartley her ginger ale," he said. He spoke rather hurriedly.

Jerry, who was nearest the bar, said, "Here," and reached for the innocent bottle—a bottle, Pam thought, which looked a little smug and virtuous among the other bottles. Jerry used a silver opener, snapped off the bottle cap. The cap bounced off, tinkled against a bottle.

"Don't know your own strength," Clark said, and took the bottle and, with it, a glass into which Jerry dropped ice. "Never drinks anything stronger, the lady doesn't," Clark said, and bore away the bottle.

"And doesn't need to," Hortense Notson said, and drifted away. She could drift immaculately.

"She buys dresses," Pam said. "Wouldn't you know?"

"As distinct—?" Jerry said, and was told he knew perfectly well what Pam meant.

"Buys them for, not from," Pam said.

To this, Jerry simply said, "Oh."

It was then a little after eight, and there was a restless circulation in the long room. Pam was with Phyllis Pitt. Phyllis assured her that food would arrive soon. And hadn't old times come flooding back?

"Mm," Pam said. Pam was then with Clark Notson and, with him, talked unexpectedly of tooth paste. One never knows what will come up at a party. It appeared that Clark's firm made tooth paste. Stanley Pitt joined them. He said Clark had quite an operation there. Pam left them and drifted, dutifully, back to Fern, who sipped ginger ale. Fern's eyes were very bright. They seemed almost to glitter.

(But that's absurd, Pam thought. People's don't, only cats'.)

"It's so exciting," Fern said, and looked around the room, presumably at "it." "To meet you all again, and your nice husbands and—" She paused. "Only," she said, "I keep wondering . . ."

Pam waited. She said, "What, Fern?"

"Oh," Fern said. "Nothing dear. Nothing really. Do you remember—"

Pam did not. She listened for a time, and was relieved by Hortense, and drifted on again. For a minute or two, then, Pam North was alone and stood looking up and down the softly lighted room. Beyond the windows at the far end, lights glowed up from the garden below. The room was filled, but not harshly, with conversation—there seemed, somehow, to be more than the seven of them in it. Probably, Pam thought, memories crowded it—the red-haired girl, the stuttering boy.

Fern laughed. Her laughter was rather high in pitch. It had a little "hee" at the end. That little "hee," Pam thought idly, would identify

Fern—be something to remember her by. As Jerry's habit of running his hand through his hair would identify him if, about all else, she suddenly lost her memory. (As I've evidently begun to do, Pam North thought.) Little tricks. And Fern puts her right index finger gently to the tip of her nose, presumably when she's thinking. Why, Pam thought, she did that as a girl, and was surprised to remember.

Her host stood in front of her, wondering what he could get her. She had, Pam told him, everything.

"Including your memories?" Stanley Pitt asked her. Pam noticed a small scar on his chin. But it wasn't, of course, the same thing as —as running a hand through your hair. But everybody has something, which is one way of telling them apart.

"I seem," Pam said, "a little short of memories."

"By comparison with Miss Hartley," Stanley said, "who isn't? A pipe line to the past. Can't I get you a drink?"

He could not. Pam had had enough. So, she thought, had all of them. Not that anybody was in the least tight. But still . . .

Over the other voices, that of Fern Hartley was raised. There was excitement in it. So it isn't alcohol, Pam thought, since Fern hadn't had any. It's just getting keyed up at a party. She looked toward Fern, who was talking, very rapidly, to Jerry. No doubt, Pam thought, about what I was like in high school. Not that there's anything he shouldn't know. But still . . .

Fern was now very animated. If, Pam thought, I asked whether anyone here was one cocktail up I'd—why, I'd say Fern. Fern, of all people. Or else, Pam thought, she has some exciting surprise.

It was now eight thirty. A maid appeared at the door, waited to be noticed, and nodded to Phyllis Pitt, who said, at once, "Dinner, everybody." The dining room was downstairs, on a level with the garden. "These old stairs," Phyllis said. "Everybody be careful."

The stairs were, indeed, very steep, and the treads very narrow. But there were handrails and a carpet. The stairway ended in the dining room, where candles glowed softly on the table, among flowers.

"If you'll sit—" Phyllis said, starting with Pam North. "And you and—" They moved to the places indicated. "And Fern—" Phyllis said, and stopped. "Why," she said, "where is—"

She did not finish, because Fern Hartley stood at the top of the steep staircase. She was a slight figure in a white dress. She seemed to be staring fixedly down at them, her eyes strangely bright. Her face was flushed and she made odd, uncertain movements with her little hands.

"I'm—" Fern said, and spoke harshly, loudly, and so that the word was almost a shapeless sound. "I'm—"

And then Fern Hartley, taking both hands from the rails, pitched headfirst down the staircase. In a great moment of silence, her body made a strange, soft thudding on the stairs. She did not cry out.

At the bottom of the red-carpeted stairs she lay quite still. Her head was at a hideous angle to her body—an impossible angle to her body. That was how she died.

Fern Hartley died of a broken neck. There was no doubt. Six people had seen her fall. Now she lay at the bottom of the stairs and no one would ever forget her soft quick falling down that steep flight. An ambulance surgeon confirmed the cause of her death and another doctor from up the street—called when it seemed the ambulance would never get there—confirmed it, too.

But after he had knelt for some time by the body the second doctor beckoned the ambulance surgeon and they went out into the hallway. Then the ambulance surgeon beckoned one of the policemen who had arrived with the ambulance, and the policeman went into the hall with them. After a few minutes, the policeman returned and asked, politely enough, that they all wait upstairs. There were, he said meaninglessly, a few formalities.

They waited upstairs, in the living room. They waited for more than two hours, puzzled and in growing uneasiness. Then a thinnish man of medium height, about whom there was nothing special in appearance, came into the room and looked around at them.

"Why, *Bill!*" Pam North said.

The thinnish man looked at her, and then at Jerry North, and said, "Oh." Then he said there were one or two points.

And then Pam said, "Oh," on a note strangely flat.

How one introduces a police officer, who happens to be an old and close friend, to other friends who happen to be murder suspects —else why was Bill Weigand there?—had long been a moot question with Pam and Jerry North. Pam said, "This is Bill Weigand, everybody. Captain Weigand. He's—he's a policeman. So there must be—" And stopped.

"All right, Pam," Bill Weigand said. Then, "You all saw her fall. Tell me about it." He looked around at them, back at Pam North. It was she who told him.

Her eyes had been "staring"? Her face flushed? Her movements uncertain? Her voice hoarse? "Yes," Pam said, confirming each statement. Bill Weigand looked from one to another of the six in the room. He received nods of confirmation. One of the men—tall, dark-haired but with gray coming, a little older than the others—seemed about to speak. Bill waited. The man shook his head. Bill got them identified then. The tall man was Stanley Pitt. This was his house.

"But," Bill said, "she hadn't been drinking. The medical examiner is quite certain of that." He seemed to wait for comment.

"She said she never did," Pam told him.

"So—" Bill said.

Then Hortense Notson spoke, in a tense voice. "You act," she said, "as if you think one of us pushed her."

Weigand looked at her carefully. He said, "No. That didn't happen, Mrs. Notson. How could it have happened? You were all in the dining room, looking up at her. How could any of you have pushed her?"

"Then," Clark Notson said, and spoke quickly, with unexpected violence. "Then why all this? She . . . what? Had a heart attack?"

"Possibly," Bill said. "But the doctors—"

Again he was interrupted.

"I've heard of you," Notson said, and leaned forward in his chair. "Aren't you homicide?"

"Right," Bill said. He looked around again, slowly. "As Mr. Notson said, I'm homicide." And he waited.

Phyllis Pitt—the pretty, the very pretty, light-haired woman—had been crying. More than the rest, in expression, in movements, she showed the shock of what had happened. "Those dreadful stairs," she said, as if to herself. "Those dreadful stairs."

Her husband got up and went to her and leaned over her. He touched her bright hair and said, very softly, "All right, Phyl. All right."

"Bill," Pam said. "Fern fell downstairs and—and died. What more is there?"

"You all agree," Bill said, "that she was flushed and excited and uncertain—as if she had been drinking. But she hadn't been drinking. And . . . the pupils of her eyes were dilated. That was why she seemed to be staring. Because, you see, she couldn't see where she was going. So . . ." He paused. "She walked off into the air. I have to find out why. So what I want . . ."

It took him a long time to get what he wanted, which was all they could remember, one memory reinforcing another, of what had happened from the start of the dinner party until it ended with Fern Hartley, at the foot of the staircase, all her memories dead. Pam, listening, contributing what she could, could not see that a pattern formed—a pattern of murder.

Fern had seemed entirely normal—at least, until near the end. They agreed on that. She had always remembered much about the past and talked of it. Meeting old school friends, after long separation, she had seemed to remember everything—far more than any of the others.

"Most of it, to be honest, wasn't very interesting." That was Hortense Notson. Hortense looked at Pam, at Phyllis Pitt.

"She was so sweet," Phyllis said, in a broken voice.

"So—so interested herself." Pam said, "A good deal of it was pretty long ago, Bill."

Fern had shared her memories chiefly with the other women. But she had talked of the past, also, with the men.

"It didn't mean much to me," Stanley Pitt said. "It seemed to be all about Centertown, and I've never been in Centertown. Phyllis and I met in New York." He paused. "What's the point of this?" he said.

"I don't know," Bill Weigand told him. "Not yet. Everything she remembered seemed to be trivial? Nothing stands out? To any of you?"

"She remembered I had a black eye the first time she saw me," Clark Notson said. "Hortense and I—when we were going together—ran into her at a party. It was a long time ago. And I had a black eye, she said. I don't remember anything about it. I don't even remember the party, actually. Yes, I'd call it pretty trivial."

"My God," Stanley Pitt said. "*Is* there some point to this?"

"I don't know," Bill said again, and was patient. "Had you known Miss Hartley before, Mr. Pitt?"

"Met her for the first time yesterday," Stanley told him. "We had her to dinner and she stayed the night. Today I took her to lunch, because Phyl had things to do about the party. And—" He stopped. He shrugged and shook his head, seemingly at the futility of everything.

"I suppose," Jerry North said, "the point is—did she remember something that somebody—one of us—wanted forgotten?"

"Yes," Bill said. "It may be that."

Then it was in the open. And, with it in the open, the six looked at one another; and there was a kind of wariness in the manner of their looking. Although what on earth I've got to be wary about I don't know, Pam thought. Or Jerry, she added in her mind. She couldn't have told Jerry anything about me. Well, not anything important. At least not very . . .

"I don't understand," Phyllis said, and spoke dully. "I just don't understand at all. Fern just—just fell down those awful stairs."

It became like a game of tennis, with too many players, played in the dark. "Try to remember," Bill had told them; and it seemed they tried. But all they remembered was apparently trivial.

"There was something about a boy next door," Phyllis Pitt remembered. "A good deal older than she was—than we all were. Next door to Fern. A boy named—" She moved her hands helplessly. "I've forgotten. A name I'd never heard before. Something—she said something dreadful—happened to him. I suppose he died of something."

"No," Hortense Notson said. "She told me about him. He didn't die. He went to jail. He was always saying 'oh.'" She considered. "I think," she said, "he was named Russell something." She paused again. "Never in my life, did I hear so much about people I'd never heard of. Gossip about the past."

Stanley Pitt stood up. His impatience was evident.

"Look," he said. "This is my house, Captain. These people are my guests. Is any of this badgering getting you anywhere? And . . . where is there to get? Maybe she had a heart attack. Maybe she ate something that—" He stopped, rather abruptly; rather as if he had stumbled over something.

Weigand waited, but Pitt did not continue. Then Bill said they had thought of that. The symptoms—they had all noticed the symptoms —including the dilation of the pupils, might have been due to acute food poisoning. But she had eaten almost nothing during the cocktail period. The maid who had passed canapés was sure of that. Certainly she had eaten nothing the rest had not. And she had drunk only ginger ale, from a freshly opened bottle.

"Which," Bill said, "apparently you opened, Jerry."

Jerry North ran his right hand through his hair. He looked at Bill blankly.

"Of course you did," Pam said. "So vigorously the bottle cap flew off. Don't you—"

"Oh," Jerry said. Everybody looked at him. "Is that supposed—" But he was interrupted by Pitt, still leaning forward in his chair. "Wait," Pitt said, and put right thumb and index finger together, firmly, as if to hold a thought pinched between them. They waited.

"This place I took her to lunch," Stanley said. "It's a little place—little downstairs place, but wonderful food. I've eaten there off and on for years. But . . . I don't suppose it's too damned sanitary. Not like your labs are, Clark. And the weather's been hot. And—" He seemed to remember something else and held this new memory between thumb and finger. "Miss Hartley ate most of a bowl of ripe olives. Said she never seemed to get enough of them. And . . . isn't there something that can get into ripe olives? That can poison people?" He put the heel of one hand to his forehead. "God," he said. "Do you suppose it was that?"

"You mean food poisoning?" Weigand said. "Yes—years ago people got it from ripe olives. But not recently, that I've heard of. New methods and—"

"The olives are imported," Pitt said. "From Italy, I think. Yes. Dilated pupils—"

"Right," Bill said. "And the other symptoms match quite well. You may—"

But now he was interrupted by a uniformed policeman, who brought him a slip of paper. Bill Weigand looked at it and put it in his pocket and said, "Right," and the policeman went out again.

"Mr. Notson," Bill said, "you're production manager of the Winslow Pharmaceutical Company, aren't you?"

Notson looked blank. He said, "Sure."

"Which makes all kinds of drug products?"

Notson continued to look blank. He nodded his head.

"And Mr. Pitt," Bill Weigand said. "You're—"

He's gone off on a tangent, Pam North thought, half listening. What difference can it make that Mr. Notson makes drugs—or that Mr. Pitt tells people how to run offices and plants better—is an "efficiency engineer"? Because just a few minutes ago, somebody said something really important. Because it was wrong. Because—Oh! Pam thought. It's on the tip of my mind. If people would only be quiet, so I could think. If Bill only wouldn't go off on these—

"All kinds of drugs," Bill was saying, from his tangent, in the distance. "Including preparations containing atropine?"

She heard Clark Notson say, "Yes. Sure."

"Because," Bill said, and now Pam heard him clearly—very clearly— "Miss Hartley had been given atropine. It might have been enough to have killed her, if she had not had quick and proper treatment. She'd had enough to bring on dizziness and double vision. So that, on the verge of losing consciousness, she fell downstairs and broke her neck. Well?"

He looked around.

"The ginger ale," Jerry said. "The ginger ale I opened. That . . . opened so easily. Was that it?"

"Probably," Bill said. "The cap taken off carefully. Put back on carefully. After enough atropine sulphate had been put in. Enough to stop her remembering." Again he looked around at them; and Pam looked, too, and could see nothing—except shock—in any face. There seemed to be fear in none.

"The doctors suspected atropine from the start," Bill said, speaking slowly. "But the symptoms of atropine poisoning are very similar to those of food poisoning—or ptomaine. If she had lived to be treated, almost any physician would have diagnosed food poisoning—particularly after Mr. Pitt remembered the olives—and treated for that. Not for atropine. Since the treatments are different, she probably would not have lived." He paused. "Well," he said, "what did she remember? So that there was death for remembrance?"

Phyllis Pitt covered her eyes with both hands and shook her head slowly, dully. Hortense Notson looked at Weigand with narrowed eyes and her husband with—Pam thought—something like defiance. Stanley Pitt looked at the floor and seemed deep in thought, to be planning each thought between thumb and finger, when Weigand turned from them and said, "Yes?" to a man in civilian clothes. He went to talk briefly with the man. He returned. He said the telephone was a useful thing; he said the Centertown police were efficient.

"The boy next door," Weigand said, "was named Russell Clarkson. He was some years—fifteen, about—older than Fern Hartley. Not a boy any more, when she was in high school, but still 'the boy next door.' He did go to jail, as you said, Mrs. Notson. He helped set up a robbery of the place he worked in. A payroll messenger was killed. Clarkson got twenty years to life. And—he escaped in two years, and was never caught. And—*he was a chemist*. Mr. Notson. As you are. Mr. *Clark* Notson."

Notson was on his feet. His face was very red and he no longer looked younger than he was. He said, "You're crazy! I can prove—" His voice rose until he was shouting across the few feet between himself and Weigand.

And then it came to Pam—came with a kind of violent clarity. "Wait, Bill. *Wait!*" Pam shouted. "It wasn't 'ohs' at all. Not *saying* them. That's what was wrong."

They were listening. Bill was listening.

Then Pam pointed at Hortense. "You," she said, "the first time you said *doing* ohs. Not saying 'Oh.' You even asked how one *did* an oh. We thought it was the—the o-h kind of O. But—it was the *letter* O. And—*look at him now!* He's doing them now. *With his fingers.*"

And now she pointed at Stanley Pitt, who was forming the letter O with the thumb and index finger of his right hand; who now, violently, closed into fists his betraying hands. A shudder ran through his body. But he spoke quietly, without looking up from the floor.

"She hadn't quite remembered," he said, as if talking of something which had happened a long time ago. "Not quite." And he put the thumb and index finger tip to tip again, to measure the smallness of a margin. "But—she would have. She remembered everything. I've changed a lot and she was a little girl, but . . ."

He looked at his hands. "I've always done that, I guess," he said. He spread his fingers and looked at his hands, "Once it came up," he said, "there would be fingerprints. So—I had to try." He looked up, then, at his wife. "You see, Phyl, that I had to try?"

Phyllis covered her face with her hands.

After a moment Stanley Pitt looked again at his hands, spreading them in front of him. Slowly he began to bring together the fingertips and thumbtips of both hands; and he studied the movements of his fingers intently, as if they were new to him. He sat so, his hands moving in patterns they had never been able to forget, until Weigand told him it was time to go.

THE EMPTY HOURS:
An 87th Precinct Mystery

by Ed McBain

1

They thought she was colored at first.

The patrolman who investigated the complaint didn't expect to find a dead woman. This was the first time he'd seen a corpse, and he was somewhat shaken by the ludicrously relaxed grotesqueness of the girl lying on her back on the rug, and his hand trembled a little as he made out his report. But when he came to the blank line calling for an identification of RACE, he unhesitatingly wrote "Negro."

The call had been taken at Headquarters by a patrolman in the central Complaint Bureau. He sat at a desk with a pad of printed forms before him, and he copied down the information, shrugged because this seemed like a routine squeal, rolled the form and slipped it into a metal carrier, and then shot it by pneumatic tube to the radio room. A dispatcher there read the complaint form, shrugged because this seemed like a routine squeal, studied the precinct map on the wall opposite his desk, and then dispatched car eleven of the 87th Precinct to the scene.

The girl was dead.

She may have been a pretty girl, but she was hideous in death, distorted by the expanding gases inside her skin case. She was wearing a sweater and skirt, and she was barefoot, and her skirt had pulled back when she fell to the rug. Her head was twisted at a curious angle, the short black hair cradled by the rug, her eyes open and brown in a bloated face. The patrolman felt a sudden impulse to pull the girl's skirt down over her knees. He knew, suddenly, she would have wanted this. Death had caught her in this indecent posture, robbing her of female instinct. There were things this girl would never do again, so many things, all of which must have seemed enormously important to the girl herself. But the single universal thing was an infinitesimal detail, magnified now by death: she would never again perform the simple feminine and somehow beautiful act of pulling her skirt down over her knees.

The patrolman sighed and finished his report. The image of the dead girl remained in his mind all the way down to the squad car.

It was hot in the squadroom on that night in early August. The men working the graveyard shift had reported for duty at 6:00 P.M., and they would not go home until eight the following morning. They were all detectives and perhaps privileged members of the police force, but there were many policemen—Detective Meyer Meyer among them —who maintained that a uniformed cop's life made a hell of a lot more sense than a detective's.

"Sure, it does," Meyer insisted now, sitting at his desk in his shirt sleeves. "A patrolman's schedule provides regularity and security. It gives a man a home life."

"This squadroom is your home, Meyer," Carella said. "Admit it."

"Sure," Meyer answered, grinning. "I can't wait to come to work each day." He passed a hand over his bald pate. "You know what I like especially about this place? The interior decoration. The décor. It's very restful."

"Oh, you don't like your fellow workers, huh?" Carella said. He slid off the desk and winked at Cotton Hawes, who was standing at one of the filing cabinets. Then he walked toward the water cooler at the other end of the room, just inside the slatted railing that divided squadroom from corridor. He moved with a nonchalant ease that was deceptive. Steve Carella had never been one of those weight-lifting goons, and the image he presented was hardly one of bulging muscular power. But there was a quiet strength about the man and the way he moved, a confidence in the way he casually accepted the capabilities and limitations of his body. He stopped at the water cooler, filled a paper cup, and turned to look at Meyer again.

"No, I like my colleagues," Meyer said. "In fact, Steve, if I had my choice in all the world of who to work with, I would choose you honorable, decent guys. Sure." Meyer nodded, building steam. "In fact, I'm thinking of having some medals cast off, so I can hand them out to you guys. Boy, am I lucky to have this job! I may come to work without pay from now on. I may just refuse my salary, this job is so enriching. I want to thank you guys. You make me recognize the real values in life."

"He makes a nice speech," Hawes said.

"He should run the line-up. It would break the monotony. How come you don't run the line-up, Meyer?"

"Steve, I been offered the job," Meyer said seriously. "I told them I'm needed right here at the Eighty-seventh, the garden spot of all the precincts. Why, they offered me chief of detectives, and when I said no, they offered me commissioner, but I was loyal to the squad."

"Let's give *him* a medal," Hawes said, and the telephone rang.

Meyer lifted the receiver. "Eighty-seventh Squad, Detective Meyer. What? Yeah, just a second." He pulled a pad into place and began writing. "Yeah, I got it. Right. Right. Right. Okay." He hung up. Carella had walked to his desk. "A little colored girl," Meyer said.

"Yeah?"

"In a furnished room on South Eleventh."

"Yeah?"

"Dead," Meyer said.

2

The city doesn't seem to be itself in the very early hours of the morning.

She is a woman, of course, and time will never change that. She awakes as a woman, tentatively touching the day in a yawning, smiling stretch, her lips free of color, her hair tousled, warm from sleep, her body richer, an innocent girlish quality about her as sunlight stains the eastern sky and covers her with early heat. She dresses in furnished rooms in crumby rundown slums, and she dresses in Hall Avenue penthouses, and in the countless apartments that crowd the buildings of Isola and Riverhead and Calm's Point, in the private houses that line the streets of Bethtown and Majesta, and she emerges a different woman, sleek and businesslike, attractive but not sexy, a look of utter competence about her, manicured and polished, but with no time for nonsense, there is a long working day ahead of her. At five o'clock a metamorphosis takes place. She does not change her costume, this city, this woman, she wears the same frock or the same suit, the same high-heeled pumps or the same suburban loafers, but something breaks through that immaculate shell, a mood, a tone, an undercurrent. She is a different woman who sits in the bars and cocktail lounges, who relaxes on the patios or on the terraces shelving the skyscrapers, a different woman with a somewhat lazily inviting grin, a somewhat tired expression, an impenetrable knowledge on her face and in her eyes: she lifts her glass, she laughs gently, the evening sits expectantly on the skyline, the sky is awash with the purple of day's end.

She turns female in the night.

She drops her femininity and turns female. The polish is gone, the mechanized competence; she becomes a little scatterbrained and a little cuddly; she crosses her legs recklessly and allows her lipstick to be kissed clear off her mouth, and she responds to the male hands on her body, and she turns soft and inviting and miraculously primitive. The night is a female time, and the city is nothing but a woman.

And in the empty hours she sleeps, and she does not seem to be herself.

In the morning she will awake again and touch the silent air in a yawn, spreading her arms, the contented smile on her naked mouth. Her hair will be mussed, we will know her, we have seen her this way often.

But now she sleeps. She sleeps silently, this city. Oh, an eye open in the buildings of the night here and there, winking on, off again, silence. She rests. In sleep we do not recognize her. Her sleep is not like death, for we can hear and sense the murmur of life beneath the warm bedclothes. But she is a strange woman whom we have known intimately, loved passionately, and now she curls into an unresponsive ball beneath the sheet, and our hand is on her rich hip. We can feel life there, but we do not know her. She is faceless and featureless in the dark. She could be any city, any woman, anywhere. We touch her uncertainly. She has pulled the black nightgown of early morning around her, and we do not know her. She is a stranger, and her eyes are closed.

The landlady was frightened by the presence of policemen, even though she had summoned them. The taller one, the one who called himself Detective Hawes, was a redheaded giant with a white streak in his hair, a horror if she'd ever seen one. The landlady stood in the apartment where the girl lay dead on the rug, and she talked to the detectives in whispers, not because she was in the presence of death, but only because it was three o'clock in the morning. The landlady was wearing a bathrobe over her gown. There was an intimacy to the scene, the same intimacy that hangs alike over an impending fishing trip or a completed tragedy. Three A.M. is a time for slumber, and those who are awake while the city sleeps share a common bond that makes them friendly aliens.

"What's the girl's name?" Carella asked. It was three o'clock in the morning, and he had not shaved since 5 P.M. the day before, but his chin looked smooth. His eyes slanted slightly downward, combining with his clean-shaven face to give him a curiously oriental appearance. The landlady liked him. He was a nice boy, she thought. In her lexicon the men of the world were either "nice boys" or "louses." She wasn't sure about Cotton Hawes yet, but she imagined he was a parasitic insect.

"Claudia Davis," she answered, directing the answer to Carella whom she liked, and totally ignoring Hawes who had no right to be so big a man with a frightening white streak in his hair.

"Do you know how old she was?" Carella asked.

"Twenty-eight or twenty-nine, I think."

"Had she been living here long?"

"Since June," the landlady said.

"That short a time, huh?"

"And *this* has to happen," the landlady said. "She seemed like such a nice girl. Who do you suppose did it?"

"I don't know," Carella said.

"Or do you think it was suicide? I don't smell no gas, do you?"

"No," Carella said. "Do you know where she lived before this, Mrs. Mauder?"

"No, I don't."

"You didn't ask for references when she took the apartment?"

"It's only a furnished room," Mrs. Mauder said, shrugging. "She paid me a month's rent in advance."

"How much was that, Mrs. Mauder?"

"Sixty dollars. She paid it in cash. I never take checks from strangers."

"But you have no idea whether she's from this city, or out of town, or whatever. Am I right?"

"Yes, that's right."

"Davis," Hawes said, shaking his head. "That'll be a tough name to track down, Steve. Must be a thousand of them in the phone book."

"Why is your hair white?" the landlady asked.

"Huh?"

"That streak."

"Oh." Hawes unconsciously touched his left temple. "I got knifed once," he said, dismissing the question abruptly. "Mrs. Mauder, was the girl living alone?"

"I don't know. I mind my own business."

"Well, surely you would have seen . . ."

"I think she was living alone. I don't pry, and I don't spy. She gave me a month's rent in advance."

Hawes sighed. He could feel the woman's hostility. He decided to leave the questioning to Carella. "I'll take a look through the drawers and closets," he said, and moved off without waiting for Carella's answer.

"It's awfully hot in here," Carella said.

"The patrolman said we shouldn't touch anything until you got here," Mrs. Mauder said. "That's why I didn't open the windows or nothing."

"That was very thoughtful of you," Carella said, smiling. "But I think we can open the window now, don't you?"

"If you like. It does smell in here. Is . . . is that her? Smelling?"

"Yes," Carella answered. He pulled open the window. "There. That's a little better."

"Doesn't help much," the landlady said. "The weather's been terrible—just terrible. Body can't sleep at all." She looked down at the dead girl. "She looks just awful, don't she?"

"Yes. Mrs. Mauder, would you know where she worked, or if she had a job?"

"No, I'm sorry."

"Anyone ever come by asking for her? Friends? Relatives?"

"No, I'm sorry. I never saw any."

"Can you tell me anything about her habits? When she left the house in the morning? When she returned at night?"

"I'm sorry; I never noticed."

"Well, what made you think something was wrong in here?"

"The milk. Outside the door. I was out with some friends tonight, you see, and when I came back a man on the third floor called down to say his neighbor was playing the radio very loud and would I tell him to shut up, please. So I went upstairs and asked him to turn down the radio, and then I passed Miss Davis' apartment and saw the milk standing outside the door, and I thought this was kind of funny in such hot weather, but I figured it was *her* milk, you know, and I don't like to pry. So I came down and went to bed, but I couldn't stop thinking about that milk standing outside in the hallway. So I put on a robe and came upstairs and knocked on the door, and she didn't answer. So I called out to her, and she still didn't answer. So I figured something must be wrong. I don't know why. I just figured . . . I don't know. If she was in here, why didn't she answer?"

"How'd you know she was here?"

"I didn't."

"Was the door locked?"

"Yes."

"You tried it?"

"Yes. It was locked."

"I see," Carella said.

"Couple of cars just pulled up downstairs," Hawes said, walking over. "Probably the lab. And Homicide South."

"They know the squeal is ours," Carella said. "Why do they bother?"

"Make it look good," Hawes said. "Homicide's got the title on the door, so they figure they ought to go out and earn their salaries."

"Did you find anything?"

"A brand-new set of luggage in the closet, six pieces. The drawers and closets are full of clothes. Most of them look new. Lots of resort stuff, Steve. Found some brand-new books, too."

"What else?"

"Some mail on the dresser top."

"Anything we can use?"

Hawes shrugged. "A statement from the girl's bank. Bunch of canceled checks. Might help us."

"Maybe," Carella said. "Let's see what the lab comes up with."

The laboratory report came the next day, together with a necropsy report from the assistant medical examiner. In combination, the reports were fairly valuable. The first thing the detectives learned was that the girl was a white Caucasian of approximately thirty years of age.

Yes, white.

The news came as something of a surprise to the cops because the girl lying on the rug had certainly looked like a Negress. After all, her skin was black. Not tan, not coffee-colored, not brown, but black

—that intensely black coloration found on primitive tribes who spend a good deal of their time in the sun. The conclusion seemed to be a logical one, but death is a great equalizer not without a whimsical humor all its own, and the funniest kind of joke is a sight gag. Death changes white to black, and when that grisly old man comes marching in there's no question of who's going to school with whom. There's no longer any question of pigmentation, friend. That girl on the floor looked black, but she was white, and whatever else she was she was also stone cold dead, and that's the worst you can do to anybody.

The report explained that the girl's body was in a state of advanced putrefaction, and it went into such esoteric terms as "general distention of the body cavities, tissues, and blood vessels with gas," and "black discoloration of the skin, mucous membranes, and irides caused by hemolysis and action of hydrogen sulfide on the blood pigment," all of which broke down to the simple fact that it was a damn hot week in August and the girl had been lying on a rug which retained heat and speeded the post-mortem putrefaction. From what they could tell, and in weather like this, it was mostly a guess, the girl had been dead and decomposing for at least forty-eight hours, which set the time of her demise as August first or thereabouts.

One of the reports went on to say that the clothes she'd been wearing had been purchased in one of the city's larger department stores. All of her clothes—those she wore and those found in her apartment—were rather expensive, but someone at the lab thought it necessary to note that all her panties were trimmed with Belgian lace and retailed for twenty-five dollars a pair. Someone else at the lab mentioned that a thorough examination of her garments and her body had revealed no traces of blood, semen, or oil stains.

The coroner fixed the cause of death as strangulation.

3

It is amazing how much an apartment can sometimes yield to science. It is equally amazing, and more than a little disappointing, to get nothing from the scene of a murder when you are desperately seeking a clue. The furnished room in which Claudia Davis had been strangled to death was full of juicy surfaces conceivably carrying hundreds of latent fingerprints. The closets and drawers contained piles of clothing that might have carried traces of anything from gunpowder to face powder.

But the lab boys went around lifting their prints and sifting their dust and vacuuming with a Söderman-Heuberger filter, and they went down to the morgue and studied the girl's skin and came up with a total of nothing. Zero. Oh, not quite zero. They got a lot of prints belonging to Claudia Davis, and a lot of dust collected from all over the city and clinging to her shoes and her furniture. They also found some documents belonging to the dead girl—a birth certificate, a diploma of graduation from a high school in Santa Monica, and an expired library card. And, oh, yes, a key. The key didn't seem to fit any of the locks in the room. They sent all the junk over to the 87th, and Sam Grossman called Carella personally later that day to apologize for the lack of results.

The squadroom was hot and noisy when Carella took the call from the lab. The conversation was a curiously one-sided affair. Carella, who had dumped the contents of the laboratory envelope onto his desk, merely grunted or nodded every now and then. He thanked Grossman at last, hung up, and stared at the window facing the street and Grover Park.

"Get anything?" Meyer asked.

"Yeah. Grossman thinks the killer was wearing gloves."

"That's nice," Meyer said.

"Also, I think I know what this key is for." He lifted it from the desk.

"Yeah? What?"

"Well, did you see these canceled checks?"

"No."

"Take a look," Carella said.

He opened the brown bank envelope addressed to Claudia Davis, spread the canceled checks on his desk top, and then unfolded the yellow bank statement. Meyer studied the display silently.

"Cotton found the envelope in her room," Carella said. "The statement covers the month of July. Those are all the checks she wrote, or at least everything that cleared the bank by the thirty-first."

"Lots of checks here," Meyer said.

"Twenty-five, to be exact. What do you think?"

"I know what *I* think," Carella said.

"What's that?"

"I look at those checks, I can see a life. It's like reading somebody's diary. Everything she did last month is right here, Meyer. All the department stores she went to, look, a florist, her hairdresser, a candy shop, even her shoemaker, and look at this. A check made out to a funeral home. Now who died, Meyer, huh? And look here. She was living at Mrs. Mauder's place, but here's a check made out to a swank apartment building on the South Side, in Stewart City. And some of these checks are just made out to names, *people*. This case is crying for some people."

"You want me to get the phone book?"

"No, wait a minute. Look at this bank statement. She opened the account on July fifth with a thousand bucks. All of a sudden, bam, she deposits a thousand bucks in the Seaboard Bank of America."

"What's so odd about that?"

"Nothing, maybe. But Cotton called the other banks in the city, and Claudia Davis has a very healthy account at the Highland Trust on Cromwell Avenue. And I mean *very* healthy."

"How healthy?"

"Close to sixty grand."

"What!"

"You heard me. And the Highland Trust lists no withdrawals for the month of July. So where'd she get the money to put into Seaboard?"

"Was that the only deposit?"

"Take a look."

Meyer picked up the statement.

"The initial deposit was on July fifth," Carella said. "A thousand bucks. She made another thousand-dollar deposit on July twelfth. And another on the nineteenth. And another on the twenty-seventh."

Meyer raised his eyebrows. "Four grand. That's a lot of loot."

"And all deposited in less than a month's time. I've got to work almost a full year to make that kind of money."

"Not to mention the sixty grand in the other bank. Where do you suppose she got it, Steve?"

"I don't know. It just doesn't make sense. She wears underpants trimmed with Belgian lace, but she lives in a crumby room-and-a-half with bath. How the hell do you figure that? Two bank accounts, twenty-five bucks to cover her ass, and all she pays is sixty bucks a month for a flophouse."

"Maybe she's hot, Steve."

"No." Carella shook his head. "I ran a make with C.B.I. She hasn't got a record, and she's not wanted for anything. I haven't heard from the feds yet, but I imagine it'll be the same story."

"What about that key? You said . . ."

"Oh, yeah. That's pretty simple, thank God. Look at this."

He reached into the pile of checks and sorted out a yellow slip, larger than the checks. He handed it to Meyer. The slip read:

THE SEABOARD BANK OF AMERICA
Isola Branch
P 1698

July 5

We are charging your account as per items below. Please see that the amount is deducted on your books so that our accounts may agree.

FOR	Safe deposit rental #375	5	00
	U.S. Tax		50
	AMOUNT OF CHARGE	5	50

CHARGE	Claudia Davis	ENTERED BY
	1263 South Eleventh	*BPR*
	Isola	

"She rented a safe-deposit box the same day she opened the new checking account, huh?" Meyer said.

"Right."

"What's in it?"

"That's a good question."

"Look, do you want to save some time, Steve?"

"Sure."

"Let's get the court order *before* we go to the bank."

4

The manager of the Seaboard Bank of America was a bald-headed man in his early fifties. Working on the theory that similar physical types are *simpático*, Carella allowed Meyer to do most of the questioning. It was not easy to elicit answers from Mr. Anderson, the manager of the bank, because he was by nature a reticent man. But Detective Meyer Meyer was the most patient man in the city, if not the entire world. His patience was an acquired trait, rather than an inherited one. Oh, he had inherited a few things from his father, a jovial man named Max Meyer, but patience was not one of them. If anything, Max Meyer had been a very impatient if not downright short-tempered sort of fellow. When his wife, for example, came to him with the news that she was expecting a baby, Max nearly hit the ceiling. He enjoyed little jokes immensely, was perhaps the biggest practical joker in all Riverhead, but this particular prank of nature failed to amuse him. He had thought his wife was long past the age when bearing children was even a remote possibility. He never thought of himself as approaching dotage, but he was after all getting on in years, and a change-of-life baby was hardly what the doctor had ordered. He allowed the impending birth to simmer inside him, planning his revenge all the while, plotting the practical joke to end all practical jokes.

When the baby was born, he named it Meyer, a delightful handle which when coupled with the family name provided the infant with a double-barreled monicker: Meyer Meyer.

Now that's pretty funny. Admit it. You can split your sides laughing over that one, unless you happen to be a pretty sensitive kid who also happens to be an Orthodox Jew, and who happens to live in a predominately Gentile neighborhood. The kids in the neighborhood thought Meyer Meyer had been invented solely for their own pleasure. If they needed further provocation for beating up the Jew boy, and they didn't need any, his name provided excellent motivational fuel. "Meyer Meyer, Jew on fire!" they would shout, and then they would chase him down the street and beat hell out of him.

Meyer learned patience. It is not very often that one kid, or even one grown man, can successfully defend himself against a gang. But sometimes you can talk yourself out of a beating. Sometimes, if you're patient, if you just wait long enough, you can catch one of them alone and stand up to him face to face, man to man, and know the exultation of a fair fight without the frustration of overwhelming odds.

Listen, Max Meyer's joke was a harmless one. You can't deny an old man his pleasure. But Mr. Anderson, the manager of the bank, was fifty-four years old and totally bald. Meyer Meyer, the detective second grade who sat opposite him and asked questions, was also totally bald. Maybe a lifetime of sublimation, a lifetime of devoted patience, doesn't leave any scars. Maybe not. But Meyer Meyer was only thirty-seven years old.

Patiently he said, "Didn't you find these large deposits rather odd, Mr. Anderson?"

"No," Anderson said. "A thousand dollars is not a lot of money."

"Mr. Anderson," Meyer said patiently, "you are aware, of course, that banks in this city are required to report to the police any unusually large sums of money deposited at one time. You are aware of that, are you not?"

"Yes, I am."

"Miss Davis deposited four thousand dollars in three weeks' time. Didn't that seem unusual to you?"

"No. The deposits were spaced. A thousand dollars is not a lot of money, and not an unusually large deposit."

"To me," Meyer said, "a thousand dollars is a lot of money. You can buy a lot of beer with a thousand dollars."

"I don't drink beer," Anderson said flatly.

"Neither do I," Meyer answered.

"Besides, we *do* call the police whenever we get a very large deposit, unless the depositor is one of our regular customers. I did not feel these deposits warranted such a call."

"Thank you, Mr. Anderson," Meyer said. "We have a court order here. We'd like to open the box Miss Davis rented."

"May I see the order, please?" Anderson said. Meyer showed it to him. Anderson sighed and said, "Very well. Do you have Miss Davis' key?"

Carella reached into his pocket. "Would this be it?" he said. He put a key on the desk. It was the key that had come to him from the lab together with the documents they'd found in the apartment.

"Yes, that's it," Mr. Anderson said. "There are two different keys to every box, you see. The bank keeps one, and the renter keeps the other. The box cannot be opened without both keys. Will you come with me, please?"

He collected the bank key to safety-deposit box number 375 and led the detectives to the rear of the bank. The room seemed to be lined with shining metal. The boxes, row upon row, reminded Carella of the morgue and the refrigerated shelves that slid in and out of the wall on squeaking rollers. Anderson pushed the bank key into a slot and turned it, and then he put Claudia Davis' key into a second slot and turned that. He pulled the long, thin box out of the wall and handed it to Meyer. Meyer carried it to the counter on the opposite wall and lifted the catch.

"Okay?" he said to Carella.

"Go ahead."

Meyer raised the lid of the box.

There was $16,000 in the box. There was also a slip of note paper. The $16,000 was neatly divided into four stacks of bills. Three of the stacks held $5,000 each. The fourth stack held only $1,000. Carella picked up the slip of paper. Someone, presumably Claudia Davis, had made some annotations on it in pencil.

$$\begin{array}{rr} 7/5 & 20,000 \\ 7/5 & -1,000 \\ \hline & 19,000 \\ 7/12 & -1,000 \\ \hline & 18,000 \\ 7/19 & -1,000 \\ \hline & 17,000 \\ 7/27 & -1,000 \\ \hline & 16,000 \end{array}$$

"Make any sense to you, Mr. Anderson?"

"No. I'm afraid not."

"She came into this bank on July fifth with twenty thousand dollars in cash, Mr. Anderson. She put a thousand of that into a checking account and the remainder into this box. The dates on this slip of paper show exactly when she took cash from the box and transferred it to the checking account. She knew the rules, Mr. Anderson. She knew that twenty grand deposited in one lump would bring a call to the police. This way was a lot safer."

"We'd better get a list of these serial numbers," Meyer said.

"Would you have one of your people do that for us, Mr. Anderson?"

Anderson seemed ready to protest. Instead, he looked at Carella, sighed, and said, "Of course."

The serial numbers didn't help them at all. They compared them against their own lists, and the out-of-town lists, and the FBI lists, but none of those bills was hot.

Only August was.

5

Stewart City hangs in the hair of Isola like a jeweled tiara. Not really a city, not even a town, merely a collection of swank apartment buildings overlooking the River Dix, the community had been named after British royalty and remained one of the most exclusive neighborhoods in town. If you could boast of a Stewart City address, you could also boast of a high income, a country place on Sands Spit, and a Mercedes Benz in the garage under the apartment building. You could give your address with a measure of snobbery and pride—you were, after all, one of the elite.

The dead girl named Claudia Davis had made out a check to Management Enterprises, Inc., at 13 Stewart Place South, to the tune of $750. The check had been dated July ninth, four days after she'd opened the Seaboard account.

A cool breeze was blowing in off the river as Carella and Hawes pulled up. Late-afternoon sunlight dappled the polluted water of the Dix. The bridges connecting Calm's Point with Isola hung against a sky awaiting the assault of dusk.

"Want to pull down the sun visor?" Carella said.

Hawes reached up and turned down the visor. Clipped to the visor so that it showed through the windshield of the car was a hand-lettered card that read POLICEMAN ON DUTY CALL—87TH PRECINCT. The car, a 1956 Chevrolet, was Carella's own.

"I've got to make a sign for my car," Hawes said. "Some bastard tagged it last week."

"What did you do?"

"I went to court and pleaded not guilty. On my day off."

"Did you get out of it?"

"Sure. I was answering a squeal. It's bad enough I had to use my own car, but for Pete's sake, to get a ticket!"

"I prefer my own car," Carella said. "Those three cars belonging to the squad are ready for the junk heap."

"*Two,*" Hawes corrected. "One of them's been in the police garage for a month now."

"Meyer went down to see about it the other day."

"What'd they say? Was it ready?"

"No, the mechanic told him there were four patrol cars ahead of the sedan, and they took precedence. Now how about that?"

"Sure, it figures. I've still got a chit in for the gas I used, you know that?"

"Forget it. I've never got back a cent I laid out for gas."

"What'd Meyer do about the car?"

"He slipped the mechanic five bucks. Maybe that'll speed him up."

"You know what the city ought to do?" Hawes said. "They ought to buy some of those used taxicabs. Pick them up for two or three hundred bucks, paint them over, and give them out to the squads. Some of them are still in pretty good condition."

"Well, it's an idea," Carella said dubiously, and they entered the building. They found Mrs. Miller, the manager, in an office at the rear of the ornate entrance lobby. She was a woman in her early forties with a well-preserved figure and a very husky voice. She wore her hair piled on the top of her head, a pencil stuck rakishly into the reddish-brown heap. She looked at the photostated check and said, "Oh, yes, of course."

"You knew Miss Davis?"

"Yes, she lived here for a long time."

"How long?"

"Five years."

"When did she move out?"

"At the end of June." Mrs. Miller crossed her splendid legs and smiled graciously. The legs were remarkable for a woman of her age, and the smile was almost radiant. She moved with an expert femininity, a calculated conscious fluidity of flesh that suggested availability and yet was totally respectable. She seemed to have devoted a lifetime to learning the ways and wiles of the female and now practiced them with facility and charm. She was pleasant to be with, this woman, pleasant to watch and to hear, and to think of touching.

Carella and Hawes, charmed to their shoes, found themselves relaxing in her presence.

"This check," Carella said, tapping the photostat. "What was it for?"

"June's rent. I received it on the tenth of July. Claudia always paid her rent by the tenth of the month. She was a very good tenant."

"The apartment cost seven hundred and fifty dollars a month?"

"Yes."

"Isn't that high for an apartment?"

"Not in Stewart City," Mrs. Miller said gently. "And this was a river-front apartment."

"I see. I take it Miss Davis had a good job."

"No, no, she doesn't have a job at all."

"Then how could she afford . . . ?"

"Well, she's rather well off, you know."

"Where does she get the money, Mrs. Miller?"

"Well . . ." Mrs. Miller shrugged. "I really think you should ask *her*, don't you? I mean, if this is something concerning Claudia, shouldn't you . . . ?"

"Mrs. Miller," Carella said, "Claudia Davis is dead."

"What?"

"She's . . ."

"What? No. No." She shook her head. "Claudia? But the check . . . I . . . the check came only last month." She shook her head again. "No. No."

"She's dead, Mrs. Miller," Carella said gently. "She was strangled."

The charm faltered for just an instant. Revulsion knifed the eyes of Mrs. Miller, the eyelids flickered, it seemed for an instant that the pupils would turn shining and wet, that the carefully lipsticked mouth would crumble. And then something inside took over, something that demanded control, something that reminded her that a charming woman does not weep and cause her fashionable eye makeup to run.

"I'm sorry," she said, almost in a whisper. "I am really, really sorry. She was a nice person."

"Can you tell us what you know about her, Mrs. Miller?"

"Yes. Yes, of course." She shook her head again, unwilling to accept the idea. "That's terrible. That's terrible. Why, she was only a baby."

"We figured her for thirty, Mrs. Miller. Are we wrong?"

"She seemed younger, but perhaps that was because . . . well, she was a rather shy person. Even when she first came here, there was an air of—well, lostness about her. Of course, that was right after her parents died, so . . ."

"Where did she come from, Mrs. Miller?"

"California. Santa Monica."

Carella nodded. "You were starting to tell us . . . you said she was rather well off. Could you . . . ?"

"Well, the stock, you know."

"What stock?"

"Her parents had set up a securities trust account for her. When they died, Claudia began receiving the income from the stock. She was an only child, you know."

"And she lived on stock dividends alone?"

"They amounted to quite a bit. Which she saved, I might add. She was a very systematic person, not at all frivolous. When she received a dividend check, she would endorse it and take it straight to the bank. Claudia was a very sensible girl."

"Which bank, Mrs. Miller?"

"The Highland Trust. Right down the street. On Cromwell Avenue."

"I see," Carella said. "Was she dating many men? Would you know?"

"I don't think so. She kept pretty much to herself. Even after Josie came."

Carella leaned forward. "Josie? Who's Josie?"

"Josie Thompson. Josephine, actually. Her cousin."

"And where did *she* come from?"

"California. They both came from California."

"And how can we get in touch with this Josie Thompson?"

"Well, she . . . Don't you know? Haven't you . . . ?"

"What, Mrs. Miller?"

"Why, Josie is dead. Josie passed on in June. That's why Claudia moved, I suppose. I suppose she couldn't bear the thought of living in that apartment without Josie. It *is* a little frightening, isn't it?"

"Yes," Carella said.

DETECTIVE DIVISION SUPPLEMENTARY REPORT	SQUAD	PRECINCT	PRECINCT REPORT	DETECTIVE DIVISION REPORT NUMBER
pdcn 360 rev 25m	87	87	32-101	DD 60 R-42

NAME AND ADDRESS OF PERSON REPORTING					DATE ORIGINAL REPORT
Miller	Irene(Mrs. John)		13	Stewart Place So.	8-4-60
SURNAME	GIVEN NAME	INITIALS	NUMBER	STREET	

DETAILS

Summary of interview with Irene (Mrs. John) Miller at office of Management Enterprises, Inc., address above, in re homicide Claudia Davis. Mrs. Miller states:

Claudia Davis came to this city in June of 1955, took $750-a-month apartment above address, lived there alone. Rarely seen in company of friends, male or female. Young recluse type living on substantial income of inherited securities. Parents, Mr. and Mrs. Carter Davis, killed on San Diego Freeway in head-on collision with station wagon, April 14, 1955. L.A.P.D. confirms traffic accident, driver of other vehicle convicted for negligent operation. Mrs. Miller describes girl as medium height and weight, close-cropped brunette hair, brown eyes, no scars or birthmarks she can remember, tallies with what we have on corpse. Further says Claudia Davis was quiet, unobtrusive tenant, paid rent and all service bills punctually, was gentle, sweet, plain, childlike, shy, meticulous in money matters, well liked but unapproachable.

In April or May of 1959, Josie Thompson, cousin of deceased, arrived from Brentwood, California. (Routine check with Criminal Bureau Identification negative, no record. Checking now with L.A.P.D., and FBI.) Described as slightly older than Claudia, rather different in looks and personality. "They were like black and white," Mrs. Miller says, "but they hit it off exceptionally well." Josie moved into the apartment with cousin. Words used to describe relationship between two were "like the closest sisters," and "really in tune," and "the best of friends," etc. Girls did not date much, were constantly in each other's company, Josie seeming to pick up recluse habits from Claudia. Went on frequent trips together. Spent summer of '59 on Tortoise Island in the bay, returned Labor Day. Went away again at Christmas time to ski Sun Valley, and again in March this year to Kingston, Jamaica, for three weeks, returning at beginning of April. Source of income was fairly standard securities-income account. Claudia did not own the stock, but income on it was hers for as long as she lived. Trust specified that upon her death the stock and the income be turned over to U.C.L.A. (father's alma mater). In any case, Claudia was assured of a very, very substantial lifetime income (see Highland Trust bank account) and was apparently supporting Josie as well, since Mrs. Miller claims neither girl worked. Brought up question of possible lesbianism, but Mrs. Miller, who is knowledgeable and hip, says no, neither girl was a dike.

On June 3, Josie and Claudia left for another weekend trip. Doorman reports having helped them pack valises into trunk of Claudia's car, 1960 Cadillac convertible. Claudia did the driving. Girls did not return on Monday morning as they had indicated they would. Claudia called on Wednesday, crying on telephone. Told Mrs. Miller that Josie had had a terrible accident and was dead. Mrs. Miller remembers asking Claudia if she could help in any way. Claudia said, quote, *No, everything's been taken care of already,* unquote.

On June 17, Mrs. Miller received a letter from Claudia (letter attached—handwriting compares positive with checks Claudia signed) stating she could not possibly return to apartment, not after what had happened to her cousin. She reminded Mrs. Miller lease expired on July 4, told her she would send check for June's rent before July 10. Said moving company would pack and pick up her belongings, delivering all valuables and documents to her, and storing rest. (See Claudia Davis' check number 010, 7/14, made payable to Allora Brothers, Inc., "in payment for packing, moving, and storage.") Claudia Davis never returned to the apartment. Mrs. Miller had not seen her and knew nothing of her whereabouts until we informed her of the homicide.

DATE OF THIS REPORT
August 6

Det	2/gr	Carella	S.L.	714-56-32	Det/Lt.PeterByrnes
RANK		SURNAME	INITIALS	SHIELD NUMBER	COMMANDING OFFICER

6

The drive upstate to Triangle Lake was a particularly scenic one, and since it was August, and since Sunday was supposed to be Carella's day off, he thought he might just as well combine a little business with pleasure. So he put the top of the car down, and he packed Teddy into the front seat together with a picnic lunch and a gallon Thermos of iced coffee, and he forgot all about Claudia Davis on the drive up through the mountains. Carella found it easy to forget about almost anything when he was with his wife.

Teddy as far as he was concerned—and his astute judgment had been backed up by many a street-corner whistle—was only the most beautiful woman in the world. He could never understand how he, a hairy, corny, ugly, stupid, clumsy cop, had managed to capture anyone as wonderful as Theodora Franklin. But capture her he had, and he sat beside her now in the open car and stole sidelong glances at her as he drove, excited as always by her very presence.

Her black hair, always wild, seemed to capture something of the wind's frenzy as it whipped about the oval of her face. Her brown eyes were partially squinted against the rush of air over the windshield. She wore a white blouse emphatically curved over a full bosom, black tapered slacks form-fitted over generous hips and good legs. She had kicked off her sandals and folded her knees against her breasts, her bare feet pressed against the glove-compartment panel. There was about her, Carella realized, a curious combination of savage and sophisticate. You never knew whether she was going to kiss you or slug you, and the uncertainty kept her eternally desirable and exciting.

Teddy watched her husband as he drove, his big-knuckled hands on the wheel of the car. She watched him not only because it gave her pleasure to watch him, but also because he was speaking. And since she could not hear, since she had been born a deaf mute, it was essential that she look at his mouth when he spoke. He did not discuss the case at all. She knew that one of the Claudia Davis checks had been made out to the Fancher Funeral Home in Triangle Lake and she knew that Carella wanted to talk to the proprietor of the place personally. She further knew that this was very important or he wouldn't be spending his Sunday driving all the way upstate. But he had promised her he'd combine business with pleasure. This was the pleasure part of the trip, and in deference to his promise and his wife, he refrained from discussing the case, which was really foremost in his mind. He talked, instead, about the scenery, and their plans for the fall, and the way the twins were growing, and how pretty Teddy looked, and how she'd better button that top button of her blouse before they got out of the car, but he never once mentioned Claudia Davis until they were standing in the office of the Fancher Funeral Home and looking into the gloomy eyes of a man who called himself Barton Scoles.

Scoles was tall and thin and he wore a black suit that he had probably worn to his own confirmation back in 1912. He was so much the stereotype of a small-town undertaker that Carella almost burst out laughing when he met him. Somehow, though, the environment was not conducive to hilarity. There was a strange smell hovering over the thick rugs and the papered walls and the hanging chandeliers. It was a while before Carella recognized it as formaldehyde and then made the automatic association and, curious for a man who had stared into the eyes of death so often, suddenly felt like retching.

"Miss Davis made out a check to you on July fifteenth," Carella said. "Can you tell me what it was for?"

"Sure can," Scoles said. "Had to wait a long time for that check. She give me only a twenty-five dollar deposit. Usually take fifty, you know. I got stuck many a time, believe me."

"How do you mean?" Carella asked.

"People. You bury their dead, and then sometimes they don't pay you for your work. This business isn't *all* fun, you know. Many's the time I handled the whole funeral and the service and the burial and all, and never did get paid. Makes you lose your faith in human nature."

"But Miss Davis finally *did* pay you."

"Oh, sure. But I can tell you I was sweating that one out. I can tell you that. After all, she was a strange gal from the city, has the funeral here, nobody comes to it but her, sitting in the chapel out there and watching the body as if someone's going to steal it away, just her and the departed. I tell you, Mr. Carella . . . Is that your name?"

"Yes, Carella."

"I tell you, it was kind of spooky. Lay there two days, she did, her cousin. And then Miss Davis asked that we bury the girl right here in the local cemetery, so I done that for her, too—all on the strength of a twenty-five-dollar deposit. That's trust, Mr. Carella, with a capital T."

"When was this, Mr. Scoles?"

"The girl drowned the first weekend in June," Scoles said. "Had no business being out on the lake so early, anyways. That water's still icy cold in June. Don't really warm up none till the latter part July. She fell over the side of the boat—she was out there rowing, you know—and that icy water probably froze her solid, or give her cramps or something, drowned her anyways." Scoles shook his head. "Had no business being out on the lake so early."

"Did you see a death certificate?"

"Yep, Dr. Donneli made it out. Cause of death was drowning, all right, no question about it. We had an inquest, too, you know. The Tuesday after she drowned. They said it was accidental."

"You said she was out rowing in a boat. Alone?"

"Yep. Her cousin, Miss Davis, was on the shore watching. Jumped in when she fell overboard, tried to reach her, but couldn't make it in time. That water's plenty cold, believe me. Ain't too warm even now, and here it is August already."

"But it didn't seem to affect Miss Davis, did it?"

"Well, she was probably a strong swimmer. Been my experience most pretty girls are strong girls, too. I'll bet your wife here is a strong girl. She sure is a pretty one."

Scoles smiled, and Teddy smiled and squeezed Carella's hand.

"About the payment," Carella said, "for the funeral and the burial. Do you have any idea why it took Miss Davis so long to send her check?"

"Nope. I wrote her twice. First time was just a friendly little reminder. Second time, I made it a little stronger. Attorney friend of mine in town wrote it on his stationery; that always impresses them. Didn't get an answer either time. Finally, right out of the blue, the check came, payment in full. Beats me. Maybe she was affected by the death. Or maybe she's always slow paying her debts. I'm just happy the check came, that's all. Sometimes the live ones can give you more trouble than them who's dead, believe me."

They strolled down to the lake together, Carella and his wife, and ate their picnic lunch on its shores. Carella was strangely silent. Teddy dangled her bare feet in the water. The water, as Scoles had promised, was very cold even though it was August. On the way back from the lake Carella said, "Honey, would you mind if I make one more stop?"

Teddy turned her eyes to him inquisitively.

"I want to see the chief of police here."

Teddy frowned. The question was in her eyes, and he answered it immediately.

"To find out whether or not there were any witnesses to that drowning. *Besides* Claudia Davis, I mean. From the way Scoles was talking, I get the impression that lake was pretty deserted in June."

The chief of police was a short man with a pot belly and big feet. He kept his feet propped up on his desk all the while he spoke to Carella. Carella watched him and wondered why everybody in this damn town seemed to be on vacation from an MGM movie. A row of rifles in a locked rack was behind the chief's desk. A host of WANTED fliers covered a bulletin board to the right of the rack. The chief had a hole in the sole of his left shoe.

"Yep," he said, "there was a witness, all right."

Carella felt a pang of disappointment. "Who?" he asked.

"Fellow fishing at the lake. Saw the whole thing. Testified before the coroner's jury."

"What'd he say?"

"Said he was fishing there when Josie Thompson took the boat out. Said Claudia Davis stayed behind, on the shore. Said Miss Thompson fell overboard and went under like a stone. Said Miss Davis jumped in the water and began swimming toward her. Didn't make it in time. That's what he said."

"What else did he say?"

"Well, he drove Miss Davis back to town in her car. 1960 Caddy convertible, I believe. She could hardly speak. She was sobbing and mumbling and wringing her hands, oh, in a hell of a mess. Why, we had to get the whole story out of that fishing fellow. Wasn't until the next day that Miss Davis could make any kind of sense."

"When did you hold the inquest?"

"Tuesday. Day before they buried the cousin. Coroner did the dissection on Monday. We got authorization from Miss Davis, Penal Law 2213, next of kin being charged by law with the duty of burial may authorize dissection for the sole purpose of ascertaining the cause of death."

"And the coroner reported the cause of death as drowning?"

"That's right. Said so right before the jury."

"Why'd you have an inquest? Did you suspect something more than accidental drowning?"

"Not necessarily. But that fellow who was fishing, well, *he* was from the city, too, you know. And for all we knew him and Miss Davis could have been in this together, you know, shoved the cousin over the side of the boat, and then faked up a whole story, you know. They both coulda been lying in their teeth."

"Were they?"

"Not so we could tell. You never seen anybody so grief-stricken as Miss Davis was when the fishing fellow drove her into town. Girl would have to be a hell of an actress to behave that way. Calmed down the next day, but you shoulda seen her when it happened. And at the inquest it was plain this fishing fellow had never met her before that day at the lake. Convinced the jury he had no prior knowledge of or connection with either of the two girls. Convinced me, too, for that matter."

"What's his name?" Carella asked. "This fishing fellow."

"Courtenoy."

"What did you say?"

"Courtenoy. Sidney Courtenoy."

"Thanks," Carella answered, and he rose suddenly. "Come on, Teddy. I want to get back to the city."

7

Courtenoy lived in a one-family clapboard house in Riverhead. He was rolling up the door of his garage when Carella and Meyer pulled into his driveway early Monday morning. He turned to look at the car curiously, one hand on the rising garage door. The door stopped, halfway up, halfway down. Carella stepped into the driveway.

"Mr. Courtenoy?" he asked.

"Yes?" He stared at Carella, puzzlement on his face, the puzzlement that is always there when a perfect stranger addresses you by name. Courtenoy was a man in his late forties, wearing a cap and a badly fitted sports jacket and dark flannel slacks in the month of August. His hair was graying at the temples. He looked tired, very tired, and his weariness had nothing whatever to do with the fact that it was only seven o'clock in the morning. A lunch box was at his feet where he had apparently put it when he began rolling up the garage door. The car in the garage was a 1953 Ford.

"We're police officers," Carella said. "Mind if we ask you a few questions?"

"I'd like to see your badge," Courtenoy said. Carella showed it to him. Courtenoy nodded as if he had performed a precautionary public duty. "What are your questions?" he said. "I'm on my way to work. Is this about that damn building permit again?"

"What building permit?"

"For extending the garage. I'm buying my son a little jalopy, don't want to leave it out on the street. Been having a hell of a time getting a building permit. Can you imagine that? All I want to do is add another twelve feet to the garage. You'd think I was trying to build a city park or something. Is that what this is about?"

From inside the house a woman's voice called, "Who is it, Sid?"

"Nothing, nothing," Courtenoy said impatiently. "Nobody. Never mind, Bett." He looked at Carella. "My wife. You married?"

"Yes, sir, I'm married," Carella said.

"Then you know," Courtenoy said cryptically. "What are your questions?"

"Ever see this before?" Carella asked. He handed a photostated copy of the check to Courtenoy, who looked at it briefly and handed it back.

"Sure."

"Want to explain it, Mr. Courtenoy?"

"Explain what?"

"Explain why Claudia Davis sent you a check for a hundred and twenty dollars."

"As recompense," Courtenoy said unhesitatingly.

"Oh, recompense, huh?" Meyer said. "For what, Mr. Courtenoy? For a little cock-and-bull story?"

"Huh? What are you talking about?"

"Recompense for *what*, Mr. Courtenoy?"

"For missing three days' work, what the hell did you think?"

"How's that again?"

"No, what did you *think?*" Courtenoy said angrily, waving his finger at Meyer. "What did you think it was for? Some kind of payoff or something? Is that what you thought?"

"Mr. Courtenoy . . ."

"I lost three days' work because of that damn inquest. I had to stay up at Triangle Lake all day Monday and Tuesday and then again on Wednesday waiting for the jury decision. I'm a bricklayer. I get five bucks an hour and I lost three days' work, eight hours a day, and so Miss Davis was good enough to send me a check for a hundred and twenty bucks. Now just what the hell did you think, would you mind telling me?"

"Did you know Miss Davis before that day at Triangle Lake, Mr. Courtenoy?"

"Never saw her before in my life. What is this? Am I on trial here? What is this?"

From inside the house the woman's voice came again, sharply, "Sidney! Is something wrong? Are you all right?"

"Nothing's wrong. Shut up, will you?"

There was an aggrieved silence from within the clapboard structure. Courtenoy muttered something under his breath and then turned to face the detectives again. "You finished?" he said.

"Not quite, Mr. Courtenoy. We'd like you to tell us what you saw that day at the lake."

"What the hell for? Go read the minutes of the inquest if you're so damn interested. I've got to get to work."

"That can wait, Mr. Courtenoy."

"Like hell it can. This job is away over in . . ."

"Mr. Courtenoy, we don't want to have to go all the way downtown and come back with a warrant for your arrest."

"My *arrest!* For what? Listen, what did I . . . ?"

"Sidney? Sidney, shall I call the police?" the woman shouted from inside the house.

"Oh, shut the hell up!" Courtenoy answered. "Call the police," he mumbled. "I'm up to my ears in cops, and she wants to call the police. What do you want from me? I'm an honest bricklayer. I saw a girl drown. I told it just the way I saw it. Is that a crime? Why are you bothering me?"

"Just tell it again, Mr. Courtenoy. Just the way you saw it."

"She was out in the boat," Courtenoy said, sighing. "I was fishing. Her cousin was on the shore. She fell over the side."

"Josie Thompson."

"Yes, Josie Thompson, whatever the hell her name was."

"She was alone in the boat?"

"Yes. She was alone in the boat."

"Go on."

"The other one—Miss Davis—screamed and ran into the water, and began swimming toward her." He shook his head. "She didn't make it in time. That boat was a long way out. When she got there, the lake was still. She dove under and came up, and then dove under again, but it was too late, it was just too late. Then, as she was swimming back, I thought *she* was going to drown, too. She faltered and sank below the surface, and I waited and I thought sure she was gone. Then there was a patch of yellow that broke through the water, and I saw she was all right."

"Why didn't you jump in to help her, Mr. Courtenoy?"

"I don't know how to swim."

"All right. What happened next?"

"She came out of the water—Miss Davis. She was exhausted and hysterical. I tried to calm her down, but she kept yelling and crying, not making any sense at all. I dragged her over to the car, and I asked her for the car keys. She didn't seem to know what I was talking about at first. 'The keys!' I said, and she just stared at me. 'Your car keys!' I yelled. 'The keys to the car.' Finally she reached in her purse and handed me the keys."

"Go on."

"I drove her into town. It was me who told the story to the police. She couldn't talk, all she could do was babble and scream and cry. It was a terrible thing to watch. I'd never before seen a woman so completely off her nut. We couldn't get two straight words out of her until the next day. Then she was all right. Told the police who she was, explained what I'd already told them the day before, and told them the dead girl was her cousin, Josie Thompson. They dragged the lake and got her out of the water. A shame. A real shame. Nice young girl like that."

"What was the dead girl wearing?"

"Cotton dress. Loafers, I think. Or sandals. Little thin sweater over the dress. A cardigan."

"Any jewelry?"

"I don't think so. No."

"Was she carrying a purse?"

"No. Her purse was in the car with Miss Davis'."

"What was Miss Davis wearing?"

"When? The day of the drowning? Or when they pulled her cousin out of the lake?"

"Was she there then?"

"Sure. Identified the body."

"No, I wanted to know what she was wearing on the day of the accident, Mr. Courtenoy."

"Oh, a skirt and a blouse, I think. Ribbon in her hair. Loafers. I'm not sure."

"What color blouse? Yellow?"

"No. Blue."

"You said yellow."

"No, blue. I didn't say yellow."

Carella frowned. "I thought you said yellow earlier." He shrugged. "All right, what happened after the inquest?"

"Nothing much. Miss Davis thanked me for being so kind and said she would send me a check for the time I'd missed. I refused at first and then I thought, What the hell, I'm a hard-working man, and money doesn't grow on trees. So I gave her my address. I figured she could afford it. Driving a Caddy, and hiring a fellow to take it back to the city."

"Why didn't she drive it back herself?"

"I don't know. I guess she was still a little shaken. Listen, that was a terrible experience. Did you ever see anyone die up close?"

"Yes," Carella said.

From inside the house Courtenoy's wife yelled, "Sidney, tell those men to get out of our driveway!"

"You heard her," Courtenoy said, and finished rolling up his garage door.

8

Nobody likes Monday morning.

It was invented for hang-overs. It is really not the beginning of a new week, but only the tail end of the week before. Nobody likes it, and it doesn't have to be rainy or gloomy or blue in order to provoke disaffection. It can be bright and sunny and the beginning of August. It can start with a driveway interview at seven A.M. and grow progressively worse by nine-thirty that same morning. Monday is Monday and legislature will never change its personality. Monday is Monday, and it stinks.

By nine-thirty that Monday morning, Detective Steve Carella was on the edge of total bewilderment and, like any normal person, he blamed it on Monday. He had come back to the squadroom and painstakingly gone over the pile of checks Claudia Davis had written during the month of July, a total of twenty-five, searching them for some clue to her strangulation, studying them with the scrutiny of a typographer in a print shop. Several things seemed evident from the checks, but nothing seemed pertinent. He could recall having said: "I look at those checks, I can see a life. It's like reading somebody's diary," and he was beginning to believe he had uttered some famous last words in those two succinct sentences. For if this was the diary of Claudia Davis, it was a singularly unprovocative account that would never make the nation's best-seller lists.

Most of the checks had been made out to clothing or department stores. Claudia, true to the species, seemed to have a penchant for shopping and a checkbook that yielded to her spending urge. Calls to the various stores represented revealed that her taste ranged through a wide variety of items. A check of sales slips showed that she had purchased during the month of July alone three baby doll nightgowns, two half slips, a trenchcoat, a wrist watch, four pairs of tapered slacks in various colors, two pairs of walking shoes, a pair of sunglasses, four Bikini swimsuits, eight wash-and-wear frocks, two skirts, two cashmere sweaters, half-a-dozen best-selling novels, a large bottle of aspirin, two bottles of Dramamine, six pieces of luggage, and four boxes of cleansing tissue. The most expensive thing she had purchased was an evening gown costing $500. These purchases accounted for most of the checks she had drawn in July. There were also checks to a hairdresser, a florist, a shoemaker, a candy shop, and three unexplained checks that were drawn to individuals, two men and a woman.

The first was made out to George Badueck.

The second was made out to David Oblinsky.

The third was made out to Martha Fedelson.

Someone on the squad had attacked the telephone directory and come up with addresses for two of the three. The third, Oblinsky, had an unlisted number, but a half-hour's argument with a supervisor had finally netted an address for him. The completed list was now on Carella's desk together with all the canceled checks. He should have begun tracking down those names, he knew, but something still was bugging him.

"Why did Courtenoy lie to me and Meyer?" he asked Cotton Hawes. "Why did he lie about something as simple as what Claudia Davis was wearing on the day of the drowning?"

"How did he lie?"

"First he said she was wearing yellow, said he saw a patch of yellow break the surface of the lake. Then he changed it to blue. Why did he do that, Cotton?"

"I don't know."

"And if he lied about that, why couldn't he have been lying about everything? Why couldn't he and Claudia have done in little Josie together."

"I don't know," Hawes said.

"Where'd that twenty thousand bucks come from, Cotton?"

"Maybe it was a stock dividend."

"Maybe. Then why didn't she simply deposit the check? This was cash, Cotton, *cash*. Now where did it come from? That's a nice piece of change. You don't pick twenty grand out of the gutter."

"I suppose not."

"I know where you can get twenty grand, Cotton."

"Where?"

"From an insurance company. When someone dies." Carella nodded once, sharply. "I'm going to make some calls. Damnit, that money had to come from *some*place."

He hit pay dirt on his sixth call. The man he spoke to was named Jeremiah Dodd and was a representative of the Security Insurance Corporation, Inc. He recognized Josie Thompson's name at once.

"Oh, yes," he said. "We settled that claim in July."

"Who made the claim, Mr. Dodd?"

"The beneficiary, of course. Just a moment. Let me get the folder on this. Will you hold on, please?"

Carella waited impatiently. Over at the insurance company on the other end of the line he could hear muted voices. A girl giggled suddenly, and he wondered who was kissing whom over by the water cooler. At last Dodd came back on the line.

"Here it is," he said. "Josephine Thompson. Beneficiary was her cousin, Miss Claudia Davis. Oh, yes, now it's all coming back. Yes, this is the one."

"What one?"

"Where the girls were mutual beneficiaries."

"What do you mean?"

"The cousins," Dodd said. "There were two life policies. One for Miss Davis and one for Miss Thompson. And they were mutual beneficiaries."

"You mean Miss Davis was the beneficiary of Miss Thompson's policy and vice versa?"

"Yes, that's right."

"That's very interesting. How large were the policies?"

"Oh, very small."

"Well, how *small* then?"

"I believe they were both insured for twelve thousand five hundred. Just a moment; let me check. Yes, that's right."

"And Miss Davis applied for payment on the policy after her cousin died, huh?"

"Yes. Here it is, right here. Josephine Thompson drowned at Lake Triangle on June fourth. That's right. Claudia Davis sent in the policy and the certificate of death and also a coroner's jury verdict."

"She didn't miss a trick, did she?"

"Sir? I'm sorry, I . . ."

"Did you pay her?"

"Yes. It was a perfectly legitimate claim. We began processing it at once."

"Did you send anyone up to Lake Triangle to investigate the circumstances of Miss Thompson's death?"

"Yes, but it was merely a routine investigation. A coroner's inquest is good enough for us, Detective Carella."

"When did you pay Miss Davis?"

"On July first."

"You sent her a check for twelve thousand five hundred dollars, is that right?"

"No, sir."

"Didn't you say . . . ?"

"The policy insured her for twelve-five, that's correct. But there was a double-indemnity clause, you see, and Josephine Thompson's death was accidental. No, we had to pay the policy's limit, Detective Carella. On July first we sent Claudia Davis a check for twenty-five thousand dollars."

9

There are no mysteries in police work.

Nothing fits into a carefully preconceived scheme. The high point of any given case is very often the corpse that opens the case. There is no climactic progression; suspense is for the movies. There are only people and curiously twisted motives, and small unexplained details, and coincidence, and the unexpected, and they combine to form a sequence of events, but there is no real mystery, there never is. There is only life, and sometimes death, and neither follows a rule book. Policemen hate mystery stories because they recognize in them a control that is lacking in their own very real, sometimes routine, sometimes spectacular, sometimes tedious investigation of a case. It is very nice and very clever and very convenient to have all the pieces fit together neatly. It is very kind to think of detectives as master mathematicians working on an algebraic problem whose constants are death and a victim, whose unknown is a murderer. But many of these mastermind detectives have trouble adding up the deductions on their twice-monthly pay checks. The world is full of wizards, for sure, but hardly any of them work for the city police.

There was one big mathematical discrepancy in the Claudia Davis case.

There seemed to be $5,000 unaccounted for.

Twenty-five grand had been mailed to Claudia Davis on July 1, and she presumably received the check after the Fourth of July holiday, cashed it someplace, and then took her money to the Seaboard Bank of America, opened a new checking account, and rented a safety-deposit box. But her total deposit at Seaboard had been $20,000 whereas the check had been for $25,000, so where was the laggard five? And who had cashed the check for her? Mr. Dodd of the Security Insurance Corporation, Inc., explained the company's rather complicated accounting system to Carella. A check was kept in the local office for several days after it was cashed in order to close out the policy, after which it was sent to the main office in Chicago where it sometimes stayed for several weeks until the master files were closed out. It was then sent to the company's accounting and auditing firm in San Francisco. It was Dodd's guess that the canceled check had already been sent to the California accountants, and he promised to put a tracer on it at once. Carella asked him to please hurry. Someone had cashed that check for Claudia and, supposedly, someone also had one fifth of the check's face value.

The very fact that Claudia had not taken the check itself to Seaboard seemed to indicate that she had something to hide. Presumably, she did not want anyone asking questions about insurance company checks, or insurance policies, or double indemnities, or accidental drownings, or especially her cousin Josie. The check was a perfectly good one, and yet she had chosen to cash it *before* opening a new account. Why? And why, for that matter, had she bothered opening a new account when she had a rather well-stuffed and active account at another bank?

There are only whys in police work, but they do not add up to mystery. They add up to work, and nobody in the world likes work. The bulls of the 87th would have preferred to sit on their backsides and sip at gin-and-tonics, but the whys were there, so they put on their hats and their holsters and tried to find some becauses.

Cotton Hawes systematically interrogated each and every tenant in the rooming house where Claudia Davis had been killed. They all had alibis tighter than the closed fist of an Arabian stablekeeper. In his report to the lieutenant, Hawes expressed the belief that none of the tenants was guilty of homicide. As far as he was concerned, they were all clean.

Meyer Meyer attacked the 87th's stool pigeons. There were money-changers galore in the precinct and the city, men who turned hot loot into cold cash—for a price. If someone had cashed a $25,000 check for Claudia and kept $5,000 of it during the process, couldn't that person conceivably be one of the money-changers? He put the precinct stoolies on the ear, asked them to sound around for word of a Security Insurance Corporation check. The stoolies came up with nothing.

Detective Lieutenant Sam Grossman took his laboratory boys to the murder room and went over it again. And again. And again. He reported that the lock on the door was a snap lock, the kind that clicks shut automatically when the door is slammed. Whoever killed Claudia Davis could have done so without performing any locked-room gymnastics. All he had to do was close the door behind him when he left. Grossman also reported that Claudia's bed had apparently not been slept in on the night of the murder. A pair of shoes had been found at the foot of a large easy chair in the bedroom and a novel was wedged open on the arm of the chair. He suggested that Claudia had fallen asleep while reading, had awakened, and gone into the other room where she had met her murderer and her death. He had no suggestions as to just who that murderer might have been.

Steve Carella was hot and impatient and overloaded. There were other things happening in the precinct, things like burglaries and muggings and knifings and assaults and kids with summertime on their hands hitting other kids with ball bats because they didn't like the way they pronounced the word *"señor."* There were telephones jangling, and reports to be typed in triplicate, and people filing into the squadroom day and night with complaints against the citizenry of that fair city, and the Claudia Davis case was beginning to be a big fat pain in the keester. Carella wondered what it was like to be a shoemaker. And while he was wondering, he began to chase down the checks made out to George Badueck, David Oblinsky, and Martha Fedelson.

Happily, Bert Kling had nothing whatsoever to do with the Claudia Davis case. He hadn't even discussed it with any of the men on the squad. He was a young detective and a new detective, and the things that happened in that precinct were enough to drive a guy nuts and keep him busy forty-eight hours every day, so he didn't go around sticking his nose into other people's cases. He had enough troubles of his own. One of those troubles was the line-up.

On Wednesday morning Bert Kling's name appeared on the line-up duty chart.

10

The line-up was held in the gym downtown at Headquarters on High Street. It was held four days a week, Monday to Thursday, and the purpose of the parade was to acquaint the city's detectives with the people who were committing crime, the premise being that crime is a repetitive profession and that a crook will always be a crook, and it's good to know who your adversaries are should you happen to come face to face with them on the street. Timely recognition of a thief had helped crack many a case and had, on some occasions, even saved a detective's life. So the line-up was a pretty valuable in-group custom. This didn't mean that detectives enjoyed the trip downtown. They drew line-up perhaps once every two weeks and, often as not, line-up duty fell on their day off, and nobody appreciated rubbing elbows with criminals on his day off.

The line-up that Wednesday morning followed the classic pattern of all line-ups. The detectives sat in the gymnasium on folding chairs, and the chief of detectives sat behind a high podium at the back of the gym. The green shades were drawn, and the stage illuminated, and the offenders who'd been arrested the day before were marched before the assembled bulls while the chief read off the charges and handled the interrogation. The pattern was a simple one. The arresting officer, uniformed or plain-clothes, would join the chief at the rear of the gym when his arrest came up. The chief would read off the felon's name, and then the section of the city in which he'd been arrested, and then a number. He would say, for example, "Jones, John, Riverhead, three." The "three" would simply indicate that this was the third arrest in Riverhead that day. Only felonies and special types of misdemeanors were handled at the line-up, so this narrowed the list of performers on any given day. Following the case number, the chief would read off the offense, and then say either "Statement" or "No statement," telling the assembled cops that the thief either had or had not said anything when they'd put the collar on him. If there had been a statement, the chief would limit his questions to rather general topics since he didn't want to lead the felon into saying anything that might contradict his usually incriminating initial statement, words that could be used against him in court. If there had been *no* statement, the chief would pull out all the stops. He was generally armed with whatever police records were available on the man who stood under the blinding lights, and it was the smart thief who understood the purpose of the line-up and who knew he was not bound to answer a goddamned thing they asked him. The chief of detectives was something like a deadly earnest Mike Wallace, but the stakes were slightly higher here because this involved something a little more important than a novelist plugging his new book or a senator explaining the stand he had taken on a farm bill. These were truly "interviews in depth," and the booby prize was very often a long stretch up the river in a cozy one-windowed room.

The line-up bored the hell out of Kling. It always did. It was like seeing a stage show for the hundredth time. Every now and then somebody stopped the show with a really good routine. But usually it was the same old song and dance. It wasn't any different that Wednesday. By the time the eighth offender had been paraded and subjected to the chief's bludgeoning interrogation, Kling was beginning to doze. The detective sitting next to him nudged him gently in the ribs.

". . . Reynolds, Ralph," the chief was saying, "Isola, four. Caught burgling an apartment on North Third. No statement. How about it, Ralph?"

"How about what?"

"You do this sort of thing often?"
"What sort of thing?"
"Burglary."
"I'm no burglar," Reynolds said.
"I've got his B-sheet here," the chief said. "Arrested for burglary in 1948, witness withdrew her testimony, claimed she had mistakenly identified him. Arrested again for burglary in 1952, convicted for Burglary One, sentenced to ten at Castleview, paroled in '58 on good behavior. You're back at the old stand, huh, Ralph?"
"No, not me. I've been straight ever since I got out."
"Then what were you doing in that apartment during the middle of the night?"
"I was a little drunk. I must have walked into the wrong building."
"What do you mean?"
"I thought it was my apartment."
"Where do you live, Ralph?"
"On . . . uh . . . well . . ."
"Come on, Ralph."
"Well, I live on South Fifth."
"And the apartment you were in last night is on North Third. You must have been pretty drunk to wander that far off course."
"Yeah, I guess I was pretty drunk."
"Woman in that apartment said you hit her when she woke up. Is that true, Ralph?"
"No. No, hey, I never hit her."
"She says so, Ralph."
"Well, she's mistaken."
"Well, now, a doctor's report says somebody clipped her on the jaw, Ralph, now how about that?"
"Well, maybe."
"Yes or no?"
"Well, maybe when she started screaming she got me nervous. I mean, you know, I thought it was my apartment and all."
"Ralph, you were burgling that apartment. How about telling us the truth?"
"No, I got in there by mistake."
"How'd you get in?"
"The door was open."
"In the middle of the night, huh? The door was open?"
"Yeah."

"You sure you didn't pick the lock or something, huh?"

"No, no. Why would I do that? I thought it was my apartment."

"Ralph, what were you doing with burglar's tools?"

"Who? Who me? Those weren't burglar's tools."

"Then what were they? You had a glass cutter, and a bunch of jimmies, and some punches, and a drill and bits, and three celluloid strips, and some lock-picking tools, and eight skeleton keys. Those sound like burglar's tools to me, Ralph."

"No. I'm a carpenter."

"Yeah, you're a carpenter all right, Ralph. We searched your apartment, Ralph, and found a couple of things we're curious about. Do you always keep sixteen wrist watches and four typewriters and twelve bracelets and eight rings and a mink stole and three sets of silverware, Ralph?"

"Yeah. I'm a collector."

"Of other people's things. We also found four hundred dollars in American currency and five thousand dollars in French francs. Where'd you get that money, Ralph?"

"Which?"

"Whichever you feel like telling us about."

"Well, the U.S. stuff I . . . I won at the track. And the other, well, a Frenchman owed me some gold, and so he paid me in francs. That's all."

"We're checking our stolen-goods list right this minute, Ralph."

"So check!" Reynolds said, suddenly angry. "What the hell do you want from me? Work for your goddamn living! You want it all on a platter! Like fun! I told you everything I'm gonna . . ."

"Get him out of here," the chief said. "Next, Blake, Donald, Bethtown, two. Attempted rape. No statement . . ."

Bert Kling made himself comfortable on the folding chair and began to doze again.

11

The check made out to George Badueck was numbered 018. It was a small check, five dollars. It did not seem very important to Carella, but it was one of the unexplained three, and he decided to give it a whirl.

Badueck, as it turned out, was a photographer. His shop was directly across the street from the County Court Building in Isola. A sign in his window advised that he took photographs for chauffeurs' licenses, hunting licenses, passports, taxicab permits, pistol permits, and the like. The shop was small and crowded. Badueck fitted into the shop like a beetle in an ant trap. He was a huge man with thick, unruly black hair and the smell of developing fluid on him.

"Who remembers?" he said. "I get millions of people in here every day of the week. They pay me in cash, they pay me with checks, they're ugly, they're pretty, they're skinny, they're fat, they all look the same on the pictures I take. Lousy. They all look like I'm photographing them for you guys. You never see any of these official-type pictures? Man, they look like mug shots, all of them. So who remembers this . . . what's her name? Claudia Davis, yeah. Another face that's all. Another mug shot. Why? Is the check bad or something?"

"No, it's a good check."

"So what's the fuss?"

"No fuss," Carella said. "Thanks a lot."

He sighed and went out into the August heat. The County Court Building across the street was white and Gothic in the sunshine. He wiped a handkerchief across his forehead and thought, *Another face, that's all.* Sighing, he crossed the street and entered the building. It was cool in the high vaulted corridors. He consulted the directory and went up to the Bureau of Motor Vehicles first. He asked the clerk there if anyone named Claudia Davis had applied for a license requiring a photograph.

"We only require pictures on chauffeurs' licenses," the clerk said.

"Well, would you check?" Carella asked.

"Sure. Might take a few minutes, though. Would you have a seat?"

Carella sat. It was very cool. It felt like October. He looked at his watch. It was almost time for lunch, and he was getting hungry. The clerk came back and motioned him over.

"We've got a Claudia Davis listed," he said, "but she's already got a license, and she didn't apply for a new one."

"What kind of license?"

"Operator's."

"When does it expire?"

"Next September."

"And she hasn't applied for anything needing a photo?"

"Nope. Sorry."

"That's all right. Thanks," Carella said.

He went out into the corridor again. He hardly thought it likely that Claudia Davis had applied for a permit to own or operate a taxicab, so he skipped the Hack Bureau and went upstairs to Pistol Permits. The woman he spoke to there was very kind and very efficient. She checked her files and told him that no one named Claudia Davis had ever applied for either a carry or a premises pistol permit. Carella thanked her and went into the hall again. He was very hungry. His stomach was beginning to growl. He debated having lunch and then returning and decided, *Hell, I'd better get it done now.*

The man behind the counter in the Passport Bureau was old and thin and he wore a green eyeshade. Carella asked his question, and the old man went to his files and creakingly returned to the window.

"That's right," he said.

"What's right?"

"She did. Claudia Davis. She applied for a passport."

"When?"

The old man checked the slip of paper in his trembling hands. "July twentieth," he said.

"Did you give it to her?"

"We accepted her application, sure. Isn't us who issues the passports. We've got to send the application on to Washington."

"But you did accept it?"

"Sure, why not? Had all the necessary stuff. Why shouldn't we accept it?"

"What was the necessary stuff?"

"Two photos, proof of citizenship, filled-out application, and cash."

"What did she show as proof of citizenship?"

"Her birth certificate."

"Where was she born?"

"California."

"She paid you in cash?"

"That's right."

"Not a check?"

"Nope. She started to write a check, but the blamed pen was on the blink. We use ballpoints, you know, and it gave out after she filled in the application. So she paid me in cash. It's not all that much money, you know."

"I see. Thank you," Carella said.

"Not at all," the old man replied, and he creaked back to his files to replace the record on Claudia Davis.

The check was numbered 007, and it was dated July twelfth, and it was made out to a woman named Martha Fedelson.

Miss Fedelson adjusted her pince-nez and looked at the check. Then she moved some papers aside on the small desk in the cluttered office, and put the check down, and leaned closer to it, and studied it again.

"Yes," she said, "that check was made out to me. Claudia Davis wrote it right in this office." Miss Fedelson smiled. "If you can call it an office. Desk space and a telephone. But then, I'm just starting, you know."

"How long have you been a travel agent, Miss Fedelson?"

"Six months now. It's very exciting work."

"Had you ever booked a trip for Miss Davis before?"

"No. This was the first time."

"Did someone refer her to you?"

"No. She picked my name out of the phone book."

"And asked you to arrange this trip for her, is that right?"

"Yes."

"And this check? What's it for?"

"Her airline tickets, and deposits at several hotels."

"Hotels *where?*"

"In Paris and Dijon. And then another in Lausanne, Switzerland."

"She was going to Europe?"

"Yes. From Lausanne she was heading down to the Italian Riviera. I was working on that for her, too. Getting transportation and the hotels, you know."

"When did she plan to leave?"

"September first."

"Well, that explains the luggage and the clothes," Carella said aloud.

"I'm sorry," Miss Fedelson said, and she smiled and raised her eyebrows.

"Nothing, nothing," Carella said. "What was your impression of Miss Davis?"

"Oh, that's hard to say. She was only here once, you understand." Miss Fedelson thought for a moment, and then said, "I suppose she *could* have been a pretty girl if she tried, but she wasn't trying. Her hair was short and dark, and she seemed rather—well, withdrawn, I guess. She didn't take her sunglasses off all the while she was here. I suppose you would call her shy. Or frightened. I don't know." Miss Fedelson smiled again. "Have I helped you any?"

"Well, now we know she was going abroad," Carella said.

"September is a good time to go," Miss Fedelson answered. "In September the tourists have all gone home." There was a wistful sound to her voice. Carella thanked her for her time and left the small office with its travel folders on the cluttered desk top.

12

He was running out of checks and running out of ideas. Everything seemed to point toward a girl in flight, a girl in hiding, but what was there to hide, what was there to run from? Josie Thompson had been in that boat alone. The coroner's jury had labeled it accidental drowning. The insurance company hadn't contested Claudia's claim, and they'd given her a legitimate check that she could have cashed anywhere in the world. And yet there *was* hiding, and there *was* flight—and he couldn't understand why.

He took the list of remaining checks from his pocket. The girl's shoemaker, the girl's hairdresser, a florist, a candy shop. None of them truly important. And the remaining check made out to an individual, the check numbered 006 and dated July eleventh, and written to a man named David Oblinsky in the amount of $45.75. Carella had his lunch at two-thirty and then went downtown. He found Oblinsky in a diner near the bus terminal. Oblinsky was sitting on one of the counter stools, and he was drinking a cup of coffee. He asked Carella to join him, and Carella did.

"You traced me through that check, huh?" he said. "The phone company gave you my number and my address, huh? I'm unlisted, you know. They ain't supposed to give out my number."

"Well, they made a special concession because it was police business."

"Yeah, well, suppose the cops called and asked for Marlon Brando's number? You think they'd give it out? Like hell they would. I don't like that. No, sir, I don't like it one damn bit."

"What do you do, Mr. Oblinsky? Is there a reason for the unlisted number?"

"I drive a cab is what I do. Sure there's a reason. It's classy to have an unlisted number. Didn't you know that?"

Carella smiled. "No, I didn't."

"Sure, it is."

"Why did Claudia Davis give you this check?" Carella asked.

"Well, I work for a cab company here in this city, you see. But usually on weekends or on my day off I use my own car and I take people on long trips, you know what I mean? Like to the country, or the mountains, or the beach, wherever they want to go. I don't care. I'll take them wherever they want to go."

"I see."

"Sure. So in June sometime, the beginning of June it was, I get a call from this guy I know up at Triangle Lake, he tells me there's a rich broad there who needs somebody to drive her Caddy back to the city for her. He said it was worth thirty bucks if I was willing to take the train up and the heap back. I told him, no sir, I wanted forty-five or it was no deal. I knew I had him over a barrel, you understand? He'd already told me he checked with the local hicks and none of them felt like making the ride. So he said he would talk it over with her and get back to me. Well, he called again . . . you know, it burns me up about the phone company. They ain't supposed to give out my number like that. Suppose it was Marilyn Monroe? You think they'd give out her number? I'm gonna raise a stink about this, believe me."

"What happened when he called you back?"

"Well, he said she was willing to pay forty-five, but like could I wait until July sometime when she would send me a check because she was a little short right at the moment. So I figured what the hell, am I going to get stiffed by a dame who's driving a 1960 Caddy? I figured I could trust her until July. But I also told him, if that was the case, then I also wanted her to pay the tolls on the way back, which I don't ordinarily ask my customers to do. That's what the seventy-five cents was for. The tolls."

"So you took the train up there and then drove Miss Davis and the Cadillac back to the city, is that right?"

"Yeah."

"I suppose she was pretty distraught on the trip home."

"Huh?"

"You know. Not too coherent."

"Huh?"

"Broken up. Crying. Hysterical," Carella said.

"No. No, she was okay."

"Well, what I mean is . . ." Carella hesitated. "I assumed she wasn't capable of driving the car back herself."

"Yeah, that's right. That's why she hired me."

"Well, then . . ."

"But not because she was broken up or anything."

"Then why?" Carella frowned. "Was there a lot of luggage? Did she need your help with that?"

"Yeah, sure. Both hers and her cousin's. Her cousin drowned, you know."

"Yes. I know that."

"But anybody coulda helped her with the luggage," Oblinsky said. "No, that wasn't why she hired me. She really *needed* me, mister."

"Why?"

"Why? Because she don't know how to drive, that's why."

Carella stared at him. "You're wrong," he said.

"Oh, no," Oblinsky said. "She can't drive, believe me. While I was putting the luggage in the trunk, I asked her to start the car, and she didn't even know how to do that. Hey, you think I ought to raise a fuss with the phone company?"

"I don't know," Carella said, rising suddenly. All at once the check made out to Claudia Davis' hairdresser seemed terribly important to him. He had almost run out of checks, but all at once he had an idea.

13

The hairdresser's salon was on South Twenty-third, just off Jefferson Avenue. A green canopy covered the sidewalk outside the salon. The words ARTURO MANFREDI, INC., were lettered discreetly in white on the canopy. A glass plaque in the window repeated the name of the establishment and added, for the benefit of those who did not read either *Vogue* or *Harper's Bazaar,* that there were two branches of the shop, one here in Isola and another in "Nassau, the Bahamas." Beneath that, in smaller more modest letters, were the words "Internationally Renowned." Carella and Hawes went into the shop at four-thirty in the afternoon. Two meticulously coifed and manicured women were sitting in the small reception room, their expensively sleek legs crossed, apparently awaiting either their chauffeurs, their husbands, or their lovers. They both looked up expectantly when the detectives entered, expressed mild disappointment by only slightly raising newly plucked eyebrows, and went back to reading their fashion magazines. Carella and Hawes walked to the desk. The girl behind the desk was a blonde with a brilliant shellacked look and an English finishing school voice.

"Yes?" she said. "May I help you?"

She lost a tiny trace of her poise when Carella flashed his buzzer. She read the raised lettering on the shield, glanced at the photo on the plastic-encased I.D. card, quickly regained her polished calm, and said coolly and unemotionally, "Yes, what can I do for you?"

"We wonder if you can tell us anything about the girl who wrote this check?" Carella said. He reached into his jacket pocket, took out a folded photostat of the check, unfolded it, and put it on the desk before the blonde. The blonde looked at it casually.

"What is the name?" she asked. "I can't make it out."

"Claudia Davis."

"D-A-V-I-S?"

"Yes."

"I don't recognize the name," the blonde said. "She's not one of our regular customers."

"But she did make out a check to your salon," Carella said. "She wrote this on July seventh. Would you please check your records and find out why she was here and who took care of her?"

"I'm sorry," the blonde said.

"What?"

"I'm sorry, but we close at five o'clock, and this is the busiest time of the day for us. I'm sure you can understand that. If you'd care to come back a little later . . ."

"No, we wouldn't care to come back a little later," Carella said. "Because if we came back a little later, it would be with a search warrant and possibly a warrant for the seizure of your books, and sometimes that can cause a little commotion among the gossip columnists, and that kind of commotion might add to your international renown a little bit. We've had a long day, miss, and this is important, so how about it?"

"Of course. We're always delighted to cooperate with the police," the blonde said frigidly. "Especially when they're so well mannered."

"Yes, we're all of that," Carella answered.

"Yes. July seventh, did you say?"

"July seventh."

The blonde left the desk and went into the back of the salon. A brunette came out front and said, "Has Miss Marie left for the evening?"

"Who's Miss Marie?" Hawes asked.

"The blond girl."

"No. She's getting something for us."

"That white streak is very attractive," the brunette said. "I'm Miss Olga."

"How do you do."

"Fine, thank you," Miss Olga said. "When she comes back, would you tell her there's something wrong with one of the dryers on the third floor?"

"Yes, I will," Hawes said.

Miss Olga smiled, waved, and vanished into the rear of the salon again. Miss Marie reappeared not a moment later. She looked at Carella and said, "A Miss Claudia Davis was here on July seventh. Mr. Sam worked on her. Would you like to talk to him?"

"Yes, we would."

"Then follow me, please," she said curtly.

They followed her into the back of the salon past women who sat with crossed legs, wearing smocks, their heads in hair dryers.

"Oh, by the way," Hawes said, "Miss Olga said to tell you there's something wrong with one of the third-floor dryers."

"Thank you," Miss Marie said.

Hawes felt particularly clumsy in this world of women's machines. There was an air of delicate efficiency about the place, and Hawes—six feet two inches tall in his bare soles, weighing in at a hundred and ninety pounds—was certain he would knock over a bottle of nail polish or a pail of hair rinse. As they entered the second-floor salon, as he looked down that long line of humming space helmets at women with crossed legs and what looked like barbers' aprons covering their nylon slips, he became aware of a new phenomenon. The women were slowly turning their heads inside the dryers to look at the white streak over his left temple. He suddenly felt like a horse's ass. For whereas the streak was the legitimate result of a knifing—they had shaved his red hair to get at the wound, and it had grown back this way—he realized all at once that many of these women had shelled out hard-earned dollars to simulate identical white streaks in their own hair, and he no longer felt like a cop making a business call. Instead, he felt like a customer who had come to have his goddamned streak touched up a little.

"This is Mr. Sam," Miss Marie said, and Hawes turned to see Carella shaking hands with a rather elongated man. The man wasn't particularly tall, he was simply elongated. He gave the impression of being seen from the side seats in a movie theater, stretched out of true proportion, curiously two-dimensional. He wore a white smock, and there were three narrow combs in the breast pocket. He carried a pair of scissors in one thin, sensitive-looking hand.

"How do you do?" he said to Carella, and he executed a half-bow, European in origin, American in execution. He turned to Hawes, took his hand, shook it, and again said, "How do you do?"

"They're from the police," Miss Marie said briskly, releasing Mr. Sam from any obligation to be polite, and then left the men alone.

"A woman named Claudia Davis was here on July seventh," Carella said. "Apparently she had her hair done by you. Can you tell us what you remember about her?"

"Miss Davis, Miss Davis," Mr. Sam said, touching his high forehead in an attempt at visual shorthand, trying to convey the concept of thought without having to do the accompanying brainwork. "Let me see, Miss Davis, Miss Davis."

"Yes."

"Yes, Miss Davis. A very pretty blonde."

"No," Carella said. He shook his head. "A brunette. You're thinking of the wrong person."

"No, I'm thinking of the right person," Mr. Sam said. He tapped his temple with one extended forefinger, another piece of visual abbreviation. "I remember. Claudia Davis. A blonde."

"A brunette," Carella insisted, and he kept watching Mr. Sam.

"When she left. But when she came, a blonde."

"What?" Hawes said.

"She was a blonde, a very pretty, natural blonde. It is rare. Natural blondness, I mean. I couldn't understand why she wanted to change the color."

"You dyed her hair?" Hawes asked.

"That is correct."

"Did she say *why* she wanted to be a brunette?"

"No, sir. I argued with her. I said, 'You have *beau*-tiful hair, I can do *mar*-velous things with this hair of yours. You are a *blonde,* my dear, there are drab women who come in here every day of the week and *beg* to be turned into blondes.' No. She would not listen. I dyed it for her." Mr. Sam seemed to become offended by the idea all over again. He looked at the detectives as if they had been responsible for the stubbornness of Claudia Davis.

"What else did you do for her, Mr. Sam?" Carella asked.

"The dye, a cut, and a set. And I believe one of the girls gave her a facial and a manicure."

"What do you mean by a cut? Was her hair long when she came here?"

"Yes, beautiful long blond hair. She wanted it cut. I cut it." Mr. Sam shook his head. "A pity. She looked terrible. I don't usually say this about someone I work on, but she walked out of here looking terrible. You would hardly recognize her as the same pretty blonde who came in not three hours before."

"Maybe that was the idea," Carella said.

"I beg your pardon?"

"Forget it. Thank you, Mr. Sam. We know you're busy."

In the street outside Hawes said, "You knew before we went in there, didn't you, Mr. Steve?"

"I suspected, Mr. Cotton, I suspected. Come on, let's get back to the squad."

14

They kicked it around like a bunch of advertising executives. They sat in Lieutenant Byrnes' office and tried to find out how the cookie crumbled and which way the Tootsie rolled. They were just throwing out a life preserver to see if anyone grabbed at it, that's all. What they were doing, you see, was running up the flag to see if anyone saluted, that's all. The lieutenant's office was a four-window office because he was top man in this particular combine. It was a very elegant office. It had an electric fan all its own, and a big wide desk. It got cross ventilation from the street. It was really very pleasant. Well, to tell the truth, it was a pretty ratty office in which to be holding a top-level meeting, but it was the best the precinct had to offer. And after a while you got used to the chipping paint and the soiled walls and the bad lighting and the stench of urine from the men's room down the hall. Peter Byrnes didn't work for B.B.D. & O. He worked for the city. Somehow, there was a difference.

"I just put in a call to Irene Miller," Carella said. "I asked her to describe Claudia Davis to me, and she went through it all over again. Short dark hair, shy, plain. Then I asked her to describe the cousin, Josie Thompson." Carella nodded glumly. "Guess what?"

"A pretty girl," Hawes said. "A pretty girl with long blond hair."

"Sure. Why, Mrs. Miller practically spelled it out the first time we talked to her. It's all there in the report. She said they were like black and white in looks and personality. Black and white, sure. A brunette and a goddamn blonde!"

"That explains the yellow," Hawes said.

"What yellow?"

"Courtenoy. He said he saw a patch of yellow breaking the surface. He wasn't talking about her clothes, Steve. He was talking about her *hair*."

"It explains a lot of things," Carella said. "It explains why shy Claudia Davis was preparing for her European trip by purchasing baby doll nightgowns and Bikini bathing suits. And it explains why the undertaker up there referred to Claudia as a pretty girl. And it explains why our necropsy report said she was thirty when everybody talked about her as if she were much younger."

"The girl who drowned wasn't Josie, huh?" Meyer said. "You figure she was Claudia."

"Damn right I figure she was Claudia."

"And you figure she cut her hair afterward, and dyed it, and took her cousin's name, and tried to pass as her cousin until she could get out of the country, huh?" Meyer said.

"Why?" Byrnes said. He was a compact man with a compact bullet head and a chunky economical body. He did not like to waste time or words.

"Because the trust income was in Claudia's name. Because Josie didn't have a dime of her own."

"She could have collected on her cousin's insurance policy," Meyer said.

"Sure, but that would have been the end of it. The trust called for those stocks to be turned over to U.C.L.A. if Claudia died. A college, for God's sake! How do you suppose Josie felt about that? Look, I'm not trying to hang a homicide on her. I just think she took advantage of a damn good situation. Claudia was in that boat alone. When she fell over the side, Josie really tried to rescue her, no question about it. But she missed, and Claudia drowned. Okay. Josie went all to pieces, couldn't talk straight, crying, sobbing, real hysterical woman, we've seen them before. But came the dawn. And with the dawn, Josie began thinking. They were away from the city, strangers in a strange town. Claudia had drowned but no one *knew* that she was Claudia. No one but Josie. She had no identification on her, remember? Her purse was in the car. Okay. If Josie identified her cousin correctly, she'd collect twenty-five grand on the insurance policy, and then all that stock would be turned over to the college, and that would be the end of the gravy train. But suppose, just suppose Josie told the police the girl in the lake was Josie Thompson? Suppose she said, 'I, Claudia Davis, tell you that girl who drowned is my cousin, Josie Thompson'?"

Hawes nodded. "Then she'd still collect on an insurance policy, and also fall heir to those fat security dividends coming in."

"Right. What does it take to cash a dividend check? A bank account, that's all. A bank account with an established signature. So all she had to do was open one, sign her name as Claudia Davis, and then endorse every dividend check that came in exactly the same way."

"Which explains the new account," Meyer said. "She couldn't use Claudia's old account because the bank undoubtedly knew both Claudia *and* her signature. So Josie had to forfeit the sixty grand at Highland Trust and start from scratch."

"And while she was building a new identity and a new fortune," Hawes said, "just to make sure Claudia's few friends forgot all about her, Josie was running off to Europe. She may have planned to stay there for years."

"It all ties in," Carella said. "Claudia had a driver's license. She was the one who drove the car away from Stewart City. But Josie had to hire a chauffeur to take her back."

"And would Claudia, who was so meticulous about money matters, have kept so many people waiting for payment?" Hawes said. "No, sir. That was Josie. And Josie was broke, Josie was waiting for that insurance policy to pay off so she could settle those debts and get the hell out of the country."

"Well, I admit it adds up," Meyer said.

Peter Byrnes never wasted words. "Who cashed that twenty-five thousand-dollar check for Josie?" he said.

There was silence in the room.

"Who's got that missing five grand?" he said.

There was another silence.

"Who *killed* Josie?" he said.

15

Jeremiah Dodd of the Security Insurance Corporation, Inc., did not call until two days later. He asked to speak to Detective Carella, and when he got him on the phone, he said, "Mr. Carella, I've just heard from San Francisco on that check."

"What check?" Carella asked. He had been interrogating a witness to a knifing in a grocery store on Culver Avenue. The Claudia Davis or rather the Josie Thompson Case was not quite yet in the Open File, but it was ready to be dumped there, and was truly the farthest thing from Carella's mind at the moment.

"The check was paid to Claudia Davis," Dodd said.

"Oh, yes. Who cashed it?"

"Well, there are two endorsements on the back. One was made by Claudia Davis, of course. The other was made by an outfit called Leslie Summers, Inc. It's a regular company stamp marked 'For Deposit Only' and signed by one of the officers."

"Have any idea what sort of a company that is?" Carella asked.

"Yes," Dodd said. "They handle foreign exchange."

"Thank you," Carella said.

He went there with Bert Kling later that afternoon. He went with Kling completely by chance and only because Kling was heading downtown to buy his mother a birthday gift and offered Carella a ride. When they parked the car, Kling asked, "How long will this take, Steve?"

"Few minutes, I guess."

"Want to meet me back here?"

"Well, I'll be at 720 Hall, Leslie Summers, Inc. If you're through before me, come on over."

"Okay, I'll see you," Kling said.

They parted on Hall Avenue without shaking hands. Carella found the street-level office of Leslie Summers, Inc., and walked in. A counter ran the length of the room, and there were several girls behind it. One of the girls was speaking to a customer in French and another was talking Italian to a man who wanted lire in exchange for dollars. A board behind the desk quoted the current exchange rate for countries all over the world. Carella got in line and waited. When he reached the counter, the girl who'd been speaking French said, "Yes, sir?"

"I'm a detective," Carella said. He opened his wallet to where his shield was pinned to the leather. "You cashed a check for Miss Claudia Davis sometime in July. An insurance-company check for twenty-five thousand dollars. Would you happen to remember it?"

"No, sir, I don't think I handled it."

"Would you check around and see who did, please?"

The girl held a brief consultation with the other girls, and then walked to a desk behind which sat a corpulent, balding man with a razor-thin mustache. They talked with each other for a full five minutes. The man kept waving his hands. The girl kept trying to explain about the insurance-company check. The bell over the front door sounded. Bert Kling came in, looked around, saw Carella, and joined him at the counter.

"All done?" Carella asked.

"Yeah, I bought her a charm for her bracelet. How about you?"

"They're holding a summit meeting," Carella said.

The fat man waddled over to the counter. "What is the trouble?" he asked Carella.

"No trouble. Did you cash a check for twenty-five thousand dollars?"

"Yes. Is the check no good?"

"It's a good check."

"It looked like a good check. It was an insurance-company check. The young lady waited while we called the company. They said it was bona fide and we should accept it. Was it a bad check?"

"No, no, it was fine."

"She had identification. It all seemed very proper."

"What did she show you?"

"A driver's license or a passport is what we usually require. But she had neither. We accepted her birth certificate. After all, we *did* call the company. Is the check no good?"

"It's fine. But the check was for twenty-five thousand, and we're trying to find out what happened to five thousand of . . ."

"Oh, yes. The francs."

"What?"

"She bought five thousand dollars' worth of French francs," the fat man said. "She was going abroad?"

"Yes, she was going abroad," Carella said. He sighed heavily. "Well, that's that, I guess."

"It all seemed very proper," the fat man insisted.

"Oh, it was, it was. Thank you. Come on, Bert."

They walked down Hall Avenue in silence.

"Beats me," Carella said.

"What's that, Steve?"

"This case." He sighed again. "Oh, what the hell!"

"Yeah, let's get some coffee. What was all that business about the francs?"

"She bought five thousand dollars' worth of francs," Carella said.

"The French are getting a big play lately, huh?" Kling said, smiling. "Here's a place. This look okay?"

"Yeah, fine." Carella pulled open the door of the luncheonette. "What do you mean, Bert?"

"With the francs."

"What about them?"

"The exchange rate must be very good."

"I don't get you."

"You know. All those francs kicking around."

"Bert, what the hell are you talking about?"

"Weren't you with me? Last Wednesday?"

"With you where?"

"The line-up. I thought you were with me."

"No, I wasn't," Carella said tiredly.

"Oh, well, that's why."

"That's why what? Bert, for the love of . . ."

"That's why you don't remember him."

"Who?"

"The punk they brought in on that burglary pickup. They found five grand in French francs in his apartment."

Carella felt as if he'd just been hit by a truck.

16

It had been crazy from the beginning. Some of them are like that. The girl had looked black, but she was really white. They thought she was Claudia Davis, but she was Josie Thompson. And they had been looking for a murderer when all there happened to be was a burglar.

They brought him up from his cell where he was awaiting trial for Burglary One. He came up in an elevator with a police escort. The police van had dropped him off at the side door of the Criminal Courts Building, and he had entered the corridor under guard and been marched down through the connecting tunnel and into the building that housed the district attorney's office, and then taken into the elevator. The door of the elevator opened into a tiny room upstairs. The other door of the room was locked from the outside and a sign on it read No ADMITTANCE. The patrolman who'd brought Ralph Reynolds up to the interrogation room stood with his back against the elevator door all the while the detectives talked to him, and his right hand was on the butt of his Police Special.

"I never heard of her," Reynolds said.

"Claudia Davis," Carella said. "Or Josie Thompson. Take your choice."

"I don't know either one of them. What the hell *is* this? You got me on a burglary rap, now you try to pull in everything was ever done in this city?"

"Who said anything was done, Reynolds?"

"If nothing was done, why'd you drag me up here?"

"They found five thousand bucks in French francs in your pad, Reynolds. Where'd you get it?"

"Who wants to know?"

"Don't get snotty, Reynolds! Where'd you get that money?"

"A guy owed it to me. He paid me in francs. He was a French guy."

"What's his name?"

"I can't remember."

"You'd better start trying."

"Pierre something."

"Pierre what?" Meyer said.

"Pierre La Salle, something like that. I didn't know him too good."

"But you lent him five grand, huh?"

"Yeah."
"What were you doing on the night of August first?"
"Why? What happened on August first?"
"You tell us."
"I don't know what I was doing."
"Were you working?"
"I'm unemployed."
"You know what we mean!"
"No. What do you mean?"
"Were you breaking into apartments?"
"No."
"Speak up! Yes or no?"
"I said no."
"He's lying, Steve," Meyer said.
"Sure he is."
"Yeah, sure I am. Look, cop, you got nothing on me but Burglary One, if that. And that you gotta prove in court. So stop trying to hang anything else on me. You ain't got a chance."
"Not unless those prints check out," Carella said quickly.
"What prints?"
"The prints we found on the dead girl's throat," Carella lied.
"I was wearing . . . !"
The small room went as still as death.
Reynolds sighed heavily. He looked at the floor.
"You want to tell us?"
"No," he said. "Go to hell."
He finally told them. After twelve hours of repeated questioning he finally broke down. He hadn't meant to kill her, he said. He didn't even know anybody was in the apartment. He had looked in the bedroom, and the bed was empty. He hadn't seen her asleep in one of the chairs, fully dressed. He had found the French money in a big jar on one of the shelves over the sink. He had taken the money and then accidentally dropped the jar, and she woke up and came into the room and saw him and began screaming. So he grabbed her by the throat. He only meant to shut her up. But she kept struggling. She was very strong. He kept holding on, but only to shut her up. She kept struggling, so he had to hold on. She kept struggling as if . . . as if he'd really been trying to kill her, as if she didn't want to lose her life. But that was manslaughter, wasn't it? He wasn't trying to kill her. That wasn't homicide, was it?

"I didn't mean to kill her!" he shouted as they took him into the elevator. "She began screaming! I'm not a killer! Look at me! Do I look like a killer?" And then, as the elevator began dropping to the basement, he shouted, "I'm a burglar!" as if proud of his profession, as if stating that he was something more than a common thief, a trained workman, a skilled artisan. "I'm not a killer! I'm a burglar!" he screamed. "I'm not a killer! I'm not a killer!" And his voice echoed down the elevator shaft as the car dropped to the basement and the waiting van.

They sat in the small room for several moments after he was gone.

"Hot in here," Meyer said.

"Yeah." Carella nodded.

"What's the matter?"

"Nothing."

"Maybe he's right," Meyer said. "Maybe he's only a burglar."

"He stopped being that the minute he stole a life, Meyer."

"Josie Thompson stole a life, too."

"No," Carella said. He shook his head. "She only borrowed one. There's a difference, Meyer."

The room went silent.

"You feel like some coffee?" Meyer asked.

"Sure."

They took the elevator down and then walked out into the brilliant August sunshine. The streets were teeming with life. They walked into the human swarm, but they were curiously silent.

At last Carella said, "I guess I think she shouldn't be dead. I guess I think that someone who tried so hard to make a life shouldn't have had it taken away from her."

Meyer put his hand on Carella's shoulder. "Listen," he said earnestly. "It's a job. It's only a job."

"Sure," Carella said. "It's only a job."

THREE TIMES THREE

MYSTERY OMNIBUS

VOLUME II

THREE
TIMES
THREE

MYSTERY OMNIBUS

Edited by
HOWARD HAYCRAFT
and
JOHN BEECROFT

VOLUME II

VOLUME II

VOLUME II

ROGUE MALE

by Geoffrey Household

1

I cannot blame them. After all, one doesn't need a telescopic sight to shoot boar and bear; so that when they came on me watching the terrace at a range of 550 yards, it was natural enough that they should jump to conclusions. And they behaved, I think, with discretion. I am not an obvious anarchist or fanatic, and I don't look as if I took any interest in politics; I might perhaps have sat for an agricultural constituency in the South of England, but that hardly counts as politics. I carried a British passport, and if I had been caught walking up to the House instead of watching it I should probably have been asked to lunch. It was a difficult problem for angry men to solve in an afternoon.

They must have wondered whether I had been employed on, as it were, an official mission; but I think they turned that suspicion down. No government—least of all ours—encourages assassination. Or was I a free lance? That must have seemed very unlikely; anyone can see that I am not the type of avenging angel. Was I, then, innocent of any criminal intent, and exactly what I claimed to be—a sportsman who couldn't resist the temptation to stalk the impossible?

After two or three hours of their questions I could see I had them shaken. They didn't believe me, though they were beginning to understand that a bored and wealthy Englishman who had hunted all commoner game might well find a perverse pleasure in hunting the biggest game on earth. But even if my explanation were true and the hunt were purely formal, it made no difference. I couldn't be allowed to live.

By that time I had, of course, been knocked about very considerably. My nails are growing back but my left eye is still pretty useless. I wasn't a case you could turn loose with apologies. They would probably have given me a picturesque funeral, with huntsmen firing volleys and sounding horns, with all the bigwigs present in fancy dress, and put up a stone obelisk to the memory of a brother sportsman. They do those things well.

As it was, they bungled the job. They took me to the edge of a cliff and put me over, all but my hands. That was cunning. Scrabbling at the rough rock would have accounted—near enough—for the state of my fingers when I was found. I did hang on, of course; for how long I don't know. I cannot see why I wasn't glad to die, seeing that I hadn't a hope of living and the quicker the end the less the suffering. But I was not glad. One always hopes—if a clinging to life can be called hope. I am not too civilized to be influenced by that force which makes a rabbit run when a stoat is after him. The rabbit doesn't hope for anything, I take it. His mind has no conception of the future. But he runs. And so I hung on till I dropped.

I was doubtful whether I had died or not. I have always believed that consciousness remains after physical death (though I have no opinion on how long it lasts), so I thought I was probably dead. I had been such a hell of a time falling; it didn't seem reasonable that I could be alive. And there had been a terrifying instant of pain. I felt as if the back of my thighs and rump had been shorn off, pulled off, scraped off—off, however done. I had parted, obviously and irrevocably, with a lot of my living matter.

My second thought was a longing for death, for it was revolting to imagine myself still alive and of the consistency of mud. There was a pulped substance all around me, in the midst of which I carried on my absurd consciousness. I had supposed that this bog was me; it tasted of blood. Then it occurred to me that this soft extension of my body might really be bog; that anything into which I fell would taste of blood.

I had crashed into a patch of marsh; small, but deep. Now, I think that I am alive—to-day, that is, for I still hesitate to describe myself as alive with any permanency—because I couldn't see or feel how much damage had been dealt. It was dark, and I was quite numb. I hauled myself out by the tussocks of grass, a creature of mud, bandaged and hidden in mud. A slope of scree rose sharply from the marsh. I had evidently grazed it in my fall. I didn't feel the pain any longer. I could persuade myself that I was no more seriously hurt than when they put me over the cliff; so I determined to move off before they came to find my body.

I had, though I didn't then know it, a good deal of time to play with; they hadn't any intention of finding my body until it was stiff and there were independent witnesses with them. The unfortunate brother sportsman would be accidentally discovered with his corpse undisturbed, and the whole history of his fate perfectly plain on the nasty sloping rock from which he had slipped.

The country at the foot of the cliff was open woodland. I remember nothing except that there were thin shadows and thick shadows. The image in my mind is so vague that they might have been coverts or clouds or waves of the sea. I walked about a mile, I suppose, and chose a thick darkness to faint in. I came to a sort of consciousness several times during the night, but let it slide away. I wasn't returning to this difficult world till dawn.

When it was light, I tried to stand on my feet, but of course I couldn't. I made no second effort. Any movement of the muscles interfered with my nice cake of mud. Whenever a crust fell off I started to bleed. No, I certainly wasn't interfering with the mud.

I knew where there was water. I had never seen that stream, and my certainty of its direction may have been due to a subconscious memory of the map. But I knew where water was, and I made for it. I traveled on my belly, using my elbows for legs and leaving a track behind me like that of a wounded crocodile, all slime and blood. I wasn't going into the stream—I wouldn't have washed off that mud for anything in the world; for all I knew, my bowels were only held in by mud—but I was going to the edge.

This was the reasoning of a hunted beast; or rather, it was not reasoning at all. I don't know whether a sedentary townsman's mind would have worked the same way. I think it would, if he had been badly enough hurt. You must be badly hurt to reach that stage of extinction where you stop thinking what you ought to do, and merely do it.

I made the trail look as if I had taken to the stream. I crawled to the edge and drank, and turned myself round in a shallow, a safe two inches deep, where the signs of my wallowing would be washed out. They could track me to the cover where I had lain up for the night, and from there to the water. Where I had gone when I left the water they would have to guess.

Personally I had no doubt where I was going, and the decision must be credited to my useful ancestors. A deer would trot upstream or downstream and leave the water at some point that the hunter's nose or eyes could determine. A monkey would do nothing of the sort; he would confuse his tracks and vanish into a third dimension.

When I had turned round in the shallows, I wriggled back again—back and back along the damned snake's track I had made. It was easy to follow; indeed it looked as definite as a country lane, for my face was only six inches above the ground. Thinking about it now, I wonder that they didn't notice, when they followed me to the stream, that some of the grass was bent the wrong way and that I must have gone back on my tracks. But who the devil would think of that? There aren't any laws on what print a man leaves when he's dragging his belly—and on such a monster of a trail there was no apparent need to look for details.

The outward journey had taken me under a stand of larch, where the earth was soft and free of undergrowth. I had brushed past the trunk of one tree which I now meant to climb. The lowest branch was within two feet of the ground; above that were another and another, sweet-smelling sooty branches as close together as the rungs of a ladder. The muscles of my hands were intact; I had gone beyond worrying about the state of surfaces.

Until I was well above the level of a man's eyes I did not dare rest boots on branch; they would have left caked prints that no one could miss. I went up the first ten feet in a single burst, knowing that the longer I held on to a branch the less strength remained to reach the next. That half minute was just a compelling of one hand above the other: two pistons shooting alternately from heaven knows what cylinder of force. My friends have sometimes accused me of taking pride in the maceration of my flesh. They are right. But I did not know that I could persuade myself to such agony as that climb.

The rest was easier, for now I could let my feet bear my weight and pause as long as I wished before each hoist. My legs were not limp; they were immovable. That was no disadvantage. I couldn't fall, wedged in as I was between the little branches of that prolific tree. When I climbed into the narrowing of the cone and the boughs were thicker and smaller and greener, I got jammed. That suited me well enough, so I fainted again. It was luxury, almost sin.

When I became conscious, the tree was swaying in the light wind and smelling of peace. I felt deliciously secure, for I was not looking forward at all; I felt as if I were a parasite on the tree, grown to it. I was not in pain, not hungry, not thirsty, and I was safe. There was nothing in each passing moment of the present that could hurt me. I was dealing exclusively with the present. If I had looked forward I should have known despair, but for a hunted, resting mammal it is no more possible to experience despair than hope.

It must have been the early afternoon when I heard the search party. As they worked down the slope to the north of my tree I could watch them. The sun was in their eyes, and there was no risk of their spotting my face among the soft green feathers of the larch which I pushed aside. So far as I could tell, my legs were not bleeding; drops falling on the lower branches would be the only immediate sign of my presence. The slight bloodstains from my hands were there to be seen if anyone looked for them, but, on black boughs in the half-lit centre of a tree, not readily to be seen.

Three uniformed police were trampling down the hillside: heavy, stolid fellows enjoying the sunshine and good-humoredly following a plain-clothes man who was ranging about on my trail like a dog they had taken for a walk. I recognized him. He was the house detective who had conducted the first part of my examination. He had proposed a really obscene method of dragging the truth out of me and had actually started it when his colleagues protested. They had no objection to his technique, but they had the sense to see that it might be necessary for my corpse to be found and that it must not be found unreasonably mutilated.

When they came nearer I could hear scraps of their conversation. The policemen were looking for me with decent anxiety. They knew nothing of the truth, and were in doubt whether I had been man or woman and whether the case had been accident or attempted suicide. They had been notified, I gathered, that a cry or a fall was heard in the night; then, unobtrusively guided by the detective, they had found my knapsack and the disturbance in the patch of marsh. Of course I could not work out the situation at the time. I could only receive impressions. I was growing to my tree and aware of immense good nature as I listened to them. Later on, I made sense of their words.

Seeing my reptilian trail disappear into the stand of larch, the house detective perked up and took command. He seemed certain that I should be found under the trees. He shouted to his three companions to run round to the other side in case I should escape, and himself crawled under the low boughs. He nearly gave the show away there, for I was supposed to be eagerly awaiting help; but he wanted to find me himself and alone. If I were alive, it was necessary to finish me off discreetly.

He passed rapidly beneath my tree, and on into the open. I heard him curse when he discovered that I had not stopped in the wood. Then I heard their faint voices as they shouted to one another up and down the stream. That surprised me. I had thought of the stream, naturally, as a morning's march away.

I saw no more of the hunt. A few hours later there was a lot of splashing and excitement down by the water. They must have been dragging the pools for my body. The stream was a shallow mountain torrent, but quite fast enough to roll a man along with it until he was caught by rock or eddy.

In the evening I heard dogs, and felt really frightened. I started to tremble, and knew pain again, aches and stabs and throbbings, all the symphony of pain, all my members fiddling away to the beat of my heart, on it or off it or half a bar behind. I had come back to life, thanks to that healing tree. The dogs might have found me, but their master, whoever he was, never gave them a chance. He wasn't wasting time by putting them on a trail that he could follow himself; he was casting up and down the stream.

When night fell I came down from my tree. I could stand, and, with the aid of two sticks, I could shuffle slowly forwards, flat-footed and stiff-legged. I could think, too. None of my mental activities for the past twenty-four hours might be called thinking. I had allowed my body to take charge. It knew far more about escaping and healing than I did.

I must try to make my behavior intelligible. This confession—shall I call it?—is written to keep myself from brooding, to get down what happened in the order in which it happened. I am not content with myself. With this pencil and exercise book I hope to find some clarity. I create a second self, man of the past by whom the man of the present may be measured. Lest what I write should ever, by accident or intention, become public property, I will not mention who I am. My name is widely known. I have been frequently and unavoidably dishonored by the banners and praises of the penny press.

This shooting trip of mine started, I believe, innocently enough. Like most Englishmen, I am not accustomed to inquire very deeply into motives. I dislike and disbelieve in cold-blooded planning, whether it be suggested of me or of anyone else. I remember asking myself when I packed the telescopic sight what the devil I wanted it for; but I just felt that it might come in handy.

It is undoubtedly true that I had been speculating—a curiosity that we all share—upon the methods of guarding a great man, and how they might be circumvented. I had a fortnight's sport in Poland, and then crossed the frontier for more. I began moving rather aimlessly from place to place, and as I found myself getting a little nearer to the House with each night's lodging I became obsessed by this idea of a sporting stalk. I have asked myself once or twice since why I didn't leave the rifle behind. I think the answer is that it wouldn't have been cricket.

Police protection is based upon the assumption that an assassin is a half-crazed idiot with a clumsy, close-range weapon—the bomb, the revolver, or the knife. It is obvious that the type of man who is a really fine shot and experienced in the approaching and killing of big game would shrink from political or any other kind of murder. He probably hasn't any grievances, and, if he had, the rifle would not occur to him as a means of redressing them. I haven't any grievances myself. One can hardly count the upsetting of one's trivial private life and plans by European disturbances as a grievance. I don't see myself yowling of love like an Italian tenor and poking at the baritone with a stiletto.

A Bond Street rifle, I say, is not a weapon that the bodyguard need consider, for the potential assassin cannot train himself to use it. The secret police, who know all about the political antecedents of anyone disaffected to the regime, are not going to allow such a man to possess a good rifle, to walk about with it, or even to turn himself into a first-class shot. So the assassin is compelled to use a weapon that can be easily concealed.

Now, I argued, here am I with a rifle, with a permit to carry it, with an excuse for possessing it. Let us see whether, as an academic point, such a stalk and such a bag are possible. I went no further than that. I planned nothing. It has always been my habit to let things take their course.

I sent my baggage home by train, and covered the last hundred miles or so on foot, traveling only with a knapsack, my rifle and sight, my maps and my field glasses. I marched by night. During daylight I lay up in timber or heath. I have never enjoyed anything so much. Whoever has stalked a beast for a couple of miles would understand what a superbly exciting enterprise it was to stalk over a hundred, passing unseen through the main herds of human beings, the outliers, the young males walking unexpectedly upon hillsides. I was killing two birds with one stone; I revived in myself a sense of adventure and—well, I don't see why I wrote "two birds." There was only one bird: the fun of the stalk.

I arrived on the ground at dawn and spent the whole day in reconnaissance. It was an alarming day, for the forest surrounding the House was most efficiently patrolled. From tree to tree and gully to gully I prowled over most of the circuit, but only flat on the earth was I really safe. Often I hid my rifle and glasses, thinking that I was certain to be challenged and questioned. I never was. I might have been transparent. I have learned the trick of watching shadows, and standing motionless in such a position that they cut and dapple my outline; still, there were times when even a rhinoceros could have seen me.

Here, at any rate, they had considered the offensive possibilities of the rifle. At all points commanding the terrace and the gardens clearings had been cut; nobody, even at extreme ranges, could shoot from cover. Open spaces, constantly crossed by guards, there were in plenty. I chose the narrowest of them: a ride some fifty feet broad which ran straight through the woods and ended at the edge of a low cliff. From the grass slope above the cliff the terrace and the doors leading on to it were in full sight. I worked out the range as 550 yards.

I spent the night on a couch of pine needles, well hidden under the mother tree, and finished my provisions and slept undisturbed. A little before dawn I climbed a few feet down the cliff and squatted on a ledge where the overhang protected me from anyone who might peer over the brink. A stunted elder, clawing at the gravel with the tips of its topheavy roots, was safe enough cover from distant eyes looking upwards. In that cramped position my rifle was useless, but I could, and very clearly, see the great man were he to come out and play with the dog or smell a rose or practise gestures on the gardener.

A path ran across the bottom of the ride, just above my head, and continued along the lower edge of the woods. I timed the intervals at which I heard footsteps, and discovered that somebody crossed the ride about every fourteen minutes. As soon as I was certain of that, I came out of hiding and followed. I wanted to understand his exact routine.

He was a young guard of splendid physique with loyalty written all over him, but he had, I should think, hardly ever been out of an industrial town in his life. He couldn't have seen me if I had been under his feet. He knew perfectly well that he was not alone, for he looked over his shoulder again and again, and stared at the bush or the fold in the ground where I was; but of course he put his sensation down to nervousness or imagination. I treated him with disrespect, but I liked him; he was such a sturdy youth, with one of those fleshy open faces and the right instincts—a boy worth teaching. His eyes when he bagged his first tiger would be enough reward for putting up with a month of his naïve ideas.

After I had been round his beat with him and behind him, I knew for how many minutes, at any given time, I could occupy the grass slope and by what route I must escape. When at last the great man came out to the terrace, my young friend had just passed. I had ten minutes to play with. I was up at once on to the slope.

I made myself comfortable, and got the three pointers of the sight steady on the V of his waistcoat. He was facing me and winding up his watch. He would never have known what shattered him—if I had meant to fire, that is. Just at that moment I felt a slight breeze on my cheek. It had been dead calm till then. I had to allow for the wind. No doubt the great man's disciples would see the hand of the Almighty in that. I should not disagree with them, for providence assuredly takes special care of any lone and magnificent male. Everyone who has stalked a particularly fine head knows that. It's natural enough. The Almighty Himself is always considered to be masculine.

I heard a yell. The next thing I knew was that I was coming round from a severe blow on the back of the head, and my young friend was covering me with his revolver. He had hurled a stone at me and himself after it—immediate, instinctive action far swifter than fiddling with his holster. We stared at each other. I remember complaining incoherently that he was seven minutes early. He looked at me as if I had been the devil in person, with horror, with fear—not fear of me, but fear at the suddenly revealed depravity of this world.

"I turned back," he said. "I knew."

Well, of course he did. I should never have been such a conceited fool as to upset his nerves and his routine by following him about. He had neither heard me nor set eyes on me, but he was aware enough to make his movements irregular.

Together with his commanding officer he took me down to the House, and there, as I have already written, I was questioned by professionals. My captor left the room after disgracing his manhood—or so he thought—by being violently sick. I myself was detached. Perhaps I should not call it detachment, for my body is sensitive and there was no interruption or hiatus in its messages to my brain. But training counts.

I hold no brief for the prewar Spartan training of the English upper class—or middle class as it is now the fashion to call it, leaving the upper to the angels—since in the ordinary affairs of a conventional life it is not of the slightest value to anyone; but it is of use on the admittedly rare occasions when one needs a high degree of physical endurance. I have been through an initiation ceremony on the Rio Javary—the only way I could persuade them to teach me how their men can exercise a slight muscular control over hemorrhage—and I thought it more a disagreeable experience than any proof of maturity. It lasted only a day and a night, whereas the initiation ceremonies of the tribal English continue for the ten years of education. We torture a boy's spirit rather than his body, but all torture is, in the end, directed at the spirit. I was conditioned to endure without making an ass of myself. That is all I mean by detachment.

I suspect that resignation was a lot easier for me than for a real assassin, since I had nothing at all to give away—no confederates, no motive. I couldn't save myself by telling them anything interesting. I had no right to endanger others by irresponsible invention. So I kept on automatically repeating the truth without the slightest hope that it would be believed.

At last someone recognized my name, and my story of a sporting stalk became faintly possible; but, whether it were true or not, it was now more than ever essential that I be discreetly murdered. And that was easy. I had admitted that I had not spent a night under a roof for five days, and that nobody knew where I was. They put all my papers and possessions back into my pockets, drove me fifty miles to the north, and staged the accident.

When I came down from that blessed larch and found that my legs would carry me, I began, I say, to look forward. It would be supposed either that I was drowned or that I was lying hurt and incapable in some riverside cover where my corpse would eventually be found. The police and the authorities in neighboring villages would be warned to look out for a moribund stranger, but it was most unlikely that any description of me would have been circularized to other districts. The security officers at the House had no official knowledge of my existence and would share their unofficial knowledge with as few outsiders as possible. It was a convenience to have no existence. Had I stolen a watch instead of stalking the head of a nation my photograph would have been in all the police stations.

If I could walk, if I had new breeches, and if I could pass the danger zone without calling attention to myself, my chance of getting clear out of the country was not negligible. I had my passport, my maps, and my money. I spoke the language well enough to deceive anyone but a highly educated man listening for mistakes. Dear old Holy George—my private nickname for their ambassador in London—insists that I speak a dialect, but to him polished grammar is more important than accent. That's a superstition inseparable from foreign affairs. A well-trained diplomat is supposed to write French, for example, like an angel, but to speak it with the peculiar gutlessness of a Geneva nancy-boy.

I wish I could apologize to Holy George. He had certainly spent some hours of those last twenty-four in answering very confidential cables about me—wiring as respectfully as possible that the bodyguard of his revered master were a pack of bloody fools, and following up with a strong letter to the effect that I was a member of his club and that it was unthinkable I should be mixed up in any such business as was, he could hardly believe seriously, suggested. I fear he must have been reprimanded. The bodyguard were, on the face of it, right.

It was now, I think, Sunday night; it was a Saturday when I was caught, but I am not sure of the lapse of time thereafter. I missed a day somewhere, but whether it was in my tree or on my island I cannot tell.

I knew roughly where I was, and that, to escape from this tumbled world of rock and forest, I should follow any path which ran parallel to the stream. My journey would not have been difficult if I had had crutches, but I could find no pieces of wood of the right height and with an angle to fit under the arm. It was, when I come to think of it, a nearly impossible quest, but at the time I was angry with myself, angry to the point where I wept childish tears of impotence. I couldn't make my hands use enough pressure on a knife, and I couldn't find sticks of the right length and shape. For an hour I raged and cursed at myself. I thought my spirit had altogether broken. It was pardonable. When everything was impossible, it was unreasonable to expect myself to distinguish between the miracle that could be forced to happen and the miracle that could not happen.

Finally, of course, I had to accept a miracle that could be forced; to make myself progress without crutches. With a rough staff in each hand I managed about four miles, shuffling over even ground, and crawling for short distances over obstacles or for long distances whenever my legs became unbearably painful. I remember that common experience of carrying a heavy suitcase further than it can reasonably be carried; one changes it from arm to arm at shorter and shorter intervals until one can no longer decide whether to continue the pain in the right or change to instant pain in the left. So it was with me in my changes from crawling to walking and back again.

I thanked God for the dawn, for it meant that I need not drive myself any farther. Until I knew exactly where I was, and upon what paths men came and went, I had to hide. I collapsed into a dry ditch and lay there for hours. I heard no sounds except a lark and the crunch of cows tearing at the grass in a neighboring field.

At last I stood up and had a look at my surroundings. I was near the top of a ridge. Below me and to the left was the wooded valley along which I had come. I had not noticed in the night that I was climbing. Part of my exhaustion had been due to the rising ground.

I shuffled upwards to the skyline. The long curve of a river was spread out at my feet. The near bank was clothed in low bushes through which ran a footpath, appearing and disappearing until it crossed the mouth of my stream by an iron bridge. On the farther bank, a mile upstream, was a country town with a few small factories. Downstream there were pastures on both banks and a small islet in the centre of the river. It was tranquil and safe as any of our hidden English Avons.

I got out the map and checked my position. I was looking at a tributary which, after a course of thirty miles, ran into one of the main rivers of Europe. From this town, a provincial capital, the search for me would be directed, and to it the police, my would-be rescuers, presumably belonged. Nevertheless I had to go there. It was the centre of communications: road, river, and railway. And since I could not walk I had to find some transport to carry me to the frontier.

At intervals the breeze bore to me the faint sound of cries and splashing. I thought someone was being hurt,—a morbid fancy, natural enough in the circumstances,—but then I realized that the screaming was the collective voice of several women, and that they were bathing. It occurred to me that when commerce and education stopped for lunch men might come to swim at the same place, and I could lay my hands on a pair of trousers.

I waited until I saw the girls cross the iron footbridge on their way back to town, and then hobbled down the ridge—a stony, barren hillside where there were, thank heaven, no fences to cross and no officious small holder to ask me what I was doing. The bathing place was plain enough, a semicircle of grass with a clean drop of three feet into the river. Above and below it the bank was covered with a dense growth of willow and alder. I took to my elbows and belly again, and crawled into the thicket. There was already a sort of runway leading into it, which, at the time, I could only assume the Lord had made for my special benefit. I realized afterwards that it had been bored through the bushes by some young fellow who was curious to know the female form and too poor to arrange for it in the ordinary way. I think of him as charitably as I can. From the end of his burrow I had an excellent view of the bushes behind which a modest bather would undress.

My necessary males were not long in coming. Indeed I had a narrow shave, for I heard them yelling and singing their way along the path before I had turned myself round. They were five hefty lads: sons, I should think, of shopkeepers and petty officials. There were two pairs of shorts, two of nondescript trousers, and an old pair of riding breeches. For my build all had the waistbands too roomy and the legs too short, and I couldn't guess which pair would best fit me. It was that, I think, which gave me the brilliant idea of taking them all. To steal one pair of trousers would obviously direct attention to some passing tramp or fugitive; but if all disappeared, the theft would be put down as the practical joke of a comrade. I remember chuckling crazily as I worked my way back to the edge of the bushes.

They undressed in the open, ten yards from the water. That meant there was only one chance for me—to do the job the moment the last man had dived in and before the first came out. It was a mad risk, but I had gone long beyond caring what risks I took.

They dived in within a few seconds of each other, all but one who remained on the bank shadowboxing with his fat-bottomed, idiotic self until a friend, as fed up with his posing as I was, reached an arm for his ankles and pulled him in. I was out of my observation post on the instant and hunching myself across the grass. I got four pairs; the fifth was too far away. I just had time to slip behind a bramble bush before one of them pulled himself up the bank. He didn't look at the clothes—why should he?—and I crawled downstream with the trousers.

Now what was the one place where they would not look? To climb a second tree was unsafe; young men in high spirits naturally think of trees. As for the bushes, they would trample them down like a herd of buffalo. The best place for me was, I decided, the water. No one would expect a practical joker, presumably fully dressed, to go to such lengths as to sink himself and his friends' breeches in the river. I made for the bank and slid under the willows into a patch of still water full of scum and brushwood. Two of them were swimming quite close, but the boughs trailing in the water protected me well enough from casual glances.

I needn't have taken so much trouble, for the plan succeeded more easily than I dared hope. They dashed up the path, and I heard their voices resounding from the hillside as they yelled for one Willy. When Willy was not to be found, they draped towels round the tails of their shirts and stormed through the thicket. I don't know if they actually looked over the bank where I was. I heard one of them within a yard or two, and ducked. At last, in an evil mood, they took the path for home and Willy. They never doubted for a moment that the culprit was Willy. I hope they didn't believe his denials till he was thoroughly punished. The sort of man whom one instantly accuses of any practical joke that has been played deserves whatever is coming to him.

Together with the trousers I let myself float down to the islet which I had seen from the top of the ridge. I could use only my arms for swimming. My generation never normally learned the crawl, and my old-fashioned frog's leg-stroke was too painful to be possible. However, I managed to keep myself and my soggy raft of trousers well out into the river, and the current did the rest.

The islet was bare, but with enough low vegetation on its shores to cover me, provided I kept close to the edge, from observation by anyone on the high ground where I had lain that morning. There were four notices, neatly spaced, to the effect that it was forbidden to land. I can't conceive why. Perhaps because any idle person in a boat would naturally want to land, and anything that encourages idleness is considered immoral.

I spread out myself, my clothes, and the breeches to dry in the afternoon sun. I did not attempt to examine my body. It was enough that the soaking had separated textile from flesh with no worse result than a gentle oozing of matter.

I remained on the islet for the Monday night and all the following day. Probably I was there for the Tuesday night too. I do not know; as I say, I lost a day somewhere. It was very heaven, for I lay on the sand naked and undisturbed, and allowed the sun to start the work of healing. I was barely conscious most of the time. I would hunch myself into the half-shade of the weeds and rushes and sleep till I grew cold, and I would hunch myself back again and roast and scar my wounds. I had but those two pleasures within attaining, and both were utterly satisfying. I did not want food. I was, I suppose, running a fever, so my lack of appetite was natural. I did suffer from the cold at night, but not severely. I had all the various garments to cover me, and, at any other time, I should have thought the weather too hot and still for easy sleep.

I awoke, feeling clear-headed and ravenously hungry, at the false dawn of what turned out to be Wednesday. I chose the riding breeches —as I held them against my body they seemed roomy enough not to rub my hide—and threw shorts and trousers into the river. I hope that their small change was not too great a loss to the owners. Only one had a wallet, and that, since it stuck out from his hip pocket, I had managed to slip on top of the rest of his clothes.

I tied two bits of driftwood together with my belt, and put all my possessions on this improvised raft. I found that I could splash with more ease—though the regular motions of swimming were still beyond me—and reached the farther bank, the raft helping, without being carried more than a hundred yards downstream.

On dry land and within a stone's throw of a main road, I had to take stock of my appearance. So far my looks had mattered no more to me than the condition of its fur to an animal; but now I proposed to reënter the world of men, and the impression I made was vitally important. Only my shoes and stockings were respectable. I couldn't bend to take them off, so the river had cleaned them.

Item: I had to shave off a four days' beard. That was far from being the mere prejudice of an Englishman against appearing in public with his bristles. If a man is clean-shaved and has a well-fitting collar and tie—even reasonably dirty—he can get away with a multitude of suspicious circumstances.

Item: Gloves. The ends of my fingers had to be shown while paying money and taking goods, and they were not human.

Item: An eye patch. My left eye was in a condition that could not be verified without a mirror. The eyelid had stuck to a mess of what I hoped was only blood.

Item: A clothes brush. My tweed coat had no elbows, but it might pass provided I brushed off the mud and did not turn away from anyone I spoke to.

I had to have these things. Without them I might as well have given myself up. I had not the will to crawl and hobble night after night to the frontier, nor the agility to steal enough to eat; but if I entered so much as a village shop as I was, the proprietor would promptly escort me to the police or a hospital.

The putting on of the breeches was an interminable agony. When at last I had them up, I couldn't fasten the blasted buttons. I managed three and had to forgo the rest for fear of leaving bloodstains all over the cloth. Shirt buttons were quite impossible.

I crossed a field and stood for a moment on the empty main road. It was the hour before dawn, the sky an imperial awning fringed with blue and gold. The tarred surface of the road was blue and calm as a canal. Only the trains were alive, dashing across the flat vale as if striving to reach the mountains before day. At my disposal, as the map had told me, were river, road, and railway. I was inclined to favor escape by river. A man drifting down the current in a boat doesn't have to answer questions or fill up forms. But again there was the insuperable handicap of my appearance. I couldn't present myself as I was to buy a boat, and if I stole one and it were missed, my arrest was certain at the next village downriver.

On the far side of the road was a farm cart, backed against the edge of a field of wheat. I knelt behind it to watch the passers-by. Men were already stirring—a few peasants in the fields, a few walkers on the road. From the latter I hoped to obtain help or at least, by observing them, an inspiration how to help myself.

There was a workman bound for some small factory in the town to whom I nearly spoke. He had an honest, kindly face—but so had most of them. I had no reason at all to suppose he would protect me. Two aimless wanderers went by together. They looked to be persons who would sympathize, but their faces were those of scared rabbits. I couldn't trust them. Then there were several peasants on their way to the fields. I could only pray that they wouldn't enter mine. They would have had some sport with me before handing me over to the police; they seemed that sort. There was a wretched fellow mumbling and weeping who raised my hopes for a moment. But misery is in some way as sacred as happiness: one doesn't intrude—not, at any rate, if there is a risk that one might merely add to the misery. Then came another factory worker, and then a tall, stooping man with a fishing rod. He cut across to the river and began to fish not far from where I had landed. He had a melancholy, intellectual face with a deal of strength in it, and I decided to have another look at him.

Their tiresome conception of the state has one comforting effect: it creates so many moral lepers that no one of them, if he has a little patience, can long be lonely. The flotsam of the nation is washed together into an unrecognized, nameless, formless secret society. There isn't much that the bits of scum can do to help one another, but at least they can cling and keep silence. And dawn, I think, is the hour when the pariah goes out. Not for him is the scornful morning with its crowds pointing the fingers of their minds at him, nor the evening when all but he may rest and be merry; but the peace before sunrise cannot be taken from him. It is the hour of the outlawed, the persecuted, the damned; for no man was ever born who could not feel some shade of hope if he were in open country with the sun about to rise. I did not formulate these thoughts at the time. I have developed them in the curious and lonely circumstances under which I write. But I give them for what they are worth to account for my intuition in choosing the right face and the fact that there were so many to choose from.

There was no cover on the farther side of the road and precious little on the bank, so that I had to make up my mind about the fisherman as I slowly and silently crossed the fields towards him. He was paying more attention to his thoughts than to his rod. By the angle of his float I could see that he had hooked the bottom, but he was quite unaware of it. I walked up behind him and wished him good-morning and asked if he had had any luck. He jumped to his feet with the butt of the rod pointed towards me as if to keep me off. I expect he hadn't seen a creature like me in a long time; they haven't any tramps. Even considering me the last word in villains, he thought it best to propitiate me. He apologized for his fishing, and said he didn't think there was anything wrong in it. He did his best to look servile, but his eyes burned with courage.

I held out my hands to him and asked if he knew how that was done. He didn't answer a word, just waited for further information.

"Look here!" I said to him. "I swear there isn't a soul in this country who knows I am alive except yourself. I want gloves, shaving tackle, and a clothes brush. Don't buy them. Give me old things that have no mark on them by which they could be traced back to you if I am caught. And if you don't mind putting your hand in my inside coat pocket you will find money."

"I don't want money," he said.

His face was absolutely expressionless. He wasn't giving anything away. He might have meant that he wouldn't help a fugitive for all the money in the world or that he wouldn't take money for helping a fugitive. The next move was up to me.

"Do you speak English?" I asked.

I saw a flicker of interest in his eyes, but he made no sign that he had understood me. I carried on in English. I was completely in his power, so that there was no point in hiding my nationality. I hoped that the foreign tongue might break down his reserve.

"I won't tell you who I am or what I have done," I said, "because it is wiser that you shouldn't know. But so long as no one sees us talking together, I don't think you run the slightest risk in helping me."

"I'll help you," he answered in perfect English. "What was it you wanted?"

I repeated my requirements and asked him to throw in an eye patch and some food if he could manage it. I also told him that I was a rich man and he shouldn't hesitate to take any money he might need. He refused,—with a very sweet, melancholy smile,—but gave me an address in England to which I was to pay what I thought fit if ever I got home.

"Where shall I put the things?" he asked.

"Under the cart over there," I answered. "And don't worry. I shall be in the wheat, and I'll take care not to be seen."

He said good-bye and moved off abruptly. In one stride he had dissociated himself from me completely. He knew by experience that among the proscribed the truest courtesy was to waste no time in courtesy.

The traffic on the road was increasing, and I had to wait some minutes before I could safely cross into the shelter of the wheat. The sun rose and the landscape budded men and business—barges on the river, a battalion out for a route march on the road, and damned, silent bicycles sneaking up every time I raised my head.

The fisherman was back in an hour, but the road was too busy for him to drop a parcel under the cart unseen. He solved the problem by fetching his rod and sitting on the cart while he took it apart and packed it. When he got up he accidentally left the parcel behind.

To get possession of it was the devil of a job, for I could not see what was about to pass until the traffic was nearly opposite me. I knelt in the wheat, bobbing my head up and down like a pious old woman divided between silent prayer and the responses. At last I plucked up courage and reached the cart. A stream of cars went by, but they did not matter; the danger was a pedestrian or a cyclist who might be tempted to stop and talk. I kept my back to the road and pretended to be tinkering with the axle. A woman wished me good-morning, and that was the worst fright I had had since they pushed me over the cliff. I answered her surlily and she passed on. To wait for a clear road was exasperating, but I needed a full minute free from possible observation. I couldn't plunge boldly back into the wheat. I had to tread gently, separating the stalks so as not to leave too obvious a track behind me.

At last I knelt in peace and unpacked the parcel which that blessed fisherman had left for me. There were a bottle of milk well laced with brandy, bread, and the best part of a cold chicken. He had thought of everything, even hot shaving water in a thermos flask.

When I had finished his food I felt equal to looking in the mirror. I was cleaner than I expected; the morning swim was responsible for that. But I didn't recognize myself. It was not the smashed eye which surprised me—that was merely closed, swollen, and ugly. It was the other eye. Glaring back at me from the mirror, deep and enormous, it seemed to belong to someone intensely alive, so much more alive than I felt. My face was all pallors and angles, like that of a Christian martyr in a mediaeval painting—and I had the added villainy of bristles. I marveled how such a beastly crop could grow in so poor and spiritual a soil.

I put on my gloves,—limp leather, God reward him, and several sizes too large!—then shaved, brushed my clothes, and dressed myself more tidily. My coat and shirt were patterned in shades of brown, and the bloodstains, weakened by my swim to the island, hardly showed. When I had cleaned up and adjusted the eye patch, I came to the conclusion that I aroused pity rather than suspicion. I looked like a poor but educated man, a clerk or schoolmaster, convalescent after some nasty accident. That was evidently the right part to play.

As soon as I was ready I left the wheat, for now I did not care how wide a track I made so long as no one actually saw me emerge. The road was clearer; it had ceased to feed and empty the town, and become an artery in a greater life. Lorries and cars sped by with the leisurely roar of through traffic. Their drivers had no neighborly feelings towards that mile of road, no damned curiosity about a lonely pedestrian. I covered the mile into town, limping along as best I could and stopping frequently to rest. At need I could walk very slowly and correctly, hanging on each foot as if waiting for somebody.

I was desperately nervous when first I engaged myself between two lines of houses. There seemed to be so many windows observing me, such crowds on the streets. Looking back on it, I cannot think that I passed more than a score of people, mostly women shopping; but, at the best of times, I have a tendency to agoraphobia. Even in London I avoid crowds at all cost; to push my way through the drift of suburban idlers in Oxford Street is torment to me. The streets of that town were really no more full nor empty than those of my own county town, and normally I should not have been affected; but I seemed to have been out of human society for years.

I cut down to the river by the first turning, and came out on to a paved walk, with flower beds and a bandstand, where I could stroll at my artificial pace without making myself conspicuous. Ahead, under the bridge, were moored a dozen boats. When I came abreast of them I saw the expected notice of "Boats for Hire" on a prettily painted cottage. There was a man leaning on the fence, meditative and unbuttoned, and obviously digesting his breakfast while mistaking that process for thought.

I wished him good-day and asked if I could hire a boat. He looked at me suspiciously and remarked that he had never seen me before, as if that ended the discussion. I explained that I was a schoolmaster recovering from a motor accident and had been ordered by my doctor to spend a week in the open air. He took his pipe out of his mouth and said that he didn't hire boats to strangers. Well, had he one for sale? No, he had not. So there we were. He evidently didn't like the look of me and wasn't going to argue.

A shrill yell came from a bedroom window:—

"Sell him the punt, idiot!"

I looked up. A red face and formidable bust were hanging over the window sill, both quivering with exasperation. I bowed to her with the formality of a village teacher, and she came down.

"Sell him what he wants, dolt!" she ordered.

Her small, screaming voice came most oddly from so huge a bulk.

I imagine he had driven her voice higher and higher with impatience until it stuck permanently on its top note.

"I don't know who he is," insisted her husband with stupid surliness.

"Well, who *are* you?" she shrieked, as if I had repeatedly refused her the information.

I told my story: how I couldn't yet walk with any ease, and so had thought of spending a holiday in drifting down the river from town to town and realizing a dream of my youth.

"Where's your baggage?" asked that damned boatman.

I patted my pockets, bulging with the thermos flask and shaving tackle. I told him I needed no more than a nightshirt and a toothbrush.

That set the old girl off again. She skirled like a sucking pig separated from the litter.

"You expect him to travel with a trunk? He's a proper man, not an ignorant, shameless idler who wastes good money on clubs and uniforms and whores, and would rather go to the river than raise his hand to pull the plug. He shall have his boat! And cheap!"

She stamped down to the waterfront and showed me the punt. It was comfortable, but far too long and clumsy to be handled by a man who couldn't sit to paddle. It wasn't cheap. She asked about double its fair price. Evidently her kindness was not at all disinterested.

There was a twelve-foot dinghy with a red sail, and I inquired if it was for sale. She said it was too expensive for me.

"I shall sell it again wherever I finish the trip," I answered. "And I have a little money—compensation for my accident."

She made her husband step the mast and hoist the sail. How that man hated the pair of us! He announced with gusto that I should certainly drown myself and that his wife could take the blame. A child couldn't have drowned himself. That boat was exactly what I wanted. The sail was hardly more than a toy, but it would be a considerable help with the wind astern, and was not large enough to be a hindrance if I let go the sheet and drifted with the current. I knew that some days must pass before I felt equal to the effort of tacking.

While she raved at her husband, I got out my wallet. I didn't want them to see how much I had, nor to wonder at my fumbling with gloved hands.

"There!" I said, holding out to her a sheaf of notes. "That's all I can afford. Tell me yes or no."

I don't know whether it was less or more than she intended to ask, but it was a sight more than the little tub was worth to anyone but me. She looked astonished at my rural simplicity and began to haggle just for form's sake. I sympathized; I said that no doubt she was right, but that sum was all I could pay for a boat. She took it, of course, and gave me a receipt. In five minutes I was out on the river, and they were wondering, I suppose, why the crazy schoolmaster should kneel on the bottom boards instead of sitting on a thwart, and why he didn't have his coat decently mended.

Of the days and nights that passed on the tributary and the main river there is little to write. I was out of any immediate danger and content—far more content than I am now, though no less solitary. I didn't exist, and so long as I was not compelled to show my papers there was no reason why I should exist. Patience was all I needed, and easy enough to keep. I recovered my strength as peacefully as if I had been the convalescent I pretended; indeed, thinking myself into the part actually helped me to recover. I nearly believed in my motor accident, my elementary school, my housekeeper, and my favorite pupils about whom I prattled when I fell in with other users of the river or when I took a meal in an obscure riverside tavern.

From nightfall to dawn I moored my boat in silent reaches of the river, choosing high or marshy or thickly wooded banks where no one could burst in upon me with questions. At first I had taken to the ditches and backwaters, but the danger of that amphibian habit was impressed on me when a farmer led his horses down to drink in my temporary harbor, and insisted on regarding me as a suspicious character. Rain was the greatest hardship I had to endure. After a night's soaking I felt the chill of the morning mist. A rubber sheet was unobtainable, but I managed at last to buy a tarpaulin. It kept me dry and uncomfortably warm, but it was heavy, and hard for my hands to fold and unfold. Only the most persistent rain could force me to use it.

I made but sixty miles in the first week. My object was to heal myself rather than hurry. I took no risks and expended no effort. Until the back of my thighs had grown some sturdy scars I had to kneel while sailing or drifting, and lie on my stomach across the thwarts while sleeping. That limited my speed. I could not row.

In the second week I tried to buy an outboard motor, and only just got out of the deal in time. I found that to purchase an engine and gasoline I had to sign enough papers to ensure my arrest by every political or administrative body that had heard of me. I must say, they have made the way of the transgressor uncommonly difficult. At the next town, however, there was an old-fashioned yard where I bought a businesslike lug sail and had a small foresail fitted into the bargain.

Thereafter I carried my own stores, and never put into town or village. With my new canvas and the aid of the current I could sometimes do forty miles a day and—what was more important—I could keep out of the way of the barges and tugs that were now treating the river as their own.

All the way downriver I had considered the problem of my final escape from the country, and had arrived at three possible solutions. The first was to keep on sailing and trust to luck. This was obviously very risky, for only a fast motorboat could slip past the patrol craft off the port. I should be turned back, either as a suspicious character or as an ignorant idiot who oughtn't to be allowed in a boat—and the chances, indeed, were against my little twelve-foot tub's being able to live in the short, breaking seas of the estuary.

The second plan was to embark openly on a passenger vessel—or train, for that matter—and trust that my name and description had never been circularized to the frontier police. This, earlier, I might have tried if I had had the strength; but as my voyage crept into its third week it seemed probable that even the most extensive search for my body would have been abandoned, that it would be assumed I was alive, and that every blessed official was praying for a sight of me and promotion.

My third solution was to hang around the docks for an opportunity of stowing away or stealing a boat or seeing a yacht which belonged to some friend. But this demanded time—and I could neither sleep in a hotel without being invited to show my papers to a lodging-house keeper, nor in the open without showing them to a policeman. Whatever I did, I had to do immediately after arrival at the port.

Now, of course I was thinking stupidly. The way out of the country was laughably easy. A boy who had merely hit a policeman would have thought of it at once. But in my mind I was a convalescent schoolmaster or I was a ghost. I had divested myself of my nationality and forgotten that I could call on the loyalty of my compatriots. I had nearly thrown away my British passport on the theory that no papers whatever would be safer than my own. As soon as I came in sight of the wharfs, I saw British ships and realized that I had merely to tell a good enough story to the right man to be taken aboard.

I moored my boat to a public landing stage and went ashore. I made a bad mistake in not sinking her; it did occur to me that I should, but, quite apart from the nuisance of sailing back up the river to find a quiet spot where she could be sunk unobserved, I disliked the thought of the friendly little country tub rotting away at the disgusting bottom of an industrial river.

I bought myself a nondescript outfit of blue serge at the first slopshop I came to, and changed in a public lavatory. My old clothes I sold in another slopshop—that seeming the best way to get rid of them without a trace. If ever they were bought it must have been by the poorest of workmen. He'll find an unexpected bargain in my favorite coat; it will last him all his life.

Strolling along the quays, I got into conversation with two British seamen by means of the old and tried introduction (which has extracted many a sixpence from me)—"Got a match?" We had a drink together. Neither of them was in a ship bound for England, but they had a pal in a motor ship which was sailing for London the next day.

The pal, haled from the bar to join us on our bench, was a bit wary of me; he was inclined to think that I was a parson from the seamen's mission masquerading as an honest worker. I calmed his suspicions with two double whiskies and my most engaging dirty story, whereupon he declared that I was a "bit of orl right" and consented to talk about his officers. The captain, it seemed, was a stickler for correct detail—"thinks 'e'll lose 'is ticket if 'e forgets a muckin' ha'penny stamp." But Mr. Vaner, the First Officer, was a "one and a fair caution"; I gathered from his wry smile that pal found the mate a hard taskmaster, while admiring his flamboyant character. Mr. Vaner was obviously the man for me. And, yes, I might catch him still on board if I hurried, because he had been out late the night before.

She was a little ship, hardly more than a coaster, lying alongside an endless ribbon of wharf with her gray and white forecastle nosing up towards the load line of the huge empty tramp in front of her, like a neat fox terrier making the acquaintance of a collie.

Two dock policemen were standing near by. I kept my back to them while I hailed the deck importantly.

"Mr. Vaner on board?"

The cook, who was peeling potatoes on a hatch cover, looked up from the bucket between his knees.

"I'll see, sir."

That "sir" was curious and comforting. In spite of my shabby foreign clothing and filthy shoes, the cook had placed me at a glance in Class X. He would undoubtedly describe me as a gent, and Mr. Vaner would feel he ought to see me.

I say Class X because there is no definition of it. To talk of an upper or a ruling class is nonsense. The upper class, if the term has any meaning at all, means landed gentry who probably do belong to Class X but form only a small proportion of it. The ruling class are, I presume, politicians and servants of the state—terms which are self-contradictory.

I wish there were some explanation of Class X. We are politically a democracy—or should I say that we are an oligarchy with its ranks ever open to talent?—and the least class-conscious of nations in the Marxian sense. The only class-conscious people are those who would like to belong to Class X and don't: the suburban old-school-tie brigade and their wives, especially their wives. Yet we have a profound division of classes which defies analysis since it is in a continual state of flux.

Who belongs to Class X? I don't know till I talk to him and then I know at once. It is not, I think, a question of accent, but rather of the gentle voice. It is certainly not a question of clothes. It may be a question of bearing. I am not talking, of course, of provincial society in which the division between gentry and non-gentry is purely and simply a question of education.

I should like some socialist pundit to explain to me why it is that in England a man can be a member of the proletariat by every definition of the proletariat (that is, by the nature of his employment and his poverty) and yet obviously belong to Class X, and why another can be a bulging capitalist or cabinet minister or both and never get nearer to Class X than being directed to the Saloon bar if he enters the Public.

I worry with this analysis in the hope of hitting on some new method of effacing my identity. When I speak a foreign language I can disguise my class, background, and nationality without effort, but when I speak English to an Englishman I am at once spotted as a member of X. I want to avoid that, and if the class could be defined I might know how.

Mr. Vaner received me in his cabin. He was a dashing young man in his early twenties, with his cap on the back of a head of brown curls. His tiny stateroom was well hung with feminine photographs, some cut from the illustrated weeklies, some personally presented and inscribed in various languages. He evidently drove himself hard on land as well as sea.

As soon as we had shaken hands, he said:—

"Haven't met you before, have I?"

"No. I got your name from one of the hands. I hear you are sailing to-morrow."

"Well?" he asked guardedly.

I handed him my passport.

"Before we go any farther, I want you to satisfy yourself that I am British and really the person I pretend to be."

He looked at my passport, then up at my face and eye patch.

"That's all right," he said. "Take a seat, won't you? You seem to have been in trouble, sir."

"I have, by God! And I want to get out of it."

"A passage? If it depended on me—but I'm afraid the old man—"

I told him that I didn't want a passage, that I wouldn't put so much responsibility on either him or the captain; all I wanted was a safe place to stow away.

He shook his head and advised me to try a liner.

"I daren't risk it," I answered. "But show me where to hide, and I give you my word of honor that no one shall see me during the voyage or when I go ashore."

"You had better tell me a little more," he said.

He threw himself back in his chair and cocked one leg over the other. His face assumed a serious and judicial air, but his delightfully swaggering pose showed that he was enjoying himself.

I spun him a yarn which, so far as it went, was true. I told him that I was in deadly trouble with the authorities, that I had come down the river in a boat, and that an appeal to our consul was quite useless.

"I might put you in the storeroom," he said doubtfully. "We're going home in ballast, and there's nowhere in the hold for you to hide."

I suggested that the storeroom was too dangerous, that I didn't want to take the remotest chance of being seen and getting the ship into trouble. That seemed to impress him.

"Well," he replied, "if you can stand it, there's an empty freshwater tank which we never use, and I could prop up the cover so that you'd get some air. But I expect that you've slept in worse places, sir, now that I come to think of it."

"You recognized my name?"

"Of course. I wouldn't do this for everyone."

All the same I think he would, given a story that appealed to him. I asked when I could come aboard.

"No time like the present! I don't know who's down in the engine room, but there's nobody on deck except the cook. I'll just deal with the cops!"

He waited till the couple of police had walked two hundred yards up the wharf and then started waving and shouting good-bye as if someone had just gone away between the warehouses. The two looked round and continued their stroll; they had no reason to doubt that a visitor left the ship while they had their backs to her.

Mr. Vaner sent the cook ashore to buy a bottle of whiskey.

"You'll need something to mix with your water," he chuckled, immensely pleased that he had now committed himself to the adventure, "and I don't want him around while I open up the tank. You wait here and make yourself comfortable."

I asked him what I had better say if anyone came aboard unexpectedly and found me in his cabin.

"Say? Oh, tell 'em you're her father!" He pointed to a photograph of a giggling young girl who was bashfully displaying her legs as if to advertise silk stockings. "I should surely have urgent business elsewhere if you were. Inside the water tank myself, as likely as not!"

He settled his cap over one ear and marched out of the cabin, whistling with such an elaborate air of unconcern that any one of his young women would have known he was planning some deception. But I was pretty sure he would take no risks. His play-acting was for his own amusement and for me, his partner in crime. To the rest of the world he was the responsible ship's officer.

He was back in ten minutes.

"Hurry!" he said. "The cops have just gone round the corner."

We did have to hurry. The manhole was on a level with and in full view of the wharf, being set into the quarter-deck between the after wall of the chartroom and a lifeboat slung athwartship. We took a hasty look round and I pushed myself through into a space about the size of half a dozen coffins.

"I'll make you comfortable later on," he said. "It will be slack water in about two hours."

I was comfortable enough, more relaxed than I had been since the first week on the river. The darkness and the six walls gave me an immediate sense of safety. I had gone to ground after the hunt, and the cold iron of the closed tank was more protective than the softest grass in the open. This was the first of my dens, and I think that it provided me with the idea of the second.

At the bottom of the ebb, when the quarter-deck had sunk well below the edge of the wharf, Mr. Vaner turned up with blankets, the cushion of a settee, water, whiskey, biscuits, and a covered bucket for my personal needs.

"Snug as a bug in a rug!" he declared cheerfully. "And what's more, I've given you a safety valve."

"How's that?"

"I've disconnected the outflow. Can you see light?"

I looked down a small pipe at the bottom of the tank and did see light.

"That's on the wall of the captain's bathroom," he said. "I never knew we could get fresh water there. The worst of these laborsaving ships is that one never has time to find out all the gadgets. Now, you have that and you have the air intake, so if the old man notices the manhole and I have to screw it up for a time, you'll be all right."

"Where do you dock?" I asked.

"We're going right up the river to Wandsworth. I'll tell you when it's safe to slip ashore."

I heard steps on the deck—one heard in that tank everything that touched or struck the deck—and Mr. Vaner disappeared. I never saw him again.

I dozed uneasily until all the noises ceased; the crew, I suppose, had come on board and settled down for the night. Then I slept in good earnest and awoke to the sound of heavy boots trampling above and below me; it was morning, for I could see light at the end of my two pipes. The manhole was screwed up tight with a finality which I didn't enjoy—not that there was the slightest risk of asphyxiation, but it suddenly occurred to me that if Mr. Vaner were washed overboard I should be in the tank until the captain discovered, if he ever did discover, that he could fill his bath with fresh water by making a simple connection. That was the sort of ridiculous fear which alcohol can dispel quicker than self-control, so I poured myself a stiff whiskey and ate some biscuits.

Then we sailed—an unmistakable jangle of sounds like a hundred iron monkeys playing tag in a squash court. Some hours later my manhole was opened and propped, and a cold mutton chop, with a note attached to it instead of a frill, descended on my stomach. I ate the chop and knelt below the crack of light to read the message.

> Sorry I had to screw you down. The cops found a boat and traced it to you. They turned us inside out this morning and all other ships at the wharf. Caught four stowaways, I hear. We are outside territorial waters, so you're O.K. They know all about your eye patch. If you're likely to run into any trouble, take it off. I'll slip you a pair of dark glasses when it's time to go. Dock police reported that a chap of your build had come on board and left. I said I had been asked for a passage, and refused. If you have any papers you want to get rid of, leave them in the tank and I'll deliver them wherever you direct.
>
> R. VANER (*First Officer*)

P.S. Try not to upset anything. Have just remembered that if you do, it will run into the old man's bathroom.

I wish I could have given the dashing Mr. Vaner some convincing evidence that he was serving his country instead of a—well, I can't call myself a criminal. If there were any crimes committed, they were committed on my person. But, as I say, I do not blame them. They had every reason to think they had caught an assassin.

Their police organization is superb; but the finding of that paralyzed thing which had crawled and bled was a casual job for foresters. Only within the last day or two, I expect, when an exhaustive search for my corpse at last suggested that there might be no corpse to find, did the House extend inquiries to road, rail, and river, and learn about the boating schoolmaster who had an eye patch and always kept on his gloves. Then the police came into action. They hadn't picked me up, I should guess, for the simple reason that they had just begun to look for a boat with red sails and happened to miss the little yard where I changed them; but when some official noticed an unfamiliar dinghy moored where I probably had no right to moor her, she was at once identified.

Vaner's suggestion that my troubles might by no means be over when I reached London was disturbing. I hadn't given the matter any thought. One's instinct is against looking too far forward when the present demands all available resource.

I began to speculate on what would happen if I reappeared quite openly in England. I was perfectly certain that they would not appeal to the Foreign Office or to Scotland Yard. Whatever I might have done or intended, their treatment of me wouldn't stand publicity. They couldn't be sure how the English would react; nobody ever is. After all, we once went to war for the ear of a Captain Jenkins—though Jenkins was an obscurer person than I and had, considering the number of laws he broke, been treated with no great barbarity.

Would they, then, follow me up themselves? Mr. Vaner, with his taste for romance, appeared to think they would. I myself had assumed that once I was over the frontier, bygones would be bygones. I now saw that this was a foolishly optimistic view. They couldn't go to the police, true, but neither could I. I had committed an extraditable offense; if I complained of being molested, I might force them into telling why I was molested.

It came to this: I was an outlaw in my own country as in theirs, and if my death were required it could easily be accomplished. Even assuming they couldn't fake an accident or suicide, no motive or a wrong motive would be discovered for the crime, and no murderer or the wrong murderer would be arrested.

Then I thought that I had let myself be carried away by a casual phrase of Vaner's, and that this uneasiness was preposterous. Why on earth, I argued, should they take the unnecessary risk of removing me in my own country? Did they imagine that I was likely to put the wind up them by another of these sporting expeditions?

I reluctantly admitted that they might very well imagine it. They knew that I was an elusive person who could quite possibly return, if he chose, and upset the great man's nerves once more. As to whether I would so choose, there were among my opponents—I can't call them enemies—some notable big-game shots who would realize that the temptation was not unthinkable.

The manhole was never screwed up again, and I lay on my cushion suffering little more discomfort than I generally suffer at sea. I am a good sailor, but even in a first-class stateroom I feel gently and sleepily bilious, disinclined to do more than walk from my cabin to the library and back, or be faintly polite to a fellow passenger at the hour of the *apéritif*. On the credit side of this voyage was the fact that I hadn't got to be polite to anyone; on the debit, that I hadn't got a book. I passed my time in sleep and slightly nightmarish meditation.

The boom and thump of the Diesels, resonant and regular as distant tribal drums, signaled to me our progress up the Thames. They slowed to pick up the pilot; they were fussed and flurried by the engine-room telegraph in the crowded waters of Gravesend Reach; they handed over to the whir of electric capstans when we tied up, as I guess, somewhere below bridges (for she rode too high to pass upriver on the top of the flood); they beat slowly seven hours later, while I imagined them carrying us up through the Pool and the City, through Westminster and Chelsea, until the telegraph belled them into incoherent rhythms and Finished with the Engines.

There were bangings and tramplings, and then silence. After a while my tank settled over to port, and I assumed that we were resting on the Wandsworth mud. Another note was dropped through the manhole, accompanied by a pair of formidably dark glasses wrapped in brown paper.

> Don't go out through the gates. There's a chap watching I don't like the look of. The dinghy is under the starboard quarter. As soon as she floats I'll give you a knock, and you beat it quick.

Row across to the public steps by Hurlingham east wall. I'll take the boat back later. Best of luck.

R. VANER (*First Officer*)

He rapped on the manhole an hour or so later, and I pushed out my arms and shoulders by merely standing up; indeed I could stand up no other way. There was a light in Mr. Vaner's cabin, and a loud noise of conversation; he was assuring my privacy by entertaining the night watchman. I dropped into the dinghy, and pulled quietly across the river through the pink band of water that reflected the glare of London into the black band of water beneath the trees. My arrival was noticed only by a boy and girl, the inevitable boy and girl to be found in every dark corner of a great city. Better provision should be made for them—a Park of Temporary Affection, for example, from which lecherous clergymen and aged civil servants should be rigorously excluded. But such segregation is more easily accomplished by the uncivilized. Any competent witch doctor could merely declare the Park taboo for all but the nubile.

It was nearly ten o'clock. I walked to the King's Road and found a grillroom where I ordered about all the meat they had to be put on the bars and served to me. While I waited I entered the telephone box to call my club. I always stay there when I have to be in London, and that I should stay there this time I never doubted until the door of the box shut behind me. Then I found that I could not telephone my club.

What excuses I gave myself at the moment, I can't remember. I think I told myself that it was too late, that they wouldn't have a room, that I didn't wish to walk through the vestibule in those clothes and in that condition.

After my supper I took a bus to Cromwell Road and put up at one of those hotels designed for gentlewomen in moderately distressed circumstances. The porter didn't much care about taking me in, but fortunately I had a couple of pound notes and they had a room with a private bath; since their regular clientele could never afford such luxury, they were glad enough to let me the room. I gave them a false name and told them some absurd story to the effect that I had just arrived from abroad and had my luggage stolen. To digest my meal I read a sheaf of morning and evening papers, and then went to my room.

Their water, thank God, was hot! I had the most pleasurable bath that I ever remember. I have spent a large part of my life out of reach of hot baths; yet, when I enjoy a tub at leisure, I wonder why any man voluntarily deprives himself of so cheap and satisfying a delight. It rested and calmed me more than any sleep; indeed I had slept so much on the ship that my bath and my thoughts while lying in it had the flavor of morning rather than of night.

I understood why I had not telephoned my club. This was the first occasion on which I recognized that I had a second enemy dogging my movements—my own unjust and impossible conscience. Utterly unfair it was that I should judge myself as a potential murderer. I insist that I was always sure I could resist the temptation to press the trigger when my sights were actually on the target.

I have good reason now for a certain malaise. I have killed a man, though in self-defense. But then I had no reason at all. I may be wrong in talking of conscience; my trouble was, perhaps, merely a vision of the social effects of what I had done. This stalk of mine made it impossible for me to enter my club. How could I, for example, talk to Holy George after all the trouble I had caused him? And how could I expose my fellow members to the unpleasantness of being watched and perhaps questioned? No, I was an outlaw not because of my conscience (which, I maintain, has no right to torment me) but on the plain facts.

There was no lack of mirrors in the bathroom, and I made a thorough examination of my body. My legs and backside were an ugly mess,—I shall carry some extraordinary scars for life,—but the wounds had healed, and there was nothing any doctor could do to help. My fingers still appeared to have been squashed in a railway carriage door and then sharpened with a penknife, but they were in fact serviceable for all but very rough or very sensitive work. The eye was the only part of me that needed attention. I didn't propose to have anyone monkeying with it,—I dared not give up my freedom of movement for the sake of regular treatment or an operation,—but I wanted a medical opinion and whatever lotions would do it the most good.

In the morning I changed all the foreign money in my possession, and bought myself a passable suit off the peg. Then I got a list of eye specialists and taxied round and about Harley Street until I found a man who would see me at once. He was annoyingly inquisitive. I told him that I had hurt the eye at the beginning of a long voyage and had been out of reach of medical care ever since. When he had fully opened the lid, he fumed over my neglect, folly, and idiocy and declared that the eye had been burned as well as bruised. I agreed politely that it had and shut up; whereupon he became a doctor instead of a moralist and got down to business. He was honest enough to say that he could do nothing, that I'd be lucky if I ever perceived more than light and darkness, and that, on the whole, he recommended changing the real for a glass eye for the sake of appearance. He was wrong. My eye isn't pretty, but it functions better every day.

He wouldn't hear of my going about in dark glasses with no bandage, so I had him extend the bandages over the whole of my head. He humored me in this, evidently thinking that I might get violent if opposed; my object was to give the impression of a man who had smashed his head rather than a man with a damaged eye. He was convinced that my face was familiar to him, and I allowed him to decide that we had once met in Vienna.

The next job was to see my solicitors in Lincoln's Inn Fields. The partner who has the entire handling of my estate is a man of about my own age and an intimate friend. He disapproves of me on only two grounds: that I refuse to sit on the board of any blasted company, and that I insist upon my right to waste money in agriculture. He doesn't mind my spending it on anything else, finding a vicarious pleasure in my travels and outlandish hobbies. He himself has a longing for a less ordered life, shown chiefly in his attitude to clothes. During the day he is sombrely and richly attired, and has even taken in recent years to wearing a black silk stock. At night he puts on tweeds, a sweater, and a tie that would frighten a newspaperman. One can't make him change for dinner. He would rather refuse an invitation.

Saul greeted me with concern rather than surprise; it was as if he had expected me to turn up in a hurry and the worse for wear. He locked the door and told his office manager we were not to be disturbed.

I assured him that I was all right and that the bandage was four times as long as was necessary. I asked what he knew and who had inquired for me.

He said that there had been a pointedly casual inquiry from Holy George and that a few days later a fellow had come in to consult him about some inconceivable tangle under the Married Women's Property Act.

"He was so perfectly the retired military man from the West of England," said Saul, "that I felt he couldn't be real. He claimed to be a friend and neighbor of yours and was continually referring to you. When I cross-examined him a bit, it looked as if he had mugged up his case out of a law book and was really after information. Major Quive-Smith, he called himself. Ever heard of him?"

"Never," I replied. "He certainly isn't a neighbor of mine. Was he English?"

"I thought so. Did you expect him not to be English?"

I said I wasn't answering any of his innocent questions, that he was, after all, an Officer of the Court, and that I didn't wish to involve him.

"Tell me this much," he said. "Have you been abroad in the employ of our government?"

"No, on my own business. But I have to disappear."

"You shouldn't think of the police as tactless," he reminded me gently. "A man in your position is protected without question. You've been abroad so much that I don't think you have ever realized the power of your name. You're automatically trusted, you see."

I told him that I knew as much of my own people as he did—perhaps more, since I had been an exile long enough to see them from the outside. But I had to vanish. There was a risk that I might be disgraced.

A nasty word, that. I am not disgraced and I will not feel it.

"Can I vanish? Financially, I mean?" I asked him. "You have my power of attorney and you know more of my affairs than I do myself. Can you go on handling my estate if I am never heard of again?"

"So long as I know you are alive."

"What do you mean by that?"

"A postcard this time next year will do."

"X marks my window, and this is a palm tree?"

"Quite sufficient if in your own handwriting. You needn't even sign it."

"Mightn't you be asked for proof?" I inquired.

"No. If I say you are alive, why the devil should it ever be questioned? But don't leave me without a postcard from time to time. You mustn't put me in the position of maintaining what might be a lie."

I told him that if he ever got one postcard, he'd probably get a lot more; it was my ever living to write the first that was doubtful.

He blew up and told me I was absurd. He mingled abuse with affection in a way I hadn't heard since my father died. I didn't think he would take my disappearance so hard; I suppose he is as fond of me, after all, as I am of him, and that's saying a lot. He begged me again to let him talk to the police. I had no idea, he insisted, of the number and the subtle beauty of the strings that could be pulled.

I could only say I was awfully sorry, and after a silence I told him I wanted five thousand pounds in cash.

He produced my deed box and accounts. I had a balance of three thousand at the bank; he wrote his own check for the other two. That was like him—no nonsense about waiting for sales of stock or arranging an overdraft.

"Shall we go out and lunch while the boy is at the bank?" he suggested.

"I think I'll leave here only once," I said.

"You might be watched? Well, we'll soon settle that."

He sent for Peale, a gray little man in a gray little suit whom I had only seen emptying the waste-paper baskets or fetching cups of tea.

"Anybody taking an interest in us, Peale?"

"There is a person in the gardens between Remnant Street and here feeding the birds. He is not very successful with them, sir,—" Peale permitted himself a dry chuckle,—"in spite of the fact that he has been there for the past week during office hours. And I understand from Pruce & Fothergill that there are two other persons in Newman's Row. One of them is waiting for a lady to come out of their offices—a matrimonial case, I believe. The other is not known to us, and was observed to be in communication with the pigeon man, sir, as soon as this gentleman emerged from his taxi."

Saul thanked him, and sent him out to fetch us some beer and a cold bird.

I asked where he watched from, having a vague picture of Peale hanging over the parapet of the roof when he had nothing to do.

"Good God, he doesn't watch!" exclaimed Saul, as if I had suggested a major impropriety. "He just knows all the private detectives who are likely to be hanging around Lincoln's Inn Fields—on very good terms with them, I believe. They have to have a drink occasionally, and then they ask Peale or his counterpart in some other firm to keep his eyes open. When they see anyone who is not a member of their Trades Union, so to speak, they all know it."

Peale came back with the lunch, and a packet of information straight from the counter of the saloon bar. The birdman had been showing great interest in our windows and had twice telephoned. The chap in Newman's Row had hailed my taxi as it drove away. He would be able to trace me back to Harley Street and to the clothes shop, where, by a little adroit questioning, he could make an excuse to see the suit I discarded; my identification would be complete. It didn't much matter, since the watchers already had a strong suspicion that I was their man.

Peale couldn't tell us whether another watcher had been posted in Newman's Row or whether the other exits from Lincoln's Inn Fields were watched. I was certain that they were, and complained to Saul that all respectable firms of solicitors (who deal with far more scabrous affairs than the crooked) should have a back door. He replied that they weren't such fools as they looked, and that Peale could take me into Lincoln's Inn or the Law Courts and lose me completely.

Perhaps I should have trusted them; but I felt that, while their tricks might be good enough to lose a single private detective, I shouldn't be allowed to escape so easily. I decided to throw off the hunt in my own way.

When I kept my gloves on to eat, Saul forgot his official discretion and became an anxious friend. I think he suspected what had happened to me, though not why it had happened. I had to beg him to leave the whole subject alone.

After lunch I signed a number of documents to tidy up loose ends, and we blocked out a plan I had often discussed with him of forming a sort of Tenants' Coöperative Society. Since I never make a penny out of the land, I thought they might as well pay rent to themselves, do their own repairs, and advance their own loans, with the right to purchase their own land by installments at a price fixed by the committee. I hope it works. At any rate Saul and my land agent will keep them from quarreling among themselves. I have no other dependents.

Then I told him something of the fisherman and passed on the address that he had given me; and we arranged for an income to be paid where it would do the most good—a discreet trust that couldn't conceivably be traced to me. It appeared to come from the estate of a recently defunct old lady who had left the bulk of her money to an institution for inoculating parrots against psittacosis, and the rest to any charitable object that Saul, as sole trustee, might direct.

There was nothing further to be done but arrange my cash in a body belt, and say good-bye. I asked him, if at any time a coroner sat on my body and brought in a verdict of suicide, not to believe it but to make no attempt to reopen the case.

Peale walked with me across the square and into Kingsway by Gate Street. I observed that we were followed by a tall, inoffensive fellow in a dirty mackintosh and shabby felt hat, who was the birdman. He looked the part. We also caught sight of a cheerful military man in Remnant Street, wearing a coat cut for riding and trousers narrower than were fashionable, whom Peale at once recognized as Major Quive-Smith. So I knew two at least whom I must throw off my track.

We parted at Holborn underground station, and I took a shilling ticket with which I could travel to the remotest end of London. The birdman had got ahead of me. I passed him on the level of the Central London, and went down the escalator to the west-bound Piccadilly Tube. Ten seconds after I reached the platform, Major Quive-Smith also appeared upon it. He was gazing at the advertisements and grinning at the comic ones, as if he hadn't been in London for a year.

I pretended I had forgotten something, and shot out of the exit, up the stairs, and down a corridor to the north-bound platform. No train was in. Even if there had been a train, the major was too close behind for me to catch it and leave him standing.

I noticed that the shuttle train to the Aldwych left from the opposite side of the same platform. This offered a way of escape if ever there were two trains in at the same time.

The escalator took me back to the Central London level. The birdman was talking to the chap in a glass box at the junction of all the runways. I'd call him a ticket collector, but he never seems to collect any tickets; probably he is there to answer silly questions such as the birdman was busily engaged in asking. I took the second escalator to the surface, and promptly dashed down again.

The birdman followed me, but a bit late. We passed each other about midway, he going up and I going down and both running like hell. I thought I had him, that I could reach a Central London train before he could; but he was taking no risks. He vaulted over the division on to the stationary staircase. We reached the bottom separated only by the extra speed of my moving staircase—and that was a mere ten yards. The man in the glass box came to life and said: "'Ere! You can't do that, you know!" But that didn't worry the birdman. He was content to remain and discuss his antisocial action with the ticket-non-collector. I had already turned to the right into the Piccadilly Line and on to Major Quive-Smith's preserves.

At the bottom of the Piccadilly escalator you turn left for the north-bound trains, and continue straight on for the west-bound. To the right is the exit, along which an old lady with two wide parcels was perversely trying to force her way against the stream of outcoming passengers. Major Quive-Smith was away to the left, at the mouth of the passage to the north-bound trains; so I plunged into the stream after the old lady, and was clear of it long before he was.

I ran on to the north-bound platform. An Aldwych shuttle was just pulling in, but there was no Piccadilly train. I shot under the Aldwych line, down to the west-bound platform, into the general exit, jamming him in another stream of outcoming passengers, and back to the north-bound Piccadilly. There was a train standing, and the Aldwych shuttle had not left. I jumped into the Piccadilly train with the major so far behind that he was compelled to enter another coach just as the doors were closing and just as I stepped out again. Having thus dispatched the major to an unknown destination, I got into the Aldwych shuttle, which at once left on its half-mile journey.

This was all done at such a pace that I hadn't had time to think. I ought to have crossed to the west-bound Piccadilly and taken a train into the blue. But, naturally enough, I wanted to leave Holborn station as rapidly as possible for fear of running into the birdman or another unknown watcher if I waited. After half a minute in the Aldwych shuttle I realized that I had panicked like a rabbit in a warren. The mere couple of ferrets who had been after me had been magnified by my escape mechanism—a literal escape mechanism, this, and working much faster than my mind—into an infinity of ferrets.

When we arrived at the Aldwych station and I was strolling to the lifts, I saw that it was not yet too late to return to Holborn. The birdman would still be on the Central London level, for he might lose me if he left it for a moment. Quive-Smith couldn't have had time to telephone to anyone what had happened.

I turned back and reëntered the shuttle. The passengers were already seated in the single coach, and the platform clear; but a man in a black hat and blue flannel suit got in after me. That meant that he had turned back when I had turned back.

At Holborn I remained seated to prove whether my suspicions were correct. They were. Black Hat got out, sauntered around the platform, and got in again just before the doors closed. They had been far too clever for me! They had evidently ordered Black Hat to travel back and forth between Holborn and the Aldwych, and to go on traveling until either I entered that cursed coach or they gave him the signal that I had left by some other route. All I had done was to send Quive-Smith to Bloomsbury, whence no doubt he had already taken a taxi to some central clearing point to which all news of my movements was telephoned.

As we left again for the Aldwych, Black Hat was at the back of the coach and I was in the front. We sat as far away as possible from each other. Though we were both potential murderers, we felt, I suppose, mutual embarrassment. Mutual. I wish to God he had sat opposite me, or shown himself in some way less human than I.

The Aldwych station is a dead end. A passenger cannot leave it except by the lift or the emergency spiral staircase. Nevertheless I thought I had a wild chance of getting away. When the doors of the train opened, I dashed on to and off the platform, round a corner to the left, and up a few stairs; but instead of going ten yards further, round to the right and so to the lift, I hopped into a little blank alley that I had noticed on my earlier walk.

There was no cover of any sort, but Black Hat did just what I hoped. He came haring up the corridor, pushing through the passengers with his eyes fixed straight ahead, and jumped for the emergency staircase. The ticket collector called him back. He shouted a question whether anyone had gone up the stairs. The ticket collector, in turn, asked was it likely. Black Hat then entered the lift, and in the time it took him to get there and to glance over the passengers I was out of my alley and back on the platform.

The train was still in, but if I could catch it, so could Black Hat. The corridor was short, though with two right-angled twists, and he couldn't be more than five seconds behind me. I jumped on to the line and took refuge in the tunnel. There wasn't any employee of the Underground to see me except the driver, and he was in his box at the front of the coach. The platform, of course, was empty.

Beyond the Aldwych station there seemed to be some fifty yards of straight tube, and then a curve, its walls faintly visible in a gleam of gray light. Where the tunnel goes, or if it ends in an old shaft after the curve, I didn't have time to find out.

Black Hat looked through the coach and saw that I wasn't in it. The train pulled out, and when its roar had died away there was absolute silence. I hadn't realized that Black Hat and I would be left alone a hundred feet under London. I lay flattened against the wall in the darkest section of the tunnel.

The working of the Aldwych station is very simple. Just before the shuttle is due, the lift comes down. The departing passengers get into the train; the arriving passengers get into the lift. When the lift goes up and the train leaves, Aldwych station is deserted as an ancient mine. You can hear the drip of water and the beat of your heart.

I can still hear them, and the sound of steps and his scream and the hideous, because domestic, sound of sizzling. They echoed along that tunnel which leads Lord knows where. A queer place for a soul to find itself adrift.

It was self-defense. He had a flashlight and a pistol. I don't know if he meant to use it. Perhaps he was only as frightened of me as I was of him. I crawled right to his feet and sprang at him. By God,

I want to die in the open! If ever I have land again, I swear I'll never kill a creature below ground.

I lifted the bandages from my head and put them in my pocket; that expanse of white below my hat attracted too much attention to me. Then I came out, crossed the platform into the corridor, and climbed a turn of the emergency stairs. As soon as the lift came down, I mingled with the departing passengers and waited for the train. When it came in, I went up in the lift with the new arrivals. I gave up my shilling ticket and received a surprised glance from the collector, since the fare from Holborn was but a penny. The only alternative was to pretend I had lost my ticket and to pay; that would have meant still closer examination.

I left the station free, unwatched, unhurried, and took a bus back to the respectable squares of Kensington. Who would look for a fugitive between the Cromwell and Fulham roads? I dined at leisure, and then went to a cinema to think.

In these days of visas and identification cards it is impossible to travel without leaving a trail that can, with patience, bribery, and access to public records, be picked up. In the happy years between 1925 and 1930 you could talk yourself over any western European frontier, so long as you looked respectable and explained your movements and business with a few details that could be checked; you could treat frontier police as men of decency and common sense: two virtues that they could then afford to indulge. But now unless a traveler has some organization—subversive or benevolent—to help him, frontiers are an efficient bar to those who find it inconvenient or impossible to show their papers; and even if a frontier be crossed without record, there isn't the remotest village where a man can live without justifying himself and his reasons for being himself. Thus Europe, for me, was a mere trap with a delayed action.

Where then could I go? I thought at once of a job on a ship, for there's a shortage of seamen in these days; but it wasn't worth visiting shipping offices with my hands in the state they were. Rule out a long voyage as a stowaway. Rule out a discreet passage on a cargo ship. I could easily have got such a passage, but only by revealing my identity and presence in England to some friend. That I wanted to avoid at all costs. Only Saul, Peale, Vaner, and the admirable secret service which was hunting me knew that I wasn't in Poland. None of them would talk.

There remained a voyage on a passenger vessel. I could certainly get on to the ship without showing my passport; I might be able to get off it. But passenger lists are open to inspection, and if my name appeared on one some blasted reporter would consider it news and save my hunters trouble. They would, anyway, be watching the lists themselves.

Then I needed a false passport. In normal circumstances I have no doubt that Saul or my friends in the Foreign Office could have arranged some tactful documentation for me, but, as it was, I could not involve any of them. It was unthinkable, just as police protection was unthinkable. I could not risk embarrassing the officials of my country. If the extraordinary being at whose waistcoat I had looked through a telescopic sight were moved by his daemon or digestion to poison international relations more than they already were, a very pretty case could be built up against a government that helped me to escape.

As I sat back in that cheap cinema seat, with my eyes closed and with the meaningless noises and music forcing my mind from plan to plan, I saw that I could only disappear by not leaving England at all. I must bury myself in some farm or country pub until the search for me had slackened.

When the main feature, as I believe they call it, was at its most dramatic quarter of an hour and the lavatory was likely to be empty, I left my seat, bathed my eye with the lotion the doctor had given me, and put on my bandages again. Then I wandered westwards through the quiet squares which smelled of a London August night—that perfume of dust and heavy flowers, held down by trees into the warm, well-dug ravines between the houses.

I decided against sleeping at a hotel. My position was becoming so complicated that it seemed wise to occupy neutral territory whence I could move according to circumstance. A hotel porter might compel me into some act or lie that was unnecessary. I took a bus to Wimbledon Common; I had never been there, but knew there was a golf course and some sort of cover where corpses were very frequently discovered—indications of a considerable stretch of country that was open to the public at night.

The Common turned out to be ideal. I spent the night in a grove of silver birch where the fine soil—silver, too, it seemed to me, but the cause was probably the half-moon—held the heat of the day. There is, for me, no better resting place than the temperate forest of Europe. Can one reasonably speak of forest at half an hour from Piccadilly Circus? I think so. The trees and heath are there, and at night one sees no paper bags.

In the morning I brushed off the leaves and bought a paper in a hurry from the local tobacconist as if I were briskly on my way to the

City. In my new and too smart clothes I looked the part. ALDWYCH MYSTERY was occupying half a column of the centre page. I retired to a seat on the Common before committing myself to further dealings with the public.

The body had been discovered almost as soon as I was clear of the station. Foul play, said the paper cautiously, was suspected. In other words, the police were wondering how a man who had fallen on his back across the live rail could have suffered a smashing blow in the solar plexus.

The deceased had been identified. He was a Mr. Johns, who lived in a furnished room in those barrack squares of furnished rooms between Millbank and Victoria Station. His age, his friends, his background, were unknown (and, if he knew his job, always would be), but the paper carried an interview with his landlady. It must have been a horrible shock to be knocked up by a reporter around midnight and told that her lodger had been killed under suspicious circumstances. Or perhaps not. I have been assured by newspapermen that even close relatives forget their grief in the excitement of getting into the news; so a landlady, provided she had her rent, might not worry overmuch. Though knowing nothing whatever about the man under her roof, she had been most communicative. She said:—

"He was a real gentleman and I'm sure I don't know why anyone should have done him harm. His poor old mother will be broken-hearted."

But it appeared that nobody had discovered the address of the poor old mother. The only evidence for her existence was the landlady's statement that she would often telephone Mr. Johns, who thereupon rushed out in a great hurry to see her. I was not, of course, so cynical at the moment; but when the aged mother, such jam for journalists, was not mentioned at all in the evening papers, my conscience was easier.

The police were anxious to interview a well-dressed clean-shaven man in the early forties, with a bruised and blackened eye, who was observed to leave the Aldwych station shortly before the body was discovered, and surrendered a shilling ticket to the collector. I am not yet forty and I was not well dressed, but the description was accurate enough to be unpleasant reading.

It might have been worse. If they had wanted a man with a bandaged head, one of Saul's clerks might have let information leak, and the taxi driver, who had, no doubt, already answered a number of mysterious questions, would have gone to the police. As it was, the public were left with the impression that the man's eye had been injured in the struggle below ground. No one except Saul and Mr. Vaner could suspect that I might be the man concerned. Both of them would assume that the rights and wrongs were for my own conscience to settle rather than the police.

That confounded eye finished any chance I might have had of living in some obscure farm or inn. A wanted man with any well-marked peculiarity cannot hide in an English village. The local bobby has nothing to do but see that the pubs observe a decent discretion, if not the law, and that farmers do not too flagrantly ignore the mass of *paperasserie* that they are supposed to have read and haven't. He pushes his bicycle up the hills, dreaming of catching a real criminal, and when the usual chap with a scar or with a finger missing is wanted by the metropolitan police, every person of small means who has recently retired to a cottage (which puts him under suspicion anyway) is visited by the village bobby at unexpected times on the most improbable errands.

There was nothing for it but to live in the open. I sat on my bench on Wimbledon Common and considered what part of England to choose. The North was the wilder, but since I might have to endure a winter, the rigor of the climate was not inviting. My own county, though I carried the ordnance map in my eye and knew a dozen spots where I could go to ground, had to be avoided. I wonder what my tenants made of the gentleman who, at that time, was doubtless staying at the Red Lion, asking questions, and describing himself as a hiker who had fallen in love with the village. A hideous word—hiker. It has nothing to do with the gentle souls of my youth who wandered in tweeds and stout shoes from pub to pub. But, by God, it fits those bawling Englishwomen whose tight shorts and loose voices are turning every beauty spot in Europe into a Skegness holiday camp.

I chose southern England, with a strong preference for Dorset. It is a remote county, lying as it does between Hampshire, which is becoming an outer suburb, and Devon, which is a playground. I knew one part of the county very well indeed, and, better still, there was no reason for anyone to suppose that I knew it. I had never hunted with the Cattistock. I had no intimate friends nearer than Somerset. The business that had taken me to Dorset was so precious that I kept it to myself.

There are times when I am no more self-conscious than a chimpanzee. I had chosen my destination to within ten yards; yet, that day, I couldn't have told even Saul where I was going. This habit of thinking about myself and my motives has only grown upon me recently. In this confession I have forced myself to analyze; when I write that I did this because of that, it is true. At the time of the action, however, it was not always true; my reasons were insistent but frequently obscure.

Though the precise spot where I was going was no more nor less present in my consciousness than the dark shadows which floated before my left eye, I knew I had to have a fleece-lined, waterproof sleeping bag. I dared not return to the centre of London, so I decided to telephone and have the thing sent C.O.D. to Wimbledon station by a commissionaire.

I spoke to the shop in what I believed to be a fine disguised bass voice, but the senior partner recognized me almost at once. Either I gave myself away by showing too much knowledge of his stock, or my sentence rhythm is unmistakable.

"Another trip, sir, I suppose?"

I could imagine him rubbing his hands with satisfaction at my continued custom.

He mentioned my name six times in one minute of ejaculations. He burbled like a fatherly butler receiving the prodigal son.

I had to think quickly. To deny my identity would evidently cause a greater mystery than to admit it. I felt pretty safe with him. He was one of the few dozen black-coated, archbishoplike tradesmen of the West End—tailors, gunsmiths, bootmakers, hatters—who would die of shame rather than betray the confidence of a customer, to whom neither the law nor the certainty of a bad debt is as anything compared to the pride of serving the aristocracy.

"Can anyone hear you?" I asked him.

I thought he was probably chucking my name about for the benefit of a shop assistant or a customer. These ecclesiasts of Savile Row and Jermyn Street are about the only true dyed-in-the-wool snobs that are left.

He hesitated an instant. I imagined him looking round. I knew the telephone was in the office at the far end of the shop.

"No, sir," he said with a shade of regret that made me certain he was telling the truth.

I explained to him that I wished no one to know I was in England and that I trusted him to keep my name off his lips and out of his books. He oozed dutifulness—and thoughtfulness too, for after much humming and hawing and excusing himself he asked me if I would like him to bring me some cash together with the sleeping bag. I very possibly had not wished to visit my bank, he said. Wonderful fellow! He assumed without any misgiving at all that his discretion was greater than that of my bank manager. I wouldn't be surprised if it was.

Since I was in for it anyway, I gave him a full list of my requirements: a boy's catapult, a billhook, and the best knife he had; toilet requisites and a rubber basin; a Primus stove and a pan; flannel shirts, heavy trousers and underclothes, and a windproof jacket. Within an hour he was at Wimbledon station in person, with the whole lot neatly strapped into the sleeping bag. I should have liked a firearm of some sort, but it was laying unfair weight on his discretion to ask him not to register or report the sale.

I took a train to Guildford, and thence by slow stages to Dorchester, where I arrived about five in the afternoon. I changed after Salisbury, where a friendly porter heaved my roll into an empty carriage on a stopping train without any corridor. By the time we reached the next station I was no longer the well-dressed man. I had become a holiday-maker with Mr. Vaner's very large and dark sun glasses.

I left my kit at Dorchester station. What transport to take into the green depths of Dorset I hadn't the faintest notion. I couldn't buy a motor vehicle or a horse because of the difficulty of getting rid of them. A derelict car or a wandering horse at once arouses any amount of inquiry. To walk with my unwieldy roll was nearly impossible. To take a bus merely put off the moment when I would have to find more private conveyance.

Strolling as far as the Roman amphitheatre, I lay on the outer grass slope to watch the traffic on the Weymouth road and hope for an idea. The troops of cyclists interested me. I hadn't ridden a cycle since I was a boy, and had forgotten its possibilities. These holiday-makers carried enough gear on their backs and mudguards to last a week or two, but I didn't see how I could balance my own camping outfit on a bike.

I waited for an hour, and along came the very vehicle I wanted. I have since noticed that they are quite common on the roads, but this was the first I had seen. A tandem bicycle it was, with Pa and Ma riding and the baby slung alongside in a little sidecar. I should never have dared to carry any offspring of mine in a contraption like that, but I must admit that for a young couple with no nerves and little money it was a sensible way of taking a holiday.

I stood up and yelled to them, pointing frantically at nothing in particular. They dismounted, looked at me with surprise, then at baby, then at the back wheel.

"Sorry to stop you," I said. "But might I ask where you bought that thing? Just what I want for me and the missus and the young un!"

I thought that struck the right note.

"I made it," said Pa proudly.

He was a boy of about twenty-three or four. He had the perfect self-possession and merry eyes of a craftsman. One can usually spot them, this new generation of craftsmen. They know the world is theirs, and are equally contemptuous of the professed radical and the genteel. They definitely belong in Class X, though I suppose they must learn to speak the part before being recognized by so conservative a nation.

"Are you in the cycle trade?"

"Not me!" he answered with marked scorn for his present method of transport. "Aircraft!"

I should have guessed it. The aluminum plating and the curved, beautifully tooled ribs had the professional touch; and two projections at the front of the sidecar, which at first glance I had taken for lamps, were obviously model machine guns. I hope they were for Pa's amusement rather than for the infant's.

"He looks pretty comfortable," I said to the wife.

She was a sturdy wench in corduroy shorts no longer than trunks, and with legs so red that the golden hairs showed as continuous fur. Not my taste at all. But my taste is far from eugenic.

" 'E loves it, don't you, duck?"

She drew him from the sidecar as if uncorking a fat puppy from a riding boot. I take it that she did not get hold of him by the scruff of the neck, but my memory insists that she did. The baby chortled with joy, and made a grab for my dark glasses.

"Now, Rodney, leave the poor gentleman alone!" said his mother.

That was fine. There was a note of Pity the Blind about her voice. Mr. Vaner's glasses had no delicate tints. They turned the world dark blue.

"You wouldn't like to sell it, I suppose?" I asked, handing Pa a cigarette.

"I might when we get home," he answered cautiously. "But my home's Leicester."

I said I was ready to make him an offer for bicycle and sidecar then and there.

"And give up my holiday?" he laughed. "Not likely, mister!"

"Well, what would it cost?"

"I wouldn't let it go a penny under fifteen quid!"

"I might go to twelve pound ten," I offered—I'd have gladly offered him fifty for it, but I had to avoid suspicion. "I expect I could buy the whole thing new for that, but I like your sidecar and the way it's fixed. My wife is a bit nervous, you see, and she'd never put the nipper in anything that didn't look strong."

"It is strong," he said. "And fifteen quid would be my last word. But I can't sell it you, because what would we do?"

He hesitated and seemed to be summing up me and the bargain. A fine, quick-witted mind he had. Most people would be far too conservative to consider changing a holiday in the middle.

"Haven't anything you'd like to swap?" he asked. "An old car or rooms at the seaside? We'd like a bit of beach to sit on, but what with doctor's bills and the missus so extravagant . . ."

He gave me a broad wink, but the missus wasn't to be drawn.

"He's a one for kidding!" she informed me happily.

"I've got a beach hut near Weymouth," I said. "I'll let you have it free for a fortnight, and ten quid for the combination."

The missus gave a squeal of joy, and was sternly frowned upon by her husband.

"I don't know as I want a beach hut," he said, "and it would be twelve quid. Now we're going to Weymouth to-night. Now suppose we did a swap, could we move in right away?"

I told him he certainly could, so long as I could get there ahead of him to fix things up and have the place ready. I said I would see if there was a train.

"Oh, ask for a lift!" he said, as if it were the obvious way of traveling any short distance. "I'll soon get you one."

That chap must have had some private countersign to the freemasonry of the road. Personally, I never have the impudence to stop a car on a main road. Why, I don't know. I'm always perfectly willing to give a lift if I am driving.

He let half a dozen cars go by, remarking "Toffs!", and then stopped one unerringly. It was a battered Morris, very much occupied by a sporty-looking gent who might have been a bookmaker or a publican. He turned out to be an employee of the County Council whose job it was to inspect the steam rollers.

"Hey, mister! Can you give my pal a lift to Weymouth?"

"Look sharp, then!" answered the driver cheerily.

I arranged to meet the family at the station at seven-thirty, and got in.

He did the eight miles to Weymouth in a quarter of an hour. I explained that I was hopping ahead to get rooms for the rest of our cycling party when they arrived, and asked him if he knew of any beach huts for rent. He said there weren't any beach huts, and that, what was more, we should find it difficult to get rooms.

"A wonderful season!" he said. "Sleeping on the beach they were at Bank Holiday!"

This was depressing. I had evidently been rash in my offer for the family combination. I told him that I personally intended to stay some time in Weymouth, and what about a tent or a bungalow or even one of those caravans the steam-roller men slept in?

That amused him like anything.

"Ho!" he said. "They're county property, they are! They wouldn't let you have one of them things. But I tell you what—" he lowered his voice confidentially in the manner of the English when they are proposing a deal (it comes, I think, from the national habit of buying and selling in a public bar)—"I know a trailer you could buy cheap, if you were thinking of buying, that is."

He drove me to a garage kept by some in-law of his, where there was a whacking great trailer standing in the yard amid a heap of scrap iron. It appeared homemade by some enthusiast who had forgotten, in his passion for roominess and gadgets, that it had to be towed round corners behind a car. The in-law and the steam-roller man showed me over that trailer as if they were a couple of high-powered estate agents selling a mansion. It was a little home from home, they said. And it was! It had everything for two except the bedding, and it was mine for forty quid. I accepted their price on condition that they threw in the bedding and a cot for Rodney, and towed me then and there to a camp site. They drove me a couple of miles to the east of Weymouth where there was an open field with a dozen tents and trailers. I rented a site for six months from the landowner and told him that friends would be occupying the trailer for the moment, and that I myself hoped to get down for many weekends in the autumn. He showed no curiosity whatever; if strange beings chose to camp on his land he collected five bob a week from them in advance and never went near them again.

When we got back to the town I had a quick drink with my saviors and vanished. It was nearly eight before I could reach the station. Pa and Ma were leaning disconsolately against the railings.

"Now then, mister," said my aircraft mechanic, "time's money, and how about it?"

He was a little peeved at my being late. Evidently he had been thinking the luck too good to be true, and that he wouldn't see me again.

We walked wearily out to the camp site. The trailer was quite enchanting in the gathering dusk, and I damn near gave it to them. Well, at any rate he got his fortnight's holiday rent free and I expect he managed to replace tandem and sidecar for the twelve quid. I said that I should probably be back before the end of his fortnight, but that if I was not, he should give the key to the landowner. I don't think the trailer can be the object of any inquiry until the six months are up; and by that time I hope to be out of England.

I rode the beastly combination back to Weymouth, spilling myself into the ditch at the first left-hand corner, for it wasn't easy to get the hang of it. Then I had a meal and, finding that the snack bars and tea shops were still open, filled up the sidecar with a stock of biscuits and a ham, plenty of tinned foods and fruits, tobacco, and a few bottles of beer and whiskey. At the third shop I entered, a dry-faced spinster gazed into my glasses long and suspiciously, and remarked:—

" 'Urt your eye, 'ave you?"

I answered unctuously that it was an infliction from birth, and that I feared it was the Lord's will to take from me the sight of the other eye. She became most sympathetic after that, but I had had my warning.

I cycled through the darkness to Dorchester, arriving there dead-beat about midnight. I picked up my kit and strapped it on the sidecar. Then I pedaled a few miles north into the silence of a valley where the only moving thing was the Frome gurgling and gleaming over the pebbles. I wheeled my combination off the road and into a copse, unpacked, and slept.

The bag was delicious. In a month I had only spent half a night in bed. I slept and slept, brought up to consciousness at intervals by the stirring of leaves or insects, but seizing upon sleep again as effortlessly as pulling a blanket over one's ears.

It was after ten when I awoke. I lay in my fleece till noon, looking up through the oak leaves to a windy sky and trying to decide whether it was less risky to travel by day or night. If by day I should arouse no particular curiosity, but my vehicle was so odd that dozens of people would remember having seen it; if by night, anyone who saw me would talk about me for days. But between midnight and three nothing stirs in farm or village. I was prepared to gamble that nobody would see me.

I admitted to myself now where I was going. The road I meant to take was a narrow track along the downs, a remnant of the old Roman road from Dorchester to Exeter only used by farmers' carts. My meeting with any human being in the darkness was most improbable. Even if I were not alone on the hills I should hear before

I was heard. I remembered how in that wheat field I had cursed the silent approach of cyclists.

My temporary camp was fairly safe, though close to a road. All day I saw no one but a most human billy goat belonging to a herd of cows in the neighboring field. He had a look at the sidecar and ate some twigs of the bush under which it was resting. He spat them out again, regarding me ironically. He reminded me of some old whiskered countryman solemnly walking over a right of way which isn't the slightest use to him in order to keep it open. I like to see a billy goat accompanying the dairy herd to pasture, supposedly to bring them luck or to eat the herbs that cause abortion. I think his true function has been forgotten, but there is no object in going against ancient tradition, nor reason to suppose he has no function.

I started at midnight. The first three miles were on a well-used byroad, but I met only one car. I had time to lean my bicycle against a hedge and get over into the field myself. The Roman road was teeming with life: sheep and cows lying on it, rabbits dancing in and out of ancient pits, owls gliding and hooting over the thorn. I carried no light, and was continually upsetting in the ruts, for the space between them was only just wide enough to take my three wheels. Eventually I dismounted and walked.

What with the slow going and losing my way in a maze of tracks and gorse bushes, the hedges were beginning to take shape in the half-light when I coasted down into the vale, crossed the railway, and slipped silently through the sleeping village of Powerstock. It was time to leave the road. In the neighboring fields, so far as I could search them with one eye,—and that still unused to judging perspective,—there was little cover. When I came upon the four walls of a burned and derelict cottage, I laid the tandem in the nettles that covered the old floor and detached the sidecar, which I half hid under bricks and debris. I made no attempt to conceal myself, lying down in the long grass beside a stream. It was a warm, silent day, beginning with a September mist that hung low over the meadows. If anyone saw me, I was really sleeping or pretending to sleep with my head on my arms—a common enough sight by any stream in holiday time.

I reassembled my vehicle in the dusk, and started at eleven. There were no villages, and the only checks were at the crossing of two main roads. The dogs barked and cursed at me as I passed solitary farms and cottages, but I was out of sight before the householders could look out of their windows, if they ever did. I rode swiftly, for there was much to be done that night.

At half-past twelve I was on the ridge of a half-moon of low rabbit-cropped hills, the horns of which rested upon the sea, enclosing between them a small, lush valley. The outer or northern slopes look down upon the Marshwood Vale. Here I passed out of the chalk into the sandstone; the lanes, worn down by the pack horses of a hundred generations plodding up from the sea on to the dry, hard going of the ridges, were fifteen feet or more below the level of the fields. These trade-worn canyons of red and green upon the flanks of the hills are very dear to me.

I pushed my combination along the ridge until I came to a lane that dived down into the valley. In the dark I could hardly recognize it. I remembered it as a path, deep indeed, but dappled with sunlight; it looked to me now a cleft eroded in desert country, for its bottom was only a cart's width across, and its sides, with the banks, the hedges above them, and young oaks leaping up from the hedge, seemed fifty feet of solid blackness.

I followed it down until another lane crossed at a right angle; this led northwards back to the ridge, where it came up to the surface and branched into two farm tracks. These two tracks appear to be the end and aim of the ancient little highroad, but if you ignore them and walk across an acre of pasture you come to a thick hedge running downhill into the Marshwood Vale. In the heart of this hedge, which I had been seeking all the way from London, the lane reappears. It is not marked on the map. It has not been used, I imagine, for a hundred years.

The deep sandstone cutting, its hedges grown together across the top, is still there; anyone who wishes can dive under the sentinel thorns at the entrance and push his way through and come out in a cross hedge that runs along the foot of the hills. But who would wish? Where there is light the nettles grow as high as a man's shoulder; where there is not, the lane is choked by deadwood. The interior of the double hedge is of no conceivable use to the two farmers whose boundary fence it is, and nobody but an adventurous child would want to explore it.

That, indeed, was the manner of its finding. In love one becomes a child again. A rock is a cliff, a hedge a forest, a stream a river flowing to God knows what Arcadies. This lane was our discovery, a perilous passage made for us to force. It was only the spring of this year that I took her to England, choosing the Dorset downs to give her the first sight and feeling of the land that was to be her home. It was her last sight, too. I cannot say that we had any sense of premonition, unless the tenseness of our love. There is a desperate sweetness between man and woman when the wings of the four horsemen drone inwards from the corners of their world.

It was now my job to prevent children or lovers from pushing through that way again. I worked the sidecar into the thicket and deposited it in the first bare stretch of lane, where the foliage overhead was so thick that nothing grew but ferns. Then I unpacked the billhook and slashed at the deadwood on the inside of the hedges. I jammed the bicycle crosswise between the banks and piled over it a hedge of thorn that would have stopped a lion. At the lower end of the lane the trailing brambles were sufficient defense, and I reënforced them with a dead holly bush. That was all I dared do for the moment. The light was growing, and the strokes of my hook echoing down the hillside.

I cut steps up the western bank and up the inner side of a young elm; it had a top-heavy branch hanging low over the hedge and within reach of the ground on the farther side. This elm became my way in and out of the lane. I spent most of the day up the tree, whence I had a clear view to the north and west. I wanted to watch the routine of the neighboring farms and to see if I had overlooked any danger.

The field on the east of the lane was rough pasture. An hour after dawn the cows came wandering into it over the skyline, having been driven through a gate which I could not see. Farther to the east was a down where the short turf was only good for sheep. To the west, immediately below my tree, was a forty-acre field of wheat stubble, falling away sharply to a great, gray, prosperous farm with generous barns and a duck pond.

It was as quiet a hillside as any in England. The activities of the farm below me were chiefly in the vale. Of the inhabitants of the farm to the east I saw none, only heard the boy who called the cows home in the evening—which he did without ever entering the pasture. In the lanes of the Marshwood Vale there was little traffic. I saw the postman with his motor bike and red sidecar. I saw the school bus and an occasional car, and a couple of milk lorries bobbing about among the trees to collect the cans set out on wooden platforms by the road or on the pebble bottoms of the streams.

The section of lane that I had chosen was so damp and dark that the roots which crept over the earth were white. In the evening I moved my possessions farther down into a tiny glade of bracken where the sun shone for three hours a day. It was protected by the high banks, topped by untrimmed hedges of ash, and buttressed on the east by bushes of blackberry and sloe extending far out into the pasture.

I cut the bracken and scraped out a channel for the stream that ran down the lane after every shower. Then I slung ash poles from bank to bank,—where the distance was a bare six feet,—making a monkey's platform on top of them with twigs and bracken. A day or two later, when I stole some bricks from a tumble-down barn and propped up my poles in the middle, the platform was as strong and dry as a floor of laths.

The eastern bank was full of rabbit holes which ran into the heavy topsoil along the upper level of the sandstone. On this same night I began the work on them which has provided me with shelter from the rain and with a hearth. By morning I had made a hollow about two feet in diameter, and long enough to receive my body. The roof and sides were of earth and the floor of sandstone.

Burrowing into the stone, soft though it was, proved an interminable job; but I found that it was easy to scrape away the surface, and thus lower the floor inch by inch. In a week I had a shelter to be proud of. The roof had a high vault, packed with clay. The drip trickled down the sides and was caught on two projecting ledges which ran the length of the burrow and were channeled to lead the water into the lane. The floor was three feet below the level of the ledges and crossed by short faggots of ash which kept my sleeping bag from resting on damp stone. The hole was very much the size and shape of two large bathtubs, one inverted upon the other.

As soon as my beard had grown I walked to Beaminster and came back with a knapsack full of groceries, a grill, iron spits, and a short pick, one arm of which was shaped like a miniature battle-axe. I do not know what it was for, but it seemed admirably fitted for working sandstone in a confined space. I aroused no particular interest in Beaminster—a mere untidy holiday-maker with dark glasses—and gave out that I was camping on the hills just across the Somerset border. I had a meal in an inn and read the papers. There was only a passing reference to the Aldwych Mystery. The verdict had been murder by a person or persons unknown. When I climbed down the elm into the lane I felt that I had come home—a half-melancholy sense of slippered relaxation.

I began a routine of sleeping by day and working on the burrow at night. Working by day was too dangerous; someone might walk past the hedge while I was underground, and hear the noise of the pick. There was a morning when I was nearly caught by a party of children picking blackberries on the edge of the pasture.

I ran the hole a good ten feet back into the bank and then drove a gallery to the right, intending only to make a hearth; but I found the stone so split by tree roots and easily worked that I ended the gallery with a beehive grotto in which I could comfortably squat. After some difficult surface measurements (by sticking a pole through the hedge and climbing out to see where the tip had got to) I drove a chimney straight upwards into the centre of a blackberry bush. I could then risk a fire at night and cook fresh food.

All this while I had wondered why it was that I had no trouble with dogs. I was prepared so to frighten any dogs which investigated me that they would never come back, but it appeared that something had already scared them for me; dogs gave the lane a wide berth. The cause was Asmodeus. I observed him first as two ears and two eyes apparently attached to a black branch. When I moved my head, the ears vanished, and when I stood up the rest of him had vanished. I put out some scraps of bully beef behind the branch, and an hour later they too had vanished.

One morning when I had just gone to bed, and was lying with my head out of the burrow chewing biscuits, he slunk on to my platform and watched me, tail gripping the ground, head savage and expectant. He was a thin and powerful tomcat, black, but with many of his hairs ending in a streak of silver, like a smooth-headed Mediterranean beauty just turning gray. I don't think that in his case it was age, but a freak of coloring inherited from some silver ancestor. I threw him a biscuit; he was out of sight while it was still in the air. It had gone, of course, when I woke up, and so had half a tin of bully beef.

He began to consider me as a curious show for his leisure hours, sitting motionless at a safe distance of ten feet. In a few more days he would snatch food from my hand, hissing and bristling if I dared advance the hand to touch him. It was then that I named him Asmodeus, for he could make himself appear the very spirit of hatred and malignity.

I won his friendship with a pheasant's head, attached to the end of a string. I have noticed that what cats most appreciate in a human being is not the ability to produce food,—which they take for granted, —but his or her entertainment value. Asmodeus took to his toy enthusiastically. In another week he permitted me to stroke him, producing a raucous purr but, in order to save his face, pretending to be asleep. Soon afterwards he started a habit of sleeping in the burrow with me during the day, and hunting while I worked at night. But bully beef was the meat he preferred; no doubt it gave him the maximum nourishment for the minimum effort.

I made two more journeys to Beaminster, walking there and back at night and spending the intervening day—after doing my shopping—hidden on a hillside of gorse. From the first expedition I returned with food and paraffin for the Primus; from the second with a glue pot and a small door which I had ordered from the local carpenter.

This door or lid fitted exactly into the entrance to my burrow. On the inside was a stout handle by which I could lift and jam it into position; on the outside was camouflage. I sprinkled over a coating of glue a rough layer of sandstone dust, and on that stuck an arrangement of twigs and dead plants, some of which trailed over the edges of the door so that they masked the outline when it was in place.

As soon as I was satisfied with the door, I practised a drill for effacing myself completely from the lane. The platform was dismantled, the bricks scattered, and the poles thrust into the hedge; my latrine and rubbish pit were covered by a dead thorn, and I myself was inside in the burrow, all in ten minutes. Anyone forcing a way into the lane might or might not notice that some gypsy had been camping there, but could not guess that the place was inhabited at the moment. The only sign was an apparent rabbit hole, a bit artificial in spite of the droppings I scattered round the entrance, which gave me air while I was shut in the burrow.

The tandem bicycle could not be seen. I took it apart and propped the pieces against the bank, covering them with a mass of dead vegetation. The sidecar was a continual nuisance. I couldn't bury it or take it to bits, and the bright aluminum shone through the brushwood I heaped on it. It was so new and strong that no one could be deceived into thinking it innocently abandoned. Eventually I had to spend a night tearing down my defenses in order to get the thing out of the lane, and half wheeling, half carrying it down to the vale.

I didn't know what on earth to do with it. Wherever I put it, it might be found, and the more remote the place, the more the question as to how it came there. Nor could I waste any time; if I met anyone, he would see my gleaming and awkward burden long before I saw him. Finally I chucked it into a sheltered stream, hoping that the action of water would destroy it; I couldn't.

I am now prepared to spend the first half of the winter where I am, subject to the bottom of the lane being still invisible when the leaves have fallen—which seems probable. I cannot be seen and, if I am careful, I cannot be heard. I avoid chopping wood and risk the noise of my billhook only on one night a week when I fill the inner chamber with brushwood and burn it. This dries out the whole den and gives me a layer of hot ashes on which I can grill at one time whatever store of meat I have.

My dry and tinned food is sufficient, for I have been largely living on the country. There are cobnuts, sloes, and blackberries at my door, and from time to time I extract a bowl of milk from a red cow; she has a great liking for salt, and can be tempted to stand quietly among the domes and ramps of blackberry bush that flank the eastern hedge.

My catapult keeps me supplied with the rabbits I want. It's an inefficient weapon. As one whose hobby is the craft of ballistics, ancient and modern, I ought to be ashamed of myself for depending on rubber when a far better weapon could be made from twisted hair or cord. But I have a distaste for the whole business. I have to compel myself to shoot a rabbit in these days. After all, it is perfectly justifiable to kill for food.

I am not content, in spite of the fact that this Robinson Crusoe existence ought to suit my temperament pretty well. There is not, any longer, enough to do. I am not affected by loneliness or by the memories of this place. Asmodeus helps there. He is a ridiculous outlet for a lot of sentimentality. I am uncertain of myself. Even this journal, which I was sure would exorcise my misgivings, has settled nothing.

2

I start on this exercise book again, for I dare not leave my thoughts uncontrolled. Sitting below the ventilator, I have just enough light. It is good to hold the white page before it. My eyes as well as my mind long for some object on which to concentrate.

A month ago I wrote that I did not feel lonely. It was true, and it accounts for my folly. The essence of safety is that a hunted man should feel lonely; then his whole being throws out tendrils, as it were, towards the outer world. He becomes swift to imagine, sensitive as an animal to danger. But I, I was sunk in a gentle, moody preoccupation with my cat and my conscience. Dear God, I might as well have been a retired company director living in a solitary cottage and mildly worried whether his peculations were discovered!

I committed the supreme folly of writing to Saul to send me books. Once my earth was finished, I had too much leisure and no use for it. Besides all my other incoherent dissatisfactions, questions of sex were worrying me.

For me, sex has never been a problem. Like most normal people, I have been able to suppress my desires without difficulty. When there was no need to suppress them, my appreciation has been keen, but my emotions not deeply involved. Indeed, I begin to think that I have never known truly passionate love. I have no doubt that, say, an Italian would consider me the perfect type of frigid Anglo-Saxon.

Why then my strong resistance to coming to this lane? I take it that I showed a resistance, since I refused to admit to myself that this was my destination until I was within twenty miles of it—and that, though the double hedge was an excellent hiding place which I was eager to reach. Well, I suppose I wished to save myself pain. But I cannot even remember her face, except that her eyes appeared violet against the tawny skin. And that I know to be a trick of memory, for I have often looked for violet eyes in man and woman and never seen them. I repeat, I was never in love. The proof of it is that I so calmly accepted the destruction of my happiness. I was prepared for it. I begged her to stay in England, or at least, if she felt it her duty to return, to temper her politics with discretion. When I heard that she was dead, I really suffered very little.

I wrote to Saul for books: meaty stuff which I could reread throughout the winter, penetrating with each reading a little further into what the author meant rather than what he said. I did not, of course, sign the letter, but wrote in block capitals, asking him to send the books to Professor Foulsham at a sub post office in Lyme Regis. Foulsham was (and still is, I trust) the professor of Christian Ethics in my day, and it seemed to me that my hairy face looked rather like his. It probably didn't; but it is always well to choose and think oneself into a part.

I did not wish to use Beaminster any more. While the holiday season was still on, my three visits and my account of myself naturally passed unchallenged, but a man who claimed to be still camping on the downs in the gathering gales of October would start any amount of gossip about where he was and why. I picked Lyme Regis because the little town had a winter colony of visitors and strangers presumably attracted no attention.

I had a straggly beard that was quite as convincing as most of those one sees in Bloomsbury. My eye, as a result of continual washing in dew and lotion, was no longer swollen; it looked odd, but more like a bad glass eye than a wounded. There was nothing in my appearance of a harmless and rather dirty eccentric to arouse the curiosity of the police. As for my other enemies, they had then no more reason to search Dorset than Kamchatka.

I walked to the outskirts of the town in a couple of hours before dawn, and concealed myself during the day in the shrubbery of a large empty house. In the evening I called at the post office, introduced myself as Professor Foulsham, and asked if a parcel of books had come for me. It was one of those small, dark shops that sell stationery and tobacco, and have a back room with the inevitable pot of tea stewing by the fire.

"Sorry! There is no parcel in that name," said the postmistress.

I asked if there were a letter.

"I think there may be," she said archly, and reached under the counter for half a dozen letters.

A woman who had been examining a row of dressmaking magazines hung on strings across the window said good-night and opened the door, letting the last of the evening light into the shop. The postmistress stared at me as if her eyes had stuck—shoe-button eyes they were, sharp and nervous.

"There—there's more letters in the back room," she stammered, and edged through the door into the parlor, still watching me.

I heard frantic whispering, and a girl's voice say: "Oo, Ma, I couldn't do that!"—followed by a resounding slap.

A schoolgirl of about twelve dashed out of the back room, dived under the flap of the counter, and with one terrified glance at me bolted down the road. The postmistress remained at the threshold of her room, still fascinated by my appearance.

I didn't like the look of things, but what was wrong I couldn't imagine. I was wearing my reach-me-down suit and a muffler, and had succeeded, I thought, in impersonating a weatherproof don on his hardy way from a tea party. I had left my glasses at home, believing that I should attract less attention without those tremendous blinkers. As a matter of fact it would have made no difference whether I wore them or not.

"Now, madam," I said severely, "if you can bring yourself to attend to public business, I should like my letter."

"Don't you dare come near me!" she squeaked, shrinking back into the doorway.

It was no time for respecting His Majesty's mails. She had dropped the letters behind the wire enclosure which protected her cash and stamps. I reached over it, and took an envelope addressed to Professor Foulsham.

"Kindly satisfy yourself, madam," I said, seeing that she was mustering courage to scream, "that this letter is actually addressed to me. I regret that it will be my duty to report your extraordinary behavior. Good afternoon."

This pomposity, delivered in a most professorial tone, held her with her mouth open long enough for me to move with dignity out of the shop. I jumped on a bus that was running uphill out of the town, and got off it ten minutes later at a crossroads on the Devon and Dorset border. Safe for the moment in the thick cover of a spinney I opened my letter, hoping it would tell me why a description of me had been circulated to Dorset post offices.

The letter was typewritten and unsigned, but Saul had made his identity certain. He wrote in some such words as these:—

> The parrots paid the fisherman. I must not send you books in case they are found and traced to the buyer. If you know nothing of a caravan trailer, write to me again and I will risk it.
>
> About two weeks ago the police tried to find the owner of a trailer near Weymouth. It was a routine inquiry. The camp site was deserted, and the landlord did not wish to be held responsible for damage done by children who had broken a window and were climbing in and out of the trailer.
>
> The police established that the owner had bought and let the caravan on the same evening, that this was the evening after a man had been found killed in the Aldwych station, and that the owner wore dark glasses.
>
> They then got in touch with a family at Leicester who had rented the thing. They learned that the owner had taken, in exchange for rent, a tandem bicycle and baby's sidecar, and that he had told a lot of complicated untruths to account for himself.
>
> A woman in Weymouth from whom he bought food is sure that under his glasses one eye was worse than the other, but no one else noticed this.
>
> The man is wanted for murder, but if the case, as I think it must, depends solely on doubtful identification by a ticket collector, no jury would convict. And let me very urgently impress it on you that if the man were a person of good character, if he pleaded self-defense and gave good reason for the attack made upon him, the case would never go to court. I earnestly advise this course. The dead man was a thoroughly undesirable fellow, suspected of being in the pay of a foreign power.
>
> The owner of the trailer is certain to be found and detained, for he is known to be camping or living in the open on the

downs near Beaminster. A person who had grown a beard but otherwise answered his description was seen three times at Beaminster before any police inquiries had begun.

I have naturally kept myself fully informed of the Aldwych investigation, and you can take it as certain that the police know as much as I have told you and no more.

He ended with a request to me to burn the letter immediately, which I did.

I had little fear of my burrow being discovered, and my first reaction was to thank heaven that I now knew the worst and had been warned in time. But then I perceived the full extent of my folly, and its consequences; a desultory search which had spread over the whole of Dorset, and especially over the Dorset downs miles to the northeast of where I really was, would now be concentrated on the limited patch of country between Beaminster and Lyme Regis.

That part of me which was unconsciously looking after my safety kept count of the minutes (for I dared not stay where I was more than very few) while my conscious mind lived through hours of muddled and panicky thinking. I quite seriously considered taking Saul's advice and telling the police my real name and enough of my trip abroad to account for my disappearance and for the attack upon me in the Aldwych. I forgot that I had worse enemies than the police.

This longing to surrender was very insistent at the time, yet never really came out of the world of dreams. The knowledge that one pack was on my trail had only temporarily excluded fear of the other. There is no animal but man which can be hunted simultaneously by two different packs without the two becoming one; so it is not surprising that all one's sagacity should be at fault.

Reason took over. If I resumed my identity, death or disgrace was certain. And if some unbalanced idiots chose to regard me as a martyr, I had the makings of a first-class international incident. It was my duty to kill myself—or, easier, arrange for myself to be killed incognito—rather than seek protection.

The police were at the crossroads ten minutes after I got off the bus. Neither they nor the postmistress's daughter had wasted any time. They switched the headlights of two cars into the spinney where I was, and crashed into the undergrowth.

The immediate future didn't worry me at all. It was already dusk, and I knew that in the dark I could pass through a multitude of policemen and possibly take their boots off as well. I moved quietly away in front of them until I had to break cover, either by crossing the road or by taking to the downs on the west. I didn't want to cross the road—it meant that I should lead the chase into my own country—nor was there any point in stealing away into unknown difficulties. I decided to stay in contact with this lot of police—about five couple of them there were—so I jumped on to the stone wall that bounded the spinney and pretended to remain there indecisively. At last one of them saw me and gave a holloa. I broke away into Devonshire down a long, barren slope.

I was magnificently fit as a result of my life in the open and the brisk autumn air. I remember how easily my muscles answered the call I made on them. By God, in all this immobility and carrion thought it does me good to think of the man I was!

I intended to lie still wherever there was a scrap of not too obvious cover and to let the hunt pass me; but I didn't reckon on a young and active inspector who shed his overcoat and seemed able to do the quarter mile in well under sixty seconds. As we neared the bottom of the slope, I had no chance of playing hide and seek in the gorse or vanishing into a hedge. The lead of a hundred and fifty yards which, in the gathering dusk, I had considered ample for my purpose had been reduced to fifty.

I had to keep running—either for a gate that led into another open field, or for a gate beyond which I saw a muddy farm track with water faintly gleaming in the deep hoof marks. I chose the mud, and vaulted the gate into eighteen inches of it. I was bogged, but so would he be, and then endurance could count; he wouldn't be able to give me any more of his cinder-track stuff. I pounded along the track, spattering as much mud as a horse over myself and the hedges. He was now twenty yards behind, and wasting his breath by yelling at me to stop and come quietly.

While he was still in the wet clay, and the rest of the police had just entered it, I pulled out on to a hard surface. The wall of a farmhouse loomed up ahead; it was built in the usual shape of an E without the centre bar, the house at the back, the barns forming the two wings. It seemed an excellent place for the police to surround and search; they would be kept busy for the next few hours, and the cordon between Lyme Regis and Beaminster, through which I had to pass, would be relaxed.

I looked back. The inspector had dropped back a little; the rest of the hunt I could hear plunging and cursing in the mud. I put on a spurt and dashed round the lower bar of the E. Knowing the general layout of English farms, I was sure that my wanted patch of not too obvious cover would be right at the corner, and it was. I dropped flat on my face in a pattern of mounds and shadows. I couldn't see myself of what they consisted. My head landed in a manure heap with a smell of disinfectant—they had probably been dosing the sheep for worms—and my elbow on an old millstone; there were hurdles, and firewood; the dominating shadow was that of an old mounting block.

The inspector raced round the corner after me and into the open barns, flashing his light on the carts, the piles of fodder, and the cider barrels. As soon as he passed me, I shot out of the yard, crouching and silent, and dropped against the outer wall. I hadn't any luck in minor matters. This time I put my face in a patch of nettles.

The police, a full half minute behind us, dashed into the yard, rallying to their inspector. He was shouting to them to come on, boys, that he had the beggar cornered. The farm and its dogs woke up to the fact that there was a criminal in their midst, and I left the police to their search; it was probably long and exhausting, for there was not, from their point of view, the remotest possibility of my escaping from the three-sided trap into which I had run.

I had no intention of going home. There could be no peace for me in the lane until I had laid a false scent and knew that the police were following it to the exclusion of all others.

First: I had to make a false hiding place and satisfy the police that there I had lived, so that they wouldn't do too thorough a search between Beaminster and Lyme Regis.

Second: I must persuade the police that I had left the district for good.

I followed the main road, along which I had come in the bus, back towards Lyme Regis. I say I followed it,—I had to, since I wasn't sure of my direction in the dark,—but I didn't walk on it. I moved parallel, climbing a fence or forcing a hedge about every two hundred yards for three solid miles. It's a major feat of acrobatics to follow a main road without ever setting foot on it, and I began to feel infernally tired.

The high ground to the east of Beaminster, where a new den had to be faked, was twenty miles away. I decided to jump a lorry on the steep hill between Lyme Regis and Charmouth where I could be pretty sure of getting a lift unknown to the driver.

A mile or so outside the town I cut down into a valley and up the other side towards the steep hairpin bend where heavy traffic had to slow to walking pace. I thought this an ingenious and original scheme, but the police, more mechanically-minded than myself, had thought of it already. At the steepest part of the road was a sergeant with a bicycle, keeping careful watch.

I cursed him heartily and silently, for now I had to go down again to the bottom of the valley, draw him off, and return to the road. My knees were very weary, but there was nothing else for it. I stood in a little copse at the bottom and started yelling bloody murder in a terrified soprano—"Help!" and "Let me go!" and "God, won't anybody come?" and then a succession of hysterical screams that were horrible to hear and quite false. The screams of a terrified woman are rhythmical and wholly unnatural, and had I imitated them correctly the sergeant would have thought me a ghost or some fool yodeling.

I heard the whine of brakes hastily applied, and several dim figures ran down into the valley as I ran up. I peered over the hedge. The sergeant had gone. A grocer's van and a sports car stood empty by the side of the road. I gave up my original idea of boarding a lorry and took the sports car. I reckoned that I should have the safe use of it for at least twenty-five minutes—ten minutes before the party gave up their search of the wooded bottom, five minutes before they could reach a telephone, and ten more minutes before patrols and police cars could be warned.

Over my head and round my beard I wrapped my muffler. Then I pulled out in front of a noisy milk truck that was banging up the hill, in case the owner should recognize the engine of his own car. It was a fine car. I did the nine twisting miles to Bridport in eleven minutes and ten miles along the Dorchester road in ten minutes. I hated that speed at the time, and I'm ashamed of it. No driver has a right to average more than forty; if he wants to terrify his fellows there are always a few wars going on, and either side will be glad to let him indulge his pleasure and get some healthy exercise at the same time.

Three miles from Dorchester I turned to the left and abandoned the car in a neglected footpath, no wider than itself, between high hedges. I stuck ten pounds in the owner's license with penciled apologies (written in block capitals with my left hand) and my sincere hope that the notes would cover his night's lodging and any incidental loss.

It was now midnight. I crossed the down, slunk unseen round a village, and entered the Sydling Valley, which, by the map, appeared to be as remote a dead end as any in Dorset. I spent the rest of the night in a covered stack, sleeping warmly and soundly between the hay and the corrugated iron. The chances of the police finding the car till daylight were negligible.

After a breakfast of blackberries I struck north along the watershed. There was a main road a quarter of a mile to the west. I watched the posting of constables at two crossings. Down in the valley a police car was racing towards Sydling. They made no attempt to watch the grass tracks, being convinced, I think, that criminals from London never go far from roads. No doubt Scotland Yard had exact statistics showing what my next move would be. My theft of a car had put me into the proper gangster pigeonhole—from their point of view, a blatant, self-advertising gangster.

The downs on both sides of the Sydling Valley were country after my own heart: patches of gorse and patches of woodland, connected by straggling hedges which gave me cover from the occasional shepherd or farmer but were not thick enough to compel me to climb them. I assumed that all high ground had been picketed and reckoned—unnecessarily, I expect—on field glasses as well as eyes.

The valley ended in a great bowl of turf and woodland, crossed by no road and two miles from the village. Dry bottoms ran up from the head of the valley like the sticks of a fan. In any one of them I might very reasonably have been camping since September.

That which I chose had a wood of hazel on one side and of oak on the other. Between them the brown bracken grew waist high, and through the bracken ran a ride of turf upon which the rabbits were feeding and playing. The glade smelt of fox, turf, and rabbit, the sweet musk that lingers in dry valleys where the dew is heavy and the water flows a few feet underground. The only signs of humanity were two ruined cottages, some bundles of cut hazel rods, and a few cartridge cases scattered about the turf.

On the green track that led to the cottages tall thistles grew unbroken, showing that few ever passed that way. The gardens had been swamped by wild vegetation, but an apple tree was bearing fruit in spite of the bramble and ivy which grabbed at the low, heavily laden branches. That invaded tree and garden reminded me of the tropics.

The cottages were roofless, but in one was a hearth that ran two feet back into the thick masonry. I built a rough wall of fallen stone around it, and succeeded in making a fairly convincing nest for a fugitive, drier and more airy than my own but not so safe. While I was working I saw no one but a farmer riding through the bracken on the opposite ridge. I knew what he was looking for—a cow that had just calved. I had run across her earlier in the day, and had been encouraged by this sure sign that the farm was large and full of cover.

When night fell I lit a fire, piling it fiercely up the chimney so that the ash and soot would appear the result of many fires. While it burned I lay in the hazelwood, in case anyone should be attracted by the light and smoke. Then I sat over the ashes dozing and shivering till dawn. I was still wearing my town suit, inadequate for the cold and mist of an October night.

It was hard to make the place look as if I had lived there for weeks. I distributed widely and messily the corpse of a rabbit that was polluting the atmosphere a little way up the valley. I fouled and trampled the interior of the cottage, stripped the apple tree, and strewed apple cores and nutshells over the ground. A pile of feathers from a wood pigeon and a rook provided further evidence of my diet. Plucking the ancient remains of a hawk's dinner was the nastiest job of all.

I spent the day sitting in the bracken and waiting for the police, but they refused to find me. Possibly they thought that I had made for the coast. There was, after all, no earthly reason why I should be in the Sydling Valley more than anywhere else.

I put the night to good use. First I collected a dozen empty tins from a rubbish heap and piled them in a corner of the cottage; then I went down to sleeping Sydling and did a smash-and-grab raid on the village shop. My objects were to draw the attention of those obstinate police, and to get hold of some dried fish. In this sporting country some damned fool was sure to try bloodhounds on my scent.

In the few seconds at my disposal I couldn't find any kippers or bloaters, but I did get four tins of sardines and a small bag of fertilizer. I raced for the downs while the whole village squawked and muttered and slammed its doors. It was probably the first time in all the history of Sydling that a sudden noise had been heard at night.

As soon as I was back in my cottage I pounded the sardines and fertilizer together, tied up the mixture in the bag, and rubbed the corner of the hearth where I had sat and the wall I had built. Trailing the bag on the end of a string, I laid a drag through the hazels, over the heather on the hilltop, round the oak wood, and into the bracken overlooking the cottage. There I remained, and got some sleep.

In spite of all the assistance I had given them, it was nearly midday before the police discovered the cottages. They moved around in them as respectfully as in church, dusting all likely surfaces for fingerprints. There weren't any. I had never taken off my gloves. They must have thought they were dealing with an experienced criminal.

Half an hour later a police car came bumping over the turf and decanted an old friend of mine into the cottages. I had quite forgotten that he was now Chief Constable of Dorset. If he had looked closely at those feathers he would have seen at once that a hawk, not a man, had done the killing; but naturally he was leaving the criminology to Scotland Yard, and they weren't likely to go into the fine point of whether the birds had met their death through the plumage of back or breast.

The dry bottom began to look like a meet of the Cattistock. The couple of bloodhounds that I had expected turned up, towing a bloodthirsty maiden lady in their wake. She was encouraging them with yawps and had feet so massive that I could see them clearly at two hundred yards—great brogued boats navigating a green sea. She was followed by half the village of Sydling and a sprinkling of local gentry. Two fellows had turned out on horseback. I felt they should have paid me the compliment of pink coats.

Away went the bloodhounds on the trail of the fertilized sardines, and away I went too; I had a good half hour's law while they followed my bag through the hazels and heather. I crossed the main road—a hasty dash from ditch to ditch while the constable on watch was occupied with the distant beauty of the sea—and slid along the hedges into a great headland of gorse above Cattistock. There I wove so complicated a pattern that boat-footed Artemis must have thought her long-eared darlings were on the line of a hare. I skirted Cattistock and heard their lovely carillon most appropriately chime "D'Ye Ken John Peel" at my passage, followed by "Lead, Kindly Light." It was half-past five and the dusk was falling. I waded into the Frome, passed under the Great Western Railway, and paddled upstream for a mile or so, taking cover in the rushes whenever there was anyone to see me. Then I buried the sardines in the gravel at the bottom of the river, and proceeded under my own scent.

I have not the faintest idea what hounds can or cannot do on the trail of a man. I doubt if they could have run on my true scent from the cottages to my lane, but I had to guard against the possibility. Looking back on those two days, it cheers me to see the healthy insolence in all I did.

I moved slowly westwards, following the lanes but taking no risks —slowly, deliberately slowly, in the technique that I have developed since I became an outlaw. It was nearly four in the morning when I swung myself on to the elm branch that did duty as my front door, and climbed down into the lane. I felt Asmodeus brush against my legs but I could not see him in that safe pit of blackness. That I consider darkness safety sets me, in itself alone, apart from my fellows. Darkness is safety only on condition that all one's enemies are human.

I ate a tremendous breakfast of beef and oatmeal, and set aside my town suit to be made into bags and lashings—all it was now good for. I was relieved to be done with it; it reminded me too forcibly of the newspapers' "well-dressed man." Then I slipped into my bag, unwearing, damp-proof citadel of luxury, and slept till nightfall.

When I awoke I felt sufficiently strong and rested to attempt the second feint: to convince the police that I had left the county for good. This was rash, but necessary. I still think it was necessary. If I hadn't gone the bicycle would be in the lane, and the evidence of my presence here a deal stronger than it is.

By the light of two candles—for the battery of the head lamp had run down—I turned to the unholy job of reassembling the tandem. It was after midnight before I had the machine, entire and unpunctured, clear of the lane, and the thorns replaced in a sufficiently forbidding pattern.

I dressed myself in the warmest of my working clothes, tearing off all distinguishing marks and the maker's name. I put a flask of whiskey in my inside breast pocket, and took plenty of food. I could be away for days without worrying. Even the ventilation hole was no longer suspicious, for Asmodeus used it when the door was jammed home and had given the entrance the proper sandy, claw-worn look. I think he always treated the den as his headquarters in my absence, but, being a cleanly cat, he never left a sign of his tenancy.

I pedaled cautiously through the lanes of the Marshwood Vale and up into the hills beyond. The byroads were empty. Before crossing any main road I put the bicycle in the hedge and explored on foot and belly. Once I was nearly caught. I crawled almost into a constable whom I mistook, as he towered above me, for a tree stump. It was the fault of the massive overcoat. The same error, I believe, is frequently made by dogs.

By dawn I was past Crewkerne and well into Somerset. It was now time to let myself be seen and to put the police on a trail that obviously led north to Bristol or some little port on the Bristol Channel. I shot through two scattered villages where I gave the early risers a sight to look at and talk about for the rest of the day; then on into the Fosse Way, speeding along the arrow-straight road to Bristol and drawing cheers and laughter from the passing lorry drivers. I was too incredible a sight to be thought a criminal—muddy, bearded, and riding a tandem, as odd a creature as that amusing tramp who used to do tricks on the Halls with a collapsible bicycle.

After showing myself over a mile of main road I was more than ready to hide the bicycle for good and myself till nightfall, but the country on both sides of the great Roman highway was open and unpleasantly short of cover; indeed much of it was below the level of the road. I pedaled on and on in the hope of reaching a wood or heath or quarry. It was all flat land with well-trimmed hedges and shallow drains.

By the side of the road was an empty field of cabbages—one of those melancholy fields with a cinder track leading into them and a tumble-down hut leaning against a pile of refuse. Close to the hut and at a stone's throw from the road was a derelict car. When the only traffic was a cluster of black dots a mile or two away, I lifted the tandem on to my shoulder, to avoid leaving a track, and staggered into the shelter of the hut. I smashed the two sets of handlebars so that the bicycle would lie flat on the ground, and shoved it under the car, afterwards restoring the trampled weeds to a fairly upright position. It will not be found until the car moulders away above it, and then will be indistinguishable from the other rusty debris.

I now had to take cover myself. The hut was too obvious a place. The hedges were inadequate. I dared not risk so much as a quarter-mile walk. There was nothing for it but to lie on the clay among those blasted cabbages. In the middle of the field I was perfectly safe.

It was a disgusting day. The flats of England on a gray morning remind me of the classical hell—a featureless landscape where the peewits twitter and the half-alive remember hills and sunshine. And the asphodel of this Hades is the cabbage. To lie among cabbages in my own country should have been nothing after the pain and exposure I suffered during my escape; but it was summer then and it was autumn now. To lie still on a clay soil in a gentle drizzle was exasperating. But safe! If the owner of that vile field had been planting, he'd have stuck his dibber into me before noticing that I wasn't mud.

I was so bored that I was thankful when in the early afternoon a car stopped at the gate into the field, and a party of three policemen crunched up the cinder path. I had been expecting them for hours; they knew that I had been seen on the Fosse Way in the morning, and since then nowhere, so it was certain they would search every possible hiding place along the highway and its byroads. They looked into the hut and into that decaying car. I kept my face well down between my arms, so I don't know whether they even glanced at the cabbage field. Probably not. It was so open and innocent.

I shivered and grumbled for an eternity in that repellent field. I tried to find comfort in infinitesimal changes of position; there was none to be had, but it occupied my mind to change, for example, my head from elbow to forearm or to twist my feet from resting on the ankles to resting on the insteps. I analyzed the comparative discomforts of the various movements open to me. I made patterns out of the avenues of cabbages that spread in a quadrant before my eyes. I tortured myself (for even torture may be a diversion) by thinking of the flask of whiskey in my inner breast pocket and refusing to allow myself to touch it. I knew damn well that I dared not touch it; the wriggles necessary to get at it and the flash of the nickel plate might have given me away. There were plenty of cars and cyclists on the road, and the owner of the field, presumably advised that his hut had received a visit from the police, was leaning against it in the company of two friends and looking over his possessions with ruminative pride. I don't suppose there had been so much excitement in the villages since Monmouth's troops were flying from Sedgemoor, foundering their horses in that awful ploughland, and crawling in the muck like me and the worms.

At last the cabbage man went home to his soggy tea and dusk fell and I stood up. I drank a quarter of my flask and struck eastwards away from the road. Cross-country travel in the dark was nearly impossible. I felt my way along drains and hedges, usually circumnavigating three sides of a field before I found the way out of it—and when I did find the way out, it invariably led me into a village or back into the cabbage field.

After an hour or two of this maze, I struck straight across country, climbing or wading whatever obstacles were in my way. This was sheer obstinacy. I was wet to the armpits; I was leaving a track like a hippopotamus; and, since I didn't know where I was heading, it was all objectless. Finally I took to the lanes—or roads, I should call them, for they were narrow ribbons of Tarmac with low hedges. There I spent most of the time pretending to be a manure heap, for the roads were relatively crowded with pedestrians. The average was certainly one person for every two hundred yards. Evening entertainment in that dreary vale consists of pub-crawling to the next village and back again. If you haven't the money for beer, you lie under a mackintosh with a girl. At normal times I have only sympathy for so firm an attachment to the preliminaries of procreation, but the groups by the wayside were not recognizable as human until I had practically stepped on them. My own county is gayer and more pagan. When it rains we do our love-making in the tithe barn or the church porch or under the steps at the back of the Women's Institute, and we don't care who sees us. Trespassers are expected to guffaw and look away.

I should have been forced to spend another day in the cabbage field if I had not stumbled across a railway line which I followed towards Yeovil, stepping quietly from sleeper to sleeper. Two railway employees passed me walking homewards, but their boots on the ballast gave me ample warning of their approach. I avoided them, and the one train, by lying down at the bottom of the embankment.

A denser darkness on the horizon warned me that I was nearing the massed little houses of Yeovil. It was then about two in the morning, and the byroads were deserted; so I turned south towards the hills. When the slow autumn dawn turned night to mist I could feel the short turf under my feet and see the gleam of chalk and flint wherever man or beast had scraped the escarpment.

I drank at the piped spring which fed a cattle trough, and took refuge in the heart of a wild half acre of gorse and heather. Here I startled an old dog fox, and startled myself, when I came to consider it, a deal more. I flatter myself I am able to get as near to game as any civilized man and most savages; indeed it has been my favorite pursuit since I was given my first air rifle at the age of six, and told—an injunction which with a single exception I have obeyed—that I must never point a gun at anyone. Yet I should certainly not have backed myself to approach within three yards of a fox, even knowing where he was and deliberately stalking him. Oddly enough, it worried me that I had come to move with such instinctive quietness. I was already on the lookout for all signs of demoralization—morbidly anxious to assure myself that I was losing none of my humanity.

I chose a south bank where short heather was gradually overcoming the turf, laying black springs under its green mattress. The sun promised a mild heat, and I spread out my coat and leather jacket to dry. I dozed sweetly, awakening whenever a bird perched on the gorse or a rabbit scuttered through the runways, but instantly and easily falling asleep again.

A little after midday I woke up for good. There was nothing immediately visible to account for the sudden clarity of my senses, so I peered over the gorse. Upwind were two men strolling along the crest of the hill. One was a sergeant of the Dorset constabulary; the other a small farmer—to judge by the fact that he carried an old-fashioned hammer gun. They passed me within ten yards, the policeman pressing down with firm feet as if searching for a pavement beneath that silent and resilient turf, the farmer plodding along with the slightly bent knees of a man who seldom walks on the flat.

I decided to follow these two solemn wanderers and hear what they had to say. They were discussing me, since the farmer had remarked, apropos of nothing: " 'Tis my belief he was over to Zumerset all the time"—a final and definite pronouncement as of one who should say: I believe he went to South America and died there.

It's curious how much cover there is on the chalk downs. A body of men couldn't move unseen, but a single man can. In the vales of southern England, though they look like woodland from the top of hills, hedges and fences compel the fugitive to go the way of other men, and sooner or later he is forced, as I was, to lie down and pray for the earth to cover him. But on the bare—apparently bare—downs there are prehistoric pits and trenches, tree-grown tumps, gorse and the upper edge of coverts, lonely barns and thickets of thorn. And the hedges, where there are any, are either miniature forests or full of gaps.

It was easy to catch them up. They went at an easy pace, stopping every now and then to exchange a few words. The weighty business of conversation could not be disturbed by movement. At last they settled on a gate and leaned over it, contemplating twenty acres of steely-green mangel-wurzels which sloped down to the golden hedges of the vale. I crawled the length of a dry ditch and came within earshot.

The sergeant finished a long mumble with the word "foreigners," pronounced loudly and aggressively.

"Err, they bastards!" said the farmer.

The sergeant considered this judicially, turning with deliberation towards his companion and me. He was a uniformed servant of the state, and thus, I imagine, predisposed to diplomacy.

"I wouldn't 'ardly go so far as that," he said. "Not that I 'old with furr'ners—but I don't know as I'd go so far as that."

There was a deal more conversation which I couldn't hear because neither of them was sufficiently excited to raise his voice. The farmer, I think, must have denied that any foreigners ever came to Dorset. The suggestion that they did was almost a criticism on his county.

"I tell 'ee there's been furr'ners askin' for 'm," said the sergeant. "And I knows that, because the inspector says to me, 'e says—" Then his voice trailed away again.

"Mrs. Maydoone says 'e were a proper gent," chuckled the farmer.

The sergeant chuckled in sympathy and then showed offended dignity.

"Told me she couldn't 'ardly call 'im to mind, she did! Don't 'ee come asking questions, she says, as if the Bull were a nasty common public 'ouse, she says."

There was more laughter which turned to a full-throated giggle as both remembered the opulent Mrs. Maydoone and dug each other in their own less admirably covered ribs. She was a respectably eager widow who owned the inn in Beaminster where I had lunched. The doctors, she told me, had never seen anything like Mr. Maydoone's kidneys outside a London hospital.

My two friends marched off across the downs, while I remained in the ditch digesting the scraps of news. I was perturbed, but not surprised. It was natural enough that my enemies should get possession of Scotland Yard's clues to my whereabouts. If dear old Holy George couldn't manage it, then one of their newspaper correspondents in London could. It wasn't confidential information.

I returned to my form in the heart of the gorse. The early afternoon sun had a dying bite of summer in it, and I was glowing with the exertion of my stalk. At dusk I ate the last of my provisions and drank again at the spring. By good fortune I left untouched the half flask of whiskey that remained. I feared its effect—slight, but enough to give me confidence when my safe return to the lane and my peace of mind throughout the winter depended on moving now with the utmost caution.

I kept to the hilltops, following the ridgeways southwards till they ended on Eggardon Down. There I was lost. There was not a star showing, and, although I knew I was on Eggardon, I could not tell from what point of the compass I had immediately approached it; the tracks, ancient and modern, green and metaled, crossed and switched like the lines in a goods yard. At last I found myself in the outer ditch of the camp and, to make sure of my orientation, walked halfway round the huge circuit of earthworks until I could see far below me the faint lights of a town which had to be Bridport.

The emptiness was infinity, darkness with distance but no shape. The southwest wind swirled over the turf, and the triple line of turf ramparts hung over me like smooth seas traveling through the night. I might have been upon the eastern slopes of the Andes with an empty continent of forest at my feet. I could have wished it so. There I should have felt alone, secure, an impregnable outpost of humanity.

Eggardon affected me as a city. The camp was haunted. I didn't feel the presence of its builders, those unknown imperialists who set their cantonments on the high chalk, but I was suddenly terrified of the sleeping towns and villages that lay at my feet and clustered, waiting, around empty Eggardon. A gray mare and her foal leaped monstrously out of a ditch and galloped away. A thornbush just beyond the easy range of sight hovered between reality and a vision; it was round and black like the mouth of a tunnel. Guilt was on me. I had killed without object, and my fellows were all around me waiting lest I should kill again.

I stumbled down to the valley, compelling myself to move slowly and to look straight ahead. If there had been any living being upon Eggardon I should have walked into him. I was obsessed by this sense of all southern England crowding in upon the hill.

As I dodged and darted home from lane to lane and farmhouse to farmhouse, I couldn't get the sidecar out of my head. I wanted to know if it had been disturbed. Should the police have found it, and taken it from the stream for identification, they might disbelieve the evidence of the cottages—which was good only so long as no one questioned it—and search the country where I really was.

Although it was only a field away from a well-frequented byroad, the sidecar was in a safe place: a muddy little stream flowing between deep banks with the hawthorn arching overhead. It would remain unseen, I thought, for years unless some yokel took it into his head to wade up the bed of the stream or a cow rubbed her way through the bushes.

I entered the water at a cattle wallow, plunging up to my knees in mire, and forced my way under the hawthorn. I couldn't see the sidecar. I was sure of the place, but it wasn't there. I didn't allow myself to worry yet, but I felt, as a stab of pain, the cold of the water. I pushed on downstream, hoping that the sidecar had been shifted by the force of the current, and knowing very well, as I now remember, that nothing but a winter flood would shift it.

At last I saw it, a faint white bulk in the darkness canted up against a bank of rushes where the stream widened. I was so glad to find it that I didn't hesitate, didn't listen to the intuition that was clamoring to be heard, and being ascribed to nervousness. After Eggardon I was not allowing my imagination any play.

I was leaning over the sidecar when a voice quite softly called my name. I straightened up, so astounded and fascinated that for a second I couldn't move. A thin beam of light flashed on my face, and dropped to my heart with a roar and a smashing blow. I was knocked backwards across the baby carriage, pitching with my right side on the mud and my head half under water. I have no memory of falling, only of the light and the simultaneous explosion. I must have been unconscious while I hit the mud, for just so long, I suppose, as my heart took to recover its habit of beating.

I remained collapsed, with eyes staring, trying to pick up the continuity of life. If I had had the energy I should have cackled with crazy laughter; it seemed so very extraordinary to have a beam of light thrust through one's heart and be still alive. I heard my assassin give his ridiculous party war cry in a low, fervent voice as if praising God for the slaughter of the infidel. Then a car cruised quietly up the road, and I heard a door slam as someone got out. I lay still, uncertain whether the gunman had gone to meet the newcomer or not; he had, for I heard their voices a moment later as they approached the stream, presumably to collect my body. I crawled off through the grass and rushes on the far bank, and bolted for home. I am not ashamed to remember that I was frightened, shocked, careless. To be shot from ambush is horribly unnerving.

I jumped into my tree and down into the lane, regardless of darting pain whenever I moved my right arm. Then I shut the door of the den behind me and lay down to collect myself. When I had regained a more graceful mastery of my spirit, I lit a candle and explored the damage.

The bullet—from a .45 revolver—had turned on the nickel of the flask in my breast pocket, ploughed sideways through my leather jacket, and come to rest (point foremost, thank God!) in the fleshy part of my right shoulder. It was so near the surface that I squeezed it out with my fingers. The skin was bruised and broken right across my chest, and I felt as if I had been knocked down by a railway engine; but no serious damage had been done.

I understood why the hunter had not even taken the trouble to examine his kill. He had shot along the beam of a flash lamp, seen the bullet strike, and watched the stain of whiskey, which couldn't in artificial light be distinguished from blood, leap to the breast of my coat and spread. It wasn't necessary to pay me any further attention for the moment; he had no use for my pelt or liver.

I patched myself up and lit a pipe, thinking of the fellow who had shot me. He had used a revolver because a rifle couldn't be handled in such thick cover and at so close a range, but his technique showed that he had experience of big game. He had got into my mind. He knew that sooner or later I should have a look at that sidecar. And his gentle calling of my name to make me turn my head was perfect.

They had dispatched a redoubtable emissary. He knew, as the police did not, who I was and what sort of man I was; thus he had been suspicious of my elaborate false trails. He guessed the plain facts: that I had committed a folly in going to Lyme Regis, and that my jack-in-the-box tricks thereafter were evidence of nothing but my anxiety. Therefore I had some secure hiding place not far from Lyme Regis and almost certainly on the Beaminster side of it. His private search for the sidecar, which he may have been carrying on for weeks, was then concentrated on the right spot. That he found it was due to imagination rather than luck. It had to be near a track or lane; it was probably in wood or water. And I think if I had been he I should have voted for water. There was a pattern in my escape. I had a preference for hiding, traveling, throwing off pursuit by water. Water, as the Spanish would say, was my *querencia*.

Well, he had missed. I think I wrote in some other context which I have forgotten that the Almighty looks after the rogue male. Nevertheless this sportsman (I allow him the title, for he must have waited up two or three nights over his bait, and been prepared to wait for many more) would be content. He had discovered the bit of country were I had been hiding, and he could even be pretty sure whereabouts my lair was. My panic-stricken dash through the water meadow showed that I was bolting south. I wouldn't be camping in the marshland; therefore the only place for me was on or just over the semicircle of low hills beyond. All that he had to do was to go into the long grass, as it were, after his wounded beast. The hunt had narrowed from all England to Dorset, from Dorset to the western corner of the county, and from that to four square miles.

I had known that this fate, whether delayed for months or years, was on the way to me; but the tranquillity of my life in the lane had taken the edge off my fear. I had been inclined to brood over my motives and congratulate myself on my superior cleverness, to look back rather than forward. There was, indeed, nothing to look forward to, no activity, no object; so I clung, and cling, to what I have—this lane. I might have escaped and lived on the country, but sooner or later one pack or the other would run me to earth, and no earth could be so deep and well-disguised as this.

It was obvious that, if I stayed where I was, I must completely reverse my policy of keeping the lane closed. The thorns must go, and the place be wide open to inspection while I myself lived underground.

I started on the work immediately. A southwest gale was sweeping down the hillside carrying along with it a solid ceiling of cloud high enough for the rain to drive and sting, so low that the whole sky seemed in movement. I welcomed the rain, for it helped me to obliterate all traces of myself and it would discourage the two men in the car from attempting to follow me up until visibility was better.

The eastern hedge, beneath which my burrow ran, was as wide as a cottage and promised to be as impenetrable in winter as in summer. The western hedge, however, which bounded the ploughed field, had not been allowed to eat up so much land and formed a thinner screen. I built up the weak stretches, thus getting rid of the poles from my platform and a lot of loose brushwood. The holly bush and the larger branches of thorn I shoved into the eastern hedge, hiding the cut ends. I stamped the earth hard down over my rubbish pit, and the water that was now rushing along the bottom of the lane covered pit and floor with a smooth expanse of dead bracken and red sand. I then retired indoors, leaving it to the rain to wash out my footprints. I have never had a chance to dry the clothes in which I was working.

The obliteration was not perfect. Bracken and nettles were crushed, but, since the whole lane was filled with the dying debris of autumn, the traces of my tramplings and removals were not very plain. There was a faint but definite smell. Worst of all, there were the steps cut up the inside of the elm which could not be disguised. If the fellow who was about to go into the covert after me had an observant eye—and I knew he had—he was bound to consider the lane suspicious; but I hoped he would judge his suspicions wrong and conclude that, whether or not I had once lived between the hedges, I had taken to the open and died of my wound.

The door was a faultless piece of camouflage; I had planted around it the same weeds as were over it, and no one could tell which had died with their roots in earth and which with their roots in glue. A few trails of living ivy hung over the door from the hedge.

Thenceforth my way out of the burrow was the chimney. The diameter of its course through the solid sandstone was already sufficient to receive my body; only the last ten feet of broken stone and earth had to be widened. I completed the job that afternoon—a nightmarish job, for my shoulder was painful and I was continually knocking off to rest. Then I would begin to dream of the root or the stone or the water that was beating me, and I would get up again and go to work, half-naked and foul with the red earth, a creature inhuman in mind and body. I think that sometimes I must have worked while asleep. It was the first time that I experienced this dazed and earthy dreaming; it has since become very common.

A queer tunnel it seemed to me when I examined it after a night's sleep. I hadn't attempted to cut through any roots that were thicker than a thumb; I had gone round them. At one point I had tunneled right away from the chimney, and come back to it. This was all to the good. Though the curve demanded odd contortions to get in and out, the roots acted as the rungs of a ladder, and the slope as a sump for water. The mouth was still well hidden under the blackberry bush. The only disaster was that my inner chamber was now full of wet earth, and I had no means of dumping it elsewhere.

God! When I look back upon them those blind hours of work seem to have been happy in spite of all their muddy and evasive horror.

I had something to do. Something to do. There is no fearing dreams when they produce work. It is when they feed upon themselves that one becomes uncertain of reality, unable to distinguish between the present in one's mind and the present as it appears to the outer world.

I stared at my face to-day, hoping to see those spiritual attributes which surprised me when I first looked in the fisherman's mirror. I wanted comfort from my face, wanted to know that this torture, like the last, had refined it. I saw my eyes fouled with earth, my hair and beard dripping with blood-red earth, my skin gray and puffed as that of a crushed earthworm. It was the mask of a beast in its den, terrified, waiting.

But I must not anticipate. To preserve my sanity it is necessary that I take things in their order. That is the object of this confession: to tell things in their order, reasonably, precisely; to recover that man with his insolence, his irony, his ingenuity. By writing of him I become him for the time.

It was Major Quive-Smith who had shot me by the stream. I am sure of it because his subsequent behavior and his character (which by now I know as an old fox, outliving his contemporaries, knows the idiosyncrasies of the huntsman) correspond to those of the man who waited patiently over the sidecar, who called my name to make me turn my head.

Two days I spent recovering from the wound, light in itself but aggravated by all that sudden toil. On the third I emerged from my chimney and crawled from bush to bush along the edge of the eastern pasture until I reached an ivy-covered oak at the bottom of the lane. It was nearly dead, and a paradise of wood pigeons. From the top I could see the Marshwood Vale spread out as on a map, and I overlooked the courtyard of Patachon's farm.

Pat and Patachon are the names I have given to my two neighbors. I live unsuspected between them like an evil spirit, knowing their ways and their characters but not permitted to discover their true names. Pat, the farmer to whom the cows and the eastern hedge belong, is a tall, thin youth with a lined, brown face, a habit of muttering to himself, and a soul embittered by bad homemade cider. His little dairy farm can barely pay its way; but he has an active wife with a lot of healthy poultry which probably produce all the ready cash. On the other hand she is prolific as her hens. They have six children with expensive tastes. I judge the kids by the fact that they suck sweets at the same time as eating blackberries.

Patachon, who owns the western hedge and the great gray farm, is a chunky, red-faced old rascal, always with a tall ash plant in his hand when he hasn't a gun. His terse Dorset speech delights his laborers, and is heard, I should guess, on a number of local boards. His land runs past the lower end of the lane, and round over the top of the hill, so that Pat's pasture is an enclave in the middle of it. On warm evenings he walks his side of the hedge in the hope of picking up rabbit or wood pigeon, but the only shots he has ever fired were at Asmodeus. The old poacher was too quick for him; all you can do to Asmodeus is to shoot where he ought to be but never is.

All morning I saw nothing of interest from the tree, but in the afternoon two men in a car drove into the yard of Patachon's farm and dropped a bag and a gun case. Then they bumped along the lower edge of the stubble, following the farm track which joined the serviceable portion of my lane. I guessed that they must be bound for Pat's farm; if they had been going beyond it, they would have taken a better road. I couldn't keep them under observation, for the southern slopes were much too dangerous in daylight. There were deep lanes which had to be crossed or entered, with no possibility of avoiding other pedestrians.

In half an hour they were back at Patachon's. One of the men got out and went indoors. The other drove the car away. Someone, then, had come to stay at the farm. I remained on watch in the tree, for I didn't like the look of things.

In the evening Patachon and his visitor emerged from the farmhouse with their guns under their arms, prepared for a stroll round the estate. They started towards the low-lying thickets at the western end of the farm, and I didn't see them again for an hour. Patachon owned a lot of rough land in that direction which I had never bothered to explore. I heard a few shots. A flight of three duck shot northwards and vanished in the dusk. A wood pigeon came homing to my tree, saw me, banked against the wind, and dived sideways with brilliant virtuosity. When I caught sight of the two guns again, they were stealing along the edge of the lane, separated from me only by the width of the two hedges. Patachon's visitor was Major Quive-Smith.

The farmer picked up a stone and flung it smack into the tree, just missing my feet. No pigeon flew out of the ivy, needless to say.

"And if 'e'd a bin there," said Patachon bitterly, "'e'd a flewed t'other way."

"He would," agreed Major Quive-Smith. "By Jove! I can't think why that fellow wouldn't let his little bit of shooting!"

That explained why he had gone to see Pat. And Pat, I am sure, refused his request rudely and finally.

"Sour man, 'e is!" said the farmer. "Sour!"

"Does he shoot at all himself?"

"No. 'E baint a man for fun. But don't 'ee go botherin' 'im, Major, for there's nobbut in the 'edge this year."

"How's that?" asked Quive-Smith.

I could see the swift, suspicious turn of his head, and hear the bark in the question.

"A perishin' cat! Can't trap un. Can't shoot un."

"Very shy of man, I suppose?"

"Knows as well as we what us would do to un if us could catch un," Patachon agreed.

They strolled down to the farm for supper. I observed that the major carried one of those awkward German weapons with a rifled barrel below the two gun barrels. As a rifle, it is inaccurate at 200 yards; as a gun, unnecessarily heavy. But the three barrels were admirably adapted to his purpose of ostensibly shooting rabbits while actually expecting bigger game.

I don't yet know Quive-Smith's true nationality or name. As a retired military man he had nearly, but not quite, convinced Saul. In his present part, a nondescript gentleman amusing himself with a farm holiday and some cheap and worthless shooting, there was no fault to be found. Tall, fair, slim, and a clever actor, he could pass as a member of half a dozen different nations according to the way he cut his hair and moustache. His cheekbones are too high to be typically English, but so are my own. His nose is that unmistakable Anglo-Roman which with few exceptions—again I am one of them—seems to lead its possessor to Sandhurst. He might have been a Hungarian or Swede, and I have seen faces and figures like his among fair-haired Arabs. I think he is not of pure European origin; his hands, feet, and bone structure are too delicate.

To rent the shooting over three quarters of the country where I was likely to be was a superb conception. He had every right to walk about with a gun and to fire it. If he bagged me, the chances were a thousand to one against the murder ever being discovered. In a year or two Saul would have to assume that I was dead. But where had I died? Anywhere between Poland and Lyme Regis. And where was my body? At the bottom of the sea or in a pit of quicklime if Quive-Smith and his unknown friend with the car knew their business.

I was glad of my two unconscious protectors: Asmodeus, whose presence in the lane made my own rather improbable, and Pat, who wouldn't have trespassers on his land and wouldn't let his little bit of shooting. I know that type of dyspeptic John Bull. When he has forbidden a person to enter his ground, he is ready to desert the most urgent jobs merely to watch his boundary fence. Quive-Smith couldn't be prevented from exploring Pat's side of the hedge, but he would have to do it with discretion and preferably at night.

I returned to my burrow, now no larger than it had been in the first few weeks, and much damper. I cursed myself for not having widened the chimney before I cleaned up the lane; I could then have thrown out the earth and allowed the rain to distribute it. The inner chamber was uninhabitable and so remains.

I stayed in my sleeping bag for two wretched days. I envied Quive-Smith. He was showing great courage in hunting single-handed a fugitive whom he believed to be desperate. Twice Asmodeus came home with a rush through the ventilation hole and crouched at the back of the den, untouchable and malignant—a sure sign that somebody was in the lane. I lay still underground. Desperate I was, and am, but I want no violence.

On the third afternoon I found the immobility and dirt no longer endurable, and decided to reconnoitre. Asmodeus was out, so I knew that there was no human being in the immediate vicinity. I hoped that Quive-Smith was already paying attention to some other part of the county, or at least to some other farm, but I warned myself not to underestimate his patience. I poked my filthy head and shoulders out into the heart of the blackberry bush and remained there, listening. It was a long and intricate process to leave the bush; I had to lie flat on the ground, separating the trailing thorny stems with gloved hands and pushing myself forwards with my toes.

I sat among my green fortifications, enjoying the open air and watching Pat's field and the sheep down beyond. It wasn't much to have under observation. Behind me was my own lane, and fifty yards to my left the cross hedge in which was another lane running up to the down; there might have been a platoon of infantry in both for all that I could have seen of them or they of me. Opposite me was another hedge that separated Pat's pasture from Patachon's sheep; to my right, the skyline of the pasture.

About five o'clock Pat came into the field to drive the cows home himself—a task that hitherto he had always left to a boy—and remained for some time staring about him truculently and swinging a stick. At sunset Major Quive-Smith detached himself from a brown-scarred rabbit warren on the hillside, and put his field glasses back in their case. I had not the remotest notion that he was there, but, since I had been assuming he was everywhere, I knew he had not seen me. To let me see him I thought obliging.

He struck down the hillside into the lane leading to Patachon's farm. As soon as he was in dead ground I crawled to the corner to have a look at him while he passed beneath me. A clump of gorse covered me from observation from the pasture as I crouched in the angle of the hedges.

I waited, but he didn't come. Then it occurred to me that he must hate those deep tracks almost as much as I did; a man walking along them was completely at the mercy of anyone above him. So he was possibly behind the opposite hedge, working his way back to the farm across the fields. It seemed odd that he should take all that trouble when he could have gone home by the vale and run no risks whatever; it seemed so odd that I suddenly realized I had been outmanoeuvred. He had shown himself deliberately. If I were haunting the lane, which he suspected, and out for revenge, of which he must have been sure, then I should have waited for him just in that corner where I was.

I turned round and peered through the gorse. He was racing silently down the slope towards me. He had decoyed me into the corner of two hedges, from which there was no escape.

He hadn't seen me. He didn't know I was there; he could only hope I was there. I tried a desperate bluff.

"Git off my land!" I yelled. "Git off ut, I tell 'ee, or I'll 'ave the law on 'ee!"

It was a good enough imitation of Pat's high-pitched voice, but it wasn't very good Dorset. However, I speak my county dialect as richly as my old nurse, and we're near enough to the Bristol Channel to have the West Country burr. I hoped Quive-Smith had not learned to distinguish between one dialect and another.

The major stopped in his stride. It was quite possible that Pat was standing in the lane and looking at him through the hedge, and he didn't want to quarrel more than could be helped.

"Go round by t' ga-ate, and git off my land!" I shouted.

"I say, I'm very sorry!" said Quive-Smith in a loud and embarrassed military voice—he was acting his part every bit as well as I was acting mine. "Thought I'd be late for supper, you know. Just taking a short cut!"

"Well, cut oop ba-ack, dam' 'ee!" I yelled.

He turned, and strolled back up the field with offended dignity. I did not even wait for him to reach the skyline, for he might have lain down and continued observation. I sprinted along the twenty yards of straight hedge between the gorse and my own bramble patch, wriggled under the blackberry bush, and popped into my burrow. I remained till nightfall with my head and shoulders above ground, but heard no more of him.

I have a reasonable certainty that Quive-Smith will never discover the deception. Pat is sure to be rude and taciturn in any conversation. If the major apologizes when they next meet, Pat will accept the apologies with a grunt, and, if asked straight out whether or not he ordered the major off his land on such a day at such an hour, will allow it to be thought he did. My presence in the lane is still not proved. Suspected, yes. Before Quive-Smith got home to supper, he had no doubt kicked himself for not walking right up to the angle of the hedges.

How much did he know? He had decided, obviously, that I had not been badly wounded; I had, after all, left the stream at a pace that defied pursuit, and there had not been a spot of blood. Then where was I? He had, I presumed, explored all the cover on Patachon's farm and on the two or three others over which he was shooting. He had found no trace of me except in the lane, and he knew that at some time it had been my headquarters. Was I still there? No, but I might return; the lane was well worth watching until the police or the public reported me elsewhere.

His general routine was more or less predictable. If he made a habit of scouting around Pat's pasture in daylight, he ran a real risk of being assaulted or sued for trespass, and he had at all costs to avoid drawing attention to himself by a large local row. By day, then, he might be on the high ground or in the lane itself or on Patachon's side of it. After dusk he would explore or lie up in the pasture.

I was confident that, under these circumstances, he would not find the mouth of my earth; but on one condition—that I cleaned it up and never used it again. There must not be a stem of the bush out of place, nor a blade of grass bent, nor any loose earth scraped from my clothes.

I resigned myself to remaining in the burrow, however unendurable. I have determined not to give way to impatience. I have been underground for nine days.

I dare not smoke or cook, but I have plenty of food: a large store of nuts and most of the tinned meat and groceries that I brought back from my last trips to Beaminster. Of water I have far more than I need. It collects in the sandstone channels that run like wainscoting along the sides of the den and slops over on to the floor. Lest it should undermine the door I have driven two holes, half an inch in diameter, through to the lane, drilling with a tin-opener attached to the end of a stick. I keep them plugged during the day for fear that Quive-Smith might notice such unnatural springs.

Space I have none. The inner chamber is a tumbled morass of wet earth which I am compelled to use as a latrine. I am confined to my original excavation, the size of three large dog kennels, where I lie on or inside my sleeping bag. I cannot extend it. The noise of working would be audible in the lane.

I spend a part of each day wedged in the enlarged chimney, with my head out of the top; but that is more for change of position than for fresh air. The domed, prolific bush is so thick and so shadowed by its companions and by the hedge that I can only be sure it is day when the sun is in the east. The lifeless centre seems full of gases, unsatisfying in themselves and carrying in suspension the brown dust and debris that fall from above and the soot from my fires that has accumulated on the underside of the leaves.

Asmodeus, as always, is my comfort. It is seldom that one can give to and receive from an animal close, silent, and continuous attention. We live in the same space, in the same way, and on the same food, except that Asmodeus has no use for oatmeal, nor I for field mice. During the hours while he sits cleaning himself, and I motionless in my dirt, there is, I believe, some slight thought transference between us. I cannot "order" or even "hope" that he should perform a given act, but back and forth between us go thoughts of fear and disconnected dreams of action. I should call these dreams madness did I not know they came from him and that his mind is, by our human standards, mad.

All initiative is at an end. All luck is at an end. We are so dependent on luck, good and bad. I think of those men and women—cases faintly parallel to mine—who live in one room and eat poorly and lie in bed, since their incomes are too small for any marked activity. Their lives would be unbearable were it not for their hopes of good luck and fears of bad. They have, in fact, little of either; but illusion magnifies what there is.

I have no chance even of illusion. Luck has reached a state of equilibrium and stopped. I had one stroke of evil when that trailer innocently attracted the notice of the police, one stroke of magnificent luck when Quive-Smith's bullet hit the flask. In most other cases I have been able to account for the march of events by conscious planning or by my own instinctive and animal reactions under stress.

Now luck, movement, wisdom, and folly have all stopped. Even time has stopped, for I have no space. That, I think, is the reason why I have again taken refuge in this confession. I retain a sense of time, of the continuity of a stream of facts. I remind myself that I have extended and presumably will extend again in the time of the outer world. At present I exist only in my own time, as one does in a nightmare, forcing myself to a fanaticism of endurance. Without a God, without a love, without a hate—yet a fanatic! An embodiment of that myth of foreigners, the English gentleman, the gentle Englishman. I will not kill; to hide I am ashamed. So I endure without object.

3

I have a use for this record, so I finish it. By God, it is good to write with a purpose, good to grudge the time I must spend on it, instead of whining, as it were, up my own sleeve! This will not, I think, be a pleasant task, nor dispassionate. But I can and must be frank.

I remained in my burrow for eleven days—for a week because it was a week, for two more days to prove to myself that I was not being unduly impatient, and still two more for good measure. Eleven days seemed ample to persuade Quive-Smith that I had either died in cover or left the district; I was entitled to find out whether he had gone. Asmodeus's behavior suggested that he had. For the middle days the cat had been coming and going in dignified leisure, his ears upright and the hair along his back unruffled. For the last three I had not seen him at all. His delicate movements made the reason perfectly clear; he could not endure the dirt any longer.

Without climbing a tree or exposing myself on open ground—both too dangerous—it was impossible to spy on Quive-Smith during the day; so I decided to look for him after nightfall in the farm itself. Inch by inch I emerged from the blackberry bush and crawled on my stomach to the hedge at the top of Pat's pasture, then through it and over the close turf of the down to much the same point that the major himself had occupied. It was cold and very dark, with a slight ground mist; I was quite safe so long as I moved slowly and avoided the lanes. It was very heaven to be out on the grass and breathing. A blazing summer noon couldn't have given me more pleasure than that foul November night.

There was little wind. The countryside was utterly silent except for the drip of the trees. I could see the lights in Patachon's farm and smell the sweet wood smoke from his chimneys. I dropped down into the vale and made my way to the farm along the edge of the open road, coming to the back of the north wing across an orchard. Here there was a high wall with the sloping roof of a farm building above it. From the top of the gable I should have the yard and the whole front of the house under observation. I didn't dare to enter the yard itself. Even if the dogs neither heard nor saw me, the southwest wind, such as it was, would have carried my scent to them.

The wall was built of flints and easily climbed, but there was a gap of two feet between the top of the wall and the lower edge of the slates which gave me trouble. A rotten iron gutter ran below the slates, and it was difficult to reach the roof without momentarily putting some weight on this gutter. Eventually I got up by way of a stout iron bracket and the gable end.

I lay on the slates with my head over the coping. I could see right into the living room of the farm—a peaceful and depressing sight. Quive-Smith was playing chess with Patachon's small daughter. I was surprised to see him sitting so carelessly before a lighted window with the blind up, and all black Dorset outside; but then I understood that, as always, I had underrated him. The clever devil knew that he was safe with his head nearly touching that of the child across the board. He was teaching her the game. I saw him laugh and shake his head and show her some move she should have made.

It was a bitter shock to find him still there. The eleven days had seemed an eternity to me. To him they were just eleven days; it was even possible, I thought, that he had been enjoying himself. My disappointment turned to fury. It was the first time in the whole of this business that I lost my temper. I lay on that roof picking at the moss on the stone coping, and cursing Quive-Smith, his country, his party, and his boss in a white-hot silence. I blasted him to hell, him and his friend and Patachon and their manservants and maidservants. If my thoughts had hit those walls, I should have created a massacre that would have done credit to a plunging Jehovah called from eternity by the anathemas of a thousand infuriated priests.

It shook me out of my melancholy, that blazing, silent orgasm of rage. I didn't stop to think that I had brought all this on myself, nor to consider that if I had actually been transported to that living room I should have shown a damned silly punctilious courtesy to the lot of them. I let myself go. I don't remember anything like it since I enjoyed—certainly, enjoyed—speechless temper at the age of seven.

I was brought back to reality by a fit of shivering. I had sweated with wrath and the perspiration was cooling in the night air. It's strange that I noticed it, for all my clothes were as permanently wet as those of a seaman in the days of sail. There must be a special virtue in sweat, cooling one spiritually as well as physically.

Quive-Smith might stay for weeks. I couldn't bear the thought of returning to the burrow. I determined to take to open country again. I am not persuading myself of that. I really meant to go on the run, desperate though my chances were. Considering my appearance, to live and move at all would have been a hundred times harder than my original escape. Then I was believed to be dead and nobody was looking for me; now the police would be on me at the first rumor of my presence. But I wasn't going back. I intended to skulk around the downs, hiding in barns and in gorse, and living, if there were no other food, upon the raw meat of sheep. I could keep Quive-Smith under observation until such time as he returned to London or wherever else his undoubted ability to increase the rottenness in a rotten world should be required.

I watched the living room until the child went to bed. Then the major joined Patachon in front of the fire, and Patachon's wife entered with two huge china mugs of cider. All three settled down to newspapers. There was nothing more to be learned.

I sidled towards the gable end, the weight of my body taken on shoulder and thigh, left hand on the coping and right hand testing the slates ahead lest one should be loose. I was concerned, God help me, with the noise of a single slate sliding down the roof into the gutter! A few feet from the end there was a subsidence beneath me. The slates sagged. I seemed to be floating on a heavy liquid that moulded itself to me, suddenly became brittle and crashed to the floor of the barn. For an instant I swung from the coping and then that too gave way. Five feet of stone tile, a solid expanse of slate, and I myself roared down on to a pile of iron drinking troughs. It sounded like the collapse of a foundry.

I found later that I had reopened the wound in my shoulder and suffered various cuts and bruises, but at the time I was only shaken. I picked myself up from that welter of ironwork and dashed to the open door of the barn. I didn't go through it. Quive-Smith had thrown up the window of the living room, and his long legs were already over the sill. My only thought was that he mustn't know I was still in this part of the country. The dogs started barking and jumping against their chains. Patachon opened the front door and stumped over the threshold, flashlight in hand.

I retreated into the barn and dived under the drinking troughs. They were ranged side by side, so that there was room for me between any two, and covered by the slates and rubble from the roof. Quive-Smith and the farmer entered the barn immediately afterwards.

"Damn un," stormed Patachon, observing the damage, " 'tis that beggarin' murderer aafter my cheeses! Over t' barn and down to dairy! I knew 'e was a stealin' of 'em. Over t' barn and down to dairy!"

I don't suppose he had lost an ounce, but farmers always suspect something is being stolen from them; there are so many things to steal. Quive-Smith obligingly agreed with me.

"Oh, I don't think there was anybody on the roof," he said. "Look at that!"

I knew what he was pointing at—a broken beam. It hadn't even broken with a crack. It had just given way like a sponge of wood dust.

"Deathwatch beetle," said the major. "I met the same thing in the East Riding, by Jove! Tithe barn it was. Poor chap broke his bloody neck!"

It didn't ring quite true, but it was a gallant attempt at the right manner.

"Rotted!" agreed Patachon in a disgusted tone. "Damn un, 'e's rotted!"

"Got to happen some time," answered Quive-Smith. "We ought to be thankful no one was hurt."

"Bin there three 'underd years," grumbled Patachon, "and 'e 'as to come beggarin' down on *our* 'eads!"

"Oh, well," the major said cheerfully, "I'll turn to in the morning and give you a hand. Nothing to be done now! Nothing at all!"

I heard them leave the barn, straining my ears to analyze their two individual treads, making absolutely certain that one of them did not remain behind, or return. I heard the front door of the farm shut and bolted, and waited till the silence of the night was restored, till the faint noises of windows opening and bedroom doors closing had ceased, till the rats began to scutter over the floor of the barn. Then I crawled to the door and out, creeping like a nocturnal caterpillar along the angle between the wall and the filthy courtyard.

For what I then did I have no excuse. I had begun to think as an animal; I was afraid but a little proud of it. Instinct, saving instinct, had preserved me time and again. I accepted its power complacently, never warning myself that instinct might be deadly wrong. If it were not, the hunted could always escape the hunter, and the carnivores would be extinct as the great saurians.

Gone was my disgust with my burrow; gone my determination to take to open country whatever the difficulties of food and shelter. I didn't think, didn't reason. I was no longer the man who had challenged and nearly beaten all the cunning and loyalty of a first-class power. Living as a beast, I had become as a beast, unable to question emotional stress, unable to distinguish danger in general from a particular source of danger. I could startle a dog fox, move as quietly and sleep as lightly, but the price I paid was to be deprived of ordinary human cunning.

I had had a bad fright. I was hurt and shaken. So I went without thinking to Safety—not to the form of safety adapted to the case, but to Safety in general. And that meant my burrow—darkness, rest, freedom from pursuit. I hadn't a thought—any more than, I suppose, the fox has such a thought—that the earth might mean death. Under the influence of panic when Quive-Smith shot me I had behaved in the same way, but then it was excusable. I didn't know what the devil I was up against, and to seek general Safety was as sound as any other move. To seek it now was simply a reflex action.

I took, of course, the most beautiful and cunning route; the animal could be trusted to perform that futility to perfection. I went through water and through sheep. I waited in cover to be sure there was no pursuit. I knew finally and definitely that there was no pursuit; that I was alone on the down above my lane. Then I covered the last lap with extreme caution and entered my burrow with attention to every dead leaf and every blade of grass.

All the next day I remained underground, congratulating myself on my good fortune. The stench and dirt were revolting, but I endured them with a holy masochism. I persuaded myself that in three or four days I could open my door and cleanse and dry the den, and Asmodeus would come back and we could live peacefully until it was safe for me to hang around the ports and get out of the country. My hands were all right again, showing little deformity. The left eye was still queer, but the right was so foul, filmy, and bloodshot that the difference between them was no longer remarkable. A shave and haircut were all I needed, and then I could pass anywhere as a criminal who had just celebrated his release from prison with a two-day binge.

After nightfall I heard some activity in the lane, and sat with my ear to the ventilator. I couldn't translate the noises. There were two men, but they did not speak to each other. I expect they whispered, but owing to the curve of the little tunnel I could not hear so slight a sound. Something heavy was being moved, and once I heard a thud against the door. My thoughts played with the idea of a man trap, a log perhaps that would fall on my head; they were certainly building something in the runway I had once used. Since I used it no longer I felt very clever and secure. I told myself that I was disappointed, merely disappointed, for they would wait another week or two for the result of their trap and I should have to stay underground.

All the time, as I now see, I was conscious of extreme terror and my heart was beating as if I had been running for my life. Only by an effort did I stop myself from talking aloud. I am very clever, I was saying to myself over and over again. They'll find themselves run in for murder, I said, if they catch somebody else. And then the terror came up in my throat, for there was silence in the lane and little bits of earth were falling down my bolt hole into the inner chamber.

I lay between the two dens, watching the trickle of earth and listening to the quick strokes of a chopper. A man, as I thought, jumped or fell into the hole, and a wave of rubble rolled down to the bottom. I reached for my knife, and waited. He's at my mercy, I said, I can make what terms I like. I was obsessed with the idea of talking, not killing. A reasonable man, I told myself. He'll see sense. He plays chess.

There was no further sound, none at all. The man had stuck in the hole or died. I crept up the slope of foul earth and lay on my back, poking an ash pole up the chimney as far as the twist. It didn't meet the body I expected; it met a hard obstruction. I withdrew myself as far as I could, for fear of some trap or explosive, and poked harder. The thing felt solid with a smooth undersurface. I lit a candle and examined it. It was the sawn end of a tree trunk which had been jammed into my hole.

I crawled to the door and pushed against it; nothing moved. Then I felt a sense of panic with which was mingled relief that the end had come at last. I intended to rush out and let them shoot. A quick death, merited. I took the axe that had hollowed out the sandstone and drove it between the planks of the door. It turned. I ripped off the planks. On the far side of them was an iron plate. It rang hollow except in the centre. They had jammed it in place with a balk of timber, the other end of which rested against the opposite bank of the lane.

I don't know what happened to me then. When I heard Quive-Smith's voice I was lying on the bag with my head on my arms, pretending to myself that I was thinking things out. I was controlled, but my ears were drumming and my skin oozing cold sweat. I suppose that if one sits on hysteria long enough and hard enough, one loses consciousness. Something has to give way, and if the mind won't the body must.

Quive-Smith was saying:—

"Can you hear me?"

I pulled myself together and sloshed a handful of water over my head. There was no point in keeping silence; he must have heard me battering on the iron. The only thing to do was to answer him and play for time.

"Yes," I said, "I can hear you."

"Are you badly wounded?"

Damn him for asking that question then! I should have found it very useful later if I could have persuaded them that I was suffering from a neglected wound and incapable. As it was, I answered the truth:—

"Nothing much. You hit a whiskey flask with a leather jacket behind it."

He muttered something that I could not hear. He was speaking with his mouth close to the ventilation hole. If he jerked his head, the voice was lost.

I asked him how he had found me. He explained that he had gone straight from the barn to the lane on the off chance that I had been responsible for the broken roof and that he might see me returning to my mysterious hiding place.

"Simple," he said, "so simple that I was very much afraid that it was what you meant me to do."

I told him that I had never attempted to kill him, that I could have done it a dozen times if I had wished.

"I supposed so," he replied. "But I counted on your leaving me alone. You would only have exchanged me for the police, and it was obviously wiser to persuade me that you had gone. You did, as a matter of fact."

His voice had a weary harshness. He must have been in fear of his life all the time that he was at the farm. A braver man and a cleverer than I am, but without—I was going to write "ethics." But God knows what right I have to claim any! I have neither cruelty nor ambition, I think; but that is the only difference between Quive-Smith and myself.

"Couldn't you give me a cleaner death than this?" I asked.

"My dear fellow, I don't want you to die at all," he said, "not now. I am so glad you had the sense not to break out while I was sealing you up. This position has taken me by surprise as well as you. I can't promise you anything, but your death seems wholly unnecessary."

"The only alternative is the zoo," I answered.

He laughed at this for a nervous, uncontrollable moment. Lord, he must have been relieved to know where I was!

"Nothing so drastic," he said. "I'm afraid you wouldn't survive in captivity. No, if they take my advice, I shall be ordered to return you to your position and friends."

"On what condition?"

"Trifling—but we needn't go into that yet. Now, how are you off for food?"

"Reasonably well, thank you."

"No little delicacies I can bring you from the farm?"

I nearly lost my temper at this. The man's voice had just the right touch of concern; there was but the tiniest shade of irony to tell me that he was thoroughly enjoying his own acting. He would have brought me anything I asked, I have no doubt. For the cat-and-mouse act to be subtle enough to please his taste, it had to be hardly distinguishable from genuine kindness.

"I think not," I answered.

"All right. But there's no need for you to suffer any more."

"Look here!" I said. "You won't get any more out of me than your police did, and you can't stay here indefinitely. So why not get it over?"

"I can stay here for months," he answered quietly. "Months, you understand. I and my friend are going to study the habits and diet of the badger. The large piece of timber which is holding your door is for us to sit on. The bush placed in front of your door is a hide for the camera, and there will shortly be a camera in it. I'm afraid all these preparations are wasted since nobody ever comes into the lane. But if anyone should—well, all he will see is my friend or myself engaged in the harmless study of the life story of the badger. We might even get a nice young man with a microphone and have him tell the children what Bertie the Brock keeps under his tail."

I called him a damned fool, and told him that the whole countryside would be consumed with curiosity—that all their doings would be public property in twenty-four hours.

"I doubt it," he answered. "Nobody at the farm pays any attention to my innocent rambles. Sometimes I go out with a gun, sometimes not. Sometimes on foot, sometimes in the car. Why should they guess I am always in this lane? They have never seen you. They won't see me. As for my assistant, he has no connection with me at all. He is staying in Chideock and his landlady thinks he is a night watchman at Bridport. He isn't as careful in making his way here as I should like. But we can't expect a paid agent to have our experience, can we, my dear fellow?"

This "dear fellow" of his infuriated me. I am ashamed to remember that I rammed my axe against the door in anger.

"How about that?" I asked.

"It makes surprisingly little noise," he said coolly.

It did, even in my closed space. He explained that there were felt and plywood over the iron.

"And if you think it out," he added, "what would happen if anyone did hear you? That disagreeable peasant who owns the field over your head, for example? You would compel me to remove the pair of you, and to arrange the bodies to show murder and suicide."

It was true enough—so true, at any rate, that there was little object in pointing out that he couldn't get at me without running a grave risk himself. He held the only firearm and all the cards. He could foresee a more or less satisfactory outcome if he killed me; but if I killed him I could foresee nothing but murder on my conscience, and death or disgrace eventually at the hands of the service to which he belonged. Psychologically I was at his mercy. My mind cowered.

"We must stop talking now," he said. "No conversation in daylight will be our rule. I shall be on duty from 10 A.M. to 8 P.M., and we shall talk during the last couple of hours. My assistant will be on duty the rest of the time. Now, let me make the position perfectly clear. I cannot, I expect, prevent you from forcing your way out over the top of the door. But if you do, you'll be shot before you can shoot, and closed up again in your cosy home. Your back door is very thoroughly blocked, and if we hear you working we shall cut off your air. So be careful, my dear fellow, and don't lose heart! Quite calm—that's the watchword. Your release is certain."

I sat for hours with my ear to the ventilator. I didn't expect to learn anything, but hearing was the only one of my senses which could keep in touch with my captors. So long as I heard them, I had the illusion that I was not wholly defenseless, that I was planning, gathering data for an escape.

I heard the twittering of birds at dawn. I heard a crackle as Quive-Smith adjusted or trimmed the screen of dead thorn outside my door. Then I heard a low mutter of voices which I translated as the sound of Quive-Smith's colleague taking over the watch from him. They couldn't, of course, keep to their schedule on that first day. The major had presumably to telegraph a report.

The new man sat quite still. I imagined his figure as a silhouette thrown against the darkness of the door. I had only seen him at a distance. I thought of him as dark and thick, as a contrast to Quive-Smith, who was fair and tall. I was quite wrong.

All the time that I crouched at the ventilator, my mind had been drifting over the wildest images of escape, enveloping them, rejecting them, concentrating finally upon the two practical schemes. The first, as Quive-Smith had suggested, was to cut a passage diagonally upwards over the top of the door. I took one of my long spits and drove it through the red earth. So far as I could tell, it passed over the top of their plate; but the knowledge was useless. As he had said, if I stuck out my head I should be shot—and, by the tone of his voice, I knew he did not mean killed, but deliberately crippled. The final break-through was bound to be so noisy that the watcher would have ample warning.

The second, and far more likely, way of escape was by the bolt hole. They hadn't caged me so neatly as they thought. Their tree trunk had not blocked the whole length of my tunnel; only its vertical section between the surface and the twist. The passage quarried through the sandstone was open. All I had to do was to cut a new passage through the earth, and surely I could work at that so silently that not a sound would be heard outside.

I crawled into the choked inner chamber and began to dig with my knife. There was no room to use the axe; I was kneeling on the pile of muck and earth with my body filling the whole funnel. Very silently and carefully, catching earth and stones in my hand, spending minutes in wearing through some root that I could have cleared with a jerk, I went at the job of digging a tunnel parallel to the tree trunk. The roar of my breath, thumping and gasping like the Diesel engines that had carried me to England, was by far the loudest sound.

The air was foul, for the draught between ventilator and bolt hole no longer existed. The carbon dioxide that I breathed out collected between my shoulders and the working surface. My energy steadily diminished. I cleared a foot of clay and broken sandstone, and then had to return to the ventilator to breathe. On the next shift I cleared six inches; on the next three; on the next, again three. But there I interfered with the laws of geometrical progression, and faded out before I reached the ventilator.

I had insisted to myself that my sensation of extreme lassitude was sheer slackness; but now it was quite obvious that my body would collapse, try what I might in the way of compulsion, if I didn't allow it to obey the laws that governed its intake of oxygen. God knows what I was breathing in that muck heap! If I had the exact figures of work and rest, no doubt some chemist would be able to work it out. Since I had only moved out of the burrow for a few hours in thirteen days there must have been many gases besides carbon dioxide.

I came to after an unknown lapse of time. In the original den there was plenty of air so long as I did not work at anything too long or too fast. The ventilator was a passage some four feet long and curving down from the bank to the side of the den. It had a diameter large enough for Asmodeus to go in and out, but so small that I was always amazed he could.

It seemed to me at the time that I kept a remarkable control over myself. I concentrated on breathing in and out by the ventilator, forcing my mind to remain blank, to stay in that state where all activity is inhibited by shock and it is freed to wander through space obsessed by trivialities. I felt that I was, to use a horrid phrase, captain of my soul. I had hardly been tested. The only periods, I suspect, when a man feels captain of his soul are those when he has not the slightest need of such an organ.

For short intervals, separated by lengthy halts to breathe, I worked at the old chimney. There was no space to swing or thrust, nowhere to put the earth that fell. It was like trying to burrow through a sandhill, impossible to breathe, impossible to remove the debris. I could have obtained more air by boring another hole through to the lane (though it wouldn't have done me much good in the inner chamber), but I dared not give them a direct view into the burrow. The one strength of my position was that they could never see what I was doing.

The day passed quickly. Time drags only when one is thinking fast, and all my mental processes were slowed down. I was lying by the ventilator when night fell and Quive-Smith wished me a cheerful good-evening.

"Everything has gone splendidly," he said. "Splendidly! We'll have you out of there in an hour. Free to go home, free to live on that lovely estate of yours, free to do anything you like. I'm very glad, my dear fellow. I have a great respect for you, you know."

I replied that I doubted his respect, that I knew him to be a good party man.

"I am," he agreed. "But I can admire such an individualist as you. What I respect in you is that you have no need of any law but your own. You're prepared to rule, or to be suppressed, but you won't obey. You are able to deal with your own conscience."

"I am not. But I see what you mean," I said.

"You must be! A man in your position to commit what you described in the subsequent proceedings as a sporting stalk! And then calmly pitching a spy on the live rail at the Aldwych!"

I kept silence. I didn't know where this was leading. I hated the philosophy he was ascribing to me; it was a travesty of the truth.

"I'm not blaming you in the least for defending yourself," he went on. "The man was worthless, and got in your way. What other result could there have been? I should be disappointed—really, I mean it—to find a lot of sloppy scruples in such an anarchical aristocrat as you."

"That's your morality rather than mine," I answered.

"My dear fellow!" he protested. "There's all the difference in the world! It's the mass that we are out to discipline and educate. If an individual interferes, certainly we crush him; but for the sake of the mass—of the state, shall I say? You, you don't give a damn for the state. You obey your own taste and your own laws."

"That's true enough," I admitted. "But I have respect for the rights of other individuals."

"Of course. But none at all for the nation. Admit it now, my dear fellow—you could get along perfectly well without any state!"

"Yes, damn you!" I answered angrily—I hated his pseudo-Socratic cross-examination. "Without the shameless politicians who run this country or the incompetent idiots who would like to, or your blasted spotlight Caesars."

"There's no point in being rude," he laughed. "Limelight has just the same effect on the emotional public as Westminster Abbey and a sovereign's escort—and it's a lot cheaper. But I'm glad you have grown out of these rather childish allegiances, because we shan't have any difficulty in coming to terms."

I asked him what his terms were. He pushed a paper down the ventilator with a stick. I collected it, also with a stick.

"Just sign that, and you are free," he said. "There is only one serious restriction. You must undertake not to leave England. We leave you at complete liberty in your own country. But if you attempt to reach the Continent, this will begin all over again and we shall show no mercy. I think you'll admit that, after what you did, it's a reasonable condition."

I asked him for a light. I wasn't going to use up candles and oxygen. He poked his torch down the hole without hesitation. He knew by this time that he could force me to give it back.

The form they wished me to sign was lengthy but simple. It was a confession that on the —th August I had attempted to assassinate the great man, that I had undertaken this with the knowledge (they didn't quite dare to write "approval") of the British Government, and that I had been released without any punishment on condition that I remained in England. The document was signed by their chief of police, by witnesses, and by a London notary public attesting my signature, although it did not then exist. He was, to judge by his address, quite a reputable notary, too.

It was a good torch, and I employed it for the next quarter of an hour in getting order into my excavations. Then I gave it back to him, together with his paper. There was no object in showing indignation.

"I wouldn't try to persuade you," he said, "if you had the usual bourgeois nationalism. A man of your type would rather be a martyr. But since you don't believe in anything but yourself, why not sign?"

I told him that I cared for public opinion.

"Public opinion? Well, we shouldn't publish this document unless there was imminent danger of war, and your government was acting its usual morality play. And from what I know of the English public's temper in time of crisis, they would probably make you a popular hero."

"They possibly would," I answered. "But I don't sign lies."

"Now, now, no heroics!" he begged me in his blasted patronizing manner. "You're a good Englishman, and you know very well that truth is always relative. Sincerity is what matters."

I blame myself for being drawn into argument with him, but what else could I do? I was glad to hear a cultured human voice, even his, after so much solitary confinement. It was, in a sense, not unlike being stuck in the club with some bore whose opinions are very left or very right. You can't do anything but listen to the man. You know he is wrong, but since you argue from the standpoint of individuals and he argues about a mythical mass, there is no common ground. And it's utterly impossible to explain yourself.

I lay no stress on the great physical weariness and discomfort to which I was subject. They gave him an enormous advantage over me in intellectual power, but he had that in any case. He drove me gently from one untenable position to another. He might have been a kindly doctor investigating a moral delinquent.

"I think," he said at last, "that it would make it a lot easier for both of us if you told me why you attempted assassination."

"I told your people long ago," I retorted impatiently. "I wanted to see whether it was possible, and his death would be no great loss to the world."

"You did then intend to shoot," he said, accepting my statement quite naturally. "I couldn't really help you, you see, till you had admitted that."

I perceived that I had given myself away to him and to myself. Of course I had intended to shoot.

Their methods of interrogation are devastating to the muddle-minded—90 per cent of us, whatever class we belong to. It's easy to make a man confess the lies he tells to himself; it's far harder to make him confess the truth. And when by their technique the truth has been dragged from him, he is so plastic and demoralized that he will accept any interpretation the questioner chooses to put upon it. The process is equally immoral and effective whether used by psychoanalysts or secret police. They make us see our own motives, and in the horror of that exposure we are ready to confess to any enormity.

I had been through all this before, of course, but at the hands of much coarser and less intelligent examiners than Quive-Smith. Physical torture merely increased my obstinacy. I was so occupied in proving to myself that my spirit was superior to my body that the problem of whether my intelligence had not been hopelessly overshadowed by my emotions did not arise.

"Yes," I admitted. "I intended to shoot."

"But why?" he asked. "Surely political assassination settles nothing?"

"It has settled a good deal in history," I said.

"I see. A matter of high policy then?"

"If you wish."

"Then you must have talked it over with someone?"

"No. I went alone, on my own responsibility."

"For the sake of your country?"

"Mine and others."

"Then even though your government knew nothing about you, you were acting in a sense on their behalf?"

"I don't admit that," I said, seeing where he was heading.

"My dear fellow!" he sighed. "Now, you say you don't sign lies. Let me make your mind a little clearer, and you will see that I don't want you to. You have a number of friends in the Foreign Office, haven't you?"

"Yes."

"You sometimes give them an informal report on your return from trips abroad. I don't mean that you are an agent. But if you had any interesting impressions, you would pass them to the right man over the lunch table?"

"I have done so," I admitted.

"Then suppose you had succeeded and we had hushed the assassination up, would you have informed your friends that he was dead?"

"Yes, I expect so."

"You do, you see, consider yourself a servant of the state," he said.

"Not in this matter."

"Oh dear, oh dear!" complained Quive-Smith patiently. "A man with your experience of foreign society shouldn't have this English dislike of reasonable conversation. It is precisely and only in a matter of such importance that you consider yourself a servant of the state. In your daily routine you do not. You are an individualist obeying his own laws. Yet you admit that in this matter you acted for reasons of state and that you intended to inform the state."

I repeat that I could not escape from him, that I was imprisoned in a space eight feet long by four feet high by three feet wide. The fact that he was free and I was buried alive gave me a sense of inferiority to him. Of course it did. Obviously it did. Yet why should it have? I knew that he understood nothing which mattered to me, that he had not the faintest idea of my scale of values. Therefore, myself being sure of those values, our physical circumstances should have made no difference.

I see now that he was destroying a great deal of nonsense in my mind. It was possibly that, more than anything else, which gave me the sense of wriggling at the end of a hook.

"But I did not act at the orders of the state," I said.

"I haven't asked you to sign your name to that. 'With the knowledge of the government' is the phrase. That wouldn't be a lie at all. We needn't even stick to those words. 'With the knowledge of my friends'—how would that be?"

"It isn't true."

"I'm not suggesting you were paid. No, I think you undertook this, as you say, more or less in a sporting spirit."

"I told you so," I said.

"Ah, yes. But a sporting assassination! Now, really, you wouldn't believe it yourself, you know."

"Why not?" I asked furiously.

"Because it is incredible. I want to know why you hate us to such a degree that you were ready to murder the head of the state. What were your motives?"

"Political."

"But you have admitted that you care nothing for politics, and I believe you implicitly. Perhaps we mean the same thing. Shall we say that your motives were patriotic?"

"They were not," I answered.

"My dear fellow!" he protested. "But they were certainly not personal!"

Not personal! But what else could they be? He had made me see myself. No man would do what I did unless he were cold-drawn by grief and rage, consecrated by his own anger to do justice where no other hand could reach.

I left the ventilator, and lay down with my head at the entrance to the inner chamber; it was the most privacy I could attain. His voice murmured on, grew angry. I didn't care. I was fighting against the self-knowledge he had forced upon me. At last he was silent, and I surrendered to misery.

I will try to write of this calmly. I think that now I can. I am a man who has only loved once, and did not know it till she was dead. Perhaps that is not quite correct. I loved with all my heart, but had little self-consciousness about it—not, at any rate, compared to the ecstasy and glory which love meant to her. I was too disciplined, too civilized. I loved her as a Chinese mandarin might love a flower, beautiful in itself, unquestionably beautiful to live with.

When I heard of her death, I did not weep. I told myself immediately that love was an illusion. I grieved that so exquisite a work of nature had been destroyed. I grieved, in my conscious mind, with that same sorrow which I would have felt had my house, in which fifteen generations have lived, been burned—an irreparable, terrible sense of loss, transcending any injury, but no hot, human grief.

That, I say, is what I thought I felt. He who has learned not to intrude his emotions upon his fellows has also learned not to intrude them upon himself.

Yet I was mad with grief and hatred. I describe myself as then mad because I did not know it. The tepidity of my sorrow was not indifference; it was the blankness which descends upon me when I dare not know what I am thinking. I know that I was consumed by anger. I remember the venomous thoughts, yet at the time I was utterly unaware of them. I suppressed them as fast as they came up into my conscious mind. I would have nothing to do with them, nothing to do with grief or hatred or revenge.

When I went to Poland I considered that I was taking quite a conventional course: to go out and kill something in rough country in order to forget my troubles. I had not admitted what I meant to kill. I did not admit it till Quive-Smith destroyed all possible self-deception.

She was so swift and sensitive. She could do no other than make a generous cause her own. Impulsive, spiritual, intelligent, all at such energy that she seemed to glow. A boy who saw such things told me that sometimes there was a visible halo of light around her. To that

I am insensible. But, as I remember her, life extended beyond her body; neither touch nor sight could quite surely say, Here she begins and here she ends. Her skin was not a surface; it was an indefinite glory of the palest rose and orange that chose to mould itself to those tense limbs.

She knew, I suppose, that in our mixture of impulse and intelligence we were alike. Her emotions governed her brain; though she would support her side with devastating logic, logic had nothing to do with her devotion. I should never have suspected that of myself, yet it is true. I have never taken sides, never leaped wholeheartedly into one scale or the other; nor do I realize disappointments, provided they are severe, until the occasion is long past. Yet I am ruled by my emotions, though I murder them at birth.

They caught her and shot her. Shot her. Reasons of state. Yes, I know, but surely the preservation of such an individual is why we suffer, why we fight, why we endure this life. Causes? Politics? Religion? But the object of them is to produce such a woman—or man, if you will. To put her, her, against a wall—there is no cause that justifies an act so satanic. It is the life of such a creature which justifies any cause she chooses to adopt. What other standard have we? In all history has any man become a Christian because he was convinced by the Athanasian Creed? But how many millions have been convinced by the life of a single saint!

I declared war upon the men who could commit such sacrilege, and above all upon the man who has given them their creed. How ridiculous that one person should declare war upon a nation! That was another reason why I hid from myself what I was doing. My war was a futile cause to me, to be smiled at sympathetically just as I used to smile at her enthusiasms. Yet in fact my war is anything but futile. Its cost in lives and human suffering is low. Seek out and destroy the main body of the enemy—and I should have destroyed it but for a change of wind.

I realized that since the day I was caught I had been defeated only by the loneliness and uncertainty. How could I admit to myself that I, the mandarin, was declaring war; that I, the unfeeling lover, had been so moved by the death of my beloved? That I, the civilized, scrupulous sportsman was behaving like an ice-cream merchant with a knife?

Well, all that, as I lay in the silence of my temporary grave, was at last admitted. And so I passed to a spiritual offensive.

The offensive! Again how ridiculous for a man who hadn't the room to stand up to feel on the offensive! But I was no longer the passive sufferer. My demoralization had been appalling while I knew no cause for which I suffered. Now that I did know—my God, I remembered that there were men at Ypres in 1915 whose dugouts were smaller and damper than mine!

I do not know how long I lay there. I passed in thought over great distances of geographical space, over all the movement of my attack and retreat, but there was no activity in myself or the outer world by which time could be measured. At last I was roused by the perceptible rising of the water.

I thought at first that there must be heavy rain outside, and thrust a stick down my two drains to clear them. It met hard obstructions. Of course they had found and plugged the holes. That added to my discomfort—if anything could—but put me in no danger. The water would leak out under the door as soon as it rose to the height of the sill.

I spoke through the ventilator almost with gayety. I was buoyed up by a feeling of light-heartedness, much the same, I suppose, as that of a penitent after confession. I knew why I was in my burrow. I felt that what I had done had been worth-while.

"Anyone there?" I asked.

Quive-Smith answered me. The night had passed, and the other man had come and gone.

"You will merely succeed in giving me pneumonia, my dear fellow," I said.

"Delirium," he replied, "won't change your handwriting."

It was the first time that I had annoyed him; he let me hear the cruelty in his voice.

I started to burrow again, hoping with my new courage to get to the surface sometime after nightfall. But it was not courage that needed multiplying; it was oxygen. I had to leave the work at shorter and shorter intervals, and to allow a greater margin of safety than before. If I fainted with my head in the sea of mud on which my sleeping bag was floating, it would be all over.

When I could do no more, I rolled up the useless bag and spread a layer of tins on top of the bundle. On them I sat, crouched forward with the nape of my neck against the roof and my elbows on my knees. It was uncomfortable, but the only alternative was to lie full length in the water. That would have made me no wetter than I was, but a lot colder. I shivered continuously. Nevertheless the temperature in the den must have been well above that of the outside air. The poets are wrong when they describe the grave as cold.

In the evening, the third since my imprisonment, Quive-Smith tried to make me talk, but I would not. At last I heard his colleague take over from him. The major wished me good-night, and regretted that I should force him to increase my discomfort. I didn't understand what he meant. After that there was silence—a silence more complete than any I had experienced. Even at night and buried, my ears caught faint noises of bird and beast.

The night dragged on and on. I began to suffer from hallucinations. I remember wondering how she had got in, and begging her to be careful. I was afraid that when she left, they might think she was I, and shoot. Even while I was off my head I could not conceive that anyone would hurt her for being herself.

They passed, those dreams. It was the growing effort of breathing which drove them away. I was desperate for air. I couldn't make the man hear me when I spoke, so I hammered lightly on the door. A shaft of light showed at the angle of the ventilator. Quive-Smith had blocked it before he left.

"Stop that!" ordered a low voice.

"I thought it was still night," I answered idiotically.

I meant that I wouldn't have hammered on the door if I had known it was already morning. I didn't want some innocent person involved in the reckoning.

"I have orders to break in and shoot if you make a noise," he said stolidly.

He had the flat voice of a policeman in the witness box. From that, and from the major's description of him, I was pretty sure of his type. He wasn't in this service from ambition and love of the game itself, both of which undoubtedly counted with Quive-Smith; he was a paid hand.

I told him that I was a wealthy man and that if I escaped I could make him independent for life.

"Stop that!" he answered again.

I thought of pushing a fat bank note up the ventilator, but it was too dangerous to let him know I had money; he would have been in a position to force unlimited sums from me and give nothing in return.

"All right," I said. "I won't talk any more. But I want you to know that when they let me out I won't forget any little favors you can show me."

He made no answer, but he didn't put back the obstruction.

I hunched my rolled bag towards the ventilator, and sat down with my face pressed to it. The sun was shining outside. I could not see it, but in the curve of that imitation rabbit hole the deep orange crystals of the sandstone were glowing with light. There was an illusion of warmth and space. The twenty-four inches of sand, being so close to and directly under my eyes, lost perspective. The minute irregularities became sandhills, and the tunnel a desert with the sun still bathing the horizon and the dark clouds of the khamsin gathering overhead.

My watch had stopped, but I think it must have been nearly midday before Quive-Smith came on duty. The first I heard of him was a shot—so close that I was sure he had potted something in the lane —and then the laughter of both men.

When dusk fell, he began to examine me for the fourth time. His approach was cordial and ingenious. He gave me a précis of the news in the morning paper, then talked of football, and so came round to his boyhood; he had, he said, been educated in England.

His personal reminiscences were frank, though he implied a lot more than he said. His mother had been an English governess. She felt socially inferior and morally superior to his father—a horrid combination—and had tried to make her son a good little Briton by waving the Union Jack and driving in patriotism with the back of a hairbrush—with the natural result that his affection for his mother's country never rose higher than the point of contact. He gave away nothing about his father; I gathered that he was some obscure baron. When, later, I came to know Quive-Smith's real name I remembered that his restless family had a habit of marrying odd foreign women, and had consequently been cold-shouldered by their peers. He had a Syrian for his grandmother. That accounted for the almost feminine delicacy of his bone structure.

He led me on to talk of my own boyhood, but as soon as I felt myself affected by the confidential atmosphere that he was creating I dried up. I knew his methods by now. There was never a chance that he could make me sign that paper of his, but he could—and it shows amazing technique—still make me wonder whether I wasn't being absurdly quixotic in refusing.

He threatened to block the ventilator again if I did not talk to him. I retorted that if he stuffed up that hole I should die; and, in case that should encourage him, I added that asphyxiation appeared to be a pleasanter death than any I could give myself.

I had not, in fact, the least thought of committing suicide now that I knew the object of my existence. Even during the first lost and hopeless days suicide had only been a possibility to which I gave as much consideration as to each of a dozen other plans. One does not, I think, kill oneself without a definite desire to do so. It is hardly ever an act to which a man must key himself up; it is a temptation which he must struggle against. I have more than my fair share of mental diseases, but the black suicidal depression doesn't happen to be one of them.

He laughed and said he would give me all the air I wanted, all the air I wanted through the sort of filter that was fit for me. He dropped his English manner completely. It cheered me enormously to know that I was getting on his nerves.

I heard him push some bulky object into the hole and ram it well down towards the curve. I didn't much care. I knew from experience that there was enough air stored in the burrow and leaking under the door to keep me going for many hours.

I remained quiet, considering whether or not to pull the obstruction down into the burrow. I could get at it. The tunnel was the shape of my arm bent at the elbow, and half as long again. But the risk was serious. If he caught and fixed my left arm as it groped upwards, he would not thereafter be so dainty in his methods of cross-examination.

I poked with a stick, and found the thing to be soft and stiff. I advanced my fingers inch by inch until they brushed against it and I snatched back my hand. I had touched, as I thought, an arrangement of wires and teeth, but before my arm was fairly out of the tunnel I realized what it really was. The simultaneous mixture of terror and relief and anger made me violently sick.

Taking Asmodeus's head in my hand, I drew his remains into the den. Poor old boy, he had been shot at close quarters full in the chest. It was my fault. People who sat quietly in the lane were, in his only experience, friendly and had bully beef. He had been shot as he confidently sat up to watch them.

I was choking with sorrow and rage. Yes, I know—or one side of me knows—that it was the idiotic, indefensible love of an Anglo-Saxon for his animal. But Asmodeus's affection had been of so much harder price than that of a creature which one has fed and brought up from birth. Our companionship had a stern quality, as of the deep love between two people who have met in middle age, each looking back to an utterly unshared and independent life.

Quive-Smith cackled with laughter and told me that, really, I had only myself to blame; that he hoped I wouldn't be too proud to talk to him on the following evening. He couldn't, of course, have known that Asmodeus was my cat, but he had quite correctly calculated that I should draw his obstruction into the den and that I could never push it back. By God, if he had known the atmosphere I lived in he would never have thought that a dead cat could make it any worse!

When the other man had come on duty, I set about disentangling my stiffened body. While moving my roll of bedding I felt that I could not have stood up even if there had been headroom. I knelt in the mud with my hands on the doorsill and tried to straighten my legs. My impression had been right—I had set with my knees two feet from my chin.

I had no need of sleep, for I had passed some hours of every twenty-four half dozing, half unconscious. During the night I worked on my body, and when at last it consented to open up I supported myself on toes and hands and practised those exercises which, I believe, businessmen are ordered to perform before breakfast. I stopped shivering and ate a solid meal of oatmeal moistened with whiskey. I wished that I had thought of limited exercise before, but I had been demoralized by the filth of my condition. And there was no object for physical strength.

It seems ridiculous to say that by shooting Asmodeus Quive-Smith condemned himself to death; it was in a sense so slight a crime. Patachon would have shot the old poacher without hesitation. I should have grieved for him no less, but admitted Patachon's right. In the same way I admitted Quive-Smith's right to shoot me by the stream. I can neither defend nor explain the effect that the shooting of this cat had upon me. It released me. I had intended to escape by the chimney without bloodshed. From then on all my plans were directed towards a swift and deadly break-through into the lane. I was at last able to admit that all my schemes for escaping without violence were impossible. The only practical method was to kill the man on duty before, not after, I started digging.

The ventilator was my only means of physical contact with them. I meditated a number of ingenious decoys to persuade the major to thrust his arm down the hole. This idea of a trap had not, apparently, occurred to him, and it might work. But it would do me no good, I decided, even if I caught Quive-Smith. You can't kill a man quickly with only his arm to work on. He would yell for help.

To kill him through the ventilator? Well, there was only one way, and that was to straighten the curve so that I could shoot a missile up the tunnel. It was useless to poke at him with some improvised spear; to give instantaneous death I had to deliver a heavy weapon at a high initial velocity.

An iron spit at once suggested itself as the weapon. It would fly true for the short range of some three and a half feet between the point and his head; but it could not be fired from my catapult or from any rearrangement of its rubber. I had to have something in the nature of a bow.

None of my bits of wood served. There was no room to handle an ash pole of such length that its bending would have the necessary force. A bow proper, or any method of propulsion by the resiliency of wood, was excluded. Bent steel or twisted rope might have done, but I had neither.

I looked over my full and empty tins in the hope of finding another source of power. Some were on my rolled sleeping bag; some under Asmodeus. I had laid his carcass on a platform of tins. A last tribute of sentimentality. He could never have endured the mud. When I laid my hand on him I realized that in his body was power. He could take his own revenge.

I skinned Asmodeus and cut his hide into strips. I have always been interested in the mechanics of obsolete weapons, and guilty of boring my friends by maintaining the supremacy of the Roman artillery over any other up to the Napoleonic Wars. The engine that I now contrived was an extremely crude model of a hand-drawn ballista. I remember considering something of the sort for use on rabbits, but, since I felt more sympathy for them alive than dead, I never constructed it.

I made a square frame of which the uprights were two bricks and the horizontal bars two stout billets of ash fitting into roughly scraped grooves at the tops and bottoms of the bricks. Parallel to the bricks and on the inner side of them I twisted two columns of rawhide. Through the centre of each column was driven a long peg, which projected three or four inches beyond the brick. A wide thong was attached to the tips of the two pegs as a bowstring joins the ends of a bow. The twisting and shrinkage of the strips of hide held the whole frame rigid and forced the pegs hard back against the bricks.

On the farther side of the bricks and lashed to them by square lashings was a strip of wood from a packing case, in the centre of which I cut a semi-circular aperture. The method of firing the ballista was to lie on my back with my feet on the outer edges of this wooden strip. The point of the spit passed through, and was supported by, the aperture; the ring of the spit was gripped in the centre of the thong by the thumb and forefinger of the right hand. Thus, by the pull between hand and feet the pegs were drawn towards my chest against the torsion of the columns of hide. When the spit was discharged, the pegs thudded back on the bricks, which were padded with cloth at the point of contact.

By the time I had made the machine it was morning, or later, and Quive-Smith was on duty again. I dared not practise for fear of noise, so I slept as best I could and waited for the evening examination. I intended to be polite, for I wanted information about the major's assistant. I hadn't the faintest idea what to do with him,—I was in no position to take prisoners,—but I had a feeling that he might be more useful to me alive than dead.

At the hour when Pat, Patachon, and their laborers had all retired to their respective firesides, Quive-Smith opened the conversation. After we had exchanged a few guarded commonplaces, he said:—

"You're unreasonable, really unreasonable. I'm surprised at a man of your sense enduring such conditions!"

I noticed a touch of impatience in his voice. He had begun to realize that watching badgers in a damp lane on November evenings was not an amusement that anyone would want to carry on for long. He must have wished that he had never thought of that invaluable confession.

"I can endure them," I answered. "You're the man who is suffering for nothing. I've come to the conclusion that if I sign that document of yours, you'll never have occasion to publish it. There isn't going to be any war. So it doesn't matter whether I sign or not."

I thought that would appeal to him as a piece of British casuistry: to deny that I was uncomfortable, but to produce a hypocritical justification for getting more comfort. It was a textbook illustration good enough to take in the foreigner.

As a matter of fact no Englishman that I know would have signed his bloody paper—refusing partly from honor but chiefly from sheer obstinacy. He's a neurotic creature, the modern John Bull, when compared to the beef-and-ale yeoman of a hundred years ago; but he has lost none of great-grandfather's pigheadedness.

"You're perfectly right, my dear fellow," said Quive-Smith. "Your signature is a mere necessary formality. The thing will probably stay at the bottom of the archives till the end of time."

"Yes, but look here!" I answered. "I trust you not to talk. I don't know who you are, but you must be pretty high up in your service and have a sense of responsibility. But what about this other fellow? I may lay myself open to blackmail, or he may change sides."

"He doesn't know who you are," replied Quive-Smith.

"How can I be sure of that?"

"Oh, use your head, man!" he answered contemptuously—I was pleased that his voice no longer had its usual note of ironical but genuine respect. "Is it likely? He doesn't even know who I am, let alone you. This morning he did his best to find out. I expect you tried to bribe him."

"Is he English?" I asked.

"No, Swiss. A people, my dear fellow, of quite extraordinary stupidity and immorality. A very rare combination which only a long experience of democratic government could have produced. A Swiss agent is the perfect type of Shakespeare's Second Murderer."

I refrained from the obvious gibe. Nobody could cast Quive-Smith as a First Murderer. He was definitely in the employing class.

I wanted to keep him talking, so that he wouldn't insist on my signing his document immediately. I asked him what was the matter with democracy.

He read me a long lecture, which degenerated into a philippic against the British Empire. I slipped in a provocative word here and there to encourage him. He hated us like hell, considered us (he said it himself) as the Goths must have considered the Roman Empire, a corrupt bunch of moralizing luxury lovers who could only hold their frontiers by exploiting—and that inefficiently—the enormous wealth and the suffering millions behind them. In fact it was a speech that would have gone equally well in the mouth of his boss's opposite number on the other side of Poland.

He even had the effrontery to invite me to join the winning side. He said that they needed in all countries natural leaders like myself; I had only to sign, and bygones would be bygones, and I should be given every chance to satisfy my will to power. I didn't tell him that natural leaders don't have any will to power. He wouldn't have understood what I meant.

I dare say he was sincere. I should have been a very useful tool, completely in their power. When you find an agitator who hasn't suffered poverty, it's sound to ask whether he has ever been in my position and what he has done that our police don't know and a foreign police do.

"I'll sign in the morning," I said.

"Why not now?" he answered. "Why suffer another night?"

I asked him where on earth I could go. I told him that before I could be let loose on the public, he would have to bring me clothes, and, when I was decently dressed, take me to his farm to wash. All that couldn't be done at a moment's notice without arousing a lot of curiosity.

"I see your point," he said. "Yes, I'll bring you clothes in the morning."

"And get that Swiss of yours away before we talk! That's what worries me most. I don't trust him a yard."

"My dear fellow," he protested, "I wish you would give me credit for some discretion."

When the Second Murderer had come on duty and settled down for the night, I started to practise with the ballista, stuffing a coat into my end of the ventilator so that the thud of the pegs could not be heard. The strips of hide had shrunk into even tighter coils. It was a more powerful weapon than I needed, and the devil to pull; I had to use both hands, my left on the shaft of the spit, my right gripping the ring, held horizontally so that it did not catch as it flew through the aperture. At a range of four feet the spit drilled clean through two tins of tomatoes and buried itself six inches in the earth. I shot it off less than a dozen times, for the construction was none too strong.

I unstopped the ventilator and fanned for an hour to change the air. Heaven knows whether it really made any difference, but it was worth trying since my next task was to persuade the Swiss to shut up his end of the ventilator, and keep it shut while I straightened the tunnel.

I began moaning and mumbling to shake his nerves a bit. When he ordered me to stop it, I said I would if he told me the time.

"Half-past two," he answered sulkily.

I stayed quiet for another hour, and then went off my head again—sobs and maniac laughter and appeals to him to let me out. He endured my noises with annoying patience (hoping perhaps for that hypothetical reward) and compelled me to such a show of hysteria before he plugged the hole that I managed to get on my own nerves into the bargain. My acting was good enough to be a genuine release for my feelings.

The straightening of the tunnel was easy and quite silent. I dug with my knife and gathered the earth handful by handful. At intervals I let off some moans to discourage him from removing the plug. The curve vanished, and in its place was an empty hollow, like a rabbit's nest, with two mouths. His plug was a piece of sacking. I opened out its folds on my side without disturbing its position. I could breathe without difficulty and hear every sound in the lane.

I arranged my rolled sleeping bag under my shoulder blades, and lay on my back in the mud with the engine presented and the spit fitted to the thong. I had to be ready to fire the moment that a man's head appeared at the hole. The removal of the sacking would give me time to draw, and if anyone looked into the hole and noticed that its shape had been altered, that would be the last thing he ever noticed.

I hoped that the Swiss would leave the sacking alone. I felt no compunction in killing him, but if he removed the plug immediately before Quive-Smith's arrival I might not be able to cut my way out in time to surprise the major. I kept up enough muttering to prove that

I was a nuisance and alive, but not so much that he would be tempted to pull out the sacking and curse me.

The light of morning gleamed through the folds. I waited. I waited, it seemed to me, till long after midday before Quive-Smith arrived. As a matter of fact, he was early—if, that is, he usually came at 10 A.M.

For the first time I could hear all their conversation. At that hour in the morning they spoke in low voices and as little as possible.

"He has gone mad, sir," reported the Swiss stolidly.

"Oh, I don't expect so," answered Quive-Smith. "He's just avoiding the crisis. He'll soon be calm."

"Usual time to-night, sir?"

"If not, I will let you know. Your woman has been warned that you may be leaving?"

"Yes, sir."

I heard his heavy steps sploshing off through the mud. All this time I was lying on my back and staring at the hole.

I cannot remember the slightest effort in drawing the ballista. There was a flash of light as Quive-Smith withdrew the plug. I started, and that slight jerk of my muscles seemed to pull the thong. Immediately afterwards his head appeared. I noticed the surprise in his eyes, but by that time I think he was dead. The spit took him square above the nose. He looked, when he vanished, as if someone had screwed a ring into his forehead.

I hacked at my end of the ventilator until it was large enough to receive my body, then crawled inside and burst through into the lane with a drive of head and shoulders. Quive-Smith was lying on his back watching me. I had my thumbs on his windpipe before I realized what had happened. The foot of spit that projected behind his skull was holding up his head in a most lifelike manner. He hadn't brought any spare clothes. Perhaps he didn't intend me to live after he had my signature; perhaps he didn't believe that I would sign. The latter is the more charitable thought. He had a loaded revolver in his pocket, but that is no proof one way or the other.

I burned that scandalous document, then stretched myself and peered through the hedge over the once familiar fields. Pat was nowhere in sight, and his cows were grazing peacefully. Patachon was talking to his shepherd on the down. It was a damp November day, windless, sunless, of so soft a neutrality that, coming to it straight from disinterment, I couldn't tell whether the temperature was ten or thirty degrees above freezing point. By Quive-Smith's watch it was only eleven. I ate his lunch. Behold, Sisera lay dead, and the nail was in his temples.

I destroyed his screen of bushes and his camera (thorough though I knew him to be, I was surprised that he had really set the scene for his badger watching) and folded up the heavy motor rug which kept him warm. Then I shifted the log that was jammed between both banks of the lane, and opened the door of the burrow. The stench was appalling. I had been out only half an hour, but that was enough for me to notice, as if it had been created by another person, the atmosphere in which I had been living.

Boiling some muddy water on the Primus, I sponged my body—a gesture rather than a wash. It was heaven to feel dry and warm when I had changed into his clothes. He had heavy whipcord riding breeches, a short fur-lined shooting coat—Central European rather than English, but the ideal garment for his job—over his tweeds, and a fleece-lined trench coat over the lot.

When I was dressed I went through his papers. He had the party and identity documents of his own nation, with his real name on them. He also had a British passport. It was not in the name of Quive-Smith. He had put on that name and character for this particular job. His occupation was given as Company Director, almost as noncommittal as Author. Anybody can qualify for either description, as every police-court magistrate knows; but they look impressive.

In a belt round his waist I found £200 in gold and a second passport. It had twice been extended by obscure consulates, but had neither stamps nor visas on it, showing that it had never yet been used for travel. That this passport was his own private affair was a fair assumption. The photograph showed his face and hair darkened with stain, and without a moustache. If I were in Quive-Smith's game, I should take care to have a similar passport; should he have a difference of opinion with his employers, he could disappear completely and find a home in a very pleasant little Latin country.

I held up any definite plans until after I should have interviewed the Swiss, but when I cut my hair and shaved I left myself a moustache exactly like the major's and brushed my hair, as his, straight back from the forehead. The name and identity of the Company Director might suit me very well.

I removed what was left of Asmodeus and buried him in the lane where he had lived and hunted, with a tin of beef to carry him through till he learned the movements of game over his new ground. I plugged the ragged hole made by my escape with my old clothes, my bedding, and earth, and took from the den my money and the exercise book that contained the two first parts of this journal. Then I replaced the original door, and laid the iron plate against the bank of the lane, covering it with earth and debris. When the nettles and bracken grow up in the spring—and thick they will grow on that turned earth—there will be no trace of any of us.

I propped up Quive-Smith's body against a bush, where it was out of the way. Not a pretty act, but his siege had destroyed my sensibility. I had room for no feeling but immense relief. After dusk I walked round Pat's pasture to accustom my legs to exercise. I was very weak, and probably a bit lightheaded. It didn't matter. Since all that remained was to take crazy risks, to be a little crazy was no disadvantage.

The tracks in the mud told me that the Swiss always entered and left by the top of the lane. There was no mistaking the prints left by Quive-Smith's abnormally small feet. I had been compelled to keep my own shoes, and the heels of his stockings were lumps under my soles.

I squatted against the bank in the darkest section of the lane and waited. I heard the fellow a quarter of a mile away. He was moving reasonably quietly where the lanes were dry, but had no patience with mud.

When he was a few paces from me I flashed Quive-Smith's torch on his face and ordered him to put his hands up. I have never seen such a badly frightened man. From his point of view he had been held up in the middle of nowhere by a maniac with a considerable grudge against him.

I made him keep his face to the hedge while I removed his documents, his pistol, and his trouser buttons. I had read of that trick, but never seen it done. It's effective. A man with his trousers round his ankles is not only hindered; his morale is destroyed.

He carried a passport on him. I suppose those chaps always do. A glance at the first page showed me that his name was Müller, that he was naturalized English, and that he was a hotel porter. He was a big man, fair-haired, with a fair moustache waxed to points. He looked as if he had modeled himself upon some ex-N.C.O. of the Corps of Commissionaires.

"Is he dead?" the man stammered.

I told him to turn round and look, keeping him covered while I flashed the light on Quive-Smith's naked body. Then I put him back with his face to the hedge. He was shaking with fear and cold. His legs pulsated. He exhibited all the other involuntary reactions of panic. I had thrown his imagination out of control.

He kept on saying: "What . . . what . . . what . . ."
He meant, I think, to ask what I was going to do to him.
"Who am I?" I asked.
"I don't know."
"Think again, Müller!"

I placed the cold flat of my knife against his naked thighs. God knows what he thought it was, or what he imagined I meant to do! He collapsed on the ground, whimpering. I wanted him to keep his clothes reasonably clean, so I picked him up by one ear, and propped him against the hawthorn alongside Quive-Smith.

"Who am I?" I asked again.
"The Aldwych . . . the . . . police wanted you."
"Who is the man whose clothes I am wearing?"
"Number 43. I never met him before this job. I know him as Major Quive-Smith."
"Why didn't Major Quive-Smith hand me over to the police?"
"He said you were one of his agents, and you knew too much."

That sounded a true piece of Quive-Smith ingenuity; it explained to a simple intelligence why it was necessary to put me out of the way, and why they were working independently of the police; it also ensured the Second Murderer's zealous cooperation.

"What were you going to do with my body that night?"
"I don't know," he sobbed. "I swear I don't know. I had orders to stay in the car every night until I heard a shot and then to join him."
"Where did you get the iron plate?"
"I had it cut in Bridport on the morning when he first discovered you were here. I used to meet him outside the farm for orders."
"How many years have you worked in hotels?"
"Ten years. Two as night porter."
"Any dependents?"
"A wife and two tiny tots, sir," he said piteously.

I suspected he was lying; there was a whine in his voice. And I felt that, considering the varied human material at their disposal, his employers wouldn't have chosen a family man for a job of indefinite duration.

"Where does your wife think you are?" I asked.
"Relieving at—at Torquay."
"Does she believe that?"
"Yes."
"She doesn't mind getting no letters from you?"
"No."

"Doesn't it ever occur to her that you might be with another woman?"

"No."

"Careful, Müller!" I said.

I merely raised the revolver to the level of his eyes. He shrieked that he had been lying. He pawed the air with his right hand as if he could catch the bullet in its flight. The wretched fellow feared death as he would a ghost. I admit that death is a horrid visitor, but surely distinguished? Even a man going to the gallows feels that he should receive the guest with some attempt at dignity.

"From whom do you take your orders?" I asked.

"The hotel manager."

"No one else?"

"Nobody else, I swear!"

"What hotel?"

He gave me the name of the hotel and its manager. I won't repeat it here. It ought to be above suspicion, but for that reason, if no other, I have little doubt that our people suspect it. If they don't, they have only to check which of them in the last week of October lost a night porter who never returned.

"What crime did you commit?" I asked.

It was obvious that they had some hold on him in order to make of him so obedient and unquestioning a tool. Night porters, in my experience, are remarkable for their brusque independence.

"Assault," he muttered, evidently ashamed of himself.

"How?"

"She invited me to her room—at least I thought she did. I shouldn't have done it. I know that. But I was going off duty. And then—then I went for her a bit rough-like. I thought she'd been leading me on, you see. And she screamed and the manager and her father came in. She looked a child. I thought I'd taken leave of my senses. She had just been laughing at me friendly, sir, when she came in of an evening, and I'd thought . . . I could have sworn that . . ."

"I know what you thought," I said. "Why didn't they charge you?"

"For the sake of the hotel, sir. The manager hushed it up."

"And they didn't sack you?"

"No, the manager made me sign a confession and they all witnessed it."

"So you have done what you were told ever since?"

"Yes."

"Why didn't you get another job?"

"They wouldn't give me any references, sir, and I don't blame them."

He was genuinely ashamed. He had come out of the realms of a panic-stricken imagination as soon as he was reminded of the real trouble of his everyday life. They had a double grip on the poor devil. They had not only ensured his obedience, but shattered his self-respect.

"Don't you see that they framed you?" I asked.

I was sure of it. Any really competent little bitch of seventeen could have managed those enigmatic smiles and performed that disconcerting change from temptress to horrified child.

"I'd like to believe it, sir," he said, shaking his head.

No wonder Quive-Smith was exasperated by him!

I myself became a human being again. Müller might, for all I knew, have been a gangster of the most savage, and therefore cowardly, type. I had to break him down. It wasn't only acting; I should have killed him without hesitation if he hadn't proved useful. But I was almost as relieved as he when I could lay brutality aside. I told him to pull up his pants, and gave him a bit of string to hold them, and a cigarette. I kept the revolver in sight, of course, just to remind him that all in the garden was not yet roses.

"They know you at the farm?" I asked.

"Yes. I drove the major over there."

"In what capacity? His servant?"

"Yes. He told them I was taking my own holiday on the coast."

"Have you been at the farm since?"

"Once. I had lunch there the day that . . . that . . ."

"That you buried me alive."

"Oh, sir! If only I had known!" he cried. "I thought you were one of them—honest, I did! I didn't care if they murdered each other. It was a case of the more the merrier, if you see what I mean."

"You seem to be pretty sure now that I'm not one of them," I said.

"I know you're not. A gentleman like you wouldn't be against his own country."

Wouldn't he? I don't know. I distrust patriotism; the reasonable man can find little in these days that is worth dying for. But dying against—there's enough iniquity in Europe to carry the most urbane or decadent into battle.

However, I saw what use Müller had been to his employers. A night porter must be able to sum up his customers on mighty little evidence, especially when they arrive without any baggage. He must, for example, know the difference between a duke and a stock pusher, though they speak with the same accent and the latter be much better dressed than the former.

I explained to him that he might consider himself out of danger so long as his nerve did not fail; he was going down to the farm to tell Patachon that Quive-Smith had been called back to London, to pack up his things, and to take them away in the car.

Quive-Smith had almost certainly warned his hosts that he might be off any day, so the plan was not outrageously daring. Müller had the right air of authority; with the rug over his arm, he looked trained and respectable in spite of being somewhat muddy. He was dressed in such a way that he could pass for a night watchman in Chideock or a manservant on a holiday: a stout tweed suit, an old pull-over of suède, and a stiff white collar.

The chief risk was that Müller, when he found himself in the farm, would decide that his late employers were more to be feared than I. That point I put to him with the utmost frankness. I told him that if he wasn't out of the house in a quarter of an hour I should come and fetch him and claim to be the major's brother. I also told him that he was useful to me just so long as nobody knew the major was dead, and that the moment when his usefulness ceased, whether in ten minutes or two weeks, would be his last.

"But if you are loyal to me for the next few days," I added, "you can forget that matter of criminal assault. I'll give you money to go abroad and never see your late employers again. They'll leave you in peace. You're no further use to them, and you don't know enough to be worth following. So there you are! Give me away, and I'll kill you! Play straight with me, and there's a new life open to you wherever you want to lead it!"

There were a good many holes in the argument, but he was in no state for analytical thinking. He was deeply impressed and became maudlin with relief. Quive-Smith was quite right about him; he was the perfect Second Murderer. He attached himself with doglike simplicity and asked only to be allowed to obey.

He took the major's head while I took his heels, and we moved cautiously down into the road that ran along the foot of the hill. There, thankfully and immediately, we dropped our white burden in the ditch. I saw the sweat burst out on the back of Müller's thick neck as soon as he was convinced that we had not been seen.

At the five-bar gate where Patachon's private track swung across the home paddock to the farm we stopped. I told Müller that I should wait for him there, and should enter the car when he got out to open the gate. I gave him Quive-Smith's keys and I gave him a story to tell. The major was dining with friends in Bridport. He had learned that he had to go abroad at once. His address for forwarding letters was Barclay's Bank, Cairo. I knew from a letter in his pocket that he kept an account with a branch of Barclay's—and Cairo is a complicated town through which to trace a man's passage.

"But what will I do if they don't believe me?" he asked.

"Of course they'll believe you," I answered. "Why the devil shouldn't they?"

I was none too sure of that, but his best chance of success was to show the utmost confidence.

I gave him a pound to tip the girl who had made the major's bed—if there were such a girl—and another which he was to hand to Mrs. Patachon for her daughter's savings bank.

"You know the little daughter?" I asked.

"Yes—Marjorie."

"Give Marjorie a message from Major Quive-Smith: that she must remember not to bring her queen out too soon."

"I don't understand," he said.

"All the better. Explain to her that you don't understand what it means. But she will, and she'll laugh. Tell her not to bring her queen out too soon."

It was perfectly safe advice to give a beginner at chess, and it would establish Müller's *bona fides*.

I let him cross the paddock and go round the corner of the barns into the yard; then I followed to watch, so far as possible, over my fate. This time there was no need to take extreme pains to hide myself —the dogs had an excuse to bark. I squatted behind a tree whence I could see the front door.

Mrs. Patachon received the caller with surprise but no hesitation. She shut the door and there was no movement for five minutes— which I spent wishing I had cut the telephone wires. Then an oil lamp was lit in an upper room, and I saw Müller pass back and forth across the window. He came out with a suitcase in his hand, followed by Patachon with a gun case, Marjorie with the rug, and Mrs. Patachon with a packet of sandwiches. The whole party were chattering gayly —except Müller, who was far too glum—and sending messages to the major. They entered the stable to watch Müller load and start the car, and I ran back to the gate.

"Where to, sir?" asked Müller.

In spite of his grip on the wheel his elbows were quivering like the gills of a fish—partly from reaction and partly from fear that his usefulness had come to an end. I was sorry to appear again as a ruthless killer, but there was a risk that he might try to rush the gate.

I told him to drive to Liverpool and to go easy with the traffic laws. Southampton was too close, and London too full of eyes. We picked up Quive-Smith and put him in the back of the car under a rug.

My plans were straightening out. I was sure that nobody would call at the farm until letters and telegrams had remained a week or more without reply; anxiety would have to be very strong before any of the major's subordinates or superiors—if he had any superiors— ventured to intrude upon his discreet movements. When they did, and visited the lane, they could take their choice of three theories: that I had got away with Quive-Smith and Müller hard on my heels; that I had bribed the pair of them to let me go; or that they had killed me and in some way aroused the curiosity of the police.

We stopped for petrol at Bristol and Shrewsbury. On the way I wired an assortment of ironmongery to Quive-Smith, and dropped him into the Severn. I have no regrets. Reluctantly, belatedly, but finally I have taken on the mentality of war; and I risk for myself a death as violent and unpleasant as any he could wish for me.

We reached Liverpool in time for an early breakfast. The town was in its vilest mood, and I was glad that the major had dressed himself for exposure to the elements. A northeast wind gathered the soot, dust, and paper from the empty streets, iced them, and flung them into the Mersey. The sullen yellow water gave a more bitter impression of cold than the blue of the Arctic. I felt greater confidence in the wretched Müller. On such a morning it was inconceivable that anyone would betray a person who intended to have him out of England before nightfall.

Putting up at a hotel, we breakfasted in our room. While Müller dropped off to sleep in front of the fire, I spent a couple of hours practising the signature on Quive-Smith's passport. For convenience I still write of him and think of him as Quive-Smith, though there is possibly no one but myself, Saul, Müller, and a handful of people in a corner of Dorset who ever knew him by that name. The signature I practised and the identity I had taken were those of his normal British self—the nondescript company director.

This English name of his was signed in a spidery, flowing script which, with a fine nib, was not at all difficult to imitate. My forgery wouldn't have taken in a bank manager, but it was good enough for an embarkation form or a customs declaration—especially since it would be written on cheap paper with an office pen.

The passport photograph was not very like me, but near enough.

No shipping clerk would question it. The common type of Quive-Smith and myself is manifestly respectable and responsible.

I woke up Müller and offered him a drink. He turned out to be a teetotaler—another advantage, I suppose, to his employers. I took him with me to the bathroom, and while I washed off the accumulated filth of weeks (keeping the revolver handy on the soap dish) I made him sit on the lavatory seat and read me the shipping news.

We had ships sailing that afternoon for New York; for the West Indies; for Gibraltar and Mediterranean ports; for Madeira and South America; for Tangier and the East. All countries for which I needed a visa were excluded, and all voyages longer than a week. Gibraltar, Madeira, and Tangier remained—and Madeira was a dead end, to be avoided if possible.

How to lose Müller was a difficult problem. I had promised him his life and freedom, but it was going to be a hard promise to keep. He had only one set of documents; he was too stupid to ship himself as a stowaway without being caught; he hadn't the sense or presence to bluff. Whatever port he entered and left would be sure to have full particulars of him. I didn't much care whether he were traced or not; I was sure that his employers would take no further interest in him after he had answered their questions, but I wanted to put off that questioning as long as possible.

I wondered what Quive-Smith would have done had he found himself saddled with Müller as the only witness to murder or bribery. The answer was not far to seek. He would have pushed Müller overboard on the night before reaching port, and concealed his absence. That seemed an admirable solution. It would convince them that I really was Quive-Smith—in case they doubted it—and would put an end to all search for the hotel porter.

This, then, was my plan; but instead of pushing him overboard wherever was convenient, I had to push him overboard within reach of land and with the means of landing. There were two places where that could be done—the point near the mouth of the Tagus where the Cintra Hills come down to the sea, and Cape St. Vincent.

I sent for a barber to give me a decent haircut, and, as soon as we left the hotel, bought a monocle which disguised, or rather emphasized and accounted for, the glassy stare of my left eye. Then I led Müller round the shipping offices—an eccentric holiday-maker and his secretary-valet. I asked as many silly questions as a Cook's tourist; I hoped, I said, to be able to wave to an old friend who lived in Portugal. The shipping clerks explained to me patiently that it depended where my friend lived, that Portugal had a long seaboard, and that in any case the largest of handkerchiefs could not be seen at a couple of miles. They were surprisingly polite; they must, after all, spend much more time instructing prospective customers in elementary geography than in selling them tickets.

I found out what I wanted to know. The Gibraltar ship wouldn't do; it passed the Tagus in the morning, and Cape St. Vincent shortly after sunset. The Tangier ship, a slow old tub with one class only, was more suitable. It passed the Tagus between 9 P.M. and midnight.

I had a look at the plans. The steering gear was aft on the main deck, and between its housing and the stern was the usual small and private space where lovers park their chairs, provided they can endure the exaggerated motion of the ship. There would be no room for lovers on this trip. The company director and his companion were going to spread themselves and their deck chairs over that space, and be rude to anyone who disturbed their privacy.

We booked two adjoining staterooms with a bath between, and then did our shopping. I provided Müller and myself with bags and necessaries for the voyage. I bought a collapsible rubber boat with a bicycle pump to inflate it, a pair of strong paddles in two pieces, and a hundred feet of light rope, all packed in a large suitcase. Müller, naturally, thought the boat was for my own escape; I didn't disillusion him. Then I put the car into storage for a year, and we went on board.

Down St. George's Channel and across the Bay I had no need to trouble myself about Müller's whereabouts. He had never made an ocean voyage. The ship was a mere 8000 tons. The sea was very rough. I occupied the vile heaving rail at the stern, just to establish a squatter's rights over it, and after a painful morning acquired my sea legs. It was a blessing to have none of my usual biliousness. I was free to spend my time eating, drinking, and washing; I needed as much of the three pleasures as the ship provided.

On the third night out from Liverpool we passed Finistierra, and awoke to a pale blue world with a rapidly falling swell; the gray-green hills of Portugal lay along the eastern horizon. I routed my secretary-valet out of bed, and fed him breakfast. Then we occupied the two deck chairs at the stern. I spread out my rugs and legs as awkwardly as possible, and through my monocle stared offensively at anyone who dared to pick his way over them. None of the passengers showed the slightest desire to join us.

In the late afternoon I gave Müller a couple of lemonades to brace his courage, and asked him what he wanted to do. Would he rather return to London and report himself, or vanish off the face of the earth? He was very nervous at the thought of not going back to tell what he knew of Quive-Smith's death.

"You'll have to explain why you told so many lies at the farm," I reminded him. "The family can bear witness to the fact that you were alone. Nothing prevented you from telephoning to London."

He promptly begged me to take him with me wherever I was going. The man was quite incapable of standing by himself. As soon as he was detached from one support, he began waving frantic tentacles in the hope of gripping another.

I replied that I couldn't take him; he would have to disappear by his own individual route.

"They would follow me!" he cried. "I would never have any peace, sir."

"They won't follow you if they think you are dead," I said.

I explained to him the plan: that he and the rubber boat were to be thrown overboard when we were a couple of miles from shore, and that I would give him £500 with which to start a new life. He brightened up a bit at the thought of money, but then was appalled by the difficulties facing him when he reached the shore.

Well, there was one thing Müller could be trusted to do: to follow orders. So I gave them.

"Your clothes will be in the boat," I said. "When you land, put them on. Rip the boat to bits, and hide them under a rock. Walk to Cascaes and take the electric train to Lisbon. Don't go to a hotel. Spend the night where you do not have to register. If you drink a coffee at any of the bars in the centre of the town, I expect some way of passing a discreet and pleasant night will occur to you. In the morning go to the docks to meet an imaginary friend who is arriving by ship. Pass back again through the customs as if you came off the boat and get your passport stamped. Then buy yourself a visa and a ticket for any country you want to visit, and leave at once by another ship."

"But suppose they look for me in Lisbon," he said. "They will see that I entered and left."

I explained to him that I should make it clear he was dead; once they were sure he had never landed in Tangier, they wouldn't look for him in Lisbon or anywhere else.

He seemed to think that he was a person of importance, and that they would ransack the world to find him. I repeated that so long as they thought Quive-Smith alive, they would not spend an hour or a fiver hunting for a useless agent whom they believed to be dead.

"I know too much," he protested.

"You don't know a damn thing," I answered. "I doubt if you even know what country you were working for."

"I do, sir," he said, and mentioned it.

By God, it was the wrong one! I suppose it's a commonplace that the underlings of a secret service should not even know the nationality of their employers, but it seemed to me remarkably clever.

I told him he was wrong, and proved it by the major's papers. After that I had no more trouble except his natural funk of the sea.

We were a little ahead of schedule, and the Cintra Hills were in sight at sunset. That suited me well enough; we could get the job over while the passengers were at dinner. So that no one should be sent in search of us, I told the chief steward that I wasn't feeling well, and that my secretary would be looking after me.

Müller undressed in the cabin, and I tied the money round his neck in a fold of oilskin. As soon as the alleyways were clear we took the suitcase on deck, and unpacked and inflated the boat in the shelter of the deckhouse. We could see lights on shore, so he knew in which direction to row. I made Müller repeat his orders. He had them pat, and he put them crudely. Then I lashed his clothes and the paddles to the bottom of the boat, and looped the other end of the long line around his wrist.

The wash of a ship isn't inviting. The poor devil sat on the rail shivering with cold and panic. I didn't give him time to think, but hurled the boat over and snapped at him that he would drown if he let the line tauten. I saw the boat, a dark patch bobbing on the white wash, and I saw him come to the surface. A second later, the only sign that he had ever existed was a dressing gown lying on the deck. Good luck to him! With the right job and a positive boss, his qualities of Second Murderer should ensure for him a secure and happy life.

I returned to my stateroom with the suitcase and dressing gown, and went to bed—his bed till midnight and my own till morning. When the cabin steward called us, he naturally assumed that my secretary was already up and about.

The day was abominably long. There was some doubt whether we should arrive at Tangier in time for passengers to land that night; if we didn't, I had no hope of keeping Müller's disappearance secret. I missed breakfast and passed the morning in concealment, acting on the general principle that nobody would think of us if neither was seen, but that, if one were seen, there might be inquiries about the other. At lunchtime I entered the saloon to tip my table steward, but refused to eat. I told him that both I and my secretary had been badly upset by our food, and that I had prescribed for us a short period of starvation. There was nothing like starvation, I boomed pompously, for putting the stomach right; that had always been our experience in India.

While the cabin steward was off duty between two and four, I packed the bags and took them on deck. Cape Spartel was in sight. The purser confirmed that we should certainly be able to leave the ship before the customs closed. I collected the two landing cards. Then again I went into hiding until we dropped anchor.

As soon as the tender arrived and the baggage had been carried off the ship, I visited and tipped the cabin steward in a great hurry. He was not exactly suspicious, but he felt it his duty to ask a question.

"Is Mr. Müller all right, sir?"

"Good heavens, yes!" I answered. "He packed up for me and took everything on deck. He's on the tender now with the baggage."

"I hadn't seen him all day, sir," he explained, "so I thought I had better ask."

"I haven't seen much of him myself," I replied testily. "I understand he found an old friend in the engineers' department."

He let it go at that. Müller was my servant. I was eminently respectable. If I saw nothing wrong, nothing could be wrong.

The worst danger was on me now. Lest the tally should be wrong I had to surrender two landing cards while appearing to surrender only one. I am no conjurer; the simplest card trick defeats me if it demands sleight of hand. This confounded business worried me far more than the job of throwing Müller overboard. I loitered near the head of the gangway, hoping there would be a rush of passengers descending to the tender. There never was. Most had already left the ship. The rest came one by one.

I dashed into the smoking room and stuck the two landing cards lightly together with the gum from a penny stamp; they were of thin cardboard, and I hoped that the Assistant Purser who was collecting them wouldn't notice that I had shoved two into his hand. If he did notice, I proposed to say that Müller was already on the tender and that he must have gone down the gangway without surrendering his card. If someone then had a look at the tender and found he wasn't there, I could only show amazement and pray that I didn't find myself in the dock on a capital charge.

I went through the entire murder trial while I stuck those two cards together: the black and incontrovertible evidence that I had concealed Müller's absence, the discovery of my identity, and so on. My fantasy had developed as far as shooting my way out of the magistrate's court when I walked down the gangway and the Assistant Purser received my two cards without a glance. Ten minutes later I was on the Tangier mole, surrounded by a yelling mob of coffee-colored porters draped in burnooses of sacking.

Passing through customs, I had my entry carefully noted. I took pains to see that the French immigration official wrote down the company director's name correctly spelled. From then on there could be no shadow of doubt that Major Quive-Smith had duly entered Tangier, and alone.

As for Müller, his late employers' discreet inquiries at the offices of the line would be duly passed on to the ship. The stewards would remember that Müller had not been seen for twenty-four hours. The Assistant Purser would remember that when he checked the landing cards he found two suspiciously stuck together. The engineers' department—if the steward remembered my remark—would say they had never heard of Müller. And it would be reported back to Liverpool that there was indeed grave reason to fear that something had happened to Mr. Müller. Whoever had put the inquiry on foot, having found out what he wanted to know, would then laugh at the serious faces of the directors, and explain that Mr. Müller was perfectly safe and sound, and that—well, any yarn would do! Mr. Müller, for example, had feared to be cited as corespondent and had taken steps to conceal his movements.

I drove to a hotel, deposited my baggage, and booked a room for a week, telling the proprietor that I had a little friend in Tangier, and that, if I didn't turn up for two or three nights, he was not to be surprised. I had an enormous meal at his excellent restaurant. Then I put a razor, a bottle of hair dye, and another of stain into my pocket, and walked off into the deserted hills. Besides money, the only thing I carried out of my past life was this confession, for I began to see in what manner it might be useful.

I do not think that in all my life I have known such relief and certainty as in a valley between those sun-dried hills, where the water trickled down the irrigation channels from one hand-dug, well-loved terrace to another, and no light showed but the blazing stars. My escape was over; my purpose decided; my conscience limpid. I was at war—and no one is so aware of the tranquillity of nature as a soldier resting between one action and the next.

I buried that company director's passport and my own, with which I have probably finished forever. I shaved off my moustache, stained my face and body, and dyed my hair. Then I slept till dawn, my face in the short grass by the water's edge, my body drawing strength from that warm and ancient earth.

In the morning I strolled to the upper town, where I had not been the night before, and completed my change of identity. I bought a thoroughly Latin suit, spats, and some beastly pointed shoes, posting my other clothes in a parcel addressed to the Public Assistance Committee, Rangoon. I trust there is such a committee. I went to a barber who duly doused me with Eau de Cologne and brushed my luscious black hair straight back from my forehead. When this was over, my resemblance to the photograph on Quive-Smith's passport was a lot closer than my resemblance to the company director.

The regular packet was leaving that day for Marseille. I got a French visa on my passport (my new fatherland is as awkward as all other American countries—I can travel nowhere without a visa) and bought a ticket in my new name. Since I had no baggage, it was easy to bluff my way on to the ship without passing the control. Thus there was no record for inquisitive eyes that this courteous and scented gentleman had either entered or left Tangier, and no means of connecting him with Quive-Smith. I think they will be looking for their vanished agent between Atlas and the Niger.

EXTRACT FROM THE LETTER WHICH ACCOMPANIED THIS MANUSCRIPT

My dear Saul,

I write this from a pleasant inn where I am accustoming myself to a new avatar. I must not, of course, give you any clue to it; nor would the trail of the gentleman I describe as Latin—even assuming it could be followed—lead to where or what I am.

I want these papers published. If necessary, have them brushed up by some competent hack and marketed under his name. You won't, of course, mention mine, nor the name of the country to which I went from Poland and to which I am about to return. Let the public take its choice!

My reason for publishing is twofold. First, I have committed two murders, and the facts must be placed on record in case the police ever got hold of the wrong man. Second, if I am caught, there can never again be any possible question of the complicity of H. M. Government. Every statement of mine can, at need, be checked, amplified, and documented. The three parts of the journal (two written accidentally and the last deliberately) form an absolute answer to any accusation from any quarter that I have involved my own nation.

Forgive me for never telling you of my engagement nor of the happy weeks we lived in Dorset. I first met her in Spain a couple of years ago. We hadn't reached the point of an announcement in *The Times* and we didn't give a damn about it anyway.

The ethics of revenge? The same as the ethics of war, old boy! Unless you are a conscientious objector, you cannot condemn me. Unsporting? Not at all. It is one of the two or three most difficult shots in the world.

I begin to see where I went wrong the first time. It was a mistake to make use of my skill over the sort of country I understood. One should always hunt an animal in its natural habitat; and the natural habitat of man is—in these days—a town. Chimney pots should be the cover, and the method, snapshots at two hundred yards. My plans are far advanced. I shall not get away alive, but I shall not miss; and that is really all that matters to me any longer.

SILENT NIGHT

by Baynard Kendrick

On Friday, Dec. 20th, a week to the day since six year old Ronnie Connatser had been kidnapped from Miss Murray's School, Arnold Cameron, Special Agent in Charge of the New York F.B.I., telephoned early in the morning to make an appointment with Capt. Duncan Maclain. It was arranged for 10:00 A.M. in Maclain's penthouse office twenty-six stories above 72nd Street and Riverside Drive. Cameron arrived promptly, bringing with him Special Agent Hank Weeks and Alan Connatser, Ronnie's father. The men were silent, grim.

Capt. Maclain, an ex-Intelligence Officer blinded in World War I, had carried on the work of a Private Investigator with the aid of his partner, Spud Savage, for nearly forty years. To him being a Licensed P.I. was a dedicated profession. He hoped by developing his remaining four senses, hearing, feeling, taste, and smell to the highest point of proficiency to prove to the world before he died that a blind man with sufficient intelligence could be just as good, if not a little bit better, than millions of people who had eyes with which to see.

Waiting for Cameron, the Captain had a gratified feeling that maybe after all these years he had at last succeeded. Duncan Maclain was no superman. He had certain peculiar talents that had proved most useful through the years to various law-enforcement agencies, among them the New York Police Department, and on several occasions the F.B.I.

He had known Arnold Cameron for a long time, and worked with him before Cameron became S.A.C. of the New York office. The Captain was the first to admit that neither he, nor any private operator, no matter where he worked, could get to first base without the co-operation of the local police or the F.B.I.

Cameron hadn't said what this case was about, except that it concerned the kidnapping of Connatser's six year old son. The Captain had heard about Alan Connatser, President and Treasurer of Connatser Products, Inc., the big plant that sprawled over acres on the edge of Long Island City. It was one of those industrial mushrooms that had grown in importance since World War II, mainly through Connatser's personality and engineering genius. The company did a lot of top security defense work, but the F.B.I. was quite capable of handling any violations of security on their own. Kidnapping, too, for that matter.

Why go on guessing? Speculation was always fruitless and a waste of time. He'd know the details soon enough. Whatever they were he hoped he could help. It was flattering that Arnold Cameron had dealt him in.

At 9:55 Rena, the Captain's secretary showed the three men in. Maclain shook hands around. Cameron's grip was friendly as usual. Special Agent Hank Weeks was properly official, neither cold nor warm, with an element of doubt in it as though he didn't intend to commit himself even on the say-so of the S.A.C. unless he was shown. Maclain suppressed a grin. He was skeptical himself about people who claimed they saw everything—even when they had 20-20 vision.

Alan Connatser wrung the Captain's hand with a grip that was full of despairing appeal. "Mr. Cameron thinks that you can help us, Captain Maclain. My son's been gone for a week now—more like a lifetime to Evelyn, my wife, and me. She has collapsed and is under a doctor's care. It isn't a question of money—I can pay a million and not be hurt. It's the life of my boy—our only child and we can never have another."

A very strong man, Alan Connatser, the Captain judged. Six foot, slow spoken, powerful as flexible steel, and younger than one would imagine. From his voice—not yet forty. And right now he was on the verge of flying into little pieces.

Maclain released himself wordlessly from the clinging grip and went to the bar set in the paneled wall near the diamond-paned doors to the terrace. He sloshed a liberal portion of cognac into a bell goblet and took it to the red leather divan where Connatser had slumped down.

"Slug it!" His face was grave with deep concern. "Your hand is as cold as a frozen fish. It won't help your boy if you crack up now and have a chill."

"Thanks. I guess you're right." Connatser downed the burning brandy in a gulp. "I'm afraid we're saddling you with a hopeless task."

"The world considers blindness hopeless. I haven't found it so." The Captain walked to his broad flat-top desk and sat down. "You say your son has been missing for a week?"

"He was kidnapped last Friday, Dec. 13th at ten past three," Arnold Cameron said. "He'd been to a Christmas party at his school. Miss Murray's at 66th Street and Fifth Avenue. The Connatsers live in a duplex at 82nd and Fifth—sixteen blocks away. Miss Murray saw Ronnie get into his father's Chrysler Imperial in front of the school at three-ten. The car was driven by a substitute chauffeur, who called himself Jules Rosine.

"Rosine stuck up Leon Gerard, who has driven for the family for years, in Gerard's apartment on East 82nd Street—right across the street from the garage where the Chrysler is kept. That was about eleven the night before. Rosine wore a stocking mask. He forced Leon to telephone at gun-point. Leon talked to Mrs. Murchison, the Connatser's housekeeper, said he was ill, and would send a reliable man to take his place the next day. Nobody thought it suspicious since it had happened a few times before. Leon is getting along in years and his health isn't too good."

Cameron paused. The Captain said, "If you fellows believe his story then I do, too."

"We don't believe anything until we've convinced ourselves that it's true," Cameron went on. "Weeks released Leon in his apartment shortly after the kidnapping was reported to us on the evening of the thirteenth. The poor old guy was trussed up like a turkey with adhesive. Anyhow, nothing has been seen of Ronnie, or this Jules Rosine since ten past three in the afternoon a week ago."

A hopeless task, Connatser had said! The Captain ran a hand through his dark graying hair. The details of Charles A. Lindbergh, Jr., Bobby Greenlease, Jr., and the tiny month old Peter Weinberger, all coolly murdered by their kidnappers, were much too vivid in his mind not to realize that Connatser's fears were far from being groundless.

He kept his repellent thoughts to himself and tried to speak reassuringly: "I've known Arnold Cameron for many years, Mr. Connatser. Neither he nor the F.B.I. consider this hopeless or he wouldn't have brought you here to talk with me." His dark sightless eyes, so perfect that many people thought he could see, turned from Connatser to fix themselves on the S.A.C. "You must have some very good reason for thinking Ronnie is still alive, Arnold."

"We happen, in this case, to know he was alive on Tuesday or Wednesday, and probably yesterday."

"What proof?"

"The sound of his voice, Captain, plus an answer to a couple of questions asked by Ronnie's mother—answers that only Ronnie would know."

"Then you must have made contact by phone." The Captain's expressive eyebrows went up a fraction.

"No. They're the ones who have been in touch," Cameron said. "One-way touch, by Audograph records. Three of them. You've told me often that you live in a world of sound. I also know that you're the best man living on identification of voices. Furthermore, you work with an Audograph all the time and are familiar with its sounds and foibles. Isn't that true?"

Maclain nodded. "I have one right here in my desk drawer." He referred to a compact efficient dictating machine used in thousands of business offices. Not more than nine inches square and five inches high, it records dictation on a flexible blue disc, and the dictation can be played back through its built in loud-speaker, or through plugged-in headphones at the flip of a lever.

"Here's the first of the three. The first word from Ronnie's captors, for that matter, from Friday to Monday. Let the family suffer. Die a thousand deaths. It softens them up. I could—"

He broke off abruptly, leaned forward and put a brown manila envelope on the Captain's blotter. It was a standard mailing envelope for the feather light discs. Seven inches square. Printed on the front was: GRAY AUDOGRAM FOR—a space for the address—and below that the words PLEASE DO NOT FOLD. The envelopes, like the discs, could be obtained from any Audograph dealer in cities throughout the country.

For an instant the Captain stared at the envelope as though by sheer intentness, he might develop some superhuman power to penetrate its secret.

"That was mailed to Mrs. Connatser at her home," Cameron explained. "Air mail. It's postmarked: Miami, Florida, Dec. 15th. That was last Sunday."

Maclain touched it gingerly with his forefinger. "I know what a working over you must have given these things. I was wondering about handwriting, or typing, on the address."

"Not this bird, Captain! He hasn't forgotten that we went through two million specimens of handwriting before we nailed LaMarca as kidnapper of the Weinberger baby. There's not even typewriting. No return address, of course. Mrs. Connatser's name and address has been stamped on with one of those kid's rubber stamps that has separate removable rubber letters. You can buy them in any toy store or Five-and-ten."

The Captain took his Audograph machine from the deep bottom left-hand desk drawer. He put it on the desk, then brought up a hand microphone which he plugged into a six-slotted receptacle on the left hand side of the machine. A switch in the handle of the mike controlled the playing of the record, turning it on when pressed in. For continuous playing, a flick of the thumb could lock the switch.

He took the record from the envelope, felt for the grooved side with his finger-nail, and turning it upward put the record on the machine. Unlike a regular phonograph record, the Audograph recorded from the center to the edge.

The Captain slid it into place, turned on the machine, and pushed a lever over to LISTEN. A red indicator light glowed. When recording, the light showed green. He locked the switch on the hand mike and laid the mike gently on the blotter beside the machine.

Out of nowhere the boyish treble of Ronnie Connatser's voice began to speak. Maclain reached out and turned the volume higher, as though that might help to bring the six-year-old closer to his home.

> *"Mommy, Mommy, can you hear me? The man says to tell you that I'm all right and that if I talk in here you can hear me. He says that Daddy can hear me, too, and that if you do what the man says he'll bring me home. Mommy, please tell Daddy to do what the man says. I'm all right, but I'm scared, Mommy. I don't want to spend Christmas here. I'm doing just what the man tells me to. Please hurry and do what the man says. I don't want to spend Christmas here. I don't like it and the man says he'll bring me home. So, please hurry."*

Ronnie's voice quit abruptly. For an endless length of time—actually a few short seconds—the record revolved in mechanical silence. Cameron lit a cigarette. Smoke reached the Captain's nostrils. Leather squeaked as Connatser moved uneasily on the red divan. A man's voice took up where the child's voice had stopped:

> *"Your son's been kidnapped, but he hasn't been harmed. It's to prove that that I'm letting him talk to you. You'll be better off if you keep the police out of this as well as the F.B.I. Press me too hard and you'll never hear his voice again, let alone see him. If you follow out instructions to the letter you'll have him back very shortly. In case you don't think that's your son who was speaking, I'm going to offer you further proof. Ask him*

any two questions you want—questions that only he can answer. Put it in a Personal in the New York Times of Tuesday December the seventeenth. Sign it 'E.C.' You'll be answered by Ronnie on the next record we send to you. That's all for now. You'll never see me. Just call me: Junior."

"Is that all?" The Captain sat up straight in his chair, his face grim.

"End of Record One," Cameron told him.

Maclain swiftly adjusted the disc to play the last few lines a second time.

Faintly, but clearly, through the man's last few words had come the sound of chimes pealing the opening bars of "Silent Night." Then a singer had begun:

> "Silent Night,
> Holy Night,
> All is—"

The song had ended with the click of the mike as the man said "Junior."

"The musical interlude," Cameron said glumly, "is the first song on Side One of Bing Crosby's Decca Recording DL-8128, entitled 'Merry Christmas.' Sales to date about two million. On the last report from our bunion-ridden Agents in Miami, they have found some two hundred radio, record, and music shops, super-markets, drive-ins, and various other publicity-minded places of business, including second-hand-car lots that have P.A. systems working overtime. They have been deafening the public for a week or more to let them know the time of year. No. 1 on the Hit Parade is Bing's little dose of Christmas Cheer." He viciously snubbed out his cigarette.

"We don't think Ronnie's in Miami, anyhow. This Jules Rosine—who is trying hard to make us believe that that's his name by calling himself Junior from the initials J.R.—just doesn't strike me as the type, Captain, who would mail a letter or anything from a city where he has that boy. As a matter of fact, he jumps around the country like a twelve legged flea. The second record is from Kansas City and the third one is from Cleveland."

The Captain sat pinching his upper lip and saying nothing.

Cameron put the second envelope on his desk. "Here's the one where Ronnie answers his mother's questions. Mailed Wednesday, December the eighteenth. Air mail from K.C."

There was a tremor in the Captain's sensitive fingers as he removed the first record and put the second on.

> "Mommy the man says that you and Daddy can hear me if I talk in here, but I don't see how you can hear me if I can't see you. He said I was to tell you what picture Ted Schuyler and I were going to see with Mrs. Murchison, and what I call my electric engine that pulls the train, and if I didn't tell you I wouldn't get back home. I thought you knew that Ted and I were going to see 'Snow White and the Seven Dwarfs'—except Daddy wanted me to come to the plant to meet him and I drank the Pepsi-Cola the chauffeur got me and got so sleepy. And you know my engine is called the Camel because it has a hump-back in its middle. I know you told me not to repeat things, but the man said unless I told you that and unless Daddy did just what he says, I won't get home for Christmas. I don't want to stay here. There's nobody to play with and I want to come home."

The man's voice took it up from there:

> "That answers the questions you had in the *Times* and proves beyond doubt that your son's alive. Nobody is trying to torture you. You'll see when we write again that we're not after money. It's possible that we have even more of that than you. The next will tell you what we want. We know what you want, but don't think we're fooling. Stay away from the police and the F.B.I. and do exactly what I tell you or your precious son is going to die. Cheerio! Junior."

"Junior seems to have split himself in two," the Captain said as he took off the record. "The *man* has become *we*. Do you think it's merely a cover-up, Arnold, or is there really someone else involved beside the man?"

"Anywhere from two to two million. They're after something more precious than money." He put the third record on the desk. "Listen to this one and you'll see."

Agent Hank Weeks said, "I'm betting there's a woman. Purely because they've kept Ronnie harping on *the man*."

The Captain nursed his chin for a moment. "I'm inclined to agree." He put the final record on.

"Do you mind if I have another brandy?" Alan Connatser's voice was tight and dry.

"Drink it all," the Captain said. "Ronnie isn't my son, but nevertheless these records are really getting me."

Connatser poured his drink and returned to his seat. "They're somehow worse than ransom notes to Evelyn and me. They're sadistic. Mean. I find myself wanting to answer Ronnie. Scream at him: 'Tell me where you are!'—as though he were hiding away in some ghostly world of his own. It's unbearable."

"I'd merely sound inane if I tried to express my sympathy." A sharp cold fury was setting the Captain's skin to tingling, turning him into a ruthless inhuman machine. His mind was being honed to a razor edge on a whetstone of revenge and implacability. "This is the one from Cleveland?"

"Mailed air mail yesterday. Thursday the nineteenth. It arrived in New York this morning at seven. We have a tag out for them at the Post Office. They notified us right away."

The Captain flipped the lever to LISTEN and started the disc to play.

> "Mommy did you hear what I told you about the picture show? The Seven Dwarfs? And my engine, the Camel, on the electric train? I wish that you and Daddy would come for me, or answer me if you heard me, like the man said. He says he's telling Daddy exactly what to do right now, and if Daddy does it I'll come back home. Mommy tell him to hurry, please. Hurry and do it because I miss you so much and I want to see the Macy's parade and get my presents."

More unbearable silence then until the man cut in:

> "At six-o'-clock, P. M.—eighteen hours Service Time—you and your pilot, Steven Donegan, will take off from the air strip at your plant on Long Island, flying your Cessna Twin. You will file no flight plan with anyone. At your regular cruising speed of two-hundred-and-ten miles per hour, flying at eight thousand feet, you will follow the regular plane route from New York to Philadelphia. From Philadelphia to Baltimore. From Baltimore to Washington. From Washington to Richmond. From Richmond to Wilmington, North Carolina. From Wilmington to Charleston, South Carolina. From Charleston to Savannah, Georgia. From Savannah to Jacksonville, Florida. From Jacksonville to Daytona. From Daytona to Vero Beach, and from Vero Beach to Miami.
>
> Be on the alert. Somewhere between two of the places named

you will be contacted by radio. When contact is made, if you broadcast an alarm your son will be killed. Remember we'll be tuned in on you, too. We want the complete plans of the *SF-800T Missile.* Those plans consist of forty-four sheets of blueprints that were delivered to you by the Navy a month ago. You are the only one living who has immediate access to them all. Those forty-four blueprints are the price of your son. Particularly the details of the cone.

Once they are received they will be checked immediately by engineers just as competent as you. If they are not approved, or any attempt at trickery is discovered, your boy will die. The clearer those specifications are, the quicker you get your son. Remember, it's his life that's at stake.

Put the plans in a large portmanteau—not a dispatch-case—and weight the portmanteau with a couple of sash-weights. Paint the portmanteau with phosphorescent paint and be ready to drop it on a moment's notice. You will be contacted by the words: *'Cessna come down!'* and will immediately start descending to a thousand feet still holding your course. Watch the ground. One minute before the drop you will be contacted again. Answer: *Roger, Junior!* and look for a red flasher that will turn on on top of a car. When you spot it say: *Condition red!* and drop the portmanteau as close as possible to the flasher. You will be directed if you have to make a second try. Follow the straightest compass course between points and there will be no trouble. Another record will tell you where to pick up your boy. If weather reports are generally bad don't attempt to start. That's your hard luck and you'll have to make another try. Happy landings! Junior."

"Sounds like something from out of the wild blue yonder," Maclain said as he stopped the record. "A modern Chekov nightmare manufactured in Moscow. What are the chances of pulling off such a scheme?"

"My pilot, Steve, says there's a damn good chance," Connatser told him. "I'm a pilot, myself, with some missions behind me, and I'm afraid I agree. Junior knows that we'll break our necks to drop that luminous suitcase on his head, if possible. He also knows that the SF-800T is an ace we have in the hole. So I'm supposed to stake the life of my son against the safety of my country."

The Captain gnawed at his clipped mustache. "At least the Soviets have one weakness that will never change: We know that it's impossible to fathom their way of thinking—but they fully believe that they know the thinking of every other country in the world. Now, it's the life of a child against the lives of untold millions. Tomorrow night! That's not much time to make up forty-four sheets of phony blueprints. What does the F.B.I. think, Arnold? What are you going to do?"

"Mr. Connatser is going to drop the plans as ordered," Cameron said promptly. "You're right about Soviet thinking. We've learned a lot since the days of Klaus Fuchs and Harry Gold. Naval Intelligence draws up two sets of plans, today—when the design is for anything as vital as the SF-800T. The second set is slightly different. To discover the bugs in it might take a corps of scientists a half a year. That's the set we're feeding to Junior tomorrow night."

"Leaving three people only on the hot seat: Ronnie, my wife, and me!" Connatser's voice was low and deadly. "They're not going to keep Ronnie alive for six months. So they may find some bugs in a couple of days, and kill him then. Then there's always the chance when they get the plans that they'll consider it safer to murder him anyhow."

"So we better get busy with what we have, Mr. Connatser: Three records, the sound of a kidnapper's voice, and a snatch of song from a P.A. speaker." Maclain shook his head. "It's not very much, but somehow among us we've got to put it together. Before those plans are examined at all, we've got to find your boy. There is no other alternative."

"Knowing you as well as I do," Arnold Cameron said, "I have a vague uneasy feeling that you may be on to something that we've managed to overlook. God only knows, I hope so."

"I have some questions." There were lines creased on Maclain's forehead and his mobile face was set in a look of concentration as though his mind were far away. "Why did this man pick Audograph records?"

"We have fifteen Audographs in our office at the plant," Connatser explained. "I also have one for dictation at home."

"Do you think he was an ex-employee, Arnold?"

"That's a possibility that we're checking. We're getting a rundown on everyone who has worked at Connatser Products since the war. It's a big job, but it's a top-security plant so it shouldn't be impossible. But it is going to take plenty of time."

"Of which we have none," Connatser grunted. "Personally, I think it more likely that Junior called in as a salesman and saw the machines. Employees in our place are too closely checked for comfort."

"How would he know you had one home?"

"Maybe he didn't, but he knew I could always get one and take it home, since he's addressing his records to Evelyn there."

"Okay," Maclain said shortly. "I'm going to start just as though I knew what I was talking about: the same voices made all those records—Ronnie's and Junior's. Let's take it for granted that it's the same man who picked up Ronnie, and drove you to work under the name of Jules Rosine. Would you know him again, Mr. Connatser, if you saw him?"

Connatser gave it a little thought. "I doubt it. He wore a chauffeur's livery. He was dark, I believe, seemed personable enough, slightly built—that is, he didn't impress me as being particularly big and strong. I didn't see him standing up. From the few words he spoke, I'd say he had a French accent. On the drive to Long Island, after dropping Ronnie at school in the morning, I was reading the paper and busy with some figures in the back seat of the car. Since I was occupied, I didn't give him too much thought really."

"He is French, according to Leon Gerard," Hank Weeks stated positively. "He spoke fluent French to Leon when he held him up in his room and forced him to phone the housekeeper."

"So his speech on the records, while marking him as an educated man, has words in it that are British as a dish of bubble-and-squeak," Maclain declared. "'Phosphorescent paint'—'portmanteau'—'dispatch case.' We'd say briefcase, or luminous suitcase. But his accent isn't really British—just the words he uses. Let's mark him as a French Canadian—Quebec, or Montreal. Do you agree?"

"I think I'll buy that Canadian angle right now," Weeks said. "Since Igor Gouzenko skipped the Russian Embassy in Ottawa, in 1946, and turned up Klaus Fuchs, they've had troubles aplenty with certain Reds in Canada."

"What would you guess his age to be?" the Captain asked.

"Between thirty and forty at a guess." Connatser sounded a little unsure.

"Well, later if nothing happens, it might pay you to run back through the Year Books of Graduates in Engineering at McGill—University of Toronto, too. A picture just might jog your memory enough to spot him. There's another point I'd like to get clear: Ronnie certainly wasn't kidnapped in your own car—that is I don't think they'd chance driving him very far."

"Just across the Queensboro Bridge," Cameron said. "The police found Mr. Connatser's Imperial parked under the approach to the bridge on the Long Island side at 6:20. Ronnie was going to a picture show with another boy, Ted Schuyler, at four. You heard that."

Maclain nodded. "I'm interested as to how this Rosine got him to come along without a fuss, and then transferred him to another car. That's not easy in New York City between three and four in the afternoon."

"You know as much as we do, Captain. From what Ronnie says on the records, the kidnapper gave him a line that Mr. Connatser wanted Ronnie to meet him at the plant. He bought Ronnie a bottle of Pepsi-Cola on the way. The police found the bottle still in the car and analyzed what was left. It showed Ronnie must have drunk three or four grains of Seconal. That would have put him out cold in fifteen minutes to half-an-hour, and he would have stayed out for eight to ten hours, maybe longer, according to the Medical Examiner. Of course they could have given him more on the trip if they were driving far."

Maclain took a box of paper-clips from his middle desk drawer and slowly began to chain them together.

"That's what I was trying to figure—how long would they drive Ronnie and how far. Let's say four hundred miles—ten hours driving. That would put them where they were going about four in the early morning. I think Junior lives there and owns a house most likely. It's not easy to rent a place to hide a child. It must be fairly large—the town, I mean, or the city. Far too dangerous to take him to a small town—"

"What about an isolated farm?" Agent Weeks broke in on the Captain's audible reverie.

"Not close enough to a Post Office and an airport." The Captain put his clips back in the drawer and closed it with a snap of certainty. "Let's consider these records: It's obvious that nobody is flying around the country with a kidnapped boy. So the boy's in one place—probably guarded by Junior's wife or paramour. Women are better with children, anyhow. Now, listen to this." He found the Miami record and put it on, keeping his hand held up for silence until it was through.

"That record was made by Ronnie and the man on the machine, and at the same time. The machine may be old, or defective, for there's a murmuring drone in the background that records itself all the way through. Junior didn't notice it, so it must be a noise that he's used to. He noticed the start of 'Silent Night' quick enough and shut off the machine."

"The record was mailed from Miami, Captain," Cameron reminded him.

"That's my point, Arnold—nearness to an airport. The woman's mailing records to him. I believe that record was made Saturday evening, giving Ronnie time to come around and get instructions as to what he should say. Then Junior took it with him as soon as it was finished and caught a flight to Miami. In his suitcase he was carrying another Audograph machine. He mailed the record from Miami on Sunday. That would check as to time—ample time for him to stop off and make arrangements for the pick-up with some Deputy Sheriff, or town constable confederate, at any point along the way."

"You're right there," Cameron said glumly. "Deputy Sheriffs and Constables are a dime a dozen, and a police car is made to order—two way telephone, flasher and all. We can't police every point between here and Miami."

"So again the best bet is to find the woman and the boy," Maclain said. "She'll talk, I believe, if Junior has told her anything. We can be sure if he'd made arrangements in Miami the record wouldn't have been mailed from there, any more than if Ronnie was there. Anyhow, we know that after the record was mailed, he hopped the first flight for Kansas City."

"Typical Commie technique, that hopping about," Hank Weeks remarked. "The Boss, in his book 'Masters of Deceit' says they call it 'dry cleaning'—driving three hundred miles to cover thirty so no one will know where you've been or where you are."

"Go on, Captain!" Cameron sounded impatient. "You've got this Commie Canuck with his Audograph in K.C. now. Where do we go from there—outside of Cleveland?"

Without replying, Maclain put on the second record and played it to the end. "I know that Ronnie made this record on the same machine that recorded record No. 1. All the time that Ronnie is speaking you can hear that noise that runs through the first one. As soon as Junior starts to speak, the noise is gone. We must assume that the woman mailed this record to Junior in K.C., and he filled his part in on the Audograph he has with him. The New York Times is available in most cities the same, or the following day. The woman could have seen the personal and told Ronnie what to say, or Junior could have seen it and could have called her long-distance."

"Still more dry cleaning," Cameron said, "to help us Special Agents earn our pay, and put us through a wringer like we're going through today. Let's hear No. 3."

The Cleveland record just served to clinch the Captain's beliefs more firmly. A background noise when Ronnie was speaking, while Junior's words were clear.

"Could that noise come from a car or a plane?" Connatser asked. "I've used an Audograph in both, but I haven't been conscious of anything like that in the playbacks. Still, I might have overlooked it just like Junior has."

"It just won't hold water." The Captain's agile fingers beat a tattoo on the desk top. "I don't believe that Ronnie and his captor made that first record while driving in a car. There's that 'Silent Night' music, for one thing. Can you picture a man with a kidnapped boy in his car dictating a record and telling the boy what to say? Then a stop in front of a music store where there's a blaring P.A.?"

Hank Weeks said, "Hell no! Nor can I picture the kid being flown around to make records in a plane."

Maclain stood up abruptly. "Let's get what we can from the horse's mouth—the Sound Engineer at Gray Audograph. Let him hear these and see what he has to say."

In less than an hour they were in the Gray Audograph offices at 521 Fifth Ave., talking to Carl Schantz, the company's Chief Sound Engineer. Schantz, a stocky, phlegmatic, brilliant German, listened to Cameron, then played the three records through without comment.

Finished, he sat down in his desk chair and stared from one to another of his visitors through his gold-rimmed glasses. "The boy's voice and the man's—all of record one—was dictated to the same machine. The man's voice on records two and three was dictated to another machine. I'd say that both machines were old. Probably our Model Three, but there's nothing the matter with either of them. I'm certain of that."

"How do you know that?" Cameron asked. "The differences in the machines, I mean."

Schantz gave a slow smile. "You know from your work in the F.B.I. that there's a difference in every typewriter. Well, there's a difference in the needles of every dictating machine. They cut grooves of different depths on the records. The difference in those grooves is infinitesimal, but it shows up on a tape made by the electric-micrometer on our testing machine—the one I just played those on." He handed the S.A.C. a wide piece of ruled paper marked in purple ink with three wavy parallel lines. "Look for yourself."

All of the line made by record one, and the two lines made by Ronnie's voice on two and three were noticeably similar. There was a difference when Junior started to speak on the Kansas City and

Cleveland records, but it still could be seen with the naked eye that those two lines were similar to each other.

"Does this mean that if we find those two machines and bring them in you can identify them for us?" Cameron's voice was eager.

"You bring them in. We'll give it a try!"

"What about that noise in the background?"

Schantz shrugged his heavy shoulders. "I'm afraid I can't help you there. Frankly, I don't know."

"Could it come from a nearby power plant or high-tension lines, something like that?" the Captain asked him.

Schantz shook his head. "We have Audographs running in offices with air-conditioners, calculators, and IBM sorting machines, sometimes right in the same room, and there's nothing but voice on the dictated record. Now and then, if you're not careful, you can get a loose connection in the six-hole receptacle where the mike plugs in. That will cause a nasty roar—but you can't dictate to the machine." He thought a moment. "The nearest thing to that noise I've heard was on a record dictated in an auto running at high speed with the windows open. The machine didn't pick up the motor, but it picked up the sound of the wind rushing by. That sound you have is steady like that, but deeper. It's almost like the lad was speaking through some distant hurricane." He sighed. "I'm really sorry I can't help you more."

"About those few lines of 'Silent Night'—have you any ideas there?" the Captain asked as Schantz was showing them out.

"I thought of a radio in another room, but it's too muffled. It's probably from outside the house from a juiced-up P.A. system. If that's it, the place is right next door, or at the most right across the street. Anyhow, it must be very near."

All afternoon, the Captain sat in his penthouse office listening to the records that Cameron had left with him. He had played them back through the Audograph speaker; listened to them with headphones on and finally using a jackplug, hopped them up to deafening volume on his hi-fi machine.

That background sound was all enveloping. The longer he listened to it, the more it took possession of him, until he almost believed what Schantz had said about a distant hurricane.

He thought of the ocean. It could keep people awake the first night, and in a day or two the noise would be gone. But the ocean wouldn't record like that unless it might be a wind-lashed sea.

Could they have the boy on a ship at sea? In a seven day storm?

And mailing records air-mail to Junior in Kansas City? It showed how feeble the mind could get if you worked it on and on!

He kept coming back to that power plant. Why, when Schantz had said it wouldn't record? Could Schantz be wrong? Or could he, Maclain, whose ears had replaced his eyes, be clutching at straws and building into roaring volume some tiny wisp of sound? Was that noise, that should be a thousand jet planes busy ripping the skies, merely the hum of a washing machine, or an electric dryer? It had to be more.

Power! Overwhelming power! It had to be. With the life of a six year old boy at stake, he didn't dare to be wrong.

He'd stick to his own obsessions, too: They'd taken the boy, maybe dressed as a girl, on a single trip of ten hours. Four hundred miles at least. Then why not into Canada? If Junior was a Canadian, his car could have Canadian tags. It would be easy to cross the International Bridge in the middle of the night with a sleeping little girl accompanied by her father and mother . . .

The Captain jumped from the red divan, shut off the Audograph, and took his Braille map of New York State from a flat cabinet drawer. Moving faster than the eye could follow, he traced a line from New York City to Buffalo. Just three hundred and seventy-five miles!

Five minutes later he had Arnold Cameron on the phone. "I've got a fix, Arnold. Two points of sound, like when you're hunting down a hidden radio. Crosby singing 'Silent Night'—and the noise of the biggest power plant in the whole wide world. Now it's up to you to go get that boy!" For a minute more he stammered on.

"Don't tell us how to run our business," Cameron cut in. "Get off the line so I can phone the Border Patrol of the Royal Canadian Mounted Police. It should be twice as easy to get a boy, since they're the chaps who always get their man!"

Just outside of the city limits, running at right angles to the river between Stanley Ave. and the Parkway, is a short street with eight neat houses on it. Five on one side and three on the other. On the side with the three houses and not quite forming a corner with the Parkway stands the Maple Leaf Tavern, boasting ten spotless bedrooms on the second floor, and downstairs a very good restaurant and a bar.

At seven o'clock, on Friday, Dec. 20th, Mr. Burns, who had owned and run the Maple Leaf for forty years, left his wife to superintend the cooking of dinner in the kitchen. He came into the bar to start his pick-up with Bing Crosby's "Merry Christmas" record. The first few chimes introducing "Silent Night" had scarcely pealed forth from the loud speaker over the Maple Leaf's front door, when Det. Sgt. McMurtrie, of the Ontario Provincial Police walked into the bar.

He and Burns were old friends. McMurtrie, tall and cadaverous with sad black eyes, was a startling contrast to the sandy-haired Burns, a Scot grown fat with good living through the years.

They shook hands. McMurtrie ordered an ale and sat down at a table in the empty bar. Burns joined him a moment later carrying two bottles and glasses.

"I'll have an ale wi' ye, Mac."

"On me, if ye like. Looks to me, Matey, like you've driven all your trade away wi' that racket over the front door."

"A racket ye call it! Don't be blasphemous, Mac. 'Tis one of God's songs, and there's others to come. I've been playing it every night now, except Sundays, for the past ten nights. 'Tis weather that's driven the trade away and not my offering passers-by a bit of warmth and Christmas cheer."

"Hmph!" McMurtrie swallowed some ale, his Adam's apple moving up and down. "And would ye have a permit, Burns, to play that thing? Seems to me the good folks on this street would be kicking with you disturbing their TV and their sleep."

"'Tis you who know perfectly well I have a permit, McMurtrie. Even though I'm outside of the city line, who but you has poked his long nose in here every chance he gets, checking every license and permit. And as for the folks on this street kicking, they're all good customers and friends of mine and glad of a little music."

"All?" Det. McMurtrie narrowed his bushy brows. "Now there was one I recalled that you turned in for making subversive talk here during the war. What was his name?"

"Zwicker," Burns said. "Francois Zwicker." Burns held up his glass of sparkling ale and looked at the bubbles against the light. "He owns the house right across the street. Number 3. God be praised, a year ago he lost his job at the Electric, where he was engineer, and moved away. The house stood vacant for a spell; then was rented for three months in the summer, to be vacant again until just this last Saturday."

"Rented?"

"No, he and his missus are back, but it won't be for long, mark me. He'll hold a job nowhere with his anarchistic tongue. I've forbid him my place. His missus is no prize, either. Louise is her name, a Frenchie like him. Quebec or Three Rivers. She's there by herself right now. He's off again, hunting another job, I'll say. Not that he'll keep it long."

A party of four came in. Burns finished his ale and got up to greet them. "The ale's on me, Mac. Drop in again, and a Merry Christmas to ye!"

Outside, the detective got in a big black car where four men were waiting for him. "Let's go and get the search warrant," he said. "Zwicker's the name. The house is No. 3." The car moved off.

An hour later to the accompaniment of Bing's voice singing, "I'll Be Home for Christmas," McMurtrie rang the doorbell of No. 3. The door was opened finally by a white-faced woman with burning black eyes and raven hair.

"Provincial Police, Mrs. Zwicker," McMurtrie said. "There are four men posted about the house, and we have a search warrant. Let me in, please. We've come to get the boy."

At 6:00 P.M., on Saturday, Dec. 21st, Alan Connatser's Cessna Twin took off from the air strip at Connatser Products, on Long Island. With Steven Donegan, and Connatser, at the twin controls, it headed south as ordered. Instead of a phosphorescent-painted portmanteau, it was carrying Special Agent Hank Weeks, member of the F.B.I.

Ronnie, safely home with his mother, had made it in time for Macy's Christmas Parade.

Contact by radio was made at 8:20, and almost instantly a red flasher was turned-on on the ground in a large open area some twenty miles north of New Bern, North Carolina. As the Cessna headed for a point directly over the flasher, Hank Weeks spoke into the microphone:

"Zwicker, hear this now! This is a Special Agent of the F.B.I. speaking to you from the Cessna. Your wife has been arrested and we have the boy. She gave us the name of Walter Vollmer, the County Official who is with you now in that Patrol Car. You were followed, and we know exactly where you are—in between Vanceboro and Blount Creek. You are hopelessly trapped, for cars are posted all along U.S. 17 and along State Road 33, as well as the country road you came in on. They have heard this and are closing in right now. That's all! There's no use your trying to escape."

The Cessna began to climb. "There's just one thing that gripes me, Hank," Connatser said disgruntledly. "Think of all the trouble you'd have saved if you'd done what Steve and I wanted to—loaded that portmanteau with just one little ol' bomb!"

Way up north in the Maple Leaf Tavern, Mr. Burns turned over the "Merry Christmas" record for the third time and started "Silent

Night" again. On guard in the empty house across the street, in the event that plans went wrong and Zwicker returned to his home, two members of the Ontario Provincial Police were engaged in a game of Rummy.

"It would be a silent night if Burns would shut that blasted thing off," one said to the other, slapping a card on the table.

"Aye," said the other, "still as the dead, if you're asking me!"

They went on playing unaware of the noise that filled every room, every cranny and every house and every street for miles around. They had lived in the midst of its deep reverberation far too long to hear it —the stunning boom of the Horseshoe Falls of Niagara, dumping its endless deafening millions of gallons down a drop of a hundred and fifty-eight feet just a half block away.

DEATH BY INVISIBLE HANDS

by John Dickson Carr

He could never understand afterward why he felt uneasiness, even to the point of fear, before he saw the beach at all.

Night and fancies? But how far can fancies go?

It was a steep track down to the beach. The road, however, was good, and he could rely on his car. And yet, halfway down, before he could even taste the sea-wind or hear the rustle of the sea, Dan Fraser felt sweat on his forehead. A nerve jerked in the calf of his leg over the foot brake.

"Look, this is damn silly!" he thought to himself. He thought it with a kind of surprise, as when he had first known fear in wartime long ago. But the fear had been real enough, no matter how well he concealed it, and they believed he never felt it.

A dazzle of lightning lifted ahead of him. The night was too hot. This enclosed road, bumping the springs of his car, seemed pressed down in an airless hollow.

After all, Dan Fraser decided, he had everything to be thankful for. He was going to see Brenda; he was the luckiest man in London. If she chose to spend week-ends as far away as North Cornwall, he was glad to drag himself there—even a day late.

Brenda's image rose before him, as clearly as the flash of lightning. He always seemed to see her half laughing, half pouting, with light on her yellow hair. She was beautiful; she was desirable. It would only be disloyalty to think any trickiness underlay her intense, naive ways.

Brenda Lestrange always got what she wanted. And she had wanted him, though God alone knew why: he was no prize package at all. Again, in imagination, he saw her against the beat and shuffle of music in a night club. Brenda's shoulders rose from a low-cut silver gown, her eyes as blue and wide-spaced as the eternal Eve's.

You'd have thought she would have preferred a dasher, a roaring bloke like Toby Curtis, who had all the women after him. But that, as Joyce had intimated, might be the trouble. Toby Curtis couldn't see Brenda for all the rest of the crowd. And so Brenda preferred—

Well, then, what was the matter with him?

He would see Brenda in a few minutes. There ought to have been joy bells in the tower, not bats in the—

Easy!

He was out in the open now, at sea level. Dan Fraser drove bumpingly along scrub grass, at the head of a few shallow terraces leading down to the private beach. Ahead of him, facing seaward, stood the overlarge, overdecorated bungalow which Brenda had rather grandly named "The King's House."

And there wasn't a light in it—not a light showing at only a quarter past ten.

Dan cut the engine, switched off the lights, and got out of the car. In the darkness he could hear the sea charge the beach as an army might have charged it.

Twisting open the handle of the car's trunk, he dragged out his suitcase. He closed the compartment with a slam which echoed out above the swirl of water. This part of the Cornish coast was too lonely, too desolate, but it was the first time such a thought had ever occurred to him.

He went to the house, round the side and toward the front. His footsteps clacked loudly on the crazy-paved path on the side. And even in a kind of luminous darkness from the white of the breakers ahead, he saw why the bungalow showed no lights.

All the curtains were drawn on the windows—on this side, at least.

When Dan hurried round to the front door, he was almost running. He banged the iron knocker on the door, then hammered it again. As he glanced over his shoulder, another flash of lightning paled the sky to the west.

It showed him the sweep of gray sand. It showed black water snakily edged with foam. In the middle of the beach, unearthly, stood the small natural rock formation—shaped like a low-backed armchair, eternally facing out to sea—which for centuries had been known as King Arthur's Chair.

The white eye of the lightning closed. Distantly there was a shock of thunder.

This whole bungalow couldn't be deserted! Even if Edmund Ireton and Toby Curtis were at the former's house some distance along the coast, Brenda herself must be here. And Joyce Ray. And the two maids.

Dan stopped hammering the knocker. He groped for and found the knob of the door.

The door was unlocked.

He opened it on brightness. In the hall, rather overdecorated like so many of Brenda's possessions, several lamps shone on gaudy furniture and a polished floor. But the hall was empty too.

With the wind whisking and whistling at his back Dan went in and kicked the door shut behind him. He had no time to give a hail. At the back of the hall a door opened. Joyce Ray, Brenda's cousin, walked toward him, her arms hanging limply at her sides and her enormous eyes like a sleepwalker's.

"Then you did get here," said Joyce, moistening dry lips. "You did get here, after all."

"I—"

Dan stopped. The sight of her brought a new realization. It didn't explain his uneasiness or his fear—but it did explain much.

Joyce was the quiet one, the dark one, the unobtrusive one, with her glossy black hair and her subdued elegance. But she was the poor relation, and Brenda never let her forget it. Dan merely stood and stared at her. Suddenly Joyce's eyes lost their sleepwalker's look. They were gray eyes, with very black lashes; they grew alive and vivid, as if she could read his mind.

"Joyce," he blurted, "I've just understood something. And I never understood it before. But I've got to tell—"

"Stop!" Joyce cried.

Her mouth twisted. She put up a hand as if to shade her eyes.

"I know what you want to say," she went on. "But you're not to say it! Do you hear me?"

"Joyce, I don't know why we're standing here yelling at each other. Anyway, I—I didn't mean to tell you. Not yet, anyway. I mean, I must tell Brenda—"

"You can't tell Brenda!" Joyce cried.

"What's that?"

"You can't tell her anything, ever again," said Joyce. "Brenda's dead."

There are some words which at first do not even shock or stun. You just don't believe them. They can't be true. Very carefully Dan Fraser put his suitcase down on the floor and straightened up again.

"The police," said Joyce, swallowing hard, "have been here since early this morning. They're not here now. They've taken her away to the mortuary. That's where she'll sleep tonight."

Still Dan said nothing.

"Mr.—Mr. Edmund Ireton," Joyce went on, "has been here ever since it happened. So has Toby Curtis. So, fortunately, has a man named Dr. Gideon Fell. Dr. Fell's a bumbling old duffer, a very learned man or something. He's a friend of the police; he's kind; he's helped soften things. All the same, Dan, if *you'd* been here last night—"

"I couldn't get away. I told Brenda so."

"Yes, I know all that talk about hard-working journalists. But if you'd only been here, Dan, it might not have happened at all."

"Joyce, for God's sake!"

Then there was a silence in the bright, quiet room. A stricken look crept into Joyce's eyes.

"Dan, I'm sorry. I'm terribly sorry. I was feeling dreadful and so, I suppose, I had to take it out on the first person handy."

"That's all right. But how did she die?" Then desperately he began to surmise. "Wait, I've got it! She went out to swim early this morning, just as usual? She's been diving off those rocks on the headland again? And—"

"No," said Joyce. "She was strangled."

"*Strangled?*"

What Joyce tried to say was "murdered." Her mouth shook and faltered round the syllables; she couldn't say them; her thoughts, it seemed, shied back and ran from the very word. But she looked at Dan steadily.

"Brenda went out to swim early this morning, yes."

"Well?"

"At least, she must have. I didn't see her. I was still asleep in that back bedroom she always gives me. Anyway, she went down there in a red swim suit and a white beach robe."

Automatically Dan's eyes moved over to an oil painting above the fireplace. Painted by a famous R.A., it showed a scene from classical antiquity; it was called *The Lovers,* and left little to the imagination. It had always been Brenda's favorite because the female figure in the picture looked so much like her.

"Well!" said Joyce, throwing out her hands. "You know what Brenda always does. She takes off her beach robe and spreads it out over King Arthur's Chair. She sits down in the chair and smokes a cigarette and looks out at the sea before she goes into the water.

"The beach robe was still in that rock chair," Joyce continued with an effort, "when I came downstairs at half-past seven. But Brenda wasn't. She hadn't even put on her bathing cap. Somebody had strangled her with that silk scarf she wore with the beach robe. It was twisted so tightly into her neck they couldn't get it out. She was lying on the sand in front of the chair, on her back, in the red swim suit, with her face black and swollen. You could see her clearly from the terrace."

Dan glanced at the flesh tints of *The Lovers,* then quickly looked away.

Joyce, the cool and competent, was holding herself under restraint.

"I can only thank my lucky stars," she burst out, "I didn't run out there. I mean, from the flagstones of the lowest terrace out across the sand. They stopped me."

" 'They' stopped you? Who?"

"Mr. Ireton and Toby. Or, rather, Mr. Ireton did; Toby wouldn't have thought of it."

"But—"

"Toby, you see, had come over here a little earlier. But he was at the back of the bungalow, practising with a .22 target rifle. I heard him once. Mr. Ireton had just got there. All three of us walked out on the terrace at once. And saw her."

"Listen, Joyce. What difference does it make whether or not you ran out across the sand? Why were you so lucky they stopped you?"

"Because if they hadn't, the police might have said I did it."

"Did it?"

"Killed Brenda," Joyce answered clearly. "In all that stretch of sand, Dan, there weren't any footprints except Brenda's own."

"Now hold on!" he protested. "She—she *was* killed with that scarf of hers?"

"Oh, yes. The police and even Dr. Fell don't doubt that."

"Then how could anybody, anybody at all, go out across the sand and come back without leaving a footprint?"

"That's just it. The police don't know and they can't guess. That's why they're in a flat spin, and Dr. Fell will be here again tonight."

In her desperate attempt to speak lightly, as if all this didn't matter, Joyce failed. Her face was white. But again the expression of the dark-fringed eyes changed, and she hesitated.

"Dan—"

"Yes?"

"You do understand, don't you, why I was so upset when you came charging in and said what you did?"

"Yes, of course."

"Whatever you had to tell me, or thought you had to tell me—"

"About—us?"

"About anything! You do see that you must forget it and not mention it again? Not ever?"

"I see why I can't mention it now. With Brenda dead, it wouldn't even be decent to think of it." He could not keep his eyes off that mocking picture. "But is the future dead too? If I happen to have been an idiot and thought I was head over heels gone on Brenda when all the time it was really—"

"*Dan!*"

There were five doors opening into the gaudy hall, which had too many mirrors. Joyce whirled round to look at every door, as if she feared an ambush behind each.

"For heaven's sake keep your voice down," she begged. "Practically every word that's said can be heard all over the house. I said never, and I meant it. If you'd spoken a week ago, even twenty-four hours ago, it might have been different. Do you think I didn't want you to? But now it's too late!"

"Why?"

"May *I* answer that question?" interrupted a new, dry, rather quizzical voice.

Dan had taken a step toward her, intensely conscious of her attractiveness. He stopped, burned with embarrassment, as one of the five doors opened.

Mr. Edmund Ireton, shortish and thin and dandified in his middle-fifties, emerged with his usual briskness. There was not much gray in his polished black hair. His face was a benevolent satyr's.

"Forgive me," he said.

Behind him towered Toby Curtis, heavy and handsome and fair-haired, in a bulky tweed jacket. Toby began to speak, but Mr. Ireton's gesture silenced him before he could utter a sound.

"Forgive me," he repeated. "But what Joyce says is quite true. Every word can be overheard here, even with the rain pouring down. If you go on shouting and Dr. Fell hears it, you will land that girl in serious danger."

"Danger?" demanded Toby Curtis. He had to clear his throat. "What danger could *Dan* get her into?"

Mr. Ireton, immaculate in flannels and shirt and thin pullover, stalked to the mantelpiece. He stared up hard at *The Lovers* before turning round.

"The Psalmist tells us," he said dryly, "that all is vanity. Has none of you ever noticed—God forgive me for saying so—that Brenda's most outstanding trait was her vanity?"

His glance flashed toward Joyce, who abruptly turned away and pressed her hands over her face.

"Appalling vanity. Scratch that vanity deeply enough and our dearest Brenda would have committed murder."

"Aren't you getting this backwards?" asked Dan. "Brenda didn't commit any murder. It was Brenda—"

"Ah!" Mr. Ireton pounced. "And there might be a lesson in that, don't you think?"

"Look here, you're not saying she strangled herself with her own scarf?"

"No—but hear what I do say. Our Brenda, no doubt, had many passions and many fancies. But there was only one man she loved or ever wanted to marry. It was not Mr. Dan Fraser."

"Then who was it?" asked Toby.

"You."

Toby's amazement was too genuine to be assumed. The color drained out of his face. Once more he had to clear his throat.

"So help me," he said, "I never knew it! I never imagined—"

"No, of course you didn't," Mr. Ireton said even more dryly. A goatish amusement flashed across his face and was gone. "Brenda, as a rule, could get any man she chose. So she turned Mr. Fraser's head and became engaged to him. It was to sting you, Mr. Curtis, to make you jealous. And you never noticed. While all the time Joyce Ray and Dan Fraser were eating their hearts out for each other; and *he* never noticed either."

Edmund Ireton wheeled round.

"You may lament my bluntness, Mr. Fraser. You may want to wring my neck, as I see you do. But can you deny one word I say?"

"No." In honesty Dan could not deny it.

"Well! Then be very careful when you face the police, both of you, or they will see it too. Joyce already has a strong motive. She is Brenda's only relative, and inherits Brenda's money. If they learn she wanted Brenda's *fiancé*, they will have her in the dock for murder."

"That's enough!" blurted Dan, who dared not look at Joyce. "You've made it clear. All right, stop there!"

"Oh, I had intended to stop. If you are such fools that you won't help yourselves, I must help you. That's all."

It was Toby Curtis who strode forward.

"Dan, don't let him bluff you!" Toby said. "In the first place, they can't arrest anybody for this. You weren't here. I know—"

"I've heard about it, Toby."

"Look," insisted Toby. "When the police finished measuring and photographing and taking casts of Brenda's footprints, I did some measuring myself."

Edmund Ireton smiled. "Are *you* attempting to solve this mystery, Mr. Curtis?"

"I didn't say that." Toby spoke coolly. "But I might have a question or two for you. Why have you had your knife into me all day?"

"Frankly, Mr. Curtis, because I envy you."

"You—*what?*"

"So far as women are concerned, young man, I have not your advantages. *I* had no romantic boyhood on a veldt-farm in South Africa. *I* never learned to drive a span of oxen and flick a fly off the leader's ear with my whip. *I* was never taught to be a spectacular horseman and rifle shot."

"Oh, turn it up!"

"'Turn it up?' Ah, I see. And was that the sinister question you had for me?"

"No. Not yet. You're too tricky."

"My profoundest thanks."

"Look, Dan," Toby insisted. "You've seen that rock formation they call King Arthur's Chair?"

"Toby, I've seen it fifty times," Dan said. "But I still don't understand—"

"And I don't understand," suddenly interrupted Joyce, without turning round, "why they made me sit there where Brenda had been sitting. It was horrible."

"Oh, they were only reconstructing the crime." Toby spoke rather grandly. "But the question, Dan, is how anybody came near that chair without leaving a footprint?"

"Quite."

"Nobody could have," Toby said just as grandly. "The murderer, for instance, couldn't have come from the direction of the sea. Why? Because the highest point at high tide, where the water might have blotted out footprints, is more than twenty feet in front of the chair. More than twenty feet!"

"Er—one moment," said Mr. Ireton, twitching up a finger. "Surely Inspector Tregellis said the murderer must have crept up and caught her from the back? Before she knew it?"

"That won't do either. From the flagstones of the terrace to the back of the chair is at least twenty feet, too. Well, Dan? Do you see any way out of that one?"

Dan, not normally slow-witted, was so concentrating on Joyce that he could think of little else. She was cut off from him, drifting away from him, forever out of reach just when he had found her. But he tried to think.

"Well . . . could somebody have jumped there?"

"Ho!" scoffed Toby, who was himself a broad jumper and knew better. "That was the first thing they thought of."

"And that's out, too?"

"Definitely. An Olympic champion in good form might have done it, if he'd had any place for a running start and any place to land. But he hadn't. There was *no* mark in the sand. He couldn't have landed on the chair, strangled Brenda at his leisure, and then hopped back like a jumping bean. Now could he?"

"But somebody did it, Toby! It happened!"

"How?"

"I don't know."

"You seem rather proud of this, Mr. Curtis," Edmund Ireton said smoothly.

"Proud?" exclaimed Toby, losing color again.

"These romantic boyhoods—"

Toby did not lose his temper. But he had declared war.

"All right, gaffer. I've been very grateful for your hospitality, at that bungalow of yours, when we've come down here for week-ends. All the same, you've been going on for hours about who I am and what I am. Who are *you?*"

"I beg your pardon?"

"For two or three years," Toby said, "you've been hanging about with us. Especially with Brenda and Joyce. Who are you? What are you?"

"I am an observer of life," Mr. Ireton answered tranquilly. "A student of human nature. And—shall I say?—a courtesy uncle to both young ladies."

"Is that all you were? To either of them?"

"Toby!" exclaimed Joyce, shocked out of her fear.

She whirled round, her gaze going instinctively to Dan, then back to Toby.

"Don't worry, old girl," said Toby, waving his hand at her. "This is no reflection on you." He kept looking steadily at Mr. Ireton.

"Continue," Mr. Ireton said politely.

"You claim Joyce is in danger. She isn't in any danger at all," said

Toby, "as long as the police don't know how Brenda was strangled."

"They will discover it, Mr. Curtis. Be sure they will discover it!"

"You're trying to protect Joyce?"

"Naturally."

"And that's why you warned Dan not to say he was in love with her?"

"Of course. What else?"

Toby straightened up, his hand inside the bulky tweed jacket.

"Then why didn't you take him outside, rain or no, and tell him on the quiet? Why did *you* shout out that Dan was in love with Joyce, and she was in love with him, and give 'em a motive for the whole house to hear?"

Edmund Ireton opened his mouth, and shut it again.

It was a blow under the guard, all the more unexpected because it came from Toby Curtis.

Mr. Ireton stood motionless under the painting of *The Lovers*. The expression of the pictured Brenda, elusive and mocking, no longer matched his own. Whereupon, while nerves were strained and still nobody spoke, Dan Fraser realized that there was a dead silence because the rain had stopped.

Small night-noises, the creak of woodwork or a drip of water from the eaves, intensified the stillness. Then they heard footsteps, as heavy as those of an elephant, slowly approaching behind another of the doors. The footfalls, heavy and slow and creaking, brought a note of doom.

Into the room, wheezing and leaning on a stick, lumbered a man so enormous that he had to maneuver himself sideways through the door.

His big mop of gray-streaked hair had tumbled over one ear. His eyeglasses, with a broad black ribbon, were stuck askew on his nose. His big face would ordinarily have been red and beaming, with chuckles animating several chins. Now it was only absent-minded, his bandit's mustache outthrust.

"Aha!" he said in a rumbling voice. He blinked at Dan with an air of refreshed interest. "I think you must be Mr. Fraser, the last of this rather curious week-end party? H'm. Yes. Your obedient servant, sir. I am Gideon Fell."

Dr. Fell wore a black cloak as big as a tent and carried a shovel-hat in his other hand. He tried to bow and make a flourish with his stick, endangering all the furniture near him.

The others stood very still. Fear was as palpable as the scent after rain.

"Yes, I've heard of you," said Dan. His voice rose in spite of himself. "But you're rather far from home, aren't you? I suppose you had some—er—antiquarian interest in King Arthur's Chair?"

Still Dr. Fell blinked at him. For a second it seemed that chuckles would jiggle his chins and waistcoat, but he only shook his head.

"Antiquarian interest? My dear sir!" Dr. Fell wheezed gently. "If there were any association with a semi-legendary King Arthur, it would be at Tintagel much farther south. No, I was here on holiday. This morning, Inspector Tregellis fascinated me with the story of a fantastic murder. I returned tonight for my own reasons."

Mr. Ireton, at ease again, matched the other's courtesy. "May I ask what these reasons were?"

"First, I wished to question the two maids. They have a room at the back, as Miss Ray has; and this afternoon, you may remember, they were still rather hysterical."

"And that is all?"

"H'mf. Well, no." Dr. Fell scowled. "Second, I wanted to detain all of you here for an hour or two. Third, I must make sure of the motive for this crime. And I am happy to say that I have made very sure."

Joyce could not control herself. "Then you did overhear everything!"

"Eh?"

"Every word that man said!"

Despite Dan's signals, Joyce nodded toward Mr. Ireton and poured out the words. "But I swear I hadn't anything to do with Brenda's death. What I told you today was perfectly true: I don't want her money and I won't touch it. As for my—my private affairs," and Joyce's face flamed, "everybody seems to know all about them except Dan and me. Please, please pay no attention to what that man has been saying."

Dr. Fell blinked at her in an astonishment which changed to vast distress.

"But, my dear young lady!" he rumbled. "We never for a moment believed you did. No, no! Archons of Athens, no!" exclaimed Dr. Fell, as though at incredible absurdity. "As for what your friend Mr. Ireton may have been saying, I did not hear it. I suspect it was only what he told me today, and it did supply the motive. But it was not your motive."

"Please, is this true? You're not trying to trap me?"

"Do I really strike you," Dr. Fell asked gently, "as being that sort of person? Nothing was more unlikely than that you killed your cousin, especially in the way she was killed."

"Do you know how she was killed?"

"Oh, *that,*" grunted Dr. Fell, waving the point away too. "That was the simplest part of the whole business."

He lumbered over, reflected in the mirrors and put down stick and shovel-hat on a table. Afterward he faced them with a mixture of distress and apology.

"It may surprise you," he said, "that an old scatterbrain like myself can observe anything at all. But I have an unfair advantage over the police. I began life as a schoolmaster: I have had more experience with habitual liars. Hang it all, think!"

"Of what?"

"The facts!" said Dr. Fell, making a hideous face. "According to the maids, Sonia and Dolly, Miss Brenda Lestrange went down to swim at ten minutes to seven this morning. Both Dolly and Sonia were awake, but did not get up. Some eight or ten minutes later, Mr. Toby Curtis began practising with a target rifle some distance away behind the bungalow."

"Don't look at me!" exclaimed Toby. "That rifle has nothing to do with it. Brenda wasn't shot."

"Sir," said Dr. Fell with much patience, "I am aware of that."

"Then what are you hinting at?"

"Sir," said Dr. Fell, "you will oblige me if you too don't regard every question as a trap. I have a trap for the murderer, and the murderer alone. You fired a number of shots—the maids heard you and saw you." He turned to Joyce. "I believe you heard too?"

"I heard one shot," answered the bewildered Joyce, "as I told Dan. About seven o'clock, when I got up and dressed."

"Did you look out of the windows?"

"No."

"What happened to that rifle afterwards? Is it here now?"

"No," Toby almost yelled. "I took it back to Ireton's after we found Brenda. But if the rifle had nothing to do with it, and I had nothing to do with it, then what the hell's the point?"

Dr. Fell did not reply for a moment. Then he made another hideous face. "We know," he rumbled, "that Brenda Lestrange wore a beach robe, a bathing suit, and a heavy silk scarf knotted round her neck. Miss Ray?"

"Y-yes?"

"I am not precisely an authority on women's clothes," said Dr. Fell. "As a rule I should notice nothing odd unless I passed Madge

Wildfire or Lady Godiva. I have seen men wear a scarf with a beach robe, but is it customary for women to wear a scarf as well?"

There was a pause.

"No, of course it isn't," said Joyce. "I can't speak for everybody, but I never do. It was just one of Brenda's fancies. She always did."

"Aha!" said Dr. Fell. "The murderer was counting on that."

"On what?"

"On her known conduct. Let me show you rather a grisly picture of a murder."

Dr. Fell's eyes were squeezed shut. From inside his cloak and pocket he fished out an immense meerschaum pipe. Firmly under the impression that he had filled and lighted the pipe, he put the stem in his mouth and drew at it.

"Miss Lestrange," he said, "goes down to the beach. She takes off her robe. Remember that, it's very important. She spreads out the robe in King Arthur's Chair and sits down. She is still wearing the scarf, knotted tightly in a broad band round her neck. She is about the same height as you, Miss Ray. She is held there, at the height of her shoulders, by a curving rock formation deeply bedded in sand."

Dr. Fell paused and opened his eyes.

"The murderer, we believe, catches her from the back. She sees and hears nothing until she is seized. Intense pressure on the carotid arteries, here at either side of the neck under the chin, will strike her unconscious within seconds and dead within minutes. When her body is released, it should fall straight forward. Instead, what happens?"

To Dan, full of relief ever since danger had seemed to leave Joyce, it was as if a shutter had flown open in his brain.

"She was lying on her back," Dan said. "Joyce told me so. Brenda was lying flat on her back with her head towards the sea. And that means—"

"Yes?"

"It means she was twisted or spun round in some way when she fell. It has something to do with that infernal scarf—I've thought so from the first. Dr. Fell! Was Brenda killed with the scarf?"

"In one sense, yes. In another sense, no."

"You can't have it both ways! Either she was killed with the scarf, or she wasn't."

"Not necessarily," said Dr. Fell.

"Then let's all retire to a loony bin," Dan suggested, "because nothing makes any sense at all. The murderer still couldn't have walked out there without leaving tracks. Finally, I agree with Toby: what's the point of the rifle? How does a .22 rifle figure in all this?"

"Because of its sound."

Dr. Fell took the pipe out of his mouth. Dan wondered why he had ever thought the learned doctor's eyes were vague. Magnified behind the glasses on the broad black ribbon, they were not vague at all.

"A .22 rifle," he went on in his big voice, "has a distinctive noise. Fired in the open air or anywhere else, it sounds exactly like the noise made by the real instrument used in this crime."

"Real instrument? What noise?"

"The crack of a blacksnake whip," replied Dr. Fell.

Edmund Ireton, looking very tired and ten years older, went over and sat down in an easy chair. Toby Curtis took one step backward, then another.

"In South Africa," said Dr. Fell, "I have never seen the very long whip which drivers of long ox spans use. But in America I have seen the blacksnake whip, and it can be twenty-four feet long. You yourselves must have watched it used in a variety turn on the stage."

Dr. Fell pointed his pipe at them.

"Remember?" he asked. "The user of the whip stands some distance away facing his girl assistant. There is a vicious crack. The end of the whip coils two or three times round the girl's neck. She is not hurt. But she would be in difficulties if he pulled the whip towards him. She would be in grave danger if she were held back and could not move.

"Somebody planned a murder with a whip like that. He came here early in the morning. The whip, coiled round his waist, was hidden by a loose and bulky tweed jacket. Please observe the jacket Toby Curtis is wearing now."

Toby's voice went high when he screeched out one word. It may have been protest, defiance, a jeer, or all three.

"Stop this!" cried Joyce, who had again turned away.

"Continue, I beg," Mr. Ireton said.

"In the dead hush of morning," said Dr. Fell, "he could not hide the loud crack of the whip. But what could he do?"

"He could mask it," said Edmund Ireton.

"Just that! He was always practising with a .22 rifle. So he fired several shots, behind the bungalow, to establish his presence. Afterwards nobody would notice when the crack of the whip—that single, isolated 'shot' heard by Miss Ray—only seemed to come from behind the house."

"Then, actually, he was—?"

"On the terrace, twenty feet behind a victim held immovable in the curve of a stone chair. The end of the whip coiled round the scarf.

Miss Lestrange's breath was cut off instantly. Under the pull of a powerful arm she died in seconds.

"On the stage, you recall, a lift and twist dislodges the whip from the girl-assistant's neck. Toby Curtis had a harder task; the scarf was so embedded in her neck that she seemed to have been strangled with it. He *could* dislodge it. But only with a powerful whirl and lift of the arm which spun her up and round, to fall face upwards. The whip snaked back to him with no trace in the sand. Afterwards he had only to take the whip back to Mr. Ireton's house, under pretext of returning the rifle. He had committed a murder which, in his vanity, he thought undetectable. That's all."

"But it can't be all!" said Dan. "Why should Toby have killed her? His motive—"

"His motive was offended vanity. Mr. Edmund Ireton as good as told you so, I fancy. He had certainly hinted as much to me."

Edmund Ireton rose shakily from the chair.

"I am no judge or executioner," he said. "I—I am detached from life. I only observe. If I guessed why this was done—"

"You could never speak straight out?" Dr. Fell asked sardonically.

"No!"

"And yet that was the tragic irony of the whole affair. Miss Lestrange wanted Toby Curtis, as he wanted her. But, being a woman, her pretense of indifference and contempt was too good. He believed it. Scratch her vanity deeply enough and she would have committed murder. Scratch *his* vanity deeply enough—"

"Lies!" said Toby.

"Look at him, all of you!" said Dr. Fell. "Even when he's accused of murder, he can't take his eyes off a mirror."

"*Lies!*"

"She laughed at him," the big voice went on, "and so she had to die. Brutally and senselessly he killed a girl who would have been his for the asking. That is what I meant by tragic irony."

Toby had retreated across the room until his back bumped against a wall. Startled, he looked behind him; he had banged against another mirror.

"Lies!" he kept repeating. "You can talk and talk and talk. But there's not a single damned thing you can prove!"

"Sir," inquired Dr. Fell, "are you sure?"

"Yes!"

"I warned you," said Dr. Fell, "that I returned tonight partly to detain all of you for an hour or so. It gave Inspector Tregellis time to search Mr. Ireton's house, and the Inspector has since returned. I further warned you that I questioned the maids, Sonia and Dolly, who today were only incoherent. My dear sir, you underestimate your personal attractions."

Now it was Joyce who seemed to understand. But she did not speak.

"Sonia, it seems," and Dr. Fell looked hard at Toby, "has quite a fondness for you. When she heard that last isolated 'shot' this morning, she looked out of the window again. You weren't there. This was so strange that she ran out to the front terrace to discover where you were. She saw you."

The door by which Dr. Fell had entered was still open. His voice lifted and echoed through the hall.

"Come in, Sonia!" he called. "After all, you are a witness to the murder. You, Inspector, had better come in too."

Toby Curtis blundered back, but there was no way out. There was only a brief glimpse of Sonia's swollen, tear-stained face. Past her marched a massive figure in uniform, carrying what he had found hidden in the other house.

Inspector Tregellis was reflected everywhere in the mirrors, with the long coils of the whip over his arm. And he seemed to be carrying not a whip but a coil of rope—gallows rope.

AFTER-DINNER STORY

by William Irish (Cornell Woolrich)

MacKenzie got on the elevator at the thirteenth floor. He was a water-filter salesman and had stopped in at his home office to make out his accounts before going home for the day. Later on that night he told his wife, half-laughingly, that that must have been why it happened to *him,* his getting on at the thirteenth floor. A lot of buildings omit them.

The red bulb bloomed and the car stopped for him. It was an express, omitting all floors, both coming and going, below the tenth. There were two other men in it when he got on, not counting the operator. It was late in the day, and most of the offices had already emptied themselves. One of the passengers was a scholarly looking man with rimless glasses, tall and slightly stooped. The time came when MacKenzie learned all their names. This was Kenshaw. The other was stout and cherubic looking, one of two partners in a struggling concern that was trying to market fountain pens with tiny light bulbs in their barrels—without much success. He was fiddling with one of his own samples on the way down, clicking it on and off with an air of proud ownership. He turned out to be Lambert.

The car was very efficient looking, very smooth running, sleek with bronze and chromium. It appeared very safe. It stopped at the next floor down, the twelfth, and a surly looking individual with bushy brows stepped in, Prendergast. Then the number eleven on the operator's call board lit up, and it stopped there too. A man about MacKenzie's own age and an older man with a trim white mustache were standing there side by side when the door opened. However, only the young man got on; the elder man gripped him by the arm in parting and turned away remarking loudly, "Tell Elinor I was asking for her."

The younger answered, "'By, Dad," and stepped in. Hardecker was his name. Almost at the same time ten was flashing.

The entry from eleven had turned to face the door, as all passengers are supposed to do in an elevator for their own safety. MacKenzie happened to glance at the sour-pussed man with the bushy brows at that moment; the latter was directly behind the newest arrival. He was glaring at the back of Hardecker's head with baleful intensity; in fact MacKenzie had never seen such a hundred-watt glower anywhere before except on a movie "heavy." The man's features, it must be admitted, lent themselves to just such an expression admirably; he had a swell head-start even when his face was in repose.

MacKenzie imagined this little by-play was due to the newcomer's having inadvertently trodden on the other's toe in turning to face forward. As a matter of fact, he himself was hardly conscious of analyzing the whole thing thus thoroughly; these were all just disconnected thoughts.

Ten was still another single passenger, a bill collector judging by the sheaf of pink, green, and canary slips he kept riffling through. He hadn't, by the gloomy look he wore, been having much luck today; or maybe his feet hurt him. This one was Megaffin.

There were now seven people in the car, counting the operator, standing in a compact little group facing the door, and no more stops due until it reached street level. Not a very great crowd; certainly far from the maximum the mechanism was able to hold. The framed notice, tacked to the panel just before MacKenzie's eyes, showed that it had been last inspected barely ten days before.

It never stopped at the street floor.

MacKenzie, trying to reconstruct the sequence of events for his wife that night, said that the operator seemed to put on added speed as soon as they had left the tenth floor behind. It was an express, so he didn't think anything of it. He remembered noticing at this point that the operator had a boil on the back of his neck, just above his uniform collar, with a Maltese cross of adhesive over it. He got that peculiar sinking sensation at the pit of his stomach many people get from a too-precipitate drop. The man near him, the young fellow from the eleventh, turned and gave him a half-humorous, half-pained look, so he knew that he must be feeling it too. Someone farther back whistled slightly to show his discomfort.

The car was a closed one, all metal, so you couldn't see the shaft doors flashing up. They must have been ticking off at a furious rate, just the same. MacKenzie began to get a peculiar ringing in his ears, like when he took the subway under the East River, and his knee-joints seemed to loosen up, trying to buckle under him.

But what really first told him—and all of them—that something had gone wrong and this was not a normal descent, was the sudden, futile, jerky way the operator was wangling the control lever to and fro. It traveled the short arc of its orbit readily enough, but the car refused to answer to it. He kept slamming it into the socket at one end of the groove, marked Stop for all eyes to read, and nothing happened. Fractions of seconds, not minutes, were going by.

They heard him say in a muffled voice, "Look out! We're going to hit!" And that was all there was time for.

The whole thing was a matter of instants. The click of a camera-shutter. The velocity of the descent became sickening; MacKenzie felt as if he were going to throw up. Then there was a tremendous bang like a cannon, an explosion of blackness, and of bulb-glass showering down as the light went out.

They all toppled together in a heap, like a bunch of ninepins. Mac-Kenzie, who had gone over backward, was the luckiest of the lot; he could feel squirming bodies bedded under him, didn't touch the hard-rubber floor of the car at all. However, his hip and shoulder got a bad wrench, and the sole of his foot went numb, through shoe and all, from the stinging impact it got flying up and slapping the bronze wall of the car.

There was no opportunity to extricate one's self, to try to regain one's feet. They were going up again—on springs or something. It was a little sickening too, but not as bad as the coming down had been. It slackened, reversed into a drop, and they banged a second time. Not with the terrific impact of the first, but a sort of cushioned bang that scrambled them up even more than they were already. Somebody's shoe grazed MacKenzie's skull. He couldn't see it but quickly caught it and warded it aside before it kicked him and gave him a fracture.

A voice near him was yelling, "Stop it! Cut it out!" half-hysterically, as though the jockeying up and down could be controlled. Even MacKenzie, badly frightened and shaken up as he was, hadn't lost his head to that extent.

The car finally settled, after a second slight bounce that barely cleared the springs under it at all, and a third and almost unnoticeable jolt. The rest was pitch darkness, a sense of suffocation, a commingling of threshing bodies like an ant heap, groans from the badly hurt and an ominous sigh or two from those even beyond groaning.

Somebody directly under MacKenzie was not moving at all. He put his hand on him, felt an upright, stiff collar, and just above it a small swelling, crisscrossed by plaster. The operator was dead.

There was an inertness that told MacKenzie, and the rubber matting beneath the operator's skull was sticky.

He felt then for the sleek metal wall of the enclosure that had buried them all alive, reached up it like a fly struggling up glass, with the heels of his hands and the points of his elbows. He squirmed the rest of his body up after these precarious grips. Upright again, he leaned against cold bronze.

The voice, there's always one in every catastrophe or panic, that had been pleading to "Cut it out!" was now begging with childish vehemence: "Get me outa here! For the love of Mike, I've got a wife and kids. Get me outa here!"

MacKenzie had the impression it was the surly looking fellow with the bushy eyebrows. The probabilities, he felt, were all for it. Such visible truculence and toughness are usually all hollow inside, a mask of weakness.

"Shut up," he said, "I've got a wife too. What's that got to do with it?"

The important thing, he recognized, was not the darkness, nor their trapped position at the bottom of a sealed-up shaft, nor even any possible injuries any of them had received. But the least noticeable of all the many corollaries of their predicament was the most dangerous. It was that vague sense of stuffiness, of suffocation. Something had to be done about that at once. The operator had opened the front panel of the car at each floor, simply by latch-motion. There was no reason why that could not be repeated down here, even though there was no accompanying opening in the shaft wall facing it. Enough air would filter down the crack between the jammed-in car and the wall, narrow though it was, to keep them breathing until help came. They were going to need that air before this was over.

MacKenzie's arms executed interlocking circles against the satiny metal face of the car, groping for the indented grip used to unlatch it. "Match," he ordered. "Somebody light a match. I'm trying to get this thing open. We're practically airtight in here."

The immediate, and expected, reaction was a howl of dismay from the tough-looking bird, like a dog's craven yelp.

Another voice, more self-controlled, said, "Wait a minute." Then nothing happened.

"Here I am; here, hand 'em to me," said MacKenzie, shoveling his upturned hand in and out through the velvety darkness.

"They won't strike, got all wet. Glass must have cut me." And then an alarmed "My shirt's all covered with blood!"

"All right, it mayn't be yours," said MacKenzie steadyingly. "Feel yourself before you let loose. If it is, hold a handkerchief to it. That bulb glass isn't strong enough to pierce very deep." And then in exasperation he hollered out, "For the love of—! Six men! Haven't any of you got a match to give me?" Which was unfair, considering that he himself had run short just before he left his office, and had been meaning to get a folder at the cigar store when he got off the car. "Hey, you, the guy that was fiddling with that trick fountain pen coming down, how about that gadget of yours?"

A new voice, unfrightened but infinitely crestfallen, answered disappointedly, "It—it broke." And then with a sadness that betokened there were other, greater tragedies than what had happened to the car: "It shows you can't drop it without breakage. And that was the chief point of our whole advertising campaign." Then an indistinct mumble: "Fifteen hundred dollars capital! Wait'll Belman hears what a white elephant we've got on our hands." Which, under the circumstances, was far funnier than was intended.

At least he's not yellow, whoever he is, thought MacKenzie. "Never mind," he exclaimed suddenly. "I've got it." His fingertips had found the slot at the far end of the seamless cast-bronze panel. The thing didn't feel buckled in any way but if the concussion had done that to it, if it refused to open—

He pulled back the latch, leaning over the operator's lifeless body to do so, and tugged at the slide. It gave, fell back about a third of its usual orbit along the groove, then stalled unmanageably. That was sufficient for their present needs, though there was no question of egress through it. The rough-edged bricks of the shaft wall were a finger's width beyond the lips of the car's orifice; not even a venturesome cat could have gotten a paw between without jamming it. What mattered was that they wouldn't asphyxiate now, no matter how long it took to free the mechanism, raise it.

"It's all right, fellows," he called reassuringly to those behind him, "I've got some air into the thing now."

If there was light farther up the shaft, it didn't reach down this far. The shaft wall opposite the opening was as black as the inside of the car itself.

He said, "They've heard us. They know what's happened. No use yelling at the top of your voice like that, only makes it tougher for the rest of us. They'll get an emergency crew on the job. We'll just have to sit and wait, that's all."

The nerve-tingling bellows for help, probably the tough guy again, were silenced shamefacedly. A groaning still kept up intermittently from someone else. "My arm, oh, Gawd, it hurts!" The sighing, from an injury that had gone deeper still, had quieted suspiciously some time before. Either the man had fainted, or he, too, was dead.

MacKenzie, matter-of-factly but not callously, reached down for the operator's outflung form, shifted it into the angle between two of the walls, and propped it upright there. Then he sat himself down in the clear floor space provided, tucked up his legs, wrapped his arms around them. He wouldn't have called himself a brave man; he was just a realist.

There was a momentary silence from all of them at once, one of those pauses. Then, because there was also, or seemed to be, a complete stillness from overhead in the shaft, panic stabbed at the tough guy again. "They gonna leave us here all night?" he whimpered. "What you guys sit there like that for? Don't you wanna get out?"

"For Pete's sake, somebody clip that loud-mouth on the chin!" urged MacKenzie truculently.

There was a soundless indrawn whistle. "My arm! Oh, my arm!"

"Must be busted," suggested MacKenzie sympathetically. "Try wrapping your shirt tight around it to kill the pain."

Time seemed to stand still, jog forward a few notches at a time every so often, like something on a belt. The rustle of a restless body, a groan, an exhalation of impatience, an occasional cry from the craven in their midst, whom MacKenzie sat on each time with increasing acidity as his own nerves slowly frayed.

The waiting, the sense of trapped helplessness, began to tell on them, far more than the accident had.

"They may think we're all dead and take their time," someone said.

"They never do in a case like this," MacKenzie answered shortly. "They're doing whatever they're doing as fast as they can. Give 'em time."

A new voice, that he hadn't heard until then, said to no one in particular, "I'm glad my father didn't get on here with me."

Somebody chimed in, "I wish I hadn't gone back after that damn phone call. It was a wrong number, and I coulda ridden down the trip before this."

MacKenzie sneered, "Ah, you talk like a bunch of ten-year-olds! It's happened; what's the good of wishing about it?"

He had a watch with a luminous dial on his wrist. He wished that he hadn't had, or that it had gone out of commission like the other man's trick fountain pen. It was too nerve-racking; every minute his eyes sought it, and when it seemed like half an hour had gone by, it was only five minutes. He wisely refrained from mentioning it to any of the others; they would have kept asking him, "How long is it now?" until he went screwy.

When they'd been down twenty-two and one-half minutes from the time he'd first looked at it, and were all in a state of nervous instability bordering on frenzy, including himself, there was a sudden unexpected, unannounced thump directly overhead, as though something heavy had landed on the roof of the car.

This time it was MacKenzie who leaped up, pressed his cheek flat against the brickwork outside the open panel, and funneled up the paper-thin gap: "Hello! Hello!"

"Yeah," a voice came down, "we're coming to you, take it easy!"

More thumping for a while, as though somebody were jigging over their heads. Then a sudden metallic din, like a boiler factory going full blast. The whole car seemed to vibrate with it, it became numbing to touch it for long at any one point. The confined space of the shaft magnified the noise into a torrent of sound, drowning out all their remarks. MacKenzie couldn't stand it, finally had to stick his palms up flat against his ears. A blue electric spark shot down the narrow crevice outside the door from above. Then another, then a third. They all went out too quickly to cast any light inside.

Acetylene torches! They were having to cut a hole through the car roof to get at them. If there was a basement opening in the shaft, and there must have been, the car must have plunged down even beyond that, to sub-basement level, wound up in a dead end cul-de-sac at pit bottom. There was apparently no other way.

A spark materialized eerily through the ceiling. Then another, then a semicircular gush of them. A curtain of fire descended halfway into their midst, illuminating their faces wanly for a minute. Luckily it went out before it touched the car floor.

The noise broke off short and the silence in its wake was deafening. A voice shouted just above them: "Look out for sparks, you guys below, we're coming through. Keep your eyes closed, get back against the walls!"

The noise came on again, nearer at hand, louder than before. MacKenzie's teeth were on edge from the incessant vibration. Being rescued was worse than being stuck down there. He wondered how the others were standing it, especially that poor guy with the broken wing. He thought he heard a voice scream: "Elinor! Elinor!" twice, like that, but you couldn't be sure of anything in that infernal din.

The sparks kept coming down like a dripping waterfall; MacKenzie squinted his eyes cagily, kept one hand shielded up over them to protect his eyesight. He thought he saw one spark shoot across horizontally, instead of down vertically, like all the others; it was a different color too, more orange. He thought it must be an optical illusion produced by the alternating glare and darkness they were all being subjected to; either that, or a detached splinter of combusted metal from the roof, ricocheting off the wall. He closed his eyes all the way, just to play safe.

There wasn't much more to it after that. The noise and sparks stopped abruptly. They pried up the crescent-shaped flap they had cut in the roof with crowbars, to keep it from toppling inward and crushing those below. The cool, icy beams of torches flickered through. A cop jumped down into their midst and ropes were sent snaking down after him. He said in a brisk, matter-of-fact way, "All right, who's first now? Who's the worst hurt of yez all?"

His torch showed three forms motionless at the feet of the others in the confined space. The operator, huddled in the corner where MacKenzie had propped him; the scholarly looking man with the rimless glasses (minus them now, and a deep gash under one eye to show what had become of them) lying senseless on his side; and the young fellow who had got on at the eleventh, tumbled partly across him, face down.

"The operator's dead," MacKenzie answered as spokesman for the rest, "and these two're out of their pain just now. There's a guy with a busted arm here, take him first."

The cop deftly looped the rope under the armpits of the ashen-faced bill collector, who was knotting the slack of one sleeve tightly in his other hand and sweating away like a fish in the torchlight.

"Haul away!" the cop shouted toward the opening. "And take your time, the guy's hurt."

The bill collector went up through the ceiling, groaning, legs drawn up under him like a trussed-up fowl.

The scholarly looking man went next, head bobbing down in unconsciousness. When the noose came down empty, the cop bent over to fasten it around the young fellow still on the floor.

MacKenzie saw him change his mind, pry open one eyelid, pass the rope on to the tough-looking mug who had been such a crybaby, and who was shaking all over from the nervous reaction to the fright he'd had.

"What's the matter with him?" MacKenzie butted in, pointing to the floor.

"He's dead," the cop answered briefly. "He can wait, the living come first."

"Dead! Why, I heard him say he was glad his father didn't get on with him, long after we hit!"

"I don't care what you heard him say!" the cop answered. "He coulda said it, and still be dead now! Nuts. Are you telling me my business? You seem to be pretty chipper for a guy that's just come through an experience like this!"

"Skip it," said MacKenzie placatingly. He figured it was no business of his anyway, if the guy had seemed all right at first and now was dead. He might have had a weak heart.

He and the disheartened fountain pen entrepreneur seemed to be the only two out of the lot who were totally unharmed. The latter, however, was so brokenhearted over the failure of his appliance to stand up under an emergency, that he seemed hardly to care whether he went up or stayed down or what became of him. He kept examining the defective gadget even on his way up through the aperture in the car roof, with the expression of a man who has just bitten into a very sour lemon.

MacKenzie was the last one up the shaft, except the two fatalities. He was pulled in over the lip of the basement opening, from which the sliding doors had been taken down bodily. It was a bare four feet above the roof of the car; in other words the shaft continued on down past it for little more than the height of the car. He couldn't understand why it had been built that way, and not ended flush with the basement, in which case their long imprisonment could have been avoided. It was explained to him later, by the building superintendent, that it was necessary to give the car additional clearance underneath, else it would have run the risk of jamming each time it came down to the basement.

There were stretchers there in the basement passageway, and the bill collector and the studious looking man were being given first aid by a pair of interns. The hard-looking egg was gulping down a large glass of spirits of ammonia between clicking teeth. MacKenzie let one of the interns look him over, at the latter's insistence; was told what he knew already, that he was okay. He gave his name and address to the lieutenant of police in charge, and walked up a flight of stairs to the street level, thinking, "The old-fashioned way's the best after all."

He found the lobby of the building choked with a milling crowd, warded off a number of ambulance chasers who tried to tell him how badly hurt he was. "There's money in it, buddy, don't be a sucker!"

MacKenzie phoned his wife from a near-by booth to shorten her anxiety, then he left the scene for home.

His last fleeting impression was of a forlorn figure standing there in the lobby, a man with a trim white mustache, the father of the young fellow lying dead below, buttonholing every cop within reach, asking over and over again, "Where's my son? Why haven't they brought my son up yet?" And not getting any answer from any of them—which was an answer in itself. MacKenzie pushed out into the street.

Friday, that was four days later, the doorbell rang right after supper and he had a visitor. "MacKenzie? You were in that elevator Monday night, weren't you, sir?"

"Yes," MacKenzie grinned, he sure was.

"I'm from Police Headquarters. Mind if I ask you a few questions? I've been going around to all of 'em checking up."

"Come in and sit down," said MacKenzie interestedly. His first guess was that they were trying to track down labor sabotage, or some violation of the building laws. "Matter, anything phony about it?"

"Not for our money," said the dick, evidently because this was the last leg of what was simply a routine questioning of all the survivors, and he refused to differ from his superiors. "The young fellow that was lying dead there in the bottom of the car—not the operator but young Wesley Hardecker—was found by the examiner to have a bullet embedded in his heart."

MacKenzie, jolted, gave a long-drawn whistle that brought his Scotty to the door questioningly. "Whew! You mean somebody shot him while we were all cooped up down there in that two-by-four?"

The dick showed, without being too pugnacious about it, that he was there to ask the questions, not answer them. "Did you know him at all?"

"Never saw him in my life before, until he got on the car that night. I know his name by now, because I read it in the papers next day; I didn't at the time."

The visitor nodded, as though this was the answer he'd gotten from all the others too. "Well, did you hear anything like a shot while you were down there?"

"No, not before they started the blowtorches. And after that, you couldn't have heard one anyway. Matter of fact, I had my hands over my ears at one time. I did see a flash, though," he went on eagerly. "Or at least I remember seeing one of the sparks shoot *across* instead of dropping down, and it was more orange in color."

Again the dick nodded. "Yeah, a couple of others saw that too. That was probably it, right there. Did it light up anyone's face behind it, anything like that?"

"No," MacKenzie admitted, "my eyes were all pinwheels, between the coal blackness and these flashing sparks coming down through the roof; we'd been warned, anyway, to keep them shut a minute before." He paused thoughtfully, went on: "It doesn't seem to hang together, does it? Why should anyone pick such a time and place to—"

"It hangs together beautifully," contradicted the dick. "It's his old man, the elder Hardecker, that's raising a stink, trying to read something phony into it. It's suicide while of unsound mind, and has been all along; and that's what the findings of the coroner's inquest are going to be too. We haven't turned up anything that throws a doubt on that. Old man Hardecker himself hasn't been able to identify a single one of you as having ever known or seen his son—or himself— before six o'clock last Monday evening. The gun was the fellow's own, and he had a license for it. He had it with him when he got in the car. It was under his body when it was picked up. The only fingerprints brought out on it were his. The examiner finds the wound a contact wound, powder burns all around it."

"The way we were crowded together down there, any kind of a shot at anyone would have been a contact," MacKenzie tried to object.

The dick waved this aside. "The nitrate test shows that his fingers fired the shot. It's true that we neglected to give it to anyone else at the time, but since there'd been only one shot fired out of the gun, and no other gun was found, that don't stack up to much. The bullet, of course, was from that gun and no other, ballistics has told us. The guy was a nervous, high-strung young fellow. He went hysterical down there, cracked up, and when he couldn't stand it any more, took himself out of it. And against this, his old man is beefing that he was happy, he had a lovely wife, they were expecting a kid and he had everything to live for."

"Well, all right," objected MacKenzie mildly, "but why should he do it when they were already working on the roof over us, and it was just a matter of minutes before they got to us. Why not before? That don't sound logical. Matter of fact, his voice sounded calm and unfrightened enough while we were waiting."

The detective got up, as though the discussion were ended, but condescended to enlighten him on his way to the door. "People don't crack up at a minute's notice; it was after he'd been down there twenty minutes, half an hour, it got him. When you heard him say that, he was probably trying to hold himself together, kid himself he was brave or something. Any psychiatrist will tell you what noise'll do to someone already under a strain or tension. The noise of the blowtorches gave him the finishing touch; that's why he did it then, couldn't think straight any more. As far as having a wife and expecting a kid is concerned, that would only make him lose his head all the quicker. A man without ties or responsibilities is always more cold-blooded in an emergency."

"It's a new one on me, but maybe you're right. I only know water-filters."

"It's my job to be right about things like that. Good night, Mr. Mac-Kenzie."

The voice on the wire said, "Mr. MacKenzie? Is this the Mr. Stephen MacKenzie who was in an elevator accident a year ago last August? The newspapers gave—"

"Yes, I was."

"Well, I'd like you to come to dinner at my house next Saturday evening, at exactly seven o'clock."

MacKenzie cocked his brows at himself in the wall mirror. "Hadn't you better tell me who you are, first?"

"Sorry," said the voice, crisply. "I thought I had. I've been doing this for the past hour or so, and it's beginning to tell on me. This is Harold Hardecker, I'm head of the Hardecker Import and Export Company."

"Well, I still don't place you, Mr. Hardecker," MacKenzie said levelly. "Are you one of the men who was on that elevator with me?"

"No, my son was. He lost his life."

"Oh," said MacKenzie. He remembered now. A man with a trim white mustache, standing in the milling crowd, buttonholing the cops as they hurried by. . . .

"Can I expect you then at seven next Saturday, Mr. MacKenzie? I'm at —— Park Avenue."

"Frankly," said MacKenzie, who was a plain soul not much given to social hypocrisy, "I don't see any point to it. I don't believe we've ever spoken to one another before. Why do you single me out?"

Hardecker explained patiently, even good-naturedly, "I'm not singling you out, Mr. MacKenzie. I've already contacted each of the others who were on the car that night with my son, and they've all agreed to be there. I don't wish to disclose what I have in mind beforehand; I'm giving this dinner for that purpose. However, I might mention that my son died intestate, and his poor wife passed away in childbirth in the early hours of the following morning. His estate reverted to me, and I am a lonely old man, without friends or relatives, and with more money already than I know what to do with. It occurred to me to bring together five perfect strangers, who shared a common hazard with my son, who were with him during the last few moments of his life." The voice paused, insinuatingly, to let this sink in. Then it resumed, "If you'll be at my house for dinner Saturday at seven, I'll have an announcement of considerable importance to make. It's to your interest to be present when I do."

MacKenzie scanned his water-filter-salesman's salary with his mind's eye, and found it altogether unsatisfactory, as he had done not once but many times before. "All right," he agreed, after a moment's consideration.

Saturday at six he was still saying, "You can't tell me. The guy isn't in his right mind, to do a thing like this. Five people that he don't know from Adam, and that don't know each other. I wonder if it's a practical joke?"

"Well, if you feel that way, why didn't you refuse him?" said his wife, brushing off his dark-blue coat.

"I'm curious to find out what it's all about. I want to see what the gag is." Curiosity is one of the strongest of human traits. It's almost irresistible. The expectation of getting something for nothing is no slouch either. MacKenzie was a good guy, but he was a guy after all, not an image on a stained glass window.

At the door she said with belated anxiety, "Steve, I know you can take care of yourself and all that, but if you don't like the looks of things, I mean if none of the others show up, don't stay there alone."

He laughed. He'd made up his mind by now, had even spent the windfall ahead of time, already. "You make me feel like one of those innocents in the old silent pictures, that were always being invited to a big blowout and when they got there they were alone with the villain and just supper for two. Don't worry, Toots, if there's no one else there, I turn around and come back."

The building had a Park Avenue address, but was actually on one of the exclusive side streets just off that thoroughfare. A small ultra-ultra co-operative, with only one apartment to a floor. "Mr. Harold Hardecker?" asked Mr. MacKenzie in the lobby. "Stephen MacKenzie."

He saw the hallman take out a small typed list of five names, four of which already had been penciled out, and cross out the last one. "Go right up, Mr. MacKenzie. Third floor."

A butler opened the single door in the elevator foyer for him, greeted him by name and took his hat. A single glance at the money this place spelled would have been enough to restore anyone's confidence. People that lived like this were perfectly capable of having five strangers in to dinner, subdividing a dead son's estate among them, and chalking it off as just that evening's little whimsey. The sense of proportion alters above a certain yearly income.

He remembered Hardecker readily enough as soon as he saw him coming toward him along the central gallery that seemed to bisect the place like a bowling alley. It took him about three and a half minutes to get up to him, at that. The man had aged appreciably from the visual snapshot that was all he'd had of him at the scene of the accident. He was slightly stooped, very thin at the waist, looked as though he'd suffered. But the white mustache was as trim and needle-pointed as ever, and he had on one of the new turned-over soft collars under his dinner jacket, which gave him a peculiarly boyish look in spite of the almost blinding white of his undiminished hair, cropped close as a Prussian's.

Hardecker held out his hand, said with just the right mixture of dignity and warmth, "How do you do, Mr. MacKenzie, I'm very glad to know you. Come in and meet the others and have a pickup."

There were no women present in the living room, just the four men sitting around at ease. There was no sense of strain, of stiffness; an advantage that stag gatherings are apt to have over mixed parties anyway, not through the fault of women, but through men's consciousness of them.

Kenshaw, the scholarly looking man, had a white scar still visible under his left eye where his glasses had broken. The cherubic Lambert had deserted the illuminated fountain pen business, he hurriedly confided, unasked, to MacKenzie, for the ladies' foundation-girdle business. No more mechanical gadgets for him. Or as he put it, unarguably, "A brassiere they gotta have, or else. But who needs a fountain pen?" The hard-bitten mug was introduced as Prendergast, occupation undisclosed. Megaffin, the bill collector, was no longer a bill collector. "I send out my own now," he explained, swiveling a synthetic diamond around on his pinky.

MacKenzie selected Scotch, and when he'd caught up with the rest the butler came to the door, almost as though he'd been timing him through a knothole. He just looked in, then went away again.

"Let's go and get down to business now, gentlemen, shall we?" Hardecker grinned. He had the happy faculty, MacKenzie said to himself, of making you feel perfectly at home, without overdoing it, getting in your hair. Which looks easier than it is.

No flowers, candles, or fripperies like that were on the table set for six; just good substantial man's board. Hardecker said, "Just sit down anywhere you choose, only keep the head for me." Lambert and Kenshaw took one side, Prendergast and Megaffin on the other. MacKenzie sat down at the foot. It was obvious that whatever announcement their host intended making was being kept for the end of the meal, as was only fitting.

The butler had closed a pair of sliding doors beyond them after they were all in, and he stayed outside. The waiting was done by a man. It was a typical bachelor's repast, plain, marvelously cooked, without dainty or frivolous accessories to detract from it, salads, vegetables, things like that. Each course had its vintage corollary. And at the end no cloying sweets—Roquefort cheese and coffee with the blue flame of Courvoisier flickering above each glass. It was a masterpiece. And each one, as it ended, relaxed in his chair in a haze of golden daydreams. They anticipated coming into money, money they hadn't had to work for, maybe more money than they'd ever had before. It wasn't such a bad world after all.

One thing had struck MacKenzie, but since he'd never been waited on by servants in a private home before, only in restaurants, he couldn't determine whether it was unusual or customary. There was an expensive mahogany buffet running across one side of the dining room, but the waiter had done no serving or carving on it, had brought in each portion separately, always individually, even the roast. The coffee and the wines, too, had been poured behind the scenes, the glasses and the cups brought in already filled. It gave the man a lot more work and slowed the meal somewhat, but if that was the way it was done in Hardecker's house, that was the way it was done.

When they were already luxuriating with their cigars and cigarettes, and the cloth had been cleared of all but the emptied coffee cups, an additional dish was brought in. It was a silver chalice, a sort of stemmed bowl, holding a thick yellowish substance that looked like mayonnaise. The waiter placed it in the exact geometrical center of the table, even measuring with his eye its distance from both sides, and from the head and foot, and shifting its position to conform. Then he took the lid off and left it open. Threads of steam rose sluggishly from it. Every eye was on it interestedly.

"Is it well mixed?" they heard Hardecker ask.

"Yes, sir," said the waiter.

"That will be all, don't come in again."

The man left by the pantry door he had been using, and it clicked slightly after it had closed behind him.

Somebody—Megaffin—asked cozily, "What's *that* got in it?" evidently on the lookout for still more treats.

"Oh, quite a number of things," Hardecker answered carelessly, "whites of eggs, mustard, as well as certain other ingredients all beaten up together."

MacKenzie, trying to be funny, said, "Sounds like an antidote."

"It is an antidote," Hardecker answered, looking steadily down the table at him. He must have pushed a call button or something under the table, for the butler opened the sliding doors and stood between them, without coming in.

Hardecker didn't turn his head. "You have that gun I gave you? Stand there, please, on the other side of those doors and see that no one comes out of here. If they try it, you know what to do."

The doors slipped to again, effaced him, but not before MacKenzie, facing that way, had seen something glimmer in his hand.

Tension was slow in coming on, the change was too abrupt, they had been too steeped in the rosy afterglow of the meal and their own imminent good fortune. Then too, not all of them were equally alert mentally, particularly Megaffin, who had been on such a fourth dimensional plane of unaccustomedness all evening he couldn't tell menace from hospitality, even when a gun was mentioned.

Its first focal point was Hardecker's own face—that went slowly white, grim, remorseless. From there it darted out to MacKenzie and Lambert, caught at them, paled them too. The rest grew allergic to it one by one, until there was complete silence at the table.

Hardecker spoke. Not loudly, not angrily, but in a steely, pitiless voice. "Gentlemen, there's a murderer in our midst."

Five breaths were sharply indrawn together, making a fearful "Ffff!" sound around the table. Not so much aghast at the statement itself, as aghast at the implication of retribution that lurked just behind it. And behind that was the shadowy suspicion that it had already been exacted.

No one said anything.

The hard, remorseless cores of Hardecker's eyes shot from face to face. He was smoking a long slim cigar, cigarette-thin. He pointed it straight out before him, indicated them all with it without moving it much, like a dark finger of doom. "Gentlemen, one of you killed my son." Pause. "On August 30, 1936." Pause. "And hasn't paid for it yet."

The words were like a stone going down into a deep pool of transparent water, and the ripples spreading out from them spelled fear.

MacKenzie said slowly, "You setting yourself above the properly constituted authorities? The findings of the coroner's inquest were suicide while of unsound mind. Why do you hold them incompe—"

Hardecker cut him short like a whip. "This isn't a discussion. It's—" a long pause, then very low, but very audible, "an execution."

There was another of those strangling silences. They took it in a variety of ways, each according to his temperament. MacKenzie just kept staring at him, startled, apprehensive. Apprehensive, but not inordinately frightened, any more than he had been that night on the elevator. The scholarly looking Kenshaw had a rebuking look on his face, that of a teacher for an unruly pupil, and the scar on his cheek stood out whitely. Megaffin looked shifty, like some small weasel at bay, planning its next move. The pugnacious-looking guy was going to cave in again in a minute, judging by the wavering of his facial lines. Lambert pinched the bridge of his nose momentarily, dropped his hand, mumbled something that sounded like, *"Oy,* I give up my pinochle club to come here, yet!"

Hardecker resumed, as though he hadn't said anything unusual just now. "I know who the man is. I know which one among you the man is. It's taken me a year to find out, but now I know, beyond the shadow of a doubt." He was looking at his cigar now, watching the ash drop off of its own weight onto his coffee saucer. "The police wouldn't listen to me, they insisted it was suicide. The evidence was insufficient to convince them the first time, and for all I know it still may be." He raised his eyes. "But I demand justice for the taking of my son's life." He took an expensive, dime-thin, octagonal watch out of his pocket, placed it face up on the table before him. "Gentlemen, it's now nine o'clock. In half an hour, at the most, one of you will be dead. Did you notice that you were all served separately just now? One dish, and one alone out of all of them, was deadly. It's putting in its slow, sure work right as we sit here." He pointed to the silver tureen, equidistant from all of them. "There's the answer. There's the antidote. I have no wish to set myself up as executioner above the law. Let the murderer be the chooser. Let him reach out and save his life and stand convicted before all of you. Or let him keep silent and go down to his death without confessing, privately executed for what can't be publicly proved. In twenty-five minutes collapse will come without warning. Then it will be too late."

It was Lambert who voiced the question in all their minds. "But are you sure you did this to the right—"

"I haven't made any mistake, the waiter was carefully rehearsed, you are all perfectly unharmed but the killer."

Lambert didn't seem to derive much consolation from this. "Now he tells us! A fine way to digest a meal," he brooded aloud. "Why didn't you serve the murderer first, so then the rest of us could eat in peace at least?"

"Shut up," somebody said, terrifiedly.

"Twenty minutes to go," Hardecker said, tonelessly as a chime signal over the radio.

MacKenzie said, without heat, "You can't be sane, you know, to do a thing like this."

"Did you ever have a son?" was the answer.

Something seemed to snap in Megaffin. His chair jolted back. "I'm gettin' out of here," he said hoarsely.

The doors parted about two inches, silently as water, and a black metal cylinder peered through. "That man there," directed Hardecker. "Shoot him where he stands if he doesn't sit down."

Megaffin shrank down in his seat again like a whipped cur, tried to shelter himself behind Prendergast's shoulder. The doors slipped together again into a hairline crack.

"I couldn't," sighed the cherubic-faced Lambert, "feel more at home if I was in the Brown House at Munich!"

"Eighteen minutes," was the comment from the head of the table.

Prendergast suddenly grimaced uncontrollably, flattened his forearms on the table, and ducked his head onto them. He sniveled aloud. "I can't stand it! Lemme out of here! *I* didn't do it!"

A wave of revulsion went around the table. It was not because he'd broken down, analyzed MacKenzie, it was just that he didn't have the face for it. It should have been Lambert with his kewpie physiognomy, if anyone. The latter, however, was having other troubles. He touched the side of his head, tapped himself on the chest. "Whoof!" he murmured. "What heartburn! He should live so long, I don't take this up with my lawyer!"

"This is no way," said MacKenzie surlily. "If you had any kind of a case—"

"This is my way," was Hardecker's crackling answer. "I've given the man his choice. He needn't have it this way; he has his alternative. Fourteen minutes. Let me remind you, the longer the antidote's delayed, the more doubtful its efficiency will be. If it's postponed too long, it may miss altogether."

Conscious of a sticking sensation in his stomach, as though a mass of concrete had lodged there, MacKenzie felt a burning sensation shoot out from it. There is such a thing as nervous indigestion, he knew, but— He eyed the silver goblet reflectively.

But they were all doing that almost incessantly. Prendergast had raised his head again, but it remained a woebegone mask of infantile fretfulness. Megaffin was green in the face and kept moistening his lips. Kenshaw was the most self-controlled of the lot; he had folded his arms and just sat there, as though waiting to see which one of the others would reach for the salvation in the silver container.

MacKenzie could feel a painful pulsing under his solar plexus now; he was in acute discomfort that verged on cramp. The thought of what this might be was bringing out sweat on his forehead.

Lambert reached out abruptly, and they all quit breathing for a minute. But his hand dodged the silver tureen, plunged into a box of perfectos to one side of it. He grabbed up two, stuck one in his breast pocket, the other between his teeth. "On you," he remarked resentfully to Hardecker.

Somebody gave a strained laugh at the false alarm they had all had. Kenshaw took off his glasses, wiped them ruefully, as though disappointed it hadn't been the payoff after all.

MacKenzie said, "You're alienating whatever sympathy's due you, by pulling a stunt like this."

"I'm not asking for sympathy," was Hardecker's coldly ferocious answer. "It's atonement I want. Three lives were taken from me: My only son, my daughter-in-law, their prematurely born child. I demand payment for that!"

Lambert said aloud for his own benefit, "Jennie wouldn't believe this when I tell her."

Prendergast clutched his throat all at once, whimpered, "I can't breathe! He's done it to *me,* so help me!"

MacKenzie, hostile now to Hardecker, tried to steady him just on general principle. "Gas around the heart, maybe. Don't fall for it if you're not sure."

"Don't fall for it," was the ungrateful yelp, "and if I drop dead are *you* gonna bring me back?"

"He ought to be arrested for this," said Kenshaw, displaying emotion for the first time. His glasses had clouded over, giving him a peculiarly sightless look.

"Arrested?" snapped Lambert. He wagged his head from side to side. "He's going to be sued like no one was ever sued before! When I get through with him he'll go on relief."

Hardecker threw him a contemptuous look. "About ten minutes," he said. "He seems to prefer the more certain way. Stubborn, eh? He'd rather die than admit it."

MacKenzie gripped the seat of his chair, his churning insides heaving. He thought, *If this is the McCoy that I'm feeling now, I'm going to bash his head in with a chair before I go. I'll give him something to poison innocent people about!*

Megaffin was starting to swear at their tormentor, in a whining, guttural singsong.

"*Mazzeltov,*" seconded Lambert, with a formal nod of approval. "Your breath, but my ideas."

"Five minutes. It will almost certainly fail if it's not downed within the next thirty seconds." Hardecker pocketed his watch, as though there were no further need for consulting it.

MacKenzie gagged, hauled at the knot of his tie, undid his collar-button. A needle of suffocating pain had just splintered into his heart.

Only the whites of Prendergast's eyes showed; he was going off into some fit or fainting spell. Even Lambert quit pulling at his cigar, as though it sickened him. Kenshaw took off his glasses for the third time in five minutes, to clear them.

A pair of arms suddenly shot out, grasped the silver bowl, swung it. It was uptilted over someone's face and there was a hollow, metallic groaning coming from behind it, infinitely gruesome to hear. It had happened so quickly, MacKenzie couldn't be sure who it was for a minute, long as he had been sitting at the macabre table with all of them. He had to do it by a quick process of elimination. Man sitting beside Lambert—Kenshaw, the scholarly looking one, the man who had had the least to say since the ordeal had begun! He was gulping with a convulsive rising and falling of his Adam's apple, visible in the shadow just below the lower rim of the bowl.

Then suddenly he flung it aside, his face was visible again, the drained receptacle clanged against the wall where he'd cast it, dropped heavily to the floor. He couldn't talk for a minute or two, and neither could anyone else, except possibly Hardecker, and he didn't. Just sat staring at the self-confessed culprit with pitiless eyes.

Finally Kenshaw panted, cheeks twitching, "Will it—will it—save me?"

Hardecker folded his arms, said to the others, but without taking his eyes off Kenshaw, "So now you know. So now you see whether I was right or not."

Kenshaw was holding his hands pressed tightly to the sides of his head. A sudden flood of words was unloosed from him, as though he found it a relief to talk now, after the long unbearable tension he'd been through. "Sure you were right, and I'd do it over again! I'm glad he's gone. The rich man's son that had everything. But that wasn't enough for him, was it? He had to show off how good he was —Horatio Alger stuff, paddle your own canoe from riches to more riches! He couldn't take a job with your own firm, could he? No, people might say you were helping him. He had to come to the place *I* worked and ask for a job. Not just anonymously. No, he had to mention whose son he was, to swing the scales in his favor! They were afraid to offend you, they thought maybe they'd get a pull with you, through him. It didn't count that I'd been with them all the best years of my life, that I had someone home too, just like he had, that I couldn't go anywhere else and mention the name of an influential father! They fired me."

His voice rose shrilly. "D'you know what happened to me? D'you know or care how I tramped the streets in the rain, at my age, looking for work? D'you know my wife had to get down on her knees and scrub dirty office corridors? D'you know how I washed dishes, carried sandwich-boards through the streets, slept on park benches, all on account of a smart-aleck with Rover Boy ideas? Yes, it preyed on my mind, why wouldn't it? I suppose you found the threatening letters I wrote him, that's how you knew."

Hardecker just shook his head slightly in denial.

"Then he got on the elevator that day. He didn't see me, probably wouldn't have known me if he had, but I saw him. I knew him. Then we fell—and I hoped he was dead, I hoped he was dead! But he wasn't. The idea took hold of me slowly, waiting down there in the dark. The torches started making noise, and I grabbed him, I was going to choke him. But he wrenched himself free and took out his gun to defend himself against what I guess he thought was a fear-crazed man. I wasn't fear-crazed, I was revenge-crazed, I knew what I was doing!

"I grabbed his hand. Not the gun, but the hand that was holding it. I turned it around the other way, into his own heart. He said 'Elinor, Elinor!' but that didn't save him; that was the wrong name, that was *his* wife not mine. I squeezed the finger he had on the trigger with my own, and he fired his own weapon. So the police were right, it was suicide in a way.

"He leaned against me, there wasn't room enough in there to fall. I flung myself down first under him, so they'd find us that way, and eased him down on top of me. He bled on me a little while and then he quit. And when they came through I pretended I'd fainted."

Hardecker said, "Murderer. Murderer." Like drops of ice water. "He didn't *know* he'd done all that to you; oh, why didn't you give him a chance at least, why weren't you a man? Murderer! Murderer!"

Kenshaw started reaching downward to the floor, where he'd dropped his glasses when he had seized the antidote. His face was on a level with the table top. He scowled: "No matter what they've all heard me say just now, you'll never be able to prove I did it. Nobody saw me. Only the dark."

A whisper sounded: "And that's where you're going. Into the dark."

Kenshaw's head vanished suddenly below the table. The empty back of his chair whirled over sidewise, cracked against the floor.

They were all on their feet now, bending over him. All but Hardecker. MacKenzie got up from his knees. "He's dead!" he said. "The antidote didn't work in time!"

Hardecker said, "That wasn't the antidote, that was the poison itself. He hadn't been given any until he gulped that down. He convicted himself and carried out sentence upon himself with one and the same gesture. I hadn't known which one of you it was until then. I'd only known it hadn't been my son's own doing, because, you see, the noise of those torches wouldn't have affected him much, he was partly deaf from birth."

He pushed his chair back and stood up. "I didn't summon you here under false pretenses; his estate will be divided in equal parts among the four of you that are left. And now I'm ready to take my own medicine. Call the police, let them and their prosecutors and their courts of law decide whether I killed him or his own guilty conscience did!"

DEAD MAN'S MIRROR

by Agatha Christie

1

The flat was a modern one. The furnishings of the room were modern, too. The armchairs were squarely built, the upright chairs were angular. A modern writing-table was set squarely in front of the window and at it sat a small, elderly man. His head was practically the only thing in the room that was not square. It was egg-shaped.

M. Hercule Poirot was reading a letter:

Station: Whimperley.
Telegrams: Harborough
St. John.

Hamborough Close,
Hamborough St. Mary,
Westshire.

September 24th

M. Hercule Poirot,
Dear Sir,
    A matter has arisen which requires handling with great delicacy and discretion. I have heard good accounts of you and have decided to entrust the matter to you. I have reason to believe that I am the victim of fraud, but for family reasons I do not wish to call in the police. I am taking certain measures of my own to deal with the business, but you must be prepared to come down here immediately on receipt of a telegram. I should be obliged if you will not answer this letter.
                            Yours faithfully,
                            Gervase Chevenix-Gore.

The eyebrows of M. Hercule Poirot climbed slowly up his forehead until they nearly disappeared into his hair.

"And who, then," he demanded of space, "is this Gervase Chevenix-Gore?"

He crossed to a bookcase and took out a large, fat book.
He found what he wanted easily enough:

> Chevenix-Gore, Sir Gervase Francis Xavier, 10th Bt. cr. 1694; formerly Captain 17th Lancers; b. 18th May 1878; e.s. of Sir Guy Chevenix-Gore, 9th Bt. and Lady Claudia Bretherton, 2nd d. of 8th Earl of Wallingford. S. father, 1911; m. 1912, Vanda Elizabeth, e.d. of Colonel Frederick Arbuthnot, q.v.; educ. Eton. Served European War 1914-'18. Recreations: traveling, big game hunting. Address: Hamborough Close, Hamborough St. Mary, Westshire, and 218 Lowndes Square, S.W.1. Clubs: Cavalry, Travelers.

Poirot shook his head in a slightly dissatisfied manner. For a moment or two he remained lost in thought, then he went to the desk, pulled open a drawer, and took out a little pile of invitation cards.

His face brightened.

"*A la bonne heure!* Exactly my affair! He will certainly be there."

A duchess greeted M. Hercule Poirot in fulsome tones:

"So you could manage to come after all, M. Poirot! Why, that's splendid."

"The pleasure is mine, madame," murmured Poirot, bowing.

He escaped from several important and splendid beings—a famous diplomat, an equally famous actress and a well-known sporting peer —and found at last the person he had come to seek, that invariably "also present" guest, Mr. Satterthwaite.

Mr. Satterthwaite twittered amiably:

"The dear Duchess—I always enjoy her parties. . . . Such a *personality,* if you know what I mean. I saw a lot of her in Corsica some years ago. . . ."

Mr. Satterthwaite's conversation was apt to be unduly burdened by mentions of his titled acquaintances. It is possible that he *may* sometimes have found pleasure in the company of Messrs. Jones, Brown or Robinson, but if so, he did not mention the fact. And yet, to describe Mr. Satterthwaite as a mere snob and leave it at that would have been to do him an injustice. He was a keen observer of human nature, and if it is true that the looker-on knows most of the game, Mr. Satterthwaite knew a good deal.

"You know, my dear fellow, it is really ages since I saw you. I always feel myself privileged to have seen you work at close quarters in the Crow's Nest business. I feel since then that I am in the know, so to speak. I saw Lady Mary only last week, by the way. A charming creature—potpourri and lavender!"

After passing lightly on one or two scandals of the moment—the indiscretions of an Earl's daughter, and the lamentable conduct of a Viscount—Poirot succeeded in introducing the name of Gervase Chevenix-Gore.

Mr. Satterthwaite responded immediately:

"Ah, now, there *is* a character, if you like! The Last of the Baronets—that's his nickname."

"*Pardon,* I do not quite comprehend—?"

Mr. Satterthwaite unbent indulgently to the lower comprehension of a foreigner.

"It's a joke, you know—a *joke*. Naturally, he's not *really* the last Baronet in England—but he *does* represent the end of an era. The Bold Bad Baronet—the mad harum-scarum Baronet so popular in the novels of the last century—the kind of fellow who laid impossible wagers and won 'em."

He went on to expound what he meant in more detail. In younger years, Gervase Chevenix-Gore had sailed around the world in a windjammer. He had been on an expedition to the Pole; he had challenged a racing peer to a duel. For a wager he had ridden his favorite mare up the staircase of a ducal house. He had once leapt from a box to the stage, and carried off a well-known actress in the middle of her rôle. The anecdotes of him were innumerable.

"It's an old family," went on Mr. Satterthwaite. "Sir Guy Chevenix-Gore went on the first crusade. Now, alas, the line looks like coming to an end. Old Gervase is the last Chevenix-Gore."

"The estate, it is impoverished?"

"Not a bit of it. Gervase is fabulously wealthy. Owns valuable house-property—coal-fields—and in addition, he staked out a claim to some mine in Peru or somewhere in South America, when he was a young man, which has yielded him a fortune. An amazing man. Always fortunate in everything he's undertaken."

"He is now an elderly man, of course?"

"Yes, poor old Gervase." Mr. Satterthwaite sighed, shook his head. "Most people would describe him to you as mad as a hatter. It's true, in a way. He *is* mad—not in the sense of being certifiable or having delusions—but mad in the sense of being abnormal. He's always been a man of great originality of character."

"And originality becomes eccentricity as the years go by?" suggested Poirot.

"Very true. That's exactly what's happened to poor old Gervase."

"He has, perhaps, a swollen idea of his own importance?"

"Absolutely. I should imagine that, in Gervase's mind, the world has always been divided into two parts—the Chevenix-Gores—and the other people!"

"An exaggerated sense of family!"

"Yes. The Chevenix-Gores are all arrogant as the devil—a law unto themselves. Gervase, being the last of them, has got it badly. He is—well, really, you know, to hear him talk, you might imagine him to be —er, the Almighty!"

Poirot nodded his head slowly and thoughtfully.

"Yes, I imagined that. I have had, you see, a letter from him. It was an unusual letter. It did not demand. It summoned!"

"A royal command," said Mr. Satterthwaite, tittering a little.

"Precisely. It did not seem to occur to this Sir Gervase that I, Hercule Poirot, am a man of importance, a man of infinite affairs! That it was extremely unlikely that I should be able to fling everything aside and come hastening like an obedient dog—like a mere nobody, gratified to receive a commission!"

Mr. Satterthwaite bit his lip in an effort to suppress a smile. It may have occurred to him that where egoism was concerned, there was not much to choose between Hercule Poirot and Gervase Chevenix-Gore.

He murmured:

"Of course, if the cause of the summons was urgent—?"

"It was not!" Poirot's hands rose in the air in an emphatic gesture. "I was to hold myself at his disposition, that was all, *in case* he should require me! *Enfin, je vous demande!*"

Again the hands rose eloquently, expressing better than words could do M. Hercule Poirot's sense of utter outrage.

"I take it," said Mr. Satterthwaite, "that you refused?"

"I have not yet had the opportunity," said Poirot slowly.

"But you will refuse?"

A new expression passed over the little man's face. His brow furrowed itself perplexedly.

He said:

"How can I express myself? To refuse—yes, that was my first instinct. But I do not know. . . . One has, sometimes, a feeling. Faintly, I seem to smell the fish. . . ."

Mr. Satterthwaite received this last statement without any sign of amusement.

"Oh?" he said. "That is interesting. . . ."

"It seems to me," went on Hercule Poirot, "that a man such as you have described might be very vulnerable—"

"Vulnerable?" queried Mr. Satterthwaite. For the moment he was surprised. The word was not one that he would naturally have associated with Gervase Chevenix-Gore. But he was a man of perception, quick in observation. He said slowly:

"I think—I see what you mean."

"Such a one is encased, is he not, in an armor—such an armor! The armor of the crusaders was nothing to it—an armor of arrogance, of pride, of complete self-esteem. This armor, it is in some ways a protection, the arrows, the everyday arrows of life glance off it. But there is this danger. *Sometimes a man in armor might not even know he was being attacked.* He will be slow to see, slow to hear—slower still to feel."

He paused, then asked with a change of manner:

"Of what does the family of this Sir Gervase consist?"

"There's Vanda—his wife. She was an Arbuthnot—very handsome girl. She's still quite a handsome woman. Frightfully vague, though. Devoted to Gervase. She's got a leaning towards the occult, I believe. Wears amulets and scarabs and gives out that she's the reincarnation of an Egyptian Queen. . . . Then there's Ruth—she's their adopted daughter. They've no children of their own. Very attractive girl in the modern style. That's all the family. Except, of course, for Hugo Trent. He's Gervase's nephew. Pamela Chevenix-Gore married Reggie Trent and Hugo was their only child. He's an orphan. He can't inherit the title, of course, but I imagine he'll come in for most of Gervase's money in the end. Good-looking lad; he's in the Blues."

Poirot nodded his head thoughtfully. Then he asked:

"It is a grief to Sir Gervase, yes, that he has no son to inherit his name?"

"I should imagine that it cuts pretty deep."

"The family name, it is a passion with him?"

"Yes."

Mr. Satterthwaite was silent a moment or two. He was very intrigued. Finally he ventured:

"You see a definite reason for going down to Hamborough Close?"

Slowly, Poirot shook his head.

"No," he said. "As far as I can see, there is no reason at all. But all the same, I fancy I shall go."

2

Hercule Poirot sat in the corner of a first-class carriage speeding through the English countryside.

Meditatively he took from his pocket a neatly folded telegram, which he opened and re-read.

> *Take 4.30 from St. Pancras instruct guard have express stopped at Whimperley. Chevenix-Gore.*

He folded up the telegram again and put it back in his pocket.

The guard on the train had been obsequious. The gentleman was going to Hamborough Close? Oh, yes, Sir Gervase Chevenix-Gore's guests always had the express stopped at Whimperley. "A special kind of prerogative I think it is, sir."

Since then the guard had paid two visits to the carriage: the first in order to assure the traveler that everything would be done to keep the carriage for himself, the second to announce that the express was running ten minutes late.

The train was due to arrive at 7.50, but it was exactly two minutes past eight when Hercule Poirot descended onto the platform of the little country station and pressed the expected half-crown in the attentive guard's hand.

There was a whistle from the engine and the Northern Express began to move once more. A tall chauffeur in dark green uniform stepped up to Poirot.

"Mr. Poirot? For Hamborough Close?"

He picked up the detective's neat valise and led the way out of the station. A big Rolls was waiting. The chauffeur held the door open for Poirot to get in, arranged a sumptuous fur rug over his knees and they drove off.

After some ten minutes of cross-country driving, round sharp corners and down country lanes, the car turned in at a wide gateway flanked with huge stone griffons.

They drove through a park and up to the house. The door of it was opened as they drew up, and a butler of imposing proportions showed himself upon the front step.

"Mr. Poirot? This way, sir."

He led the way along the hall and threw open a door halfway along it on the right.

"Mr. Hercule Poirot," he announced.

The room contained a number of people in evening dress, and as

Poirot walked in, his quick eyes perceived at once that his appearance was not expected. The eyes of all present rested on him in unfeigned surprise.

Then a tall woman, whose dark hair was threaded with gray, made an uncertain advance towards him.

Poirot bowed over her hand.

"My apologies, madame," he said. "I fear that my train was late."

"Not at all," said Lady Chevenix-Gore vaguely. Her eyes still stared at him in a puzzled fashion. "Not at all, Mr.—er—I didn't quite hear—"

"Hercule Poirot."

He said the name clearly and distinctly.

Somewhere behind him he heard a sudden sharp intake of breath.

At the same time he realized clearly that his host could not be in the room. He murmured gently:

"You knew I was coming, madame?"

"Oh—oh, yes. . . ." Her manner was not convincing. "I think—I mean I suppose so, but I am so terribly impractical, M. Poirot. I forget everything." Her tone held a melancholy pleasure in the fact. "I am told things. I appear to take them in—but they just pass through my brain and are gone! Vanished! As though they had never been."

Then, with a slight air of performing a duty long overdue, she glanced round her vaguely and murmured:

"I expect you know everybody."

Though this was patently not the case, the phrase was clearly a well-worn formula by means of which Lady Chevenix-Gore spared herself the trouble of introduction and the strain of remembering people's right names.

Making a supreme effort to meet the difficulties of this particular case, she added:

"My daughter—Ruth."

The girl who stood before him was also tall and dark, but she was of a very different type. Instead of the flattish, indeterminate features of Lady Chevenix-Gore, she had a well-chiseled nose, slightly aquiline, and a clear, sharp line of jaw. Her black hair swept back from her face into a mass of little tight curls. Her coloring was of carnation clearness and brilliance and owed little to make-up. She was, so Hercule Poirot thought, one of the loveliest girls he had seen.

He recognized, too, that she had brains as well as beauty, and guessed at certain qualities of pride and temper. Her voice, when she spoke, came with a slight drawl that struck him as deliberately put on.

"How exciting," she said, "to entertain M. Hercule Poirot! The Old Man arranged a little surprise for us, I suppose."

"So you did not know I was coming, mademoiselle?" he said quickly.

"I hadn't an idea of it. As it is, I must postpone getting my autograph book until after dinner."

The notes of a gong sounded from the hall, then the butler opened the door and announced:

"Dinner is served."

And then, almost before the last word, "served," had been uttered, something very curious happened. The pontifical domestic figure became, just for one moment, a highly astonished human being. . . .

The metamorphosis was so quick, and the mask of the well-trained servant was back again so soon, that anyone who had not happened to be looking would not have noticed the change. Poirot, however, *had* happened to be looking. He wondered.

The butler hesitated in the doorway. Though his face was again correctly expressionless, an air of tension hung about his figure.

Lady Chevenix-Gore said uncertainly:

"Oh, dear—this is most extraordinary—really, I—one hardly knows what to do."

Ruth said to Poirot:

"This singular consternation, M. Poirot, is occasioned by the fact that my father, for the first time for at least twenty years, is late for dinner."

"It is most extraordinary—" wailed Lady Chevenix-Gore. "Gervase never—"

An elderly man of upright soldierly carriage came to her side. He laughed genially.

"Good old Gervase! Late at last! Upon my word, we'll rag him over this. Elusive collar-stud, d'you think? Or is Gervase immune from our common weaknesses?"

Lady Chevenix-Gore said in a low, puzzled voice:

"But Gervase is *never* late."

It was almost ludicrous, the consternation caused by this simple *contretemps*. And yet, to Hercule Poirot, it was *not* ludicrous. . . . Behind the consternation he felt uneasiness—perhaps even apprehension. And he, too, found it strange that Gervase Chevenix-Gore should not appear to greet the guest he had summoned in such a mysterious manner.

In the meantime, it was clear that nobody knew quite what to do.

An unprecedented situation had arisen with which nobody knew how to deal.

Lady Chevenix-Gore at last took the initiative, if initiative it could be called. Certainly her manner was vague in the extreme.

"Snell," she said, "is your master—?"

She did not finish the sentence, merely looked at the butler expectantly.

Snell, who was clearly used to his mistress's methods of seeking information, replied promptly to the unspecified question.

"Sir Gervase came downstairs at five minutes to eight, m'lady, and went straight to the study."

"Oh, I see—" Her mouth remained open, her eyes seemed far away. "You don't think—I mean—he heard the gong?"

"I think he must have done so m'lady, the gong being immediately outside the study door. I did not, of course, know that Sir Gervase was still in the study, otherwise I should have announced to him that dinner was ready. Shall I do so now, m'lady?"

Lady Chevenix-Gore seized on the suggestion with manifest relief.

"Oh, thank you, Snell. Yes, please do. Yes, certainly."

She said, as the butler left the room:

"Snell is such a treasure. I rely on him absolutely. I really don't know what I should *do* without Snell."

Somebody murmured a sympathetic assent, but nobody spoke. Hercule Poirot, watching that room full of people with suddenly sharpened attention, had an idea that one and all were in a state of tension. His eyes ran quickly over them, tabulating them roughly. Two elderly men, the soldierly one who had spoken just now, and a thin, spare, gray-haired man with closely pinched legal lips. Two youngish men —very different in type from each other. One with a mustache and an air of modest arrogance, he guessed to be possibly Sir Gervase's nephew, the one in the Blues. The other, with sleek brushed-back hair and a rather obvious style of good looks, he put down as of a definitely inferior social class. There was a small middle-aged woman with pince-nez and intelligent eyes, and there was a girl with flaming red hair.

Snell appeared at the door. His manner was perfect, but once again the veneer of the impersonal butler showed signs of the perturbed human being beneath the surface.

"Excuse me, m'lady, the study door is locked."

"Locked?"

It was a man's voice—young, alert, with a ring of excitement in it.

It was the good-looking young man with the slicked-back hair who had spoken. He went on, hurrying forward:

"Shall I go and see—?"

But very quietly, Hercule Poirot took command. He did it so naturally that no one thought it odd that this stranger, who had just arrived, should suddenly assume charge of the situation.

"Come," he said. "Let us go to the study."

He continued, speaking to Snell:

"Lead the way, if you please."

Snell obeyed. Poirot followed close behind him and, like a flock of sheep, everyone else followed.

Snell led the way through the big hall, past the great branching curve of the staircase, past an enormous grandfather clock and a recess in which stood a gong, along a narrow passage which ended in a door.

Here Poirot passed Snell and gently tried the handle. It turned, but the door did not open. Poirot rapped gently with his knuckles on the panel of the door. He rapped louder and louder. Then, suddenly desisting, he dropped to his knees and applied his eye to the keyhole.

Slowly he rose to his feet and looked round. His face was stern.

"Gentlemen," he said, "this door must be broken open immediately!"

Under his direction the two young men, who were both tall and powerfully-built, attacked the door. It was no easy matter. The doors of Hamborough Close were solidly built.

At last, however, the lock gave, and the door swung inwards with a noise of splintering, rending wood.

And then, for a moment, everyone stood still, huddled in the doorway looking at the scene inside. The lights were on. Along the left-hand wall was a big writing-table, a massive affair of solid mahogany. Sitting, not at the table, but sideways to it, so that his back was directly towards them, was a big man slouched down in a chair. His head and the upper part of his body hung down over the right side of the chair, and his right hand and arm hung limply down. Just below it on the carpet was a small, gleaming pistol. . . .

There was no need of speculation. The picture was clear. Sir Gervase Chevenix-Gore had shot himself.

3

For a moment or two, the group in the doorway stood motionless, staring at the scene. Then Poirot strode forward.

At the same moment Hugo Trent said crisply:

"My God, the Old Man's shot himself!"

And there was a long, shuddering moan from Lady Chevenix-Gore.

"Oh, Gervase—Gervase!"

Over his shoulder Poirot said sharply:

"Take Lady Chevenix-Gore away. She can do nothing here."

The elderly soldierly man obeyed. He said:

"Come, Vanda. Come, my dear. You can do nothing. It's all over. Ruth, come and look after your mother."

But Ruth Chevenix-Gore had pressed into the room and stood close by Poirot's side as he bent over the dreadful sprawled figure in the chair—the figure of a man of Herculean build with a Viking beard.

She said in a low tense voice, curiously restrained and muffled:

"You're quite sure he's—dead?"

Poirot looked up.

The girl's face was alive with some emotion—an emotion sternly checked and repressed—that he did not quite understand. It was not grief—it seemed more like a kind of half-fearful excitement.

The little woman with the pince-nez murmured:

"Your mother, my dear— Don't you think—?"

In a high, hysterical voice the girl with the red hair cried out:

"Then it *wasn't* a car or a champagne-cork! It was a *shot* we heard. . . ."

Poirot turned and faced them all.

He said:

"Somebody must communicate with the police—"

Ruth Chevenix-Gore cried out violently:

"No!"

The elderly man with the legal face said:

"Unavoidable, I am afraid. Will you see to that, Burrows? Hugo—"

Poirot said:

"You are Mr. Hugo Trent?" to the tall young man with the mustache. "It would be well, I think, if everyone except you and I were to leave this room."

Again his authority was not questioned. The lawyer shepherded the others away. Poirot and Hugo Trent were left alone.

The latter said, staring:

"Look here—who *are* you? I mean, I haven't the foggiest idea. What are you doing here?"

Poirot took a card-case from his pocket and selected a card.

Hugo Trent said, staring at it:

"Private detective—eh? Of course, I've heard of you. . . . But I still don't see what you are doing *here?*"

"You did not know that your uncle—he was your uncle, was he not—?"

Hugo's eyes dropped for a fleeting moment to the dead man.

"The Old Man? Yes, he was my uncle all right."

"You did not know that he had sent for me?"

Hugo shook his head. He said slowly:

"I'd no idea of it."

There was an emotion in his voice that was rather hard to classify. His face looked wooden and stupid—the kind of expression, Poirot thought, that made a useful mask in times of stress.

Poirot said quietly:

"We are in Westshire, are we not? I know your Chief Constable, Major Riddle, very well."

Hugo said:

"Riddle lives about half-a-mile away. He'll probably come over himself."

"That," said Poirot, "will be very convenient."

He began prowling gently round the room. He twitched aside the window curtains and examined the French windows, trying them gently. They were closed.

On the wall behind the desk there hung a round mirror. The mirror was shivered. Poirot bent and picked up a small object.

"What's that?" asked Hugo Trent.

"The bullet."

"It passed straight through his head and struck the mirror?"

"It seems so."

Poirot replaced the bullet meticulously where he had found it. He came up to the desk. Some papers were arranged neatly stacked in heaps. On the blotting-pad itself there was a loose sheet of paper with the word *SORRY* printed across it in large, shaky handwriting.

Hugo said: "He must have written that just before he—did it."

Poirot nodded thoughtfully.

He looked again at the smashed mirror, then at the dead man. His brow creased itself a little as though in perplexity. He went over to the door, where it hung crookedly with its splintered lock. There was no key in the door, as he knew—otherwise he would not have been able to see through the keyhole. There was no sign of it on the floor. Poirot leaned over the dead man and ran his fingers over him.

"Yes," he said. "The key is in his pocket."

Hugo drew out a cigarette case and lighted a cigarette. He spoke rather hoarsely.

"It seems all quite clear," he said. "My uncle shut himself up in here, scrawled that message on a piece of paper, and then shot himself."

Poirot nodded meditatively. Hugo went on:

"But I don't understand why he sent for you? What was it all about?"

"That is rather more difficult to explain. While we are waiting, Mr. Trent, for the authorities to arrive, perhaps you will tell me exactly who all the people are whom I saw tonight when I arrived?"

"Who they are?" Hugo spoke almost absently. "Oh, yes, of course. Sorry. Shall we sit down?" He indicated a settee in the farthest corner of the room from the body. He went on, speaking jerkily: "Well, there's Vanda—my aunt, you know. And Ruth, my cousin. But you know them. Then the other girl is Susan Cardwell. She's just staying here. And there's Colonel Bury. He's an old friend of the family. And Ogilvie Forbes. He's an old friend, too, besides being the family lawyer and all that. Both the old boys had a passion for Vanda when she was young, and they still hang round in a faithful, devoted sort of way. Ridiculous, but rather touching. Then there's Godfrey Burrows, the Old Man's—I mean my uncle's—secretary, and Miss Lingard, who's here to help him write a history of the Chevenix-Gores. She mugs up historical stuff for writers. That's the lot, I think."

Poirot nodded. Then he said:

"And I understand you actually heard the shot that killed your uncle?"

"Yes, we did. Thought it was a champagne-cork—at least, I did. Susan and Miss Lingard thought it was a car back-firing outside—the road runs quite near, you know."

"When was this?"

"Oh! about ten past eight. Snell had just sounded the first gong."

"And where were you when you heard it?"

"In the hall. We—we were laughing about it—arguing, you know, as to where the sound came from. I said it came from the dining-room, and Susan said it came from the direction of the drawing-room, and Miss Lingard said it sounded like upstairs, and Snell said it came from the road outside, only it came through the upstairs windows. And Susan said, any more theories? And I laughed and said there was always murder! Seems pretty rotten to think of now."

His face twitched nervously.

"It did not occur to anyone that Sir Gervase might have shot himself?"

"No, of course not."

"You have, in fact, no idea why he should have shot himself?"

Hugo said slowly:

"Oh, well, I shouldn't say that—"

"You *have* an idea?"

"Yes—well—it's difficult to explain. Naturally I didn't expect him to commit suicide, but all the same, I'm not frightfully surprised. The truth of it is that my uncle was as mad as a hatter, M. Poirot. Everyone knew that."

"That strikes you as a sufficient explanation?"

"Well, people do shoot themselves when they're a bit balmy."

"An explanation of an admirable simplicity."

Hugo stared.

Poirot got up again and wandered aimlessly round the room. It was comfortably furnished, mainly in a rather heavy Victorian style. There were massive bookcases, huge armchairs, and some upright chairs of genuine Chippendale. There were not many ornaments, but some bronzes on the mantelpiece attracted Poirot's attention and apparently stirred his admiration. He picked them up one by one, carefully examining them before replacing them with care. From the one on the extreme left he detached something with a fingernail.

"What's that?" asked Hugo, without much interest.

"Nothing very much. A tiny sliver of looking-glass."

Hugo said:

"Funny the way that mirror was smashed by the shot. A broken mirror means bad luck. Poor old Gervase. . . . I suppose his luck had held a bit too long."

"Your uncle was a lucky man?"

Hugo gave a short laugh.

"Why, his luck was proverbial! Everything he touched turned to gold! If he backed an outsider, it romped home! If he invested in a doubtful mine, they struck a vein of ore at once! He's had the most amazing escapes from the tightest of tight places. His life's been saved by a kind of miracle more than once. He was rather a fine old boy, in his way, you know. He'd certainly 'been places and seen things'— more than most of his generation."

Poirot murmured in a conversational tone:

"You were attached to your uncle, Mr. Trent?"

Hugo Trent seemed a little startled by the question.

"Oh—er—yes, of course," he said rather vaguely. "You know, he was a bit difficult at times. Frightful strain to live with, and all that. Fortunately I didn't have to see much of him."

"*He* was fond of *you?*"

"Not so that you'd notice it! As a matter of fact, he rather resented my existence, so to speak."

"How was that, Mr. Trent?"

"Well, you see, he had no son of his own—and he was pretty sore about it. He was mad about family and all that sort of thing. I believe it cut him to the quick to know that when he died the Chevenix-Gores would cease to exist. They've been going ever since the Norman Conquest, you know. The Old Man was the last of them. I suppose it *was* rather rotten from his point of view."

"You yourself do not share that sentiment?"

Hugo shrugged his shoulders.

"All that sort of thing seems to me rather out-of-date."

"What will happen to the estate?"

"Don't really know. I might get it. Or he may have left it to Ruth. Probably Vanda has it for her lifetime."

"Your uncle did not definitely declare his intentions?"

"Well, he had his pet idea."

"And what was that?"

"His idea was that Ruth and I should make a match of it."

"That would doubtless have been very suitable."

"Eminently suitable. But Ruth—well, Ruth has very decided views of her own about life. Mind you, she's an extremely attractive young woman, and she knows it. She's in no hurry to marry and settle down."

Poirot leaned forward.

"But you yourself would have been willing, M. Trent?"

Hugo said in a bored tone of voice:

"I really can't see it makes a ha'p'orth of difference who you marry nowadays. Divorce is so easy. If you're not hitting it off, nothing is easier than to cut the tangle and start again."

The door opened and Ogilvie Forbes entered with a tall, spruce-looking man.

The latter nodded to Trent.

"Hullo, Hugo. I'm extremely sorry about this. Very rough on all of you."

Hercule Poirot came forward.

"How do you do, Major Riddle? You remember me?"

"Yes, indeed." The Chief Constable shook hands. "So *you're* down here?"

There was a meditative note in his voice. He glanced curiously at Hercule Poirot.

4

"Well?" said Major Riddle.

It was twenty minutes later. The Chief Constable's interrogative "Well" was addressed to the police-surgeon, a lank elderly man with grizzled hair.

The latter shrugged his shoulders.

"He's been dead over half-an-hour—but not more than an hour. You don't want technicalities, I know, so I'll spare you them. The man was shot through the head, the pistol being held a few inches from the right temple. Bullet passed right through the brain and out again."

"Perfectly compatible with suicide?"

"Oh, perfectly. The body then slumped down in the chair and the pistol dropped from his hand."

"You've got the bullet?"

"Yes." The doctor held it up.

"Good," said Major Riddle. "We'll keep it for comparison with the pistol. Glad it's a clear case and no difficulties."

Hercule Poirot asked gently:

"You are sure there *are* no difficulties, doctor?"

The doctor replied slowly:

"Well, I suppose you might call one thing a little odd. When he shot himself he must have been leaning slightly over to the right. Otherwise the bullet would have hit the wall *below* the mirror, instead of plumb in the middle."

"An uncomfortable position in which to commit suicide," said Poirot.

The doctor shrugged his shoulders.

"Oh, well—comfort—if you're going to end it all . . ." He left the sentence unfinished.

Major Riddle said:

"The body can be moved now?"

"Oh, yes. I've done with it until the post mortem."

"What about you, Inspector?" Major Riddle spoke to a tall impassive-faced man in plain clothes.

"O.K., sir, we've got all we want. Only the deceased's fingerprints on the pistol."

"Then you can get on with it."

The mortal remains of Gervase Chevenix-Gore were removed. The Chief Constable and Poirot were left together.

"Well," said Riddle. "Everything seems quite clear and aboveboard. Door locked, window fastened, key of door in dead man's pocket. Everything according to Cocker—but for one circumstance."

"And what is that, my friend?" inquired Poirot.

"*You!*" said Riddle bluntly. "What are *you* doing down here?"

By way of reply, Poirot handed to him the letter he had received from the dead man a week ago, and the telegram which had finally brought him there.

"Humph!" said the Chief Constable. "Interesting. We'll have to get to the bottom of this. I should say it had a direct bearing upon his suicide."

"I agree."

"We must check up on who is in the house."

"I can tell you their names. I have just been making inquiries of Mr. Trent."

He repeated the list of names.

"Perhaps you, Major Riddle, know something about these people?"

"I know something of them, naturally. Lady Chevenix-Gore is quite as mad in her own way as old Sir Gervase. They were devoted to each other—and both quite mad. She's the vaguest creature that ever lived, with an occasional uncanny shrewdness that strikes the nail on the head in the most surprising fashion. People laugh at her a good deal. I think she knows it, but she doesn't care. She's absolutely no sense of humor."

"Miss Chevenix-Gore is only their adopted daughter, I understand?"

"Yes."

"A very handsome young lady."

"She's a devilishly attractive girl. Has played havoc with most of the young fellows round here. Leads them all on and then turns round and laughs at them. Good seat on a horse, and wonderful hands."

"That, for the moment, does not concern us."

"Er—no, perhaps not. . . . Well, about the other people; I know old Bury, of course. He's here most of the time. Almost a tame cat about the house. Kind of A.D.C. to Lady Chevenix-Gore. He's a very old friend. They've known him all their lives. I think he and Sir Gervase were both interested in some company of which Bury was a director."

"Ogilvie Forbes; do you know anything of him?"

"I rather believe I've met him once."

"Miss Lingard?"

"Never heard of her."

"Miss Susan Cardwell?"

"Rather a good-looking girl with red hair? I've seen her about with Ruth Chevenix-Gore the last few days."

"Mr. Burrows?"

"Yes, I know him. Chevenix-Gore's secretary. Between you and me I don't take to him much. He's good-looking and knows it. Not quite out of the top drawer."

"Had he been with Sir Gervase long?"

"About two years, I fancy."

"And there is no one else—?"

Poirot broke off.

A tall, fair-haired man in a lounge suit came hurrying in. He was out of breath and looked disturbed.

"Good evening, Major Riddle. I heard a rumor that Sir Gervase had shot himself and I hurried up here. Snell tells me it's true. It's incredible! I can't believe it!"

"It's true enough, Lake. Let me introduce you. This is Captain Lake, Sir Gervase's agent for the estate. M. Hercule Poirot, of whom you may have heard."

Lake's face lit up with what seemed a kind of delighted incredulity.

"M. Hercule Poirot? I'm most awfully pleased to meet you. At least—" He broke off, the quick charming smile vanished—he looked disturbed and upset. "There isn't anything—fishy—about this suicide, is there, sir?"

"Why should there be anything 'fishy,' as you call it?" asked the Chief Constable sharply.

"I mean, because M. Poirot is here. Oh! and because the whole business seems so incredible!"

"No, no," said Poirot quickly. "I am not here on account of the death of Sir Gervase. I was already in the house—as a guest."

"Oh, I see. Funny, he never told me you were coming when I was going over accounts with him this afternoon."

Poirot said quietly:

"You have twice used the word 'incredible,' Captain Lake. Are you then so surprised to hear of Sir Gervase committing suicide?"

"Indeed I am. Of course, he was mad as a hatter, everyone would agree about that. But all the same, I simply can't imagine his thinking the world would be able to get on without him."

"Yes," said Poirot. "It is a point, that." And he looked with appreciation at the frank, intelligent countenance of the young man.

Major Riddle cleared his throat.

"Since you are here, Captain Lake, perhaps you will sit down and answer a few questions."

"Certainly, sir."

Lake took a chair opposite the other two.

"When did you last see Sir Gervase?"

"This afternoon, just before three o'clock. There were some accounts to be checked and the question of a new tenant for one of the farms."

"How long were you with him?"

"Perhaps half-an-hour."

"Think carefully, and tell me whether you noticed anything unusual in his manner?"

The young man considered.

"No, I hardly think so. He was, perhaps, a trifle excited—but that wasn't unusual with him."

"He was not depressed in any way?"

"Oh, no, he seemed in good spirits. He was enjoying himself very much just now, writing up a history of the family."

"How long had he been doing this?"

"He began it about six months ago."

"Is that when Miss Lingard came here?"

"No. She arrived about two months ago when he had discovered that he could not manage the necessary research work by himself."

"And you consider he was enjoying himself?"

"Oh, simply enormously! He really didn't think that anything else mattered in the world except his family."

There was a momentary bitterness in the young man's tone.

"Then, as far as you know, Sir Gervase had no worries of any kind?"

There was a slight—a very slight—pause, before Captain Lake answered:

"No."

Poirot suddenly interposed a question:

"Sir Gervase was not, as far as you know, worried about his daughter in any way?"

"His daughter?"

"That is what I said."

"Not as far as I know," said the young man, stiffly.

Poirot said nothing further. Major Riddle said:

"Well, thank you, Lake. Perhaps you'd stay around in case I might want to ask you anything?"

"Certainly, sir." He rose. "Anything I can do?"

"Yes, you might send the butler here. And perhaps you'd find out for me how Lady Chevenix-Gore is, and if I could have a few words with her presently, or if she's too upset."

The young man nodded and left the room with a quick, decisive step.

"An attractive personality," said Hercule Poirot.

"Yes, nice fellow, and good at his job. Everyone likes him."

5

"Sit down, Snell," said Major Riddle in a friendly tone. "I've a good many questions to ask you, and I expect this has been a shock to you."

"Oh, it has indeed, sir. Thank you, sir." Snell sat down with such a discreet air that it was practically the same as though he had remained on his feet.

"Been here a good long time, haven't you?"

"Sixteen years, sir, ever since Sir Gervase—er—settled down, so to speak."

"Ah, yes, of course, your master was a great traveler in his day."

"Yes, sir. He went on an expedition to the Pole and many other interesting places."

"Now, Snell, can you tell me when you last saw your master this evening?"

"I was in the dining-room, sir, seeing that the table arrangements were all complete. The door into the hall was open and I saw Sir Gervase come down the stairs, cross the hall, and go along the passage to the study."

"That was at what time?"

"Just before eight o'clock. It might have been as much as five minutes before eight."

"And that was the last you saw of him?"

"Yes, sir."

"Did you hear a shot?"

"Oh, yes, indeed, sir, but of course I had no idea at the time—how should I have had?"

"What did you think it was?"

"I thought it was a car, sir. The road runs quite near the Park wall. Or it might have been a shot in the woods—a poacher perhaps. I never dreamed—"

Major Riddle cut him short.

"What time was that?"

"It was exactly eight minutes past eight, sir."

The Chief Constable said sharply:

"How is it you can fix the time to a minute?"

"That's easy, sir. I had just sounded the first gong."

"The first gong?"

"Yes, sir. By Sir Gervase's orders a gong was always to be sounded seven minutes before the actual dinner gong. Very particular he was, sir, that everyone should be assembled ready in the drawing-room when the second gong went. As soon as I had sounded the second gong, I went to the drawing-room and announced dinner and everyone went in."

"I begin to understand," said Hercule Poirot, "why you looked so surprised when you announced dinner this evening. It was usual for Sir Gervase to be in the drawing-room?"

"I'd never known him not be there before, sir. It was quite a shock. I little thought—"

Again Major Riddle interrupted adroitly:

"And were the others also usually there?"

Snell coughed.

"Anyone who was late for dinner, sir, was never asked to the house again."

"H'm, very drastic."

"Sir Gervase, sir, employed a chef who was formerly with the Emperor of Moravia. He used to say, sir, that dinner was as important as a religious ritual."

"And what about his own family?"

"Lady Chevenix-Gore was always very particular not to upset him, sir, and even Miss Ruth dared not be late for dinner."

"Interesting," murmured Hercule Poirot.

"I see," said Riddle. "So, dinner being at a quarter-past-eight, you sounded the first gong at eight minutes past, as usual?"

"That is so, sir—but it wasn't as usual. Dinner was usually at eight. Sir Gervase gave orders that dinner was to be a quarter-of-an-hour later this evening as he was expecting a gentleman by the late train."

Snell made a little bow towards Poirot as he spoke.

"When your master went to the study, did he look upset or worried in any way?"

"I could not say, sir. It was too far for me to judge of 'is expression. I just noticed him, that was all."

"Was he alone when he went to the study?"

"Yes, sir."

"Did anyone go to the study after that?"

"I could not say, sir. I went to the butler's pantry after that and was there until I sounded the first gong at eight minutes past eight."

"That was when you heard the shot?"

"Yes, sir."

Poirot gently interposed a question.

"There were others, I think, who also heard the shot?"

"Yes, sir. Mr. Hugo and Miss Cardwell. And Miss Lingard."

"These people were also in the hall?"

"Miss Lingard came out from the drawing-room and Miss Cardwell and Mr. Hugo were just coming down the stairs."

Poirot asked:

"Was there any conversation about the matter?"

"Well, sir, Mr. Hugo asked if there was champagne for dinner. I told him that sherry, hock and burgundy were being served."

"He thought it was a champagne cork?"

"Yes, sir."

"But nobody took it seriously?"

"Oh, no, sir. They all went into the drawing-room talking and laughing."

"Where were the other members of the household?"

"I could not say, sir."

Major Riddle said:

"Do you know anything about this pistol?" He held it out as he spoke.

"Oh, yes, sir. That belonged to Sir Gervase. He always kept it in the drawer of his desk in here."

"Was it usually loaded?"

"I couldn't say, sir."

Major Riddle laid down the pistol and cleared his throat.

"Now, Snell, I'm going to ask you a rather important question. I hope you will answer it as truthfully as you can. *Do you know of any reason which might lead your master to commit suicide?*"

"No, sir. I know of nothing."

"Sir Gervase had not been odd in his manner of late? Not depressed? Or worried?"

Snell coughed apologetically.

"You'll excuse my saying it, sir, but Sir Gervase was always what might have seemed to strangers a little odd in his manner. He was a highly original gentleman, sir."

"Yes, yes, I am quite aware of that."

"Outsiders, sir, did not always Understand Sir Gervase."

Snell gave the phrase a definite value of capital letter.

"I know. I know. But there was nothing that *you* would have called unusual?"

The butler hesitated.

"I think, sir, that Sir Gervase was worried about something," he said at last.

"Worried and depressed?"

"I shouldn't say depressed, sir. But worried, yes."

"Have you any idea of the cause of that worry?"

"No, sir."

"Was it connected with any particular person, for instance?"

"I could not say at all, sir. In any case, it is only an impression of mine."

Poirot spoke again.

"You were surprised at his suicide?"

"Very surprised, sir. It had been a terrible shock to me. I never dreamed of such a thing."

Poirot nodded thoughtfully.

Riddle glanced at him, then said:

"Well, Snell, I think that is all we want to ask you. You are quite sure that there is nothing else you can tell us—no unusual incident, for instance, that has happened in the last few days?"

The butler, rising to his feet, shook his head.

"There is nothing, sir, nothing whatever."

"Then you can go."

"Thank you, sir."

Moving towards the doorway, Snell drew back and stood aside. Lady Chevenix-Gore floated into the room.

She was wearing an oriental-looking garment of purple and orange silk wound tightly round her body. Her face was serene and her manner collected and calm.

"Lady Chevenix-Gore." Major Riddle sprang to his feet.

She said:

"They told me you would like to talk to me, so I came."

"Shall we go into another room? This must be painful for you in the extreme."

Lady Chevenix-Gore shook her head and sat down on one of the Chippendale chairs. She murmured:

"Oh, no, what does it matter?"

"It is very good of you, Lady Chevenix-Gore, to put your feelings aside. I know what a frightful shock this must have been and—"

She interrupted him.

"It was rather a shock at first," she admitted. Her tone was easy and conversational. "But there is no such thing as Death, really, you know, only Change." She added: "As a matter of fact, Gervase is standing just behind your left shoulder now. I can see him distinctly."

Major Riddle's left shoulder twitched slightly. He looked at Lady Chevenix-Gore rather doubtfully.

She smiled at him, a vague, happy smile.

"You don't believe, of course! So few people will. To me, the spirit world is quite as real as this one. But please ask me anything you like and don't worry about distressing me. I'm not in the least distressed. Everything, you see, is Fate. One cannot escape one's Karma. It all fits in—the mirror—everything."

"The mirror, madame?" asked Poirot.

She nodded her head towards it vaguely.

"Yes. It's splintered, you see. A symbol! You know Tennyson's poem? I used to read it as a girl—though, of course, I didn't realize then the esoteric side of it. *'The mirror cracked from side to side; "The curse is come upon me!" cried the Lady of Shalott.'* That's what happened to Gervase. The Curse came upon him suddenly. I think, you know, most very old families have a curse. . . . The mirror cracked. He knew that he was doomed! *The Curse had come!*"

"But, madame, it was not a curse that cracked the mirror—it was a bullet!"

Lady Chevenix-Gore said, still in the same sweet vague manner:

"It's all the same thing really. . . . It was Fate."

"But your husband shot himself."

Lady Chevenix-Gore smiled indulgently.

"He shouldn't have done that, of course. But Gervase was always impatient. He could never wait. His hour had come—he went forward to meet it. It's all so simple, really."

Major Riddle, clearing his throat in exasperation, said sharply:

"Then you weren't surprised at your husband's taking his own life? Had you been expecting such a thing to happen?"

"Oh, no." Her eyes opened wide. "One can't always foresee the future. Gervase, of course, was a very strange man, a very unusual man. He was quite unlike anyone else. He was one of the Great Ones born again. I've known that for some time. I think he knew it himself. He found it very hard to conform to the silly little standards of the everyday world." She added, looking over Major Riddle's shoulder: "He's smiling now. He's thinking how foolish we all are. So we are really. Just like children. Pretending that life is real and that it matters. . . . Life is only one of the Great Illusions."

Feeling that he was fighting a losing battle, Major Riddle asked desperately:

"You can't help us at all as to *why* your husband should have taken his life?"

She shrugged her thin shoulders.

"Forces move us—they move us. . . . You cannot understand. You move only on the material plane."

Poirot coughed.

"Talking of the material plane, have you any idea, madame, as to how your husband has left his money?"

"Money?" She stared at him. "I never think of money."

Her tone was disdainful.

Poirot switched to another point.

"At what time did you come downstairs to dinner tonight?"

"Time? What is Time? Infinite, that is the answer. Time is infinite."

Poirot murmured:

"But your husband, madame, was rather particular about time—especially, so I have been told, as regards the dinner hour."

"Dear Gervase," she smiled indulgently. "He was very foolish about that. But it made him happy. So we were never late."

"Were you in the drawing-room, madame, when the first gong went?"

"No, I was in my room then."

"Do you remember who was in the drawing-room when you did come down?"

"Nearly everybody, I think," said Lady Chevenix-Gore vaguely. "Does it matter?"

"Possibly not," admitted Poirot. "Then there is something else. Did your husband ever tell you that he suspected he was being robbed?"

Lady Chevenix-Gore did not seem much interested in the question.

"Robbed? No, I don't think so."

"Robbed, swindled—victimized in some way—?"

"No—no—I don't think so. . . . Gervase would have been very angry if anybody had dared to do anything like that."

"At any rate he said nothing about it to you?"

"No—no." Lady Chevenix-Gore shook her head, still without much real interest. "I should have remembered. . . ."

"When did you last see your husband alive?"

"He looked in, as usual, on his way downstairs before dinner. My maid was there. He just said he was going down."

"What has he talked about most in the last few weeks?"

"Oh, the family history. He was getting on so well with it. He found that funny old thing, Miss Lingard, quite invaluable. She looked up things for him in the British Museum—all that sort of thing. She worked with Lord Mulcaster on his book, you know. And she was tactful—I mean, she didn't look up the wrong things. After all, there are ancestors one doesn't want raked up. Gervase was very sensitive. She helped me, too. She got a lot of information for me about Hatshepsut. I am a reincarnation of Hatshepsut, you know."

Lady Chevenix-Gore made this announcement in a calm voice.

"Before that," she went on, "I was a Priestess in Atlantis."

Major Riddle shifted a little in his chair.

"Er—er—very interesting," he said. "Well, really, Lady Chevenix-Gore, I think that will be all. Very kind of you—"

Lady Chevenix-Gore rose, clasping her oriental robes about her.

"Good night," she said. And then, her eyes shifting to a point behind Major Riddle: "Good night, Gervase dear. I wish you could come, but I know you have to stay here." She added in an explanatory fashion: "You have to stay in the place where you've passed over for at least twenty-four hours. It's some time before you can move about freely and communicate."

She trailed out of the room.

Major Riddle wiped his brow.

"Phew," he murmured. "She's a great deal madder than I ever thought. Does she really believe all that nonsense?"

Poirot shook his head thoughtfully.

"It is possible that she finds it helpful," he said. "She needs, at this moment, to create for herself a world of illusion so that she can escape the stark reality of her husband's death."

"She seems almost certifiable to me," said Major Riddle. "A long farago of nonsense without one word of sense in it."

"No, no, my friend. The interesting thing is, as Mr. Hugo Trent casually remarked to me, that amidst all the vaporing there is an occasional shrewd thrust. She showed it by her remark about Miss

Lingard's tact in not stressing undesirable ancestors. Believe me, Lady Chevenix-Gore is no fool."

He got up and paced up and down the room.

"There are things in this affair that I do not like. No, I do not like them at all."

Riddle looked at him curiously.

"You mean the motive for his suicide?"

"Suicide—suicide! It is all wrong, I tell you. *It is wrong psychologically*. How did Chevenix-Gore think of himself? As a Colossus, as an immensely important person, as the center of the Universe! Does such a man destroy himself? Surely not. He is far more likely to destroy someone else—some miserable, crawling ant of a human being who has dared to cause him annoyance. . . . Such an act he might regard as necessary—as sanctified! But self-destruction? The destruction of such a Self?"

"It's all very well, Poirot. But the evidence is clear enough. Door locked, key in his own pocket. Window closed and fastened. I know these things happen in books—but I've never come across them in real life. Anything else?"

"But, yes, there is something else." Poirot sat down in the chair. "Here I am. I am Chevenix-Gore. I am sitting at my desk. I am determined to kill myself because—because, let us say, I have made a discovery concerning some terrific dishonor to the family name. It is not very convincing, that, but it must suffice.

"*Eh bien*, what do I do? I scrawl on a piece of paper the word SORRY. Yes, that is quite possible. Then I open the drawer of the desk, take out the pistol which I keep there, load it, if it is not loaded, and then—do I proceed to shoot myself? No, I first turn my chair round—so, and I lean over a little to the right—so—and then—*then* I put the pistol to my temple and fire!"

Poirot sprang up from his chair, and wheeling round demanded:

"I ask you, does that make sense? *Why* turn the chair round? If, for instance, there had been a picture on the wall there, then, yes, there might be an explanation. Some portrait which a dying man might wish to be the last thing on earth his eyes would see, but a window-curtain—*ah non*, that does not make sense."

"He might have wished to look out of the window. Last view out over the estate."

"My dear friend, you do not suggest that with any conviction. In fact, you know it is nonsense. At eight minutes past eight it was dark, and in any case the curtains are drawn. No, there must be some other explanation. . . ."

"There's only one as far as I can see. Gervase Chevenix-Gore was mad."

Poirot shook his head in a dissatisfied manner.

Major Riddle rose.

"Come," he said. "Let us go and interview the rest of the party. We may get at something that way."

6

After the difficulties of getting a direct statement from Lady Chevenix-Gore, Major Riddle found considerable relief in dealing with a shrewd lawyer like Ogilvie Forbes.

Mr. Forbes was extremely guarded and cautious in his statements, but his replies were all directly to the point.

He admitted that Sir Gervase's suicide had been a great shock to him. He should never have considered Sir Gervase the kind of man who would take his own life. He knew nothing of any cause for such an act.

"Sir Gervase was not only my client, but was a very old friend. I have known him since boyhood. I should say that he had always enjoyed life."

"In the circumstances, Mr. Forbes, I must ask you to speak quite candidly. You did not know of any secret anxiety or sorrow in Sir Gervase's life?"

"No. He had minor worries, like most men, but there was nothing of a serious nature."

"No illness? No trouble between him and his wife?"

"No. Sir Gervase and Lady Chevenix-Gore were devoted to each other."

Major Riddle said cautiously:

"Lady Chevenix-Gore appears to hold somewhat curious views."

Mr. Forbes smiled—an indulgent, manly smile.

"Ladies," he said, "must be allowed their fancies."

The Chief Constable went on:

"You managed all Sir Gervase's legal affairs?"

"Yes, my firm, Forbes, Ogilvie and Spence, have acted for the Chevenix-Gore family for well over a hundred years."

"Were there any—scandals in the Chevenix-Gore family?"

Mr. Forbes' eyebrows rose.

"Really, I fail to understand you?"

"M. Poirot, will you show Mr. Forbes the letter you showed me?"

In silence Poirot rose and handed the letter to Mr. Forbes with a little bow.

Mr. Forbes read it and his eyebrows rose still more.

"A most remarkable letter," he said. "I appreciate your question now. No, so far as my knowledge went, there was nothing to justify the writing of such a letter."

"Sir Gervase said nothing of this matter to you?"

"Nothing at all. I must say I find it very curious that he should not have done so."

"He was accustomed to confide in you?"

"I think he relied on my judgment."

"And you have no idea as to what this letter refers?"

"I should not like to make any rash speculations."

Major Riddle appreciated the subtlety of this reply.

"Now, Mr. Forbes, perhaps you can tell us how Sir Gervase has left his property?"

"Certainly. I see no objection to such a course. To his wife Sir Gervase left an annual income of six thousand pounds chargeable on the estate, and the choice of the Dower House or the town house in Lowndes Square, whichever she should prefer. There were, of course, several legacies and bequests, but nothing of an outstanding nature. The residue of his property was left to his adopted daughter, Ruth, on condition that, if she married, her husband should take the name of Chevenix-Gore."

"Was nothing left to his nephew, Mr. Hugo Trent?"

"Yes. A legacy of five thousand pounds."

"And I take it that Sir Gervase was a rich man?"

"He was extremely wealthy. He had a vast private fortune apart from the estate. Of course, he was not quite so well off as in the past. Practically all invested incomes have felt the strain. Also, Sir Gervase had dropped a good deal of money over a certain company— The Paragon Synthetic Rubberine Company in which Colonel Bury persuaded him to invest a good deal of money."

"Not very wise advice."

Mr. Forbes sighed.

"Retired soldiers are the worst sufferers when they engage in financial operations. I have found that their credulity far exceeds that of widows—and that is saying a good deal."

"But these unfortunate investments did not seriously affect Sir Gervase's income?"

"Oh, no, not seriously. He was still an extremely rich man."

"When was this will made?"

"Two years ago."

Poirot murmured:

"This arrangement, was it not possibly a little unfair to Mr. Hugo Trent, Sir Gervase's nephew? He is, after all, Sir Gervase's nearest blood relation."

Mr. Forbes shrugged his shoulders.

"One has to take a certain amount of family history into account."

"Such as—?"

Mr. Forbes seemed slightly unwilling to proceed.

Major Riddle said:

"You mustn't think we're unduly concerned with raking up old scandals or anything of that sort. But this letter of Sir Gervase's to M. Poirot has got to be explained."

"There is certainly nothing scandalous in the explanation of Sir Gervase's attitude to his nephew," said Mr. Forbes quickly. "It was simply that Sir Gervase always took his position as head of the family very seriously. He had a younger brother and sister. The brother, Anthony Chevenix-Gore, was killed in the War. The sister, Pamela, married, and Sir Gervase disapproved of the marriage. That is to say, he considered that she ought to have obtained his consent and approval before marrying. He thought that Captain Trent's family was not of sufficient prominence to be allied with a Chevenix-Gore. His sister was merely amused by his attitude. As a result, Sir Gervase has always been inclined to dislike his nephew. I think that dislike may have influenced him in deciding to adopt a child."

"There was no hope of his having children of his own?"

"No. There was a still-born child about a year after his marriage. The doctors told Lady Chevenix-Gore that she would never be able to have another child. About two years later he adopted Ruth."

Poirot asked:

"And who *was* Mademoiselle Ruth? How did they come to settle upon her?"

"She was, I believe, the child of a distant connection."

"That I had guessed," said Poirot. He looked up at the wall which was hung with family portraits. "One can see that she was of the same blood—the nose, the line of the chin. It repeats itself on these walls many times."

"She inherits the temper, too," said Mr. Forbes, drily.

"So I should imagine. How did she and her adopted father get on?"

"Much as you might imagine. There was a fierce clash of wills more than once. But, in spite of these quarrels, I believe there was also an underlying harmony."

"Nevertheless, she caused him a good deal of anxiety?"

"Incessant anxiety. But I can assure you not to the point of causing him to take his own life."

"Ah, that, no," agreed Poirot. "One does not blow one's brains out because one has a headstrong daughter! And so Mademoiselle inherits! Sir Gervase, he never thought of altering his will?"

"Ahem!" Mr. Forbes coughed to hide a little discomposure. "As a matter of fact, I took instructions from Sir Gervase on my arrival here (two days ago, that is to say) as to the drafting of a new will."

"What's this?" Major Riddle hitched his chair a little closer. "You didn't tell us this."

Mr. Forbes said quickly:

"You merely asked me what the terms of Sir Gervase's will were. I gave you the information for which you asked. The new will was not even properly drawn up—much less signed."

"What were its provisions? They may be some guide to Sir Gervase's state of mind."

"In the main, they were the same as before, but Miss Chevenix-Gore was only to inherit on condition that she married Mr. Hugo Trent."

"Aha," said Poirot. "But there is a very decided difference there."

"I did not approve of the clause," said Mr. Forbes. "And I felt bound to point out that it was quite possible it might be contested successfully. The Court does not look upon conditional bequests with approval. Sir Gervase, however, was quite decided."

"And if Miss Chevenix-Gore (or, incidently, Mr. Trent) refused to comply?"

"If Mr. Trent was not willing to marry Miss Chevenix-Gore, then the money went to her unconditionally. But if *he* was willing and *she* refused, then the money went to him instead."

"Odd business," said Major Riddle.

Poirot leaned forward. He tapped the lawyer on the knee.

"But what is behind it? What was in the mind of Sir Gervase when he made that stipulation? There must have been something very definite. . . . There must, I think, have been the image of another man . . . a man of whom he disapproved. I think, M. Forbes, that *you* must know who that man was?"

"Really, M. Poirot, I have no information."

"But you could make a guess?"

"I never guess," said Mr. Forbes, and his tone was scandalized.

Removing his pince-nez, he wiped them with a silk handkerchief and inquired:

"Is there anything else that you desire to know?"

"At the moment, no," said Poirot. "Not, that is, as far as I am concerned."

Mr. Forbes looked as though, in his opinion, that was not very far, and bent his attention on the Chief Constable.

"Thank you, Mr. Forbes. I think that's all. I should like, if I may, to speak to Miss Chevenix-Gore."

"Certainly. I think she is upstairs with Lady Chevenix-Gore."

"Oh, well, perhaps I'll have a word with—what's his name?—Burrows, first, and the family history woman."

"They're both in the library. I will tell them."

7

"Hard work, that," said Major Riddle as the lawyer left the room. "Extracting information from these old-fashioned legal wallahs takes a bit of doing. The whole business seems to me to center about the girl."

"It would seem so—yes."

"Ah, here comes Burrows."

Godfrey Burrows came in with a pleasant eagerness to be of use. His smile was discreetly tempered with gloom and showed only a fraction too much teeth. It seemed more mechanical than spontaneous.

"Now, Mr. Burrows, we want to ask you a few questions."

"Certainly, Major Riddle. Anything you like."

"Well, first and foremost, to put it quite simply, have you any ideas of your own about Sir Gervase's suicide?"

"Absolutely none. It was the greatest shock to me."

"You heard the shot?"

"No; I must have been in the library at the time, as far as I can make out. I came down rather early and went to the library to look up a reference I wanted. The library's right the other side of the house from the study, so I shouldn't hear anything."

"Was anyone with you in the library?" asked Poirot.

"No one at all."

"You've no idea where the other members of the household were at that time?"

"Mostly upstairs dressing, I should imagine."

"When did you come to the drawing-room?"

"Just before M. Poirot arrived. Everybody was there then—except Sir Gervase, of course."

"Did it strike you as strange that he wasn't there?"

"Yes, it did, as a matter of fact. As a rule he was always in the drawing-room before the first gong sounded."

"Have you noticed any difference in Sir Gervase's manner lately? Has he been worried? Or anxious? Depressed?"

Godfrey Burrows considered.

"No—I don't think so. A little—well, preoccupied, perhaps."

"But he did not appear to be worried about any one definite matter?"

"Oh, no."

"No—financial worries of any kind?"

"He was rather perturbed about the affairs of one particular company—the Paragon Synthetic Rubberine Company, to be exact."

"What did he actually say about it?"

Again Godfrey Burrows' mechanical smile flashed out, and again it seemed slightly unreal.

"Well—as a matter of fact—what he said was: 'Old Bury's either a fool or a knave. A fool, I suppose. I must go easy with him for Vanda's sake.'"

"And why did he say that—*for Vanda's sake?*" inquired Poirot.

"Well, you see, Lady Chevenix-Gore was very fond of Colonel Bury, and he worshiped her. Followed her about like a dog."

"Sir Gervase was not—jealous at all?"

"Jealous?" Burrows stared and then laughed. "Sir Gervase jealous? He wouldn't know how to set about it. Why, it would never have entered his head that anyone could ever prefer another man to him. Such a thing just couldn't be, you understand."

Poirot said gently:

"You did not, I think, like Sir Gervase Chevenix-Gore very much?"

Burrows flushed.

"Oh, yes, I did. At least—well, all that sort of thing strikes one as rather ridiculous nowadays."

"All what sort of thing?" asked Poirot.

"Well, the feudal motif, if you like. This worship of ancestry and personal arrogance. Sir Gervase was a very able man in many ways, and had led an interesting life, but he would have been more interesting if he hadn't been so entirely wrapped up in himself and his own egoism."

"Did his daughter agree with you there?"

Burrows flushed again—this time a deep purple.

He said:

"I should imagine Miss Chevenix-Gore is quite one of the moderns! Naturally, I shouldn't discuss her father with her."

"But the moderns *do* discuss their fathers a good deal!" said Poirot. "It is entirely in the modern spirit to criticize your parents!"

Burrows shrugged his shoulders.

Major Riddle asked:

"And there was nothing else—no other financial anxiety? Sir Gervase never spoke of having been *victimized?*"

"Victimized?" Burrows sounded very astonished. "Oh, no."

"And you yourself were on quite good terms with him?"

"Certainly I was. Why not?"

"I am asking you, Mr. Burrows."

The young man looked sulky.

"We were on the best of terms."

"Did you know that Sir Gervase had written to M. Poirot asking him to come down here?"

"No."

"Did Sir Gervase usually write his own letters?"

"No, he nearly always dictated them to me."

"But he did not do so in this case?"

"No."

"Why was that, do you think?"

"I can't imagine."

"You can suggest no reason why he should have written this particular letter himself?"

"No, I can't."

"Ah!" said Major Riddle, adding smoothly: "Rather curious. When did you last see Sir Gervase?"

"Just before I went to dress for dinner. I took him some letters to sign."

"What was his manner then?"

"Quite normal. In fact, I should say he was feeling rather pleased with himself about something."

Poirot stirred a little in his chair.

"Ah!" he said. "So that was your impression, was it? That he was pleased about something. And yet, not so very long afterwards, he shoots himself. It is odd, that!"

Godfrey Burrows shrugged his shoulders.

"I'm only telling you my impressions."

"Yes, yes, they are very valuable. After all, you are probably one of the last people who saw Sir Gervase alive."

"Snell was the last person to see him."

"To see him, yes, but not to speak to him."

Burrows did not reply.

Major Riddle said:

"What time was it when you went up to dress for dinner?"

"About five minutes past seven."

"What did Sir Gervase do?"

"I left him in the study."

"How long did he usually take to change?"

"He usually gave himself a full three-quarters of an hour."

"Then, if dinner was at a quarter-past eight, he would probably have gone up at half-past seven at the latest?"

"Very likely."

"You yourself went to change early?"

"Yes, I thought I would change and then go to the library and look up the references I wanted."

Poirot nodded thoughtfully. Major Riddle said:

"Well, I think that's all for the moment. Will you send Miss What's-her-name along?"

Little Miss Lingard tripped in almost immediately. She was wearing several chains which tinkled a little as she sat down and looked inquiringly from one to the other of the two men.

"This is all very—er—sad, Miss Lingard," began Major Riddle.

"Very sad, indeed," said Miss Lingard decorously.

"You came to this house—when?"

"About two months ago. Sir Gervase wrote to a friend of his in the Museum—Colonel Fotheringay it was—and Colonel Fotheringay recommended me. I have done a good deal of historical research work."

"Did you find Sir Gervase difficult to work for?"

"Oh, not really. One had to humor him a little, of course. But then I always find one has to do that with men."

With an uneasy feeling that Miss Lingard was probably humoring him at this moment, Major Riddle went on:

"Your work here was to help Sir Gervase with the book he was writing?"

"Yes."

"What did that involve?"

For a moment, Miss Lingard looked quite human. Her eyes twinkled as she replied:

"Well, actually, you know, it involved writing the book! I looked up all the information and made notes, and arranged the material. And then, later, I revised what Sir Gervase had written."

"You must have had to exercise a good deal of tact, mademoiselle," said Poirot.

"Tact and firmness. One needs them both," said Miss Lingard.

"Sir Gervase did not resent your—er—firmness?"

"Oh, not at all. Of course I put it to him that he mustn't be bothered with all the petty detail."

"Oh, yes, I see."

"It was quite simple, really," said Miss Lingard. "Sir Gervase was perfectly easy to manage if one took him the right way."

"Now, Miss Lingard, I wonder if you know anything that can throw light on this tragedy?"

Miss Lingard shook her head.

"I'm afraid I don't. You see, naturally he wouldn't confide in me at all. I was practically a stranger. In any case, I think he was far too proud to speak to anyone of family troubles."

"But you think it *was* family troubles that caused him to take his life?"

Miss Lingard looked rather surprised.

"But, of course! Is there any other suggestion?"

"You feel sure that there were family troubles worrying him?"

"I know that he was in great distress of mind."

"Oh, you know that?"

"Why, of course."

"Tell me, mademoiselle, did he speak to you of the matter?"

"Not explicitly."

"What did he say?"

"Let me see. I found that he didn't seem to be taking in what I was saying—"

"One moment. *Pardon*. When was this?"

"This afternoon. We usually worked from three to five."

"Pray go on."

"As I say, Sir Gervase seemed to be finding it hard to concentrate —in fact, he said as much, adding that he had several grave matters preying on his mind. And he said—let me see—something like this— (of course, I can't be sure of the exact words): '*It's a terrible thing, Miss Lingard, when a family has been one of the proudest in the land, that dishonor should be brought on it.*'"

"And what did you say to that?"

"Oh, just something soothing. I think I said that every generation had its weaklings—that that was one of the penalties of greatness— but that their failings were seldom remembered by posterity."

"And did that have the soothing effect you hoped?"

"More or less. We got back to Sir Roger Chevenix-Gore. I had found a most interesting mention of him in a contemporary manuscript. But Sir Gervase's attention wandered again. In the end he said he would not do any more work that afternoon. He said he had had a shock."

"A shock?"

"That is what he said. Of course, I didn't ask any questions. I just said: 'I am sorry to hear it, Sir Gervase.' And then he asked me to tell Snell that M. Poirot would be arriving and to put off dinner until 8.15, and send the car to meet the 7.50 train."

"Did he usually ask you to make these arrangements?"

"Well—no—that was really Mr. Burrows' business. I did nothing but my own literary work. I wasn't a secretary in any sense of the word."

Poirot asked:

"Do you think Sir Gervase had a definite reason for asking you to make these arrangements, instead of asking Mr. Burrows to do so?"

Miss Lingard considered.

"Well, he may have had. . . . I did not think of it at the time. I thought it was just a matter of convenience. Still, it's true now I come to think of it, that he *did* ask me not to tell anyone that M. Poirot was coming. It was to be a surprise, he said."

"Ah! he said that, did he? Very curious, very interesting. And *did* you tell anyone?"

"Certainly not, M. Poirot. I told Snell about dinner and to send the chauffeur to meet the 7.50 as a gentleman was arriving by it. I didn't mention your name at all."

"Did Sir Gervase say anything else that may have had a bearing on the situation?"

Miss Lingard thought.

"No—I don't think so—he was very much strung-up—I do remember that just as I was leaving the room, he said: *'Not that it's any good his coming now. It's too late.'*"

"And you have no idea at all what he meant by that?"

"N-no."

Just the faintest suspicion of indecision about the simple negative. Poirot repeated with a frown:

"*'Too late.'* That is what he said, is it? *'Too late.'*"

Major Riddle said:

"You can give us no idea, Miss Lingard, as to the nature of the circumstance that so distressed Sir Gervase?"

Miss Lingard said slowly:

"I have an idea that it was in some way connected with Mr. Hugo Trent."

"With Hugo Trent? Why do you think that?"

"Well, it was nothing definite, but yesterday afternoon we were just touching on Sir Hugo de Chevenix (who, I'm afraid, didn't bear too good a character in the War of the Roses) and Sir Gervase said: 'My sister *would* choose the family name of Hugo for her son! It's always been an unsatisfactory name in our family. She might have known no Hugo would turn out well.'"

"What you tell us there is suggestive," said Poirot. "Yes, it suggests a new idea to me."

"Sir Gervase said nothing more definite than that?" asked Major Riddle.

Miss Lingard shook her head.

"No, and of course it wouldn't have done for me to say anything. Sir Gervase was really just talking to himself. He wasn't really speaking to me."

"Quite so."

Poirot said:

"Mademoiselle, you, a stranger, have been here for two months. It would be, I think, very valuable if you were to tell us quite frankly your impressions of the family and household."

Miss Lingard took off her pince-nez and blinked reflectively.

"Well, at first, quite frankly, I felt as though I'd walked straight into a madhouse! What with Lady Chevenix-Gore continually seeing things that weren't there, and Sir Gervase behaving like—like a King—and dramatizing himself in the most extraordinary way—well, I really did think they were the queerest people I had ever come across. Of course, Miss Chevenix-Gore was perfectly normal, and I soon found that Lady Chevenix-Gore was really an extremely kind, nice woman. Nobody could be kinder or nicer to me than she has been. Sir Gervase—well, I really think he *was* mad. His egomania—isn't that what you call it?—was getting worse and worse every day."

"And the others?"

"Mr. Burrows had rather a difficult time with Sir Gervase, I should imagine. I think he was glad that our work on the book gave him a little more breathing space. Colonel Bury was always charming. He was devoted to Lady Chevenix-Gore and he managed Sir Gervase quite well. Mr. Trent, Mr. Forbes and Miss Cardwell have only been here a few days, so of course I don't know much about them."

"Thank you, mademoiselle. And what about Captain Lake, the agent?"

"Oh, he's very nice. Everybody likes him."

"Including Sir Gervase?"

"Oh, yes. I've heard him say Lake was much the best agent he'd had. Of course, Captain Lake had his difficulties with Sir Gervase, too—but he managed pretty well, on the whole. It wasn't easy."

Poirot nodded thoughtfully. He murmured: "There was something—something—that I had in mind to ask you—some little thing. . . . What was it now?"

Miss Lingard turned a patient face towards him.

Poirot shook his head vexedly.

"Tchah! It is on the tip of my tongue."

Major Riddle waited a minute or two, then as Poirot continued to frown perplexedly, he took up the interrogation once more.

"When was the last time you saw Sir Gervase?"

"At tea-time, in this room."

"What was his manner then? Normal?"

"As normal as it ever was."

"Was there any sense of strain among the party?"

"No, I think everybody seemed quite ordinary."

"Where did Sir Gervase go after tea?"

"He took Mr. Burrows with him into the study, as usual."

"That was the last time you saw him?"

"Yes. I went to the small morning-room where I worked, and typed a chapter of the book from the notes I had gone over with Sir Gervase, until seven o'clock, when I went upstairs to rest and dress for dinner."

"You actually heard the shot, I understand?"

"Yes, I was in this room. I heard what sounded like a shot and I went out into the hall. Mr. Trent was there, and Miss Cardwell. Mr. Trent asked Snell if there was champagne for dinner, and made rather a joke of it. It never entered our heads to take the matter seriously, I'm afraid. We made sure it must have been a car backfiring."

Poirot said:

"Did you hear Mr. Trent say: *'There's always murder'?*"

"I believe he did say something like that—joking, or course."

"What happened next?"

"We all came in here."

"Can you remember the order in which the others came down to dinner?"

"Miss Chevenix-Gore was the first, I think, and then Mr. Forbes. Then Colonel Bury and Lady Chevenix-Gore together, and Mr. Burrows immediately after them. I think that was the order, but I can't be quite sure because they more or less came in all together."

"Gathered by the sound of the first gong?"

"Yes. Everyone always hustled when they heard that gong. Sir Gervase was a terrible stickler for punctuality in the evening."

"What time did he himself usually come down?"

"He was nearly always in the room before the first gong went."

"Did it surprise you that he was not down on this occasion?"

"Very much."

"Ah, I have it!" cried Poirot.

As the other two looked inquiringly at him, he went on:

"I have remembered what I wanted to ask. This evening, mademoiselle, as we all went along to the study on Snell's reporting it to be locked, you stooped and picked something up."

"I did?" Miss Lingard seemed very surprised.

"Yes, just as we turned into the straight passage to the study. Something small and bright."

"How extraordinary—I don't remember. Wait a minute—yes, I do. Only I wasn't thinking. Let me see—it must be in here."

Opening her black satin bag, she poured the contents on a table.

Poirot and Major Riddle surveyed the collection with interest. There were two handkerchiefs, a powder compact, a small bunch of keys, a spectacle case and one other object on which Poirot pounced eagerly.

"A bullet, by Jove!" said Major Riddle.

The thing was indeed shaped like a bullet, but it proved to be a small pencil.

"That's what I picked up," said Miss Lingard. "I'd forgotten all about it."

"Do you know who this belongs to, Miss Lingard?"

"Oh, yes, it's Colonel Bury's. He had it made out of a bullet that hit him—or rather, didn't hit him, if you know what I mean—in the South African War."

"Do you know when he had it last?"

"Well, he had it this afternoon when they were playing bridge, because I noticed him writing with it on the score when I came in to tea."

"Who was playing bridge?"

"Colonel Bury, Lady Chevenix-Gore, Mr. Trent and Miss Cardwell."

"I think," said Poirot gently, "we will keep this and return it to the Colonel ourselves."

"Oh, please do. I am so forgetful, I might not remember to do so."

"Perhaps, mademoiselle, you would be so good as to ask Colonel Bury to come here now?"

"Certainly. I will go and find him at once."

She hurried away. Poirot got up and began walking aimlessly around the room.

"We begin," he said, "to reconstruct the afternoon. It is interesting. At half-past two Sir Gervase goes over accounts with Captain Lake. *He is slightly preoccupied.* At three, he discusses the book he is writing with Miss Lingard. *He is in great distress of mind.* Miss Lingard associates that distress of mind with Hugo Trent on the strength of a chance remark. At tea-time *his behavior is normal.* After tea, Godfrey Burrows tells us *he was in good spirits over something.* At five minutes to eight he comes downstairs, goes to his study, scrawls '*Sorry*' on a sheet of paper, and shoots himself!"

Riddle said slowly:

"I see what you mean. It isn't consistent."

"Strange alternations of moods in Sir Gervase Chevenix-Gore! He is preoccupied—he is seriously upset—he is normal—he is in high spirits! There is something very curious here! And then that phrase he used: 'Too late.' That I should get here. 'Too late.' Well, it is true, that. I *did* get here too late—*to see him alive.*"

"I see. You really think—?"

"I shall never know now why Sir Gervase sent for me! That is certain!"

Poirot was still wandering round the room. He straightened one or two objects on the mantelpiece; he examined a card table that stood against a wall, he opened the drawer of it and took out the bridge markers. Then he wandered over to the writing-table and peered into the wastepaper-basket. There was nothing in it but a paper bag. Poirot took it out, smelt it, murmured "Oranges" and flattened it out, reading the name on it. "Carpenter and Sons, Fruiterers, Hamborough St. Mary." He was just folding it neatly into squares when Colonel Bury entered the room.

8

The Colonel dropped into the chair, shook his head, sighed and said:

"Terrible business, this, Riddle. Lady Chevenix-Gore is being wonderful—wonderful. Grand woman! Full of courage!"

Coming softly back to his chair, Poirot said:

"You have known her very many years, I think?"

"Yes, indeed, I was at her coming-out dance. Wore rosebuds in her hair, I remember. And a white fluffy dress. . . . Wasn't anyone to touch her in the room!"

His voice was full of enthusiasm. Poirot held out the pencil to him.

"This is yours, I think?"

"Eh? What? Oh, thank you; had it this afternoon when we were playing bridge. Amazing, you know, I held a hundred honors in spades three times running. Never done such a thing before."

"You were playing bridge before tea, I understand?" said Poirot. "What was Sir Gervase's frame of mind when he came in to tea?"

"Usual—quite usual. Never dreamed he was thinking of making away with himself. Perhaps he was a little more excitable than usual, now I come to think of it."

"When was the last time you saw him?"

"Why, then! Tea-time! Never saw the poor chap alive again."

"You didn't go to the study at all after tea?"

"No, never saw him again."

"What time did you come down to dinner?"

"After the first gong went."

"You and Lady Chevenix-Gore came down together?"

"No, we—er—met in the hall. I think she'd been into the dining-room to see to the flowers—something like that."

Major Riddle said:

"I hope you won't mind, Colonel Bury, if I ask you a somewhat personal question. Was there any trouble between you and Sir Gervase over the question of the Synthetic Paragon Rubberine Company?"

Colonel Bury's face became suddenly purple. He spluttered a little.

"Not at all. Not at all. Old Gervase was an unreasonable sort of fellow. You've got to remember that. He always expected everything he touched to turn out trumps! Didn't seem to realize that the whole world was going through a period of crisis. All stocks and shares bound to be affected."

"So there *was* a certain amount of trouble between you?"

"No trouble. Just damned unreasonable of Gervase!"

"He blamed you for certain losses he had sustained?"

"Gervase wasn't normal! Vanda knew that. But she could always handle him. I was content to leave it all in her hands."

Poirot coughed and Major Riddle, after glancing at him, changed the subject.

"You are a very old friend of the family, I know, Colonel Bury. Had you any knowledge as to how Sir Gervase had left his money?"

"Well, I should imagine the bulk of it would go to Ruth. That's what I gathered from what Gervase let fall."

"You don't think that was at all unfair to Hugo Trent?"

"Gervase didn't like Hugo. Never could stick him."

"But he had a great sense of family. Miss Chevenix-Gore was, after all, only his adopted daughter."

Colonel Bury hesitated, then after humming and hawing a moment, he said:

"Look here, I think I'd better tell you something. Strict confidence, and all that."

"Of course—of course."

"Ruth's illegitimate, but she's a Chevenix-Gore all right. Daughter of Gervase's brother, Anthony, who was killed in the War. Seemed he'd had an affair with a typist. When he was killed, the girl wrote to Vanda. Vanda went to see her, girl was expecting a baby. Vanda took it up with Gervase, she'd just been told that she herself could never have another child. Result was they took over the child when it was born, adopted it legally. The mother renounced all rights in it. They've brought Ruth up as their own daughter and to all intents and purposes, she *is* their own daughter, and you've only got to look at her to realize she's a Chevenix-Gore all right!"

"Aha!" said Poirot. "I see. That makes Sir Gervase's attitude very much clearer. But if he did not like Mr. Hugo Trent, why was he so anxious to arrange a marriage between him and Mademoiselle Ruth?"

"To regularize the family position. It pleased his sense of fitness."

"Even though he did not like or trust the young man?"

Colonel Bury snorted.

"You don't understand old Gervase. He couldn't regard people as human beings. He arranged alliances as though the parties were Royal Personages! He considered it fitting that Ruth and Hugo should marry, Hugo taking the name of Chevenix-Gore. What Hugo and Ruth thought about it didn't matter."

"And was Mademoiselle Ruth willing to fall in with this arrangement?"

Colonel Bury chuckled.

"Not she! She's a tartar!"

"Did you know that shortly before his death Sir Gervase was drafting a new will by which Miss Chevenix-Gore would inherit only on condition that she should marry Mr. Trent?"

Colonel Bury whistled.

"Then he really *had* got the wind up about her and Burrows—"

As soon as he had spoken, he bit the words off, but it was too late. Poirot had pounced upon the admission.

"There was something between Mademoiselle Ruth and young Monsieur Burrows?"

"Probably nothing in it—nothing in it at all."

Major Riddle coughed and said:

"I think, Colonel Bury, that you must tell us all you know. It might have a direct bearing on Sir Gervase's state of mind."

"I suppose it might," said Colonel Bury, doubtfully. "Well, the truth of it is, young Burrows is not a bad-looking chap—at least, women seem to think so. He and Ruth seem to have got as thick as thieves just lately, and Gervase didn't like it—didn't like it at all. Didn't like to sack Burrows for fear of precipitating matters. He knows what Ruth's like. She won't be dictated to in any way. So I suppose he hit on this scheme. Ruth's not the sort of girl to sacrifice everything for love. She's fond of the fleshpots and she likes money."

"Do you yourself approve of Mr. Burrows?"

The Colonel delivered himself of the opinion that Godfrey Burrows was slightly hairy at the heel, a pronouncement which baffled Poirot completely, but made Major Riddle smile into his mustache.

A few more questions were asked and answered, and then Colonel Bury departed.

Riddle glanced over at Poirot who was sitting absorbed in thought.

"What do you make of it all, M. Poirot?"

The little man raised his hands.

"I seem to see a pattern—a purposeful design."

Riddle said: "It's difficult."

"Yes, it is difficult. . . . But more and more one phrase, lightly uttered, strikes me as significant."

"What was that?"

"That laughing sentence spoken by Hugo Trent: *'There's always murder'* . . ."

Riddle said sharply:

"Yes, I can see that you've been leaning that way all along."

"Do you not agree, my friend, that the more we learn, the less and less motive we find for suicide? But for murder, we begin to have a surprising collection of motives!"

"Still, you've got to remember the facts—door locked, key in dead man's pocket. Oh, I know there are ways and means. Bent pins, strings—all sorts of devices. It would, I suppose, be *possible*. . . . But do those things really work? That's what I very much doubt."

"At all events, let us examine the position from the point of view of murder, not of suicide."

"Oh, all right. As *you* are on the scene, it probably *would* be murder!"

For a moment Poirot smiled.

"I hardly like that remark."

Then he became grave once more.

"Yes, let us examine the case from the standpoint of murder. The shot is heard, four people are in the hall, Miss Lingard, Hugo Trent, Miss Cardwell and Snell. Where are all the others?

"Burrows was in the library, according to his own story. No one to check that statement. The others were presumably in their rooms, but who is to know if they were really there? Everybody seems to have come down separately. Even Lady Chevenix-Gore and Bury only met in the hall. Lady Chevenix-Gore came from the dining-room. Where did Bury come from? Isn't it possible that he came, not from upstairs, but *from the study?* There's that pencil.

"Yes, the pencil is interesting. He showed no emotion when I produced it, but that might be because he did not know where I found it and was unaware himself of having dropped it. Let us see, who else was playing bridge when the pencil was in use? Hugo Trent and Miss Cardwell. They're out of it. Miss Lingard and the butler can vouch for their alibis. The fourth was Lady Chevenix-Gore."

"You can't seriously suspect her."

"Why not, my friend? I tell you, me, I can suspect everybody! Supposing that, in spite of her apparent devotion to her husband, it is the faithful Bury she really loves?"

"H'm," said Riddle. "In a way it has been a kind of *ménage à trois* for years."

"And there is some trouble about this company between Sir Gervase and Colonel Bury."

"It's true that Sir Gervase might have been meaning to turn really nasty. We don't know the ins-and-outs of it. It might fit in with that summons to you. Say Sir Gervase suspects that Bury has deliberately fleeced him, but he doesn't want publicity because of a suspicion that his wife may be mixed up in it. Yes, that's possible. That gives either of those two a possible motive. And it *is* a bit odd really that Lady Chevenix-Gore should take her husband's death so calmly. All this spirit business may be acting!"

"Then there is the other complication," said Poirot. "Miss Chevenix-Gore and Burrows. It is very much to their interest that

Sir Gervase should not sign the new will. As it is, she gets everything on condition that her husband takes the family name—"

"Yes, and Burrows' account of Sir Gervase's attitude this evening is a bit fishy. High spirits, pleased about something! That doesn't fit with anything else we've been told."

"There is, too, Mr. Ogilvie Forbes. Most correct, most severe, of an old and well-established firm. But lawyers, even the most respectable, have been known to embezzle their clients' money when they themselves are in a hole."

"You're getting a bit too sensational, I think, Poirot."

"You think what I suggest is too like the pictures? But life, Major Riddle, is often amazingly like the pictures."

"It hasn't been, so far, in Westshire," said the Chief Constable. "We'd better finish interviewing the rest of them, don't you think? It's getting late. We haven't seen Ruth Chevenix-Gore yet, and she's probably the most important of the lot."

"I agree. There is Miss Cardwell, too. Perhaps we might see her first, since that will not take long, and interview Miss Chevenix-Gore last."

"Quite a good idea."

9

Earlier that evening Poirot had only given Susan Cardwell a fleeting glance. He examined her now more attentively. An intelligent face, he thought, not strictly good-looking, but possessing an attraction that a merely pretty girl might envy. Her hair was magnificent, her face skillfully made-up. Her eyes, he thought, were watchful.

After a few preliminary questions, Major Riddle said:

"I don't know how close a friend you are of the family, Miss Cardwell."

"I don't know them at all. Hugo arranged that I should be asked down here."

"You are, then, a friend of Hugo Trent's?"

"Yes, that's my position; Hugo's girl-friend." Susan Cardwell smiled as she drawled out the words.

"You have known him a long time?"

"Oh, no, just a month or so."

She paused and then added:

"I'm by way of being engaged to him."

"And he brought you down here to introduce you to his people?"

"Oh, dear no, nothing like that. We were keeping it very hush-hush. I just came down to spy out the land. Hugo told me the place was just like a madhouse. I thought I'd better come and see for myself. Hugo, poor sweet, is a perfect pet, but he's got absolutely no brains. The position, you see, was rather critical. Neither Hugo nor I have any money, and old Sir Gervase, who was Hugo's main hope, had set his heart on Hugo making a match of it with Ruth. Hugo's a bit weak, you know. He might agree to this marriage and count on being able to get out of it later."

"That idea did not commend itself to you, mademoiselle?" inquired Poirot gently.

"Definitely not. Ruth might have gone all peculiar and refused to divorce him or something. I put my foot down. No trotting off to St. Paul's, Knightsbridge, until I could be there dithering with a sheaf of lilies."

"So you came down to study the situation for yourself?"

"Yes."

"Eh bien!" said Poirot.

"Well, of course, Hugo was right! The whole family were bughouse! Except Ruth, who seems perfectly sensible. She'd got her own boy-friend and wasn't any keener on the marriage idea than I was."

"You refer to M. Burrows?"

"Burrows? Of course not. Ruth wouldn't fall for a bogus person like that."

"Then who was the object of her affection?"

Susan Cardwell paused, stretched for a cigarette, lit it, and remarked:

"You'd better ask her that. After all, it isn't my business."

Major Riddle asked:

"When was the last time you saw Sir Gervase?"

"At tea."

"Did his manner strike you as peculiar in any way?"

The girl shrugged her shoulders.

"Not more than usual."

"What did you do after tea?"

"Played billiards with Hugo."

"You didn't see Sir Gervase again?"

"No."

"What about the shot?"

"That was rather odd. You see, I thought the first gong had gone, so I hurried up with my dressing, came dashing out of my room, heard, as I thought, the second gong and fairly raced down the stairs. I'd been one minute late for dinner the first night I was here and Hugo told me it had about wrecked our chances with the Old Man, so I fairly hared down. Hugo was just ahead of me and then there was a queer kind of pop-bang and Hugo said it was a champagne cork, but Snell said 'No' to that and, anyway, I didn't think it had come from the dining-room. Miss Lingard thought it came from upstairs, but anyway we agreed it was a backfire and we trooped into the drawing-room and forgot about it."

"It did not occur to you for one moment that Sir Gervase might have shot himself?" asked Poirot.

"I ask you, should I be likely to think of such a thing? The Old Man seemed to enjoy himself throwing his weight about. I never imagined he'd do such a thing. I can't think why he did it. I suppose just because he was nuts."

"An unfortunate occurrence."

"Very—for Hugo and me. I gather he's left Hugo nothing at all, or practically nothing."

"Who told you that?"

"Hugo got it out of old Forbes."

"Well, Miss Cardwell—" Major Riddle paused a moment—"I think that's all. Do you think Miss Chevenix-Gore is feeling well enough to come down and talk to us?"

"Oh, I should think so. I'll tell her."

Poirot intervened.

"A little moment, mademoiselle. Have you seen this before?"

He held out the bullet pencil.

"Oh, yes, we had it at bridge this afternoon. Belongs to old Colonel Bury, I think."

"Did he take it when the rubber was over?"

"I haven't the faintest idea."

"Thank you, mademoiselle. That is all."

"Right, I'll tell Ruth."

Ruth Chevenix-Gore came into the room like a queen. Her color was vivid, her head held high. But her eyes, like the eyes of Susan Cardwell, were watchful. She wore the same frock she had on when Poirot arrived. It was a pale shade of apricot. On her shoulder was pinned a deep salmon-pink rose. It had been fresh and blooming an hour earlier, now it drooped.

"Well?" said Ruth.

"I'm extremely sorry to bother you . . ." began Major Riddle.

She interrupted him:

"Of course you have to bother me. You have to bother everyone. I can save you time, though. I haven't the faintest idea why the Old Man killed himself. All I can tell you is that it wasn't a bit like him."

"Did you notice anything amiss in his manner today? Was he depressed, or unduly excited—was there anything at all abnormal?"

"I don't think so. I wasn't noticing—"

"When did you see him last?"

"Tea-time."

Poirot spoke:

"You did not go to the study—later?"

"No. The last I saw of him was in this room. Sitting there."

She indicated a chair.

"I see. Do you know this pencil, mademoiselle?"

"It's Colonel Bury's."

"Have you seen it lately?"

"I don't really remember."

"Do you know anything of a—disagreement between Sir Gervase and Colonel Bury?"

"Over the Paragon Rubberine Company, you mean?"

"Yes."

"I should think so. The Old Man was rabid about it!"

"He considered, perhaps, that he had been swindled?"

Ruth shrugged her shoulders.

"He didn't understand the first thing about finance."

Poirot said:

"May I ask you a question, mademoiselle—a somewhat impertinent question?"

"Certainly, if you like."

"It is this—are you sorry that your—father is dead?"

She stared at him.

"Of course I'm sorry. I don't indulge in sob-stuff. But I shall miss him. . . . I was fond of the Old Man. That's what we called him, Hugo and I, always. The 'Old Man'—you know—something of the primitive-anthropoid-ape-original-Patriarch-of-the-tribe business. It sounds disrespectful, but there's really a lot of affection behind it. Of course, he was really the most complete muddle-headed old ass that ever lived!"

"You interest me, mademoiselle."

"The Old Man had the brains of a louse! Sorry to have to say it, but it's true. He was incapable of any kind of headwork. Mind you, he was a character. Fantastically brave and all that! Could go careering off to the Pole, or fighting duels. I always think that he blustered such a lot because he really knew that his brains weren't up to much. Anyone could have got the better of him."

Poirot took the letter from his pocket.

"Read this, mademoiselle."

She read it through and handed it back to him.

"So that's what brought you here!"

"Does it suggest anything to you, that letter?"

She shook her head.

"No. It's possibly quite true. Anyone could have robbed the poor old pet. John says the last agent before him swindled him right and left. You see, the Old Man was so grand and so pompous that he never really condescended to look into details! He was an invitation to crooks."

"You paint a different picture of him, mademoiselle, from the accepted one."

"Oh, well—he put up a pretty good camouflage. Vanda (my mother) backed him for all she was worth. He was so happy stalking round pretending he was God Almighty. That's why, in a way, I'm glad he's dead. It's the best thing for him."

"I do not quite follow you, mademoiselle."

Ruth said broodingly:

"It was growing on him. One of these days he would have had to be locked up. . . . People were beginning to talk as it was."

"Did you know, mademoiselle, that he was contemplating a will whereby you could only inherit his money if you married Mr. Trent?"

She cried:

"How absurd! Anyway, I'm sure that could be set aside by law. . . . I'm sure you can't dictate to people about whom they shall marry."

"If he had actually signed such a will, would you have complied with its provisions, mademoiselle?"

She stared.

"I—I—"

She broke off. For two or three minutes she sat irresolute, looking down at her dangling slipper. A little piece of earth detached itself from the heel and fell on the carpet.

Suddenly Ruth Chevenix-Gore said:

"Wait!"

She got up and ran out of the room. She returned almost immediately with Captain Lake by her side.

"It's got to come out," she said rather breathlessly. "You might as well know now. John and I were married in London three weeks ago."

10

Of the two of them, Captain Lake looked far the more embarrassed.

"This is a great surprise, Miss Chevenix-Gore—Mrs. Lake, I should say," said Major Riddle. "Did no one know of this marriage of yours?"

"No, we kept it quite dark. John didn't like that part of it much."

Lake said, stammering a little:

"I—I know that it seems rather a rotten way to set about things. I ought to have gone straight to Sir Gervase—"

Ruth interrupted:

"And told him you wanted to marry his daughter, and have been kicked out on your head, and he'd probably have disinherited me, raised hell generally in the house, and we could have told each other how beautifully we'd behaved! Believe me, my way was better! If a thing's done, it's done. There would still have been a row—but he'd have come round."

Lake still looked unhappy. Poirot asked:

"When did you intend to break the news to Sir Gervase?"

Ruth answered:

"I was preparing the ground. He'd been rather suspicious about me and John, so I pretended to turn my attentions to Godfrey. Naturally, he was ready to go quite off the deep-end about that. I figured it out that the news I was married to John would come almost as a relief!"

"Did anybody at all know of this marriage?"

"Yes, I told Vanda in the end. I wanted to get her on my side."

"And you succeeded in doing so?"

"Yes. You see, she wasn't very keen about my marrying Hugo—because he was a cousin, I think. She seemed to think the family was so batty already that we'd probably have completely batty children. That was probably rather absurd, because I'm only adopted, you know. I believe I'm some quite distant cousin's child."

"You are sure Sir Gervase had no suspicion of the truth?"

"Oh, no."

Poirot said:

"Is that true, Captain Lake? In your interview with Sir Gervase this afternoon, are you quite sure the matter was not mentioned?"

"No, sir. It was not."

"Because, you see, Captain Lake, there is certain evidence to show that Sir Gervase was in a highly excitable condition after the time he spent with you, and that he spoke once or twice of family dishonor."

"The matter was not mentioned," Lake repeated. His face had gone very white.

"Was that the last time you saw Sir Gervase?"

"Yes, I have already told you so."

"Where were you at eight minutes past eight this evening?"

"Where was I? In my house. At the end of the village, about half-a-mile away."

"You did not come up to Hamborough Close round about that time?"

"No."

Poirot turned to the girl.

"Where were you, mademoiselle, when your father shot himself?"

"In the garden."

"In the garden? You heard the shot?"

"Oh, yes. But I didn't think about it particularly. I thought it was someone out shooting rabbits, although now I remember I did think it sounded quite close at hand."

"You returned to the house—which way?"

"I came in through this window."

Ruth indicated with a turn of her head the window behind her.

"Was anyone in here?"

"No. But Hugo and Susan and Miss Lingard came in from the hall almost immediately. They were talking about shooting and murders and things."

"I see," said Poirot. "Yes, I think I see now. . . ."

Major Riddle said rather doubtfully:

"Well—er—thank you. I think that's all for the moment."

Ruth and her husband turned and left the room.

"What the devil—" began Major Riddle, and ended rather hopelessly: "It gets more and more difficult to keep track of this business."

Poirot nodded. He had picked up the little piece of earth that had fallen from Ruth's shoe and was holding it thoughtfully in his hand.

"It is like the mirror smashed on the wall," he said. "The dead man's mirror. Every new fact we come across shows us some different angle of the dead man. He is reflected from every conceivable point of view. We shall have soon a complete picture. . . ."

He rose and put the little piece of earth tidily in the wastepaper-basket.

"I will tell you one thing, my friend. The clue to the whole mystery is the mirror. Go into the study and look for yourself, if you do not believe me."

Major Riddle said decisively:

"If it's murder, it's up to you to prove it. If you ask me, I say it's definitely suicide. Did you notice what the girl said about a former agent having swindled old Gervase? I bet Lake told that tale for his own purposes. He was probably helping himself a bit, Sir Gervase suspected it, and sent for you because he didn't know how far things had gone between Lake and Ruth. Then this afternoon Lake told him they were married. That broke Gervase up. It was 'too late' now for anything to be done. He determined to get out of it all. In fact, his brain, never very well-balanced at the best of times, gave way. In my opinion that's what happened. What have you got to say against it?"

Poirot stood still in the middle of the room.

"What have I to say? This. I have nothing to say against your theory—but it does not go far enough. There are certain things it does not take into account."

"Such as?"

"The discrepancies in Sir Gervase's moods today, the finding of Colonel Bury's pencil, the evidence of Miss Cardwell (which is very important), the evidence of Miss Lingard as to the order in which people came down to dinner, the position of Sir Gervase's chair when he was found, the paper bag which had held oranges and, finally, the all-important clue of the broken mirror."

Major Riddle stared.

"Are you going to tell me that that rigmarole makes *sense?*" he asked.

Hercule Poirot replied softly:

"I hope to make it do so—by tomorrow."

It was just after dawn when Hercule Poirot awoke on the following morning. He had been given a bedroom on the east side of the house.

Getting out of bed, he drew aside the window-blind and satisfied himself that the sun had risen and that it was a fine morning.

He began to dress with his usual meticulous care. Having finished his toilet, he wrapped himself up in a thick overcoat and wound a muffler round his neck.

Then he tiptoed out of his room and through the silent house down to the drawing-room. He opened the French windows noiselessly and passed out into the garden.

The sun was just showing now. The air was misty, with the mist of a fine morning. Hercule Poirot followed the terraced walk round the side of the house until he came to the windows of Sir Gervase's study. Here he stopped and surveyed the scene.

Immediately outside the window was a strip of grass that ran parallel with the house. In front of that was a wide herbaceous border. The Michaelmas daisies still made a fine show. In front of the border was the flagged walk where Poirot was standing. A strip of grass ran from the grass walk behind the border to the terrace. Poirot examined it carefully, then shook his head. He turned his attention to the border on either side of it.

Very slowly he nodded his head. In the right-hand bed, distinct in the soft mold, there were footprints.

As he stared down at them, frowning, a sound caught his ears and he lifted his head sharply.

Above him a window had been pushed up. He saw a red head of hair. Framed in an aureole of golden red he saw the intelligent face of Susan Cardwell.

"What on earth are you doing at this hour, M. Poirot? A spot of sleuthing?"

Poirot bowed with the utmost correctitude.

"Good morning, mademoiselle. Yes, it is as you say. You now behold a detective—a great detective, I may say—in the act of detecting!"

The remark was a little flamboyant. Susan put her head on one side.

"I must remember this in my memoirs," she remarked. "Shall I come down and help?"

"I should be enchanted."

"I thought you were a burglar at first. Which way did you get out?"

"Through the drawing-room window."

"Just a minute and I'll be with you."

She was as good as her word. To all appearances Poirot was exactly in the same position as when she had first seen him.

"You are awake very early, mademoiselle?"

"I haven't been to sleep really properly. I was just getting that desperate feeling that one does get at five in the morning."

"It is not quite so early as that!"

"It feels like it! Now then, my super-sleuth, what are we looking at?"

"But observe, mademoiselle, footprints."

"So they are."

"Four of them," continued Poirot. "See, I will point them out to you. Two going towards the window, two coming from it."

"Whose are they? The gardener's?"

"Mademoiselle, mademoiselle. Those footmarks are made by the small dainty high-heeled shoes of a woman. See, convince yourself. Step, I beg of you, in the earth here beside them."

Susan hesitated a minute, then placed a foot gingerly onto the mold in the place indicated by Poirot. She was wearing small high-heeled slippers of dark brown leather.

"You see, yours are nearly the same size. Nearly, but not quite. These others are made by a rather longer foot than yours. Perhaps Miss Chevenix-Gore's—or Miss Lingard's—or even Lady Chevenix-Gore's."

"Not Lady Chevenix-Gore—she's got tiny feet. People did in those days—manage to have small feet, I mean. And Miss Lingard wears queer, flat-heeled things."

"Then they are the marks of Miss Chevenix-Gore. Ah, yes, I remember she mentioned having been out in the garden yesterday evening."

He led the way back round the house.

"Are we still sleuthing?" asked Susan.

"But, certainly. We will go now to Sir Gervase's study."

He led the way. Susan Cardwell followed him.

The door still hung in a melancholy fashion. Inside, the room was as it had been last night. Poirot pulled the curtain and admitted the daylight.

He stood there looking out a minute or two, then he said:

"You have not, I presume, mademoiselle, much acquaintance with burglars?"

Susan Cardwell shook her red head regretfully.

"I'm afraid not, M. Poirot."

"The Chief Constable, he, too, has not had the advantages of a friendly relationship with them. His connection with the criminal classes has always been strictly official. With me that is not so. I had a very pleasant chat with a burglar once. He told me an interesting thing about French windows—a trick that could sometimes be employed if the fastening was sufficiently loose."

He turned the handle as he spoke, the middle shaft came up out of the hole in the ground and Poirot was able to pull the two doors of the window towards him. Having opened them wide, he closed them again—closed them without turning the handle, so as not to send the shaft down into its socket. He let go of the handle, waited a moment, then struck a quick, jarring blow high up on the center of the shaft. The jar of the blow sent the shaft down into the socket in the ground—the handle turned of its own accord.

"You see, mademoiselle?"

"I think I do."

Susan had gone rather pale.

"The window is now closed. It is impossible to *enter* a room when the window is closed, but it *is* possible to *leave* a room, pull the doors to from outside, then hit it as I did, and the bolt goes down into the ground, turning the handle. The window then is firmly closed and anyone looking at it would say it had been closed from the *inside*."

"Is that—" Susan's voice shook a little—"is that what happened last night?"

"I think so, yes, mademoiselle."

Susan said violently:

"I don't believe a word of it."

Poirot did not answer. He walked over to the mantelpiece. He wheeled sharply round.

"Mademoiselle, I have need of you as a witness. I have already one witness, Mr. Trent. He saw me find this tiny sliver of looking-glass last night. I spoke of it to him. I left it where it was for the police. I even told the Chief Constable that a valuable clue was the broken mirror. But he did not avail himself of my hint. Now, you are a witness that I place this sliver of looking-glass (to which, remember, I have already called Mr. Trent's attention) into a little envelope—

so." He suited the action to the word. "And I write on it—so—and seal it up. You are a witness, mademoiselle?"

"Yes—but—but I don't know what it means."

Poirot walked over to the other side of the room. He stood in front of the desk and stared at the shattered mirror on the wall in front of him.

"I will tell you what it means, mademoiselle. If you had been standing here last night, looking into this mirror, you could have seen in it *murder being committed*. . . ."

12

For once in her life Ruth Chevenix-Gore—now Ruth Lake—came down to breakfast in good time. Hercule Poirot was in the hall and drew her aside before she went into the dining-room.

"I have a question to ask you, madame."

"Yes?"

"You were in the garden last night. Did you at any time step in the flowerbed outside Sir Gervase's study window?"

Ruth stared at him.

"Yes, twice."

"Ah! *twice*. How twice?"

"The first time I was picking Michaelmas daisies. That was about seven o'clock."

"Was it not rather an odd time of day to pick flowers?"

"Yes, it was, as a matter of fact. I'd done the flowers yesterday morning, but Vanda said after tea that the flowers on the dinner-table weren't good enough. I had thought they would be all right, so I hadn't done them fresh."

"But your mother requested you to do them? Is that right?"

"Yes; so I went out just before seven. I took them from that part of the border because hardly anyone goes round there, and so it didn't matter spoiling the effect."

"Yes, yes, but the *second* time. You went there a *second* time, you said?"

"That was just before dinner. I had dropped a spot of brilliantine on my dress—just by the shoulder. I didn't want to bother to change and none of my artificial flowers went with the yellow of that dress. I remembered I'd seen a late rose when I was picking the Michaelmas daisies, so I hurried out and got it and pinned it on my shoulder."

Poirot nodded his head slowly.

"Yes, I remember that you wore a rose last night. What time was it, madame, when you picked that rose?"

"I don't really know."

"But it is *essential,* madame. Consider—reflect—"

Ruth frowned. She looked swiftly at Poirot and then away again.

"I can't say exactly," she said at last. "It must have been—oh, of course—it must have been about five minutes past eight. It was when I was on my way back round the house that I heard the gong go, and then that funny bang. I was hurrying because I thought it was the second gong and not the first."

"Ah! So you thought that—and did you not try the study window when you stood there in the flowerbed?"

"As a matter of fact, I did. I thought it might be open and it would be quicker to come in that way. But it was fastened."

"So everything is explained. I congratulate you, madame."

She stared at him.

"What do you mean?"

"That you have an explanation for everything, for the mold on your shoes, for your footprints in the flowerbed, for your fingerprints on the outside of the window. It is very convenient, that."

Before Ruth could answer, Miss Lingard came hurrying down the stairs. There was a queer purple flush on her cheeks and she looked a little startled at seeing Poirot and Ruth standing together.

"I beg your pardon," she said. "Is anything the matter?"

Ruth said angrily:

"I think M. Poirot has gone mad!"

She swept by them and into the dining-room. Miss Lingard turned an astonished face on Poirot.

He shook his head.

"After breakfast," he said, "I will explain. I should like everyone to assemble in Sir Gervase's study at ten o'clock."

He repeated this request on entering the dining-room.

Susan Cardwell gave him a quick glance, then transferred her gaze to Ruth. When Hugo said:

"Eh? what's the idea?" she gave him a sharp nudge in the side, and he shut up obediently.

When he had finished his breakfast, Poirot rose and walked to the door. He turned and drew out a large old-fashioned watch.

"It is five minutes to ten. In five minutes—in the study."

Poirot looked round him. A circle of interested faces stared back at him. Everyone was there, he noted, with one exception, and at that very moment the exception swept into the room. Lady Chevenix-Gore came in with a soft, gliding step. She looked haggard and ill.

Poirot drew forward a big chair for her, and she sat down.

She looked up at the broken mirror, shivered, and pulled her chair a little way round.

"Gervase is still here," she remarked in a matter-of-fact tone. "Poor Gervase. . . . He will soon be free now."

Poirot cleared his throat and announced:

"I have asked you all to come here so that you may hear the true facts of Sir Gervase's suicide."

"It was Fate," said Lady Chevenix-Gore. "Gervase was strong, but his Fate was stronger."

Colonel Bury moved forward a little.

"Vanda—my dear."

She smiled up at him, then put up her hand. He took it in his. She said softly: "You are such a comfort, Ned."

Ruth said sharply:

"Are we to understand, M. Poirot, that you have definitely ascertained the cause of my father's suicide?"

Poirot shook his head.

"No, madame."

"Then what is all this rigmarole about?"

Poirot said quietly:

"I do not know the cause of Sir Gervase Chevenix-Gore's suicide, *because Sir Gervase Chevenix-Gore did not commit suicide*. He did not kill himself. *He was killed. . . .*"

"Killed?" Several voices echoed the word. Startled faces were turned in Poirot's direction. Lady Chevenix-Gore looked up, said, "Killed? Oh, no!" and gently shook her head.

"Killed, did you say?" It was Hugo who spoke now. "Impossible. There was no one in the room when we broke in. The window was fastened. The door was locked on the inside and the key was in my uncle's pocket. How could he have been killed?"

"Nevertheless, he was killed."

"And the murderer escaped through the keyhole, I suppose?" said Colonel Bury skeptically. "Or flew up the chimney?"

"The murderer," said Poirot, "went out through the window. I will show you how."

He repeated his maneuvers with the window.

"You see?" he said. "That was how it was done! From the first I could not consider it likely that Sir Gervase had committed suicide. He had a pronounced egomania and such a man does not kill himself.

"And there were other things! Apparently, just before his death, Sir Gervase had sat down at his desk, scrawled the word SORRY on a sheet of notepaper and had then shot himself. But before this last action he had, for some reason or other, altered the position of his chair, turning it so that it was sideways to the desk. Why? There must be some reason. I began to see light when I found, sticking to the base of a heavy bronze statuette, a tiny sliver of looking-glass. . . .

"I asked myself, how does a sliver of broken looking-glass come to be there?—and an answer suggested itself to me. The mirror had been broken, not by a bullet, *but by being struck with the heavy bronze figure.* That mirror had been broken *deliberately.*

"But why? I returned to the desk and looked down at the chair. Yes, I saw now. It was all wrong. No suicide would turn his chair round, lean over the edge of it, and then shoot himself. The whole thing was arranged. The suicide was a fake!

"And now I come to something very important. The evidence of Miss Cardwell. Miss Cardwell said that she hurried downstairs last night because she thought that the *second* gong had sounded. That is to say, she thought that she had already heard the *first* gong.

"Now observe, *if* Sir Gervase is sitting at his desk in the normal fashion when he was shot, where would the bullet go? Traveling in a straight line, it would pass through the door, if the door were open, and finally *hit the gong!*

"You see now the importance of Miss Cardwell's statement? No one else heard that first gong, but then her room is situated immediately above this one, and she was in the best position for hearing it. It would consist of only one single note, remember.

"There could be no question of Sir Gervase's shooting himself. A dead man cannot get up, shut the door, lock it and arrange himself in a convenient position! Somebody else was concerned, and therefore it was not suicide, but murder. Someone whose presence was easily accepted by Sir Gervase, stood by his side talking to him. Sir Gervase was busy writing perhaps. The murderer brings the pistol up to the right side of his head and fires. The deed is done! Then quick, to work! The murderer slips on gloves. The door is locked, the key put in Sir Gervase's pocket. But supposing that one loud note of the gong has been heard? Then it will be realized that the door was *open,* not *shut,* when the shot was fired. So the chair is turned, the body rearranged, the dead man's fingers pressed on the pistol, the mirror deliberately smashed. Then the murderer goes out through the window, jars it shut, steps, not on the grass, but in the flowerbed where footprints can be smoothed out afterwards; then round the side of the house and into the drawing-room."

He paused and said:

"*There was only one person who was out in the garden when the shot was fired.* That same person left her footprints in the flowerbed and her fingerprints on the outside of the window."

He came towards Ruth.

"And there was a motive, wasn't there? Your father had learnt of your secret marriage. He was preparing to disinherit you."

"It's a lie!" Ruth's voice came scornful and clear. "There's not a word of truth in your story. It's a lie from start to finish!"

"The proofs against you are very strong, madame. A jury *may* believe you. It may *not!*"

"She won't have to face a jury."

The others turned—startled. Miss Lingard was on her feet. Her face had altered. She was trembling all over.

"*I* shot him. I admit it! I had my reasons. I—I've been waiting for some time. M. Poirot is quite right. I followed him in here. I had taken the pistol out of the drawer earlier. I stood beside him talking about the book—and I shot him. That was just after eight. The bullet struck the gong. I never dreamt it would pass right through his head like that. There wasn't time to go out and look for it. I locked the door and put the key in his pocket. Then I swung the chair round, smashed the mirror and, after scrawling 'sorry' on a piece of paper, I went out through the window and shut it the way M. Poirot showed you. I stepped in the flowerbed, but I smoothed out the footprints with a little rake I had put there ready. Then I went round to the drawing-room. I had left the window open. I didn't know Ruth had gone out through it. She must have come round the front of the house while I went round the back. I had to put the rake away, you see, in a shed. I waited in the drawing-room till I heard someone coming downstairs and Snell going to the gong, and then—"

She looked at Poirot.

"You don't know what I did then?"

"Oh, yes, I do. I found the bag in the wastepaper-basket. It was very clever, that idea of yours. You did what children love to do. You blew up the bag and then hit it. It made a satisfactory big bang. You threw the bag into the wastepaper-basket and rushed out into the hall. You had established the time of the suicide—and an alibi for yourself. But there was still one thing that worried you. You had not had time to pick up the bullet. It must be somewhere near the gong. It was essential that the bullet should be found in the study somewhere near the mirror. I don't know when you had the idea of taking Colonel Bury's pencil—"

"It was just then," said Miss Lingard. "When we all came in from the hall. I was surprised to see Ruth in the room. I realized she must have come from the garden through the window. Then I noticed Colonel Bury's pencil lying on the bridge table. I slipped it into my bag. If, later, anyone saw me pick up the bullet, I could pretend it was the pencil. As a matter of fact, I didn't think anyone saw me pick up the bullet. I dropped it by the mirror while you were looking at the body. When you tackled me on the subject, I was very glad I had thought of the pencil."

"Yes, that was clever. It confused me completely."

"I was afraid someone must hear the real shot, but I knew everyone was dressing for dinner and would be shut away in their rooms. The servants were in their quarters. Miss Cardwell was the only one at all likely to hear it, and she would probably think it was a backfire. What she did hear was the gong. I thought—I thought everything had gone without a hitch. . . ."

Mr. Forbes said slowly in his precise tones:

"This is a most extraordinary story. There seems no motive—"

Miss Lingard said clearly: "There *was* a motive. . . ."

She added fiercely:

"Go on, ring up the police! What are you waiting for?"

Poirot said gently:

"Will you all please leave the room? Mr. Forbes, ring up Major Riddle. I will stay here till he comes."

Slowly, one by one, the family filed out of the room. Puzzled, uncomprehending, shocked, they cast abashed glances at the trim upright figure with its neatly-parted gray hair.

Ruth was the last to go. She stood, hesitating in the doorway.

"I don't understand." She spoke angrily, defiantly, accusing Poirot. "Just now, you thought *I* had done it."

"No, no." Poirot shook his head. "No, I never thought that."

Ruth went out slowly.

Poirot was left with the prim little middle-aged woman who had just confessed to a cleverly-planned and cold-blooded murder.

"No," said Miss Lingard. "You didn't think she had done it. You accused *her* to make *me* speak. That's right, isn't it?"

Poirot bowed his head.

"While we're waiting," said Miss Lingard in a conversational tone, "you might tell me what made you suspect *me?*"

"Several things. To begin with, your account of Sir Gervase. A proud man like Sir Gervase would never speak disparagingly of his nephew to an outsider, especially someone in your position. You wanted to strengthen the theory of suicide. You also went out of your way to suggest that the cause of the suicide was some dishonorable trouble connected with Hugo Trent. That, again, was a thing Sir Gervase would never have admitted to a stranger. Then, there was the object you picked up in the hall, and the very significant fact that you did not mention that Ruth, when she entered the drawing-room, did so *from the garden*. And then I found the paper bag—a most unlikely object to find in the wastepaper-basket in the drawing-room of a house like Hamborough Close! You were the only person who had been in the drawing-room when the 'shot' was heard. The paper bag trick was one that would suggest itself to a woman—an ingenious homemade device. So everything fitted in. The endeavor to throw suspicion on Hugo, and to keep it away from Ruth. The mechanism of crime—and its motive."

The little gray-haired woman stirred.

"You know the motive?"

"I think so. Ruth's happiness—that was the motive! I fancy that you had seen her with John Lake—you knew how it was with them. And then with your easy access to Sir Gervase's papers, you came across the draft of his new will—Ruth disinherited unless she married Hugo Trent. That decided you to take the law into your own hands, using the fact that Sir Gervase had previously written to me. You probably saw a copy of that letter. What muddled feeling of suspicion and fear had caused him to write originally, I do not know. He must have suspected either Burrows or Lake of systematically robbing him. His uncertainty regarding Ruth's feelings made him seek a private investigation. You used that fact and deliberately set the stage for suicide, backing it up by your account of his being very distressed over something connected with Hugo Trent. You sent a telegram to me and reported Sir Gervase as having said I should arrive 'too late.'"

Miss Lingard said fiercely:

"Gervase Chevenix-Gore was a bully, a snob, and a windbag! I wasn't going to have him ruin Ruth's happiness."

Poirot said gently:

"Ruth is your daughter?"

"Yes—she is my daughter. I've often—thought about her. When I heard Sir Gervase Chevenix-Gore wanted someone to help him with a family history, I jumped at the chance. I was curious to see my—my girl. I knew Lady Chevenix-Gore wouldn't recognize me. It was years ago—I was young and pretty then, and I changed my name after that time. Besides, Lady Chevenix-Gore is too vague to know anything definitely. I liked her, but I hated the Chevenix-Gore family. They treated me like dirt. And there was Gervase going to ruin Ruth's life with his pride and snobbery. But I determined that she should be happy. And she *will* be happy—*if she never knows about me!*"

It was a plea—not a question.

Poirot bent his head gently.

"No one shall know from me."

Miss Lingard said quietly:

"Thank you."

Later, when the police had come and gone, Poirot found Ruth Lake with her husband in the garden.

She said challengingly:

"Did you really think that I had done it, M. Poirot?"

"I knew, madame, that you could *not* have done it—because of the Michaelmas daisies."

"The Michaelmas daisies? I don't understand."

"Madame, there were four footprints and four footprints *only* in the border. But if you had been picking flowers there would have been many more. That meant that between your first visit and your second, *someone had smoothed all those footsteps away*. That could only have been done by the guilty person, and since your footprints had *not* been removed, you were *not* the guilty person. You were automatically cleared."

Ruth's face lightened.

"Oh, I see. You know—I suppose it's dreadful, but I feel rather sorry for that poor woman. After all, she did confess rather than let me be arrested—or at any rate, that is what she thought. That was —rather noble in a way. I hate to think of her going through a trial for murder."

Poirot said gently:

"Do not distress yourself. It will not come to that. The doctor, he tells me that she has serious heart trouble. She will not live many weeks."

"I'm glad of that." Ruth picked an autumn crocus and pressed it idly against her cheek.

"Poor woman. I wonder why she did it. . . ."

THREE TIMES THREE

MYSTERY OMNIBUS

VOLUME III

THREE TIMES THREE

MYSTERY OMNIBUS

Edited by
HOWARD HAYCRAFT
and
JOHN BEECROFT

VOLUME III

VOLUME III

MURDER IS NO JOKE

by Rex Stout

1

I was a little disappointed in Flora Gallant when she arrived that Tuesday morning for her eleven-o'clock appointment with Nero Wolfe. Her getup was a letdown. One of my functions as Wolfe's factotum is checking on people who phone for an appointment with him, and when I had learned that Flora Gallant was one of the staff of her brother Alec's establishment on East Fifty-fourth Street, and remembered remarks a friend of mine named Lily Rowan had made about Alec Gallant, I had phoned Lily for particulars.

And got them. Gallant was crowding two others for top ranking in the world of high fashion. He thumbed his nose at Paris and sneered at Rome, and was getting away with it. He had refused to finish three dresses for the Duchess of Harwynd because she postponed flying over from London for fittings. He declined to make anything whatever for a certain famous movie actress because he didn't like the way she handled her hips when she walked. He had been known to charge as little as eight hundred dollars for an afternoon frock, but it had been for a favorite customer so he practically gave it away.

And so forth. Therefore when I opened the door to admit his sister Flora that Tuesday morning it was a letdown to see a dumpy middle-aged female in a dark gray suit that was anything but spectacular. It needed pressing, and the shoulders were too tight, and her waist wasn't where it thought it was. As I ushered her down the hall to the office and introduced her to Wolfe, I was thinking that if the shoemaker's son went barefoot I supposed his sister could too, but all the same I felt cheated.

Her conversation was no more impressive than her costume, at least at the beginning. Seated on the edge of the red leather chair beyond the end of Wolfe's desk, the fingers of both hands gripping the rim of the gray leather bag on her lap, she apologized, in a low meek mumble with just a trace of a foreign accent, for asking such an important man as Nero Wolfe to give any of his valuable time to her and her troubles. That didn't sound promising, indicating as it did that she was looking for a bargain. As she went on with it Wolfe started a frown going, and soon he cut her off by saying that it would take less of his time if she would tell him what her troubles were.

She nodded. "I know. I just wanted you to understand that I don't expect anything for myself. I'm not anybody myself, but you know who my brother is? My brother Alec?"

"Yes. Mr. Goodwin has informed me. An illustrious dressmaker."

"He is not merely a dressmaker. He is an artist, a great artist." She wasn't arguing, just stating a fact. "This trouble is about him, and that's why I must be careful with it. That's why I come to you, and also"—she sent me a glance and then back to Wolfe—"also Mr. Archie Goodwin, because I know that although you are private detectives, you are gentlemen. I know you are worthy of confidence."

She stopped, apparently for acknowledgment. Wolfe obliged her. "Umph."

"Then it is understood I am trusting you?"

"Yes. You may."

She looked at me. "Mr. Goodwin?"

"Right. Whatever Mr. Wolfe says. I only work here."

She hesitated, seeming to consider if that was satisfactory, decided it was, and returned to Wolfe. "So I'll tell you. I must explain that in France, where my brother and I were born and brought up, our name was not 'Gallant.' What it was doesn't matter. I came to this country in nineteen-thirty-seven, when I was twenty-five years old, and Alec only came in nineteen-forty-five, after the war was over. He had changed his name to Gallant and entered legally under that name. Within seven years he had made a reputation as a designer, and then— Perhaps you remember his fall collection in nineteen-fifty-three?"

Wolfe grunted no.

Her right hand abandoned its grip on the bag to gesture. "But of course you are not married, and you have no mistress, feeling as you do about women. That collection showed what my brother was—an artist, a true creator. He got financial backing, more than he needed, and opened his place on Fifty-fourth Street. I had quit my job four years earlier—my job as a governess—in order to work with him and help him, and had changed my name to have it the same as his. From nineteen-fifty-three on it has been all a triumph, many triumphs. I will not say I had a hand in them, but I have been trying to help in my little way. The glory of great success has been my brother's, but I have been with him, and so have others. But now trouble has come."

Both hands were gripping the bag again. "The trouble," she said, "is a woman. A woman named Bianca Voss."

Wolfe made a face. She saw it and responded to it. "No, not an *affaire d'amour,* I'm sure it's not that. Though my brother has never married, he is by no means insensible to women, he is very healthy about women, but since you are worthy of confidence I may tell you that he has an *amie intime,* a young woman who is of importance in his establishment. It is impossible that Bianca Voss has attracted him that way. She first came there a little more than a year ago. My brother had told us to expect her, so he had met her somewhere. He designed a dress and a suit for her, and they were made there in the shop, but no bill was ever sent her. Then he gave her one of the rooms, the offices, on the third floor, and she started to come every day, and then the trouble began. My brother never told us she had any authority, but she took it and he allowed her to. Sometimes she interferes directly, and sometimes through him. She pokes her nose into everything. She got my brother to discharge a fitter, a very capable woman, who had been with him for years. She has a private telephone line in her office upstairs, but no one else has. About two months ago some of the others persuaded me to try to find out about her, what her standing is, and I asked my brother, but he wouldn't tell me. I begged him to, but he wouldn't."

"It sounds," Wolfe said, "as if she owns the business. Perhaps she bought it."

Flora Gallant shook her head. "No, she hasn't. I'm sure she hasn't. She wasn't one of the financial backers in nineteen-fifty-three, and since then there have been good profits, and anyway my brother has control. But now she's going to ruin it and he's going to let her, we don't know why. She wants him to design a factory line to be promoted by a chain of department stores using his name. She wants him to sponsor a line of Alec Gallant cosmetics on a royalty basis. And other things. We're against all of them, and my brother is too, really, but we think he's going to give in to her, and that will ruin it."

Her fingers tightened on the bag. "Mr. Wolfe, I want you to ruin *her*."

Wolfe grunted. "By wiggling a finger?"

"No, but you can. I'm sure you can. I'm sure she has some hold on him, but I don't know what. I don't know who she is or where she came from. I don't know what her real name is. She speaks with an accent, but not French; I'm not sure what it is. I don't know when she came to America; she may be here illegally. She may have known my brother in France, during the war. You can find out. If she has a hold on my brother you can find out what it is. If she is blackmailing him, isn't that against the law? Wouldn't that ruin her?"

"It might. It might ruin him too."

"Not unless you betrayed him." She swallowed that and added hastily, "I don't mean that, I only mean I am trusting you, you said I could, and you could make her stop and that's all you would have to do. Couldn't you just do that?"

"Conceivably." Wolfe wasn't enthusiastic. "I fear, madam, that you're biting off more than you can chew. The procedure you suggest would be prolonged, laborious, and extremely expensive. It would probably require elaborate investigation abroad. Aside from my fee, which would not be modest, the outlay would be considerable and the outcome highly uncertain. Are you in a position to undertake it?"

"I am not rich myself, Mr. Wolfe. I have some savings. But my brother—if you get her away, if you release him from her—he is truly *généreux*—excuse me—he is a generous man. He is not stingy."

"But he isn't hiring me, and your assumption that she is galling him may be groundless." Wolfe shook his head. "No. Not a reasonable venture. Unless, of course, your brother himself consults me. If you care to bring him? Or send him?"

"Oh, I couldn't!" She gestured again. "You must see that isn't possible! When I asked him about her, I told you, he wouldn't tell me anything. He was annoyed. He is never abrupt with me, but he was then. I assure you, Mr. Wolfe, she is a villain. You are *sagace*—excuse me—you are an acute man. You would know it if you saw her, spoke with her."

"Perhaps." Wolfe was getting impatient. "Even so, my perception of her villainy wouldn't avail. No, madam."

"But you would know I am right." She opened her bag, fingered in it with both hands, came out with something, left her chair to step to Wolfe's desk, and put the something on his desk pad in front of him. "There," she said, "that is one hundred dollars. For you that is nothing, but it shows how I am in earnest. I can't ask her to come so you can speak with her, she would merely laugh at me, but you can. You can tell her you have been asked in confidence to discuss a matter with her and ask her to come to see you. You will not tell her what it is. She will come, she will be afraid not to, and that alone will show you she has a secret, perhaps many secrets. Then when she comes you will ask her whatever occurs to you. For that you do not need my suggestions. You are an acute man."

Wolfe grunted. "Everybody has secrets."

"Yes," she agreed, "but not secrets that would make them afraid not to come to see Nero Wolfe. When she comes and you have spoken with her, we shall see. That may be all or it may not. We shall see."

I do not say that the hundred bucks there on his desk in used twenties was no factor in Wolfe's decision. Even though income tax would reduce it to sixteen dollars, that would buy four days' supply of beer. Another factor was plain curiosity: would she come or wouldn't she? Still another was the chance that it might develop into a decent fee. But what really settled it was her saying, "We shall see" instead of "We'll see" or "We will see." He will always stretch a point, within reason, for people who use words as he thinks they should be used. So he muttered at her, "Where is she?"

"At my brother's place. She always is."

"Give Mr. Goodwin the phone number."

"I'll get it. She may be downstairs." She started a hand for the phone on Wolfe's desk, but I told her to use mine and left my chair, and she came and sat, lifted the receiver, and dialed.

In a moment she spoke. "Doris? Flora. Is Miss Voss around? . . . Oh. I thought she might have come down. . . . No, don't bother, I'll ring her there."

She pushed the button down, told us, "She's up in her office," waited a moment, released the button, and dialed again. When she spoke it was another voice, as she barely moved her lips and brought it out through her nose: "Miss Bianca Voss? Hold the line, please. Mr. Nero Wolfe wishes to speak with you. . . . Mr. Nero Wolfe, the private detective."

She looked at Wolfe and he got at his phone. Having my own share of curiosity, I extended a hand for my receiver, and she let me take it and left my chair. As I sat and got it to my ear Wolfe was speaking.

"This is Nero Wolfe. Is this Miss Bianca Voss?"

"Yes." It was more like "yiss." "What do you want?" The "wh" and the "w" were off.

"If my name is unknown to you, I should explain—"

"I know your name. What do you want?"

"I want to invite you to call on me at my office. I have been asked to discuss certain matters with you, and—"

"Who asked you?"

"I am not at liberty to say. I shall—"

"What matters?" The "wh" was more off.

"If you will let me finish. The matters are personal and confidential, and concern you closely. That's all I can say on the telephone. I am sure you—"

A snort stopped him, a snort that might be spelled "Tzchaahh!" followed by: "I know your name, yes! You are scum, I know, in your stinking sewer! Your slimy little ego in your big gob of fat! And you dare to—*owulggh!*"

That's the best I can do at spelling it. It was part scream, part groan, and part just noise. It was followed immediately by another noise, a mixture of crash and clatter, then others, faint rustlings, and then nothing. I looked at Wolfe and he looked at me. I spoke to my transmitter. "Hello hello hello. *Hello!* Hello?"

I cradled it and so did Wolfe. Flora Gallant was asking, "What is it? She hung up?"

We ignored her. Wolfe said, "Archie? You heard."

"Yes, sir. If you want a guess, something hit her and she dragged the phone along as she went down and it struck the floor. The other noises, not even a guess, except that at the end either she put the receiver back on and cut the connection or someone else did. I don't— Okay, Miss Gallant. Take it easy." She had grabbed my arm with both hands and was jabbering, "What is it? What happened?" I put a hand on her shoulder and made it emphatic. "Take a breath and let go. You heard what I told Mr. Wolfe. Apparently something fell on her and then hung up the phone."

"But it couldn't! It is not possible!"

"That's what it sounded like. What's the number? The one downstairs?"

She just gawked at me. I looked at Wolfe and he gave me a nod, and I jerked my arm loose, sat at my desk, got the Manhattan book, flipped to the Gs and got the number, PL2-0330, and dialed it.

A cultured female voice came. "Alec Gallant Incorporated."

"This is a friend of Miss Voss," I told her. "I was just speaking to her on the phone, in her office, and from the sounds I got I think something may have happened to her. Will you send someone up to see? Right away. I'll hold the wire."

"Who is this speaking, please?"

"Never mind that. Step on it. She may be hurt."

I heard her calling to someone, then apparently she covered the transmitter. I sat and waited. Wolfe sat and scowled at me. Flora Gallant stood for a good five minutes at my elbow, staring down at me, then turned and went to the red leather chair and lowered herself onto its edge. I looked at my wristwatch: 11:40. It had said 11:31 when the connection with Bianca Voss had been cut. More waiting, and then a male voice came.

"Hello?"

"Hello."

"This is Carl Drew. What is your name, please?"

"My name is Watson, John H. Watson. Is Miss Voss all right?"

"May I have your address, Mr. Watson, please?"

"What for? Miss Voss knows my address. Is she all right?"

"I must have your address, Mr. Watson. I must insist. You will understand the necessity when I tell you that Miss Voss is dead. She was assaulted in her office and is dead. Apparently, from what you said, the assault came while she was on the phone with you, and I want your address. I must insist."

I hung up, gently not to be rude, swiveled, and asked Flora Gallant, "Who is Carl Drew?"

"He's the business manager. What happened?"

I went to Wolfe. "My guess was close. Miss Voss is dead. In her office. He said she was assaulted, but he didn't say with what or by whom."

He glowered at me, then turned to let her have it. She was coming up from the chair, slow and stiff. When she was erect she said, "No. No. It isn't possible."

"I'm only quoting Carl Drew," I told her.

"It isn't possible. He said that?"

"Distinctly."

"But how—" She let it hang. She said, "But how—" stopped again, turned, and was going. When Wolfe called to her, "Here, Miss Gallant, your money," she paid no attention but kept on, and he poked it at me, and I took it and headed for the hall. I caught up with her halfway to the front door, but when I offered it she just kept going, so I blocked her off, took her bag and opened it and dropped the bills in and closed it, handed it back, and went and pulled the door open. She hadn't said a word. I stood on the sill and watched, thinking she might stumble going down the seven steps of the stoop, but she made it to the sidewalk and turned east, toward Ninth Avenue. When I got back to the office Wolfe was sitting with his eyes closed, breathing down to his big round middle. I went to my desk and put the phone book away.

"She is so stunned with joy," I remarked, "that she'll probably get run over. I should have gone and put her in a taxi."

He grunted.

"One thing," I remarked, "Miss Voss's last words weren't exactly *généreux*. I would call them catty."

He grunted.

"Another thing," I remarked, "in spite of the fact that I was John H. Watson on the phone, we'll certainly be called on by either Sergeant Stebbins or Inspector Cramer or both. When they go into whereabouts Flora will have to cough it up for her own protection. And we actually heard it. Also we'll have the honor of being summoned to the stand. Star witnesses."

He opened his eyes. "I'm quite aware of it," he growled. "Confound it. Bring me the records on Laelia gouldiana."

No orchid ever called a genius a slimy little ego in a big gob of fat. I remarked that too, but to myself.

2

"Sure I appreciate it," Cramer declared. "Why shouldn't I? Very thoughtful of you. Saves me time and trouble. So it was eleven-thirty-one when you heard the blow?"

Inspector Cramer, big and brawny with a round red face and all his hair, half of it gray, had nothing to be sarcastic about as he sat in the red leather chair at six-thirty that Tuesday afternoon, and he knew it, but he couldn't help it. It was his reaction, not to the present circumstances, but to his memory of other occasions, other experiences he had undergone in that room. He had to admit that we had saved him time and trouble when I had anticipated his visit by typing out a complete report of the session with Flora Gallant that morning, including the dialogue verbatim, and having it ready for him in duplicate, signed by both Wolfe and me. He had skimmed through it first, and then read it slowly and carefully.

"We heard no blow, identifiably," Wolfe objected. His bulk was comfortably arranged in his oversize chair back of his desk. "Mr. Goodwin wrote that statement, but I read it, and it does not say that we heard a blow."

Cramer found the place on page four and consulted it. "Okay. You heard a groan and a crash and rustles. But there *was* a blow. She was hit in the back of the head with a chunk of marble, a paperweight, and then a scarf was tied around her throat to stop her breathing. You say here at eleven-thirty-one."

"Not when we heard the groan," I corrected. "After that there were the other noises, then the connection went, and I said hello a few times, which was human but dumb. It was when I hung up that I looked at my watch and saw eleven-thirty-one. The groan had been maybe a minute earlier. Say eleven-thirty. If a minute is important."

"It isn't. But you didn't hear the blow?"

"Not to recognize it, no."

He went back to the statement, frowning at it, reading the whole first page and glancing at the others. He looked up, at Wolfe. "I know how good you are at arranging words. This implies that Flora Gallant was a complete stranger to you, that you had never had anything to do with her or her brother or any of the people at that place, but it doesn't say so in so many words. I'd like to know."

"The implication is valid," Wolfe told him. "Except as related in that statement, I have never had any association with Miss Gallant or her brother, or, to my knowledge, with any of their colleagues. Nor has Mr. Goodwin. Archie?"

"Right," I agreed.

"Okay." Cramer folded the statement and put it in his pocket. "Then you had never heard Bianca Voss's voice before and you couldn't recognize it on the phone."

"Of course not."

"And you can't hear it now, since she's dead. So you can't swear it was her talking to you."

"Obviously."

"And that raises a point. If it was her talking to you, she was killed at exactly half past eleven. Now there are four important people in that organization who had it in for Bianca Voss. They have admitted it. Besides Flora Gallant, there is Anita Prince, fitter and designer, been with Gallant eight years; Emmy Thorne, in charge of contacts and promotion, been with him four years; and Carl Drew, business manager, been with him five years. None of them killed Bianca Voss at half past eleven. From eleven-fifteen on, until the call came from a man who said he was John H. Watson, Carl Drew was down on the main floor, constantly in view of four people, two of them customers. From eleven o'clock on Anita Prince was on the top floor, the workshop, with Alec Gallant and two models and a dozen employees. At eleven-twenty Emmy Thorne called on a man by appointment at his office on Forty-sixth Street, and was with him and two other men until a quarter to twelve. And Flora Gallant was here with you. All airtight."

"Very neat," Wolfe agreed.

"Yeah. Too damn neat. Of course there may be others who wanted Bianca Voss out of the way, but as it stands now those four are out in front. And they're all—"

"Why not five? Alec Gallant himself?"

"All right, five. They're all in the clear, including him, if she was killed at eleven-thirty. So suppose she wasn't. Suppose she was killed earlier, half an hour or so earlier. Suppose when Flora Gallant phoned her from here and put you on to talk with her, it wasn't her at all, it was someone else imitating her voice, and she pulled that stunt, the groan and the other noises, to make you think you had heard the murder at that time."

Wolfe's brows were up. "With the corpse there on the floor."

"Certainly."

"Then you're not much better off. Who did the impersonation? Their alibis still hold for eleven-thirty."

"I realize that. But there were nineteen women around there altogether, and a woman who wouldn't commit a murder might be willing to help cover up after it had been committed. You know that."

Wolfe wasn't impressed. "It's very tricky, Mr. Cramer. If you are supposing Flora Gallant killed her, it was elaborately planned. Miss Gallant phoned here yesterday morning to make an appointment for eleven this morning. Did she kill Miss Voss, station someone there beside the corpse to answer the phone, rush down here, and maneuver me into ringing Miss Voss's number? It seems a little far-fetched."

"I didn't say it was Flora Gallant." Cramer hung on. "It could have been any of them. He or she didn't have to know you were going to ring that number. He might have intended to call it himself, before witnesses, to establish the time of the murder, and when your call came, whoever it was there by the phone got rattled and went ahead with the act. There are a dozen different ways it could have happened. Hell, I know it's tricky. I'm not asking you to work your brain on it. You must know why I brought it up."

Wolfe nodded. "Yes, I think I do. You want me to consider what I heard—and Mr. Goodwin. You want to know if we are satisfied that those sounds were authentic. You want to know if we will concede that they might have been bogus."

"That's it. Exactly."

Wolfe rubbed his nose with a knuckle, closing his eyes. In a moment he opened them. "I'm afraid I can't help you, Mr. Cramer. If they were bogus they were well executed. At the time, hearing them, I had no suspicion that it was flummery. Naturally, as soon as I learned that they served to fix the precise moment of a murder, I knew they were open to question, but I can't challenge them intrinsically. Archie?"

I shook my head. "I pass." To Cramer: "You've read the statement, so you know that right after I heard it my guess was that something hit her and she dragged the phone along as she went down and it struck the floor. I'm not going to go back on my guess now. As for our not hearing the blow, read the statement. It says that it started out as if it was going to be a scream but then it was a groan. She might have seen the blow coming and was going to scream, but it landed and turned it into a groan, and in that case we wouldn't hear the blow. A chunk of marble hitting a skull wouldn't make much noise. As for supposing she was killed half an hour or so earlier, I phoned within three minutes, or John H. Watson did, and in another six or seven minutes Carl Drew was talking to me, so he must have seen the body, or someone did, not more than five minutes after we heard the groan. Was she twitching?"

"No. You don't twitch long with a scarf as tight as that around your throat."

"What about the ME?"

"He got there a little after twelve. With blood he might have timed it pretty close, but there wasn't any. That's out."

"What about the setup? Someone left that room quick after we heard the sounds. If it was the murderer, he or she had to cradle the phone and tie the scarf, but that wouldn't take long. If it was a fill-in, as you want to suppose, all she had to do was cradle the phone. Whichever it was, wasn't there anyone else around?"

"No. If there was, they're saving it. As you know, Bianca Voss wasn't popular around there. Anyway, that place is a mess, with three different elevators, one in the store, one at the back for service and deliveries, and one in an outside hall with a separate entrance so they can go up to the offices without going through the store."

"That makes it nice. Then it's wide open."

"As wide as a barn door." Cramer stood up. To Wolfe: "So that's the best you can do. You thought the sounds were open to question."

"Not intrinsically. Circumstantially, of course."

"Yeah. Much obliged." He was going. After two steps he turned. "I don't like gags about homicide, murder is no joke, but I can mention that Bianca Voss had you wrong. Scum. Stinking sewer. Orchids don't smell." He went.

Apparently he hadn't really swallowed it that she was already dead when we heard the sounds.

3

The next morning, Wednesday, eating breakfast in the kitchen with the *Times* propped up in front of me, which is routine, of course I read the account of the Bianca Voss murder. There were various details that were news to me, but nothing startling or even helpful. It included the phone call from John H. Watson, but didn't add that he had been identified as Archie Goodwin, and there was no mention of Nero Wolfe. I admit that the cops and the DA have a right to save something for themselves, but it never hurts to have your name in the paper, and I had a notion to phone Lon Cohen at the *Gazette* and give him an exclusive. However, I would have to mention it to Wolfe first, so it would have to wait until eleven o'clock.

As a matter of fact, another item in the *Times* came closer to me. Sarah Yare had committed suicide. Her body had been found Tuesday evening in her little walk-up apartment on East Thirteenth Street. I had never written a fan letter to an actress, but I had been tempted to a couple of years back when I had seen Sarah Yare in *Thumb a Ride*. The first time I saw it I had a companion, but the next three times I was alone. The reason for repeating was that I had the impression I was infatuated and I wanted to wear it down, but when the impression still stuck after three tries I quit. Actresses should be seen and heard, but not touched. At that, I might have given the impression another test in a year or two if there had been an opportunity, but there wasn't. She quit *Thumb a Ride* abruptly some months later, and the talk was that she was an alco and done for.

So I read that item twice. It didn't say that it had been pronounced suicide officially and finally, since she had left no note, but a nearly empty bourbon bottle had been there on a table, and on the floor by the couch she had died on there had been a glass with enough left in it to identify the cyanide. The picture of her was as she had been when I had got my impression. I asked Fritz if he had ever seen Sarah Yare, and he asked what movies she had been in, and I said none, she was much too good for a movie.

I didn't get to suggest phoning Lon Cohen to Wolfe because when he came down from the plant rooms at eleven o'clock I wasn't there. As I was finishing my second cup of coffee a phone call came from the District Attorney's office inviting me to drop in, and I went and spent a couple of hours at Leonard Street with an assistant DA named Brill. When we got through I knew slightly more than I had when we started, but he didn't. He had a copy of our statement on his desk, and what could I add to that? He had a lot of fun, though. He would pop a question at me and then spend nine minutes studying the statement to see if I had tripped.

Getting home a little before noon, I was prepared to find Wolfe grumpy. He likes me to be there when he comes down from the plant rooms to the office, and while he can't very well complain when the DA calls me on business that concerns us, this wasn't our affair. We had no client and no case and no fee in prospect. But I got a surprise. He wasn't grumpy; he was busy. He had the phone book open before him on his desk. He had actually gone to my desk, stooped to get the book, lifted it, and carried it around to his chair. Unheard of.

"Good morning," I said. "What's the emergency?"

"No emergency. I needed to know a number."

"Can I help?"

"Yes. I have instructions."

I sat. He wants you at his level because it's too much trouble to tilt his head back. "Nothing new," I said, "at the DA's office. Do you want a report?"

"No. You will go to Alec Gallant's place on Fifty-fourth Street and speak with Mr. Gallant, his sister, Miss Prince, Miss Thorne, and Mr. Drew. Separately if possible. You will tell each of them— You read the *Times* this morning as usual?"

"Certainly."

"You will tell each of them that I have been engaged to make certain inquiries about Miss Sarah Yare, and that I shall be grateful for any information they may be able and willing to furnish. I would like to see any communications they may have received from her, say in the past month. Don't raise one brow like that. You know it disconcerts me."

"I've never seen you disconcerted yet." I let the brow down a little. "If they ask me who engaged you what do I say?"

"That you don't know. You are merely following instructions."

"If I ask you who engaged you what do you say?"

"I tell you the truth. No one. Or more accurately, I have engaged myself. I think I may have been hoodwinked and I intend to find out. You may be fishing where there are no fish. They may all say they have never had any association with Sarah Yare, and they may be telling the truth or they may not. You will have that in mind and form your conclusions. If any of them acknowledge association with her, pursue it enough to learn the degree of intimacy, but don't labor it. That can wait until we bait a hook. You are only to discover if there are any fish."

"Now?"

"Yes. The sooner the better."

I stood up. "It may take a while if the cops and the DA are working on them, and they probably are. How urgent is it? Do you want progress reports by phone?"

"Not unless you think it necessary. You must get all five of them."

"Right. Don't wait dinner for me." I went.

On the way uptown in the taxi I was using my brain. I will not explain at this point why Wolfe wanted to know if any of the subjects had known Sarah Yare, and if so how well, for two reasons: first, you have certainly spotted it yourself; and second, since I am not as smart as you are, I had not yet come up with the answer. It was underneath. On top, what I was using my brain for, was the phone book. Unquestionably it was connected with his being hoodwinked, since that was what was biting him, and therefore it probably had some bearing on the call that had been made from his office to Bianca Voss, but what could he accomplish by consulting the phone book? For that I had no decent guess, let alone an answer, by the time I paid the hackie at Fifty-fourth and Fifth Avenue.

Alec Gallant Incorporated, on the north side of the street near Madison Avenue, was no palace, either outside or in. The front was maybe thirty feet, and five feet of that was taken by the separate entrance to the side hall. The show window, all dark green, had just one exhibit: a couple of yards of plain black fabric, silk or rayon or nylon or Orlon or Dacron or cottonon or linenon, draped on a little rack. Inside, nothing whatever was in sight—that is, nothing to buy. The wall-to-wall carpet was the same dark green as the show window. There were mirrors and screens and tables and ashtrays, and a dozen or more chairs, not fancy, more to sit in than to look at. I had taken three steps on the carpet when a woman standing with a man by a table left him to come to meet me. I told her my name and said I would like to see Mr. Gallant. The man, approaching, spoke.

"Mr. Gallant is not available. What do you want?"

That didn't strike me as a very tactful greeting to a man who, for all he knew, might be set to pay eight hundred dollars for an afternoon frock, but of course he had had a tough twenty-four hours, so I kept it pleasant. "I'm not a reporter," I assured him, "or a cop, or a lawyer drumming up trade. I'm a private detective named Archie Goodwin, sent by a private detective named Nero Wolfe to ask Mr. Gallant a couple of harmless questions—not connected with the death of Bianca Voss."

"Mr. Gallant is not available."

I hadn't heard his voice in person before, only on the phone, but I recognized it. Also he looked like a business manager, with his neat well-arranged face, his neat well-made dark suit, and his neat shadow-stripe four-in-hand. He was a little puffy around the eyes, but the city and county employees had probably kept him from getting much sleep.

"May I ask," I asked, "if you are Mr. Carl Drew?"

"Yes. I am."

"Then I'm in luck. I was instructed to see five different people here—Mr. Gallant, Miss Gallant, Miss Prince, Miss Thorne, and Mr. Carl Drew. Perhaps we could sit down?"

He ignored that. "See us about what?"

The woman had left us. She was in earshot if her hearing was good, but this was certainly no secret mission, with five of them on the list. "To get information," I told him, "if you have any, about a woman who died yesterday. Not Bianca Voss. Miss Sarah Yare."

"Oh." He blinked. "Yes. That was tragic. Information? What kind of information?"

"I don't exactly know." I was apologetic. "All I know is that someone has engaged Mr. Wolfe to make inquiries about her, and he sent me to ask you people if you had any messages or letters from her in the past month or so, and if so will you let him see them."

"Messages or letters?"

"Right."

"That seems a little— Who engaged him?"

"I don't know." I was not permitting my face or voice to show that I had caught sight of a fish. "If you have had messages or letters, and would like to know who wants to see them before you produce them, I suppose Mr. Wolfe would tell you. He would have to."

"I have no messages or letters."

I was disappointed. "None at all? I said the past month or so, but before that would help. Any time."

He shook his head. "I never have had any. I doubt if she ever wrote a letter—that is, to anyone here—or any messages, except phone messages. She always did everything by telephone. And for the past month, longer than that, more than a year, she hasn't been—uh—she hasn't been around."

"I know." I was sympathetic, and I meant it, though not for him. "Anyway, I don't think Mr. Wolfe would be interested in letters about clothes. I think it's personal letters he wants, and he thought you might have known her well enough personally to have some."

"Well, I haven't. I can't say I didn't know her personally—she was a very fine customer here for two years, and she was a very personal person. But I never had a personal letter from her."

I had to resist temptation. I had him talking, and there was no telling if or when I would get at the others. But Wolfe had said not to labor it, and I disobey instructions only when I have reason to think I know more about it than he does, and at that moment I didn't even know why he had been consulting the phone book. So I didn't press.

I thanked him and said I would appreciate it if he would tell me when Mr. Gallant would be available. He said he would find out, and left me, going to the rear and disappearing around the end of a screen, and soon I heard his voice, but too faint to get any words. There was no other voice, so, being a detective, I figured it out that he was on a phone. That accomplished, I decided to detect whether the woman, who was seated at a table going through a portfolio, was either Anita Prince or Emmy Thorne. I voted no, arriving at it by a process so subtle and complicated that I won't go into it.

Drew reappeared, and I met him in the middle of the room. He said that Mr. Gallant was in his office with Miss Prince and could let me have five minutes. Another fish. Certainly Drew had told Gallant what my line was, and why did I rate even five seconds? As Drew led me to an elevator and entered with me, and pushed the button marked "2," I had to remember to look hopeful instead of smug.

The second-floor hall was narrow, with bare walls, and not carpeted. As I said, not a palace. After following Drew down six paces and through a door, I found myself in a pin-up paradise. All available space on all four walls was covered with women, drawings and prints and photographs, both black-and-white and color, all sizes, and in one respect they were all alike: none of them had a stitch on. It hadn't occurred to me that a designer of women's clothes should understand female anatomy, but I admit it might help. The effect was so striking that it took me four or five seconds to focus on the man and woman seated at a table. By that time Drew had pronounced my name and gone.

Though the man and woman were fully clothed, they were striking too. He reminded me of someone, but I didn't remember who until later: Lord Byron—a picture of Lord Byron in a book in my father's library that had impressed me at an early age. It was chiefly Gallant's dark curly hair backing up a wide sweeping forehead, but the nose and chin were in it too. The necktie was all wrong; instead of Byron's choker he was sporting a narrow ribbon tied in a bow with long ends hanging.

The woman didn't go with him. She was small and trim, in a tailored suit that had been fitted by an expert, and her face was all eyes. Not that they popped, but they ran the show. In spite of Alec Gallant's lordly presence, as I approached the table I found myself aiming at Anita Prince's eyes.

Gallant was speaking. "What's this? About Sarah Yare?"

"Just a couple of questions." He had eyes too, when you looked at them. "It shouldn't take even five minutes. I suppose Mr. Drew told you?"

"He said Nero Wolfe is making an inquiry and sent you. What about? About how she died?"

"I don't think so, but I'm not sure. The fact is, Mr. Gallant, on this I'm just an errand boy. My instructions were to ask if you got any messages or letters from her in the past month or so, and if so will you let Mr. Wolfe see them."

"My God." He closed his eyes, tilted his head back, and shook it —a lion pestered by a fly. He looked at the woman. "This is too much. Too much!" He looked at me. "You must know a woman was assassinated here yesterday. Of course you do!" He pointed at the door. "There!" His hand dropped to the desk like a dead bird. "And after that calamity, now this, the death of my old and valued friend. Miss Yare was not only my friend; in mold and frame she was perfection, in movement she was music, as a mannequin she would have been divine. My delight in her was completely pure. I never had a letter from her." His head jerked to Anita Prince. "Send him away," he muttered.

She put fingers on his arm. "You gave him five minutes, Alec, and he has only had two." Her voice was smooth and sure. The eyes came to me. "So you don't know the purpose of Mr. Wolfe's inquiry?"

"No, Miss Prince, I don't. He only tells me what he thinks I need to know."

"Nor who hired him to make it?"

So Drew had covered the ground. "No. Not that either. He'll probably tell you, if you have what he wants, letters from her, and you want to know why he wants to see them."

"I have no letters from her. I never had any. I had no personal relations with Miss Yare." Her lips smiled, but the eyes didn't. "Though I saw her many times, my contact with her was never close. Mr. Gallant preferred to fit her himself. I just looked on. It seems—" She stopped for a word, and found it. "It seems odd that Nero Wolfe should be starting an inquiry immediately after her death. Or did he start it before?"

"I couldn't say. The first I knew, he gave me this errand this morning. This noon."

"You don't know much, do you?"

"No, I just take orders."

"Of course you do know that Miss Yare committed suicide?"

I didn't get an answer in. Gallant, hitting the table with a palm, suddenly shouted at her, "Name of God! Must you? Send him away!"

"I'm sorry, Mr. Gallant," I told him. "I guess my time's up. If you'll tell me where to find your sister and Miss Thorne, that will—"

I stopped because his hand had darted to an ashtray, a big metal one that looked heavy, and since he wasn't smoking he was presumably going to let fly with it. Anita Prince beat him to it. With her left hand she got his wrist, and with her right she got the ashtray and moved it out of reach. It was very quick and deft. Then she spoke, to me. "Miss Gallant is not here. Miss Thorne is busy, but you can ask Mr. Drew downstairs. You had better go."

I went. In more favorable circumstances I might have spared another five minutes for a survey of the pin-ups, but not then, not if I had to dodge ashtrays.

In the hall, having pulled the door shut, the indicated procedure, indicated both by the situation and by Miss Prince's suggestion, was to take the elevator down and see Drew again, but a detective is supposed to have initiative. So when I heard a voice, female, floating out through an open door, I went on past the elevator, to the door, for a look. Not only did I see, I was seen, and a voice, anything but female, came at me.

"You. Huh?"

I could have kicked myself. While, as I said, my mission couldn't be called secret with five people on the list, certainly Wolfe had intended it to be private, and there was Sergeant Purley Stebbins of Homicide West, glaring at me.

"Sightseeing?" he asked. Purley's idea of humor is a little primitive. "The scene of the crime?"

I descended to his level. "Just morbid," I told him, crossing the sill. "Compulsion neurosis. Is this it?"

Evidently it was. The room was about the same size as Alec Gallant's, but while his had been dominated by women without clothes, this one ran to clothes without women. There were coats, suits, dresses, everything. They were on dummies, scattered around; on hangers, strung on a pole along a wall; and piled on a table. At my right one dummy, wearing a skirt, was bare from the waist up; she might have blushed if she had had a face to blush with. There was one exception: a well-made tan wool dress standing by a corner of a desk contained a woman—a very attractive specimen in mold and frame, and in movement she could have been music. Standing beside her was Carl Drew. Seated at the desk was Sergeant Purley Stebbins, with a paper in his hand and other papers on the desk. Also on the desk, at his left, was a telephone—the one, presumably, that Wolfe and I had heard hit the floor.

What I had stumbled into was obvious. Purley was examining the effects, including papers, probably the second time over, of Bianca Voss, deceased, under surveillance on behalf of Alec Gallant Incorporated.

"Actually," I said, advancing past the immodest dummy, "this is one homicide I have no finger in. I'm on a fishing trip." I moved my eyes. "Would you tell me, Mr. Drew, where I can find Miss Thorne?"

"Right here," the tan wool dress said. "I am Miss Thorne."

"I'm Archie Goodwin of Nero Wolfe's office. May I have a word with you?"

She exchanged glances with Carl Drew. Her glance told me that Drew had told her about me; and his, if I am half as bright as I ought to be, told me that if he was not on a more personal basis with her than he had been with Sarah Yare it wasn't his fault. If he wasn't he would like to be.

"Go ahead," Drew told her. "I'll stick around." She moved toward the door, and I was following when Purley pronounced my name, my last name. He has on occasion called me Archie, but not when I suddenly appeared, uninvited, when he was working on a homicide. I turned.

"Who are you fishing for?" he demanded.

"If I knew," I said, "I might tell you, but don't hold your breath." There was no point in trying to sugar him. The damage, if any, had been done the second he saw me. "See you in court."

Emmy Thorne led me down the hall to a door, the next one, and opened it. Walking, she could have been music at that, if her heels had had any purchase. She held the door for me to enter, shut it, went to a chair behind a desk, and sat. The room was less than half the size of the others and displayed neither women nor clothes.

"Sit down," she said. "What is this nonsense about letters from Sarah Yare?"

I took the chair at the end of her desk. "You know," I said, "my tie must be crooked or I've got a grease spot. Mr. Drew resented me, and Mr. Gallant was going to throw an ashtray at me. Now you. Why is it nonsense to ask a simple question politely and respectfully?"

"Maybe 'nonsense' isn't the word. Maybe I should have said 'gall.' What right have you to march in here and ask questions at all? Polite or not."

"None. It's not a right, it's a liberty. I have no right to ask you to have dinner with me this evening, which might not be a bad idea, but I'm at liberty to, and you're at liberty to tell me you'd rather dine at the automat with a baboon, only that wouldn't be very polite. Also when I ask if you have any letters from Sarah Yare you're at liberty to tell me to go climb a tree if you find the question ticklish. I might add that I would be at liberty to climb a pole instead of a tree. Have you any letters from Sarah Yare?"

She laughed. She had fine teeth. She stopped laughing abruptly. "Good Lord," she said, "I didn't think I would laugh for a year. This mess, what happened here yesterday, and then Sarah. No, I have no letters from her. You don't have to climb a tree." The laughter was all gone, and her gray eyes, straight at me, were cool and keen. "What else?"

Again I had to resist temptation. With Drew the temptation had been purely professional; with her it was only partly professional and only partly pure. Cramer had said she was in charge of contacts, and one more might be good for her.

Having resisted, I shook my head. "Nothing else, unless you know of something. For instance, if you know of anyone who might have letters."

"I don't." She regarded me. "Of course I'm curious, if you want to call it that. I was very fond of Sarah, and this coming after all her trouble, naturally I'm wondering why you came here. You say Nero Wolfe is making an inquiry?"

"Yes, he sent me. I don't know who his client is, but my guess would be that it's some friend of Miss Yare's." I stood up. "Someone else may be curious. Thank you, Miss Thorne. I'm glad I don't have to climb a tree."

She got up and offered a hand. "You might tell me who it is."

"I might if I knew." Her hand was cool and firm and I kept it for a second. "I'm sorry I interrupted you in there." That was absolutely true. "By the way, one more liberty: is Miss Gallant around?"

She said no and came with me to the hall and left me, heading for the scene of the crime. I went the other way, to the elevator. Down on the main floor the woman was there alone, at a table with a portfolio. Not at all like Macy's main floor. Emerging, I turned left, found a phone booth on Madison Avenue, dialed the number I knew best, got Fritz, and asked for Wolfe.

His voice came. "Yes, Archie?"

"It's full of fish. Swarming. Sarah Yare bought her clothes there for two years and they all loved her. I'm phoning to ask about Flora Gallant. I've seen all the others, but Flora isn't around. My guess is that she's at the DA's office. Do I stick until she comes?"

"No. Satisfactory."

"Any further instructions?"

"No. Come home."

4

In the office, after a late lunch of corned-beef hash with mushrooms, chicken livers, white wine, and grated cheese, which Fritz apologized for because he had had to keep it warm too long, I gave Wolfe a full report of the fishing trip, including all dialogue. When I had finished he nodded, took in air through his nose all the way down, and let it out through his mouth.

"Very well," he said, "that settles it. You will now go—"

"Just a minute," I cut in. "It doesn't settle it for me. It was bad enough up there, not knowing the score, and before I do any more going I want a little light. Why did you pick on Sarah Yare, and where did the phone book come in?"

"I have an errand for you."

"Yeah. Will it keep for ten minutes?"

"I suppose so."

"Then why?"

He leaned back. "As I told you this morning, I thought I might have been hoodwinked and I intended to find out. It was quite possible that that performance here yesterday—getting us on the phone just in time to hear a murder committed—was flummery. Indeed, it was more than possible. Must I expound that?"

"No. Even Cramer suspected it."

"So he did. But his theory that Bianca Voss had been killed earlier and that another woman, not the murderer, was there beside the corpse waiting for a phone call, was patently ridiculous. Must I expound that?"

"No, unless it was a lunatic. Anyone who would do that, even the murderer, with the chance that someone might come in any second, would be batty."

"Of course. But if she wasn't killed at the time we heard those sounds she must have been killed earlier, since you phoned almost immediately and sent someone to that room. Therefore the sounds didn't come from there. Miss Gallant did not dial that number. She dialed the number of some other person whom she had persuaded to perform that hocus-pocus."

He turned a hand over. "I had come to that conclusion, or call it surmise, before I went to bed last night, and I had found it intolerable. I will not be mistaken for a jackass. Reading the *Times* at breakfast this morning, the item about the death of Sarah Yare, my attention was caught by the fact that she had been an actress. An actress can act a part. Also she had been in distress. Also she had died. If she had been persuaded to act *that* part, it would be extremely convenient—for the one who persuaded her—for her to die before she learned that a murder had been committed and she had been an accessory after the fact. Certainly that was mere speculation, but it was not idle, and when I came down to the office I looked in the phone book to see if Sarah Yare was listed, found that she was, and dialed her number. Algonquin nine, one-eight-four-seven."

"What for? She was dead."

"I didn't lift the receiver. I merely dialed it, to hear it. Before doing so I strained my memory. I had to recall an experience that was filed somewhere in my brain, having reached it through my ears. As you know, I am trained to attend, to observe, and to register. So are you. That same experience is filed in your brain. Close your eyes and find it. Take your ears back to yesterday, when you were standing there, having surrendered your chair to Miss Gallant, and she was at the phone, dialing. Not the first number she dialed; you dialed that one yourself later. The second one, when, according to her, she was dialing the number of the direct line to Bianca Voss's office. Close your eyes and let your ears and brain take you back. Insist on it."

I did so. I got up and stood where I had stood while she was dialing, shut my eyes, and brought it back. In ten seconds I said, "Okay."

"Keep your eyes closed. I'm going to dial it. Compare."

The sound came of his dialing. I held my breath till the end, then opened my eyes and said positively, "No. Wrong. The first and third and fourth were wrong. The second might—"

"Close your eyes and try it again. This will be another number. Say when."

I shut my eyes and took five seconds. "Go."

The dialing sound came, the seven units. I opened my eyes. "That's more like it. That was it, anyway the first four. Beyond that I'm a little lost. But in that case—"

"Satisfactory. The first four were enough. The first number, which you rejected, as I did this morning, was Plaza two, nine-oh-two-two, the number of Bianca Voss's direct line according to the phone book —the number which Miss Gallant pretended to be dialing. The second was Sarah Yare's number, Algonquin nine, one-eight-four-seven."

"Well." I sat down. "I'll be damned."

"So it was still a plausible surmise, somewhat strengthened, but no more than that. If those people, especially Miss Gallant, could not be shown to have had some association with Sarah Yare, it was untenable. So I sent you to explore, and what you found promoted the surmise to an assumption, and a weighty one. What time is it?"

He would have had to twist his neck a whole quarter-turn to look at the wall clock, whereas I had only to lower my eyes to see my wrist. I obliged. "Five to four."

"Then instructions for your errand must be brief, and they can be. You will go to Sarah Yare's address on Thirteenth Street and look at her apartment. Her phone might have been discontinued since that book was issued. I need to know that the instrument is still there and operable before I proceed. If I intend to see that whoever tried to make a fool of me regrets it, I must take care not to make a fool of myself. Have I furnished the light you wanted?"

I told him it was at least a glimmer and departed on the errand. If you think I might have shown fuller appreciation of his dialing display, I beg to differ. There is no point in assuring a man that he is a genius when he already knows it. Besides, I was too busy being sore at me. I should have thought of it myself. I certainly should have caught on when I saw him with the phone book.

It was not my day. At the address of the late Sarah Yare on East Thirteenth Street I stubbed my toe again. One thing I think I'm good at is sizing up people, and I was dead wrong about the janitor of that old walk-up. He looked as if anything would go, so I merely told him to let me into Sarah Yare's apartment to check the telephone, and the bum insisted on seeing my credentials. So I misjudged him again. I offered him a sawbuck and told him I only wanted two minutes for a look at the phone with him at my elbow, and when he turned me down I showed him a twenty. He just sneered at it. By that time we were bitter enemies, and if I had showed him a C he would probably have spit on it. The upshot was that I went back home for an assortment of keys, returned, posted myself across the street, waited nearly an hour to be sure the enemy was not peeking, and broke and entered, technically.

I won't describe it; it was too painful. It was a hell of a dump for a Sarah Yare, even for a down-and-outer who had once been Sarah Yare. But the telephone was there, and it was working. I dialed to make sure, and got Fritz, and told him I just wanted to say hello and would be home in fifteen minutes, and he said that would please Mr. Wolfe because Inspector Cramer was there.

"No," I said.

"Yes," he said.

"When did he come?"

"Ten minutes ago. At six o'clock. Mr. Wolfe said to admit him and is with him in the office. Hurry home, Archie."

I did so.

I got a hackie who liked to take advantages, and it took a little less than the fifteen minutes. I ascended the stoop and let myself in, not banging the door, and tiptoed down the hall and stopped short of the office door, thinking to get a sniff of the atmosphere before entering. I got it. Wolfe's voice came.

". . . and I didn't say I have never known you to be wrong, Mr. Cramer. I said I have never known you to be more wrong. That is putting it charitably, under provocation. You have accused me of duplicity. Pfui!"

"Nuts." Cramer had worked up to his grittiest rasp. "I have accused you of nothing. I have merely stated facts. The time of the murder was supposed to be established by you and Goodwin hearing it on the phone. Is that a fact? Those five people all have alibis for that time. One of them was here with you. Is that a fact? When I put it to you yesterday that that phone business might have been faked, that she might have been killed earlier, all I got was a runaround. You could challenge it circumstantially but not intrinsically, whatever the hell that means. Is that a fact? So that if you and Goodwin got to the witness stand you might both swear that you were absolutely satisfied that you had heard her get it at exactly half past eleven. Is that a fact? Giving me to understand that you weren't interested, you weren't concerned, you had no—"

"No," Wolfe objected. "That was not broached."

"Nuts. You know damn well it was implied. You said you had never had any association with any of those people besides what was in your statement, so how could you be concerned, with Bianca Voss dead? Tell me this, did any of them approach you, directly or indirectly, between seven o'clock yesterday and noon today?"

"No."

"But—" He bore down on the 'but.' "*But* you sent Goodwin there today. He told Stebbins he was on a fishing trip. He talked with Drew, and Gallant, and Miss Prince, and he actually took Miss Thorne from under Stebbins' nose, took her out to talk with her. Is that a fact? And they all refuse to tell what Goodwin said to them or what they said to him. That *is* a fact. They say it was a private matter and had nothing to do with the murder of Bianca Voss. And when I come and ask you what you sent Goodwin there for, ask you plainly and politely, you say that you will— What are you laughing at?"

It wasn't a laugh, I just barely caught it, it was hardly even a chuckle, but all the same it could get under your skin. I knew.

"It escaped me, Mr. Cramer. Your choice of adverbs. Your conception of politeness. Pray continue."

"All right, I asked you. And you said you will probably be ready to tell me within twenty-four hours. And what I said was absolutely justified. I did not accuse you of duplicity. You know what I said."

"I do indeed, Mr. Cramer." I couldn't see Wolfe, but I knew he had upturned a palm. "This is childish and futile. If a connection is established between your murder investigation and the topic of Mr. Goodwin's talks with those people today, it will be only because I formed a conjecture and acted on it. I hope to establish it within twenty-four hours, and meanwhile it will do no harm to give you a hint. Have you any information on the death of a woman named Sarah Yare?"

"Some, yes. Presumed a suicide, but it's being checked. I have two men on it. What about it?"

"I suggest that you assign more men to it, good ones, and explore it thoroughly. I think we will both find it helpful. I may soon have a more concrete suggestion, but for the present that should serve. You know quite well—"

The doorbell rang. I about-faced and looked through the one-way glass panel of the front door. It wasn't a visitor on the stoop, it was a mob. All five of them were there: Gallant, his sister, Anita Prince, Emmy Thorne, and Carl Drew. Fritz appeared from the kitchen, saw me, and stopped. I got my notebook and pen from pockets and wrote:

That phone works. The five subjects are outside wanting in.

AG

I told Fritz to stand by, tore out the sheet, entered the office and crossed to Wolfe's desk, and handed it to him.

Wolfe read it, frowned at it for three seconds, turned his head and called, "Fritz!"

Fritz appeared at the door. "Yes, sir?"

"Put the chain-bolt on and tell those people they will be admitted shortly. Stay there."

"Yes, sir." Fritz went.

Wolfe looked at Cramer. "Mr. Gallant, his sister, Miss Prince, Miss Thorne, and Mr. Drew have arrived, uninvited and unexpected. You'll have to leave without being seen. In the front room until they have entered. I'll communicate with you later."

"Like hell I'll leave." Cramer was on his feet. "Like hell they're unexpected." He was moving, toward the hall, his intention plain—taking over as receptionist.

"Mr. Cramer!" It snapped at his back, turning him. "Would I lie so clumsily? If they had been expected would I have let you in? Would I have sat here bickering with you? Either you leave or I do. If you admit them you'll have them to yourself, and I wish you luck."

Cramer was glaring. "You think I'm going to sneak out and sit on your goddam stoop until you whistle?"

"That *would* be unseemly," Wolfe conceded. "Very well." He pointed at a picture on the wall to his left behind him—a pretty waterfall. "You know about that. You may take that station, but only if you engage not to disclose yourself unless you are invited. Unequivocally."

The waterfall covered a hole in the wall. On the other side, in a wing of the hall across from the kitchen, the hole was covered by nothing, and you could not only see through but also hear through. Cramer had used it once before, a couple of years ago.

Cramer stood, considering. Wolfe demanded, "Well? They're waiting. For you or for me?"

Cramer said, "Okay, we'll try it your way," turned and marched to the hall, and turned left.

Wolfe told me, "All right, Archie. Bring them in."

5

Lord Byron, alias Alec Gallant, and the red leather chair went together fine. He sat well back, unlike most people I have seen there. Usually they are either too mad or too upset. Any of the other four probably would have been; they looked it. They were on yellow chairs that I had moved up to make a row facing Wolfe, with Emmy Thorne nearest me, then Anita Prince, then Carl Drew, then Flora Gallant. That put Flora nearest her brother, which seemed appropriate.

Wolfe was turned to Gallant. "You ask me, sir, why I sent Mr. Goodwin to ask you people about Sarah Yare. Of course I'm under no compulsion to reply, and I'm not sure that I am prepared to. Instead, I may ask why his questions, certainly not provocative, so disturbed you. Apparently they have even impelled you to call on me in a body. Why?"

"Talk," Gallant said. *"Vent.* Wind." There was an ashtray on the little table at his elbow, but not a heavy one.

Anita Prince put in, "The police have insisted on knowing why he was there, what he wanted."

Wolfe nodded. "And you refused to say. Why?"

"Because," Emmy Thorne declared, "it was none of their business. And we have a right to know why you sent him, whether his questions were provocative or not." That girl was strong on rights.

Wolfe's eyes went from right to left and back again. "There's no point," he said, "in dragging this out. I'll grant your question priority and we'll go on from there. I sent Mr. Goodwin to see you because I suspected I had been gulled and wanted to find out; and further, because I had guessed that there was a connection between Sarah Yare, and her death, and the murder of Bianca Voss. By coming here en masse you have made that guess a conviction, if any doubt had remained."

"I knew it," Flora Gallant mumbled.

"*Tais-toi*," her brother commanded her. To Wolfe: "I'll tell you why we came here. We came for an explanation. We came—"

"For an understanding," Carl Drew cut in. "We're in trouble, all of us, you know that, and we need your help, and we're ready to pay for it. First we have to know what the connection is between Sarah Yare and what happened to Bianca Voss."

Wolfe shook his head. "You don't mean that. You mean you have to know whether I have established the connection, and if so, how. I'm willing to tell you, but before I do so I must clarify matters. There must be no misunderstanding. For instance, I understand that all of you thought yourselves gravely endangered by Miss Voss's presence. You, Miss Prince, you, Miss Thorne, and you, Mr. Drew —your dearest ambitions were threatened. Your future was committed to the success and glory of that enterprise, and you were convinced that Miss Voss was going to cheapen it, and perhaps destroy it. Do you challenge that?"

"Of course not." Emmy Thorne was scornful. "Everybody knew it."

"Then that's understood. That applies equally to you, Miss Gallant, but with special emphasis. You also had a more intimate concern, for your brother. You told me so. As for you, Mr. Gallant, you are not a man to truckle, yet you let that woman prevail. Presumably you were under severe constraint. Were you?"

Gallant opened his mouth and closed it. He looked at his sister, returned to Wolfe, and again opened his mouth and closed it. He was under constraint now, no doubt about that.

He forced it out. "I was under her heel." He clamped his jaw. He unclamped it. "The police know. They found out enough, and I have told them the rest. She was a bad woman. I met her in France, during the war. We were in the Resistance together when I married her. Only afterward I learned that she was *perfide*. She had been a traitor to France—I couldn't prove it, but I knew it. I left her and changed my name and came to America—and then last year she found me and made demands. I was under her heel."

Wolfe grunted. "That won't do, Mr. Gallant. I doubt if it has satisfied the police, and it certainly doesn't satisfy me. In that situation you might have killed her, but surely you wouldn't have let her take charge of your business and your life. What else was there?"

"Nothing. Nothing!"

"Pfui. Of course there was. And if the investigation is prolonged the police will discover it. I advise you to disclose it and let me get on and settle this affair. Didn't her death remove her heel?"

"Yes. Thank God, it did." Gallant hit the arms of the chair with his palms. "With her gone there is no evidence to fear. She had two brothers, and they, like her, were traitors, and I killed them. I would have killed her too, but she escaped me. During the war it would have been merely an episode, but it was later, much later, when I found out about them, and by then it was a crime. With her evidence I was an *assassin,* and I was doomed. Now she is gone, thank God, but I did not kill her. You know I did not. At half past eleven yesterday morning I was in my workshop with Miss Prince and many others, and you can swear that she was killed at that moment. That is why we came to see you, to arrange to pay—"

"Hold it, Alec." Anita Prince headed him off. "Mr. Wolfe wants to clarify matters. Let him."

"The cat's head is out," Wolfe told her, "but I had already heard it scratch. Let's get on. I cannot swear that Bianca Voss was killed 'at that moment.' On the contrary, I'm sure she wasn't, for a variety of reasons. There are such minor ones as the extraordinary billingsgate she spat at me on the phone, quite gratuitous; and her calling me a gob of fat. A woman who still spoke the language with so marked an accent would not have the word 'gob' so ready, and probably wouldn't have it at all."

He waved "gob" away. "But the major reasons are more cogent. In the first place, it was too pat. Since the complexities of nature permit a myriad of coincidences we cannot reject one offhand, but we can discriminate. That one—that the attack had come just at the moment when Miss Gallant had got Mr. Goodwin and me on the phone with her—was highly suspect. Besides, it was indiscreet to strike just then. Why not wait until she had hung up? Whoever was talking with her would certainly hear the sounds and take alarm. As I told Mr. Cramer, it was open to challenge circumstantially, though not intrinsically. However, there was another challenge, on surer ground. Miss Gallant did not dial Plaza two, nine-oh-two-two, Miss Voss's number, as she pretended. She dialed Algonquin nine, one-eight-four-seven, Sarah Yare's number."

A noise, a sort of low growl, came from the waterfall. I was farthest away, and I heard it distinctly, so it must have reached their ears too, but Wolfe's last words had so riveted their attention that it didn't register.

It did with Wolfe, and he added hastily, "I didn't know that yesterday. I became certain of it only after you rang my doorbell, when Mr. Goodwin handed me this note." He tapped it, there on his desk. "Its first words are 'That phone works.' I had sent him to learn if Sarah Yare's phone was in operation. Obviously, Miss Gallant had arranged with Miss Yare to impersonate Bianca Voss, and it is a reasonable—"

"Wait a minute." Gallant had come forward in the red leather chair. "You can't prove that."

"Directly, no. Inferentially, yes."

"And how do you know she dialed Sarah Yare's number? You weren't where you could see the dial, and neither was Goodwin."

Wolfe nodded. "Evidently you have discussed it with her. You're quite right, Mr. Gallant; we couldn't see the dial. Nevertheless, we can supply evidence, and we think it will be persuasive. I am not—"

"What kind of evidence?"

"That's no good, Alec." It was Emmy Thorne, the contact girl. "You can't push Nero Wolfe. He has his teeth in it, you can see that. You know what we decided."

"I'm not sure," Anita Prince objected, "that we decided right."

"I am. Carl?"

"Yes." Drew was chewing his lip. "I think so. Yes."

"Flora? It's up to you."

"I guess so." Flora's voice was cracked, and she tried again. "I guess so." A little better.

Emmy nodded. "Go ahead, Alec. You can't push him."

"My God." Gallant looked at his sister, and back at Wolfe. "All right. We will pay you to help us. *I* will pay you. My sister is innocent and she must not suffer. It would be an offense against nature, against God Himself. She has told me all about it, and she was stupid, but she is innocent. She did arrange with Sarah Yare, as you said, but only to move you. She had read much about you and had a great opinion of your abilities. She was desperate about Bianca Voss. She knew you demanded high fees, much beyond her resources, so she conceived a plan. She would persuade you to talk with Bianca Voss on the phone, and she would get Sarah instead, and Sarah would abuse you with such violence that you would be offended and resent it, and you would be moved to act against Bianca Voss. It was stupid, yes, very stupid, but it was not criminal."

Wolfe's eyes, at him, were half closed. "And you want to pay me to help her."

"Yes. When I told her you had sent your man to inquire about Sarah Yare I saw she was frightened and asked her why, and she told me. I consulted the others, and it was apparent that you knew something, and that was dangerous. We decided to come and ask you to help. My sister must not suffer."

Wolfe's eyes moved. "Miss Gallant. You heard your brother. Did he quote you correctly?"

"Yes!" That time it was too loud.

"You did those things? As he related them?"

"Yes!"

Wolfe returned to Gallant. "I agree with you, sir, that your sister was stupid, but you are not the one to proclaim it. You say that she arranged with Sarah Yare to abuse me on the phone, but Miss Yare didn't stop at that. She ended by making noises indicating that she had been violently attacked, and jerked the phone off onto the floor, and made other noises, and then hung up the phone and cut the connection. Was that on her own initiative? Her own idea? Your sister's stupidity can bow to yours if you expected me to overlook that point—or worse, if you missed it yourself."

"I am not stupid, Mr. Wolfe."

"Then you are devious beyond my experience."

"Devious?"

"*Rusé. Subtil.*"

"No. I am not." Gallant clamped his jaw. He released it. "*Bien.* Suppose, only to suppose, she arranged that too, that comedy. Suppose even that she killed Bianca Voss. Was that a crime? No; it was justice; it was the hand of God. Bianca Voss was an evil woman. She was *vilaine.* Are you so virtuous that you must crucify my sister? Are you a paragon? For she is in your hands, at your mercy. You know about Sarah Yare, but the police do not. You know she dialed that number, but the police do not, and they will not unless you tell them. By your word it can be that my sister was here with you at the time that Bianca Voss was killed. As I have said, I will pay you. It will be a great service from you, and it deserves payment. I will trust you. I will pay you now."

Wolfe grunted. "That was quite a speech."

"It was not a speech. I do not make speeches. It was an appeal to your charity. From my heart."

"And to my cupidity." Wolfe shook his head. "No. I am not a paragon. I am not even a steward of the law. But you have ignored two important factors: one, my self-esteem. Even if Bianca Voss deserved to die, I will not permit a murderer to take me for a simpleton. Two, another woman died too. Was Sarah Yare also evil? Was she *vilaine?*"

"But she—Sarah killed herself!"

"No. I don't believe it. That's another coincidence I reject. Granted that she may have been wretched enough for that extreme, why did she choose that particular moment? Again too pat. According to the published account, she died between ten o'clock yesterday morning and two in the afternoon, but I can narrow it a little. Since she spoke with me on the phone at eleven-thirty, she died between that hour and two o'clock. I believe that the person who killed Bianca Voss at some time prior to eleven-thirty, and arranged with Sarah Yare to enact that comedy, as you call it, went to Sarah Yare's apartment later and killed her. Indeed, prudence demanded it. So you ask too much of my charity. If only Bianca Voss had died—"

"No!" Gallant exploded. "Impossible! Totally impossible! My sister loved Sarah! She killed her? Insane!"

"But you believe she killed Bianca Voss. You came here believing that. That was stupid too. She didn't."

Gallant gawked at him. Lord Byron shouldn't gawk, but he did. So did the others. Also they made noises. Carl Drew demanded, "Didn't? You say she *didn't?*" Emmy Thorne asked coolly, "What's this, Mr. Wolfe? A game?"

"No, madam, not a game. Nor a comedy—Mr. Gallant's word. As a man I know said yesterday, murder is no joke." Wolfe's eyes went to Flora. "There was much against you, Miss Gallant, especially the fact that you dialed that other number before you dialed Sarah Yare's, and asked someone you called Doris if Miss Voss was around. Are you too rattled to remember that?"

"No." She was clutching the rim of her bag with both hands. "I remember."

"Of course the reason for it was obvious, if you had killed Bianca Voss before you came here; you had to know that the body had not been found before you proceeded with your stratagem. Since you had *not* killed Bianca Voss, why did you make that call?"

"I wanted to make sure that she hadn't gone out. That she was there in her office. You might call her again after I left and find out she hadn't been there. I didn't care if you called her and she denied she had talked to you like that. I thought you would think she was lying. I suppose that was stupid." Her mouth worked. "How did you know I didn't kill her?"

"You told me. You showed me. If you had devised that elaborate humbug, certainly you would have decided how to act at the moment of crisis. You would have decided to be alarmed, and shocked, and even perhaps a little dazed. But it wasn't like that. You were utterly stunned with bewilderment. When Mr. Goodwin told us what Mr. Drew had said, what did you say? You said, 'But how—' And repeated it, 'But how—' If you had killed Bianca Voss you would have had to be a master dramatist to write such a line, and an actress of genius to deliver it as you did; and you are neither."

Wolfe waved it away. "But that was for me. For others, for a judge and jury, I must do better, and think I can. If you are innocent, someone else is guilty. Someone else learned of the arrangement you had made with Sarah Yare, either from you or from her, and persuaded her to add a dramatic climax. Someone else killed Bianca Voss and then established an invulnerable alibi for the crucial period. Someone else had secured the required amount of cyanide—it doesn't take much. Someone else, having established the alibi, went to Sarah Yare's apartment and poisoned her glass of whisky. That was done before two o'clock, and that should make it simple. Indeed, it *has* made it simple. Shortly before you came I learned from Mr. Cramer of the police that you arrived at your brother's place yesterday a few minutes after noon. Since you left here at a quarter of twelve, you hadn't had time to go first to Thirteenth Street and dispose of Sarah Yare; and you were continuously under the eyes of policemen the rest of the afternoon. That is correct?"

"Yes." Flora's eyes were wet but she hadn't used a handkerchief. "I wanted to go and see what had happened to Sarah, but I was afraid—I didn't know—"

"It's a good thing you didn't, madam. I also learned from Mr. Cramer that you, Mr. Gallant, you, Mr. Drew, and you, Miss Prince, were also constantly under surveillance, for hours, from the time the police arrived. That leaves you, Miss Thorne." His eyes were narrowed at her. "You were with three men in an office on Forty-sixth Street from eleven-twenty until a quarter to twelve. You arrived at Mr. Gallant's place, and found the police there, shortly before three o'clock. You may be able to account for the interim satisfactorily. Do you want to try?"

"I don't have to try." Emmy Thorne's gray eyes were not as cool and keen as they had been when she had told me I didn't have to climb a tree. She had to blink to keep them at Wolfe. "So it *is* a game."

"Not one you'll enjoy, I fear. Nor will I; I'm out of it now. To disclose your acquisition of the cyanide you would need for Sarah Yare; to show that you entered Bianca Voss's room yesterday morning, or could have, before you left for your business appointment; to find evidence of your visit to Thirteenth Street after your business appointment; to decide which homicide you will be put on trial for— all that is for others. You must see now that it was a mistake— *Archie!*"

I was up and moving, but halted. Gallant, out of his chair and advancing, wasn't going to touch her. His fists were doubled, but not to swing; they were pressed against his chest. He stopped square in front of her and commanded, "Look at me, Emmy."

To do so she would have had to move her head, tilt it back, and she moved nothing.

"I have loved you," he said. "Did you kill Sarah?"

Her lips moved but no sound came.

His fists opened for his fingers to spread on his chest. "So you heard us that day, and you knew I couldn't marry you because I was married to her, and you killed her. That I can understand, for I loved you. But that you killed Sarah, no. No! And even that is not the worst! Today, when I told you and the others what Flora had told me, you accepted it, you allowed us to accept it, that she had killed Bianca. You would have let her suffer for it. Look at me! You would have let my sister—"

Flora was there, tugging at his sleeve, sputtering at him, "You love her, Alec, don't hurt her now, don't—"

Gallant jerked loose, backed up, folded his arms, and breathed; and Emmy Thorne moved. She came up out of her chair, stood rigid long enough to give Gallant a straight, hard look, shook her head, spun away from him, and headed for the door, brushing against Flora. Her route took her past Anita Prince, who tilted her head back to look up at her, and past Carl Drew, who had to pull his feet back not to trip her.

I didn't budge, thinking I wasn't needed, and I was right. In movement she might have been music, but if so, the music got stopped. As she made the hall and turned toward the front a hand gripped her arm—a hand that had had plenty of practice gripping arms.

"Take it easy, Miss Thorne," Cramer said. "We'll have to have a talk."

"Grand Dieu," Gallant groaned, and covered his face with his hands.

IS BETSEY BLAKE STILL ALIVE?

by Robert Bloch

In April, Steve rented a little cottage down at the beach. Strictly speaking, it wasn't "down" at all; it stood right on the edge of a steep cliff, and you had to walk almost a quarter of a mile until you got to the nearest steps. But Steve didn't care. He hadn't come to the beach to go swimming.

He'd holed up here for a dual purpose. He wanted to lick his wounds and he wanted to write. Things hadn't gone too well for Steve during the past year—six weeks as a junior writer at one of the major studios, but no contract, and two originals picked up by small independent producers on option, only both options had lapsed without anybody getting excited. So Steve had broken with his agent after one of those standard "To hell with Hollywood!" routines and retreated to the beach. Sometimes he thought he was going to write the Great American Novel. At other times, when the fog rolled in, he'd stand at the window and gaze down at the water, thinking how easy it would be to jump.

Then he met Jimmy Powers, and things got worse.

Jimmy Powers had a cottage right down the line from the one Steve had rented. He came rolling up four or five nights a week in a big new Buick convertible. He had a nice collection of Italian silk suits, but when he was at the beach he preferred to lounge around in matching shorts-and-shirts outfits, all of which had his initials monogrammed on the pockets. Often he came for the weekend, hauling a case of champagne in the trunk of the car. On such occasions Jimmy was usually accompanied by a stock-contract girl from the studio where he was employed as a public relations man.

The thing that got Steve down was the fact that Jimmy Powers (Buick, silk suits, monogrammed shirts, champagne and starlets) was only twenty-three.

"How does he do it?" Steve asked himself over and over. "The guy's got nothing on the ball. He can't write for sour apples. He's not even a good front man. It isn't charm, or personality, or good looks, or anything like that. What's his secret?"

But Jimmy Powers never talked about his work at the studio; and whenever Steve brought up the subject, he'd switch to another topic. But one evening, when both of them had half a load on, Steve tried again.

"How long you had this job, Jimmy?"

This time it worked.

"Almost three years."

"You mean you started when you were twenty? Just walked into one of the biggest outfits in the business and snagged a public relations job?"

"That's right."

"No previous experience? And right away they let you do promotion puffs on their top stars?"

"That's the way the ball bounced."

"I don't get it." Steve stared at him. "How does a guy fall into something like that?"

"Oh, it isn't so much, really," Jimmy told him. "Only three bills a week."

"*Only* three bills." Steve grunted. "For a kid like you? I've never come close to a steady three hundred a week, and I've knocked around the Industry for years. What gives, Jimmy? Level with me. Do you know where the body is buried?"

"Something like that," Jimmy answered. He gave Steve a kind of funny look and changed the subject, fast.

After that evening, Jimmy Powers wasn't very friendly any more. There were no further invitations to the handsomely furnished cottage. Then for about three weeks Jimmy stopped coming down to the beach altogether. By this time Steve was actually in production, grinding away at a book.

He was hard at it that evening in June when Jimmy Powers knocked on his door.

"Hi, sweetheart," he said. "Mind if I barge in?"

At first Steve thought Jimmy was drunk, but a double-take convinced him that the guy was just terribly excited. Powers paced up and down, snapping his fingers like a cornball juvenile in an expectant-father routine.

"Still writing the Great American Novel, huh?" Jimmy said. "Come off it, chum. Maybe I can steer you onto some real moola."

"Like three bills a week?" Steve asked.

"Peanuts. I'm talking about big money. The minute I hit this angle I thought of you."

"Very kind, I'm sure. What do I have to do—help you stick up the Bank of America?"

Jimmy ignored the gag. "You know where I just come from? M.P.'s office. That's right—for the last five hours, solid, I've been sitting in Mr. Big's office preaching the Word. Ended up with cart blank to handle the whole deal. Any way I want."

"What deal?"

Jimmy sat down then, and when he spoke again his voice was softer.

"You know what happened to Betsey Blake?" he asked.

Steve nodded. He knew what had happened to Betsey Blake, all right. Every man, woman, and child in the United States had been bombarded for the past two weeks with news reports about the Betsey Blake tragedy.

It had been one of those freak accidents. Betsey Blake, the Screen's Blonde Baby, the one and only Miss Mystery, was piloting her speedboat just outside Catalina Channel around twilight on the evening of June 2nd. According to the reports, she was preparing to enter the annual racing event the following Sunday, to try for her fourth straight win. Nobody knew just what had happened because there were no witnesses, but apparently her speedboat rammed into another boat head-on, killing a Mr. Louis Fryer of Pasadena. And herself.

Both boats had gone down immediately, and divers were still making half-hearted efforts to recover them from the deep water outside the choppy channel when, two days later, Fryer's body was washed up on a lonely beach. The next day Betsey Blake's corpse made a farewell appearance in the same place.

Betsey's identification took another few days to be established definitely enough to satisfy authorities, but there was no doubt about it. The Blonde Baby was no more.

It was a big story, because The Blonde Baby had been up there for a long time. The "Miss Mystery" tag had been pinned on her when she first rose to prominence in pictures, and she'd always lived up to it, taking unusual care to conceal her private life, which rumor had it was just one lurid escapade after another.

So the papers had had a field day digging up her past. They managed to ring in the name of virtually every important male star of the past twenty years. Some of the scandal sheets hinted that they could also mention the names of most of the studio set-dressers, gaffers, and truck-drivers over the same period.

"What happened?" Steve asked Powers. "Did your boss have a heart attack?"

Jimmy nodded. "Just about. Her death puts us on a real spot. The Friday before, she'd just finished her part in *Splendor*. Studio wrapped the picture up, four million bucks' worth of Technicolor, Super-Cinemascope, three top stars—the works. It's all finished, no more retakes, the sets are struck, the film is in the can. And then Betsey kicks off."

"So?"

"So? M.P. is sitting there with a very cold turkey. Sure, if he could push *Splendor* out to the exhibitors right away, maybe he could capitalize on the headlines a little. But this is our biggest picture for the year. We already set it up for late Fall release, around November, to catch the holiday trade and make a bid for the Awards. You begin to see the grief? Comes November, and Betsey Blake will be dead six months. By that time all the excitement is over. Who's going to plunk down a dollar-twenty to see somebody who's putting out free lunch to the worms? M.P. has to gross at least five million to break even. How's he going to do it? So for the past two weeks he's been nursing a real headache. Takes a lot of aspirin to cure a headache like that."

"But where do you come in?"

"With the U.S. Marines," Jimmy said. "Here M.P. and all the big wheels have been batting their brains out trying to come up with an angle—naturally, they had to junk the whole publicity campaign—and all they've got for their pains is sweat. Well, I got busy, and today I walked into M.P.'s office and laid five million potatoes right in his lap—maybe seven or eight."

"You found a solution?" Steve asked.

"Damned right I found a solution! It was sitting there staring them in the face all the time. I say it—right on M.P.'s wall. I walked over and pointed to the picture. That's all, brother."

"Picture on the wall?" Steve said. "Whose picture?"

Jimmy made with the dramatic pause.

"Valentino."

"Come again?"

"Rudolph Valentino. You've heard of him?"

"Sure I've heard of him."

"Yeah. Well, chances are you wouldn't have if some bright boy hadn't pulled the same stunt back in '26."

"What stunt?"

"Valentino went up like a skyrocket, but he was coming down fast. Then, just when he'd finished *The Son of the Sheik*—bingo! he gets appendicitis or something and croaks. So there the studio sits —with a dead star and a dead flicker. That's when some genius pulled a rabbit out of the hat."

Jimmy Powers snapped his fingers again. "They staged the most sensational funeral you ever saw. Poured out the puffs about the passing of the screen's Greatest Lover. Filled the newspapers, jammed the magazines, flooded the country with Valentino. Made out that all the dames who used to flip over him on the screen were soaking their handkerchiefs now that he was gone. By the time his picture was released they had everybody so hot to see it there was no holding them. The picture and the re-releases made so much dough that even the Valentino estate paid its debts and showed a profit. How did they do it? Women weeping at the grave, rumors cropping up that Rudy was still alive—publicity. Publicity—with a capital P."

Jimmy Powers grinned. "Well, I guess you get my angle. M.P. sure latched onto it! And I pointed out to him that we had an even better deal going for us. Because we had this Miss Mystery gimmick to play with, and a real mysterious death. We can even start a story that Betsey Blake is still alive—stuff like that."

"But she was positively identified—"

"I know, I know! So was Booth, and Mata Hari, and this Anasthesia dame, or whatever her name was, over in Russia. But the suckers go for that angle. *Is Betsey Blake Still Alive?* We plant articles in all the rags. Maybe even pony up some loot to get out special one-shots. *The Betsey Blake Magazine.* You know, like they did on this kid Presley, and a lot of others. Hire some kids to start Betsey Blake fan clubs. Get some of the high-priced talent to write sob stuff for the women's magazines. Like how Betsey Blake was a symbol of American girlhood."

"But she wasn't a symbol," Steve objected. "And she wasn't exactly a girl, either."

"Sure, sure, she was past forty. And I happen to know M.P. was going to axe her the minute her contract ran out. But she was well-preserved, you got to admit that, and a lot of the kids still went for her. We can build it up—yes sir, man, we can build it up!"

No doubt about it, Jimmy Powers was very excited. "And think of what we can do with her past! Nobody has dope on her real name, or just how she got started in show biz back in the Thirties. Wait'll we get to work on *The Real Betsey Blake* and *The Betsey Blake Nobody Knows*."

The excitement was contagious. In spite of himself Steve found himself saying, "Say, that's a possibility, isn't it? You might be able to uncover all sorts of things. Didn't I once hear a rumor that she'd had an illegitimate child by some producer? And that she was once married to—"

Jimmy Powers shook his head.

"No, that isn't the kind of stuff we want at all! You hear that stuff about everybody in the Industry. I'm giving strict orders to lay off any investigation, get me? We'll cook up our own stories. Make any kind of a past we want. Maybe get her mixed up with some of these mystic cults, you know what I mean. Hint foul play, too. Oh, we'll have a ball!"

"We? I thought this was just your baby."

"It is—M.P. gave me the green light all the way. But it's a big job, Steve. That's why I thought of you, sweetheart. You'd be a natural on this kind of promotion—doing some of the high-class stuff—like, say, for those women's rags I mentioned. So how's about it, Stevie-burger? How'd you like to be a great big legend-maker?"

Steve sat there for a moment without opening his mouth. And when finally he did open it, he had no idea what was going to come out.

"You knew Betsey Blake when she was alive?" he asked.

"Of course I did. Handled most of her promotion—Stalzbuck was in charge, really, but I did a lot of the work. I thought you knew that."

"I wasn't sure." Steve hesitated. "What kind of person was she, really?"

Jimmy Powers shrugged. "An oddball. What difference does it make?"

"Was she friendly? Would you say she was a kind person?"

"In a way. Yes, she was. So why the District Attorney bit?"

"Because she's dead, Jimmy. Dead and gone, in a tragic accident. And the dead should be allowed to rest in peace. You can't just go and pitch a sideshow over her grave."

"Who says I can't?"

It was Steve's turn to shrug. "All right. I suppose you can. And nothing I say is going to stop you, is it?"

"Damned right it won't!"

Steve nodded. "Then go ahead. But, in the classic phrase, include me out. And thanks all the same. I can't be a ghoul."

Jimmy stared at him. "So I'm a ghoul, huh?" he muttered. "Well, I've got news for you. I'm a ghoul and you're a fool. A damned fool."

"Knock it off, please."

"Okay." Jimmy paused at the door. "You were always asking me what it takes to get along in this racket. Well, Stevie, it takes guts, that's what it takes. Guts to see your big opportunity when it comes along, and guts to follow through. Guts that you haven't got, Stevie-boy."

"Maybe I was brought up differently."

Jimmy laughed harshly. "You can say that again! Brother, if you only knew *how* differently! I got the perfect training for this particular job, believe me. And just you watch how I make good on it."

Then he was gone, and Steve tried to go back to work.

Jimmy stayed away from the beach for a long time—right through the height of the summer season. Steve figured he was working on his promotion, but there was no word from him.

Then the news started trickling in. The trickle became a stream, the stream became a flood.

The Betsey Blake legend burst upon the American public during the latter part of August. By September the first magazines hit the stands, carrying their planted stories. By October the specials were out, the fan clubs were formed, and the television people were combing their files for old kinescopes of Betsey Blake's few live shows.

The whole thing was just as Jimmy Powers had outlined it, only more so. *I Was Betsey Blake's Last Date* vied for attention with *The Loves of Betsey*. And there was *The Truth About—,* and *The Real—,* and *What They Don't Dare Print About—,* and a hundred others. The studio, meanwhile, was doing an indefatigable job tying in *Splendor.*

Betsey Blake in her last and greatest performance! The greatest actress of the American screen!

On a different level there was the *Betsey Blake—The Woman Nobody Knew* approach. In this series it was possible to learn that Betsey Blake had herself been the daughter of a reigning celebrity of the silent screen, or of royal European blood, or merely a youngster out of Hollywood High School who deliberately set out to fashion a career for herself.

There were as many, and as conflicting, details as to her love life. And there was much speculation about why she had maintained such an air of secrecy concerning her personal affairs. She was a devout churchgoer, she was a freethinker, she was a secret Satanist, she dabbled in astrology, she attended Voodoo ceremonies in Haiti, she was really an old woman who had discovered the secret of eternal youth. She was secretly an intellectual and her lovers included most of the celebrated literary figures of our generation; she was actually a shy, sensitive person who couldn't face her own image on the screen; she was a devoted student of the drama who had planned to retire from the screen and establish her own repertory theater. She loved children and wanted to adopt half a dozen, she had been jilted as a girl and still cherished the memory of her one real love, she was on the verge of a nervous breakdown and spent all her money on psychiatrists.

All this, and much more, could be learned by any reader during early fall.

But Jimmy Powers had prophesied correctly when he said that the mystery angle would prove to be the most attractive part of the legend. There was the *Betsey Blake Did Not Die!* theory, which played up the "strange circumstances" surrounding the case, the "unexplained disappearance" of the two boats, the "reluctance" of the studio to exhibit the body in a public funeral. This angle fastened on every conceivable circumstance, real or rumored, which could be offered as "proof."

As November approached, the volume and tempo of the articles neared a crescendo. For now the Betsey Blake legend was public property, and the fake fan clubs had given way to real fan clubs. Some of the scandal rags were printing the "inside story" and the "real lowdown"—Betsey Blake had been a tramp, she had been an alcoholic, she had started out posing for "art studies" and worse—but none of these allegations affected the legend. Rather, they served to strengthen it. To her growing army of devotees came the teen-agers, and that was the final victory. Everyone from eight to eighty was breathlessly awaiting the advent of *Splendor* on their local screens.

It was early one night in November, as Steve sat typing the second draft of his novel, that Jimmy Powers reappeared.

Once again he hailed Steve from the doorway, and once again Steve thought he might be drunk.

This time, however, he had more grounds for his suspicion, because as Jimmy entered the room he brought an alcoholic aura with him.

"How ya doing, boy?" he shouted.

Steve started to tell him, but Powers wasn't really listening.

"Guess I don't have to tell you how I'm doing," he exclaimed. "We open nation-wide next week. Nation-wide, get me? No previews, no test spots, no New York first run—just solid bookings straight across the board. Every key city, and the highest percentage of the gross we ever sold a picture for! And who did it, Stevie-burger? Me, that's who."

Steve lit a cigarette to avoid having to make any comment.

"And don't think the Industry doesn't know it! Man, are the offers pouring in. Of course, M.P.'s a smart old buzzard—he's not going to let me get away from him. Two grand a week, five years noncancellable, and that's not all. When the pic opens I get a bonus. Fifty Gs under the table. You imagine that? Fifty Gs, cash, that nobody will ever know about. No taxes, nothing. Let me tell you, M.P. knows how to make a gesture. Of course, it's worth it to him. I been sweating blood on this thing, Stevie. Nobody will ever know the throats I had to cut—"

"Don't tell me," Steve said.

"Still playing it simon-pure, huh? Well, that's okay by me, no hard feelings. I just wanted you to know what you missed out on, sweetheart. This was the biggest coup of the century."

"You can say that again."

Both Jimmy Powers and Steve stared at the woman in the doorway. She was short, brown-haired, and plump enough to fill out the rather bedraggled slacks-and-sweater combination she was wearing. Her feet were bare, and she had some difficulty balancing on them, because she was obviously tight as a tick.

"What the hell—?" Jimmy began as she weaved toward him with a smirk.

"Saw you leave your shack just as I came along," she said. "So I just sneaked in there by myself and had a little drinkie. I could hear you talking over here, so I thought why not come over and join the party?"

"Mind telling me who you are?" Steve asked, a premonition growing in him.

The woman grinned and pointed at Jimmy Powers. "Ask him," she said.

Jimmy Powers just stood there, his face going from red to white. "No," he said. "No, it isn't—it can't be—"

"The hell it isn't," said the woman. "You know better than to try and get away with that."

"But what happened? Where have you been?"

"Took myself a little trip." The woman giggled. "It's kind of a long sh-story." She turned to Steve. "Got anything to drink?"

Before Steve could answer, Jimmy stepped forward. "You've had enough," he said. "Tell your story and make it fast."

"All right, all right, hold your horses." The woman flopped into an armchair and for a moment stared at the floor.

"I saw the papers, of course," she said. "They got it all wrong."

"Then why didn't you do something?" Jimmy growled.

"Because I was on a trip, remember? I mean I saw them all right, but they were a couple of months old." She paused. "You going to let me tell this my way?"

"Go ahead."

"Sure, I cracked into this other boat, like they said. Damn thing running without a light, motor throttled down so's I never heard a thing. This Louis Fryer was on board, like they said—I knew old Louie from 'way back. What the papers didn't know, of course, is that he wasn't alone. He must have picked up some tramp off the beach, some blonde floozy hanging around the Yacht Club. Anyway, when we hit she got it, too. At least that's the way it figures. She got it and when her body came up they identified her as me."

"And what happened to—?"

"I'm coming to that part. I passed out, I guess. But I had sense enough to hang onto the boat."

"The boat went down. They never found it."

"The boat didn't go down. And the reason they never found it was that it got picked up that night. With me with it. Little Mexican freighter spotted us just outside the channel and hauled us on board. Me and the boat. I was out cold—guess I had a concussion. When I came to, I was on my way to Chile."

"Chile?"

The woman nodded. "Sure, Chile. That's in South America, you know? Valparaiso, Santiago—we went everywhere. Those little wildcat freighters, they take their own good-natured time when they make a trip. Besides, I sold the boat down there for a good price. Made enough to pay my way and plenty left over for tequila. Captain was a good friend of mine. Whole crew, for that matter. You see, they didn't ever catch on to who I was. All they could see was a blonde. At least, after I got another bottle of rinse and touched it up a bit." The woman gestured toward her tousled hair. "You know how they flip for a blonde." She giggled again.

Jimmy Powers stood up. "You mean to tell me you've spent the last five months helling around on a freighter with a bunch of Mex greasemonkeys?" he shouted.

"And why not? First real vacation I've had in years. And believe me, it was one long party. When I found out in Santiago what the score was, I thought the hell with it, let 'em suffer. This was my big chance to get off the hook for a while and live a little. So I lived. But we ran out of cash, the Captain and I, so when we docked at Long Beach today I came ashore. I knew M.P. would blow his stack if I walked in on him cold. I figured I'd see you first. Maybe we can cook up a publicity angle together, so when we hit M.P. he won't go through the roof."

The woman turned to Steve. "You sure you haven't got a drinkie?" she asked. "Jeez, look at my hair. Got to get to a beauty parlor right away. Nobody'd recognize me. Isn't that right, pal? Go ahead, admit it —you didn't recognize me either at first, did you? Gained fifteen pounds, hair grown out. And next week the picture opens—"

"That's right," Jimmy Powers said. "Next week the picture opens."

The woman stood up, swaying. "One thing I got to hand you," she said. "You did a wonderful promotion job. Even in Chile they knew all about it. And when I hit town today, first thing I did was hike over to the magazine racks. There I am, all over the place. A wonnerful job."

"Yeah," said Jimmy.

"Well, don't just stand there. Now you gotta do even a more wonnerful job. Because I'm back. That's the real topper, isn't it? Wait until this one hits the good old public!"

"Yeah," said Jimmy.

"Of course, this time I'll be around to help you. I got a line all cooked up. The Captain, he won't do any talking—he's shoving off again for Mexico tomorrow morning. We can handle it any way we like. Hah, I can just see the look on the face of old Louie Fryer's wife when she finds out he had a blonde on board! But it's a *wonnerful* story. It'll be a big needle for the picture."

"Yeah," said Jimmy.

She turned away and faced Steve again. "How about that drinkie, lover-boy?"

"I'll give you a drink," Jimmy Powers said. "Over at my place. Come along now."

"Betcha."

He placed his arm around the woman and guided her toward the door. Then he paused and looked at Steve. "Stick around, will you?" he said. "I want to talk to you later."

Steve nodded.

He saw them disappear into Jimmy's cabin. It was the only other cottage with lights on all along the beach—November is off-season.

He could even have listened and caught some of their conversation. But Steve couldn't concentrate. He was too busy calling himself names.

Was this the woman he'd been too noble to help turn into a legend? Was her reputation worth protecting at the sacrifice of his own future? Jimmy had been right—the trouble with him was he had no guts. His chance had come and he'd muffed it. For what?

Steve was too wrapped up in name calling to notice what time it was Jimmy and the woman left. When he finally glanced across the way he saw that the lights of the cottage had gone out.

Jimmy Powers had said he was coming back. Where was he? Steve started for the door. He was quite sure Jimmy hadn't driven away, because he would have heard the sound of the car.

Just then Jimmy came stumbling up the walk. He seemed to have taken on quite a bit more to drink.

Steve said, "What's the matter? Where's Betsey Blake?"

"Who?" Jimmy staggered in the doorway, then steadied himself against the side of the screen. "You mean the old bat who barged in here? I hope you didn't go for that line of malarkey she tried to hand out."

"But it figures, Jimmy. You can check up on it—"

"I don't have to. When I got her over to my place I started asking a few questions and she broke down. She was just running a bluff—

made the whole thing up. She's no more Betsey Blake than you are."

"What!"

Jimmy Powers wiped his forehead. "I think she was figuring on a shakedown. You know—come out with the story just before the picture's set to break, and threaten to queer the works unless the studio pays off." He shook his head. "Anyway, it doesn't matter, now."

"You scared her off?"

"No." Jimmy gulped. "Don't get me wrong, pal. Nobody *scared* her. She just left of her own free will, and under her own steam. You got to get that straight, see? Because I—I think there's been sort of an accident."

"Accident?"

Steve stiffened, and Jimmy went limp.

"I'm not sure yet. That's why I came over. I wanted you to come with me and look—"

"Look at what? Where is she?"

"Well, you must have noticed, she was crocked, wasn't she? I happened to be at the back window after she left, and I saw her stumbling along the edge of the cliff, like. I was all set to holler at her—listen to what I'm telling you, Stevie-boy, you got to get this—I was all set to holler at her when she sort of fell. Bingo, like that, she's gone."

"You mean she . . . But that's a sixty-foot drop!"

Jimmy gulped again. "I know. I haven't looked. I'm afraid to, alone."

"We'd better call the cops," Steve said.

"Yeah, sure. But I wanted to talk to you first. Alone, see? I mean, we call them, right away they'll ask a lot of questions. Who was she, where did she come from, what did she want around here? You know cops."

"Tell them the truth."

"And queer the picture?"

"But you say she wasn't Betsey Blake."

"She wasn't, but the minute they find out she *claimed* to be, the whole campaign is in the soup. Don't you understand, Steve? People will start wondering—was she or wasn't she? I worked my tail off building up a legend, and now it can all tumble down just because some dizzy old bag takes a header off a cliff."

Steve tried to get Jimmy Powers to meet his stare, but the bloodshot eyes kept rolling. "What I mean to say," he was muttering, "is why not just forget the whole thing?"

"But we've got to notify the authorities. Who knows? She may still be alive down there." Steve started for the phone.

"I know, I know. You got to tell them. But she isn't alive, she couldn't be. And all I want is that you don't say anything about her coming here tonight. Or that she said anything. Make believe it never happened. I just looked out the window before I went to bed and I noticed this beach bum stagger over the edge. That's the way it was. No harm done, is there, Steve? I mean, look at all that's at stake."

"I'm looking," Steve said. "And I'll think about it." He went to the phone and dialed. "Hello, get me police headquarters. I want to report an accident . . ."

He didn't waste words. No details—a woman had apparently fallen over the cliff, such-and-such an address; yes, he'd be waiting for them.

When Steve hung up, the publicity man expelled his breath in a deep sigh.

"That's the way to do it," he said. "You handled it just right. I won't forget you, Stevie-boy."

"I'm still thinking," Steve said. "When they get here I'll make up my mind what to say."

"Now, listen—"

"You listen to me. What makes you so sure that woman wasn't who she claimed to be? No, don't give me that blackmail argument again. Nobody gets drunk when they're out to pull a shakedown." He walked over to Jimmy Powers. "Let me ask you another question. Suppose she really was Betsey Blake. Then what? Why couldn't you have made the announcement tomorrow, the way she said? Think of the sensation it would have made, what it would have done for the picture."

Jimmy drew back against the door. "To hell with the picture," he said. "It's me I'm thinking about. Don't you understand that, meathead? This is *my* promotion, mine all the way. I cooked it up. I nursed it. It's my baby, and everybody in this town knows it. The picture's gonna be a smash, and who gets the credit? Me, that's who.

"Figure it your way and see what happens. So she breaks the story, and there's a sensation all right. Maybe even a bigger sensation, a real sockeroo. But it's not going to do the picture any more good—we've got it made already, just the way it is. And so Betsey Blake turns up alive, then what? She's still an old bag—she can't play leads any more, not even if they photograph her through a scrim to take the wrinkles out. Alive, she's just a middle-aged tramp who hits the sauce. Dead, she's a legend. She's right up there with Valentino and Harlow and James Dean. Her old pictures are worth a fortune in re-run rights. I tell you, it adds up!

"Besides, if she breaks the story, what happens to me? I'm the fair-haired boy right now. But if she tops me, then she gets the credit. You heard her say it yourself, how 'we' were gonna figure out an angle together. I know that 'together' line from way back! She'd take all the bows, steal all the scenes. Believe me, Steve, I know! She was always like that, couldn't stand to have anyone else share the spot with her. It was Betsey Blake, first, last, and always. The things she pulled with me personally! I would have rotted in the publicity department the rest of my life if this break hadn't come along. You don't get this kind of a chance often out here, Steve. I took it, and I worked on it, and nobody's gonna grab it away from me at the last minute. I wouldn't let her—"

Steve put his hand on the man's shoulder. "You told me what I wanted to know," he said. "She *was* Betsey Blake, wasn't she?"

"I ain't saying. And you don't have to say anything either, when the cops come. I mean, Steve, have a heart—what good can it do now? You don't know anything about it, that's all you tell 'em. I've got five grand I can bring over here tomorrow morning. Five grand in cash that says you don't know anything. Hell, ten grand. And a job at the studio—"

"So she was Betsey Blake," Steve murmured. "And she just walked out of your place and fell off the cliff."

"Those things happen, you know how it is, a drunk dame and her foot slips. It was an accident, I swear it was! All right, if you must know, I was with her—I didn't want to tell you that part. I was with her, I was going to drive her home, and then she let go of my arm and stumbled off."

"There'll be footprints in the sand," Steve said. "And they'll check anyway, they always do. They'll find out who she really is, and they'll investigate from start to finish. They'll go all the way back—"

Jimmy Powers wilted. Steve had to hold him up.

"I never figured," he said. "Sure, they'll go all the way back."

"You shouldn't have killed her."

"Don't say that, Stevie!"

"It's true, isn't it? You did kill her. You knew she was Betsey Blake, but you killed her anyway, because you thought she'd queer your big deal."

Jimmy didn't answer. Instead he hit out at Steve, and Steve twisted and brought up his arm. Jimmy sagged. Steve held him there, listening for the sound of a siren in the distance.

"Fifty grand," Jimmy whispered. "I told you I had it coming. Fifty grand, all in cash. Nobody'd ever know."

Steve sighed. "When I heard about the money I was ready to kick myself," he said. "I thought I was a sucker because I didn't have your kind of guts. But now I know what it means to have them. It means you don't stop at anything, not even killing."

"You don't understand," Jimmy whimpered. "I wanted to live it up, I wanted my chance to be a big shot. She never gave it to me while she was alive, and when she disappeared I thought my big break had finally come. But what's the use now? Like you say, they'll find out sooner or later. I ought to have doped it out. I couldn't get away with it. And now it'll kill the legend, too."

"Never mind the legend," Steve said. "You killed a woman." The sirens were close now; he could hear the tires squealing to a halt. "I guess I don't understand at that," Steve said. "I don't understand your breed of rat at all. Call yourself a big-shot publicity man, do you? Why, you'd murder your own mother for a story."

Jimmy Powers gave him a funny look as the cops came in. "That's right," he whispered. "How'd you guess?"

THE ADVENTURE OF THE GETTYSBURG BUGLE

by Ellery Queen

This is a very old story as Queen stories go. It happened in Ellery's salad days, when he was tossing his talents about like a Sunday chef and a redheaded girl named Nikki Porter had just attached herself to his typewriter. But it has not staled, this story; it has an unwithering flavor which those who partook of it relish to this day.

There are gourmets in America whose taste buds leap at any concoction dated 1861–1865. To such, the mere recitation of ingredients like Bloody Angle, Minié balls, Little Mac, "Tenting Tonight," the brand of Ulyss Grant's whisky, not to mention Father Abraham, is sufficient to start the passionate flow of juices. These are the misty-hearted to whom the Civil War is "the War" and the blue-gray armies rather more than men. Romantics, if you will; garnishers of history. But it is they who pace the lonely sentrypost by the night Potomac, they who hear the creaking of the ammunition wagons, the snap of campfires, the scream of the thin gray line and the long groan of the battlefield. They personally flee the burning hell of the Wilderness as the dead rise and twist in the flames; under lanterns, in the flickering mud, they stoop compassionately with the surgeons over quivering heaps. It is they who keep the little flags flying and the ivy ever green on the graves of the old men.

Ellery is of this company, and that is why he regards the case of the old men of Jacksburg, Pennsylvania, with particular affection.

Ellery and Nikki came upon the village of Jacksburg as people often come upon the best things, unpropitiously. They had been driving back to New York from Washington, where Ellery had had some sleuthing to do among the stacks of the Library of Congress.

Perhaps the Potomac, Arlington's eternal geometry, giant Lincoln frozen in sadness brought their weight to bear upon Ellery's decision to veer towards Gettysburg, where murder had been national. And Nikki had never been there, and May was coming to its end. There was a climate of sentiment.

They crossed the Maryland-Pennsylvania line and spent timeless hours wandering over Culp's Hill and Seminary Ridge and Little Round Top and Spangler's Spring among the watchful monuments. It is a place of everlasting life, where Pickett and Jeb Stuart keep charging to the sight of those with eyes to see, where the blood spills fresh if colorlessly, and the highpitched tones of a tall and ugly man still ring out over the graves. When they left, Ellery and Nikki were in a mood of wonder, unconscious of time or place, oblivious to the darkening sky and the direction in which the nose of the Duesenberg pointed. So in time they were disagreeably awakened by the alarm clock of nature. The sky had opened on their heads, drenching them to the skin instantly. From the horizon behind them Gettysburg was a battlefield again, sending great flashes of fire through the darkness to the din of celestial cannon. Ellery stopped the car and put the top up, but the mood was drowned when he discovered that something ultimate had happened to the ignition system. They were marooned in a faraway land, Nikki moaned; making Ellery angry, for it was true.

"We can't go on in these wet clothes, Ellery!"

"Do you suggest that we stay here in them? I'll get this crackerbox started if . . ." But at that moment the watery lights of a house wavered on somewhere ahead, and Ellery became cheerful again.

"At least we'll find out where we are and how far it is to where we ought to be. Who knows? There may even be a garage."

It was a little white house on a little swampy road marked off by a little stone fence covered with rambler rose vines, and the man who opened the door to the dripping wayfarers was little, too, little and weatherskinned and gallused, with eyes that seemed to have roots in the stones and springs of the Pennsylvania countryside. He smiled hospitably, but the smile became concern when he saw how wet they were.

"Won't take no for an answer," he said in a remarkably deep voice, and he chuckled. "That's doctor's orders, though I expect you didn't see my shingle—mostly overgrown with ivy. Got a change of clothing in your car?"

"Oh, yes!" said Nikki abjectly.

Ellery, being a man, hesitated. The house looked neat and clean, there was an enticing fire, and the rain at their backs was coming down with a roar. "Well, thank you . . . but if I might use your phone to call a garage—"

"You just give me the keys to your car trunk."

"But we can't turn your home into a tourist house—"

"It's that, too, when the good Lord sends a wanderer my way. Now see here, this storm's going to keep up most of the night and the roads hereabout get mighty soupy." The little man was bustling into waterproof and overshoes. "I'll get Lew Bagley over at the garage to pick up your car, but for now let's have those keys."

So an hour later, while the elements warred outside, they were toasting safely in a pleasant little parlor, full of Dr. Martin Strong's homemade poppy-seed twists, scrapple, and coffee. The doctor, who lived alone, was his own cook. He was also, he said with a chuckle, mayor of the village of Jacksburg and its chief of police.

"Lot of us in the village run double harness. Bill Yoder of the hardware store's our undertaker. Lew Bagley's also the fire chief. Ed MacShane—"

"Jacksburger-of-all-trades you may be, Dr. Strong," said Ellery, "but to me you'll always be primarily the Good Samaritan."

"Hallelujah," said Nikki, piously wiggling her toes.

"And make it Doc," said their host. "Why, it's just selfishness on my part, Mr. Queen. We're off the beaten track here, and you do get a hankering for a new face. I guess I know every dimple and wen on the five hundred and thirty-four in Jacksburg."

"I don't suppose your police chiefship keeps you very busy."

Doc Strong laughed. "Not any. Though last year—" His eyes puckered and he got up to poke the fire. "Did you say, Miss Porter, that Mr. Queen is sort of a detective?"

"Sort of a!" began Nikki. "Why, Dr. Strong, he's solved some simply unbeliev—"

"My father is an inspector in the New York police department," interrupted Ellery, curbing his new secretary's enthusiasm with a glance. "I stick my nose into a case once in a while. What about last year, Doc?"

"What put me in mind of it," said Jacksburg's mayor thoughtfully, "was your saying you'd been to Gettysburg today. And also you being interested in crimes . . ." Dr. Strong said abruptly, "I'm a fool, but I'm worried."

"Worried about what?"

"Well . . . Memorial Day's tomorrow, and for the first time in my life I'm not looking forward to it. Jacksburg makes quite a fuss about Memorial Day. It's not every village can brag about three living veterans of the Civil War."

"Three?" exclaimed Nikki. "How thrilling."

"Gives you an idea what the Jacksburg doctoring business is like," grinned Doc Strong. "We run to pioneer-type women and longevity . . . I ought to have said we *had* three Civil War veterans—Caleb Atwell, ninety-seven, of the Atwell family, there are dozens of 'em in the county; Zach Bigelow, ninety-five, who lives with his grandson Andy and Andy's wife and seven kids; and Abner Chase, ninety-four, Cissy Chase's great-grandpa. This year we're down to two. Caleb Atwell died last Memorial Day."

"A,B,C," murmured Ellery.

"What's that?"

"I have a bookkeeper's mind, Doc. Atwell, Bigelow, and Chase. Call it a spur-of-the-moment mnemonic system. A died last Memorial Day. Is that why you're not looking forward to this one? B following A sort of thing?"

"Didn't it always?" said Doc Strong with defiance. "Though I'm afraid it ain't—isn't as simple as all that. Maybe I better tell you how Caleb Atwell died.

"Every year Caleb, Zach, and Abner have been the star performers of our Memorial Day exercises, which are held at the old burying ground on the Hookerstown road. The oldest of the three—"

"That would be A. Caleb Atwell."

"That's right. As the oldest, Caleb always blew taps on a cracked old bugle that's 'most as old as he was. Caleb, Zach, and Abner were in the Pennsylvania Seventy-second of Hancock's Second Corps, Brigadier General Alexander S. Webb commanding. They covered themselves with immortal glory—the Seventy-second, I mean—at Gettysburg when they fought back Pickett's charge, and that bugle played a big part in their fighting. Ever since it's been known as the Gettysburg bugle—in Jacksburg, anyway."

The little mayor of Jacksburg looked softly down the years. "It's been a tradition, the oldest living vet tootling that bugle, far back as I remember. I recollect as a boy standing around with my mouth open watching the G.A.R.s—there were lots more then—take turns in front of Maroney Offcutt's general store . . . been dead thirty-eight years, old Offcutt . . . practicing on the bugle, so any one of 'em would be ready when his turn came." Doc Strong sighed. "And Zach Bigelow, as the next oldest to Caleb Atwell, he'd be the standard bearer, and Ab Chase, as the next-next oldest, he'd lay the wreath on the memorial monument in the burying ground.

"Well, last Memorial Day, while Zach was holding the regimental colors and Ab the wreath, Caleb blew taps the way he'd done nigh onto twenty times before. All of a sudden, in the middle of a high note, Caleb keeled over. Dropped in his tracks deader than church on Monday."

"Strained himself," said Nikki sympathetically. "But what a poetic way for a Civil War veteran to die."

Doc Strong regarded her oddly. "Maybe," he said. "If you like that kind of poetry." He kicked a log, sending sparks flying up his chimney.

"But surely, Doc," said Ellery with a smile, for he was young in those days, "surely you can't have been suspicious about the death of a man of ninety-seven?"

"Maybe I was," muttered their host. "Maybe I was because it so happened I'd given old Caleb a thorough physical checkup only the day before he died. I'd have staked my medical license he'd live to break a hundred and then some. Healthiest old copperhead I ever knew. Copperhead! I'm blaspheming the dead. Caleb lost an eye on Cemetery Ridge . . . I know—I'm senile. That's what I've been telling myself for the past year."

"Just what was it you suspected, Doc?" Ellery forbore to smile now, but only because of Dr. Strong's evident distress.

"Didn't know what to suspect," said the country doctor shortly. "Fooled around with the notion of an autopsy, but the Atwells wouldn't hear of it. Said I was a blame jackass to think a man of ninety-seven would die of anything but old age. I found myself agreeing with 'em. The upshot was we buried Caleb whole."

"But Doc, at that age the human economy can go to pieces without warning like the one-hoss shay. You must have had another reason for uneasiness. A motive you knew about?"

"Well . . . maybe."

"He was a rich man," said Nikki sagely.

"He didn't have a pot he could call his own," said Doc Strong.

"But somebody stood to gain by his death just the same. That is, if the old yarn's true."

"You see, there's been kind of a legend in Jacksburg about those three old fellows, Mr. Queen. I first heard it when I was running around barefoot with my tail hanging out. Folks said then, and they're still saying it, that back in '65 Caleb and Zach and Ab, who were in the same company, found some sort of treasure."

"Treasure . . ." Nikki began to cough.

"Treasure," repeated Doc Strong doggedly. "Fetched it home to Jacksburg with them, the story goes, hid it, and swore they'd never tell a living soul where it was buried. Now there's lots of tales like that came out of the War"—he fixed Nikki with a stern and glittering eye—"and most folks either cough or go into hysterics, but there's something about this one I've always half-believed. So I'm senile on two counts. Just the same, I'll breathe a lot easier when tomorrow's ceremonies are over and Zach Bigelow lays Caleb Atwell's bugle away till next year. As the oldest survivor Zach does the tootling tomorrow."

"They hid the treasure and kept it hidden for considerably over half a century?" Ellery was smiling again. "Doesn't strike me as a very sensible thing to do with a treasure, Doc. It's only sensible if the treasure is imaginary. Then you don't have to produce it."

"The story goes," mumbled Jacksburg's mayor, "that they'd sworn an oath—"

"Not to touch any of it until they all died but one," said Ellery, laughing outright now. "Last-survivor-takes-all department. Doc, that's the way most of these fairy tales go." Ellery rose, yawning. "I think I hear the featherbed in that other guest room calling. Nikki, your eyeballs are hanging out. Take my advice, Doc, and follow suit. You haven't a thing to worry about but keeping the kids quiet tomorrow while you read the Gettysburg Address!"

As it turned out, the night shared prominently in Doc Martin Strong's Memorial Day responsibilities. Ellery and Nikki awakened to a splendid world, risen from its night's ablutions with a shining eye and a scrubbed look; and they went downstairs within seconds of each other to find the mayor of Jacksburg, galluses dangling on his pants bottom, pottering about the kitchen.

"Morning, morning," said Doc Strong, welcoming but abstracted. "Just fixing things for your breakfast before catching an hour's nap."

"You lamb," said Nikki. "But what a shame, Doctor. Didn't you sleep well last night?"

"Didn't sleep at all. Tossed around a bit and just as I was dropping off my phone rings and it's Cissy Chase. Emergency sick call. Hope it didn't disturb you."

"Cissy Chase." Ellery looked at their host. "Wasn't that the name you mentioned last night of—?"

"Of old Abner Chase's great-granddaughter. That's right, Mr. Queen. Cissy's an orphan and Ab's only kin. She's kept house for the old fellow and taken care of him since she was ten." Doc Strong's shoulders sloped.

Ellery said peculiarly: "It was old Abner . . . ?"

"I was up with Ab all night. This morning, at six-thirty, he passed away."

"On Memorial Day!" Nikki sounded like a little girl in her first experience with a fact of life.

There was a silence, fretted by the sizzling of Doc Strong's bacon. Ellery said at last, "What did Abner Chase die of?"

Doc Strong looked at him. He seemed angry. But then he shook his head. "I'm no Mayo brother, Mr. Queen, and I suppose there's a lot about the practice of medicine I'll never get to learn, but I do know a cerebral hemorrhage when I see one, and that's what Ab Chase died of. In a man of ninety-four, that's as close to natural death as you can come . . . No, there wasn't any funny business in this one."

"Except," mumbled Ellery, "that—again—it happened on Memorial Day."

"Man's a contrary animal. Tell him lies and he swallows 'em whole. Give him the truth and he gags on it. Maybe the Almighty gets tired of His thankless job every once in an eon and cuts loose with a little joke." But Doc Strong said it as if he were addressing, not them, but himself. "Any special way you like your eggs?"

"Leave the eggs to me, Doctor," Nikki said firmly. "You go on up those stairs and get some sleep."

"Reckon I better if I'm to do my usual dignified job today," said the mayor of Jacksburg with a sigh. "Though Abner Chase's death is going to make the proceedings solemner than ordinary. Bill Yoder says he's not going to be false to an ancient and honorable profession by doing a hurry-up job undertaking Ab, and maybe that's just as well. If we added the Chase funeral to today's program, even old

Abe's immortal words would find it hard to compete! By the way, Mr. Queen, I talked to Lew Bagley this morning and he'll have your car ready in an hour. Special service, seeing you're guests of the mayor." Doc Strong chuckled. "When you planning to leave?"

"I *was* intending . . ." Ellery stopped with a frown. Nikki regarded him with a sniffy look. She had already learned to detect the significance of certain signs peculiar to the Queen physiognomy. "I wonder," murmured Ellery, "how Zach Bigelow's going to take the news."

"He's already taken it, Mr. Queen. Stopped in at Andy Bigelow's place on my way home. Kind of a detour, but I figured I'd better break the news to Zach early as possible."

"Poor thing," said Nikki. "I wonder how it feels to learn you're the only one left." She broke an egg viciously.

"Can't say Zach carried on about it," said Doc Strong dryly. "About all he said, as I recall, was: 'Doggone it, now who's goin' to lay the wreath after I toot the Gettysburg bugle!' I guess when you reach the age of ninety-five, death don't mean what it does to young squirts of sixty-three like me. What time 'd you say you were leaving, Mr. Queen?"

"Nikki," muttered Ellery, "are we in any particular hurry?"

"I don't know. Are we?"

"Besides, it wouldn't be patriotic. Doc, do you suppose Jacksburg would mind if a couple of New York Yanks invited themselves to your Memorial Day exercises?"

The business district of Jacksburg consisted of a single paved street bounded at one end by the sightless eye of a broken traffic signal and at the other by the twin gas pumps before Lew Bagley's garage. In between, some stores in need of paint sunned themselves, enjoying the holiday. Red, white, and blue streamers crisscrossed the thoroughfare overhead. A few seedy frame houses, each decorated with an American flag, flanked the main street at both ends.

Ellery and Nikki found the Chase house exactly where Doc Strong had said it would be—just around the corner from Bagley's garage, between the ivy-hidden church and the firehouse of the Jacksburg Volunteer Pump and Hose Company No. 1. But the mayor's directions were a superfluity; it was the only house with a crowded porch.

A heavy-shouldered young girl in a black Sunday dress sat in a rocker, the center of the crowd. Her nose was as red as her big hands, but she was trying to smile at the cheerful words of sympathy winged at her from all sides.

"Thanks, Mis' Plum . . . That's right, Mr. Schmidt, I know . . . But he was such a spry old soul, Emerson, I can't believe . . ."

"Miss Cissy Chase?"

Had the voice been that of a Confederate spy, a deeper silence could not have drowned the noise. Jacksburg eyes examined Ellery and Nikki with cold curiosity, and feet shuffled.

"My name is Queen and this is Miss Porter. We're attending the Jacksburg Memorial Day exercises as guests of Mayor Strong"—a warming murmur, like a zephyr, passed over the porch—"and he asked us to wait here for him. I'm sorry about your great-grandfather, Miss Chase."

"You must have been very proud of him," said Nikki.

"Thank you, I was. It was so sudden— Won't you set? I mean— Do come into the house. Great-grandpa's not here . . . he's over at Bill Yoder's, on some ice . . ."

The girl was flustered and began to cry, and Nikki took her arm and led her into the house. Ellery lingered a moment to exchange appropriate remarks with the neighbors who, while no longer cold, were still curious; and then he followed. It was a dreary little house, with a dark and damp parlor.

"Now, now, this is no time for fussing—may I call you Cissy?" Nikki was saying soothingly. "Besides, you're better off away from all those folks. Why, Ellery, she's only a child!"

And a very plain child, Ellery thought, with a pinched face and empty eyes; and he almost wished he had gone on past the broken traffic light and turned north.

"I understand the parade to the burying ground is going to form outside your house, Cissy," he said. "By the way, have Andrew Bigelow and his grandfather Zach arrived yet?"

"Oh, I don't know," said Cissy Chase dully. "It's all such a dream, seems like."

"Of course. And you're left alone. Haven't you any family at all, Cissy?"

"No."

"Isn't there some young man—?"

Cissy shook her head bitterly. "Who'd marry me? This is the only decent dress I got, and it's four years old. We lived on Great-grandpa's pension and what I could earn hiring out by the day. Which ain't much, nor often. Now . . ."

"I'm sure you'll find something to do," said Nikki, very heartily.

"In Jacksburg?"

Nikki was silent.

"Cissy." Ellery spoke casually, and she did not even look up. "Doc Strong mentioned something about a treasure. Do you know anything about it?"

"Oh, that." Cissy shrugged. "Just what Great-grandpa told me, and he hardly ever told the same story twice. But near as I was ever able to make out, one time during the War him and Caleb Atwell and Zach Bigelow got separated from the army—scouting, or foraging, or something. It was down South somewhere, and they spent the night in an old empty mansion that was half-burned down. Next morning they went through the ruins to see what they could pick up, and buried in the cellar they found the treasure. A big fortune in money, Great-grandpa said. They were afraid to take it with them, so they buried it in the same place in the cellar and made a map of the location and after the War they went back, the three of 'em, and dug it up again. Then they made the pact."

"Oh, yes," said Ellery. "The pact."

"Swore they'd hold onto the treasure till only one of them remained alive, I don't know why, then the last one was to get it all. Leastways, that's how Great-grandpa told it. That part he always told the same."

"Did he ever say how much of a fortune it was?"

Cissy laughed. "Couple of hundred thousand dollars. I ain't saying Great-grandpa was cracked, but you know how an old man gets."

"Did he ever give you a hint as to where he and Caleb and Zach hid the money after they got it back North?"

"No, he'd just slap his knee and wink at me."

"Maybe," said Ellery suddenly, "maybe there's something to that yarn after all."

Nikki stared. "But Ellery, you said—! Cissy, did you hear that?"

But Cissy only drooped. "If there is, it's all Zach Bigelow's now."

Then Doc Strong came in, fresh as a daisy in a pressed blue suit and a stiff collar and a bow tie, and a great many other people came in, too. Ellery and Nikki surrendered Cissy Chase to Jacksburg.

"If there's anything to the story," Nikki whispered to Ellery, "and if Mayor Strong is right, then that old scoundrel Bigelow's been murdering his friends to get the money!"

"After all these years, Nikki? At the age of ninety-five?" Ellery shook his head.

"But then what—?"

"I don't know." But when the little mayor happened to look their way, Ellery caught his eye and took him aside and whispered in his ear.

The procession—near every car in Jacksburg, Doc Strong announced proudly, over a hundred of them—got under way at exactly two o'clock.

Nikki had been embarrassed but not surprised to find herself being handed into the leading car, an old but brightly polished touring job contributed for the occasion by Lew Bagley; for the moment Nikki spied the ancient, doddering head under the Union Army hat in the front seat she detected the fine Italian whisper of her employer. Zach Bigelow held his papery frame fiercely if shakily erect between the driver and a powerful red-necked man with a brutal face who, Nikki surmised, was the old man's grandson, Andy Bigelow. Nikki looked back, peering around the flapping folds of the flag stuck in the corner of the car. Cissy Chase was in the second car in a black veil, weeping on a stout woman's shoulder. So the female Yankee from New York sat back between Ellery and Mayor Strong, against the bank of flowers in which the flag was set, and glared at the necks of the two Bigelows, having long since taken sides in this matter. And when Doc Strong made the introductions, Nikki barely nodded to Jacksburg's sole survivor of the Grand Army of the Republic, and then only in acknowledgment of his historic importance.

Ellery, however, was all deference and cordiality, even to the brute grandson. He leaned forward, talking into the hairy ear.

"How do I address your grandfather, Mr. Bigelow? I don't want to make a mistake about his rank."

"Gramp's a general," said Andy Bigelow loudly. "Ain't you, Gramp?" He beamed at the ancient, but Zach Bigelow was staring proudly ahead, holding fast to something in a rotted musette bag on his lap. "Went through the War a private," the grandson confided, "but he don't like to talk about that."

"General Bigelow—" began Ellery.

"That's his deef ear," said the grandson. "Try the other one."

"General Bigelow!"

"Hey?" The old man turned his trembling head, glaring. "Speak up, bub. Ye're mumblin'."

"General Bigelow," shouted Ellery, "now that all the money is yours, what are you going to do with it?"

"Hey? Money?"

"The treasure, Gramp," roared Andy Bigelow. "They've even heard about it in New York. What are you goin' to do with it, he wants to know?"

"Does, does he?" Old Zach sounded grimly amused. "Can't talk, Andy. Hurts m' neck."

"How much does it amount to, General?" cried Ellery.

Old Zach eyed him. "Mighty nosy, ain't ye?" Then he cackled. "Last time we counted it—Caleb, Ab, and me—came to nigh on a million dollars. Yes, sir, one million dollars." The old man's left eye, startlingly, drooped. "Goin' to be a big surprise to the smart-alecks and the doubtin' Thomases. You wait an' see."

Andy Bigelow grinned, and Nikki could have strangled him.

"According to Cissy," Nikki murmured to Doc Strong, "Abner Chase said it was only two hundred thousand."

"Zach makes it more every time he talks about it," said the mayor unhappily.

"I heard ye, Martin Strong!" yelled Zach Bigelow, swiveling his twig of a neck so suddenly that Nikki winced, expecting it to snap. "You wait! I'll show ye, ye durn whippersnapper, who's a lot o' wind!"

"Now, Zach," said Doc Strong pacifyingly. "Save your wind for that bugle."

Zach Bigelow cackled and clutched the musette bag in his lap, glaring ahead in triumph, as if he had scored a great victory.

Ellery said no more. Oddly, he kept staring not at old Zach but at Andy Bigelow, who sat beside his grandfather grinning at invisible audiences along the empty countryside as if he, too, had won—or was on his way to winning—a triumph.

The sun was hot. Men shucked their coats and women fanned themselves with handkerchiefs and pocketbooks.

"*It is for us the living, rather, to be dedicated . . .*"

Children dodged among the graves, pursued by shushing mothers. On most of the graves there were fresh flowers.

"—*that from these honored dead* . . ."

Little American flags protruded from the graves, too.

". . . *gave the last full measure of devotion* . . ."

Doc Martin Strong's voice was deep and sure, not at all like the voice of that tall ugly man, who had spoken the same words apologetically.

". . . *that these dead shall not have died in vain* . . ."

Doc was standing on the pedestal of the Civil War Monument, which was decorated with flags and bunting and faced the weathered stone ranks like a commander in full-dress uniform.

"—*that this nation, under God* . . ."

A color guard of the American Legion, Jacksburg Post, stood at attention between the mayor and the people. A file of Legionnaires carrying old Sharps rifles faced the graves.

"—*and that government of the people* . . ."

Beside the mayor, disdaining the simian shoulder of his grandson, stood General Zach Bigelow. Straight as the barrel of a Sharps, musette bag held tightly to his blue tunic.

". . . *shall not perish from the earth.*"

The old man nodded impatiently. He began to fumble with the bag.

"*Comp-'ny! Present—arms!*"

"Go ahead, Gramp!" Andy Bigelow bellowed.

The old man muttered. He was having difficulty extricating the bugle from the bag.

"Here, lemme give ye a hand!"

"Let the old man alone, Andy," said the mayor of Jacksburg quietly. "We're in no hurry."

Finally the bugle was free. It was an old army bugle, as old as Zach Bigelow, dented and scarred in a hundred places.

The old man raised it to his earth-colored lips.

Now his hands were not shaking.

Now even the children were quiet.

Now the Legionnaires stood more rigidly.

And the old man began to play taps.

It could hardly have been called playing. He blew, and out of the bugle's bell came cracked sounds. And sometimes he blew and no sounds came out at all. Then the veins of his neck swelled and his face turned to burning bark. Or he sucked at the mouthpiece, in and out, to clear it of his spittle. But still he blew, and the trees in the burying ground nodded in the warm breeze, and the people stood at attention listening as if the butchery of sound were sweet music.

And then, suddenly, the butchery faltered. Old Zach Bigelow stood with bulging eyes. The Gettysburg bugle fell to the pedestal with a tinny clatter.

For an instant everything seemed to stop—the slight movements of the children, the breathing of the people, even the rustling of the leaves.

Then into the vacuum rushed a murmur of horror, and Nikki unbelievingly opened the eyes which she had shut to glimpse the last of Jacksburg's G.A.R. veterans crumpling to the feet of Doc Strong and Andy Bigelow.

"You were right the first time, Doc," Ellery said.

They were in Andy Bigelow's house, where old Zach's body had been taken from the cemetery. The house was full of chittering woman and scampering children, but in this room there were only a few, and they talked in low tones. The old man was laid out on a settee with a patchwork quilt over him. Doc Strong sat in a rocker beside the body, looking very old.

"It's my fault," he mumbled. "I didn't examine Caleb's mouth last year. I didn't examine the mouthpiece of that bugle. It's my fault, Mr. Queen."

Ellery soothed him. "It's not an easy poison to spot, Doc, as you know. And after all, the whole thing was so ludicrous. You'd have caught it in autopsy, but the Atwells laughed you out of it."

"They're all gone. All three." Doc Strong looked up fiercely. "Who poisoned their bugle?"

"God Almighty, don't look at me," said Andy Bigelow. "Anybody could of, Doc."

"Anybody, Andy?" the mayor cried. "When Caleb Atwell died, Zach took the bugle and it's been in this house for a year!"

"Anybody could of," said Bigelow stubbornly. "The bugle was hangin' over the fireplace and anybody could of snuck in durin' the night . . . Anyway, it wasn't here before old Caleb died; *he* had it up to last Memorial Day. Who poisoned it in *his* house?"

"We won't get anywhere on this tack, Doc," Ellery murmured. "Bigelow. Did your grandfather ever let on where that Civil War treasure is hidden?"

"Suppose he did." The man licked his lips, blinking, as if he had been surprised into the half-admission. "What's it to you?"

"That money is behind the murders, Bigelow."

"Don't know nothin' about that. Anyway, nobody's got no right to that money but me." Andy Bigelow spread his thick chest. "When Ab Chase died, Gramp was the last survivor. That money was Zach Bigelow's. I'm his next o' kin, so now it's mine!"

"You know where it's hid, Andy." Doc was on his feet, eyes glittering. "Where?"

"I ain't talkin'. Git outen my house!"

"I'm the law in Jacksburg, too, Andy," Doc said softly. "This is a murder case. Where's that money?"

Bigelow laughed.

"You didn't know, Bigelow, did you?" said Ellery.

"Course not." He laughed again. "See, Doc? He's on your side, and he says I don't know, too."

"That is," said Ellery, "until a few minutes ago."

Bigelow's grin faded. "What are ye talkin' about?"

"Zach Bigelow wrote a message this morning, immediately after Doc Strong told him about Abner Chase's death."

Bigelow's face went ashen.

"And your grandfather sealed the message in an envelope—"

"Who told ye that?" yelled Bigelow.

"One of your children. And the first thing you did when we got home from the burying ground with your grandfather's corpse was to sneak up to the old man's bedroom. Hand it over."

Bigelow made two fists. Then he laughed again. "All right, I'll let ye see it. Hell, I'll let ye dig the money up for me! Why not? It's mine by law. Here, read it. See? He wrote my name on the envelope!"

And so he had. And the message in the envelope was also written in ink, in the same wavering hand:

> Dere Andy now that Ab Chase is ded to—if sumthin happins to me you wil find the money we been keepin all these long yeres in a iron box in the coffin *wich we beried Caleb Atwell in.* I leave it all to you my beluved grandson cuz you been sech a good grandson to me. Yours truly Zach Bigelow.

"In Caleb's coffin," choked Doc Strong.

Ellery's face was impassive. "How soon can you get an exhumation order, Doc?"

"Right now," exclaimed Doc. "I'm also deputy coroner of this district!"

And they took some men and they went back to the old burying ground, and in the darkening day they dug up the remains of Caleb Atwell and they opened the casket and found, on the corpse's knees, a flattish box of iron with a hasp but no lock. And, while two strong men held Andy Bigelow to keep him from hurling himself at the crumbling coffin, Doctor-Mayor-Chief of Police-Deputy Coroner Martin Strong held his breath and raised the lid of the iron box.

And it was crammed to the brim with moldy bills of large denominations.

In Confederate money.

No one said anything for some time, not even Andy Bigelow.

Then Ellery said, "It stood to reason. They found it buried in the cellar of an old Southern mansion—would it be Northern greenbacks? When they dug it up again after the War and brought it up to Jacksburg they probably had some faint hope that it might have some value. When they realized it was worthless, they decided to have some fun with it. This has been a private joke of those three old rascals since, roughly, 1865. When Caleb died last Memorial Day, Abner and Zach probably decided that, as the first of the trio to go, Caleb ought to have the honor of being custodian of their Confederate treasure in perpetuity. So one of them managed to slip the iron box into the coffin before the lid was screwed on. Zach's note bequeathing his 'fortune' to his 'beloved grandson'—in view of what I've seen of his beloved grandson today—was the old fellow's final joke."

Everybody chuckled; but the corpse stared mirthlessly and the silence fell again, to be broken by a weak curse from Andy Bigelow and Doc Strong's puzzled: "But Mr. Queen, that doesn't explain the murders."

"Well, now, Doc, it does," said Ellery; and then he said in a very different tone: "Suppose we put old Caleb back the way we found him, for your re-exhumation later for autopsy, Doc—and then we'll close the book on your Memorial Day murders."

Ellery closed the book in town, in the dusk, on the porch of Cissy Chase's house, which was central and convenient for everybody. Ellery and Nikki and Doc Strong and Cissy and Andy Bigelow—still clutching the iron box dazedly—were on the porch, and Lew Bagley and Bill Yoder and everyone else in Jacksburg, it seemed, stood about on the lawn and sidewalk, listening. And there was a touch of sadness to the soft twilight air, for something vital and exciting in the life of the village had come to an end.

"There's no trick to this," began Ellery, "and no joke, either, even though the men who were murdered were so old that death had grown tired waiting for them. The answer is as simple as the initials of their last names. Who knew that the supposed fortune was in Confederate money and therefore worthless? Only the three old men. One or another of the three would hardly have planned the deaths of the other two for possession of some scraps of valueless paper. So the murderer has to be someone who believed the fortune was legitimate and who—since until today there was no clue to the money's hiding place—knew he could claim it legally.

"Now of course that last-survivor-take-all business was pure moonshine, invented by Caleb, Zach, and Abner for their own amusement and the mystification of the community. But the would-be murderer didn't know that. The would-be murderer went on the assumption that the *whole* story was true, or he wouldn't have planned murder in the first place.

"Who would be able to claim the fortune legally if the last of the three old men—the survivor who presumably came into possession of the fortune on the deaths of the other two—died in his turn?"

"Last survivor's heir," said Doc Strong, and he rose.

"And who is the last survivor's heir?"

"*Zach Bigelow's grandson, Andy.*" And the little mayor of Jacksburg stared hard at Bigelow, and a grumbling sound came from the people below, and Bigelow shrank against the wall behind Cissy, as if to seek her protection. But Cissy only looked at him and moved away.

"You thought the fortune was real," Cissy said scornfully, "so you killed Caleb Atwell and my great-grandpa so your grandfather'd be the last survivor so you could kill him the way you did today and get the fortune."

"That's it, Ellery," cried Nikki.

"Unfortunately, Nikki, that's not it at all. You all refer to Zach Bigelow as the last survivor—"

"Well, he was," said Nikki in amazement.

"How could he not be?" said Doc Strong. "Caleb and Abner died first—"

"Literally, that's true," said Ellery, "but what you've all forgotten is that Zach Bigelow was the last survivor *only by accident*. When Abner Chase died early this morning, was it through poisoning, or some other violent means? No, Doc, you were absolutely positive he'd died of a simple cerebral hemorrhage—not by violence, but a natural death. Don't you see that if Abner Chase hadn't died a natural death early this morning, *he'd still be alive this evening?* Zach Bigelow would have put the bugle to his lips this afternoon, just as he did, just as Caleb Atwell did a year ago . . . *and at this moment Abner Chase would have been the last survivor.*

"And who was Abner Chase's only living heir, the girl who would have fallen heir to Abner's 'fortune' when, in time, or through her assistance, he joined his cronies in the great bivouac on the other side?

"You lied to me, Cissy," said Ellery to the shrinking girl in his grip, as a horror very like the horror of the burying ground in the afternoon came over the crowd of mesmerized Jacksburgers. "You pretended you didn't believe the story of the fortune. But that was only after your great-grandfather had inconsiderately died of a stroke just a few hours before old Zach would have died of poisoning, and you couldn't inherit that great, great fortune, anyway!"

Nikki did not speak until they were twenty-five miles from Jacksburg. Then all she said was, "And now there's nobody left to blow the Gettysburg bugle," and she continued to stare into the darkness toward the south.

THE ORDERLY WORLD OF MR. APPLEBY

by Stanley Ellin

Mr. Appleby was a small, prim man who wore rimless spectacles, parted his graying hair in the middle, and took sober pleasure in pointing out that there was no room in the properly organized life for the operations of Chance. Consequently, when he decided that the time had come to investigate the most efficient methods for disposing of his wife he knew where to look.

He found the book, a text on forensic medicine, on the shelf of a second-hand bookshop among several volumes of like topic, and since all but one were in a distressingly shabby and dog-eared state which offended him to his very core, he chose the only one in reasonably good condition. Most of the cases it presented, he discovered on closer examination, were horrid studies of the results (vividly illustrated) of madness and lust—enough to set any decent man wondering at the number of monsters inhabiting the earth. One case, however, seemed to be exactly what he was looking for, and this he made the object of his most intensive study.

It was the case of Mrs. X (the book was replete with Mrs. X's, and Mr. Y's, and Miss Z's) who died after what was presumably an accidental fall on a scatter rug in her home. However, a lawyer representing the interests of the late lamented charged her husband with murder, and at a coroner's investigation was attempting to prove his charge when the accused abruptly settled matters by dropping dead of a heart attack.

All this was of moderate interest to Mr. Appleby whose motive, a desire to come into the immediate possession of his wife's estate, was strikingly similar to the alleged motive of Mrs. X's husband. But more important were the actual details of the case. Mrs. X had been in the act of bringing him a glass of water, said her husband, when the scatter rug, as scatter rugs will, had suddenly slipped from under her feet.

In rebuttal the indefatigable lawyer had produced a medical authority who made clear through a number of charts (all of which were handsomely reproduced in the book) that in the act of receiving the glass of water it would have been child's play for the husband to lay one hand behind his wife's shoulder, another hand along her jaw, and with a sudden thrust produce the same drastic results as the fall on the scatter rug, without leaving any clues as to the nature of his crime.

It should be made clear now that in studying these charts and explanations relentlessly Mr. Appleby was not acting the part of the greedy man going to any lengths to appease that greed. True, it was money he wanted, but it was money for the maintenance of what he regarded as a holy cause. And that was the Shop: *Appleby, Antiques and Curios*.

The Shop was the sun of Mr. Appleby's universe. He had bought it twenty years before with the pittance left by his father, and at best it provided him with a poor living. At worst—and it was usually at worst—it had forced him to draw on his mother's meagre store of good will and capital. Since his mother was not one to give up a penny lightly, the Shop brought about a series of pitched battles which, however, always saw it the victor—since in the last analysis the Shop was to Mr. Appleby what Mr. Appleby was to his mother.

This unhappy triangle was finally shattered by his mother's death, at which time Mr. Appleby discovered that she had played a far greater role in maintaining his orderly little world than he had hitherto realized. This concerned not only the money she occasionally gave him, but also his personal habits.

He ate lightly and warily. His mother had been adept at toasting and boiling his meals to perfection. His nerves were violently shaken if anything in the house was out of place, and she had been a living assurance he would be spared this. Her death, therefore, left a vast and uncomfortable gap in his life, and in studying methods to fill it he was led to contemplate marriage, and then to the act itself.

His wife was a pale, thin-lipped woman so much like his mother in appearance and gesture that sometimes on her entrance into a room he was taken aback by the resemblance. In only one respect did she fail him: she could not understand the significance of the Shop, nor his feelings about it. That was disclosed the first time he broached the subject of a small loan that would enable him to meet some business expenses.

Mrs. Appleby had been well in the process of withering on the vine when her husband-to-be had proposed to her, but to give her full due she was not won by the mere prospect of finally making a marriage. Actually, though she would have blushed at such a blunt statement of her secret thought, it was the large, mournful eyes behind his rimless spectacles that turned the trick, promising, as they did, hidden depths of emotion neatly garbed in utter respectability. When she learned very soon after her wedding that the hidden depths were evidently too well hidden ever to be explored by her, she shrugged the matter off and turned to boiling and toasting his meals with good enough grace. The knowledge that the impressive *Appleby, Antiques and Curios* was a hollow shell she took in a different spirit.

She made some brisk investigations and then announced her findings to Mr. Appleby with some heat.

"Antiques and curios!" she said shrilly. "Why, that whole collection of stuff is nothing but a pile of junk. Just a bunch of worthless dust-catchers, that's all it is!"

What she did not understand was that these objects, which to the crass and commercial eye might seem worthless, were to Mr. Appleby the stuff of life itself. The Shop had grown directly from his childhood mania for collecting, assorting, labeling, and preserving anything he could lay his hands on. And the value of any item in the Shop increased proportionately with the length of time he possessed it; whether a cracked imitation of Sèvres, or clumsily faked Chippendale, or rusty sabre made no difference. Each piece had won a place for itself; a permanent, immutable place, as far as Mr. Appleby was concerned; and strangely enough it was the sincere agony he suffered in giving up a piece that led to the few sales he made. The customer who was uncertain of values had only to get a glimpse of this agony to be convinced that he was getting a rare bargain. Fortunately, no customer could have imagined for a moment that it was the thought of the empty space left by the object's departure—the brief disorder which the emptiness made—and not a passion for the object itself that drew Mr. Appleby's pinched features into a mask of pain.

So, not understanding, Mrs. Appleby took an unsympathetic tack. "You'll get my mite when I'm dead and gone," she said, "and only when I'm dead and gone."

Thus unwittingly she tried herself, was found wanting, and it only remained for sentence to be executed. When the time came Mr. Appleby applied the lessons he had gleaned from his invaluable textbook and found them accurate in every detail. It was over quickly, quietly, and, outside of a splash of water on his trousers, neatly. The Medical Examiner growled something about those indescribable scatter rugs costing more lives than drunken motorists; the policeman in charge kindly offered to do whatever he could in the way of making funeral arrangements; and that was all there was to it.

It had been so easy—so undramatic, in fact—that it was not until a week later when a properly sympathetic lawyer was making him an accounting of his wife's estate that Mr. Appleby suddenly understood the whole, magnificent new world that had been opened up to him.

Discretion must sometimes outweigh sentiment, and Mr. Appleby was, if anything, a discreet man. After his wife's estate had been cleared, the Shop was moved to another location far from its original setting. It was moved again after the sudden demise of the second Mrs. Appleby, and by the time the sixth Mrs. Appleby had been disposed of, the removals were merely part of a fruitful pattern.

Because of their similarities—they were all pale, thin-featured women with pinched lips, adept at toasting and boiling, and adamant on the subjects of regularity and order—Mr. Appleby was inclined to remember his departed wives rather vaguely *en masse*. Only in one regard did he qualify them: the number of digits their bank accounts totaled up to. For that reason he thought of the first two Mrs. Applebys as Fours; the third as a Three (an unpleasant surprise); and the last three as Fives. The sum would have been a pretty penny by anyone else's standards, but since each succeeding portion of it had been snapped up by the insatiable *Appleby, Antiques and Curios*—in much the way a fly is snapped up by a hungry lizard—Mr. Appleby found himself soon after the burial of the sixth Mrs. Appleby in deeper and warmer financial waters than ever. So desperate were his circumstances that although he dreamed of another Five he would have settled for a Four on the spot. It was at this opportune moment that Martha Sturgis entered his life, and after fifteen minutes' conversation with her he brushed all thoughts of Fours and Fives from his mind.

Martha Sturgis, it seemed, was a Six.

It was not only in the extent of her fortune that she broke the pattern established by the woman of Mr. Appleby's previous experience.

The Orderly World of Mr. Appleby 625

Unlike them, Martha Sturgis was a large, rather shapeless woman who in person, dress, and manner might almost be called (Mr. Appleby shuttered a little at the word) blowzy.

It was remotely possible that properly veneered, harnessed, coiffured, and appareled she might have been made into something presentable, but from all indications Martha Sturgis was a woman who went out of her way to defy such conventions. Her hair, dyed a shocking orange-red, was piled carelessly on her head; her blobby features were recklessly powdered and painted entirely to their disadvantage; her clothes, obviously worn for comfort, were, at the same time, painfully garish; and her shoes gave evidence of long and pleasurable wear without corresponding care being given their upkeep.

Of all this and its effect on the beholder Martha Sturgis seemed totally unaware. She strode through *Appleby, Antiques and Curios* with an energy that set movable objects dancing in their places; she smoked incessantly, lighting one cigarette from another, while Mr. Appleby fanned the air before his face and coughed suggestively; and she talked without pause, loudly and in a deep, hoarse voice that dinned strangely in a Shop so accustomed to the higher, thinner note.

In the first fourteen minutes of their acquaintance, the one quality she displayed that led Mr. Appleby to modify some of his immediate revulsion even a trifle was the care with which she priced each article. She examined, evaluated, and cross-examined in detail before moving on with obvious disapproval, and he moved along with her with mounting assurance that he could get her out of the Shop before any damage was done to the stock or his patience. And then in the fifteenth minute she spoke the Word.

"I've got half a million dollars in the bank," Martha Sturgis remarked with cheerful contempt, "but I never thought I'd get around to spending a nickel of it on this kind of stuff."

Mr. Appleby had his hand before his face preparatory to waving aside some of the tobacco smoke that eddied about him. In the time it took the hand to drop nervelessly to his side his mind attacked an astonishing number of problems. One concerned the important finger on her left hand which was ringless; the others concerned certain mathematical problems largely dealing with short-term notes, long-term notes, and rates of interest. By the time the hand touched his side, the problems, as far as Mr. Appleby was concerned, were well on the way to solution.

And it may be noted there was an added fillip given the matter by the very nature of Martha Sturgis' slovenly and strident being. Looking at her after she had spoken the Word, another man might perhaps have seen her through the sort of veil that a wise photographer casts over the lens of his camera in taking the picture of a prosperous, but unprepossessing, subject. Mr. Appleby, incapable of such self-deceit, girded himself instead with the example of the man who carried a heavy weight on his back for the pleasure it gave him in laying it down. Not only would the final act of a marriage to Martha Sturgis solve important mathematical problems, but it was an act he could play out with the gusto of a man ridding the world of an unpleasant object.

Therefore he turned his eyes, more melancholy and luminous than ever, on her and said, "It's a great pity, Mrs. . . ."

She told him her name, emphasizing the *Miss* before it, and Mr. Appleby smiled apologetically.

"Of course. As I was saying, it's a great pity when someone of refinement and culture—" (the *like yourself* floated delicately unsaid on the air) "—should never have known the joy in possession of fine works of art. But, as we all learn, it is never too late to begin, is it?"

Martha Sturgis looked at him sharply and then laughed a hearty bellow of laughter that stabbed his eardrums painfully. For a moment Mr. Appleby, a man not much given to humor, wondered darkly if he had unwittingly uttered something so excruciatingly epigrammatic that it was bound to have this alarming effect.

"My dear man," said Martha Sturgis, "if it is your idea that I am here to start cluttering up my life with your monstrosities, perish the thought. What I'm here for is to buy a gift for a friend, a thoroughly infuriating and loathsome person who happens to have the nature and disposition of a bar of stainless steel. I can't think of a better way of showing my feelings toward her than by presenting her with almost anything displayed in your shop. If possible, I should also like delivery arranged so that I can be on the scene when she receives the package."

Mr. Appleby staggered under this, then rallied valiantly. "In that case," he said, and shook his head firmly, "it is out of the question. Completely out of the question."

"Nonsense," Martha Sturgis said. "I'll arrange for delivery myself if you can't handle it. Really, you ought to understand that there's no point in doing this sort of thing unless you're on hand to watch the results."

Mr. Appleby kept tight rein on his temper. "I am not alluding to the matter of delivery," he said. "What I am trying to make clear is that I cannot possibly permit anything in my Shop to be bought in such a spirit. Not for any price you could name."

Martha Sturgis's heavy jaw dropped. "What was that you said?" she asked blankly.

It was a perilous moment, and Mr. Appleby knew it. His next words could set her off into another spasm of that awful laughter that would devastate him completely; or, worse, could send her right out of the Shop forever; or could decide the issue in his favor then and there. But it was a moment that had to be met, and, thought Mr. Appleby desperately, whatever else Martha Sturgis might be, she was a Woman.

He took a deep breath. "It is the policy of this Shop," he said quietly, "never to sell anything unless the prospective purchaser shows full appreciation for the article to be bought and can assure it the care and devotion to which it is entitled. That has always been the policy, and always will be as long as I am here. Anything other than that I would regard as desecration."

He watched Martha Sturgis with bated breath. There was a chair nearby, and she dropped into it heavily so that her skirts were drawn tight by her widespread thighs, and the obscene shoes were displayed mercilessly. She lit another cigarette, regarding him meanwhile with narrowed eyes through the flame of the match, and then fanned the air a little to dispel the cloud of smoke.

"You know," she said, "this is very interesting. I'd like to hear more about it."

To the inexperienced the problem of drawing information of the most personal nature from a total stranger would seem a perplexing one. To Mr. Appleby, whose interests had so often been dependent on such information, it was no problem at all. In very short time he had evidence that Martha Sturgis' estimate of her fortune was quite accurate, that she was apparently alone in the world without relatives or intimate friends, and—that she was not averse to the idea of marriage.

This last he drew from her during her now regular visits to the Shop where she would spread herself comfortably on a chair and talk to him endlessly. Much of her talk was about her father to whom Mr. Appleby evidently bore a striking resemblance.

"He even dressed like you," Martha Sturgis said reflectively. "Neat as a pin, and not only about himself either. He used to make an inspection of the house every day—march through and make sure everything was exactly where it had to be. And he kept it up right to the end. I remember an hour before he died how he went about straightening pictures on the wall."

Mr. Appleby, who had been peering with some irritation at a picture that hung slightly awry on the Shop wall, turned his attentions reluctantly from it.

"And you were with him to the end?" he asked sympathetically.

"Indeed I was."

"Well," Mr. Appleby said brightly, "one does deserve some reward for such sacrifice, doesn't one? Especially—and I hope this will not embarrass you, Miss Sturgis—when one considers that such a woman as yourself could undoubtedly have left the care of an aged father to enter matrimony almost at will. Isn't that so?"

Martha Sturgis sighed. "Maybe it is, and maybe it isn't," she said, "and I won't deny that I've had my dreams. But that's all they are, and I suppose that's all they ever will be."

"Why?" asked Mr. Appleby encouragingly.

"Because," said Martha Sturgis sombrely, "I have never yet met the man who could fit those dreams. I am not a simpering schoolgirl, Mr. Appleby; I don't have to balance myself against my bank account to know why any man would devote himself to me, and, frankly, his motives would be of no interest. But he must be a decent, respectable man who would spend every moment of his life worrying about me and caring for me; and he must be a man who would make the memory of my father a living thing."

Mr. Appleby rested a hand lightly on her shoulder.

"Miss Sturgis," he said gravely, "you may yet meet such a man."

She looked at him with features that were made even more blobby and unattractive by her emotion.

"Do you mean that, Mr. Appleby?" she asked. "Do you really believe that?"

Faith glowed in Mr. Appleby's eyes as he smiled down at her. "He may be closer than you dare realize," he said warmly.

Experience had proved to Mr. Appleby that once the ice is broken the best thing to do is take a deep breath and plunge in. Accordingly, he let very few days elapse before he made his proposal.

"Miss Sturgis," he said, "there comes a time to every lonely man when he can no longer bear his loneliness. If at such a time he is fortunate enough to meet the one woman to whom he could give unreservedly all his respect and tender feelings, he is a fortunate man indeed. Miss Sturgis—I am that man."

"Why, Mr. Appleby!" said Martha Sturgis, coloring a trifle. "That's really very good of you, but . . ."

At this note of indecision his heart sank. "Wait!" he interposed hastily. "If you have any doubts, Miss Sturgis, please speak them now so that I may answer them. Considering the state of my emotions, that would only be fair, wouldn't it?"

"Well, I suppose so," said Martha Sturgis. "You see, Mr. Appleby, I'd rather not get married at all than take the chance of getting someone who wasn't prepared to give me exactly what I'm looking for in marriage: absolute, single-minded devotion all the rest of my days."

"Miss Sturgis," said Mr. Appleby solemnly, "I am prepared to give you no less."

"Men say these things so easily," she sighed. "But—I shall certainly think about it, Mr. Appleby."

The dismal prospect of waiting an indefinite time for a woman of such careless habits to render a decision was not made any lighter by the sudden receipt a few days later of a note peremptorily requesting Mr. Appleby's presence at the offices of Gainsborough, Gainsborough, and Golding, attorneys-at-law. With his creditors closing in like a wolf pack, Mr. Appleby could only surmise the worst, and he was pleasantly surprised upon his arrival at Gainsborough, Gainsborough, and Golding to find that they represented, not his creditors, but Martha Sturgis herself.

The elder Gainsborough, obviously very much the guiding spirit of the firm, was a short, immensely fat man with pendulous dewlaps that almost concealed his collar, and large fishy eyes that goggled at Mr. Appleby. The younger Gainsborough was a duplicate of his brother, with jowls not quite so impressive, while Golding was an impassive young man with a hatchet face.

"This," said the elder Gainsborough, his eyes fixed glassily on Mr. Appleby, "is a delicate matter. Miss Sturgis, an esteemed client—" the younger Gainsborough nodded at this—"has mentioned entering matrimony with you, sir."

Mr. Appleby sitting primly on his chair was stirred by a pleased excitement. "Yes?" he said.

"And," continued the elder Gainsborough, "while Miss Sturgis is perfectly willing to concede that her fortune may be the object of attraction in any suitor's eyes—" he held up a pudgy hand to cut short Mr. Appleby's shocked protest—"she is also willing to dismiss that issue—"

"To ignore it, set it aside," said the younger Gainsborough sternly.

"—if the suitor is prepared to meet all other expectations in marriage."

"I am," said Mr. Appleby fervently.

"Mr. Appleby," said the elder Gainsborough abruptly, "have you been married before?"

Mr. Appleby thought swiftly. Denial would make any chance word about his past a deadly trap; admission, on the other hand, was a safeguard against that, and a thoroughly respectable one.

"Yes," he said.

"Divorced?"

"Good heavens, no!" said Mr. Appleby, genuinely shocked.

The Gainsboroughs looked at each other in approval. "Good," said the elder, "very good. Perhaps, Mr. Appleby, the question seemed impertinent, but in these days of moral laxity . . ."

"I should like it known in that case," said Mr. Appleby sturdily, "that I am as far from moral laxity as any human being can be. Tobacco, strong drink, and—ah—"

"Loose women," said the younger Gainsborough briskly.

"Yes," said Mr. Appleby reddening, "—are unknown to me."

The elder Gainsborough nodded. "Under any conditions," he said, "Miss Sturgis will not make any precipitate decision. She should have her answer for you within a month, however, and during that time, if you don't mind taking the advice of an old man, I suggest that you court her assiduously. She is a woman, Mr. Appleby, and I imagine that all women are much alike."

"I imagine they are," said Mr. Appleby.

"Devotion," said the younger Gainsborough. "Constancy. That's the ticket."

What he was being asked to do, Mr. Appleby reflected in one of his solitary moments, was to put aside the Shop and the orderly world it represented and to set the unappealing figure of Martha Sturgis in its place. It was a temporary measure, of course; it was one that would prove richly rewarding when Martha Sturgis had been properly wed and sent the way of the preceding Mrs. Applebys; but it was not made any easier by enforced familiarity with the woman. It was inevitable that since Mr. Appleby viewed matters not only as a prospective bridegroom, but also as a prospective widower, so to speak, he found his teeth constantly set on edge by the unwitting irony which crept into so many of her tedious discussions on marriage.

"The way I see it," Martha Sturgis once remarked, "is that a man who would divorce his wife would divorce any other woman he ever married. You take a look at all these broken marriages today, and I'll bet that in practically every case you'll find a man who's always shopping around and never finding what he wants. Now, the man *I* marry," she said pointedly, "must be willing to settle down and stay settled."

"Of course," said Mr. Appleby.

"I have heard," Martha Sturgis told him on another, and particularly trying, occasion, "that a satisfactory marriage increases a woman's span of years. That's an excellent argument for marriage, don't you think?"

"Of course," said Mr. Appleby.

It seemed to him that during that month of trial most of his conversation was restricted to the single phrase "of course," delivered with varying inflections; but the tactic must have been the proper one since at the end of the month he was able to change the formula to "I do," in a wedding ceremony at which Gainsborough, Gainsborough, and Golding were the sole guests.

Immediately afterward, Mr. Appleby (to his discomfort) was borne off with his bride to a photographer's shop where innumerable pictures were made under the supervision of the dour Golding, following which, Mr. Appleby (to his delight) exchanged documents with his wife which made them each other's heirs to all properties, possessions, *et cetera,* whatsoever.

If Mr. Appleby had occasionally appeared rather abstracted during these festivities, it was only because his mind was neatly arranging the program of impending events. The rug (the very same one that had served so well in six previous episodes) had to be placed; and then there would come the moment when he would ask for a glass of water, when he would place one hand on her shoulder, and with the other . . . It could not be a moment that took place without due time passing; yet it could not be forestalled too long in view of the pressure exercised by the Shop's voracious creditors. Watching the pen in his wife's hand as she signed her will, he decided there would be time within a few weeks. With the will in his possession there would be no point in waiting longer than that.

Before the first of those weeks was up, however, Mr. Appleby knew that even this estimate would have to undergo drastic revision. There was no question about it: he was simply not equipped to cope with his marriage.

For one thing, her home (and now his), a brownstone cavern inherited from her mother, was a nightmare of disorder. On the principle, perhaps, that anything flung casually aside was not worth picking up since it would only be flung aside again, an amazing litter had accumulated in every room. The contents of brimming closets and drawers were recklessly exchanged, mislaid, or added to the general litter, and over all lay a thin film of dust. On Mr. Appleby's quivering nervous system all this had the effect of a fingernail dragging along an endless blackboard.

The one task to which Mrs. Appleby devoted herself, as it happened, was the one which her husband prayerfully wished she would spare herself. She doted on cookery, and during mealtimes would trudge back and forth endlessly between kitchen and dining-room laden with dishes outside any of Mr. Appleby's experience.

At his first feeble protests his wife had taken pains to explain in precise terms that she was sensitive to any criticism of her cooking, even the implied criticism of a partly emptied plate; and thereafter, Mr. Appleby, plunging hopelessly through rare meats, rich sauces, and heavy pastries, found added to his tribulations the incessant pangs of dyspepsia. Nor were his pains eased by his wife's insistence that he prove himself a trencherman of her mettle. She would thrust plates heaped high with indigestibles under his quivering nose, and, bracing himself like a martyr facing the lions, Mr. Appleby would empty his portion into a digestive tract that cried for simple fare properly boiled or toasted.

It became one of his fondest waking dreams, that scene where he returned from his wife's burial to dine on hot tea and toast and, perhaps, a medium-boiled egg. But even that dream and its sequel—where he proceeded to set the house in order—were not sufficient to buoy him up each day when he awoke and reflected on what lay ahead of him.

Each day found his wife more insistent in her demands for his attentions. And on that day when she openly reproved him for devoting more of those attentions to the Shop than to herself, Mr.

Appleby knew the time had come to prepare for the final act. He brought home the rug that evening and carefully laid it in place between the living room and the hallway that led to the kitchen. Martha Appleby watched him without any great enthusiasm.

"That's a shabby-looking thing, all right," she said. "What is it, Appie, an antique or something?"

She had taken to calling him by that atrocious name and seemed cheerfully oblivious to the way he winced under it. He winced now.

"It is not an antique," Mr. Appleby admitted, "but I hold it dear for many reasons. It has a great deal of sentimental value to me."

Mrs. Appleby smiled fondly at him. "And you brought it for me, didn't you?"

"Yes," said Mr. Appleby, "I did."

"You're a dear," said Mrs. Appleby. "You really are."

Watching her cross the rug on slipshod feet to use the telephone, which stood on a small table the other side of the hallway, Mr. Appleby toyed with the idea that since she used the telephone at about the same time every evening he could schedule the accident for that time. The advantages were obvious: since those calls seemed to be the only routine she observed with any fidelity, she would cross the rug at a certain time, and he would be in a position to settle matters then and there.

However, thought Mr. Appleby as he polished his spectacles, that brought up the problem of how best to approach her under such circumstances. Clearly the tried and tested methods were best, but if the telephone call and the glass of water could be synchronized . . .

"A penny for your thoughts, Appie," said Mrs. Appleby brightly. She had laid down the telephone and crossed the hallway so that she stood squarely on the rug. Mr. Appleby replaced his spectacles and peered at her through them.

"I wish," he said querulously, "you would not address me by that horrid name. You know I detest it."

"Nonsense," his wife said briefly. "I think it's cute."

"I do not."

"Well, I like it," said Mrs. Appleby with the air of one who has settled a matter once and for all. "Anyhow," she pouted, "that couldn't have been what you were thinking about before I started talking to you, could it?"

It struck Mr. Appleby that when this stout, unkempt woman pouted, she resembled nothing so much as a wax doll badly worn by time and handling. He pushed away the thought to frame some suitable answer.

"As it happens," he said, "my mind was on the disgraceful state of my clothes. Need I remind you again that there are buttons missing from practically every garment I own?"

Mrs. Appleby yawned broadly. "I'll get to it sooner or later."

"Tomorrow perhaps?"

"I doubt it," said Mrs. Appleby. She turned toward the stairs. "Come to sleep, Appie. I'm dead tired."

Mr. Appleby followed her thoughtfully. Tomorrow, he knew, he would have to get one of his suits to the tailor if he wanted to have anything fit to wear at the funeral.

He had brought home the suit and hung it neatly away; he had eaten his dinner; and he had sat in the living room listening to his wife's hoarse voice go on for what seemed interminable hours, although the clock was not yet at nine.

Now with rising excitement he saw her lift herself slowly from her chair and cross the room to the hallway. As she reached for the telephone Mr. Appleby cleared his throat sharply. "If you don't mind," he said, "I'd like a glass of water."

Mrs. Appleby turned to look at him. "A glass of water?"

"If you don't mind," said Mr. Appleby, and waited as she hesitated, then set down the telephone, and turned toward the kitchen. There was the sound of a glass being rinsed in the kitchen, and then Mrs. Appleby came up to him holding it out. He laid one hand appreciatively on her plump shoulder, and then lifted the other as if to brush back a strand of untidy hair at her cheek.

"Is that what happened to all the others?" said Mrs. Appleby quietly.

Mr. Appleby felt his hand freeze in mid-air and the chill from it run down into his marrow. "Others?" he managed to say. "What others?"

His wife smiled grimly at him, and he saw that the glass of water in her hand was perfectly steady. "Six others," she said. "That is, six by my count. Why? Were there any more?"

"No," he said, then caught wildly at himself. "I don't understand what you're talking about!"

"Dear Appie. Surely you couldn't forget six wives just like that. Unless, of course, I've come to mean so much to you that you can't bear to think of the others. That would be a lovely thing to happen, wouldn't it?"

"I *was* married before," Mr. Appleby said loudly. "I made that quite clear myself. But this talk about six wives!"

"Of course you were married before, Appie. And it was quite easy to find out to whom—and it was just as easy to find out about the one before that—and all the others. Or even about your mother, or where you went to school, or where you were born. You see, Appie, Mr. Gainsborough is really a very clever man."

"Then it was Gainsborough who put you up to this!"

"Not at all, you foolish little man," his wife said contemptuously. "All the time you were making your plans I was unmaking them. From the moment I laid eyes on you I knew you for what you are. Does that surprise you?"

Mr. Appleby struggled with the emotions of a man who has picked up a twig to find a viper in his hand. "How could you know?" he gasped.

"Because you were the image of my father. Because in everything —the way you dress, your insufferable neatness, your priggish arrogance, the little moral lectures you dote on—you are what he was. And all my life I hated him for what he was, and what it did to my mother. He married her for her money, made her every day a nightmare, and then killed her for what was left of her fortune."

"Killed her?" said Mr. Appleby, stupefied.

"Oh, come," his wife said sharply. "Do you think you're the only man who was ever capable of that? Yes, he killed her—murdered her, if you prefer—by asking for a glass of water, and then breaking her neck when she offered it to him. A method strangely similar to yours, isn't it?"

Mr. Appleby found the incredible answer rising to his mind, but refused to accept it. "What happened to him?" he demanded. "Tell me what happened! Was he caught?"

"No, he was never caught. There were no witnesses to what he did, but Mr. Gainsborough had been my mother's lawyer, a dear friend of hers. He had suspicions and demanded a hearing. He brought a doctor to the hearing who made it plain how my father could have killed her and made it look as if she had slipped on a rug, but before there was any decision my father died of a heart attack."

"That was the case—the case I read!" Mr. Appleby groaned, and then was silent under his wife's sardonic regard.

"When he was gone," she went on inexorably, "I swore I would some day find a man exactly like him, and I would make that man live the life my father should have lived. I would know his every habit and every taste, and none of them should go satisfied. I would know he married me for my money, and he would never get a penny of it until I was dead and gone. And that would be a long, long time, because he would spend his life taking care that I should live out my life to the last possible breath."

Mr. Appleby pulled his wits together, and saw that despite her emotion she had remained in the same position. "How can you make him do that?" he asked softly, and moved an inch closer.

"It does sound strange, doesn't it, Appie?" she observed. "But hardly as strange as the fact that your six wives died by slipping on a rug—very much like this one—while bringing you a glass of water—very much like this one. So strange, that Mr. Gainsborough was led to remark that too many coincidences will certainly hang a man. Especially if there is reason to bring them to light in a trial for murder."

Mr. Appleby suddenly found the constriction of his collar unbearable. "That doesn't answer my question," he said craftily. "How can you make sure that I would devote my life to prolonging yours?"

"A man whose wife is in a position to have him hanged should be able to see that clearly."

"No," said Mr. Appleby in a stifled voice, "I only see that such a man is forced to rid himself of his wife as quickly as possible."

"Ah, but that's where the arrangements come in."

"Arrangements? What arrangements?" demanded Mr. Appleby.

"I'd like very much to explain them," his wife said. "In fact, I see the time has come when it's imperative to do so. But I do find it uncomfortable standing here like this."

"Never mind that," said Mr. Appleby impatiently, and his wife shrugged.

"Well, then," she said coolly, "Mr. Gainsborough now has all the documents about your marriages—the way the previous deaths took place, the way you always happened to get the bequests at just the right moment to pay your shop's debts.

"Besides this, he has a letter from me, explaining that in the event of my death an investigation be made immediately and all necessary action be taken. Mr. Gainsborough is really very efficient. The fingerprints and photographs . . ."

"Fingerprints and photographs!" cried Mr. Appleby.

"Of course. After my father's death it was found that he had made all preparations for a quick trip abroad. Mr. Gainsborough has assured me that in case you had such ideas in mind you should get rid of them. No matter where you are, he said, it will be quite easy to bring you back again."

"What do you want of me?" asked Mr. Appleby numbly. "Surely you don't expect me to stay now, and—"

"Oh, yes, I do. And since we've come to this point I may as well tell you I expect you to give up your useless shop once and for all, and make it a point to be at home with me the entire day."

"Give up the Shop!" he exclaimed.

"You must remember, Appie, that in my letter asking for a full investigation at my death, I did not specify death by any particular means. I look forward to a long and pleasant life with you always at my side, and perhaps—mind you, I only say *perhaps*—some day I shall turn over that letter and all the evidence to you. You can see how much it is to your interest, therefore, to watch over me very carefully."

The telephone rang with abrupt violence, and Mrs. Appleby nodded toward it. "Almost as carefully," she said softly, "as Mr. Gainsborough. Unless I call him every evening at nine to report I am well and happy, it seems he will jump to the most shocking conclusions."

"Wait," said Mr. Appleby. He lifted the telephone, and there was no mistaking the voice that spoke.

"Hello," said the elder Gainsborough. "Hello, Mrs. Appleby?"

Mr. Appleby essayed a cunning move. "No," he said, "I'm afraid she can't speak to you now. What is it?"

The voice in his ear took on an unmistakable cold menace. "This is Gainsborough, Mr. Appleby, and I wish to speak to your wife immediately. I will give you ten seconds to have her at this telephone, Mr. Appleby. Do you understand?"

Mr. Appleby turned dully toward his wife and held out the telephone. "It's for you," he said, and then saw with a start of terror that as she turned to set down the glass of water the rug skidded slightly under her feet. Her arms flailed the air as she fought for balance, the glass smashed at his feet drenching his neat trousers, and her face twisted into a silent scream. Then her body struck the floor and lay inertly in the position with which he was so familiar.

Watching her, he was barely conscious of the voice emerging tinnily from the telephone in his hand.

"The ten seconds are up, Mr. Appleby," it said shrilly. "Do you understand? *Your time is up!*"

NIGHT AT THE VULCAN

by Ngaio Marsh

CAST OF CHARACTERS

Martyn Tarne
Bob Grantley, business manager
Fred Badger, night-watchman
Clem Smith, stage-manager
Bob Cringle, dresser to Adam Poole
Adam Poole, actor-manager
Helena Hamilton, leading lady
Clark Bennington, her husband
Gay Gainsford, his niece
J. G. Darcey, character actor
Parry Percival, juvenile
Jacques Doré, designer and assistant to Adam Poole
Dr. John James Rutherford, playwright

} of the Vulcan Theatre

Chief Detective-Inspector Alleyn
Detective-Inspector Fox
Detective-Sergeant Gibson
Detective-Sergeant Bailey, finger-print expert
Detective-Sergeant Thompson, photographer
P. C. Lord Michael Lamprey
Dr. Curtis

} of the Criminal Investigation Department, New Scotland Yard

CHAPTER I
THE VULCAN

As she turned into Carpet Street the girl wondered at her own obstinacy. To what a pass it had brought her, she thought. She lifted first one foot and then the other, determined not to drag them. They felt now as if their texture had changed: their bones, it seemed, were covered by sponge and burning wires.

A clock in a jeweller's window gave the time as twenty-three minutes to five. She knew by the consequential scurry of its second-hand that it was alive. It was surrounded by other clocks that made mad dead statements of divergent times as if, she thought, to set before her the stages of that day's fruitless pilgrimage. Nine o'clock, the first agent. Nine thirty-six, the beginning of the wait for auditions at the Unicorn; five minutes past twelve, the first dismissal. "Thank you, Miss—ah— Thank you, dear. Leave your name and address. Next, please." No record of her flight from the smell of restaurants, but it must have been about ten to two, a time registered by a gilt carriage-clock in the corner, that she had climbed the stairs to Garnet Marks's Agency on the third floor. Three o'clock exactly at the Achilles where the auditions had already closed, and the next hour in and out of film agencies. "Leave your picture if you like, dear. Let you know if there's anything." Always the same. As punctual as time itself. The clocks receded, wobbled, enlarged themselves and at the same time spread before their dials a tenuous veil. Beneath the arm of a bronze nude that brandished an active swinging dial, she caught sight of a face: her own. She groped in her bag, and presently in front of the mirrored face a hand appeared and made a gesture at its own mouth with the stub of a lipstick. There was a coolness on her forehead, something pressed heavily against it. She discovered that this was the shop-window.

Behind the looking-glass was a man who peered at her from the shop's interior. She steadied herself with her hand against the window, lifted her suitcase and turned away.

The Vulcan Theatre was near the bottom of the street. Although she did not at first see its name above the entry, she had, during the past fortnight, discovered a sensitivity to theatres. She was aware of them at a distance. The way was downhill: her knees trembled and she resisted with difficulty an impulse to break into a shamble. Among the stream of faces that approached and sailed past there were now some that, on seeing hers, sharpened into awareness and speculation. She attracted notice.

The stage-door was at the end of an alleyway. Puddles of water obstructed her passage and she did not altogether avoid them. The surface of the wall was crenellated and damp.

"She knows," a rather shrill uncertain voice announced inside the theatre, "but she *mustn't* be told." A second voice spoke unintelligibly. The first voice repeated its statement with a change of emphasis: "She *knows* but she mustn't be *told*," and after a further interruption added dismally: "Thank you very much."

Five young women came out of the stage-door and it was shut behind them. She leant against the wall as they passed her. The first two muttered together and moved their shoulders petulantly, the third stared at her and at once she bent her head. The fourth passed by quickly with compressed lips. She kept her head averted and heard, but did not see, the last girl halt beside her.

"Well, for God's sake!" She looked up and saw, for the second time that day, a too-large face, over-painted, with lips that twisted downwards, tinted lids, and thickly mascaraed lashes.

She said: "I'm late, aren't I?"

"You've had it, dear. I gave you the wrong tip at Marks's. The show here, with the part I told you about, goes on this week. They were auditioning for a tour— 'That'll be all for to-day, ladies, thank you. What's the hurry, here's your hat!' For what it's worth, it's all over."

"I lost my way," she said faintly.

"Too bad." The large face swam nearer. "Are you all right?" it demanded.

She made a slight movement of her head. "A bit tired. All right, really."

"You look shocking. Here: wait a sec. Try this."

"No, no. Really. Thank you so much but—"

"It's O.K. A chap who travels for a French firm gave it to me. It's marvellous stuff: cognac. Go *on*."

A hand steadied her head. The cold mouth of the flask opened her lips and pressed against her teeth. She tried to say: "I've had nothing to eat," and at once was forced to gulp down a burning stream. The voice encouraged her: "Do you a power of good. Have the other half."

She shuddered, gasped and pushed the flask away. "No, please!"

"Is it doing the trick?"

"This is wonderfully kind of you. I am so grateful. Yes, I think it must be doing the trick."

"Gra-a-a-nd. Well, if you're sure you'll be O.K. . . ."

"Yes, indeed. I don't even know your name."

"Trixie O'Sullivan."

"I'm Martyn Tarne."

"Look nice in the programme, wouldn't it? If there's nothing else I can do . . ."

"Honestly. I'll be fine."

"You look better," Miss O'Sullivan said doubtfully. "We may run into each other again. The bloody round, the common task." She began to move away. "I've got a date, actually, and I'm running late."

"Yes, of course. Good-bye, and thank you."

"It's open in front. There's a seat in the foyer. Nobody'll say anything. Why not sit there for a bit?" She was half-way down the alley. "Hope you get fixed up," she said. "God, it's going to rain. What a life!"

"What a life," Martyn Tarne echoed, and tired to sound gay and ironic.

"I hope you'll be all right. 'Bye."

"Good-bye and thank you."

The alley was quiet now. Without moving she took stock of herself. Something thrummed inside her head and the tips of her fingers tingled but she no longer felt as if she were going to faint. The brandy glowed at the core of her being, sending out ripples of comfort. She tried to think what she should do. There was a church, back in the Strand: she ought to know its name. One could sleep there, she had been told, and perhaps there would be soup. That would leave two and fourpence for to-morrow: all she had. She lifted her suitcase—it was heavier than she had remembered—and walked to the end of the alleyway. Half a dozen raindrops plopped into a puddle. People hurried along the footpath with upward glances and opened their umbrellas. As she hesitated, the rain came down suddenly and decisively. She turned towards the front of the theatre and at first thought it was shut. Then she noticed that one of the plate-glass doors was ajar.

She pushed it open and went in.

The Vulcan was a new theatre, fashioned from the shell of an old one. Its foyer was an affair of geranium-red leather, chromium steel and double glass walls housing cacti. The central box-office, marked RESERVED TICKETS ONLY, was flanked by doors and beyond them, in the corners, were tubular steel and rubber-foam seats. She crossed the heavily carpeted floor and sat in one of these. Her feet and legs, released from the torment of supporting and moving her body, throbbed ardently.

Facing Martyn, on a huge easel, was a frame of photographs under a printed legend:

Opening at this theatre
on
THURSDAY, MAY 11TH
THUS TO REVISIT
A New Play
by
JOHN JAMES RUTHERFORD

She stared at two large familiar faces and four strange smaller ones. Adam Poole and Helena Hamilton: those were famous faces. Monstrously enlarged, they had looked out at the New Zealand and Australian public from hoardings and from above cinema entrances. She had stood in queues many times to see them, separately and together. They were in the centre, and surrounding them were Clark Bennington with a pipe and stick and a look of faded romanticism in his eyes, J. G. Darcey with pince-nez and hair *en brosse,* Gay Gainsford, young and intense, and Parry Percival, youngish and dashing. The faces swam together and grew dim.

It was very quiet in the foyer and beginning to get dark. On the other side of the entrance doors the rain drove down slantways, half-blinding her vision of homeward-bound pedestrians and the traffic of the street beyond them. She saw the lights go on in the top of a bus, illuminating the passive and remote faces of its passengers. The glare of headlamps shone pale across the rain. A wave of loneliness, excruciating in its intensity, engulfed Martyn and she closed her eyes. For the first time since her ordeal began, panic rose in her throat and sickened her. Phrases drifted with an aimless rhythm on the tide of her desolation: "You're sunk, you're sunk, you're utterly sunk, you asked for it, and you've got it. What'll happen to you now?"

She was drowning at night in a very lonely sea. She saw lights shine on some unattainable shore. Pieces of flotsam bobbed indifferently against her hands. At the climax of despair, metallic noises, stupid and commonplace, set up a clatter in her head.

Martyn jerked galvanically and opened her eyes. The whirr and click of her fantasy had been repeated behind an obscured-glass wall on her left. Light glowed beyond the wall and she was confronted by the image of a god, sand-blasted across the surface of the glass and beating at a forge under the surprising supervision, it appeared, of Melpomene and Thalia. Further along, a notice in red light, DRESS CIRCLE AND STALLS, jutted out from an opening. Beyond the hammer-blows of her heart a muffled voice spoke peevishly.

". . . not much use to *me*. What? Yes, I know, old boy, but that's not the point."

The voice seemed to listen. Martyn thought: "This is it. In a minute I'll be turned out."

". . . something pretty bad," the voice said irritably. "She's gone to hospital. . . . They *said* so but nobody's turned up. . . . Well, you know what she's like, old boy, don't you? We've been snowed under all day and *I* haven't been able to do anything about it . . . auditions for the northern tour of the old piece . . . yes, yes, that's all fixed but . . . Look, another thing: the *Onlooker* wants a story and pictures for this week . . . yes, on stage. In costume. Nine-thirty in the morning and everything still in the boxes. . . . Well, can't you think of *anyone*? . . . Who? . . . Oh, God, I'll give it a pop. All right, old boy, thanks."

To Martyn, dazed with brandy and sleep, it was a distortion of a day-dream. Very often had she dreamt herself into a theatre where all was confusion because the leading actress had laryngitis and the understudy was useless. She would present herself modestly: "I happen to know the lines. I could perhaps . . ." The sudden attentiveness, when she began to speak the lines . . . the opening night . . . the grateful tears streaming down the boiled shirts of the management . . . the critics . . . no image had been too gross for her.

"Eileen?" said the voice. "Thank God! Listen, darling, it's Bob Grantley here. Listen, Eileen, I want you to do something terribly kind. I know it's asking a hell of a lot but I'm in trouble and you're my last hope. Helena's dresser's ill. Yes, indeed, poor old Tansley. Yes, I'm afraid so. Just this afternoon, and we haven't been able to raise anybody. First dress rehearsal tomorrow night and a photograph call in the morning and nothing unpacked or anything. I know what a good soul you are and I wondered . . . Oh, God! I see. Yes, I see. No, of course. Oh, well, never mind. I know you would. Yes. 'Bye."

Silence. Precariously alone in the foyer, she meditated an advance upon the man beyond the glass wall and suppressed a dreadful impulse in herself towards hysteria. This was her day-dream in terms of reality. She must have slept longer than she had thought. Her feet were sleeping still. She began to test them, tingling and pricking, against the floor. She could see her reflection in the front doors, a dingy figure with a pallid face and cavernous shadows for eyes.

The light behind the glass wall went out. There was, however, still a yellow glow coming through the box-office door. As she got to her feet and steadied herself, the door opened.

"I believe," she said, "you are looking for a dresser."

ii

As he had stopped dead in the lighted doorway she couldn't see the man clearly but his silhouette was stocky and trim.

He said with what seemed to be a mixture of irritation and relief: "Good Lord, how long have you been here?"

"Not long. You were on the telephone. I didn't like to interrupt."

"Interrupt!" he ejaculated as if she talked nonsense. He looked at his watch, groaned, and said rapidly: "You've come about this job? From Mrs. Greenacres, aren't you?"

She wondered who Mrs. Greenacres could be? An employment agent? She hunted desperately for the right phrase, the authentic language.

"I understood you required a dresser and I would be pleased to apply." Should she have added "sir"?

"It's for Miss Helena Hamilton," he said rapidly. "Her own dresser who's been with her for years—for a long time—has been taken ill. I explained to Mrs. Greenacres. Photograph call for nine in the morning and first dress rehearsal to-morrow night. We open on Thursday. The dressing's heavy. Two quick changes and so on. I suppose you've got references?"

Her mouth was dry. She said: "I haven't brought—" and was saved by the telephone bell. He plunged back into the office and she heard him shout "Vulcan!" as he picked up the receiver. "Grantley, here," he said. "Oh, hullo, darling. Look, I'm desperately sorry, but I've been held up or I'd have rung you before. For God's sake apologize for me. Try and keep them going till I get there. I know, I know. Not a smell of one until—" The voice became suddenly muffled: she caught isolated words. "I think so . . . yes, I'll ask . . . yes . . . Right. 'Bye, darling."

He darted out, now wearing a hat and struggling into a raincoat. "Look," he said, "Miss—"

"Tarne."

"Miss Tarne. Can you start right away? Miss Hamilton's things are in her dressing-room. They need to be unpacked and hung out tonight. There'll be a lot of pressing. The cleaners have been in but the room's not ready. You can finish in the morning but she wants the things that can't be ironed—I wouldn't know—hung out. Here are the keys. We'll see how you get on and fix up something definite tomorrow if you suit. The night-watchman's there. He'll open the room for you. Say I sent you. Here!"

He fished out a wallet, found a card and scribbled on it. "He's a bit of a stickler: you'd better take this."

She took the card and the keys. "To-night?" she said. "Now?"

"Well, can you?"

"I—yes. But—"

"Not worrying about after-hours are you?"

"No."

For the first time he seemed, in the darkish foyer, to be looking closely at her. "I suppose," he muttered, "it's a bit—" and stopped short.

Martyn said in a voice that to herself sounded half-choked: "I'm perfectly trustworthy. You spoke of references. I have—"

"Oh, yes, yes," he said. "Good. That'll be O.K. then. I'm late. Will you be all right? You can go through the house. It's raining outside. Through there, will you? Thank you. Good night."

Taking up her suitcase, she went through the door he swung open and found herself in the theatre.

She was at the back of the stalls, standing on thick carpet at the top of the ramp and facing the centre aisle. It was not absolutely dark. The curtain was half-raised and a bluish light filtered in from offstage through some opening—a faintly discerned window—in the scenery. This light was dimly reflected on the shrouded boxes. The dome was invisible, lost in shadow, and so far above that the rain, hammering on the roof beyond it, sounded much as a rumour of drums to Martyn. The deadened air smelt of naphthalene and plush.

She started off cautiously down the aisle. "I forgot," said Mr. Grantley's voice behind her. She managed to choke back a yelp. "You'd better get some flowers for the dressing-room. She likes roses. Here's another card."

"I don't think I've—"

"Florian's at the corner," he shouted. "Show them the card."

The door swung to behind him and a moment later she heard a more remote slam. She waited for a little while longer, to accustom herself to the dark. The shadows melted and the shape of the auditorium filtered through them like an image on a film in the darkroom. She thought it beautiful: the curve of the circle, the fan-like shell that enclosed it, the elegance of the proscenium and modesty of the ornament—all these seemed good to Martyn, and her growing sight of them refreshed her. Though this encouragement had an unreal, rather dream-like character, yet it did actually dispel something of her physical exhaustion so that it was with renewed heart that she climbed a little curved flight of steps on the Prompt side of the proscenium, pushed open the pass-door at the top and arrived back-stage.

She was on her own ground. A single blue working-light, thick with dust, revealed a baize letter-rack and hinted at the batten-and-canvas backs of scenery fading upwards into yawning blackness. At her feet a litter of flex ran down into holes in the stage. There were vague, scarcely discernible shapes that she recognized as stacked flats, light bunches, the underside of perches, a wind machine and rain box. She smelt paint and glue size. As she received the assurance of these familiar signs she heard a faint scuffling noise—a rattle of paper, she thought. She moved forward.

In the darkness ahead of her a door opened on an oblong of light which widened to admit the figure of a man in an overcoat. He stood with bent head, fumbled in his pocket and produced a torch. The beam shot out, hunted briefly about the set and walls and found her. She blinked into a dazzling white disc and said: "Mr. Grantley sent me round. I'm the dresser."

"Dresser?" the man said hoarsely. He kept his torchlight on her face and moved towards her. "I wasn't told about no dresser," he said.

She held Mr. Grantley's card out. He came closer and flashed his light on it without touching it. "Ah," he said with a sort of grudging cheerfulness, "that's different. Now I know where I am, don't I?"

"I hope so," she said, trying to make her voice friendly. "I'm sorry to bother you. Miss Hamilton's dresser has been taken ill and I've got the job."

"*Aren't* you lucky," he said with obvious relish and added, "Not but what she isn't a lady when she takes the fit for it."

He was eating something. The movement of his jaws, the succulent noises he made and the faint odour of food were an outrage. She could have screamed her hunger at him. Her mouth filled with saliva.

" 'E says to open the star room," he said. "Come on froo while I get the keys. I was 'avin' me bit er supper."

She followed him into a tiny room choked with junk. A kettle stuttered on a gas ring by a sink clotted with dregs of calcimine and tea leaves. His supper was laid out on a newspaper—bread and an open tin of jam. He explained that he was about to make a cup of tea and suggested she should wait while he did so. She leant against the door and watched him. The fragrance of freshly brewed tea rose above the reek of stale size and dust. She thought, "If he drinks it now I'll have to go out."

"Like a drop of char?" he said. His back was turned to her.

"Very much."

He rinsed out a stained cup under the tap.

Martyn said loudly: "I've got a tin of meat in my suitcase. I was saving it. If you'd like to share it and could spare some of your bread . . ."

He swung round and for the first time she saw his face. He was dark and thin and his eyes were brightly impertinent. Their expression changed as he stared at her.

" 'Ullo, 'ullo!" he said. "Who give *you* a tanner and borrowed 'alf-a-crahn? What's up?"

"I'm all right."

"*Are* you? Your looks don't flatter you, then."

"I'm a bit tired and—" Her voice broke and she thought in terror that she was going to cry. "It's nothing," she said.

" 'Ere!" He dragged a box out from under the sink and not ungently pushed her down on it. "Where's this remarkable tin of very pertikler meat? Give us a shine at it."

He shoved her suitcase over and while she fumbled at the lock busied himself with pouring out tea. "Nothin' to touch a drop of the old char when you're browned off," he said. He put the reeking cup of dark fluid beside her and turned away.

"With any luck," Martyn thought, folding back the garments in her case, "I won't have to sell these now."

She found the tin and gave it to him. "Coo!" he said. "Looks lovely, don't it? Tongue and veal and a pitcher of sheep to show there's no deception. Very tempting."

"Can you open it?"

"Can I open it? Oh, dear."

She drank her scalding tea and watched him open the tin and turn its contents out on a more than dubious plate. Using his clasp knife he perched chunks of meat on a slab of bread and held it out to her. "You're in luck," he said. "Eat it slow."

She urged him to join her but he said he would set his share aside for later. They could both, he suggested, take another cut at it tomorrow. He examined the tin with interest while Martyn consumed her portion. She had never before given such intense concentration to a physical act. She would never have believed that eating could bring so fierce a satisfaction.

"Comes from Australia, don't it?" her companion said, still contemplating the tin.

"New Zealand."

"Same thing."

Martyn said: "Not really. There's quite a big sea in between."

"Do you come from there?"

"Where?"

"Australia."

"No. I'm a New Zealander."

"Same thing."

She looked up and found him grinning at her. He made the gesture of wiping the smile off his face. "Oh, dear," he said.

Martyn finished her tea and stood up. "I must start my job," she said.

"Feel better?"

"Much, much better."

"Would it be quite a spell since you ate anything?"

"Yesterday."

"I never fancy drinkin' on an empty stomach, myself."

Her face burnt against the palms of her hands. "But I don't . . . I mean, I know. I mean I was a bit faint and somebody . . . a girl . . . she was terribly kind . . ."

"Does yer mother know yer aht?" he asked ironically, and took a key from a collection hung on nails behind the door. "If you *must* work," he said.

"Please."

"Personally escorted tour abaht to commence. Follow in single file and don't talk to the guide. I thank you."

She followed him to the stage and round the back of the set. He warned her of obstructions by bobbing his torchlight on them and, when she stumbled against a muffled table, took her hand. She was disquieted by the grip of his fingers, calloused and wooden, and by the warmth of his palm, which was unexpectedly soft. She was oppressed with renewed loneliness and fear.

"End of the penny section," he said, releasing her. He unlocked a door, reached inside and switched on a light.

"They call this the Greenroom," he said. "That's what it was in the old days. It's been done up. Guv'nor's idea."

It was a room without a window, newly painted in green. There were a number of armchairs in brown leather, a round table littered with magazines, a set of well-stocked bookshelves and a gas fire. Groups of framed Pollock's prints decorated the walls: "Mr. Dale as Claude Amboine," "Mr. T. Hicks as Richard I," "Mr. S. French as Harlequin." This last enchanted Martyn because the diamonds of Mr. French's costume had been filled in with actual red and green sequins and he glittered in his frame.

Above the fireplace hung a largish sketch—it was little more than that—of a man of about thirty-five in mediaeval dress, with a hood that he was in the act of pushing away from his face. The face was arresting. It had great purity of form, being wide across the eyes and heart-shaped. The mouth, in particular, was of a most subtle character, perfectly masculine but drawn with extreme delicacy. It was well done: it had both strength and refinement. Yet it was not these qualities that disturbed Martyn. Reflected in the glass that covered the picture she saw her own face lying ghost-wise across the other; their forms intermingled like those in a twice-exposed photograph. It seemed to Martyn that her companion must be looking over her shoulder at this double image and she moved away from him and nearer to the picture. The reflection disappeared. Something was written faintly in one corner of the sketch. She drew closer and saw that it was a single word: *Everyman*.

"Spittin' image of 'im, ain't it?" said the night-watchman behind her.

"I don't know," she said quickly. "Is it?"

"*Is* it! Don't you know the Guv'nor when you see 'im?"

"The Governor?"

"'Strewth you're a caution and no error. Don't you know who owns this show? That's the great Mr. Adam Poole, that is."

"Oh," she murmured after a pause, and added uneasily: "I've seen him in the pictures, of course."

"Go on!" he jeered. "Where would that be? Australia? Fancy!"

He had been very kind to her, but she found his remorseless vein of irony exasperating. It would have been easier and less tedious to have let it go but she found herself embarked on an explanation. Of course she knew all about Mr. Adam Poole, she said. She'd seen his photograph in the foyer. All his pictures had been shown in New Zealand. She knew he was the most distinguished of the younger contemporary actor-managers. She was merely startled by the painting because . . . But it was impossible to explain why the face in the painting disturbed her and the unfinished phrase trailed away into an embarrassed silence.

Her companion listened to this rigmarole with an equivocal grin and when she gave it up merely remarked: "Don't apologize. It's the same with all the ladies. 'E fair rocks 'em. Talk about 'aving what it takes."

"I don't mean that at all," she shouted angrily.

"You should see 'em clawing at each other to get at 'im rahnd the stage-door, first nights. Something savage! Females of the speeches? Disgrace to their sexes more like. There's an ironing board etceterer in the wardrobe-room further along. You can plug in when you're ready. 'Er royal 'ighness is over the way."

He went out, opened a further door, switched on a light and called to her to join him.

iii

As soon as she crossed the threshold of the star dressing-room she smelt greasepaint. The dressing-shelf was bare, the room untenanted, but the smell of cosmetics mingled with the faint reek of gas. There were isolated dabs of colour on the shelves and the looking-glass; the lamp bulbs were smeared with cream and red where sticks of greasepaint had been warmed at them; and on a shelf above the wash-basin somebody had left a miniature frying-pan of congealed mascara in which a hair-pin was embedded.

It was a largish room, windowless and dank, with an air of submerged grandeur about it. The full-length cheval-glass swung from a gilt frame. There was an Empire couch, an armchair and an ornate stool before the dressing-shelf. The floor was carpeted in red with a florid pattern that use had in part obliterated. A number of dress-boxes bearing the legend *Costumes by Pierrot et Cie* were stacked in the middle of the room, and there were two suitcases on the shelf. A gas heater stood against one wall and there was a caged jet above the wash-basin.

"Here we are," said the night-watchman. "All yer own."

She turned to thank him and encountered a speculative stare. "Cosy," he said, "ain't it?" and moved nearer. "Nice little hidey hole, ain't it?"

"You've been very kind," Martyn said. "I'll manage splendidly, now. Thank you very much indeed."

"Don't mention it. Any time." His hand reached out clumsily to her arm. "Been aht in the rain," he said thickly. "Naughty girl."

"It'll soon dry off. I'm quite all right."

She moved behind the pile of dress-boxes and fumbled with the string on the top one. There was a hissing noise. She heard him strike a match and a moment later was horribly jolted by an explosion from the gas heater. It forced an involuntary cry from her.

"'Ullo, '*ullo!*" her companion said. "Ain't superstitious, are we?"

"Superstitious?"

He made an inexplicable gesture towards the gas fire. "*You* know," he said, grinning horridly at her.

"I'm afraid I don't understand?"

"Don't tell me you never 'eard abaht the great Jupiter case! Don't they learn you nothing in them anty-podes?"

The heater reddened and purred.

"Come to think of it," he said, "it'd be before your time. I wasn't 'ere myself when it occurred, a-course, but them that was don't give you a chance to forget it. Not that they mention it direct-like, but it don't get forgotten."

"What was it?" Martyn asked against her will.

"Sure yer not superstitious?"

"No, I'm not."

"You ain't been long in this business, then. Nor more am I. Shake 'ands.' He extended his hand so pointedly that she was obliged to put her own in it and had some difficulty in releasing herself.

"It must be five years ago," he said, "all of that. A bloke in Number Four dressing-room did another bloke in, very cunning, by blowing dahn the tube of 'is own gas fire. Like if I went nex' door and blew dahn the tube, this fire'd go aht. And if you was dead drunk, like you might of been if this girl-friend of yours'd been very generous with 'er brandy, you'd be commy-tose and before you knew where you was you'd be dead. Which is what occurred. It made a very nasty impression and the theatre was shut dahn for a long while until they 'ad it all altered and pansied up. The Guv'nor won't 'ave it mentioned. 'E changed the name of the 'ouse when 'e took it on. But call it what you like, the memory, as they say, lingers on. Silly, though, ain't it? You and me don't care. That's right, ain't it? We'd rather be cosy. Wouldn't we?" He gave a kind of significance to the word "cosy." Martyn unlocked the suitcases. Her fingers were unsteady and she turned her back in order to hide them from him. He stood in front of the gas fire and began to give out a smell of hot dirty cloth. She took sheets from a suitcase, hung them under the clothes pegs round the walls, and began to unpack the boxes. Her feet throbbed cruelly and she surreptitiously shuffled them out of her wet shoes.

"That's the ticket," he said. "Dry 'em orf, shall we?"

He advanced upon her and squatted to gather up the shoes. His hand, large and prehensile, with a life of its own, darted out and closed over her foot. " 'Ow abaht yer stockings?"

Martyn felt not only frightened but humiliated and ridiculous—wobbling, dead tired, on one foot. It was as if she were half-caught in some particularly degrading kind of stocks.

She said: "Look here, you're a good chap. You've been terribly kind. Let me get on with the job."

His grip slackened. He looked up at her without embarrassment, his thin London face sharp with curiosity. "O.K.," he said. "No offence meant. Call it a day, eh?"

"Call it a day."

"You're the boss," he said, and got to his feet. He put her shoes down in front of the gas fire and went to the door. "Live far from 'ere?" he asked. A feeling of intense desolation swept through her and left her without the heart to prevaricate.

"I don't know," she said. "I've got to find somewhere. There's a women's hostel near Paddington, I think."

"Broke?"

"I'll be all right, now I've got this job."

His hand was in his pocket. " 'Ere," he said.

"No, no. Please."

"Come orf it. We're pals, ain't we?"

"No, really. I'm terribly grateful but I'd rather not. I'm all right."

"You're the boss," he said again, and after a pause: "I can't get the idea, honest I can't. The way you speak and be'ave and all. What's the story? 'Ard luck or what?"

"There's no story, really."

"Just what you say yourself. No questions asked." He opened the door and moved into the passage. "Mind," he said over his shoulder, "it's against the rules but I won't be rahnd again. My mate relieves me at eight ack emma but I'll tip 'im the wink if it suits you. Them chairs in the Greenroom's not bad for a bit of kip and there's the fire. I'll turn it on. Please yourself, a-course."

"Oh," she said, "could I? *Could* I?"

"Never know what you can do till you try. Keep it under your titfer, though, or I'll be in trouble. So long. Don't get down'earted. It'll be all the same in a fahsand years."

He had gone. Martyn ran into the passage and saw his torchlight bobbing out on the stage. She called after him: "Thank you—thank you so much! I don't know your name, but thank you and good night."

"Badger's the name," he said, and his voice sounded hollow in the empty darkness. "Call me Fred."

The light bobbed out of sight. She heard him whistling for a moment and then a door slammed and she was alone.

With renewed heart she turned back to her job.

iv

At ten o'clock she had finished. She had traversed with diligence all the hazards of fatigue: the mounting threat of sleep, the clumsiness that makes the simplest action an ordeal, the horror of inertia and the temptation to let go the tortured muscles and give up, finally and indifferently, the awful struggle.

Five carefully ironed dresses hung sheeted against the walls, the make-up was laid out on the covered dressing-shelf. The boxes were stacked away, the framed photographs set out. It only remained to buy roses in the morning for Miss Helena Hamilton. Even the vase was ready and filled with water.

Martyn leant heavily on the back of a chair and stared at two photographs of the same face in a double leather case. They were not theatre photographs but studio portraits, and the face looked younger than the face in the Greenroom: younger and more formidable, with the mouth set truculently and the gaze withdrawn. But it had the same effect on Martyn. Written at the bottom of each of these photographs, in a small incisive hand, was: *Helena from Adam, 1950.* "Perhaps," she thought, "he's married to her."

Hag-ridden by the fear that she had forgotten some important detail, she paused in the doorway and looked round the room. No, she thought, there was nothing more to be done. But as she turned to go she saw herself, cruelly reflected in the long cheval-glass. It was not, of course, the first time she had seen herself that night; she had passed before the looking-glasses a dozen times and had actually polished them, but her attention had been ruthlessly fixed on the job in hand and she had not once focussed her eyes on her own image. Now she did so. She saw a girl in a yellow sweater and dark skirt with black hair that hung in streaks over her forehead. She saw a white, heart-shaped face with smudges under the eyes and a mouth that was normally firm and delicate but now drooped with fatigue. She raised her hand, pushed the hair back from her face and stared for a moment or two longer. Then she switched off the light and blundered across the passage into the Greenroom. Here, collapsed in an armchair with her overcoat across her, she slept heavily until morning.

CHAPTER II

IN A GLASS DARKLY

Martyn slept for ten hours. A wind got up in the night and found its way into the top of the stagehouse at the Vulcan. Up in the grid old back-cloths moved a little and, since the Vulcan was a hemp-house, there was a soughing among the forest of ropes. Flakes of paper, relics of some Victorian snowstorm, were dislodged from the top of a batten and fluttered down to the stage. Rain, driven fitfully against the theatre, ran in cascades down pipes and dripped noisily from ledges into the stage-door entry. The theatre mice came out, explored the contents of paste-pots in the sink-room and scuttled unsuccessfully about a covered plate of tongue and veal. Out in the auditorium there arose at intervals a vague whisper, and in his cubby-hole off the dock Fred Badger dozed and woke uneasily. At one o'clock he went on his rounds. He padded down corridors, flicking his torchlight on framed sketches for décor and costumes, explored the foyer and examined the locked doors of the offices. He climbed the heavily carpeted stairs and, lost in meditation, stood for a long time in the dress circle among shrouded rows of seats and curtained doorways. Sighing dolorously he returned back-stage and made a stealthy entrance onto the set. Finally he creaked to the Greenroom door and, impelled by who knows what impulse, furtively opened it.

Martyn lay across the chair, her knees supported by one of its arms and her head by the other. The glow from the gas fire was reflected in her face. Fred Badger stood for quite a long time eyeing her and scraping his chin with calloused fingers. At last he backed out, softly closed the door and tiptoed to his cubby-hole, where he telephoned the fire-station to make his routine report.

At dawn the rain stopped and cleaning-vans swept the water down Carpet Street with their great brushes. Milk-carts clinked past the Vulcan and the first bus roared by. Martyn heard none of them. She woke to the murmur of the gas fire, and the confused memory of a dream in which someone tapped gently at a door. The windowless room was still dark but she looked at her watch in the fire-glow and found it was eight o'clock. She got up stiffly, crossed the room and opened the door on grey diffused daylight. A cup of tea with a large sandwich balanced on it had been left on the floor of the passage. Underneath it was a torn scrap of paper on which was scrawled: *Keep your pecker up matey see you some more.*

With a feeling of gratitude and timid security she breakfasted in the Greenroom, and afterwards explored the empty passage, finding at the far end an unlocked and unused dressing-room. To this room she brought her own suitcase and here, with a chair propped under the door-handle, she stripped and washed in icy water. In clean clothes, with her toilet complete, and with a feeling of detachment, as if she herself looked on from a distance at these proceedings, she crossed the stage and went out through the side door and up the alleyway into Carpet Street.

It was a clean sunny morning. The air struck sharply at her lips and nostrils and the light dazzled her. A van had drawn up outside the Vulcan and men were lifting furniture from it. There were cleaners at work in the foyer and a telegraph boy came out whistling. Carpet Street was noisy with traffic. Martyn turned left and walked quickly downhill until she came to a corner shop called Florian. In the window a girl in a blue coverall was setting out a large gilt basket of roses. The door was still locked but Martyn, emboldened by fresh air and a sense of freedom and adventure, tapped on the window and when the girl looked up pointed to the roses and held up Mr. Grantley's card. The girl smiled and, leaving the window, came to let her in.

Martyn said: "I'm sorry to bother you, but Mr. Grantley at the Vulcan told me to get some roses for Miss Helena Hamilton. He didn't give me any money and I'm afraid I haven't got any. Is all this very irregular and tiresome?"

"That will be quayte O.K.," the girl said in a friendly manner. "Mr. Grantley has an account."

"Perhaps you know what sort of roses I should get," Martyn suggested. She felt extraordinarily light and rather loquacious. "You see, I'm Miss Hamilton's dresser but I'm new and I don't know what she likes."

"Red would be quayte in order, I think. There are some lovely Bloody Warriors just in." She caught Martyn's eye and giggled. "Well, they do think of the weirdest names, don't they? Look: aren't they lovelies?"

She held up a group of roses with drops of water clinging to their half-opened petals. "Gorgeous," she said, "aren't they? Such a colour."

Martyn, appalled at the price, took a dozen. The girl looked curiously at her and said: "Miss Hamilton's dresser. Fancy! Aren't you lucky?" and she was vividly reminded of Fred Badger.

"I feel terribly lucky this morning," she said and was going away when the girl, turning pink under her make-up, said: "Pardon me asking, but I don't suppose you could get me Miss Hamilton's autograph. I'd be ever so thrilled."

"I haven't even seen her yet but I'll do my best."

"You *are* a duck. Thanks a million. Of course," the girl added, "I'm a real fan. I never miss any of her pictures and I do think Adam Poole —pardon me, Mr. Poole—is simply mawvellous. I mean to say I just think he's mawvellous. They're so mawvellous together. I suppose he's crazy about her in real life, isn't he? I always say they couldn't act together like that—you know, so gorgeously—unless they had a pretty hot clue on the sayde. Don't you agree?"

Martyn said she hadn't had a chance of forming an opinion as yet and left the florist in pensive contemplation of the remaining Bloody Warriors.

When she got back to the theatre its character had completely changed: it was alive and noisy. The dock-doors were open and sunlight lay in incongruous patches on painted canvas and stacked furniture. Up in the grid there was a sound of hammering. A back-cloth hung diagonally in mid-air and descended in jerks, while a man in shirt-sleeves shouted: "Down on yer long. Now yer short. Now bodily. Right-oh! Dead it. Now find yer Number Two."

A chandelier lay in a heap in the middle of the stage, and above it was suspended a batten of spotlights within reach of an elderly mechanic who fitted pink and straw-coloured mediums into their frames. Near the stage-door a group of men stared at a small Empire desk from which a stage-hand had removed a cloth wrapping. A tall young man in spectacles, wearing a red pullover and corduroy trousers, said irritably: "It's too bloody chi-chi. Without a shadow of doubt, he'll hate its guts."

He glanced at Martyn and added: "Put them in her room, dear, will you?"

She hurried to the dressing-room passage and found that here too there was life and movement. A vacuum-cleaner hummed in the Greenroom, a bald man in overalls was tacking cards on the doors, somewhere down the passage an unseen person sang cheerfully and the door next to Miss Hamilton's was open. These signs of preparation awakened in Martyn a sense of urgency. In a sudden fluster she unwrapped her roses and thrust them into the vase. The stalks were too long and she had nothing to cut them with. She ran down the passage to the empty room, and reflected as she rootled in her suitcase that she would be expected to have sewing materials at hand. Here was the housewife an aunt had given her when she left New Zealand but it was depleted and in a muddle. She ran back with it, sawed at the rose stems with her nail-scissors and, when someone in the next room tapped on the wall, inadvertently jammed the points into her hand.

"And how," a disembodied voice inquired, "is La Belle Tansley this morning?"

Sucking her left hand and arranging roses with her right, Martyn wondered how she should respond to this advance. She called out tentatively: "I'm afraid it's not Miss Tansley."

"What's that?" the voice said vaguely, and a moment later she heard the brisk sound of a clothes-brush at work.

The roses were done at last. She stood with the ends of the stalks in her hand and wondered why she had become so nervous.

"Here we go again," a voice said in the doorway. She spun round to face a small man in an alpaca coat with a dinner-jacket in his hands. He stared at her with his jaw dropped. "Pardon me," he said. "I thought you was Miss Tansley."

Martyn explained. "Well!" he said. "That'll be her heart, that will. She ought to have given up before this. I warned her. In hospital, too? T'ch, t'ch, t'ch." He wagged his head and looked, apparently in astonishment, at Martyn. "So that's the story," he continued, "and you've stepped into the breach. Fancy that! Better introduce ourselves, hadn't we? The name's Cringle but Bob'll do as well as anything else. I'm 'is lordship's dresser. How are you?"

Martyn gave him her name and they shook hands. He had a pleasant face covered with a cobweb of fine wrinkles. "Been long at this game?" he asked, and added: "Well, that's a foolish question, isn't it? I should have said: Will this be your first place, or Are you doing it in your school holidays, or something of that sort."

"Do you suppose," Martyn said anxiously, "Miss Hamilton will think I'm too young?"

"Not if you give satisfaction, she won't. She's all right if you give satisfaction. Different from my case. Slave meself dizzy, I can, and if 'is lordship's in one of 'is moods, what do I get for it? Spare me days, I don't know why I put up with it and that's a fact. But *she's* all right if she likes you." He paused and added tentatively: "But you know all about that, I dare say." Martyn was silent and felt his curiosity reach out as if it were something tangible. At last she said desperately: "I'll try. I want to give satisfaction."

He glanced round the room. "Looks nice," he said. "Are you pressed and shook out? Yes, I can see you are. Flowers too. Very nice. Would you be a friend of hers? Doing it to oblige, like?"

"No, no. I've never seen her. Except in the pictures, of course."

"Is that a fact?" His rather bird-like eyes were bright with speculation. "Young ladies," he said, "have to turn their hands to all sorts of work these days, don't they?"

"I suppose so. Yes."

"No offence, I hope, but I was wondering if you come from one of those drama-schools. Hoping to learn a bit, watching from the side, like."

A kind of sheepishness that had hardened into obstinacy prevented her from telling him in a few words why she was there. The impulse of a fortnight ago to rush to somebody—the ship's captain, the High Commissioner for her own country, anyone—and unload her burden of disaster had given place almost at once to a determined silence. This mess was of her own making, she had decided, and she herself would see it out. And throughout the loneliness and panic of her ordeal, to this resolution she had stuck. It had ceased to be a reasoned affair with Martyn: the less she said, the less she wanted to say. She had become crystallized in reticence.

So she met the curiosity of the little dresser with an evasion. "It'd be wonderful," she said, "if I did get the chance."

A deep voice with an unusually vibrant quality called out on the stage. "Bob! Where the devil have you got to? Bob!"

"Cripes!" the little dresser ejaculated. "Here we are *and* in one of our tantrums. *In here, sir! Coming, sir!*"

He darted towards the doorway but before he reached it a man appeared there, a man so tall that for a fraction of a second he looked down over the dresser's head directly into Martyn's eyes.

"This young lady," Bob Cringle explained with an air of discovery, "is the new dresser for Miss Hamilton. I just been showing her the ropes, Mr. Poole, sir."

"You'd much better attend to your work. I want you." He glanced again at Martyn. "Good morning," he said and was gone. "Look at this!" she heard him say angrily in the next room. "Where *are* you!"

Cringle paused in the doorway to turn his thumbs down and his eyes up. "Here we are, sir. What's the little trouble?" he was saying pacifically as he disappeared.

Martyn thought: "The picture in the Greenroom is more like him than the photographs." Preoccupied with this discovery she was only vaguely aware of a fragrance in the air and a new voice in the passage. The next moment her employer came into the dressing-room.

ii

An encounter with a person hitherto only seen and heard on the cinema screen is often disconcerting. It is as if the two-dimensional and enormous image had contracted about a living skeleton and in taking on substance had acquired an embarrassing normality. One is not always glad to change the familiar shadow for the strange reality.

Helena Hamilton was a blonde woman. She had every grace. To set down in detail the perfections of her hair, eyes, mouth and complexion, her shape and the gallantry of her carriage would be to reiterate merely that which everyone had seen in her innumerable pictures. She was, in fact, quite astonishingly beautiful. Even the circumstance of her looking somewhat older than her moving shadow could not modify the shock of finding her its equal in everything but this.

Coupled with her beauty was her charm. This was famous. She could reduce press conferences to a conglomerate of eager, even naïve, males. She could make a curtain-speech that every leading woman in every theatre in the English-speaking world had made before her and persuade the last man in the audience that it was original. She could convince bit-part actresses playing maids in first acts that there, but for the grace of God, went she.

On Martyn, however, taken off her balance and entirely by surprise, it was Miss Hamilton's smell that made the first impression. At ten guineas a moderately sized bottle, she smelt like Master Fenton, all April and May. Martyn was very much shorter than Miss Hamilton but this did not prevent her from feeling cumbersome and out-of-place, as if she had been caught red-handed with her own work in the dressing-room. This awkwardness was in part dispelled by the friendliness of Miss Hamilton's smile and the warmth of her enchanting voice.

"You've come to help me, haven't you?" she said. "Now, that *is* kind. I know all about you from Mr. Grantley and I fully expect we'll get along famously together. The only thing I *don't* know, in fact, is your name."

Martyn wondered if she ought to give only her Christian name or only her surname. She said: "Tarne. Martyn Tarne."

"But what a charming name!" The brilliant eyes looked into Martyn's face and their gaze sharpened. After a fractional pause she repeated: "Really charming," and turned her back.

It took Martyn a moment or two to realize that this was her cue to remove Miss Hamilton's coat. She lifted it from her shoulders—it was made of Persian lamb and smelt delicious—and hung it up. When she turned round she found that her employer was looking at her. She smiled reassuringly at Martyn and said: "You've got everything arranged very nicely. Roses, too. Lovely."

"They're from Mr. Grantley."

"Sweet of him but I bet he sent you to buy them."

"Well—" Martyn began and was saved by the entry of the young man in the red sweater with a dressing-case for which she was given the keys. While she was unpacking it the door opened and a middle-aged, handsome man with a raffish face and an air of boldness came in. She remembered the photographs in the foyer. This was Clark Bennington. He addressed himself to Miss Hamilton.

"Hullo," he said, "I've been talking to John Rutherford."

"What about?" she asked and sounded nervous.

"About that kid. Young Gay. He's been at her again. So's Adam." He glanced at Martyn. "I wanted to talk to you," he added discontentedly.

"Well, so you shall. But I've got to change now, Ben. And look, this is my new dresser, Martyn Tarne."

He eyed Martyn with more attention. "Quite a change from old Tansley," he said. "And a very nice change, too." He turned away. "Is Adam down?" He jerked his head at the wall.

"Yes."

"I'll see you later, then."

"All right, but—yes, all right."

He went out, leaving a faint rumour of alcohol behind him.

She was quite still for a moment after he had gone. Martyn heard her fetch a sigh, a sound half-impatient, half-anxious. "Oh, well," she said, "let's get going, shall we?"

Martyn had been much exercised about the extent of her duties. Did, for instance, a dresser undress her employer? Did she kneel at her feet and roll down her stockings? Did she unhook and unbutton? Or did she stand capably aside while these rites were performed by the principal herself? Miss Hamilton solved the problem by removing her dress, throwing it to Martyn and waiting to be inserted into her dressing-gown. During these operations a rumble of male voices sounded at intervals in the adjoining room. Presently there was a tap at the door. Martyn answered it and found the little dresser with a florist's box in his hands. "Mr. Poole's compliments," he said and winked broadly before retiring.

Miss Hamilton by this time was spreading a yellow film over her face. She asked Martyn to open the box and, on seeing three orchids that lay crisp and fabulous on their mossy bed, sang "Darling!" on two clear notes.

The voice beyond the wall responded. "Hullo?"

"They're quite perfect. Thank you, my sweet."

"Good," the voice said. Martyn laid the box on the dressing-table and saw the card: *Until to-morrow. Adam.*

She got through the next half hour pretty successfully, she hoped. There seemed to be no blunders and Miss Hamilton continued charming and apparently delighted. There were constant visitors. A tap on the door would be followed by a head looking round and always by the invitation to come in. First there was Miss Gay Gainsford, a young and rather intense person with a pretty air of deference, who seemed to be in a state of extreme anxiety.

"Well, darling," Miss Hamilton said, glancing at her in the glass. "Everything under strict control?"

Miss Gainsford said unevenly: "I suppose so. I'm trying to be good and sort of *biddable,* do you know, but underneath I realize that I'm seething like a cauldron. Butterflies the size of *bats* in the stomach."

"Well, of course. But you mustn't be terrified, really, because whatever happens we all know John's written a good play, don't we?"

"I suppose we do."

"We do indeed. And Gay—you're going to make a great personal success in this part. I want you to tell yourself you are. Do you know? *Tell* yourself."

"I wish I could believe it." Miss Gainsford clasped her hands and raised them to her lips. "It's not very easy," she said, "when he—John —Dr. Rutherford—so obviously thinks I'm a misfit. Everybody keeps telling me it's a marvellous part, but for me it's thirteen sides of hopeless hell. Honestly, it is."

"Gay, what *nonsense!* John may seem hard—"

"*Seem!*"

"Well, he may *be* hard, then. He's famous for it, after all. But you'll get your reward, my dear, when the time comes. Remember," said Miss Hamilton with immense gravity, "we all have faith in you."

"Of course," said Miss Gainsford with an increased quaver in her voice, "it's too marvellous your feeling like that about it. You've been so miraculously kind. And Uncle Ben, of course. Both of you. I can't get over it."

"But, my dear, that's utter nonsense. You're going to be one of our rising young actresses."

"You do *really* think so!"

"But yes. We all do." Her voice lost a little colour and then freshened. "We all do," she repeated firmly and turned back to her glass.

Miss Gainsford went to the door and hesitated there. "Adam doesn't," she said loudly.

Miss Hamilton made a quick expressive gesture toward the next dressing-room and put her finger to her lips. "He'll be *really* angry if he hears you say that," she whispered, and added aloud with somewhat forced casualness: "Is John down this morning?"

"He's on-stage. I think he said he'd like to speak to you."

"I want to see him particularly. Will you tell him, darling?"

"Of course, Aunty Helena," Miss Gainsford said rather miserably, and added: "I'm sorry, I forgot. Of course, Helena, darling." With a wan smile she was gone.

"Oh, dear!" Miss Hamilton sighed and catching Martyn's eye in the looking-glass made a rueful face. "If only—" she began and stopped unaccountably, her gaze still fixed on Martyn's image. "Never mind," she said.

There was a noisy footfall in the passage followed by a bang on the door, and, with scarcely a pause for permission, by the entry of a large, florid and angry-looking man wearing a sweater, a leather waistcoat, a muffler and a very old duffel coat.

"Good morning, John darling," said Miss Hamilton gaily and extended her hand. The new-comer planted a smacking kiss on it and fixed Martyn with a china-blue and bulging pair of eyes. Martyn turned away from this embarrassing regard.

"What have we here?" he demanded. His voice was loud and rumbling.

"My new dresser. Dr. Rutherford, Martyn."

"Stay me with flagons!" said Dr. Rutherford. He turned on Miss Hamilton. "That fool of a wench Gainsford said you wanted me," he said. "What's up?"

"John, *what* have you been saying to that child?"

"I? Nothing. Nothing to what I could, and, mark you, what I ought to say to her. I merely asked her if, for the sake of my sanity, she'd be good enough to play the central scene without a goddam simper on her fat and wholly unsuitable dial."

"You're frightening her."

"She's terrifying me. She may be your niece, Helena—"

"She's not my niece. She's Ben's niece."

"If she was the Pope's niece she'd still be a goddam pain in the neck. I wrote this part for an intelligent actress who could be made to look reasonably like Adam. What do you give me? A moronic amateur who looks like nothing on God's earth."

"She's extremely pretty."

"Lollypops! Adam's too damn easy on her. The only hope lies in shaking her up. Or kicking her out and I'd do that myself if I had my way. It ought to have been done a month back. Even now—"

"Oh, my *dear* John! We open in two days, you might remember."

"An actress worth her salt'd memorize it in an hour. I told her—"

"I do beg you," she said, "to leave her to Adam. After all he is the producer, John, and he's very wise."

Dr. Rutherford pulled out of some submerged pocket a metal box. From this he extracted a pinch of snuff, which he took with loud and uncouth noises.

"In a moment," he said, "you'll be telling me the author ought to keep out of the theatre."

"That's utter nonsense."

"Let them try to keep *me* out," he said and burst into a neighing laugh.

Miss Hamilton slightly opened her mouth, hardened her upper lip, and with the closest attention painted it a purplish red. "Really," she said briskly, "you'd much better behave prettily, you know. You'll end by having her on your hands with a nervous breakdown."

"The sooner the better if it's a good one."

"Honestly, John, you are the rock *bottom* when you get like this. If you didn't write the plays you do write—if you weren't the greatest dramatist since—"

"Spare me the raptures," he said, "and give me some actors. And while we're on the subject, I may as well tell you that I don't like the way Ben is shaping in the big scene. If Adam doesn't watch him he'll be up to some bloody leading-man hocus-pocus, and by God if he tries that on I'll wring his neck for him."

She turned and faced him. "John, he *won't*. I'm sure he won't."

"No, you're not. You can't be sure. Nor can I. But if there's any sign of it to-night, and Adam doesn't tackle him, I will. I'll tickle his catastrophe, by God I will. As for that Mongolian monstrosity, that discard from the waxworks, Mr. Parry Percival, what devil—will you answer me—what inverted sadist foisted it on my play?"

"Now, look here, John—" Miss Hamilton began with some warmth, and was shouted down.

"Have I not stipulated from the beginning of my disastrous association with this ill-fated playhouse that I would have none of these abortions in my works? These Things. These foetid Growths. These Queers."

"Parry isn't one."

"Yah! He shrieks it. I have an instinct, my girl. I nose them as I go into the lobby."

She made a gesture of despair. "I give up," she said.

He helped himself to another pinch of snuff. "Hooey!" he snorted. "You don't do anything of the sort, my sweetie-pie. You're going to rock 'em, you and Adam. Think of that and preen yourself. And leave all the rest—to *me*."

"Don't quote from *Macbeth*. If Gay Gainsford heard you doing that she really would go off at the deep end."

"Which is precisely where I'd like to push her."

"Oh, go away," she cried out impatiently but with an air of good nature. "I've had enough of you. You're wonderful and you're hopeless. Go away."

"The audience is concluded?" He scraped the parody of a Regency bow.

"The audience is concluded. The door, Martyn."

Martyn opened the door. Until then, feeling wretchedly in the way, she had busied herself with the stack of suitcases in the corner of the room and now, for the first time, came absolutely face to face with the visitor. He eyed her with an extraordinary air of astonishment.

"Here!" he said. "Hi!"

"No, John," Miss Hamilton said with great determination. "No!"

"*Eureka!*"

"Nothing of the sort. Good morning."

He gave a shrill whistle and swaggered out. Martyn turned back to find her employer staring into the glass. Her hands trembled and she clasped them together. "Martyn," she said, "I'm going to call you Martyn because it's such a nice name. You know, a dresser is rather a particular sort of person. She has to be as deaf as a post and as blind as a bat to almost everything that goes on under her very nose. Dr. Rutherford is, as I expect you know, a most distinguished and brilliant person. Our Greatest English Playwright. But like many brilliant people," Miss Hamilton continued, in what Martyn couldn't help thinking a rather too special voice, "he is *eccentric*. We all understand and we expect you to do so too. Do you know?"

Martyn said she did.

"Good. Now, put me into that pink thing and let us know the worst about it, shall we?"

When she was dressed she stood before the cheval-glass and looked with cold intensity at her image. "My God," she said, "the lighting had better be good."

Martyn said: "Isn't it right? It looks lovely to me."

"My poor girl!" she muttered. "You run to my husband and ask him for cigarettes. He's got my case. I need a stimulant."

Martyn hurried into the passage and tapped at the next door. "So they are married," she thought. "He must be ten years younger than she is but they're married and he still sends her orchids in the morning."

The deep voice shouted impatiently: "Come!" and she opened the door and went in.

The little dresser was putting Poole into a dinner jacket. Their backs were turned to Martyn. "Yes?" Poole said.

"Miss Hamilton would like her cigarette case, if you please."

"I haven't got it," he said and shouted: "Helena!"

"Hullo, darling?"

"I haven't got your case."

There was a considerable pause. The voice beyond the wall called: "No, no. Ben's got it. Mr. Bennington, Martyn."

"I'm so sorry," Martyn said, and made for the door, conscious of the little dresser's embarrassment and of Poole's annoyance.

Mr. Clark Bennington's room was on the opposite side of the passage and next the Greenroom. On her entrance Martyn was abruptly and most unpleasantly transported into the immediate past—into yesterday with its exhaustion, muddle and panic, to the moment of extreme humiliation when Fred Badger had smelt brandy on her breath. Mr. Bennington's flask was open on his dressing-shelf and he was in the act of entertaining a thick-set gentleman with beautifully groomed white hair, wearing a monocle in a strikingly handsome face. This person set down his tumbler and gazed in a startled fashion at Martyn.

"It's not," he said, evidently picking up with some difficulty the conversation she had interrupted, "it's not that I would for the world interfere, Ben, dear boy. Nor do I enjoy raising what is no doubt a delicate subject in these particular circumstances. But I feel for the child damnably, you know. Damnably. Moreover, it does rather appear that the Doctor never loses an opportunity to upset her."

"I couldn't agree more, old boy, and I'm bloody angry about it. Yes, dear, wait a moment, will you?" Mr. Bennington rejoined, running his speeches together and addressing them to no one in particular. "This is my wife's new dresser, J.G."

"Really?" Mr. J. G. Darcey responded and bowed politely to Martyn. "Good morning, child. See you later, Ben, my boy. Thousand thanks."

He rose, looked kindly at Martyn, dropped his monocle, passed his hand over his hair and went out, breaking into operatic song in the passage.

Mr. Bennington made a half-hearted attempt to put his flask out of sight and addressed himself to Martyn.

"And what," he asked, "can I do for the new dresser?"

Martyn delivered her message. "Cigarette case? Have I got my wife's cigarette case? God, I don't know. Try my overcoat, dear, will you? Behind the door. Inside pocket. No secrets," he added obscurely. "Forgive my asking you. I'm busy."

But he didn't seem particularly busy. He twisted round in his chair and watched Martyn as she made a fruitless search of his overcoat pockets. "This your first job?" he asked. She said it was not and he added: "As a dresser, I mean."

"I've worked in the threatre before."

"And where was that?"

"In New Zealand."

"*Really?*" he said, as if she had answered some vitally important question.

"I'm afraid," Martyn went on quickly, "it's not in the overcoat."

"God, what a bore! Give me my jacket then, would you? The grey flannel."

She handed it to him and he fumbled through the pockets. A pocket-book dropped on the floor, spilling its contents. Martyn gathered them together and he made such a clumsy business of taking them from her that she was obliged to put them on the shelf. Among them was an envelope bearing a foreign stamp and postmark. He snatched it up and it fluttered in his fingers. "Mustn't lose track of that one, must we?" he said and laughed. "All the way from Uncle

Tito." He thrust it at Martyn. "Look," he said and steadied his hand against the edge of the shelf. "What d'you think of *that*? Take it."

Troubled at once by the delay and by the oddness of his manner Martyn took the envelope and saw that it was addressed to Bennington.

"Do you collect autographs," Bennington asked with ridiculous intensity—"or signed letters?"

"No, I'm afraid I don't," she said and put the letter face-down on the shelf.

"There's someone," he said with a jab of his finger at the envelope, "who'd give a hell of a lot for *that* one in there. A hell of a lot."

He burst out laughing, pulled a cigarette case out of the jacket and handed it to her with a flourish. "Purest gold," he said. "Birthday present but not from me. I'm her husband, you know. What the hell! Are you leaving me? Don't go."

Martyn made her escape and ran back to Miss Hamilton's room, where she found her in conference with Adam Poole and a young man of romantic appearance whom she recognized as the original of the last of the photographs in the foyer—Mr. Parry Percival. The instinct that makes us aware of a conversation in which we ourselves have in our absence been involved warned Martyn that they had been talking about her and had broken off on her entrance. After a moment's silence, Mr. Percival, with far too elaborate a nonchalance, said: "Yes. Well, there you have it," and it was obvious that there was a kind of double significance in this remark. Miss Hamilton said: "My poor Martyn, where *have* you been?" with a lightness that was not quite cordial.

"I'm sorry," Martyn said. "Mr. Bennington had trouble in finding the case." She hesitated for a moment and added, "Madam."

"That," Miss Hamilton rejoined, looking at Adam Poole, "rings dismally true. Would you believe it, darling, I became so furious with him for taking it that, most reluctantly, I gave him one for himself. He lost it instantly, of course, and now swears he didn't and mine is his. If you follow me."

"With considerable difficulty," Poole said, "I do."

Parry Percival laughed gracefully. He had a winning, if not altogether authentic, air of ingenuousness, and at the moment seemed to be hovering on the edge of some indiscretion. "I am afraid," he said ruefully to Miss Hamilton, "I'm rather in disgrace myself."

"With me, or with Adam?"

"I hope not with either of you. With Ben." He glanced apologetically at Poole, who did not look at him. "Because of the part, I mean. I suppose I spoke out of turn, but I really did think I could play it— still do for a matter of that, but there it is."

It was obvious that he was speaking at Poole. Martyn saw Miss Hamilton look from one man to the other before she said lightly, "I think you could too, Parry, but as you say, there it is. Ben *has* got a flair, you know."

Percival laughed. "He has indeed," he said. "He has had it for twenty years. Sorry. I shouldn't have said that. Honestly, I *am* sorry."

Poole said: "I dislike post mortems on casting, Parry."

"I know, I *do* apologize." Percival turned ingratiatingly, and the strong light caught his face sideways. Martyn saw with astonishment that under the thin film of greasepaint there was a system of incipient lines, and she realized that he was not, after all, a young man. "I know," he repeated, "I'm being naughty."

Poole said: "We open on Thursday. The whole thing was thrashed out weeks ago. Any discussion now is completely fruitless."

"That," said Miss Hamilton, "is what I have been trying to tell the Doctor."

"John? I heard him bellowing in here," Poole said. "Where's he gone? I want a word with him. And with you, Parry, by the way. It's about that scene at the window in the second act. You're not making your exit line. You must top Ben there. It's most important."

"Look, old boy," Mr. Percival said with agonized intensity, "I *know*. It's just another of those things. Have you *seen* what Ben does? Have you seen that business with my handkerchief? He won't take his hands off me. The whole exit gets messed up."

"I'll see what can be done."

"John," said Miss Hamilton, "is worried about it too, Adam."

Poole said: "Then he should talk to me."

"You know what the Doctor is."

"We all do," said Parry Percival, "and the public, I fear, is beginning to find out. God, there I go again."

Poole looked at him. "You'll get along better, I think, Parry, if you deny yourself these cracks against the rest of the company. Rutherford has written a serious play. It'd be a pity if any of us should lose faith in it."

Percival reddened and made towards the door. "I'm just being a nuisance," he said. "I'll take myself off and be photographed like a good boy." He made an insinuating movement of his shoulders towards Miss Hamilton, and fluttered his hand at her dress. "Marvellous," he said—"a triumph, if the bit-part actor may be allowed to say so."

The door shut crisply behind him, and Miss Hamilton said: "Darling, aren't you rather high and grand with poor Parry?"

"I don't think so. He's behaving like an ass. He couldn't play the part. He was born to be a feed."

"He'd *look* it."

"If all goes well Ben will *be* it."

"If all goes well! Adam, I'm terrified. He's—"

"Are you dressed, Helena? The cameras are ready."

"Shoes, please, Martyn," said Miss Hamilton. "Yes, darling. I'm right."

Martyn fastened her shoes and then opened the door. Miss Hamilton swept out, lifting her skirts with great elegance. Martyn waited for Poole to follow, but he said: "You're meant to be on-stage. Take make-up and a glass and whatever Miss Hamilton may need for her hair."

She thanked him and in a flurry gathered the things together. Poole took the Persian lamb coat and stood by the door. She hesitated, expecting him to precede her, but found that he was looking at the cheval-glass. When she followed his gaze it was to be confronted by their images, side by side in the mirror.

"Extraordinary," he said abruptly, "isn't it?" and motioned her to go out.

iii

When Martyn went out on the stage, she was able for the first time to see the company assembled together, and found it consisted, as far as the players were concerned, of no more than the six persons she had already encountered: first in their fixed professional poses in the show-frame at the front of the house, and later in their dressing-rooms. She had attached mental tags to them and found herself thinking of Helena Hamilton as the Leading Lady, of Gay Gainsford as the Ingenue, of J. G. Darcey as the Character Actor, of Parry Percival as the Juvenile, of Clark Bennington regrettably, perhaps unjustly, as the Drunken Actor, and of Adam Poole—but as yet she had found no label for Poole, unless it was the old-fashioned one of

"Governor," which pleased her by its vicarious association with the days of the Victorian actor-managers.

To this actual cast of six she must add a number of satellite figures —the author, Dr. John Rutherford, whose eccentricities seemed to surpass those of his legend, with which she was already acquainted; the man in the red sweater, who was the stage-manager, and was called Clem Smith; his assistant, a morose lurking figure; and the crew of stage-hands, who went about their business or contemplated the actors with equal detachment.

The actors were forming themselves now into a stage "picture," moving in a workman-like manner under the direction of Adam Poole, and watched with restless attentiveness by an elderly, slack-jointed man, carrying a paint pot and brushes. This man, the last of all the figures to appear upon the stage that morning, seemed to have no recognizable jobs but to be concerned in all of them. He was dressed in overalls and a tartan shirt, from which his long neck emerged, bird-like and crepe-y, to terminate in a head that wobbled slightly as if its articulation with the top of the spine had loosened with age. He was constantly addressed with exasperated affection as Jacko. Under his direction, bunches of lights were wheeled into position, camera men peered and muttered, and at his given signal the players, by an easy transition in behaviour and appearance, became larger than life. A gap was left in the middle of the group, and into this when all was ready floated Helena Hamilton, ruffling her plumage, and becoming at once the focal point of the picture.

"Darling," she said, "it's not going to be a flash, is it, with all of you looking like village idiots, and me like the Third Witch on the morning after the cauldron scene?"

"If you can hold it for three seconds," Adam Poole said, "it needn't be a flash."

"I can hold anything, if you come in and help me."

He moved in beside her. "All right," he said, "let's try it. The end of the first act"; and at once she turned upon him a look of tragic and burning intensity. The elderly man wandered across and tweaked at her skirts. Without changing pose or expression, she said: "Isn't it shameful the way Jacko can't keep his hands off me." He grinned and ambled away. Adam Poole said "Right"; the group froze in postures of urgency that led the eye towards the two central figures and the cameras clicked.

Martyn tried, as the morning wore on, to get some idea of the content of the play, but was unable to do so. Occasionally the players would speak snatches of dialogue leading up to the moment when a photograph was to be taken, and from these she gathered that the major conflict of the theme was between the characters played by Adam Poole and Clark Bennington and that this conflict was one of ideas. About a particular shot there was a great deal of difficulty. In this Poole and Gay Gainsford confronted each other, and it was necessary that her posture, the arrested gesture of her hand, and even her expression should be an exact reflection of his.

To Martyn, Poole had seemed to be a short-tempered man, but with Gay Gainsford he showed exemplary patience. "It's the old story, Gay," he said. "You're over-anxious. It's not enough for you to look like me. Let's face it—" he hesitated for a moment and said quickly: "We've had all this, haven't we—but it's worth repeating—you can't look strikingly like me, although Jacko's done wonders. What you've got to do is to *be* me. At this moment, don't you see, you're my heredity, confronting me like a threat. As far as the photograph is concerned, we can cheat—the shot can be taken over your shoulder, but in the performance there can be no cheating, and that is why I'm making such a thing of it. Now let's take it with the line. Your head's on your arms, you raise it slowly to face me. Ready now. Right, up you come."

Miss Gainford raised her face to his as he leaned across the writing desk and whispered: "Don't you like what you see?" At the same moment there was a cascade of laughter from Miss Hamilton. Poole's voice cracked like a whip-lash: "Helena, please," and she turned from Parry Percival to say: "Darling, I'm so sorry," and in the same breath spoke her line of dialogue: "But it's you, don't you see? You can't escape from it. It's you." Gay Gainsford made a hopeless little gesture and Poole said: "Too late, of course. Try again."

They tried several times, in an atmosphere of increasing tension. The amiable Jacko was called in to make an infinitesimal change in Gay's make-up, and Martyn saw him blot away a tear. At this juncture a disembodied voice roared from the back of the circle:

> "Madam, have comfort: all of us have cause
> To wail the dimming of our shining star!"

Poole glanced into the auditorium. "Do shut up like a good chap, John," he said.

"Pour all your tears! I am your sorrow's nurse,
And I will pamper it with la-men-ta-ti-ons."

The man called Jacko burst out laughing and was instantly dismissed to the dressing-rooms by Poole.

There followed a quarter of an hour of mounting hysteria on the part of Gay Gainsford and of implacable persistence from Adam Poole. He said suddenly: "All right, we'll cheat. Shift the camera."

The remaining photographs were taken without a great deal of trouble. Miss Gainsford, looking utterly miserable, went off to her dressing-room. The man called Jacko reappeared and ambled across to Miss Hamilton. There was an adjustment in make-up while Martyn held up the mirror.

"Maybe it's lucky," he said, "you don't have to look like somebody else."

"Are you being nice or beastly, Jacko?"

He put a cigarette between her lips and lit it. "The dresses are good," he said. He had a very slight foreign accent.

"You think so, do you?"

"Naturally. I design them for *you*."

"Next time," she said grimly, "you'd better write the play as well."

He was a phenomenally ugly man, but a smile of extraordinary sweetness broke across his face.

"All these agonies!" he murmured. "And on Thursday night everyone will be kissing everyone else and at the Combined Arts Ball we are in triumph and on Friday morning you will be purring over your notices. And you must not be unkind about the play. It is a good play." He grinned again, more broadly. His teeth were enormous and uneven. "Even the little niece of the great husband cannot entirely destroy it."

"Jacko!"

"You may say what you like, it is not intelligent casting."

"Please, Jacko."

"All right, all right. I remind you instead of the Combined Arts Ball, and that no one has decided in what costume we go."

"Nobody has any ideas. Jacko, you must invent something marvellous."

"And in two days I must also create out of air eight marvellous costumes."

"Darling Jacko, how beastly we are to you. But you know you love performing your little wonders."

"I suggest then, that we are characters from Tchekhov as they would be in Hollywood. You absurdly gorgeous, and the little niece still grimly ingenue. Adam perhaps as Vanya if he were played by Boris Karloff. And so on."

"Where shall I get my absurdly gorgeous dress?"

"I paint the design on canvas and cut it out and if I were introduced to your dresser I would persuade her to sew it up." He took the glass from Martyn and said: "No one makes any introductions in this theatre, so we introduce ourselves to each other. I am Jacques Doré, and you are the little chick whom the stork has brought too late, or dropped into the wrong nest. Really," he said, rolling his eyes at Miss Hamilton, "it is the most remarkable coincidence, if it is a coincidence. I am dropping bricks," he added. "I am a very privileged person but one day I drop an outsize brick, and away I go." He made a circle of his thumb and forefinger and looked through it, as though it were a quizzing-glass, at Martyn. "All the same," he said, "it is a pity you are a little dresser and not a little actress."

iv

Between the photograph call and the dress rehearsal, which was timed for seven o'clock, a state of uneven ferment prevailed at the Vulcan. During the rare occasions on which she had time to reflect, Martyn anticipated a sort of personal zero hour, a moment when she would have to take stock, to come to a decision. She had two and fourpence and no place of abode, and she had no idea when she would be paid, or how much she would get. This moment of reckoning, however, she continually postponed. The problem of food was answered for the moment by the announcement that it would be provided for everyone whose work kept them in the theatre throughout the day. As Miss Hamilton had discovered a number of minor alterations to be made in her dresses, Martyn was of this company. Having by this time realized the position of extraordinary ubiquity held by Jacko, she was not surprised to find him cooking a mysterious but savoury mess over the gas ring in Fred Badger's sink-room.

This concoction was served in enamel mugs, at odd intervals, to anyone who asked for it, and Martyn found herself eating her share in company with Bob Cringle, Mr. Poole's dresser. From him she learnt more about Mr. Jacques Doré. He was responsible for the décor and dressing of all Poole's productions. His official status was that of assistant to Mr. Poole, but in actual fact he seemed to be a kind of superior odd-job man.

"General dogsbody," Cringle gossiped, "that's what Mr. Jacko is. 'Poole's Luck,' people call him, and if the Guv'nor was superstitious about anything, which 'e is *not,* it would be about Mr. Jacko. The lady's the same. Can't do without 'im. As a matter of fact it's on 'er account 'e sticks it out. You might say 'e's 'er property, a kind of pet, if you like to put it that way. Joined up with 'er and 'is nibs when they was in Canada and the Guv'nor still doing the child-wonder at 'is posh college. 'E's a Canadian-Frenchy, Mr. Jacko is. Twenty years ago that must 'ave been, only don't say I said so. It's what they call dog-like devotion, and that's no error. To 'er, *not* to 'is nibs."

"Do you mean Mr. Bennington?" Martyn ventured.

"Clark Bennington, the distinguished character actor, that's right," said Cringle dryly. Evidently he was not inclined to elaborate this theme. He entertained Martyn, instead, with a lively account of the eccentricities of Dr. John Rutherford. "My oaff," he said, "what a daisy! Did you 'ear 'im chi-iking from the front this morning? Typical! We done three of 'is pieces up to date and never a dull moment. Rows and ructions, ructions and rows from the word go. The Guv'nor puts up with it on account he likes the pieces and what a time 'e 'as with 'im, oh dear! It's something shocking the way Doctor cuts up. Dynamite! This time it's the little lady and 'is nibs and Mr. Parry Profile Percival 'e's got it in for. Can't do nothing to please 'im. You should 'ear 'im at rehearsals. 'You're bastardizing my play,' 'e 'owls. 'Get the 'ell aht of it,' 'e shrieks. You never see such an exhibition. Shocking! Then the Guv'nor shuts 'im up and 'e 'as an attack of the willies or what-have-you and keeps aht of the theaytre for a couple of days. Never longer, though, which is very unfortunate for all concerned."

Martyn tried to find out from Cringle what the play was about. He was not very illuminating. "It's 'igh-brow," he said. "Intellectually, it's clarse. 'A Modern Morality' he calls it, the Doctor does. It's all about whether you're brought up right makes any difference to what your old pot 'ands on to you. ' 'Eredity versus environment' they call it. The Guv'nor's environment, and all the rest of 'em's 'eredity. And like it always is in clarse plays, the answer's a lemon. Well, I must go on me way rejoicing."

To Martyn, held as she was in a sort of emotional suspension, the lives and events enclosed within the stage walls and curtain of the Vulcan Theatre assumed a greater reality than her own immediate problem. Her existence since five o'clock the previous afternoon, when she had walked into the theatre, had much of the character and substance of a dream with all the shifting values, the passages of confusion and extreme clarity, which make up the texture of a dream. She was in a state of semi-trauma and found it vaguely agreeable. Her jobs would keep her busy all the afternoon and to-night there was the first dress rehearsal.

She could, she thought, tread water indefinitely, half in and half out of her dream, as long as she didn't come face to face with Mr. Adam Poole in any more looking-glasses.

CHAPTER III

FIRST DRESS REHEARSAL

Martyn's official jobs were all finished by about three o'clock, but by some curious process of which she herself was scarcely aware she had by that time turned into a sort of odd-job girl, particularly where Jacko was concerned. He was engaged in re-painting a piece of very modern decoration above the main and central entrance of the second act set.

"It was lousy in the design," he said, "and it was therefore twelve times lousier when it was twelve times bigger, so now I make it a little worse. Before the first dress rehearsal it is a good thing to be at one's wits' ends, or else one would lose them altogether. When there is not a job, I invent it, because after all there must be someone sane to watch the dress rehearsal. Now if you pass me up the pot of pink, I make a very civilized little flourish in the mode of the second act, and we take time off for you to tell me how clever I am, and why you are such a simpleton as to turn yourself into a dresser."

"I wish," Martyn said, "I knew what the play was about. Is it really a modern morality and do you think it good?"

"All good plays are moralities," said Jacko sententiously, and he leant so far back on the top of his step-ladder that Martyn hurriedly grasped it. "And this is a good play with a very old theme." He hesitated for a moment and she wondered if she only imagined that he looked worried. "Here is a selected man with new ideas in conflict with people who have very old ones. Adam is the selected man. He has been brought up on an island by a community of idealists; he represents the value of environment. By his own wish he returns to his original habitat, and there he is confronted by his heredity, in the persons of his great-uncle, who is played by J. G. Darcey, his brilliant but unstable cousin, who is played by Clark Bennington, this cousin's wife, who is Helena, and with whom he falls in love, and their daughter, who is freakishly like him, but vicious, and who represents therefore his inescapable heredity. This wretched girl," Jacko continued with great relish, looking at Martyn out of the corner of his eyes, "is engaged to a nonentity but finds herself drawn by a terrible attraction to Adam himself. She is played by Gay Gainsford. Receive again from me the pink pot, and bestow upon me the brown. As I have recited it to you so baldly, without nuance and without detail, you will say perhaps if Ibsen or Kafka or Brecht or even Sartre had written this play it would be a good one."

Inexplicably, he again seemed to be in some sort of distress. "It has, in fact," he said, "a continental flavour. But for those who have ears to hear and eyes to see, it has a wider implication than I have suggested. It is a tale, in point of fact, about the struggle of the human being in the detestable situation in which from the beginning he has found himself. Now I descend." He climbed down his step-ladder, groaning lamentably. "And now," he said, "we have some light, and we see if what I have done is good. Go out into the front of the house and in a moment I join you."

By the time Martyn reached the sixth row of the stalls the stage was fully illuminated, and for the first time she saw the set for Act II as Jacko had intended it.

It was an interior, simple in design and execution, but with an air of being over-civilized and stale. "They are," Jacko explained, slumping into a seat beside her, "bad people who live in it. They are not bad of their own volition, but because they have been set down in this place by their heredity and cannot escape. And now you say, all this is pretentious nonsense, and nobody will notice my set except perhaps a few oddities who come to first nights and in any case will get it all wrong. And now we wash ourselves and go out to a place where I am known, and we eat a little, and you tell me why you look like a puppy who has found his tail but dare not wag it. Come."

The restaurant where Jacko was known turned out to be hard by the theatre, and situated in a basement. He insisted on paying for a surprisingly good meal, and Martyn's two and fourpence remained in her pocket. Whereas the curiosity of Fred Badger and Bob Cringle, and in some degree of the actors, had been covert and indirect, Jacko's was unblushing and persistent.

"Now," he said, over their coffee, "I ask you my questions. If there is a secret you tell me so, and with difficulty I shut myself up. If not, you confide in me, because everybody in the Vulcan makes me their confidant and I am greatly flattered by this. In any case we remain friends, no bones broken, and we repeat our little outings. How old do you think I am?"

With some embarrassment, Martyn looked at his scrawny neck, at the thin lichen-like growth of fuzz on his head, and at his heavily scored and indented face. "Fifty-seven," she ventured.

"Sixty-two," said Jacko complacently. "I am sixty-two years old, and a bit of a character. I have not the talent to make a character of myself for the people who sit in front, so instead I play to actors. A wheel within wheels. For twenty years I have built up my role of confidant, and now if I wanted to I couldn't leave off. For example, I can speak perfect English, but my accent is a feature of the role of Papa Jacko and must be sustained. Everybody knows it is a game and, amiably, everyone pretends with me. It is all rather ham and jejune, but I hope that you are going to play too."

Martyn thought: "It would be pleasant to tell him: I'm sure he's very nice and so why don't I do it? I suppose it's because he looks so very odd." And whether with uncanny intuition or else by a queer coincidence he said: "I'm not nearly as peculiar as I look."

Martyn said tentatively: "But I honestly don't know what you want me to tell you."

On the opposite wall of the restaurant there was a tarnished looking-glass, upon the surface of which someone had half-heartedly painted a number of water-lilies and leaves. Among this growth, as if drowned in Edwardiana, Jacko's and Martyn's faces were reflected. He pointed to hers.

"See," he said. "We rehearse a play for which it is necessary a secondary-part actress should resemble, strikingly, the leading man. We have auditions, and from the hundreds of anxious ingenues we select the one who is least unlike him, but she is still very unlike him. Incidentally," Jacko continued, looking Martyn very hard in the eye, "she is the niece of Clark Bennington. She is not very like him, either, which is neither here nor there and perhaps fortunate for her. It is her unlikeness to Adam that we must deplore. Moreover, although I am a genius with make-up, there is very little I can do about it. So we depend instead on reflected emotions and echoed mannerisms. But although she is a nice little actress with a nice small talent, she cannot do this very well either. In the meantime our author, who is a person of unbridled passion where his art is in question, becomes incensed with her performance and makes scenes and everybody except her Uncle Bennington retires into corners and tears pieces of their hair out. The little actress also retires into corners and weeps and is comforted by her Uncle Bennington, who nevertheless knows she is not good.

"Upon this scene there enters, in the guise of a dresser—" he jabbed his finger at the fly-blown mirror—"this. Look at it. If I set out to draw the daughter or the young sister of the leading man, that is what I should draw. Everybody has a look at her and retires again into corners to ask what it is about. Because obviously, she is not a dresser. Is she perhaps—and there are many excited speculations. 'A niece for a niece?' we ask ourselves, and there is some mention of Adam's extreme youth—you must excuse me—and the wrong side of the rosebush, and everybody says it cannot be an accident and waits to see, except Papa Jacko, whose curiosity will not permit him to wait."

Martyn cried out: "I've never seen him before, except in films in New Zealand. He knows nothing about me at all. Nothing. I came here from New Zealand a fortnight ago and I've been looking for a job ever since. I came to the Vulcan looking for a job, that's all there is about it."

"Did you come looking for the job of dresser to Miss Hamilton?"

"For any job," she said desperately. "I heard by accident about the dresser."

"But it was not to be a dresser that you came all the way from New Zealand, and yet it was to work in the theatre, and so perhaps after all you hoped to be an actress."

"Yes," Martyn said, throwing up her hands, "all right, I hoped to be an actress. But please let's forget all about it. You can't imagine how thankful I am to be a dresser, and if you think I'm secretly hoping Miss Gainsford will get laryngitis or break her leg, you couldn't be more mistaken. I don't believe in fairy-tales."

"What humbugs you all are."

"Who?" she demanded indignantly.

"All you Anglo-Saxons. You humbug even yourselves. Conceive for the moment the *mise-en-scène,* the situation, the coincidence, and have you the cheek to tell me again that you came thirteen thousand miles to be an actress and yet do not wish to play this part? Are you a good actress?"

"Don't," Martyn said, "don't. I've got a job and I'm in a sort of a trance. It makes everything very simple and I don't want to come out of it."

Jacko grinned fiendishly. "Just a little touch of laryngitis?" he suggested.

Martyn got up. "Thank you very much for my nice dinner," she said. "I ought to be getting on with my job."

"Little hypocrite. Or perhaps after all you know already you are a very bad actress."

Without answering she walked out ahead of him, and they returned in silence to the Vulcan.

ii

Timed to begin at seven, the dress rehearsal actually started at ten past eight. They were waiting, it appeared, for the author. Miss Hamilton had no changes in the first act, and told Martyn she might watch from the front. She went out and sat at the back of the stalls near the other dressers. There was a sprinkling of onlookers, two of whom were understudies, in the auditorium. About half-way down the centre-aisle Adam Poole, made up and wearing a dressing-gown, sat between Jacko and a young man whom Martyn supposed to be a secretary. Jacko had told her that Poole's first entrance came at the end of the act. The atmosphere that hangs over all dress rehearsals seeped out into the auditorium. The delay seemed interminable. Poole turned from time to time and peered up towards the circle. At last a door slammed upstairs, somebody floundered noisily down the circle steps, a seat banged and a voice—Dr. John James Rutherford's—shouted:

> "Hung be the heavens with black, yield day to night!
> Comets, importing change of times and states,
> Brandish your crystal tresses in the sky,
> And with them scourge the bad revolting stars—

Repeat," Dr. Rutherford bawled, leaning over the balustrade, "repeat: *bad revolting stars*. I'm here, my hearties. Take it away and burn it."

Martyn saw Poole grin. "You behave yourself, up there," he said. "Have you got your paper and pencil?"

"I am provided in that kind."

"Good."

The lights went up along the fringe of the curtain. Martyn's flesh began to creep. Poole called "all right," and lit a cigarette. Throughout the auditorium other little flames sprang up, illuminating from below, like miniature footlights, the faces of the watchers in front. A remote voice said: "O.K. Take it away"; a band of gold appeared below the fringe of the curtain, widened and grew to a lighted stage. Parry Percival spoke the opening line of Dr. Rutherford's new play.

Martyn liked the first act. It concerned itself with the group of figures Jacko had already described—the old man, his son, his son's wife, their daughter and her fiancé. They were creatures of convention, the wife alone possessed of some inclination to reach out beyond her enclosed and aimless existence. In his production Adam Poole, with Jacko's décor to help him, delicately underlined the playwright's symbolic treatment of his theme. It was, as all first acts should be, anticipatory in character. The group awaited the arrival of the islander, the man from outside. Their behaviour suggested that of caged creatures who were completely resigned to their confinement, and in his arrival already saw a threat to their tranquillity. Again Helena Hamilton, as the wife, alone suggested, and she did so with great artistry, a kind of awareness of their sterility and decadence. Bennington, as her hard-drinking, brilliant and completely defeated husband, was giving an exciting performance, though at times Martyn wondered if he was not playing against his author's intention. Was he not, with facile bits of business and clever, unexpected inflections, superimposing upon the part a false quality? Wouldn't the audience, against the tenor of the play, find themselves liking this man, and become increasingly tolerant of the very traits with which the author sought to disgust them? As his father, J. G. Darcey seemed to Martyn to follow adequately the somewhat conventional die-hard the author had intended. As the completely colourless, almost puppet-like juvenile, Parry Percival with his magazine-cover looks was exactly right in what actors call a most ungrateful part. She could understand his dislike of it.

Gay Gainsford's entry as the daughter was a delayed one, and try as she might not to anticipate it, Martyn felt a sinking in her midriff when at last towards the end of the act Miss Gainsford came on. It was quite a small part but one of immense importance. Of the entire group, the girl represented the third generation, the most completely lost, and in the writing of her part Rutherford displayed the influence of Existentialism. It was clear that with few lines to carry her she must make her mark, and clever production was written over everything she did. Agitated as she was by Jacko's direct attack, Martyn wondered if she only imagined that there was nothing more than production there, and if Miss Gainsford was really as ill at ease as she herself supposed. A specific gesture had been introduced and was evidently important, a sudden thrust of her fingers through her short hair, and she twice used a phrase—"That was not what I meant" —where in the context it was evidently intended to plant a barb of attention in the minds of the audience. When this moment came, Martyn sensed uneasiness among the actors. She glanced at Poole and saw him make the specific gesture he had given Miss Gainsford, a quick thrust of his fingers through his hair.

At this juncture the voice in the circle ejaculated: "Boo!"

"Quiet!" said Poole.

Miss Gainsford hesitated, looked wretchedly into the auditorium, and lost her words. She was twice prompted before she went on again. Bennington crossed the stage, put his arm about her shoulders and glared into the circle. The prompter once more threw out a line, Miss Gainsford repeated it and they were off again. Poole got up and went back-stage through the pass-door. The secretary leant forward and shakily lit one cigarette from the butt of another. For the life of her, Martyn couldn't resist glancing at Jacko. He was slumped back in his stall with his arms folded—deliberately imperturbable, she felt— putting on an act. The light from the stage caught his emu-like head and, as if conscious of her attention, he rolled his eyes round at her. She hastily looked back at the stage.

With Gay Gainsford's exit, Martyn could have sworn a wave of relaxation blessed the actors. The dialogue began to move forward compactly with a firm upward curve towards some well-designed climax. There was an increase in tempo corresponding with the rising suspense. Martyn's blood tingled and her heart thumped. Through which door would the entrance be made? The players began a complex circling movement accompanied by a sharp crescendo in the dialogue. Up and up it soared. "Now," she thought, "now!" The action of the play was held in suspense, poised and adjusted, and into the prepared silence, with judgement and precision, at the head of Jacko's twisted flight of steps, came Adam Poole.

"Is that an entrance," thought Martyn, pressing her hands together, "or is it an entrance?"

The curtain came down almost immediately. The secretary gathered his notes together and went back-stage. Dr. Rutherford shouted: "Hold your horses," thundered out of the circle, reappeared in the stalls, and plunged through the pass-door to back-stage where he could be heard cruelly apostrophizing the Almighty and the actors. Jacko stretched elaborately and slouched down the centre-aisle, saying into the air as he passed Martyn: "You had better get round for the change."

Horrified, Martyn bolted like a rabbit. When she arrived in the dressing-room she found her employer, with a set face, attempting to unhook an elaborate back fastening. Martyn bleated an apology which was cut short.

"I hope," said Miss Hamilton, "you haven't mistaken the nature of your job, Martyn. You are my dresser and as such are expected to be here, in this dressing-room, whenever I return to it. Do you understand?"

Martyn, feeling very sick, said that she did, and with trembling fingers effected the complicated change. Miss Hamilton was completely silent, and to Martyn, humiliated and miserable, the necessary intimacies of her work were particularly mortifying.

A boy's voice in the passage chanted: "Second act, please. Second act," and Miss Hamilton said: "Have you got everything on-stage for the quick change?"

"I think so, madam."

"Very well." She looked at herself coldly and searchingly in the long glass and added: "I will go out."

Martyn opened the door. Her employer glanced critically at her. "You're as white as a sheet," she said. "What's the matter?"

Martyn stammered: "Am I? I'm sorry, madam. It must have been the first act."

"Did you like it?"

"*Like* it?" Martyn repeated. "Oh yes, I liked it."

"As much as that?" As easily as if she had passed from one room into another, Miss Hamilton re-entered her mood of enchantment.

"What a ridiculous child you are," she said. "It's only actresses who are allowed to have temperaments."

She went out to the stage, and as Martyn followed her she was surprised to feel in herself a kind of resistance to this woman who could so easily command her own happiness or misery.

An improvised dressing-room had been built on the stage for the quick change, and in or near it Martyn spent the whole of the second act. She was not sure when the quick change came, and didn't like to ask anybody. She therefore spent the first quarter of an hour on tenterhooks, hearing the dialogue, but not seeing anything of the play.

After a short introductory passage the act opened with a long scene between Helena Hamilton and Adam Poole in which their attraction to each other was introduced and established, and her instinctive struggle against her environment made clear and developed. The scene was admirably played by both of them, and carried the play strongly forward. When Miss Hamilton came off she found her dresser bright-eyed and excited. Martyn managed the change without any blunders and in good time. Miss Hamilton's attention seemed to be divided between her clothes and the scene which was now being played between J. G. Darcey, Poole and her husband. This scene built up into a quarrel between Poole and Bennington which at its climax was broken by Poole saying in his normal voice, "I dislike interrupting dress rehearsals, Ben, but we've had this point over and over again. Please take the line as we rehearsed it."

There was complete silence, perhaps for five seconds, and then, unseen, so that Martyn formed no picture of what he was doing or how he looked, Bennington began to giggle. The sound wavered and bubbled into a laugh. Helena Hamilton whispered: "Oh, my *God!*" and went out toward the stage. Martyn heard the stage-hands who had been moving round the set stop dead as if in suspended animation. She saw Parry Percival, waiting off-stage, turn with a look of elaborate concern toward Miss Hamilton and mime bewilderment.

Bennington's laughter broke down into ungainly speech. "I always say," he said, "there is no future in being an actor-manager unless you arrange things your own way. I want to make this chap a human being. You and John say he's to be a monster. All right, all right, dear boy, I won't offend again. He shall be less human than Caliban, and far less sympathetic."

Evidently Poole was standing inside the entrance nearest to the dressing-room, because Martyn heard Bennington cross the stage and when he spoke again he was quite close to her, and had lowered his voice. "You're grabbing everything, aren't you?" the voice wavered. "On and off stage, as you might say—domestically and professionally. The piratical Mr. Poole."

Poole muttered: "If you are not too drunk to think, we'll go on," and pitching his voice threw out a line of dialogue: "If you knew what you wanted, if there was any object, however silly, behind anything you say or do, I could find some excuse for you—"

Martyn heard Helena Hamilton catch her breath in a sob. The next moment she had flung open the door and had made her entrance.

iii

Through the good offices of Jacko, Martyn was able to watch the rest of the act from the side. Evidently he was determined she should see as much as possible of the play. He sent her round a list, scribbled in an elaborate hand, of the warnings and cues for Miss Hamilton's entrances and exits and times when she changed her dress. *Stand in the O.P. corner,* he had written across the paper, *and think of your sins.* She wouldn't have dared to follow his advice if Miss Hamilton, on her first exit, had not said with a sort of irritated good nature: "You needn't wait in the dressing-room perpetually. Just be ready for me, that's all."

So she stood in the shadows of the O.P. corner and saw the one big scene between Adam Poole and Gay Gainsford. The author's intention was clear enough. In this girl, the impure flower of her heredity, the most hopelessly lost of all the group, he sought to show the obverse side of the character Poole presented. She was his twisted shadow, a spiritual incubus. In everything she said and did the audience must see a distortion of Poole himself, until at the end they faced each other across the desk, as in the scene that had been photographed, and Helena Hamilton re-entered to speak the line of climax: *"But it's you, don't you see? You can't escape from it. It's you,"* and the curtain came down.

Gay Gainsford was not good enough. It was not only that she didn't resemble Poole closely: her performance was too anxious, too careful a reproduction of mannerisms without a flame to light them. Martyn burnt in her shadowy corner. The transparent covering in which, like a sea-creature, she had spent her twenty-four hours respite now shrivelled away and she was exposed to the inexorable hunger of an unsatisfied player.

She didn't see Bennington until he put his hand on her arm as the curtain came down, and he startled her so much that she cried out and backed away from him.

"So you think you could do it, dear, do you?" he said.

Martyn stammered: "I'm sorry. Miss Hamilton will want me," and dodged past him towards the improvised dressing-room. He followed, and with a conventionally showy movement barred her entrance.

"Wait a minute, *wait* a minute," he said. "I want to talk to you."

She stood there, afraid of him, conscious of his smell of greasepaint and alcohol, and thinking him a ridiculous as well as an alarming person.

"I'm *so* angry," he said conversationally, "just literally *so* angry that I'm afraid you're going to find me quite a difficult man. And now we've got that ironed out perhaps you'll tell me who the bloody hell you are."

"You know who I am," Martyn said desperately. "Please let me go in."

"M'wife's dresser?"

He took her chin in his hand and twisted her face to the light. Poole came round the back of the set. Martyn thought: "He'll be sick of the sight of me. Always getting myself into stupid little scenes." Bennington's hand felt wet and hot round her chin.

"M'wife's dresser," he repeated. "And m'wife's lover's little by-blow. That the story?"

Poole's hand dropped on his arm. "In you go," he said to Martyn, and twisted Bennington away from the door. Martyn slipped through and he shut it behind her. She heard him say: "You're an offensive fellow in your cups, Ben. We'll have this out after rehearsal. Get along and change for the third act."

There was a moment's pause. The door opened and he looked in.

"Are you all right?" he asked.

"Perfectly, thank you," Martyn said, and in an agony of embarrassment added: "I'm sorry to be a nuisance, sir."

"Oh, don't be an ass," he said with great ill humour. The next moment he had gone.

Miss Hamilton, looking desperately worried, came in to change for the third act.

iv

The dress rehearsal ended at midnight in an atmosphere of acute tension. Because she had not yet been paid, Martyn proposed to sleep again in the Greenroom. So easily do our standards adjust themselves to our circumstances that whereas on her first night at the Vulcan the Greenroom had seemed a blessed haven, her hours of precarious security had bred a longing for a bed and ordered cleanliness, and she began to dread the night.

In groups and singly, the actors and stage-staff drifted away. Their voices died out in the alley and passages, and she saw, with dismay, that Fred Badger had emerged from the door of his cubby-hole and now eyed her speculatively. Desolation and fear possessed Martyn. With a show of preoccupation, she hurried away to Miss Hamilton's dressing-room, which she had already set in order. Here she would find a moment's respite. Perhaps in a few minutes she would creep down the passage and lock herself in the empty room and wait there until Fred Badger had gone his rounds. He would think she had found a lodging somewhere and left the theatre. She opened the door of Miss Hamilton's room and went in.

Adam Poole was sitting in front of the gas fire.

Martyn stammered: "I'm sorry," and made for the door.

"Come in," he said and stood up. "I want to see you for a moment."

"Well," Martyn thought sickly, "this is it. I'm to go."

He twisted the chair round and ordered rather than invited her to sit in it. As she did so she thought: "I won't be able to sleep here tonight. When he's sacked me I'll get my suitcase and ask my way to the nearest women's hostel. I'll walk alone through the streets and when I get there the hostel will be shut."

He had turned his back to her and seemed to be examining something on the dressing-shelf.

"I would very much rather have disregarded this business," he said irritably, "but I suppose I can't. For one thing, someone should apologize to you for Bennington's behaviour. He's not likely to do it for himself."

"It really didn't matter."

"Of course it mattered," he said sharply. "It was insufferable. For both of us."

She was too distressed to recognize as one of pleasure the small shock this last phrase gave her.

"You realize, of course, how this nonsense started," he was saying. "You've seen something of the play. You've seen me. It's not a matter for congratulation, I dare say, but you're like enough to be my daughter. You're a New Zealander, I understand. How old are you?"

"Nineteen, sir."

"You needn't bother to pepper your replies with this 'sir' business. It's not in character and it's entirely unconvincing. I'm thirty-eight. I toured New Zealand in my first job twenty years ago, and Bennington was in the company. That, apparently, is good enough for him. Under the circumstances, I hope you won't mind my asking you who your parents are and where you were born."

"I've no objection whatever," said Martyn with spirit. "My father was Martin Tarne. He was the son and grandson of a high-country run-holder—a sheep-farmer—in the South Island. He was killed on Crete."

He turned and looked directly at her for the first time since she had come into the room.

"I see. And your mother?"

"She's the daughter of a run-holder in the same district."

"Do you mind telling me her maiden name, if you please?"

Martyn said: "I don't see what good this will do."

"Don't you, indeed? Don't you, after all, resent the sort of conjecture that's brewing among these people?"

"I certainly haven't the smallest desire to be thought your daughter."

"And I couldn't agree more. Good Lord!" he said. "This is a fat-headed way for us to talk. Why don't you want to tell me your mother's maiden name? What was the matter with it?"

"She always thought it sounded silly. It was Paula Poole Passington."

He brought the palm of his hand down crisply on the back of her chair. "And why in the world," he asked, "couldn't you say so at once?" Martyn was silent. "Paula Poole Passington," he repeated. "All right. An old cousin of my father's—Cousin Paula—married someone called Passington and disappeared. I suppose to New Zealand. Why didn't she look me up when I went out there?"

"I believe she didn't care for theatricals," said Martyn. "She was my grandmother. The connection is really quite distant."

"You might at least have mentioned it."

"I preferred not to."

"Too proud?"

"If you like," she said desperately.

"Why did you come to England?"

"To earn my living."

"As a dresser?" She was silent. "Well?" he said.

"As best I could."

"As an actress? Oh, for God's sake," he added, "it's damnably late and I'll be obliged if you'll behave reasonably. I may tell you I've spoken to Jacko. Don't you think you're making an ass of yourself? All this mystery act!"

Martyn got up and faced him. "I'm sorry," she said. "It's a silly business but it's not an act. I didn't want to make a thing of it. I joined an English touring company in New Zealand a year ago and they took me on with them to Australia."

"What company was this? What parts did you play?"

She told him.

"I heard about the tour," he said. "They were a reasonably good company."

"They paid quite well and I did broadcasting too. I saved up enough to keep me in England for six months and got a job as assistant children's minder on a ship coming here. Perhaps I should explain that my father lost pretty well everything in the slump, and we are poor people. I had my money in traveller's cheques and the day we landed they were stolen out of my bag, together with my letters of introduction. The bank will probably be able to stop them and let me have it back, but until they decide, I'm hard up. That's all."

"How long have you been here?"

"A fortnight."

"Where have you tried?"

"Agencies. All the London theatres, I think."

"This one last? Why?"

"One of them had to be last."

"Did you know of this—connection—as you call it?"

"Yes. My mother knew of it."

"And the resemblance?"

"I—we saw your pictures—people sometimes said—"

They looked at each other, warily, with guarded interest.

"And you deliberately fought shy of this theatre because you knew I was playing here?"

"Yes."

"Did you know about this piece? The girl's part?"

Martyn was beginning to be very tired. A weariness of spirit and body seeped up through her being in a sluggish tide. She was near to tears and thrust her hand nervously through her short hair. He made some kind of ejaculation and she said at once: "I didn't mean to do that."

"But you knew about the part when you came here?"

"There's a lot of gossip at the agencies when you're waiting. A girl I stood next to in the queue at Garnet Marks's told me they wanted someone at the Vulcan who could be made up to look like you. She'd got it all muddled up with yesterday's auditions for the touring company in another piece."

"So you thought you'd try?"

"Yes. I was a bit desperate by then. I thought I'd try."

"Without, I suppose, mentioning this famous 'connection'?"

"Yes."

"And finding there was nothing for you in the piece you applied for the job of dresser?"

"Yes."

"Well," he said, "it's fantastic, but at least it's less fantastic than pure coincidence would have been. One rather respects you by the way, if it's not impertinent in a second cousin once removed to say so."

"Thank you," she said vaguely.

"The question is, what are we going to do about it?"

Martyn turned away to the ranks of dresses, and with business-like movements of her trembling hands tweaked at the sheets that covered them. She said briskly: "I realize of course that I'll have to go. Perhaps Miss Hamilton—"

"You think you ought to go?" his voice said behind her. "I suppose you're right. It's an awkward business."

"I'm sorry."

"But I'd like to—it's difficult to suggest—"

"I'll be perfectly all right," she said with savage brightness. "Please don't give it another thought."

"Why, by the way, are you still in the theatre?"

"I was going to sleep here," Martyn said loudly. "I did last night. The night-watchman knows."

"You would be paid on Friday."

"Like the actors?"

"Certainly. How much is there in the exchequer between now and Friday?" Martyn was silent and he said with a complete change of voice: "My manners, you will already have been told, are notoriously offensive, but I don't believe I was going to say anything that would have offended you."

"I've got two and fourpence."

He opened the door and shouted "Jacko!" into the echoing darkness. She heard the Greenroom door creak and in a moment or two Jacko came in. He carried a board with a half-finished drawing pinned to it. This he exhibited to Poole. "Crazy, isn't it?" he said. "Helena's costume for the ball. What must I do but waste my beauty-sleep concocting it. Everybody will have to work very hard if it is to be made. I see you are in need of my counsel. What goes on?"

"Against my better judgement," Poole said, "I'm going to follow your advice. You always think you're indispensable at auditions. Give me some light out there and then sit in front."

"It is past midnight. This child has worked and worried herself into a complete *bouleversement*. She is as pale as a Pierrot."

Poole looked at her. "Are you all right?" he asked her. "It won't take ten minutes."

"I don't understand, but I'm all right."

"There you are, Jacko," Poole said and sounded pleased. "It's over to you."

Jacko took her by the shoulders and gently pushed her down on the chair. "*Attention*," he said. "We make a bargain. I live not so far from here in an apartment house kept by a well-disposed French couple. An entirely respectable house, you understand, with no funny business. At the top one finds an attic room as it might be in a tale for children, and so small, it is but twice the size of its nice little bed. The rental is low, within the compass of a silly girl who gets herself into equivocal situations. At my recommendation she will be accommodated in the attic, which is included in my portion of the house, and will pay me the rent at the end of a week. But in exchange for my good offices she does for us a little service. Again, no funny business."

"Oh, dear!" Martyn said. She leant towards the dressing-shelf and propped her face in her hands. "It sounds so wonderful," she said and tried to steady her voice, "a nice little bed."

"All right, Jacko," Poole said. She heard the door open and shut. "I want you to relax for a few minutes," his voice went on. "Relax all over like a cat. Don't think of anything in particular. You're going to sleep sound to-night. All will be well."

The gas fire hummed, the smell of roses and cosmetics filled the warm room. "Do you smoke?" Poole asked.

"Sometimes."

"Here you are."

She drew in the smoke gratefully. He went into the passage and she watched him light his own cigarette. Her thoughts drifted aimlessly about the bony structure of his head and face. Presently a stronger light streamed down the passage. Jacko's voice called something from a great distance.

Poole turned to her. "Come along," he said.

On the stage, dust-thickened rays from pageant-lamps settled in a pool of light about a desk and two chairs. It was like an island in a vague region of blueness. She found herself seated there at the desk, facing him across it. In response to a gesture of Poole's she rested her arms on the desk and her face on her arms.

"Listen," he said, "and don't move. You are in the hall of an old house, beautiful but decaying. You are the girl with the bad heredity. You are the creature who goes round and round in her great empty cage like a stoat filled with a wicked little desire. The object of your desire is the man on the other side of the desk, who is joined to you in blood and of whose face and mind you are the ill reflection. In a moment you will raise your face to his. He will make a gesture and you will make the same gesture. Then you will say: 'Don't you like what you see?' It must be horrible and real. Don't move. Think it. Then raise your head and speak."

There was a kind of voluptuousness in Martyn's fatigue. Only the chair she sat on and the desk that propped her arms and head prevented her, she felt, from slipping to the floor. Into this defencelessness Poole's suggestions entered like those of a mesmerist, and that perfection of duality for which actors pray and which they are so rarely granted now fully invested her. She was herself and she was the girl in the play. She guided the girl and was aware of her and she governed the possession of the girl by the obverse of the man in the play. When at last she raised her face and looked at him and repeated his gesture it seemed to her that she looked into a glass and saw her own reflection and spoke to it.

"Don't you like what you see?" Martyn said.

In the pause that followed, the sound of her own breathing and Poole's returned. She could hear her heart beat.

"Can you do it again?" he said.

"I don't know," she said helplessly. "I don't know at all." She turned away and with a childish gesture hid her face in the crook of her arm. In dismay and shame she let loose the tears she had so long denied herself.

"There, now!" he said, not so much as if to comfort her as to proclaim some private triumph of his own. Out in the dark auditorium Jacko struck his hands together once.

Poole touched her shoulder. "It's nothing," he said. "These are growing pains. They will pass." From the door in the set he said: "You can have the understudy. We'll make terms to-morrow. If you prefer it, the relationship can be forgotten. Good night."

He left her alone and presently Jacko returned to the stage carrying her suitcase.

"Now," he said, "we go home."

CHAPTER IV

SECOND DRESS REHEARSAL

When Martyn opened her eyes on the second morning of her adventure it was with the sensation of having come to rest after a painful journey. At first the events of the previous night seemed to be incorporated in the sleep that had followed them, and her happiness had something of the precarious and transitory quality of a remembered dream. It was difficult to believe that nine hours ago she had faced Adam Poole across a table on the stage of the Vulcan Theatre and had done so, for the moment at least, as an actress. The subsequent drive in a taxi with the unusually silent Jacko, their entrance into a sleeping house, creaking tiptoe up the stairs, the rapture of a hot bath and her subsequent oblivion—all these events flowed together in her memory and she felt she was as yet neither asleep nor fully wakened.

She lay quiet and looked about her. It was a bright morning and the sun came in at the attic window above her bed. The room had an air of great cleanliness and freshness. She remembered now that Jacko had told her he occasionally made use of it and indeed, tiny as it was, it bore his eccentric imprint. A set of designs for *Twelfth Night* was pinned to a wall-board. Ranged along the shelf were a number of figures dressed in paper as the persons in the play and on the wall facing her bed hung a mask of the fool, Feste, looking very like Jacko himself.

"There never was such a little room," Martyn sighed, and began to plan how she would collect and stow away her modest belongings. She was filled with gratitude and with astonished humility.

The bathroom was on the next floor and as she went downstairs she smelt coffee and fresh bread. A door on the landing opened and Jacko's clownish head looked out.

"Breakfast in ten minutes," he said. "Speed is essential."

Of all the amenities, it seemed to Martyn, a hot bath was the most beneficent, and after that a shower under which one could wash one's hair quickly. "Lucky it's short," she thought, and rubbed it dry with her towel.

She was out again in eight minutes to find Jacko on the landing.

"Good," he said. "In your woollen gown you are entirely respectable. A clean school-child. In."

He marshalled her into a largish room set out in an orderly manner as a workshop. Martyn wondered why Jacko, who showed such exquisite neatness in his work, should in his person present such a wild front to the world. He was dressed now in faded cotton trousers, a paint-stained undervest and a tattered dressing-gown. He was unshaven and uncombed and his prominent eyes were slightly bloodshot. His manner, however, was as usual amiable and disarming.

"I propose," he said, "that we breakfast together as a general rule. A light breakfast and supper are included in the arrangement. You will hand me your ration book and I shall shop with discretion. Undoubtedly I am a better cook than you and will therefore make myself responsible for supper. For luncheon you may return if you wish and forage ineffectually for yourself or make what other arrangement seems good to you. Approved?"

Martyn said carefully: "If you please, Jacko, I'm so grateful and so muddled I can't think at all sensibly. You see, I don't know what I shall be earning."

"For your dual and unusual role of understudy and dresser, I imagine about eight pounds a week. Your rental, *demi-pension,* here is two."

"It seems so little," Martyn said timidly. "The rent, I mean."

Jacko tapped the side of the coffee-pot with a spoon.

"Attention," he said. "How often must I repeat. You will have the goodness to understand I am not a dirty old man. It is true that I am virile," he continued with some complacency, "but you are not my type. I prefer the more mature, the more *mondaine,* the—" He stopped short, the spoon with which he had been gesticulating still held aloft. His eyes were fixed on the wall behind Martyn. She turned her head to see a sketch in water-colour of Helena Hamilton. When she faced Jacko again, he was grinning desperately.

"Believe me," he said, "you are in no danger of discomfort from the smallest whisper of scandal. I am notoriously pure. This morning there are eggs and therefore an omelette. Let us observe silence while I make it."

He was gay, in his outlandish fashion, from then onwards. When they had finished their admirable breakfast she helped him wash up and he gave her what he called her orders for the day. She was to go down to the theatre with him, set about her work as a dresser, and at three o'clock she would be given a formal rehearsal as understudy. At night, for the second dress rehearsal, she would again take up her duties as Miss Hamilton's dresser.

"An eccentric arrangement," Jacko said. He groped in the bosom of his undervest and produced a somewhat tattered actor's "part," typewritten and bound in paper. "Only thirteen sides," he said. "A bit-part. You will study the lines while you press and stitch and by this afternoon you are word-perfect, isn't it? You are, of course, delighted?"

"Delighted," Martyn said, "is not exactly the word. I'm flabbergasted and excited and grateful for everything and I just can't believe it's true. But it is a bit worrying to feel I've sort of got in on a fluke and that everybody's wondering what it's all about. They are, you know."

"All that," Jacko said with an ungainly sweep of his arm, "is of no importance. Gay Gainsford is still to play the part. She will not play it well but she is the niece of the leading lady's husband and she is therefore in a favourable position."

"Yes, but her uncle—"

He said quickly: "Clark Bennington was once a good actor. He is now a stencil. He drinks too much and when he is drunk he is offensive. Forget him." He turned away and with less than his usual deftness began to set out his work-table. Finally, from an adjoining room he said indistinctly: "I advise that which I find difficult to perform. Do not allow yourself to become hag-ridden by this man. It is a great mistake. I myself—" His voice was lost in the spurt of running water. Martyn heard him shout: "Run off and learn your lines. I have a job in hand."

With a feeling of unease she returned to her room. But when she opened her part and began to read the lines, this feeling retreated until it hung like a very small cloud over the hinterland of her mind. The foreground was occupied entirely by the exercise of memorizing and in a few minutes she had almost, but not quite, forgotten her anxiety.

ii

She was given her moves that afternoon by the stage-manager, and at three o'clock rehearsed her scenes with the other two understudies. The remaining parts were read from the script. Jacko pottered about back-stage intent on one of his odd jobs: otherwise the theatre seemed to be deserted. Martyn had memorized her lines but inevitably lost them from time to time in her effort to associate them with physical movement. The uncompromising half-light of a working-stage, the mechanical pacing to-and-fro of understudies, the half-muted lines raised to concert-pitch only for cues, and the dead sound of voices in an empty house—all these workaday circumstances, though she was familiar enough with them, after all, laid a weight upon her: she lost her belief in the magic of the previous night. She was oppressed by this anti-climax, and could scarcely summon up the resources of her young experience to meet it.

The positions and moves had been planned with a vivid understanding of the text and seemed to spring out of it. She learnt them readily enough. Rather to her surprise, and, she thought, that of the other understudies, they were finally taken through her scenes at concert-pitch, so that by the end of the rehearsal the visual and aural aspects of her part had fused into a whole. She had got her routine. But it was no more than a routine: she spoke and paused and moved and spoke and there was no reality at all, she felt, in anything she did. Clem Smith, the stage-manager, said nothing about interpretation but, huddled in his overcoat, merely set the moves and then crouched over the script. She was not even a failure, she was just another colourless understudy and nothing had happened.

When it was over, Clem Smith shut the book and said: "Thank you, ladies and gentlemen. Eleven in the morning, if you please." He lit a cigarette and went down into the auditorium and out through the front of the house.

Left alone on the stage, Martyn struggled with an acute attack of deflation. She tried to call herself to order. This in itself was a humiliating, if salutary, exercise. If, she thought savagely, she had been a Victorian young lady, she would at this juncture have locked herself away with a plush-bound journal and, after shedding some mortified tears, forced a confession out of herself. As it was, she set her jaw and worked it out there and then. The truth was, she told herself, she'd been at her old tricks again: she'd indulged in the most blatant kind of day-dream. She'd thought up a success-story and dumped herself down in the middle of it with half a dozen pageant-lamps bathing her girlish form. Because she looked like Poole and because last night she'd had a mild success with one line by playing it off her nerves she'd actually had the gall to imagine— Here Martyn felt her scalp creep and her face burn. "Come on," she thought, "out with it."

Very well, then. She'd dreamt up a further rehearsal with Poole. She'd seen herself responding eagerly to his production, she'd heard him say regretfully that if things had been different— She had even— At this point, overtaken with self-loathing, Martyn performed the childish exercise of throwing her part across the stage, stamping violently and thrusting her fingers through her hair.

"*Damn and blast and hell,*" said Martyn, pitching her voice to the back row of the gallery.

"Not quite as bad as all that."

Adam Poole came out of the shadowed pit and down the centre-aisle of the stalls. He rested his hands on the rail of the orchestra well. Martyn gaped at him.

"You've got the mechanics," he said. "Walk through it again by yourself before to-morrow. Then you can begin to think about the girl. Get the layout of the house into your head. Know your environment. What has she been doing all day before the play opens? What has she been thinking about? Why does she say the things she says and do the things she does? Listen to the other chaps' lines. Come down here for five minutes and we'll see what you think about acting."

Martyn went down into the house. Of all her experiences during these three days at the Vulcan Theatre, she was to remember this most vividly. It was a curious interview. They sat side by side as if waiting for the rise-of-curtain. Their voices were deadened by the plush stalls. Jacko could be heard moving about behind the set and in some distant room back-stage, somebody in desultory fashion hammered and sawed. At first Martyn was ill at ease, unable to dismiss or to reconcile the jumble of distracted notions that beset her. But Poole was talking about theatre and about problems of the actor. He talked well, without particular emphasis but with penetration and authority. Soon she listened with single hearing and with all her attention to what he had to say. Her nervousness and uncertainty were gone, and presently she was able to speak of matters that had exercised her in her own brief experience of the stage. Their conversation was adult and fruitful. It didn't even occur to her that they were getting on rather well together.

Jacko came out on the stage. He shielded his eyes with his hand and peered into the auditorium.

"Adam?" he said.

"Hullo? What is it?"

"It is Helena on the telephone to inquire why have you not rung her at four, the time being now five-thirty. Will you take it in the office?"

"Good Lord!" he ejaculated and got up. Martyn moved into the aisle to let him out.

He said: "All right, Miss Tarne. Work along the lines we've been talking about and you should be able to cope with the job. We take our understudies seriously at the Vulcan and like to feel they're an integral part of the company. You'll rehearse again to-morrow morning and—" He stopped unaccountably, and after a moment said hurriedly: "You're all right, aren't you? I mean you feel quite happy about this arrangement?"

"Yes," she said. "Very happy."

"Good." He hesitated again for a second and then said: "I must go," and was off down the aisle to the front of the house. He called out: "I'll be in the office for some time, Jacko, if anyone wants me."

A door banged. There was a long silence.

Jacko advanced to the footlights. "Where are you?" he asked.

"Here," said Martyn.

"I see you. Or a piece of you. Where is the rest? Reassemble yourself. There is work to be done."

The work turned out to be the sewing together of a fantastic garment created and tacked up by Jacko himself. It had a flamboyant design, stencilled in black and yellow, of double-headed eagles, and was made in part of scenic canvas. There was an electric sewing machine in the wardrobe-room, which was next to Mr. J. G. Darcey's at the end of the passage. Here Jacko sat Martyn down, and here for the next hour she laboured under his exacting direction while he himself crawled about the floor cutting out further garments for the Combined Arts Ball. At half past six he went out, saying he would return with food.

Martyn laboured on. Sometimes she repeated the lines of the part, her voice drowned by the clatter of the machine. Sometimes, when engaged in hand-work, it would seem in the silent room that she had entered into a new existence, as if she had at that moment been born and was a stranger to her former self. And since this was rather a frightening sensation, though not new to Martyn, she must rouse herself and make a conscious effort to dispel it. On one of these occasions, when she had just switched off the machine, she felt something of the impulse that had guided her first attempt at the scene with Poole. Wishing to retain and strengthen this experience, she set aside her work and rested her head on her arms as the scene required. She waited in this posture, summoning her resources, and when she was ready raised her head to confront her opposite.

Gay Gainsford stood on the other side of the table, watching her.

iii

Martyn's flesh leapt on her bones. She cried out and made a sweeping gesture with her arms. A pair of scissors clattered to the floor.

"I'm sorry I startled you," said Miss Gainsford. "I came in quietly. I thought you were asleep but I realize now—you were doing that scene. Weren't you?"

"I've been given the understudy," Martyn said.

"You've had an audition and a rehearsal, haven't you?"

"Yes. I was so frightful at rehearsal, I thought I'd have another shot by myself."

"You needn't," Miss Gainsford said, "try to make it easy for me."

Martyn, still shaken and bewildered, looked at her visitor. She saw a pretty face that under its make-up was sodden with tears. Even as she looked, the large photogenic eyes flooded and the small mouth quivered.

"I suppose," Miss Gainsford said, "you know what you're doing to me."

"Good Lord!" Martyn ejaculated. "What *is* all this? What have I done? I've got your understudy. I'm damn thankful to have it and so far I've made a pretty poor showing."

"It's no good taking that line with me. I know what's happening."

"Nothing's happening. Oh, *please,*" Martyn implored, torn between pity and a rising fear, "*please* don't cry. I'm nothing. I'm just any old understudy."

"That's pretty hot, I must say," Miss Gainsford said. Her voice wavered grotesquely between two registers like an adolescent boy's. "To talk about 'any old understudy' when you've got that appearance. What's everyone saying about you when they think I'm not about? 'She's got the appearance!' It doesn't matter to them that I've had to dye my hair because they don't like wigs. I still haven't got the appearance. I'm a shoulder-length natural ash-blonde, and I've had to have an urchin cut and go black and all I get is insults. In any other management," she continued wildly, "the author wouldn't be allowed to speak to the artists like that man speaks to me. In any other management an artist would be protected against that kind of treatment. Adam's worse, if anything. He's so bloody patient and persistent and half the time you don't know what he's talking about."

She drew breath, sobbed and hunted in her bag for her handkerchief.

Martyn said: "I'm so terribly sorry. It's awful when things go badly at rehearsals. But the worst kind of rehearsals *do* have a way of turning into the best kind of performances. And it's a grand play, isn't it?"

"I loathe the play. To me it's a lot of high-brow hokum and I don't care who knows it. Why the hell couldn't Uncle Ben leave me where I was, playing leads and second leads in fortnightly rep? We were a happy family in fortnightly rep; everyone had fun and games and there wasn't this ghastly graveyard atmosphere. I was miserable enough, God knows, before you came but now it's just *more* than I can stand."

"But I'm not going to play the part," Martyn said desperately.

"You'll be all right. It's just got you down for the moment. I'd be no good, I expect, anyway."

"It's what they're all saying and thinking. It's a pity, they're saying, that you came too late."

"Nonsense. You only imagine that because of the likeness."

"Do I? Let me tell you I'm not imagining *all* the things they're saying about you. And about Adam. How you *can* stay here and take it! Unless it's true. *Is* it true?"

Martyn closed her hands on the material she had been sewing. "I don't want to know what they're saying. There's nothing unkind that's true for them to say."

"So the likeness is purely an accident? There's no relationship?"

Martyn said: "It seems that we are very distantly related, so distantly that the likeness is a freak. I didn't want to tell anyone about it. It's of no significance at all. I haven't used it to get into the theatre."

"I don't know how and why you got in but I wish to God you'd get out. How you *can* hang on, knowing what they think, if it isn't true! You can't have any pride or decency. It's so cruel. It's so *damnably* cruel."

Martyn looked at the pretty tear-blubbered face and thought in terror that if it had been that of Atropos it could scarcely have offered a more dangerous threat. "Don't!" she cried out. "Please don't say that; I need this job so desperately. Honestly, *honestly* you're making a thing of all this. I'm not hurting you."

"Yes, you are. You're driving me completely frantic. I'm nervously and emotionally exhausted," Miss Gainsford sobbed, with an air of quoting somebody else. "It just needed you to send me over the border-line. Uncle Ben keeps on and on and on about it until I think I'll go mad. This is a beastly unlucky theatre anyway. Everyone knows there's something wrong about it and then you come in like a Jonah and it's the rock *bottom*. If," Miss Gainsford went on, developing a command of histrionic climax of which Martyn would scarcely have suspected her capable, "if you have *any* pity at all, *any* humanity, you'll spare me this awful ordeal."

"But this is all nonsense. You're making a song about nothing. I won't be taken in by it," Martyn said and recognized defeat in her own voice.

Miss Gainsford stared at her with watery indignation and through trembling lips uttered her final cliché. "You can't," she said, "do this thing to me," and broke down completely.

It seemed to Martyn that beyond a façade of stock emotionalism she recognized a real and a profound distress. She thought confusedly that if they had met on some common and reasonable ground she would have been able to put up a better defence. As it was they merely floundered in a welter of unreason. It was intolerably distressing to her. Her precarious happiness died, she wanted to escape, she was lost. With a feeling of nightmarish detachment she heard herself say: "All right. I'll speak to Mr. Poole. I'll say I can't do the understudy."

Miss Gainsford had turned away. She held her handkerchief to her face. Her shoulders and head had been quivering but now they were still. There was a considerable pause. She blew her nose fussily, cleared her throat, and looked up at Martyn.

"But if you're Helena's dresser," she said, "you'll still be *about*."

"You can't mean you want to turn me out of the theatre altogether."

"There's no need," Miss Gainsford mumbled, "to put it like that."

Martyn heard a voice and footsteps in the passage. She didn't want to be confronted with Jacko. She said: "I'll see if Mr. Poole's still in the theatre. I'll speak to him now if he is."

As she made for the door Miss Gainsford snatched at her arm. "Please!" she said. "I *am* grateful. But you will be really generous won't you? Really big? You won't bring me into it, will you? With Adam I mean. Adam wouldn't underst—"

Her face set as if she had been held in suspension, like a motion picture freezing into a still. She didn't even release her hold on Martyn's arm.

Martyn spun round and saw Poole, with Jacko behind him, in the passage. To her own astonishment she burst out laughing.

"No, really!" she stammered. "It's too much! This is the third time. Like the demon-king in pantomime."

"What the devil do you mean?"

"I'm sorry. It's just your flair for popping up in crises. Other people's crises. Mine, in fact."

He grimaced as if he gave her up as a bad job. "What's the present crisis?" he said and looked at Miss Gainsford, who had turned aside and was uneasily painting her mouth. "What is it, Gay?"

"Please!" she choked. "Please let me go. I'm all right, really. Quite all right. I just rather want to be alone."

She achieved a tearful smile at Poole and an imploring glance at Martyn. Poole stood away from the door and watched her go out with her chin up and with courageous suffering neatly portrayed in every inch of her body.

She disappeared into the passage and a moment later the door of the Greenroom was heard to shut.

"It is a case of mis-casting," said Jacko, coming into the room. "She should be in Hollywood. She has what it takes in Hollywood. What an exit! We have misjudged her."

"Go and see what's the matter."

"She wants," said Jacko, making a dolorous face, "to be alone."

"No, she doesn't. She wants an audience. You're it. Get along and do your stuff."

Jacko put several parcels on the table. "I am the dogsbody," he said, "to end all dogsbodies," and went out.

"Now, then," Poole said.

Martyn gathered up her work and was silent.

"What's the matter? You're as white as a sheet. Sit down. What is all this?"

She sat behind the machine.

"Come on," he said.

"I'm sorry if it's inconvenient for you but I'm afraid I've got to give notice."

"Indeed? As a dresser or as understudy?"

"As both."

"It's extremely inconvenient and I don't accept it."

"But you must. Honestly, you must. I can't go on like this: it isn't fair."

"Do you mean because of that girl?"

"Because of her and because of everything. She'll have a breakdown. There'll be some disaster."

"She doesn't imagine you're going to be given the part over her head, does she?"

"No, no, of course not. It's just that she's finding it hard anyway and the—the sight of me sort of panics her."

"The likeness?"

"Yes."

"She needn't look at you. I'm afraid she's the most complete ass, that girl," he muttered. He picked up a fold of the material Martyn had been sewing, looked absently at it and pushed the whole thing across the table. "Understand," he said, "I won't for a second entertain the idea of your going. For one thing Helena can't do without you, and for another I will not be dictated to by a minor actress in my own company. Nor," he added with a change of tone, "by anyone else."

"I'm so terribly sorry for her," Martyn said. "She feels there's some sort of underground movement against her. She really feels it."

"And you?"

"I must admit I don't much enjoy the sensation of being in the theatre on sufferance. But I was so thankful—" She caught her breath and stopped.

"Who makes you feel you're on sufferance? Gay? Bennington? Percival?"

"I used a silly phrase. Naturally, they all must think it a bit queer, my turning up. It *looks* queer."

"It'd look a damn sight queerer if you faded out again. I can't think," he said impatiently, "how you could let yourself be bamboozled by that girl."

"But it's *not* all bamboozle. She really is at the end of her tether."

Martyn waited for a moment. She thought inconsequently how strange it was that she should talk like this to Adam Poole, who two days ago had been a celebrated name, a remote legend, seen and heard and felt through a veil of characterization in his films.

"Oh, well," she thought and said aloud: "I'm thinking of the show. It's such a good play. She mustn't be allowed to fail. I'm thinking about that."

He came nearer and looked at her with a sort of incredulity. "Good Lord," he said, "I believe you are! Do you mean to say you haven't considered your own chance if she did crack up? Where's your wishful thinking?"

Martyn slapped her palm down on the table. "But of course I have. Of course I've done my bit of wishful thinking. But don't you see—"

He reached across the table and for a brief moment his hand closed over hers. "I think I do," he said. "I'm beginning, it seems, to get a taste of your quality. How do you suppose the show would get on if you had to play?"

"That's unfair," Martyn cried.

"Well," he said, "don't run out on me. That'd be unfair, if you like. No dresser. No understudy. A damn shabby trick. As for this background music, I know where it arises. It's a more complex business than you may suppose. I shall attend to it." He moved behind her chair, and rested his hands on its back. "Well," he said, "shall we clap hands and a bargain? How say you?"

Martyn said slowly: "I don't see how I can do anything but say yes."

"There's my girl!" His hand brushed across her head and he moved away.

"Though I must say," Martyn added, "you do well to quote Petruchio. And Henry the Fifth, if it comes to that."

"A brace of autocratic male animals? Therefore it must follow you are 'Kate' in two places. And—shrewd Kate, French Kate, kind Kate, but never curst Kate—you will rehearse at eleven to-morrow, hold or cut bow-strings. Agreed?"

"I am content."

"Damned if you look it, however. All right. I'll have a word with that girl. Good day to you, Kate."

"Good day, sir," said Martyn.

iv

That night the second dress rehearsal went through as for performance, without, as far as Martyn knew, any interruption during the action.

She stayed throughout in one or the other of Miss Hamilton's dressing-rooms and, on the occasions when she was in transit, contrived to be out of the way of any of the players. In the second act, her duties kept her in the improvised dressing-room on the stage and she heard a good deal of the dialogue.

There is perhaps nothing that gives one so strong a sense of theatre from the inside as the sound of invisible players in action. The disembodied and remote voices, projected at an unseen mark, the uncanny quiet off-stage, the smells and the feeling that the walls and the dust listen, the sense of a simmering expectancy; all these together make a corporate life so that the theatre itself seems to breathe and pulse and give out a warmth. This warmth communicated itself to Martyn and, in spite of all her misgivings, she glowed and thought to herself, "This is my place. This is where I belong."

Much of the effect of the girl's part in this act depended not so much on what she said, which was little, but on mime and on that integrity of approach which is made manifest in the smallest gesture, the least movement. Listening to Miss Gainsford's slight uncoloured voice, Martyn thought: "But perhaps if one watched her it would be better. Perhaps something is happening that cannot be heard, only seen."

Miss Hamilton, when she came off for her changes, spoke of nothing but the business in hand and said little enough about that. She was indrawn and formal in her dealings with her dresser. Martyn wondered uneasily how much Poole had told her of their interviews, whether she had any strong views or prejudices about her husband's niece, or shared his resentment that Martyn herself had been cast as an understudy.

The heat radiated by the strong lights of the dressing-rooms intensified their characteristic smells. With business-like precision Miss Hamilton would aim an atomizer at her person and spray herself rhythmically with scent while Martyn, standing on a chair, waited to slip a dress over her head. After the end of the second act, when she was about this business in the star-room, Poole came in. "That went very nicely, Helena," he said.

Martyn paused with the dress in her hands. Miss Hamilton extended her whitened arms, and with a very beautiful movement turned to him.

"Oh, darling," she said. "Did it? Did it really?"

Martyn thought she had never seen anyone more lovely than her employer was then. Hers was the kind of beauty that declared itself when most simply arrayed. The white cloth that protected her hair added a Holbein-like emphasis to the bones and subtly turning planes of her face. There was a sort of naïveté and warmth in her posture: a touching intimacy. Martyn saw Poole take the hands that were extended to him and she turned her head away, not liking, with the voluminous dress in her arms, to climb down from her station on the chair. She felt suddenly desolate and shrunken within herself.

"Was it *really* right?" Miss Hamilton said.

"You were, at least."

"But—otherwise?"

"Much as one would expect."

"Where's John?"

"In the circle, under oath not to come down until I say so."

"Pray God, he keep his oath!" she quoted sombrely.

"Hullo, Kate," Poole said.

"Kate?" Miss Hamilton asked. "Why Kate?"

"I suspect her," said Poole, "of being a shrew. Get on with your job, Kate. What are you doing up there?"

Miss Hamilton said: "Really, darling!" and moved away to the chair. Martyn slipped the dress over her head, jumped down and began to fasten it. She did this to a running accompaniment from Poole. He whispered to himself anxiously as if he were Martyn, muttered and grunted as if Miss Hamilton complained that the dress was tight, and thus kept up a preposterous duologue, matching his words to their actions. This was done so quaintly and with so little effort that Martyn had much ado to keep a straight face and Miss Hamilton was moved to exasperated laughter. When she was dressed she took him by the arms. "Since when, my sweet, have you become a dressing-room comedian?"

"Oh God, your only jig-maker."

"Last act, please, last act," said the call-boy in the passage.

"Come on," she said, and they went out together.

When the curtain was up, Martyn returned to the improvised dressing-room on the stage and there, having for the moment no duties, she listened to the invisible play and tried to discipline her most unruly heart.

Bennington's last exit was followed in the play by his suicide, off-stage. Jacko, who had, it seemed, a passion for even the simplest of off-stage stunts, had come round from the front of the house to supervise the gunshot. He stood near the entry into the dressing-room passage with a stage-hand who carried an effects-gun. This was fired at the appropriate moment and, as they were stationed not far from Martyn in her canvas room, she leapt at the report, which was nerve-shatteringly successful. The acrid smell of the discharge drifted into her roofless shelter.

Evidently Bennington was standing near by. His voice, carefully lowered to a murmur, sounded just beyond the canvas wall. "And that," he said, "takes me *right* off, thank God. Give me a cigarette, Jacko, will you?" There was a pause. The stage-hand moved away. A match scraped and Bennington said: "Come to my room and have a drink."

"Thank you, Ben, not now," Jacko whispered. "The curtain comes down in five minutes."

"Followed by a delicious post mortem conducted by the Great Producer and the Talented Author. Entrancing prospect! How did I go, Jacko?"

"No actor," Jacko returned, "cares to be told how he goes in anything but terms of extravagant praise. You know how clever you always are. You are quite as clever to-night as you have always been. Moreover, you showed some discretion."

Martyn heard Bennington chuckle. "There's still to-morrow," he said. "I reserve my fire, old boy. I bide my time."

There was a pause. Martyn heard one of them fetch a long sigh—Jacko, evidently, because Bennington, as if in answer to it, said: "Oh, nonsense." After a moment he added: "The kid's all right," and when Jacko didn't answer: "Don't you think so?"

"Why, yes," said Jacko.

On the stage the voices of Helena Hamilton and Adam Poole built towards a climax. The call-boy came round behind the set and went down the passage chanting: "All on for the curtain, please. All on."

Martyn shifted the chair in the dressing-room and moved noisily. There was a brief silence.

"I don't give a damn if she can hear," Bennington said more loudly. "Wait a moment. Stay where you are. I was asking you what you thought of Gay's performance. She's all right. Isn't she?"

"Yes, yes. I must go."

"Wait a bit. If the fools left her alone she'd go tremendously. I tell you what, old boy. If our Eccentric Author exercises his talent for wisecracking on that kid to-night I'll damn well take a hand."

"You will precipitate a further scene, and that is to be avoided."

"I'm not going to stand by and hear her bullied. By God, I'm not. I understand you've given harbourage, by the way, to the Mystery Maiden."

"I must get round to the side. By your leave, Ben."

"Plenty of time."

And Martyn knew that Bennington stood in the entry to the passage, barring the way.

"I'm talking," he said, "about this understudy-cum-dresser. Miss X."

"You are prolific in cryptic titles."

"Call her what you like, it's a peculiar business. What is she? You may as well tell me, you know. Some ancient indiscretion of Adam's adolescence come home to roost?"

"Be quiet, Ben."

"For tuppence I'd ask Adam himself. And that's not the only question I'd like to ask him. Do you think I relish my position?"

"They are getting near the tag. It is almost over."

"Why do you suppose I drink a bit? What would you do in my place?"

"Think before I speak," said Jacko, "for one thing."

A buzzer sounded. "There's the curtain," said Jacko. "Look out."

Martyn heard a kind of scuffle followed by an oath from Bennington. There were steps in the passage. The curtain fell with a giant whisper. A gust of air swept through the region back-stage.

"All on," said the stage-manager distantly. Martyn heard the players go on and the curtain rise and fall again.

Poole, on the stage, said: "And that's all of that. All right, everyone. Settle down and I'll take the notes. John will be round in a moment. I'll wait for you, Helena."

Miss Hamilton came into the improvised room. Martyn removed her dress and put her into her gown.

"I'll take my make-up off out there," she said. "Bring the things, Martyn, will you? Grease, towels and my cigarettes?"

Martyn had them ready. She followed Miss Hamilton out and for the first time that night went onto the set.

Poole, wearing a dark dressing-gown, stood with his back to the curtain. The other five members of the cast sat, relaxed but attentive, about the stage. Jacko and Clem Smith waited by the Prompt corner with papers and pencils. Martyn held a looking-glass before Miss Hamilton, who said: "Adam, darling, you don't mind, do you? I mustn't miss a word but I *do* rather want to get on," and began to remove her make-up.

Upon this scene Dr. John James Rutherford erupted. His arrival was prefaced in his usual manner by slammed doors, blundering footsteps and loud ejaculations. He then appeared in the central entrance, flame-headed, unshaven, overcoated, and grasping a sheaf of papers.

"Roast me," he said, "in sulphur! Wash me in steep-down gulfs of liquid fire! 'Ere I again endure the loathy torment of a dress rehearsal! What have I done, ye gods, that I should—"

"All right, John," Poole said. "Not yet. Sit down. On some heavy piece of furniture and carefully."

Clem Smith shouted: "Alf! The Doctor's chair."

A large chair with broken springs was brought on and placed with its back to the curtain. Dr. Rutherford hurled himself into it and produced his snuff-box. "I am a child to chiding," he said. "What goes on, chums?"

Poole said: "I'm going to take my stuff. If anything I have to say repeats exactly any of your own notes you might leave it out for the sake of saving time. If you've any objections, be a good chap and save them till I've finished. Agreed?"

"Can't we cut the flummery and get down to business?"

"That's just what I'm suggesting."

"Is it? I wasn't listening. Press on, then, my dear fellow. Press on."

They settled down. Jacko gave Poole a block of notes and he began to work through them. "Nothing much in Act I," he said, "until we get to—" His voice went on evenly. He spoke of details in timing, of orchestration and occasionally of stage-management. Sometimes a player would ask a question and there would be a brief discussion. Sometimes Clem Smith would make a note. For the scenes where Poole had been on, Jacko, it appeared, had taken separate notes. Martyn suddenly remembered that Jacko's official status was that of assistant to Poole, and thought it characteristic of him that he made so little of his authority.

From where she stood, holding the glass for Helena Hamilton, she could see all the players. In the foreground was the alert and beautiful face of her employer, a little older now with its make-up gone, turning at times to the looking-glass and at times, when something in his notes concerned her, towards Poole. Beyond Miss Hamilton sat J. G. Darcey, alone and thoughtfully filling his pipe. He glanced occasionally, with an air of anxious solicitude, at Miss Gainsford. At the far side Parry Percival lay in an armchair looking fretful. Bennington stood near the centre with a towel in his hands. At one moment he came behind his wife. Putting a hand on her shoulder, he reached over it, helped himself to a dollop of grease from a jar in her case and slapped it on his face. She made a slight movement of distaste and immediately afterwards a little secret grimace, as if she had caught herself out in a blunder. For a moment he retained his hold of her shoulder. Then he looked down at her, dragged his clean fingers across her neck and, smearing the grease over his face, returned to his former position and began to clean away his make-up.

Martyn didn't want to look at Gay Gainsford but was unable altogether to avoid doing so. Miss Gainsford sat, at first alone, on a smallish sofa. She seemed to have herself tolerably well in hand, but her eyes were restless and her fingers plaited and replaited the folds of her dress. Bennington watched her from a distance until he had done with his towel. Then he crossed the stage and sat beside her, taking one of the restless hands in his. He looked hard at Martyn, who was visited painfully by a feeling of great compassion for both of them and by a sensation of remorse. She had a notion, which she tried to dismiss as fantastic, that Poole sensed this reaction. His glance rested for a moment on her and she thought: "This is getting too complicated. It's going to be too much for me." She made an involuntary movement and at once Miss Hamilton put out a hand to the glass.

When Poole had dealt with the first act he turned to Dr. Rutherford, who had sat throughout with his legs extended and his chin on his chest, directing from under his brows a glare of extreme malevolence at the entire cast.

"Anything to add to that, John?" Poole asked.

"Apart from a passing observation that I regard the whole thing as a *tour de force* of understatement and with reservations that I keep to myself"—here Dr. Rutherford looked fixedly at Parry Percival—"I am mum. I reserve my fire."

"Act II, then," said Poole, and began again.

Martyn became aware after a few minutes that Dr. Rutherford, like Bennington, was staring at her. She was as horridly fascinated as a bird is said to be by the unwinking gaze of a snake. Do what she could to look elsewhere about the stage, she must after a time steal a glance at him, only to meet again his speculative and bloodshot regard. This alarmed her profoundly. She was persuaded that a feeling of tension had been communicated to the others, and that they too were aware of some kind of impending crisis. This feeling grew in intensity as Poole's voice went steadily on with his notes. He had got about half-way through the second act when Dr. Rutherford ejaculated: "Hi! Wait a bit!" and began a frenzied search through his own notes, which seemed to be in complete disorder. Finally he pounced on a sheet of paper, dragged out a pair of spectacles and, with a hand raised to enjoin silence, read it to himself with strange noises in his breathing. Having scattered the rest of his notes over his person and the floor, he now folded this particular sheet and sat on it.

"Proceed," he said. The cast stirred uneasily. Poole continued. He had come to the scene between himself and Miss Gainsford, and beyond a minor adjustment of position said nothing about it. Miss Hamilton, who had arrived at the final stage of her street make-up, dusted her face with powder, nodded good-humouredly at Martyn and turned to face Poole. Martyn thankfully shut the dressing-case and made for the nearest exit.

At the same moment Poole reached the end of his notes for the second act and Dr. Rutherford shouted: "Hold on! Stop that wench!"

Martyn, with a sensation of falling into chaos, turned in the doorway.

She saw nine faces lifted towards her own. They made a pattern against the smoke-thickened air. Her eyes travelled from one to the other and rested finally on Poole's.

"It's all right," he said. "Go home."

"No, you don't," Dr. Rutherford shouted excitedly.

"Indeed she does," said Poole. "Run away home, Kate. Good night to you."

Martyn heard the storm break as she fled down the passage.

CHAPTER V

OPENING NIGHT

From noon until half past six on the opening night of Dr. Rutherford's new play, the persons most concerned in its birth were absent from their theatre. Left to itself, the Vulcan was possessed only by an immense expectancy. It waited. In the auditorium rows of seats, stripped of their dust-cloths, stared at the curtain. The curtain itself presented its reverse side to Jacko's set, closing it in with a stuffy air of secrecy. The stage was dark. Battalions of dead lamps, focussed at crazy angles, overhung it with the promise of light. Cue-sheets, fixed to the switchboard, awaited the electrician, the prompt-script was on its shelf, the properties were ranged on trestle-tables. Everything bided its time in the dark theatre.

To enter into this silent house was to feel as if one surprised a poised and expectant presence. This air of suspense made itself felt to the occasional intruders: to the boy who from time to time came through from the office with telegrams for the dressing-rooms, to the girl from Florian's and the young man from the wig-makers, and to the piano-tuner who for an hour twanged and hammered in the covered well. And to Martyn Tarne who, alone in the ironing-room, set about the final pressing of the dresses under her care.

The offices were already active and behind their sand-blasted glass walls typewriters clattered and telephone bells rang incessantly. The blacked-out box-plan lay across Bob Grantley's desk, and stacked along the wall were rectangular parcels of programmes, fresh from the printer.

And at two o'clock the queues for the early doors began to form in Carpet Street.

ii

It was at two o'clock that Helena Hamilton, after an hour's massage, went to bed. Her husband had telephoned, with a certain air of opulence which she had learnt to dread, that he would lunch at his club and return to their flat during the afternoon to rest.

In her darkened room she followed a practised routine and, relaxing one set of muscles after another, awaited sleep. This time, however, her self-discipline was unsuccessful. If only she could hear him come in, it would be better; if only she could see into what sort of state he'd got himself. She used all her formulae for repose but none of them worked. At three o'clock she was still awake and still miserably anxious.

It was no good trying to cheer herself up by telling over her rosary of romantic memories. Usually this was a successful exercise. She had conducted her affairs of the heart, she knew, with grace and civility. She had almost always managed to keep them on a level of enchantment. She had simply allowed them to occur with the inconsequence and charm of self-sown larkspurs in an otherwise correctly ordered border. They had hung out their gay little banners for a season and then been painlessly tweaked up. Except, perhaps, for Adam. With Adam, she remembered uneasily, it had been different. With Adam, so much her junior, it had been a more deeply rooted affair. It had put an end, finally, to her living with Ben as his wife. It had made an enemy of Ben. And at once her thoughts were infested with worries about the contemporary scene at the theatre. "It's such a muddle," she thought, "and I hate muddles." They'd had nothing but trouble all through rehearsals. Ben fighting with everybody and jealous of Adam. The Doctor bawling everybody out. And that wretchedly unhappy child Gay (who, God knew, would never be an actress as long as she lived) first pitchforked into the part by Ben and now almost bullied out of it by the Doctor. And, last of all, Martyn Tarne.

She had touched the raw centre of her anxiety. Under any other conditions, she told herself, she would have welcomed the appearance out of a clear sky and—one had to face it—under very odd circumstances, of this little antipodean: this throw-back to some forebear that she and Adam were supposed to have in common. She would have been inclined to like Martyn for the resemblance instead of feeling so uncomfortably disturbed by it. Of course she accepted Adam's explanation, but at the same time she thought it rather naïve of him to believe that the girl had actually kept away from the theatre because she didn't want to make capital out of the relationship. That, Helena thought, turning restlessly on her bed, was really too simple of Adam. Moreover, he'd stirred up the already exacerbated nerves of the company by giving this girl the understudy without, until last night, making public the relationship.

There she went, thinking about last night's scene: John Rutherford demanding that even at this stage Martyn should play the part, Gay imploring Adam to release her, Ben saying he'd walk out on the show if Gay went, and Adam—Adam had done the right thing of course. He'd come down strongly with one of his rare thrusts of anger and reduced them to complete silence. He had then described the circumstances of Martyn's arrival at the theatre, and had added in a voice of ice that there was and could be no question of any change in the cast. He finished his notes and left the theatre, followed by Jacko.

This had been the signal for an extremely messy row in which everybody seemed to bring to light some deep-seated grudge. Ben had quarrelled almost simultaneously with Parry Percival (on the score of technique), with Dr. Rutherford (on the score of casting), with his niece (on the score of humanity) and, unexpectedly, with J. G. Darcey (on the score of Ben bullying Gay). Percival had responded to a witticism of the Doctor's by a stream of shrill invective which astonished everybody, himself included, and Gay had knitted the whole scene into a major climax by having a fit of hysterics from which she was restored with brutal efficiency by Dr. Rutherford himself.

The party had been broken up. J.G. sustained his new role of knightly concern by taking Gay home. Parry Percival left in a recrudescence of fury occasioned by the Doctor flinging after him a composite Shakesperian epithet: "Get you gone, you dwarf; you minimus, of hindering knot-grass made; you bead, you acorn." She herself had retired into the wings. The stage-staff had already disappeared. The Doctor and Ben, finding themselves in undisputed possession of the stage, had squared up to each other with the resolution of all-in wrestlers, and she, being desperately tired, had taken the car home and asked their man to return to the theatre for her husband. When she had awakened late in the morning she was told he had already gone out.

"I wish," a voice cried out in her mind, "I wish to God he'd never come back."

And at that moment she heard him stumble heavily upstairs.

She expected him to go straight to his room and was dismayed when he came to a halt outside her door and, with a clumsy sound that might have been intended for a knock, opened it and came in. The smell of brandy and cigars came in with him and invaded the whole room. It was more than a year since that had happened.

He walked uncertainly to the foot of the bed and leant on it—and she was frightened of him.

"Hullo," he said.

"What is it, Ben? I'm resting."

"I thought you might be interested. There'll be no more nonsense from John about Gay."

"Good," she said.

"He's calmed down. I got him to see reason."

"He's not so bad, really—old John."

"He's had some good news from abroad. About the play."

"Translation rights?"

"Something like that." He was smiling at her, uncertainly. "You look comfy," he said. "All tucked up."

"Why don't you try and get some rest yourself?" He leant over the foot of the bed and said something under his breath. "What?" she said anxiously. "What did you say?"

"I said it's a pity Adam didn't appear a bit sooner, isn't it? I'm so extraneous."

Her heart thumped like a fist inside her ribs. "Ben, *please*," she said.

"And another thing. Do you both imagine I don't see through this dresser-cum-understudy racket? Darling, I don't much enjoy playing the cuckold in your Restoration comedy, but I'm just bloody well furious when you so grossly under-estimate my intelligence. When was it? On the New Zealand tour in 1930?"

"What is this nonsense!" she said breathlessly.

"Sorry. How are you managing to-night? You and Adam?"

"My dear Ben!"

"I'll tell you. You're making shift with me for once in a blue moon. And I'm not talking about to-night."

She recognized this scene. She had dreamt it many times. His face had advanced upon her while she lay inert with terror, as one does in a nightmare. For an infinitesimal moment she was visited by the hope that perhaps after all she had slept and, if she could only scream, would awaken. But she couldn't scream. She was quite helpless.

iii

Adam Poole's telephone rang at half past four. He had gone late to rest and was wakened from a deep sleep. For a second or two he didn't recognize her voice, and she spoke so disjointedly that even when he was broad awake he couldn't make out what she was saying.

"What is it?" he said. "Helena, what's the matter? I can't hear you."

Then she spoke more clearly and he understood.

iv

At six o'clock the persons in the play began to move towards the theatre. In their lodgings and flats they bestirred themselves after their several fashions: to drink tea or black coffee, choke down pieces of bread and butter that tasted like sawdust, or swallow aspirin and alcohol. This was their zero hour: the hour of low vitality when the stimulus of the theatre and the last assault of nerves was yet to come. By a quarter past six they were all on their way. Their dressers were already in their rooms and Jacko prowled restlessly about the darkened stage. Dr. John James Rutherford, clad in an evening suit and a boiled shirt garnished with snuff, both of which dated from some distant period when he still attended the annual dinners of the B.M.A., plunged into the office and made such a nuisance of himself that Bob Grantley implored him to go away.

At twenty past six the taxi carrying Gay Gainsford and J. G. Darcey turned into Carpet Street. Darcey sat with his legs crossed elegantly and his hat perched on them. In the half-light his head and profile looked like those of a much younger man.

"It *was* sweet of you to call for me, J.G.," Gay said unevenly.

He smiled, without looking at her, and patted her hand. "I'm always petrified myself," he said, "on first nights."

"Are you? I suppose a true artist must be."

"Ah, youth, youth!" sighed J.G.—a little stagily perhaps, but, if she hadn't been too preoccupied to notice it, with a certain overtone of genuine nostalgia.

"It's worse than the usual first-night horrors for *me*," she said. "I'm just boxing on in a private hell of my own."

"My poor child."

She turned a little towards him and leant her head onto his shoulder. "Nice!" she murmured and after a moment: "I'm so frightened of him, J.G."

With the practised ease of a good actor, he slipped his arm round her. "I won't have it," he said. "By God, I won't! If he worries you again, author or no author—"

"It's not *him*," she said. "Not the Doctor. Oh, I know he's simply filthy to work with and he does fuss me dreadfully, but it's not the Doctor *really* who's responsible for all my misery."

"No? Who is then?"

"Uncle Ben!" She made a small wailing noise that was muffled by his coat. He bent his head attentively to listen. "J.G., I'm just plain *terrified* of Uncle Ben."

v

Parry Percival always enjoyed his arrival at the theatre when there was a gallery queue to be penetrated. One raised one's hat and said: "Pardon me. Thanks so much," to the gratified ladies. One heard them murmur one's name. It was a heartening little fillip to one's self-esteem.

On this occasion the stimulant didn't work with its normal magic. He was too worried to relish it wholeheartedly. For one thing his row with Dr. Rutherford still lingered like an unpleasant taste in his memory. Apart from the altogether unforgivable insults the Doctor had levelled at his art, there was one in particular which had been directed at himself as a man and this troubled him deeply. It had almost brought him to the pitch of doing something that he dreaded to do— take stock of himself. Until now he had lived in an indeterminate hinterland, drifting first towards one frontier, then the other, unsure of his impulses and not strongly propelled by them in any one direction.

He would, he thought, perhaps have turned out a happier being if he had been born a woman. "Let's face it," he thought uneasily, "I'm interested in their kind of things. I'm intuitive and sensitive in their way." It helped a little to think how intuitive and how sensitive he was. But he was not in any sense a fair target for the sort of veiled insults the Doctor had levelled at him. And as if this weren't enough of a worry, there was the immediate menace of Clark Bennington. Ben, he thought hotly, was insufferable. Every device by which a second-leading man could make a bit-part actor look foolish had been brought into play during rehearsals. Ben had up-staged him, had flurried him by introducing new business, had topped his lines and, even while he was seething with impotent fury, had reduced him to nervous giggles by looking sideways at him. It was the technique with which a schoolmaster could torture a small boy, and it revived in Parry hideous memories of his childhood.

Only partially restored by the evidence of prestige afforded by the gallery queue, he walked down the stage-door alley and into the theatre. He was at once engulfed in its warmth and expectancy.

He passed into the dressing-room passage. Helena Hamilton's door was half-open and the lights were on. He tapped, looked in and was greeted by the smell of greasepaint, powder, wet-white and flowers. The gas fire groaned comfortably. Martyn, who was spreading out towels, turned and found herself confronted by his deceptively boyish face.

"Early at work?" he fluted.

Martyn wished him good evening.

"Helena not down yet?"

"Not yet."

He hung about the dressing-room, fingering photographs and eyeing Martyn.

"I hear you come from Down Under," he said. "I nearly accepted an engagement to go out there last year, but I didn't really like the people so I turned it down. Adam played it in the year dot, I believe. Well, more years ago than he would care to remember, I dare say. Twenty, if we're going to let our back-hair down. Before you were born, I dare say."

"Yes," Martyn agreed. "Just before."

Her answer appeared to give him extraordinary satisfaction. "Just before?" he repeated. "Really?" and Martyn thought: "I mustn't let myself be worried by this."

He seemed to hover on the edge of some further observation and pottered about the dressing-room examining the great mass of flowers. "I'll swear," he said crossly, "those aren't the roses I chose at Florian's. Honestly, that female's an absolute menace."

Martyn, seeing how miserable he looked, felt sorry for him. He muttered: "I do so *abominate* first nights," and she rejoined: "They are pretty ghastly, aren't they?" Because he seemed unable to take himself off, she added with an air of finality: "Anyway, may I wish you luck for this one?"

"Sweet of you," he said. "I'll need it. I'm the stooge of this piece. Well, thanks, anyway."

He drifted into the passage, halted outside the open door of Poole's dressing-room and greeted Bob Cringle. "Governor not down yet?"

"We're on our way, Mr. Percival."

Parry inclined his head and strolled into the room. He stood close to Bob, leaning his back against the dressing-shelf, his legs elegantly crossed.

"Our little stranger," he murmured, "seems to be new-brooming away next door."

"That's right, sir," said Bob. "Settled in very nice."

"Strong resemblance," Parry said invitingly.

"To the Guv'nor, sir?" Bob rejoined cheerfully. "That's right. Quite a coincidence."

"A coincidence!" Parry echoed. "Well, not precisely, Bob. I understand there's a distant relationship. It was mentioned for the first time last night. Which accounts for the set-up, one supposes. Tell me, Bob, have you ever before heard of a dresser doubling as understudy?"

"Worked out very convenient, hasn't it, sir?"

"Oh, very," said Parry discontentedly. "Look, Bob. You were with the Governor on his New Zealand tour in 'thirty, weren't you?"

Bob said woodenly: "That's correct, sir. 'E was just a boy in them days. Might I trouble you to move, Mr. Percival? I got my table to lay out."

"Oh, sorry. I'm in the way. As usual. Quite! Quite!" he waved his hand and walked jauntily into the passage.

"Good luck for to-night, sir," said Bob and shut the door after him.

In the room opposite to Poole's and next to the Greenroom, Parry could hear Bennington's dresser moving about whistling softly through his teeth. There is a superstition in the theatre that it's unlucky to whistle in a dressing-room and Parry knew that the man wouldn't do it if Ben had arrived. He didn't much like the sound of it himself, and moved on to J. G. Darcey's room. He tapped, was answered, and went in. J.G. was already embarked on his make-up.

"Bob," said Parry, "refuses to be drawn."

"Good evening, dear boy. About what?"

"Oh, *you* know. The New Zealand tour and so on."

"Quite right," said J.G. firmly, and added: "He was the merest stripling."

"Well—eighteen," Parry began and then broke off. "I know, I know. I couldn't care less, actually." He dropped into the only other chair in the room and buried his face in his hands. "Oh, dear," he said, "I'm so bored with it all. By-blow or not, what *does* it matter!"

"It only matters," said J.G., laying down a stick of No. 5, "in so far as it's driving Gay Gainsford pretty close to a nervous breakdown, and to that I do most strongly object."

"Really?" Parry raised his head and stared at him. "How altruistic of you, J.G. Well, I mean, I'm *sorry* for her, poor child. Naturally. And one trembles for the performance, of course."

"The performance would be all right if people left her alone. Ben, in particular."

"Yes," said Parry with great satisfaction. "The situation appears to be getting under the skin of the great character actor. There is that."

"I'm told," said J.G., "there was a midnight audition. Jacko professes ecstasy."

"My dear J.G., there have been two more-or-less public auditions. The object, no doubt, being to make everything look as clean as a whistle. The second affair was this morning."

"Did you see her?"

"I happened to look in."

"What's she like?"

Parry lit a cigarette. "As you have seen," he said, "she's fantastically like *him*. Which is really the point at issue. But *fantastically* like."

"Can she give a show?"

"Oh, yes," said Parry. He leant forward and hugged his knees boyishly. "Oh, yes indeed. Indeed she can, my dear J.G. You'd be surprised."

J.G. made a non-committal sound and went on with his make-up.

"This morning," Parry continued, "the Doctor was there. And Ben.

Ben, quite obviously devoured with chagrin. I confess I couldn't help rather gloating. As I remarked, it's getting under his skin. Together, no doubt, with vast potations of brandy and soda."

"I hope to God he's all right to-night."

"It appears Gay was in the back of the house, poor thing, while it was going on."

"She didn't tell me that," J.G. said anxiously and, catching Parry's sharpened glance, he added: "I didn't really hear anything about it."

"It was a repetition of last night. Really, one feels quite dizzy. Gay rushed weeping to Adam and again implored him to let her throw in the part. The Doctor, of course, was all for it. Adam was charming, but Uncle Ben produced another temperament. He and the Doctor left simultaneously in a silence more ominous, I assure you, than last night's dog-fight. Ben's not down yet."

"Not yet," J.G. said and repeated: "I hope to God he's all right."

For a moment the two men were united in a common anxiety. J.G. said: "Christ, I wish I didn't get nervous on first nights."

"You, at least, have something to be nervous about. Whereas I half kill myself over the dimmest bit in the West End. When I first saw the part I nearly screamed the place down. I said to Adam if it wasn't that he and Helena had always been very sweet to me—"

J.G. paid this routine plaint the compliment of looking gloomily acquiescent, but he barely listened to it.

"—and anyway," Parry was saying, "what chance has any of us as long as this *fantastic* set-up continues? In Poole-Hamilton pieces the second leads go automatically to the star's husband. I suppose Adam thinks it's the least he can do. Actually, I *know* I'm too young for the part but—"

"I wouldn't say you were," J.G. said, absently. Parry shot an indignant glance at him but he was pressing powder into the sides of his nose.

"If he tries any of his up-stage fun-and-games on me to-night," Parry said, furiously hissing his sibilants, "I'll just simply bitch up his big exit for him. I could, you know. It'd be no trouble at all."

"I wouldn't, dear boy," J.G. said good-naturedly. "It never does one any good, you know. One can't afford these little luxuries, however tempting. Well, that's taken the polish off the knocker on the old front door." He took his nose delicately between his thumb and forefinger. "The play stinks," he said thoughtfully. "In my considered opinion, it stinks."

"Well, I must say you *are* a comfort to us."

"Pay no attention. I always feel like that at about half-hour time."

"Half-hour! God, have they called it?"

"They will in five minutes."

"I must dart to my paints and powders." Parry went out, but reopened the door to admit his head. "In case I don't see you again, dear J.G., all the very best."

J.G. turned and raised his hand. "And to you the best, of course, dear boy."

Left alone, he sighed rather heavily, looked closely at his carefully made-up face and, with a rueful air, shook his head at himself.

vi

Clark Bennington's dresser, a thin melancholy man, put him into his gown and hovered, expressionless, behind him.

"I shan't need you before the change," said Bennington. "See if you can help Mr. Darcey."

The man went out. Bennington knew he'd guessed the reason for his dismissal. He wondered why he could never bring himself to have a drink in front of his dresser. After all, there was nothing in taking a nip before the show. Adam, of course, chose to make a great thing of never touching it. And at the thought of Adam Poole he felt resentment and fear stir at the back of his mind. He got his flask out of his overcoat pocket and poured a stiff shot of brandy.

"The thing to do," he told himself, "is to wipe this afternoon clean out. Forget it. Forget everything except my work." But he remembered, unexpectedly, the way, fifteen years ago, he used to prepare himself for a first night. He used to make a difficult and intensive approach to his initial entrance so that when he walked out on the stage he was already possessed by a life that had been created in the dressing-room. Took a lot of concentration: Stanislavsky and all that. Hard going, but in those days it had seemed worth the effort. Helena had encouraged him. He had a notion she and Adam still went in for it. But now he'd mastered the easier way—the repeated mannerism, the trick of pause and the unexpected flattening of the voice—the technical box of tricks.

He finished his drink quickly and began to grease his face. He noticed how the flesh had dropped into sad folds under the eyes, had blurred the jawline and had sunk into grooves about the nostrils and the corners of the mouth. All right for this part, of course, where he had to make a sight of himself, but he'd been a fine-looking man. Helena had fallen for him in a big way until Adam cut him out. At the thought of Adam he experienced a sort of regurgitation of misery and anger. "I'm a haunted man," he thought suddenly.

He'd let himself get into a state, he knew, because of this afternoon. Helena's face, gaping with terror, like a fish almost, kept rising up in his mind and wouldn't be dismissed. Things always worked like that with him: remorse always turned into nightmare.

It had been a bad week altogether. Rows with everybody; with John Rutherford in particular and with Adam over that blasted little dresser. He felt he was the victim of some elaborate plot. He was fond of Gay; she was a nice friendly little thing—his own flesh and blood. Until he had brought her into this piece she had seemed to like him. Not a bad little artist either, and good enough, by God, for the artsy-craftsy part they'd thrown at her. He thought of her scene with Poole and of her unhappiness in her failure and how, in some damned cockeyed way, they all, including Gay, seemed to blame him for it. He supposed she thought he'd bullied her into hanging on. Perhaps in a way he had, but he felt so much that he was the victim of a combined assault. "Alone," he thought, "I'm so desperately *alone*," and he could almost hear the word as one would say it on the stage, making it echo, forlorn and hopeless and extremely effective.

"I'm giving myself the jim-jams," he thought. He wondered if Helena had told Adam about this afternoon. By God, that'd rock Adam, if she had. And at once a picture rose up to torture him, a picture of Helena weeping in Adam's arms and taking solace there. He saw his forehead grow red in the looking-glass and told himself he'd better steady-up. No good getting into one of his tempers with a first performance ahead of him and everything so tricky with young Gay. There he was, coming back to that girl, that phoney dresser. He poured out another drink and began his make-up.

He recognized with satisfaction a familiar change of mood, and he now indulged himself with a sort of treat. He brought out a little piece of secret knowledge he had stored away. Among this company of enemies there was one over whom he exercised almost complete power. Over one, at least, he had overwhelmingly the whip-hand, and the knowledge of his sovereignty warmed him almost as comfortably as the brandy. He began to think about his part. Ideas, brand new and as clever as paint, crowded each other in his imagination. He anticipated his coming mastery.

His left hand slid towards the flask. "One more," he said, "and I'll be fine."

vii

In her room across the passage, Gay Gainsford faced her own reflection and watched Jacko's hands pass across it. He dabbed with his finger-tips under the cheek-bones and made a droning sound behind his closed lips. He was a very good make-up; it was one of his many talents. At the dress rehearsals the touch of his fingers had soothed rather than exacerbated her nerves, but to-night evidently she found it almost intolerable.

"Haven't you finished?" she asked.

"Patience, patience. We do not catch a train. Have you never observed the triangular shadows under Adam's cheek-bones? They are yet to be created."

"Poor Jacko," Gay said breathlessly, "this must be such a bore for you! Considering everything."

"Quiet, now. How can I work?"

"No, but I mean it must be so exasperating to think that two doors away there's somebody who wouldn't need your help. Just a straight make-up, wouldn't it be? No trouble."

"I adore making up. It is my most brilliant gift."

"But she's your find in a way, isn't she? You'd like her to have the part, wouldn't you?"

He rested his hands on her shoulders. *"Ne vous dérangez pas,"* he said. "Shut up, in fact. Tranquillize yourself, idiot girl."

"But I want you to tell me."

"Then I tell you. Yes, I would like to see this little freak play your part because she is in fact a little freak. She has dropped into this theatre like an accident in somebody else's dress and the effect is fantastic. But she is well content to remain off-stage and it is you who play, and we have faith in you and wish you well with all our hearts."

"That's very nice of you," Gay said.

"What a sour voice! It is true. And now reflect. Reflect upon the minuteness of Edmund Kean, upon Sarah's one leg and upon Irving's two, upon ugly actresses who convince their audiences they are beautiful and old actors who persuade them they are young. It is all in the mind, the spirit and the preparation. What does Adam say? Think in, and then play out. Do so."

"I can't," Gay said between her teeth. "I can't." She twisted in her chair. He lifted his fingers away from her face quickly, with a wide gesture. "Jacko," she said, "there's a jinx on this night. Jacko, did you know? It was on the night of the Combined Arts Ball that it happened."

"What is this foolishness?"

"You know. Five years ago. The stage-hands were talking about it. I heard them. The gas fire case. The night that man was murdered. Everyone knows."

"Be silent!" Jacko said loudly. "This is idiocy. I forbid you to speak of it. The chatter of morons. The Combined Arts Ball has no fixed date and, if it had, shall an assembly of British bourgeoisie in bad fancy dress control our destiny? I am ashamed of you. You are altogether too stupid. Master yourself."

"It's not only that. It's everything. I can't face it."

His fingers closed down on her shoulders. "Master yourself," he said. "You must. If you cry I shall beat you and wipe your make-up across your face. I defy you to cry."

He cleaned his hands, tipped her head forward and began to massage the nape of her neck. "There are all sorts of things," he said, "that you must remember and as many more to forget. Forget the little freak and the troubles of to-day. Remember to relax all your muscles and also your nerves and your thoughts. Remember the girl in the play and the faith I have in you, and Adam and also your Uncle Bennington."

"Spare me my Uncle Bennington, Jacko. If my Uncle Bennington had left me where I belong, in fortnightly rep, I wouldn't be facing this hell. I know what everyone thinks of Uncle Ben and I agree with them. I never want to see him again. I hate him. He's made me go on with this. I wanted to throw the part in. It's not my part. I loathe it. No, I don't loathe it, that's not true. I loathe myself for letting everybody down. Oh, God, Jacko, what am I going to do?"

Across the bowed head Jacko looked at his own reflection and poked a face at it, "You shall play this part," he said through his teeth. "Mouse-heart, skunk-girl. You shall play. Think of nothing. Unbridle your infinite capacity for inertia and be dumb."

Watching himself, he arranged his face in an unconvincing glower and fetched up a Shakesperian belly-voice.

"The devil damn thee black, thou cream-faced loon! Where got'st thou that goose look?"

He caught his breath. Beneath his fingers, Gay's neck stiffened. He began to swear elaborately, in French and in a whisper.

"Jacko. *Jacko*. Where does that line come from?"

"I invented it."

"You didn't. You *didn't*. It's *Macbeth*," she wailed. *"You've quoted from* Macbeth!" and burst into a flurry of terrified weeping.

"Great suffering and all-enduring Saints of God," apostrophized Jacko, "give me some patience with this Quaking Thing."

But Gay's cries mounted in a sharp crescendo. She flung out her arms and beat with her fists on the dressing-table. A bottle of wet-white rocked to and fro, overbalanced, rapped smartly against the looking-glass and fell over. A neatly splintered star frosted the surface of the glass.

Gay pointed to it with an air of crazy triumph, snatched up her towel and scrubbed it across her make-up. She thrust her face, blotched and streaked with black cosmetic, at Jacko.

"Don't you like what you see?" she quoted, and rocketed into genuine hysteria.

Five minutes later Jacko walked down the passage towards Adam Poole's room, leaving J.G., who had rushed to the rescue in his shirt-sleeves, in helpless contemplation of the screaming Gay. Jacko disregarded the open doors and the anxious painted faces that looked out at him.

Bennington shouted from his room: "What the hell goes on? Who *is* that?"

"Listen," Jacko began, thrusting his head in at the door. He looked at Bennington and stopped short. "Stay where you are," he said and crossed the passage to Poole's room.

Poole had swung round in his chair to face the door. Bob Cringle stood beside him, twisting a towel in his hands.

"Well?" Poole said. "What is it? Is it Gay?"

"She's gone up. Sky-high. I can't do anything nor can J.G., and I don't believe anyone can. She refuses to go on."

"Where's John? Is this his doing?"

"God knows. I don't think so. He came in an hour ago and said he'd be back at five to seven."

"Has Ben tried?"

"She does nothing but scream that she never wants to see him again. In my opinion, Ben would be fatal."

"He must be able to hear all this."

"I told him to stay where he is."

Poole looked sharply at Jacko and went out. Gay's laughter had broken down in a storm of irregular sobbing that could be heard quite clearly. Helena Hamilton called out, "Adam, shall I go to her?" and he answered from the passage: "Better not, I think."

He was some time with Gay. They heard her shouting: "No! No! I won't go on! No!" over and over again like an automaton.

When he came out he went to Helena Hamilton's room. She was dressed and made up. Martyn, with an ashen face, stood inside the doorway.

"I'm sorry, darling," Poole said, "but you'll have to do without a dresser."

The call-boy came down the passage chanting: "Half-hour. Half-hour, please."

Poole and Martyn looked at each other.

"You'll be all right," he said.

CHAPTER VI

PERFORMANCE

At ten to eight Martyn stood by the entrance.

She was dressed in Gay's clothes and Jacko had made her up very lightly. They had all wished her luck: J.G., Parry Percival, Helena Hamilton, Adam Poole, Clem Smith and even the dressers and stage-hands.

There had been something real and touching in their way of doing this, so that even in her terror she had felt they were good and very kind. Bennington alone had not wished her well but he had kept right away, and this abstention, she thought, showed a certain generosity.

She no longer felt sick but the lining of her mouth and throat was harsh as if, in fact, she had actually vomited. She thought her sense of hearing must have become distorted. The actors' voices on the other side of the canvas wall had the remote quality of voices in a nightmare, whereas the hammer-blows of her heart and the rustle of her dress that accompanied them sounded exceeding loud.

She saw the frames of the set, their lashings and painted legends—ACT I, P.2—and the door which she was to open. She could look into the Prompt corner where the A.S.M. followed the lighted script with his finger, and where, high above him, the electrician leaned over his perch, watching the play. The stage lights were reflected in his face. Everything was monstrous in its preoccupation. Martyn was alone.

She tried to command the upsurge of panic in her heart, to practise an approach to her ordeal, to create, in place of these implacable realities, the reality of the house in the play and that part of it in which now, out of sight of the audience, she must already have her being. This attempt went down before the clamour of her nerves. "I'm going to fail," she thought.

Jacko came round the set. She hoped he wouldn't speak to her and, as if he sensed this wish, he stopped at a distance and waited.

"I must listen," she thought. "I'm not listening. I don't know where they've got to. I've forgotten which way the door opens. I've missed my cue." Her inside deflated and despair gripped it like a colic.

She turned and found Poole beside her.

"You're all right," he said. "The door opens on. You can do it. Now, my girl. On you go."

Martyn didn't hear the round of applause with which a London audience greets a player who appears at short notice.

She was on. She had made her entry and was engulfed in the play.

ii

Dr. Rutherford sat in the O.P. box with his massive shoulder turned to the house and his gloved hands folded together on the balustrade. His face was in shadow but the stage lights just touched the bulging curve of his old-fashioned shirt-front. He was monumentally still. One of the critics, an elderly man, said in an aside to a colleague that Rutherford reminded him of Watts's picture of the Minotaur.

For the greater part of the first act he was alone, having, as he had explained in the office, no masochistic itch to invite a guest to a Roman holiday where he himself was the major sacrifice. Towards the end of the act, however, Bob Grantley came into the box and stood behind him. Grantley's attention was divided. Sometimes he looked down through beams of spotlights at the stalls, cobbled with heads, sometimes at the stage and sometimes, sideways and with caution, at the Doctor himself. Really, Grantley thought, he was quite uncomfortably motionless. One couldn't tell what he was thinking and one hesitated, the Lord knew, to ask him.

Down on the stage Clark Bennington, Parry Percival and J. G. Darcey had opened the long crescendo leading to Helena's entrance. Grantley thought suddenly how vividly an actor's nature could be exposed on the stage: there was, for instance, a kind of bed-rock niceness about old J.G., a youthfulness of spirit that declaimed itself through the superimposed make-up, the characterization and J.G.'s indisputable middle age. And Bennington? And Percival? Grantley had begun to consider them in these terms when Percival, speaking one of his colourless lines, turned down-stage. Bennington moved centre, looked at Darcey and neatly sketched a parody of Percival's somewhat finicking movement. The theatre was filled with laughter. Percival turned quickly; Bennington smiled innocently at him, prolonging the laugh.

Grantley looked apprehensively at the Doctor.

"Is that new?" he ventured in a whisper. "That business?"

The Doctor didn't answer, and Grantley wondered if he only imagined that the great hands on the balustrade had closed more tightly over each other.

Helena Hamilton came on to a storm of applause, and with her entrance the action was roused to a new excitement and was intensified with every word she uttered. The theatre grew warm with her presence and with a sense of heightened suspense.

"Now they're all on," Grantley thought, "except Adam and the girl."

He drew a chair forward stealthily and sat behind Rutherford.

"It's going enormously," he murmured to the massive shoulder. "Terrific, old boy." And because he was nervous he added: "This brings the girl on, doesn't it?"

For the first time the Doctor spoke. His lips scarcely moved. A submerged voice uttered within him. "Hence," it said, "heap of wrath, foul indigested lump."

"Sorry, old boy," whispered Grantley, and began to wonder what hope in hell there was of persuading the distinguished author to have a drink in the office during the interval with a hand-picked number of important persons.

He was still preoccupied with this problem when a side door in the set opened and a dark girl with short hair walked out on the stage.

Grantley joined in the kindly applause. The Doctor remained immovable.

The players swept up to their major climax, Adam came on, and five minutes later the curtain fell on the first act. The hands of the audience filled the house with a storm of rain. The storm swelled prodigiously and persisted even after the lights had come up.

"Ah, good girl," Bob Grantley stammered, filled with the sudden and excessive emotion of the theatre. "Good old Adam. Jolly good show!"

Greatly daring, he clapped the Doctor on the shoulder.

The Doctor remained immovable.

Grantley edged away to the back of the box. "I must get back," he said. "Look, John, there are one or two people coming to the office for a drink who would be—"

The Doctor turned massively in his seat and faced him.

"No," he said, "thank you."

"Well, but look, dear boy, it's just one of those things. You know how it is, John, you know how—"

"Shut up," said the Doctor without any particular malice. "I'm going back-stage," he added. He rose and turned away from the audience. "I have no desire to swill tepid spirits with minor celebrities among the backsides of sand-blasted gods. Thank you, however. See you later."

He opened the pass-door at the back of the box.

"You're pleased, aren't you?" Grantley said. "You *must* be pleased."

"Must I? Must I indeed?"

"With the girl, at least? So far?"

"The wench is a good wench. So far. I go to tell her so. By your leave, Robert."

He lumbered through the pass-door and Grantley heard him plunge dangerously down the narrow stairway to the stage.

iii

Dr. Rutherford emerged in a kaleidoscopic world: a world where walls fell softly apart, landscapes ascended into darkness and stairways turned and moved aside. A blue haze rose from the stage, which was itself in motion. Jacko's first set revolved bodily, giving way to a new and more distorted version of itself, which came to rest facing the curtain. Masking pieces were run forward to frame it in. The Doctor started off for the dressing-room passage and was at once involved with moving flats. "If you please, sir." "Stand aside there, *please*." "Clear stage, *by* your leave." His bulky shape was screened and exposed again and again as he plunged forward confusedly. Warning bells rang, the call-boy began to chant: "Second act beginners, please. Second act."

"Lights," Clem Smith said.

The shifting world stood still. Circuit by circuit, the lights came on and bore down on the acting area. The last toggle-line slapped home and was made fast and the sweating stage-hands walked disinterestedly off the set. Clem Smith, with his back to the curtain, made a final check. "Clear stage," he said and looked at his watch. The curtain-hand climbed an iron ladder.

"Six minutes," said the A.S.M. He wrote it on his chart. Clem moved into the Prompt corner. "Right," he said. "Actors, please."

J. G. Darcey and Parry Percival walked onto the set and took up their positions. Helena Hamilton came out of her dressing-room. She stood with her hands clasped lightly at her waist at a little distance from the door by which she must enter. A figure emerged from the shadows near the passage and went up to her.

"Miss Hamilton," Martyn said nervously, "I'm not on for your quick change. I can do it."

Helena turned. She looked at Martyn for a moment with an odd fixedness. Then a smile of extraordinary charm broke across her face and she took Martyn's head lightly between her hands.

"My dear child," she murmured, "my ridiculous child." She hesitated for a moment and then said briskly: "I've got a new dresser."

"A new dresser?"

"Jacko. He's most efficient."

Poole came down the passage. She turned to him and linked her arm through his. "She's going to be splendid in her scene," she said. "Isn't she?"

Poole said: "Keep it up, Kate. All's well." And in the look he gave Helena Hamilton there was something of comradeship, something of compassion and something, perhaps, of gratitude.

Dr. Rutherford emerged from the passage and addressed himself to Martyn. "Here!" he said. "I've been looking for you, my pretty. You might be a lot worse, considering, but you haven't done anything yet.

When you play this next scene, my poppet, these few precepts in thy—"

"No, John," Poole and Helena Hamilton said together. "Not now."

He glowered at them. Poole nodded to Martyn, who began to move away but had not got far before she heard Rutherford say: "Have you tackled that fellow? Did you see it? Where is he? By God, when I get at him—"

"Stand by," said Clem Smith.

"Quiet, John," said Poole imperatively. "Back to your box, sir."

The curtain rose on the second act.

For the rest of her life the physical events that were encompassed by the actual performance of the play were to be almost lost for Martyn. That is to say, she was to forget all but a few desultory and quite insignificant details, such as the fact of Jacko kissing her after she came off in the second act (he smelt of toothpaste and nicotine), and of Poole, when the curtain came down, giving her his handkerchief, which surprised her until she found her face was wet with her own tears. He had said something to her, then, with a manner so unlike anything she had found in him before that it had filled her with immense surprise, but she couldn't remember his words and thought: "I shall never know what he said." She knew that when she was not playing and during the intervals, she had stood near the entry to the passage and that people had spoken to her while she was there. But these recollections had no more substance than a dream. Still more unreal was her actual performance: she thought she remembered a sense of security and command that had astonishingly blessed her, but it was as if these things had happened to someone else. Indeed, she could not be perfectly certain that they had happened at all. She might have been under hypnosis or some partial anaesthesia for all the reality they afterwards retained.

This odd condition, which was perhaps the result of some kind of physical compensation for the extreme assault on her nerves and emotions, persisted until she made her final exit in the last act. It happened some time before the curtain. The character she played was the first to relinquish its hold and to fade out of the picture. She came off and returned to her corner near the entry into the passage. The others were all on; the dressers and stage-staff, drawn by the hazards of a first night, watched from the side and Jacko was near the Prompt corner. The passage and dressing-rooms seemed deserted and Martyn was quite alone. She began to emerge from her trance-like suspension. Parry Percival came off and spoke to her.

"Darling," he said incoherently, "you were perfectly splendid. I'm just *so* angry at the moment I can't *speak,* but I do congratulate you!"

Martyn saw that he actually trembled with an emotion that was, she must suppose, fury. Out of the dream from which she was not yet fully awakened there came a memory of Gargantuan laughter and she thought she associated it with Bennington and with Percival. He said: "This settles it. I'm taking action. God, this settles it!" and darted down the passage.

Martyn thought, still confusedly, that she should go to the dressing-room and tidy her make-up for the curtain-call. But it was not her dressing-room, it was Gay's and she felt uneasy about it. While she hesitated J. G. Darcey, who had come off, put his hand on her shoulder. "Well done, child," he said. "A very creditable performance."

Martyn thanked him and, on an impulse, added: "Mr. Darcey, is Gay still here? Should I say something to her? I'd like to, but I know how she must feel and I don't want to be clumsy."

He waited for a moment, looking at her. "She's in the Greenroom," he said. "Perhaps later. Not now, I think. Nice of you."

"I won't unless you say so, then."

He made her a little bow. "I am at your service," he said and followed Percival down the passage.

Jacko came round the set with the stage-hand who was to fire the effects-gun. When he saw Martyn his whole face split in a grin. He took her hands in his and kissed them and she was overwhelmed with shyness.

"But your face," he said, wrinkling his own into a monkey's grimace. "It shines like a good deed in a naughty world. Do not touch it yourself. To your dressing-room. I come in two minutes. Away, before your ears are blasted."

He moved down-stage, applied his eye to a secret hole in the set through which he could watch the action, and held out his arm in warning to the stage-hand, who then lifted the effects-gun. Martyn went down the passage as Bennington came off. He caught her up: "Miss Tarne. Wait a moment, will you?"

Dreading another intolerable encounter, Martyn faced him. His make-up had been designed to exhibit the brutality of the character and did so all too successfully. The lips were painted a florid red, the pouches under the eyes and the sensual drag from the nostrils to the mouth had been carefully emphasized. He was sweating heavily through the greasepaint and his face glistened in the dull light of the passage.

"I just wanted to say—" he began, and at that moment the gun was fired and Martyn gave an involuntary cry. He went on talking. "—when I see it," he was saying. "I suppose you aren't to be blamed for that. You saw your chance and took it. Gay and Adam tell me you offered to get out and were not allowed to go. That may be fair enough, I wouldn't know. But I'm not worrying about that." He spoke disjointedly. It was as if his thoughts were too disordered for any coherent expression. "I just wanted to tell you that you needn't suppose what I'm going to do—you needn't think—I mean—"

He touched his shining face with the palm of his hand. Jacko came down the passage and took Martyn by the elbow. "Quick," he said. "Into your room! You want powdering, Ben. Excuse me."

Bennington went into his own room. Jacko thrust Martyn into hers, and leaving the door open followed Bennington. She heard him say: "Take care with your upper lip. It is dripping with sweat." He darted back to Martyn, stood her near the dressing-shelf and, with an expression of the most ardent concentration, effected a number of what he called running repairs to her make-up and her hair. They heard Percival and Darcey go past on their way to the stage. A humming noise caused by some distant dynamo made itself heard, the tap in the wash-basin dripped, the voices on the stage sounded intermittently. Martyn looked at Gay's make-up box, at her dressing-gown and at the array of mascots on the shelf and wished very heartily that Jacko would have done. Presently the call-boy came down the passage with his summons for the final curtain. "Come," said Jacko.

He took her round to the Prompt side.

Here she found a group already waiting: Darcey and Percival, Clem Smith, the two dressers and, at a distance, one or two stagehands. They all watched the final scene between Helena Hamilton and Adam Poole. In this scene Rutherford tied up and stated finally the whole thesis of his play. The man was faced with his ultimate decision. Would he stay and attempt, with the woman, to establish a sane and enlightened formula for living in place of the one he himself had destroyed, or would he go back to his island community and attempt a further development within himself and in a less complex environment? As throughout the play, the conflict was set out in terms of human and personal relationships. It could be played like many another love-scene, purely on those terms. Or it could be so handled that the wider implications could be felt by the audience, and in the hands of these two players that was what happened. The play ended with them pledging themselves to each other and to an incredible task. As Poole spoke the last lines, the electrician, with one eye on Clem below, played madly over his switchboard. The entire set changed its aspect, seemed to dissolve, turned threadbare, a skeleton, a wraith, while beyond it a wide stylized landscape was flooded with light and became, as Poole spoke the tag, the background upon which the curtain fell.

"Might as well be back in panto," said the electrician, leaning on his dimmers. "We got the transformation scene. All we want's the bloody fairy queen."

It was at this moment—when the applause seemed to surge forward and beat against the curtain, when Clem shouted "All on!" and Dr. Rutherford plunged out of the O.P. pass-door, when the players walked on and linked hands—that Poole, looking hurriedly along the line, said: "Where's Ben?"

One of those panic-stricken crises peculiar to the theatre boiled up on the instant. From her position between Darcey and Percival on the stage, Martyn saw the call-boy make some kind of protest to Clem Smith and disappear. Above the applause they heard him hare down the passage yelling: "Mr. Bennington! Mr. Bennington! Please! You're on!"

"We can't wait," Poole shouted. "Take it up, Clem."

The curtain rose and Martyn looked into a sea of faces and hands. She felt herself led forward into the roaring swell, bowed with the others, felt Darcey's and Percival's hands tighten on hers, bowed again and with them retreated a few steps up-stage as the first curtain fell.

"Well?" Poole shouted into the wings. The call-boy could be heard beating on the dressing-room door.

Percival said: "What's the betting he comes on for a star call?"

"He's passed out," said Darcey. "Had one or two more since he came off."

"By God, I wouldn't cry if he never came to."

"Go on, Clem," said Poole.

The curtain rose and fell again, twice. Percival and Darcey took Martyn off and it went up again on Poole and Helena Hamilton, this time to those cries of "Bravo!" that reach the actors as a long open sound like the voice of a singing wind. In the wings Clem Smith, with his eyes on the stage, was saying repeatedly: "He doesn't answer. He's locked in. The b— doesn't answer."

Martyn saw Poole coming towards her and stood aside. He seemed to tower over her as he took her hand. "Come along," he said. Darcey and Percival and the group off-stage began to clap.

Poole led her on. She felt herself resisting and heard him say: "Yes, it's all right."

So bereft was Martyn of her normal stage-wiseness that he had to tell her to bow. She did so, and wondered why there was a warm sound of laughter in the applause. She looked at Poole, found he was bowing to her and bent her head under his smile. He returned her to the wings.

They were all on again. Dr. Rutherford came out from the O.P. corner. The cast joined in the applause. Martyn's heart had begun to sing so loudly that it was like to deafen every emotion but a universal gratitude. She thought Rutherford looked like an old lion standing there in his out-of-date evening clothes, his hair ruffled, his gloved hand touching his bulging shirt, bowing in an unwieldly manner to the audience and to the cast. He moved forward and the theatre was abruptly silent—silent, but for an obscure and intermittent thudding in the dressing-room passage. Clem Smith said something to the A.S.M. and rushed away, jingling keys.

"Hah," said Dr. Rutherford with a preliminary bellow. "Hah—thankee. I'm much obliged to you, ladies and gentlemen, and to the actors. The actors are much obliged, no doubt, to you, but not necessarily to me." Here the audience laughed and the actors smiled. "I am not able to judge," the Doctor continued with a rich roll in his voice, "whether you have extracted from this play the substance of its argument. If you have done so, we may all felicitate each other with the indiscriminate enthusiasm characteristic of these occasions: if you have not, I for my part am not prepared to say where the blame should rest."

A solitary man laughed in the audience. The Doctor rolled an eye at him and, with this clownish trick, brought the house down. "The prettiest epilogue to a play that I am acquainted with," he went on, "is (as I need perhaps hardly mention to so intelligent an audience) that written for a boy actor by William Shakespere. I am neither a boy nor an actor, but I beg leave to end by quoting it to you. 'If it be true that good wine needs no bush—'"

"Gas!" Parry Percival said under his breath. Martyn, who thought the Doctor was going well, glanced indignantly at Parry and was astonished to see that he looked frightened. " '—therefore,' " the Doctor was saying arrogantly, " 'to beg will not become me—' "

"Gas!" said an imperative voice off-stage and someone else ran noisily round the back of the set.

And then Martyn smelt it. Gas.

iv

To the actors, it seemed afterwards as if they had been fantastically slow to understand that disaster had come upon the theatre. The curtain went down on Dr. Rutherford's last word. There was a further outbreak of applause. Someone off-stage shouted: "The King, for God's sake!" and at once the anthem rolled out disinterestedly in the well. Poole ran off the stage and was met by Clem Smith, who had a bunch of keys in his hand. The rest followed him.

The area back-stage reeked of gas.

It was extraordinary how little was said. The players stood together and looked about them with the question in their faces that they were unable to ask.

Poole said: "Keep all visitors out, Clem. Send them to the foyer." And at once the A.S.M. spoke into the Prompt telephone. Bob Grantley burst through the pass-door, beaming from ear to ear.

"*Stupendous!*" he shouted. "John! Helena! Adam! My God, chaps, you've done it—"

He stood, stock-still, his arms extended, the smile dying on his face.

"Go back, Bob," Poole said. "Cope with the people. Ask our guests to go on and not wait for us. Ben's ill. Clem, get all available doors open. We want air."

Grantley said: "Gas?"

"Quick," Poole said. "Take them with you. Settle them down and explain. He's ill. Then ring me here. But quickly, Bob. Quickly."

Grantley went out without another word.

"Where is he?" Dr. Rutherford demanded.

Helena Hamilton suddenly said: "Adam?"

"Go on to the stage, Helena. It's better you shouldn't be here, believe me. Kate will stay with you. I'll come in a moment."

"Here you are, Doctor," said Clem Smith.

There was a blundering sound in the direction of the passage. Rutherford said, "Open the dock-doors," and went behind the set.

Poole thrust Helena through the Prompt entry and shut the door behind her. Draughts of cold air came through the side entrances.

"Kate," Poole said, "go in and keep her there if you can. Will you? And, Kate—"

Rutherford reappeared and with him four stage-hands, bearing with difficulty the inert body of Clark Bennington. The head hung swinging upside down between the two leaders, its mouth wide open.

Poole moved quickly, but he was too late to shield Martyn.

"Never mind," he said. "Go in with Helena."

"Anyone here done respiration for gassed cases?" Dr. Rutherford demanded. "I can start but I'm not good for long."

"I can," said the A.S.M. "I was a warden."

"I can," said Jacko.

"And I," said Poole.

"In the dock, then. Shut these doors and open the outer ones."

Kneeling by Helena Hamilton and holding her hand, Martyn heard the doors roll back and the shambling steps go into the dock. The doors crashed behind them.

Martyn said: "They're giving him respiration. Dr. Rutherford's there."

Helena nodded with an air of sagacity. Her face was quite without expression and she was shivering.

"I'll get your coat," Martyn said. It was in the improvised dressing-room on the O.P. side. She was back in a moment and put Helena into it as if she were a child, guiding her arms and wrapping the fur about her.

A voice off-stage—J. G. Darcey's—said: "Where's Gay? Is Gay still in the Greenroom?"

Martyn was astonished when Helena, behind that mask that had become her face, said loudly: "Yes. She's there. In the Greenroom."

There was a moment's silence and then J.G. said: "She mustn't stay there. Good God—"

They heard him go away.

Parry Percival's voice announced abruptly that he was going to be sick. "But where?" he cried distractedly. "Where?"

"In your dressing-room, for Pete's sake," Clem Smith said.

"It'll be full of gas. Oh, *really!*" There was an agonized and not quite silent interval. "I couldn't be more sorry," Percival said weakly.

"I want," Helena said, "to know what happened. I want to see Adam. Ask him to come, please."

Martyn made for the door, but before she reached it Dr. Rutherford came in, followed by Poole. Rutherford had taken off his coat and was a fantastic sight in boiled shirt, black trousers and red braces.

"Well, Helena," he said, "this is not a nice business. We're doing everything that can be done. I'm getting a new oxygen thing in as quickly as possible. There have been some remarkable saves in these cases. But I think you ought to know it's a thinnish chance. There's no pulse and so on."

"I want," she said, holding out her hand to Poole, "to know what happened."

Poole said gently: "All right, Helena, you shall. It looks as if Ben locked himself in after his exit, and then turned the gas fire off—and on again. When Clem unlocked the door and went in he found Ben on the floor. His head was near the fire and a coat over both. He could only have been like that for quite a short time."

"This theatre," she said. "This awful theatre."

Poole looked as if he would make some kind of protest, but after a moment's hesitation he said: "All right, Helena. Perhaps it did suggest the means, but if he had made up his mind he would, in any case, have found the means."

"Why?" she said. "Why has he done it?"

Dr. Rutherford growled inarticulately and went out. They heard him open and shut the dock-doors. Poole sat down by Helena and took her hands in his. Martyn was going, but he looked up at her and said: "No, don't. Don't go, Kate," and she waited near the door.

"This is no time," Poole said, "to speculate. He may be saved. If he isn't, then we shall of course ask ourselves just why. But he was in a bad way, Helena. He'd gone to pieces and he knew it."

"I wasn't much help," she said, "was I? Though it's true to say I did try for quite a long time."

"Indeed you did. There's one thing you must be told. If it's no go with Ben, we'll have to inform the police."

She put her hand to her forehead as if puzzled. "The police?" she repeated, and stared at him. "No, darling, no!" she cried, and after a moment whispered: "They might think—oh, darling, darling, darling, the Lord knows what they might think!"

The door up-stage opened and Gay Gainsford came in, followed by Darcey.

She was in her street-clothes, and at some time during the evening had made extensive repairs to her face, which wore, at the moment, an expression oddly compounded of triumph and distraction. Before she could speak she was seized with a paroxysm of coughing.

Darcey said: "Is it all right for Gay to wait here?"

"Yes, of course," said Helena.

He went out and Poole followed him, saying he would return.

"Darling," Miss Gainsford gasped, "I knew. I knew as soon as I smelt it. There's a Thing in this theatre. Everything pointed to it. I just sat there and *knew*." She coughed again. "*Oh*, I do feel so sick," she said.

"Gay, for pity's sake, what are you talking about?" Helena said.

"It was Fate, I felt. I wasn't a bit surprised. I just knew something had to happen to-night."

"Do you mean to say," Helena murmured, and the wraith of her gift for irony was on her mouth, "that you just sat in the Greenroom with your finger raised, telling yourself it was Fate?"

"Darling Aunty—I'm sorry. I forgot. Darling Helena, wasn't it amazing?"

Helena made a little gesture of defeat. Miss Gainsford looked at her for a moment and then, with the prettiest air of compassion, knelt at her feet. "Sweet," she said, "I'm so terribly, terribly sorry. We're together in this, aren't we? He was my uncle and your husband."

"True enough," said Helena. She looked at Martyn over the head bent in devoted commiseration, and shook her own helplessly. Gay Gainsford sank into a sitting posture and leant her cheek against Helena's hand. The hand, after a courteous interval, was withdrawn.

There followed a very long silence. Martyn sat at a distance and wondered if there was anything in the world she could do to help. There was an intermittent murmur of voices somewhere off-stage. Gay Gainsford, feeling perhaps that she had sustained her position long enough, moved by gradual degrees away from her aunt by marriage, rose and, sighing heavily, transferred herself to the sofa.

Time dragged on, mostly in silence. Helena lit one cigarette from the butt of another, Gay sighed with infuriating punctuality and Martyn's thoughts drifted sadly about the evaporation of her small triumph.

Presently there were sounds of arrival. One or two persons walked round the set from the outside entry to the dock and were evidently admitted into it.

"Who can that be, I wonder?" Helena Hamilton asked idly, and after a moment: "Is Jacko about?"

"I'll see," said Martyn.

She found Jacko off-stage with Darcey and Parry Percival. Percival was saying: "Well, naturally, nobody wants to go to the party, but I must say that as one is quite evidently useless here, I don't see why one can't go home."

Jacko said: "You would be recalled by the police, I dare say, if you went."

He caught sight of Martyn, who went up to him. His face was beaded with sweat. "What is it, my small?" he asked. "This is a sad epilogue to your success story. Never mind. What is it?"

"I think Miss Hamilton would like to see you."

"Then I come. It is time, in any case."

He took her by the elbow and they went in together. When Helena saw him she seemed to rouse herself. "Jacko?" she said.

He didn't answer and she got up quickly and went to him. "Jacko? What is it? Has it happened?"

Jacko's hands, so refined and delicate that they seemed like those of another woman, touched her hair and her face.

"It has happened," he said. "We have tried very hard but nothing is any good at all, and there is no more to be done. He has taken wing."

Gay Gainsford broke into a fit of sobbing, but Helena stooped her head to Jacko's shoulder and when his arms had closed about her said: "Help me to feel something, Jacko. I'm quite empty of feeling. Help me to be sorry."

Above her head Jacko's face, glistening with sweat, grotesque and primitive, had the fixed inscrutability of a classic mask.

CHAPTER VII

DISASTER

The fact of Bennington's death had the effect of changing the values of other circumstances in the theatre. One after another the members of the company had said what they could to Helena Hamilton, and she had thanked them. She was very tremulous and uncertain of her voice, but she did not break down at any time and seemed, Martyn thought, to be in a kind of trance. At first they were all uncomfortably silent but, as the minutes slipped by, they fell into muted conversation. Most of what they said was singularly aimless. Matters of normal consequence were forgotten, details of behaviour became ridiculously important.

The question, for instance, of where they should assemble exercised the whole company. It was almost eleven o'clock and the stage was beginning to grow cold.

Clem Smith had rung up the police as soon as Dr. Rutherford said that Bennington was beyond recovery, and within five minutes a constable and sergeant had appeared at the stage-door. They went into the dock with Rutherford and then to Bennington's dressing-room, where they remained alone for some time. During this period an aimless discussion developed among the members of the company about where they should go. Clem Smith suggested the Greenroom as the warmest place, and added tactlessly that the fumes had probably dispersed and if so there was no reason why they shouldn't light the fire. Both Parry Percival and Gay Gainsford had made an outcry against this suggestion on the grounds of delicacy and susceptibility. Darcey supported Gay, the A.S.M. suggested the offices and Jacko the auditorium. Dr. Rutherford, who appeared to be less upset than anyone else, merely remarked that "All places that the eye of heaven visits are to a wise man ports and happy havens," which, as Percival said acidly, got them nowhere.

Finally, Poole asked if the central-heating couldn't be stoked up and a stage-hand was dispatched to the underworld to find out. Evidently he met with success as presently the air became less chilled.

They waited in the last-act set, much as they had waited when Poole summed up at the dress rehearsal. In this final scene, which was painted on gauze, Jacko had, by the use of grotesque perspective and exaggerated emphases, achieved a distortion of the second set, which itself was a distortion of the first. The walls and staircase seemed to lean over the actors, crushing them into too small a compass. Martyn became very much aware of this and disliked it.

The resemblance to the dress rehearsal was heightened by Jacko, who had fetched Helena's dressing-case from her room. Again she removed her make-up on the stage, but this time it was Jacko who held the glass for her. He had brought powder and her bag for Martyn and a towel for each of them. With only a spatter of desultory conversation, the players sat about the stage and cleaned their faces. And they listened.

They heard the two men come back along the passage and separate. Then the central door opened and the young constable came in.

He was a tall, good-looking youth with a charming smile.

"The sergeant," he said, "has asked me to explain that he's telephoning Scotland Yard. He couldn't be more sorry, but he's afraid he'll have to ask everybody to wait until he gets his instructions. He's sure you'll understand that it's just a matter of routine."

He might have been apologizing for his mother's late arrival at her own dinner-party.

He was about to withdraw when Dr. Rutherford said: "Hi! Sonny!"

"Yes, sir?" said the young constable obligingly.

"You intrigue me. You talk, as they say, like a book. *Non sine dis animosus infans.* You swear with a good grace and wear your boots very smooth, do you not?"

The young constable was, it seemed, only momentarily taken aback. He said: "Well, sir, for my boots, they are after the Dogberry fashion, and for my swearing, sir, it goes by the book."

The Doctor, who until now had seemed to share the general feeling of oppression and shock, appeared to cheer up with indecent haste. He was, in fact, clearly enchanted. "Define, define, well educated infant," he quoted exultantly.

"I mean that in court, sir, we swear by the book. But I'm afraid, sir," added the young constable apologetically, "that I'm not much of a hand at 'Bardinage.' My purse is empty already. If you'll excuse me," he concluded, with a civil glance round the company, "I'll just—"

He was again about to withdraw when his sergeant came in at the O.P. entrance.

"Good evening, ladies and gentlemen," the sergeant said, in what Martyn, for one, felt was the regulation manner. "Very sorry to keep you, I'm sure. Sad business. In these cases we have to do a routine check-up, as you might say. My superior officers will be here in a moment and then, I hope, we shan't be long. Thank you."

He tramped across the stage, said something inaudible to the constable and was heard to go into the dock. The constable took a chair from the Prompt corner, placed it in the proscenium entrance and, with a modest air, sat on it. His glance fell upon Martyn and he smiled at her. They were the youngest persons there and it was as if they signalled in a friendly manner to each other. In turning away from this pleasant exchange, Martyn found that Poole was watching her with fixed and, it seemed, angry glare. To her fury she found that she was very much disturbed by this circumstance.

They had by this time all cleaned their faces. Helena Hamilton with an unsteady hand put on a light street make-up. The men looked ghastly in the cold working-lights that bleakly illuminated the stage.

Parry Percival said fretfully: "Well, I must say I do *not* see the smallest point in our hanging about like this."

The constable was about to answer when they all heard sounds of arrival at the stage-door. He said: "This will be the party from the Yard, sir," and crossed to the far exit. The sergeant was heard to join him there.

There was a brief conversation off-stage. A voice said: "You two go round with Gibson then, will you? I'll join you in a moment."

The young constable reappeared to usher in a tall man in plain clothes.

"Chief Detective-Inspector Alleyn," he said.

ii

Martyn, in her weary pilgrimage round the West End, had seen men of whom Alleyn at first reminded her. In the neighbourhood of the St. James's Theatre they had emerged from clubs, from restaurants and from enchanting and preposterous shops. There had been something in their bearing and their clothes that gave them a precise definition. But when she looked more closely at Inspector Alleyn's face, this association became modified. It was a spare and scholarly face with a monkish look about it.

Martyn had formed the habit of thinking of people's voices in terms of colour. Helena Hamilton's voice, for instance, was for Martyn golden, Gay Gainsford's pink, Darcey's brown and Adam Poole's violet. When Alleyn spoke she decided that his voice was a royal blue of the clearest sort.

Reminding herself that this was no time to indulge this freakish habit of classification, she gave him her full attention.

"You will, I'm sure," he was saying, "realize that in these cases our job is simply to determine that they are, on the face of it, what they appear to be. In order to do this effectively we are obliged to make a fairly thorough examination of the scene as we find it. This takes a little time always, but if everything's quite straightforward, as I expect it will be, we won't keep you very long. Is that clear?"

He looked round his small audience. Poole said at once: "Yes, of course. We all understand. At the same time, if it's a matter of taking statements, I'd be grateful if you'd see Miss Hamilton first."

"Miss Hamilton?" Alleyn said, and after a moment's hesitation looked at her.

"I'm his wife," she said. "I'm Helena Bennington."

"I'm so sorry. I didn't know. Yes, I'm sure that can be managed. Probably the best way will be for me to see you all together. If everything seems quite clear there may be no need for further interviews. And now, if you'll excuse me, I'll have a look round and then rejoin you. There is a doctor among you, isn't there? Dr. Rutherford?" Dr. Rutherford cleared his throat portentously. "Are you he, sir? Perhaps you'll join us."

"Indubitably," said the Doctor. "I had so concluded."

"Good," Alleyn said and looked faintly amused. "Will you lead the way?"

They were at the door when Jacko suddenly said: "A moment, if you please, Chief Inspector."

"Yes?"

"I would like permission to make soup. There is a filthy small kitchen-place inhabited only by the night-watchman, where I have waiting a can of prepared soup. Everyone is very cold and fatigued and entirely empty. My name is Jacques Doré, I am dogsbody-in-waiting in this theatre and there is much virtue in my soup."

Alleyn said: "By all means. Is the kitchen-place that small sink-room near the dock with the gas jet in it?"

"But you haven't looked at the place yet!" Parry Percival ejaculated.

"I've been here before," said Alleyn. "I remember the theatre. Shall we get on, Dr. Rutherford?"

They went out. Gay Gainsford, whose particular talent from now onwards was to lie in the voicing of disquieting thoughts which her companions shared but decided to leave unspoken, said in a distracted manner: "*When* was he here before?" And when nobody answered, she said dramatically: "I can see it all! He must be the man they sent that other time." She paused and collected their reluctant attention. She laid her hand on J.G.'s arm and raised her voice. "That's why he's come again," she announced.

"Come now, dear," J.G. murmured inadequately, and Poole said quickly: "My *dear* Gay!"

"But I'm right!" she persisted. "I'm sure I'm right. Why else should he know about the sink-room?" She looked about her with an air of terrified complacency.

"*And last time,*" she pointed out, "*it was Murder.*"

"Climax," said Jacko. "Picture and Slow Curtain! Put your hands together, ladies and gentlemen, for this clever little artist."

He went out with his eyes turned up.

"Jacko's terribly hard, isn't he?" Gay said to Darcey. "After all, Uncle Ben *was* my uncle." She caught sight of Helena Hamilton. "And your husband," she said hurriedly, "of course, darling."

iii

The stage-hands had set up in the dock one of the trestle-tables used for properties. They had laid Clark Bennington's body on it and had covered it with a sheet from the wardrobe-room. The dock was a tall echoing place, concrete-floored, with stacks of old flats leaning against the walls. A solitary unprotected lamp bulb, dust-encrusted, hung above the table.

A group of four men in dark overcoats and hats stood beside this improvised bier, and it so chanced thay had taken up their places at the four corners and looked therefore as if they kept guard over it. Their hats shadowed their faces and they stood in pools of shadow. A fifth man, bareheaded, stood at the foot of the bier and a little removed from it. When the tallest of the men reached out to the margin of the sheet, his arm cast a black bar over its white and eloquent form. His gloved hand dragged down the sheet and exposed a rigid gaping face encrusted with greasepaint. He uncovered his head and the other three, a little awkwardly, followed his example.

"Well, Curtis?" he said.

Dr. Curtis, the police surgeon, bent over the head, blotting it out with his shadow. He took a flash lamp from his pocket and the face, in this changed light, stared out with an altered look as if it had secretly rearranged its expression.

"God!" Curtis muttered. "He looks pretty ghastly, doesn't he? What an atrocious make-up!"

From his removed position Dr. Rutherford said loudly: "My dear man, the make-up was required by My Play. It should, in point of fact, be a damn sight more repellent. But—*vanitas vanitatum*. Also: *Mit der Dummheit kämpfen Götter selbst vergebens.* I didn't let them fix him up at all. Thought you'd prefer not." His voice echoed coldly round the dock.

"Quite so," Curtis murmured. "Much better not."

"Smell very noticeable still," a thick-set, grizzled man observed. "Always hangs about in these cases," rejoined the sergeant, "doesn't it, Mr. Fox?"

"We worked damn hard on him," Dr. Rutherford said. "It never looked like it from the start. Not a hope."

"Well," said Curtis, drawing back, "it all seems straightforward enough, Alleyn. It doesn't call for a very extensive autopsy, but of course we'll do the usual things."

"Lend me your torch a moment," Alleyn said, and after a moment: "Very heavy make-up, isn't it? He's so thickly powdered."

"He needed it. He sweated," Dr. Rutherford said, "like a pig. Alcohol and a dicky heart."

"Did you look after him, sir?"

"Not I. I don't practise nowadays. The alcohol declared itself and he used to talk about a heart condition. Valvular trouble, I should imagine. I don't know who his medical man was. His wife can tell you."

Dr. Curtis replaced the sheet. "That," he said to Rutherford, "might account for him going quickly."

"Certainly."

"There's a mark on the jaw," Alleyn said. "Did either of you notice it? The make-up is thinner there. Is it a bruise?"

Curtis said: "I saw it, yes. It might be a bruise. We'll see better when we clean him up."

"Right. I'll look at the room," Alleyn said. "Who found him?"

"The stage-manager," said Rutherford.

"Then perhaps you wouldn't mind asking him to come along when you rejoin the others. Thank you so much, Dr. Rutherford. We're glad to have had your report. You'll be called for the inquest, I'm afraid."

"Hell's teeth, I suppose I shall. So be it." He moved to the doors. The sergeant obligingly rolled them open and he muttered "Thankee," and with an air of dissatisfaction went out.

Dr. Curtis said: "I'd better go and make professional noises at him."

"Yes, do," Alleyn said.

On their way to Bennington's room they passed Jacko and a stage-hand bearing a fragrant steaming can and a number of cups to the stage. In his cubby-hole, Fred Badger was entertaining a group of stage-hands and dressers. They had steaming pannikins in their hands and they eyed the police party in silence.

"Smells very tasty, doesn't it?" Detective-Inspector Fox observed rather wistfully.

The young constable, who was stationed by the door through which Martyn had made her entrance, opened it for the soup party and shut it after them.

Fox growled: "Keep your wits about you."

"Yes, sir," said the young constable and exhibited his note-book.

Clem Smith was waiting for them in Bennington's room. The lights were full on and a white glare beat on the dressing-shelf and walls. Bennington's street-clothes and his suit for the first act hung on coat-hangers along the wall. His make-up was laid out on a towel, and the shelf was littered with small objects that in their casual air of usage suggested that he had merely left the room for a moment and would return to take them up again. On the floor, hard by the dead gas fire, lay an overcoat from which the reek of gas, which still hung about the room, seemed to arise. The worn rug was drawn up into wrinkles.

Clem Smith's face was white and anxious under his shock of dark hair. He shook hands jerkily with Alleyn and then looked as if he wondered if he ought to have done so. "This is a pretty ghastly sort of party," he muttered, "isn't it?"

Alleyn said: "It seems that you came in for the worst part of it. Do you mind telling us what happened?"

Fox moved behind Clem and produced his note-book. Sergeant Gibson began to make a list of the objects in the room. Clem watched him with an air of distaste.

"Easy enough to tell you," he said. "He came off about eight minutes before the final curtain and I suppose went straight to this room. When the boy came round for the curtain-call, Ben didn't appear with the others. I didn't notice. There's an important light-cue at the end and I was watching for it. Then, when they all went on, he just wasn't there. We couldn't hold the curtain for long. I sent it up for the first call and the boy went back and hammered on this door. It was locked. He smelt gas and began to yell for Ben and then ran back to tell me what was wrong. I'd got the Doctor on for his speech by that time. I left my A.S.M. in charge, took the bunch of extra keys from the Prompt corner and tore round here."

He wetted his lips and fumbled in his pocket. "Is it safe to smoke?" he asked.

"I'm afraid we'd better wait a little longer," Alleyn said. "Sorry."

"O.K. Well, I unlocked the door. As soon as it opened the stink hit me in the face. I don't know why, but I expected him to be sitting at the shelf. I don't suppose, really, it was long before I saw him, but it seemed fantastically long. He was lying there by the heater. I could only see his legs and the lower half of his body. The rest was hidden by that coat. It was tucked in behind the heater, and over his head and shoulders. It looked like a tent. I heard the hiss going on underneath it." Clem rubbed his mouth. "I don't think," he said, "I was as idiotically slow as all this makes me out to be. I don't think, honestly, it was more than seconds before I went in. Honestly, I don't think so."

"I expect you're right about that. Time goes all relative in a crisis."

"Does it? Good. Well, then: I ran in and hauled the coat away. He was on his left side—his mouth—it was— The lead-in had been disconnected and it was by his mouth, hissing. I turned it off and dragged him by the heels. He sort of stuck on the carpet. Jacko—Jacques Doré bolted in and helped."

"One moment," Alleyn said. "Did you knock over that box of powder on the dressing-table? Either of you?"

Clem Smith stared at it. "That? No, I didn't go near it and I'd got him half-way to the door when Jacko came in. He must have done it himself."

"Right. Sorry. Go on."

"We lifted Ben into the passage and shut his door. At the far end of the passage there's a window, the only one near. We got it open and carried him to it. I think he was dead even then. I'm sure he was. I've seen gassed cases before, in the blitz."

Alleyn said: "You seem to have tackled this one like an old hand, at all events."

"I'm damn glad you think so," said Clem, and sounded it.

Alleyn looked at the Yale lock on the door. "This seems in good enough shape," he said absently.

"It's new," Clem said. "There were pretty extensive renovations and a sort of general clean-up when Mr. Poole took the theatre over. It's useful for the artists to be able to lock up valuables in their rooms and the old locks were clumsy and rusted up. In any case—" He stopped and then said uncomfortably: "The whole place has been repainted and modernized."

"Including the gas installations?"

"Yes," said Clem, not looking at Alleyn. "That's all new, too."

"Two of the old dressing-rooms have been knocked together to form the Greenroom?"

"Yes."

"And there are new dividing walls? And ventilators, now, in the dressing-rooms?"

"Yes," said Clem unhappily and added, "I suppose that's why he used his coat."

"It does look," Alleyn said without stressing it, "as if the general idea was to speed things up, doesn't it? All right, Mr. Smith, thank you. Would you explain to the people on the stage that I'll come as soon as we've finished our job here? It won't be very long. We'll probably ask you to sign a statement of the actual discovery as you've described it to us. You'll be glad to get away from this room, I expect."

Inspector Fox had secreted his note-book and now ushered Clem Smith out. Clem appeared to go thankfully.

"Plain sailing, wouldn't you say, Mr. Alleyn," said Fox, looking along the passage. "Nobody about," he added. "I'll leave the door open."

Alleyn rubbed his nose. "It looks like plain sailing, Fox, certainly. But in view of the other blasted affair we can't take a damn thing for granted. You weren't on the Jupiter case, were you, Gibson?"

"No, sir," said Gibson, looking up from his note-book. "Homicide dressed up to look like suicide, wasn't it?"

"It was, indeed. The place has been pretty extensively chopped up and rehashed, but the victim was on this side of the passage and in what must have been the room now taken in to make the Greenroom. Next door there was a gas fire backing on to his own. The job was done by blowing down the tube next door. This put out the fire in this room and left the gas on, of course. The one next door was then re-lit. The victim was pretty well dead-drunk and the trick worked. We got the bloke on the traces of crepe hair and greasepaint he left on the tube."

"Very careless," Fox said. "Silly chap, really."

"The theatre," Alleyn said, "was shut up for a long time. Three or four years at least. Then Adam Poole took it, renamed it the Vulcan and got a permit for renovation. I fancy this is only his second production here."

"Perhaps," Fox speculated, "the past history of the place played on deceased's mind and led him to do away with himself after the same fashion."

"Sort of superstitious?" Gibson ventured.

"Not precisely," said Fox majestically. "And yet something after that style of thing. They're a very superstitious mob, actors, Fred. Very. And if he had reason, in any case, to entertain the notion of suicide—"

"He must," Alleyn interjected, "have also entertained the very very nasty notion of throwing suspicion of foul play on his fellow-actors. If there's a gas fire back-to-back with this—"

"And there is," Fox said.

"The devil there is! So what does Bennington do? He re-creates as far as possible the whole set-up, leaves no note, no indication, as far as we can see, of his intention to gas himself, and—who's next door, Fox?"

"A Mr. Parry Percival."

"All right. Bennington pushes off, leaving Mr. Parry Percival ostensibly in the position of the Jupiter murderer. Rotten sort of suicide that'd be, Br'er Fox."

"We don't know anything yet, of course," said Fox.

"We don't, and the crashing hellish bore about the whole business lies in the all-too-obvious fact that we'll have to find out. What's on your inventory, Gibson?"

Sergeant Gibson opened his note-book and adopted his official manner.

"Dressing-table or shelf," he said. "One standing mirror. One cardboard box containing false hair, rouge, substance labelled 'nose-paste,' seven fragments of greasepaint and one unopened box of powder. Shelf. Towel spread out to serve as table-cloth. On towel, one tray containing six sticks of greasepaint. To right of tray, bottle of spirit-adhesive. Bottle containing what appears to be substance known as liquid powder. Open box of powder overturned. Behind box of powder, pile of six pieces of cotton-wool and a roll from which these pieces have been removed." He looked up at Alleyn. "Intended to be used for powdering purposes, Mr. Alleyn."

"That's it," Alleyn said. He was doubled up, peering at the floor under the dressing-shelf. "Nothing there," he grunted. "Go on."

"To left of tray, cigarette case with three cigarettes and open box of fifty. Box of matches. Ash-tray. Towel, stained with greasepaint. Behind mirror, flask—one-sixth full—and used tumbler smelling of spirits."

Alleyn looked behind the standing glass. "Furtive sort of cache," he said. "Go on."

"Considerable quantity of powder spilt on shelf and on adjacent floor area. Considerable quantity of ash. Left wall, clothes. I haven't been through the pockets yet, Mr. Alleyn. There's nothing on the floor but powder and some paper ash, original form undistinguishable. Stain as of something burnt on hearth."

"Go ahead with it then. I wanted," Alleyn said with a discontented air, "to *hear* whether I was wrong."

Fox and Gibson looked placidly at him. "All right," he said, "don't mind me. I'm broody."

He squatted down by the overcoat. "It really is the most obscene smell, gas," he muttered. "How anybody *can* always passes my comprehension." He poked in a gingerly manner at the coat. "Powder over everything," he grumbled. "Where had this coat been? On the empty hanger near the door, presumably. That's damned rum. Check it with his dresser. We'll have to get Bailey along, Fox. And Thompson. Blast!"

"I'll ring the Yard," said Fox and went out.

Alleyn squinted through a lens at the wing-taps of the gas fire. "I can see prints clearly enough," he said, "on both. We can check with Bennington's. There's even a speck or two of powder settled on the taps."

"In the air, sir, I dare say," said Gibson.

"I dare say it *was*. Like the gas. We can't go any further here until the dabs and flash party has done its stuff. Finished, Gibson?"

"Finished, Mr. Alleyn. Nothing much in the pockets. Bills. Old racing card. Cheque-book and so on. Nothing on the body, by the way, but a handkerchief."

"Come on, then. I've had my belly-full of gas."

But he stood in the doorway eyeing the room and whistling softly.

"I wish I could believe in you," he apostrophized it, "but split me and sink me if I can. No, by all that's phoney, not for one credulous second. Come on, Gibson. Let's talk to these experts."

iv

They all felt a little better for Jacko's soup, which had been laced with something that, as J. G. Darcey said (and looked uncomfortable as soon as he'd said it), went straight to the spot marked X.

Whether it was this potent soup, or whether extreme emotional and physical fatigue had induced in Martyn its familiar complement, an uncanny sharpening of the mind, she began to consider for the first time the general reaction of the company to Bennington's death. She thought: "I don't believe there's one of us who really minds very much. How lonely for him! Perhaps he guessed that was how it would be. Perhaps he felt the awful isolation of a child that knows itself unwanted and thought he'd put himself out of the way of caring."

It was a shock to Martyn when Helena Hamilton suddenly gave voice to her own thoughts. Helena had sat with her chin in her hand, looking at the floor. There was an unerring grace about her and this fireside posture had the beauty of complete relaxation. Without raising her eyes she said: "My dears, my dears, for pity's sake don't let's pretend. Don't let me pretend. I didn't love him. Isn't that sad? We all know and we try to patch up a decorous scene but it won't do. We're shocked and uneasy and dreadfully tired. Don't let's put ourselves to the trouble of pretending. It's so useless."

Gay said, "But I *did* love him!" and J.G. put his arm about her.

"Did you?" Helena murmured. "Perhaps you did, darling. Then you must hug your sorrow to yourself. Because I'm afraid nobody really shares it."

Poole said: "We understand, Helena."

With that familiar gesture, not looking at him, she reached out her hand. When he had taken it in his, she said: "When one is dreadfully tired, one talks. I do, at all events. I talk much too easily. Perhaps that's a sign of a shallow woman. You know, my dears, I begin to think I'm only capable of affection. I have a great capacity for affection, but as for my loves, they have no real permanency. None."

Jacko said gently: "Perhaps your talent for affection is equal to other women's knack of loving."

Gay and Parry Percival looked at him in astonishment, but Poole said: "That may well be."

"What I meant to say," Helena went on, "only I do sidetrack myself so awfully, is this. Hadn't we better stop being muted and mournful and talk about what may happen and what we ought to do? Adam, darling, I thought perhaps they might all be respecting my sorrow or something. What should we be talking about? What's the situation?"

Poole moved one of the chairs with its back to the curtain and sat in it. Dr. Rutherford returned and lumped himself down in the corner. "They're talking," he said, "to Clem Smith in the—they're talking to Clem. I've seen the police surgeon, a subfusc exhibit, but one that can tell a hawk from a handsaw if they're held under his nose. He agrees that there was nothing else I could have done, which is no doubt immensely gratifying to me. What are you all talking about? You look like a dress rehearsal."

"We were about to discuss the whole situation," said Poole. "Helena feels it should be discussed and I think we all agree with her."

"What situation pray? Ben's? Or ours? There is no more to be said about Ben's situation. As far as we know, my dear Helena, he has administered to himself a not too uncomfortable and effective anaesthetic which, after he had become entirely unconscious, brought about the end he had in mind. For a man who had decided to shuffle off this mortal coil he behaved very sensibly."

"Oh, *please*," Gay whispered. *"Please!"*

Dr. Rutherford contemplated her in silence for a moment and then said: "What's up, Misery?" Helena, Darcey and Parry Percival made expostulatory noises. Poole said: "See here, John, you'll either pipe down or preserve the decencies."

Gay, fortified perhaps by this common reaction, said loudly: "You might at least have the grace to remember he was my uncle."

"Grace me no grace," Dr. Rutherford quoted inevitably, "and uncle me no uncles." After a moment's reflection, he added: "All right, Thalia, have a good cry. But you must know, if the rudiments of reasoned thinking are within your command, that your Uncle Ben did you a damn shabby turn. A scurvy trick, by God. However, I digress. Get on with the post mortem, Chorus. I am dumb."

"You'll be good enough to remain so," said Poole warmly. "Very well, then. It seems to me, Helena, that Ben took this—this way out—for a number of reasons. I know you want me to speak plainly and I'm going to speak very plainly indeed, my dear."

"Oh, yes," she said. "Please, but—" For a moment they looked at each other. Martyn wondered if she imagined that Poole's head moved in the faintest possible negative. "Yes," Helena said, "very plainly, please."

"Well, then," Poole said, "we know that for the last year Ben, never a very temperate man, has been a desperately intemperate one. We know his habits undermined his health, his character and his integrity as an actor. I think he realized this very thoroughly. He was an unhappy man, who looked back at what he had once been and was appalled. We all know he did things in performance to-night that, from an actor of his standing, were quite beyond the pale."

Parry Percival ejaculated: "Well, I mean to say—oh, well. Never mind."

"Exactly," Poole said. "He had reached a sort of chronic state of instability. We all know he was subject to fits of depression. I believe he did what he did when he was at a low ebb. I believe he would have done it sooner or later by one means or another. And in my view, for what it's worth, that's the whole story. Tragic enough, God knows, but, in its tragedy, simple. I don't know if you agree."

Darcey said: "If there's nothing else. I mean," he said diffidently, glancing at Helena, "if nothing has happened that would seem like a further motive."

Helena's gaze rested for a moment on Poole and then on Darcey. "I think Adam's right," she said. "I'm afraid he was appalled by a sudden realization of himself. I'm afraid he was insufferably lonely."

"Oh, my God!" Gay ejaculated, and having by this means collected their unwilling attention she added: "I shall never forgive myself. Never."

Dr. Rutherford groaned loudly.

"I failed him," Gay announced. "I was a bitter, bitter disappointment to him. I dare say I turned the scale."

"Now in the name of all the gods at once," Dr. Rutherford began, and was brought to a stop by the entry of Clem Smith.

Clem looked uneasily at Helena Hamilton and said: "They're in the dressing-room. He says they won't keep you waiting much longer."

"It's all right, then?" Parry Percival blurted out and added in a flurry: "I mean there won't be a whole lot of formalities. I mean we'll be able to get away. I mean—"

"I've no idea about that," Clem said. "Alleyn just said they'd be here soon." He had brought a cup of soup with him and he withdrew into a corner and began to drink it. The others watched him anxiously but said nothing.

"What did he ask you about?" Jacko demanded suddenly.

"About what we did at the time."

"Anything else?"

"Well, yes. He—well, in point of fact, he seemed to be interested in the alterations to the theatre."

"To the dressing-rooms in particular?" Poole asked quickly.

"Yes," Clem said unhappily. "To them."

There was a long silence, broken by Jacko.

"I find nothing remarkable in this," he said. "Helena has shown us the way with great courage and Adam has spoken his mind. Let us all speak ours. I may resemble an ostrich but I do not propose to imitate its behaviour. Of what do we all think? There is the unpleasing little circumstance of the Jupiter case and we think of that. When Gay mentions it she does so with the air of one who opens a closet and out tumbles a skeleton. But why? It is inevitable that these gentlemen, who also remember the Jupiter case, should wish to inspect the dressing-rooms. They wish, in fact, to make very sure indeed that this is a case of suicide and not of murder. And since we are all quite certain that it is suicide we should not disturb ourselves that they do their duty."

"Exactly," Poole said.

"It's going," Darcey muttered, "to be damn bad publicity."

"Merciful Heavens!" Parry Percival exclaimed. "The Publicity! None of us thought of that!"

"Did we not!" said Poole.

"I must say," Parry complained, "I *would* like to know what's going to happen, Adam. I mean—darling Helena, I know you'll understand—but I mean, about the piece. Do we go on? Or what?"

"Yes," Helena said. "We go on. Please, Adam."

"Helena, I've got to think. There are so many—"

"We go on. Indeed, indeed we do."

Martyn felt rather than saw the sense of relief in Darcey and Percival.

Darcey said: "I'm the understudy, Lord help me," and Percival made a tiny ambiguous sound that might have been one of satisfaction or of chagrin.

"How are you for it, J.G.?" Helena asked.

"I *know* it," he said heavily.

"I'll work whenever you like. We've got the week-end."

"Thank you, Helena."

"Your own understudy's all right," said Clem.

"Good."

It was clear to Martyn that this retreat into professionalism was a great relief to them, and it was clear also that Poole didn't share in their comfort. Watching him, she was reminded of his portrait in the Greenroom: he looked withdrawn and troubled.

A lively and almost cosy discussion about re-casting had developed. Clem Smith, Jacko and Percival were all talking at once when, with her infallible talent for scenes, Gay exclaimed passionately:

"I can't bear it! I think you're all awful!"

They broke off. Having collected their attention, she built rapidly to her climax. "To sit round and talk about the show as if nothing had happened! How you can! When beyond those doors, he's lying there, forgotten. Cold and forgotten! It's the most brutal thing I've ever heard of, and if you think I'm coming near this horrible, fated, *haunted* place again, I'm telling you here and now that wild horses wouldn't drag me inside the theatre once I'm away from it. I suppose someone will find time to tell me when the funeral is going to be. I happen to be just about his only relation."

They all began to expostulate at once, but she topped their lines with the determination of a robust star. "You needn't bother to explain," she shouted. "I understand only too well, thank you." She caught sight of Martyn and pointed wildly at her. "You've angled for this miserable part, and now you've got it. I think it's extremely likely you're responsible for what's happened."

Poole said: "You'll stop at once, Gay. Stop."

"I won't! I won't be gagged! It drove my Uncle Ben to despair and I don't care who knows it."

It was upon this line that Alleyn, as if he had mastered one of the major points of stage technique, made his entrance up-stage and centre.

v

Although he must have heard every word of Gay's final outburst, Alleyn gave no sign of having done so. He and the young constable came in and, as if he had walked into somebody's flat, he took off his hat and put it on a table near the door. The young constable looked round and then went off-stage, returning with two chairs which he placed, one in a central position for Alleyn, and one in the O.P. corner for himself. To Martyn he had fantastically the air of an A.D.C. As he settled himself he gave her another of his friendly smiles.

Clem and Parry had got uncomfortably to their feet and now sat down again in a faintly huffy manner. With the exception of Dr. Rutherford, the company reorientated itself, unobtrusively, on Alleyn.

"Well, now," he said, "I'm afraid the first thing I have to say to you all won't be very pleasant news. We don't look like getting through with our side of this unhappy business as quickly as I hoped. I know you are all desperately tired and very shocked and I'm sorry. But the general circumstances aren't quite as straightforward as, on the face of it, you have probably supposed them to be."

A trickle of ice moved under Martyn's diaphragm. She thought: "No, it's not fair. I can't be made to have two goes of the jim-jams in one night."

Alleyn addressed himself specifically to Helena Hamilton.

"You'll have guessed—of course you will—that one can't overlook the other case of gas poisoning that is associated with this theatre. It must have jumped to everybody's mind, almost at once."

"Yes, of course," she said. "We've been talking about it."

The men looked uneasily at her but Alleyn said at once: "I'm sure you have. So have we. And I expect you've wondered, as we have, if the memory of that former case could have influenced your husband."

"I'm certain it did," she said quickly. "We all are."

The others made small affirmative noises. Only Dr. Rutherford was silent. Martyn saw with amazement that his chin had sunk on his rhythmically heaving bosom, his eyes were shut and his lips pursed in the manner of a sleeper who is just not snoring. He was at the back of the group and, she hoped, concealed from Alleyn.

"Have you," Alleyn asked, "any specific argument to support this theory?"

"No *specific* reason. But I know he thought a lot of that other dreadful business. He didn't *like* this theatre. Mr. Alleyn, actors are sensitive to atmosphere. We talk a lot about the theatres we play in and we get very vivid—you would probably think absurdly vivid—impressions of their 'personalities.' My husband felt there was a—an unpleasant atmosphere in this place. He often said so. In a way I think it had a rather horrible fascination for him. We'd a sort of tacit understanding in the Vulcan that its past history wouldn't be discussed among us, but I know he did talk about it. Not to us, but to people who had been concerned in the other affair."

"Yes, I see." Alleyn waited for a moment. The young constable completed a note. His back was now turned to the company. "Did anyone else notice this preoccupation of Mr. Bennington's?"

"Oh, yes!" Gay said with mournful emphasis. "*I* did. He talked to me about it, but when he saw how much it upset me—because I'm so stupidly sensitive to atmosphere—I just can't help it—it's one of those things—but I *am*—because when I first came into the theatre I just knew—you may laugh at me but these things can't be denied—"

"When," Alleyn prompted, "he saw that it upset you?"

"He stopped. I was his niece. It was rather a marvellous relationship."

"He stopped," Alleyn said. "Right." He had a programme in his hand and now glanced at it. "You must be Miss Gainsford, I think. Is that right?"

"Yes, I am. But my name's really Bennington. I'm his only brother's daughter. My father died in the war and Uncle Ben really felt we were awfully *near* to each other, do you know? That's why it's so devastating for me, because I sensed how wretchedly unhappy he was."

"Do you mind telling us why you thought him so unhappy?"

J. G. Darcey interposed quickly: "I don't think it was more than a general intuitive sort of thing, was it, Gay? Nothing special."

"Well—" Gay said reluctantly, and Helena intervened.

"I don't think any of us have any doubt about my husband's unhappiness, Mr. Alleyn. Before you came in I was saying how most, *most* anxious I am that we should be very frank with each other and of course with you. My husband drank so heavily that he had ruined his health and his work quite completely. I wasn't able to help him and we were not—" The colour died out of her face and she hesitated. "Our life together wasn't true," she said. "It had no reality at all. To-night he behaved very badly on the stage. He coloured his part at the expense of the other actors and I think he was horrified at what he'd done. He was very drunk indeed to-night. I feel he suddenly looked at himself and couldn't face what he saw. I feel that very strongly."

"One *does* sense these things," Gay interjected eagerly, "or I do at any rate."

"I'm sure you do," Alleyn agreed politely. Gay drew breath and was about to go on when he said: "Of course, if any of you can tell us any happenings or remarks or so on that seem to prove that he had this thing in mind, it will be a very great help."

Martyn heard her voice—acting, it seemed, of its own volition. "I think, perhaps—"

Alleyn turned to her and his smile reassured her. "Yes?" he said. "Forgive me, but I don't yet know all your names." He looked again at his programme and then at her. Gay gave a small laugh. Darcey put his hand over hers and said something undistinguishable.

Poole said quickly: "Miss Martyn Tarne. She is, or should be, our heroine to-night. Miss Gainsford was ill and Miss Tarne, who was the understudy, took her part at half-an-hour's notice. We'd all be extremely proud of her if we had the wits to be anything but worried and exhausted."

Martyn's heart seemed to perform some eccentric gyration in the direction of her throat and she thought: "That's done it. Now my voice is going to be ungainly with emotion."

Alleyn said: "That must have been a most terrifying and exciting adventure," and she gulped and nodded. "What had you remembered," he went on after a moment, "that might help us?"

"It was something he said when he came off in the last act."

"For his final exit in the play?"

"Yes."

"I'll be very glad to hear it."

"I'll try to remember exactly what it was," Martyn said carefully. "I was in the dressing-room passage on my way to my—to Miss Gainsford's room and he caught me up. He spoke very disjointedly and strangely, not finishing his sentences. But one thing he said—I think it was the last—I do remember quite distinctly because it puzzled me very much. He said: 'I just wanted to tell you that you needn't suppose what I'm going to do—' and then he stopped as if he was confused and added, I think: 'You needn't suppose—' and broke off again. And then Jacko—Mr. Doré—came and told me to go into the dressing-room to have my make-up attended to and, I think, said something to Mr. Bennington about his."

"I told him he was shining with sweat," said Jacko. "And he went into his room."

"Alone?" Alleyn asked.

"I just looked in to make sure he had heard me. I told him again he needed powder and then went at once to this Infant."

"Miss Tarne, can you remember anything else Mr. Bennington said?"

"Not really. I'm afraid I was rather in a haze myself just then."

"The great adventure?"

"Yes," said Martyn gratefully. "I've an idea he said something about my performance. Perhaps I should explain that I knew he must be very disappointed and upset about my going on instead of Miss Gainsford, but his manner was not unfriendly and I have the impression that he meant to say he didn't bear for me, personally, any kind of resentment. But that's putting it too definitely. I'm not at all sure what he said, except for that one sentence. Of that I'm quite positive."

"Good," Alleyn said. "Thank you. Did you hear this remark, Mr. Doré?"

Jacko said promptly: "But certainly. I was already in the passage and he spoke loudly as I came up."

"Did you form any opinion as to what he meant?"

"I was busy and very pleased with this Infant and I did not concern myself. If I thought at all it was to wonder if he was going to make a scene because the niece had not played. He had a talent for scenes. It appears to be a family trait. I thought perhaps he meant that this Infant would not be included in some scene he planned to make or be scolded for her success."

"Did he seem to you to be upset?"

"Oh, yes. Yes. Upset. Yes."

"Very much distressed, would you say?"

"All his visage wann'd?" inquired a voice in the background. "Tears in his eyes, distraction in's aspect?"

Alleyn moved his position until he could look past Gay and Darcey at the recumbent Doctor. "Or even," he said, "his whole function suiting with forms to his conceit?"

"Hah!" The Doctor ejaculated and sat up. "Upon my soul, the whirligig of time brings in his revenges. Even to the point where dull detection apes at artifice, inspectors echo with informed breath their pasteboard prototypes of fancy wrought. I am amazed and know not what to say." He helped himself to snuff and fell back into a recumbent position.

"Please don't mind him," Helena said, smiling at Alleyn. "He is a very foolish vain old man and has read somewhere that it's clever to quote in a muddled sort of way from the better known bits of the Bard."

"We encourage him too much," Jacko added gloomily.

"We have become too friendly with him," said Poole.

"And figo for thy friendship," said Dr. Rutherford.

Parry Percival sighed ostentatiously and Darcey said: "Couldn't we get on?" Alleyn looked good-humouredly at Jacko and said: "Yes, Mr. Doré?"

"I would agree," Jacko said, "that Ben was very much upset, but that was an almost chronic condition of late with poor Ben. I believe now with Miss Hamilton that he had decided there was little further enjoyment to be found in observing the dissolution of his own character and was about to take the foolproof way of ending it. He wished to assure Martyn that the decision had nothing to do with chagrin over Martyn's success or the failure of his niece. And that, if I am right, was nice of Ben."

"I don't think we need use the word 'failure,'" J.G. objected. "Gay was quite unable to go on."

"I hope you are better now, Miss Gainsford," Alleyn said.

Gay made an eloquent gesture with both hands and let them fall in her lap. "What does it matter?" she said. "Better? Oh, yes, I'm better." And with the closest possible imitation of Helena Hamilton's familiar gesture she extended her hand, without looking at him, to J. G. Darcey. He took it anxiously. "Much better," he said, patting it.

Martyn thought: "Oh, dear, he *is* in love with her. *Poor* J.G.!"

Alleyn looked thoughtfully at them for a moment and then turned to the others.

"There's a general suggestion," he said, "that none of you was very surprised by this event. May I just—sort of tally-up the general opinion as far as I've heard it? It helps to keep things tidy, I find. Miss Hamilton, you tell us that your husband had a curious, an almost morbid interest in the Jupiter case. You and Mr. Doré agree that Mr. Bennington had decided to take his life because he couldn't face the 'dissolution of his character.' Miss Gainsford, if I understand her, believes he was deeply disturbed by the *mise-en-scène* and also by her inability to go on to-night for this part. Miss Tarne's account of what was probably the last statement he made suggests that he wanted her to understand that some action he had in mind had nothing to do with her. Mr. Doré supports this interpretation and confirms the actual words that were used. This, as far as it goes, is the only tangible bit of evidence as to intention that we have."

Poole lifted his head. His face was very white and a lock of black hair had fallen over his forehead, turning him momentarily into the likeness, Martyn thought inconsequently, of Michelangelo's Adam. He said: "There's the fact itself, Alleyn. There's what he did."

Alleyn said carefully: "There's an interval of perhaps eight minutes between what he said and when he was found."

"Look here—" Parry Percival began, and then relapsed. "Let it pass," he said. "*I* wouldn't know."

"Pipe up, Narcissus," Dr. Rutherford adjured him, "the Inspector won't bite you."

"Oh, shut up!" Parry shouted, and was awarded a complete and astonished silence. He rose and addressed himself to the players. "You're all being *so* bloody frank and sensible about this suicide," he said. "You're *so* anxious to show everybody how honest you are. The Doctor's *so* unconcerned he can even spare a moment to indulge in his favourite pastime of me-baiting. I know what the Doctor thinks about me and it doesn't say much for his talents as a diagnostician. But if it's queer to feel desperately sorry for a man who was miserable enough to choke himself to death at a gas jet, if it's queer to be physically and mentally sick at the thought of it, then, by God, I'd rather be queer than normal. Now!"

There followed a silence broken only by the faint whisper of the young constable's pencil.

Dr. Rutherford struggled to his feet and lumbered down to Parry.

"Your argument, my young coxcomb," he said thoughtfully, "is as sea-worthy as a sieve. As for my diagnosis, if you're the normal man you'd have me believe, why the hell don't you show like one? You exhibit the stigmata of that water-fly whom it is a vice to know, and fly into a fit when the inevitable conclusion is drawn." He took Parry by the elbow and addressed himself to the company in the manner of a lecturer. "A phenomenon," he said, "that is not without its dim interest. I invite your attention. Here is an alleged actor who, an hour or two since, was made a public and egregious figure of fun by the deceased. Who was roasted by the deceased before an audience of a thousand whinnying nincompoops. Who allowed his performance to be prostituted by the deceased before this audience. Who before his final and most welcome exit suffered himself to be tripped up contemptuously by the deceased, and who fell on his painted face before this audience. Here is this phenomenon, ladies and gents, who now proposes himself as Exhibit A in the Compassion Stakes. I invite your—"

Poole said *"Quiet!"* and when Dr. Rutherford grinned at him added: "I meant it, John. You will be quiet if you please."

Parry wrenched himself free from the Doctor and turned on Alleyn. "You're supposed to be in charge here—" he began, and Poole said quickly: "Yes, Alleyn, I really do think that this discussion is getting quite fantastically out of hand. If we're all satisfied that this is a case of suicide—"

"Which," Alleyn said, "we are not."

They were all talking at once: Helena, the Doctor, Parry, Gay and Darcey. They were like a disorderly chorus in a verse-play. Martyn, who had been watching Alleyn, was terrified. She saw him glance at the constable. Then he stood up.

"One moment," he said. The chorus broke off as inconsequently as it had begun.

"We've reached a point," Alleyn said, "where it's my duty to tell you I'm by no means satisfied that this is, in fact, a case of suicide."

Martyn was actually conscious, in some kind, of a sense of relief. She could find no look either of surprise or of anger in any of her fellow-players. Their faces were so many white discs and they were motionless and silent. At last Clem Smith said with an indecent lack of conviction: "He was horribly careless about things like that—taps, I mean—" His voice sank to a murmur. They heard the word "accident."

"Is it not strange," Jacko said loudly, "how loath one is to pronounce the word that is in all our minds. And truth to tell, it has a soft and ugly character." His lips closed over his fantastic teeth. He used the exaggerated articulation of an old actor. "Murder," he said. "So beastly, isn't it?"

It was at this point that one of the stage-hands, following, no doubt, his routine for the night, pulled up the curtain and exhibited the scene of climax to the deserted auditorium.

CHAPTER VIII

AFTERPIECE

From this time onward, through the watches of that night, it seemed to Martyn that a second play was acted out in the Vulcan: a play that wrote itself as it went along, with many excursions into irrelevance, with countless *longueurs* and with occasional unanticipated scenes of climax. She was unable to dismiss the sense of an audience that watched in the shrouded seats, or the notion that the theatre itself was attentive to the action on its stage.

This illusion was in some sort created by the players, for it seemed to Martyn that each of them was acting a part. She was not on this account repelled by any of them, but rather felt drawn towards them all as one is to people with whom one shares a common danger. They were of one guild. Even Gay Gainsford's excesses were at first a cause only of resigned irritation, and Parry Percival's outburst, Martyn felt, was understandable. On the whole she thought the better of him for it.

When she considered them all as they sat about their own working-stage, bruised by anxiety and fatigue, Jacko's ugly word sounded not so much frightening as preposterous. It was unthinkable that it could kindle even a bat-light of fear in any of their hearts. "And yet," thought Martyn, "it has done so. There are little points of terror burning in all of us like match-flames."

After Jacko had spoken there was a long silence, broken at last by Adam Poole, who asked temperately: "Are we to understand, Alleyn, that you have quite ruled out the possibility of suicide?"

"By no means," Alleyn rejoined. "I still hope you may be able, among you, to show that there is at least a clear enough probability of suicide for us to leave the case as it stands until the inquest. But where there are strong indications that it may *not* be suicide we can't risk waiting as long as that without a pretty exhaustive look round."

"And there are such indications?"

"There are indeed."

"Strong?"

Alleyn waited a moment. "Sufficiently strong," he said.

"What are they?" Dr. Rutherford demanded.

"It must suffice," Alleyn quibbled politely, "that they are sufficient."

"An elegant sufficiency, by God!"

"But, Mr. Alleyn," Helena cried out, "what can we tell you? Except that we all most sincerely believe that Ben did this himself. Because we know him to have been bitterly unhappy. What else is there for us to say?"

"It will help, you know, when we get a clear picture of what you were all doing and where you were between the time he left the stage and the time he was found. Inspector Fox is checking now with the stage-staff. I propose to do so with the players."

"I see," she said. She leant forward and her air of reasonableness and attention was beautifully executed. "You want to find out which of us had the opportunity to murder Ben."

Gay Gainsford and Parry began an outcry, but Helena raised her hand and they were quiet. "That's it, isn't it?" she said.

"Yes," Alleyn said, "that really is it. I fancy you would rather be spared the stock evasions about routine enquiries and all the rest of it."

"Much rather."

"I was sure of it," Alleyn said. "Then shall we start with you, if you please?"

"I was on the stage for the whole of that time, Mr. Alleyn. There's a scene, before Ben's exit, between J.G.—that's Mr. Darcey over there—Parry, Adam, Ben and myself. First Parry and then J.G. goes off and Ben follows a moment later. Adam and I finish the play."

"So you, too," Alleyn said to Poole, "were here, on the stage, for the whole of this period?"

"I go off for a moment after his exit. It's a strange, rather horridly strange, coincidence that in the play he—the character he played, I mean—does commit suicide off-stage. He shoots himself. When I hear the shot I go off. The other two men have already made their exits. They remain off but I come on again almost immediately. I wait outside the door on the left from a position where I can watch Miss Hamilton, and I re-enter on a 'business' cue from her."

"How long would this take?"

"Shall we show you?" Helena suggested. She got up and moved to the centre of the stage. She raised her clasped hands to her mouth and stood motionless. She was another woman.

As if Clem had called "Clear stage"—and indeed he looked about him with an air of authority—Martyn, Jacko and Gay moved into the wings. Parry and J.G. went to the foot of the stairs and Poole crossed to above Helena. They placed themselves thus in the business-like manner of a rehearsal. The Doctor, however, remained prone on his sofa, breathing deeply and completely disregarded by everybody. Helena glanced at Clem Smith, who went to the book.

"From Ben's exit, Clem," Poole said, and after a moment Helena turned and addressed herself to the empty stage on her left.

"I've only one thing to say, but it's between the three of us." She turned to Parry and Darcey. "Do you mind?" she asked them.

Parry said: "I don't understand and I'm past minding."

Darcey said: "My head is buzzing with a sense of my own inadequacy. I shall be glad to be alone."

They went out, each on his own line, leaving Helena, Adam, and the ghost of Bennington on the stage.

Helena spoke again to vacancy. "It must be clear to you, now. It's the end, isn't it?"

"Yes," Clem's voice said. "I understand you perfectly. Good-bye, my dear."

They watched the door on the left. Alleyn took out his watch. Helena made a quick movement as if to prevent the departure of an unseen person and Poole laid his hand on her arm. They brought dead Ben back to the stage by their mime and dismissed him as vividly. It seemed that the door must open and shut for him as he went out.

Poole said: "And now I must speak to you alone." There followed a short passage of dialogue which he and Helena played *a tempo* but with muted voices. Jacko, in the wings, clapped his hands and the report was as startling as a gun-shot. Poole ran out through the left-hand door.

Helena traced a series of movements about the stage. Her gestures were made in the manner of an exercise but the shadow of their significance was reflected in her face. Finally she moved into the window and seemed to compel herself to look out. Poole re-entered.

"Thank you," Alleyn said, shutting his watch. "Fifty seconds. Will you all come on again, if you please?"

When they had assembled in their old positions, he said: "Did anyone notice Mr. Poole as he waited by the door for his re-entry?"

"The door's recessed," Poole said. "I was more or less screened."

"Someone off-stage may have noticed, however." He looked from Darcey to Percival.

"We went straight to our rooms," said Parry.

"Together?"

"I was first. Miss Tarne was in the entrance to the passage and I spoke to her for a moment. J.G. followed me, I think."

"Do you remember this, Miss Tarne?"

It had been at the time when Martyn had begun to come back to earth. It was like a recollection from a dream. "Yes," she said. "I remember. They both spoke to me."

"And went on down the passage?"

"Yes."

"To be followed in a short time by yourself and Mr. Bennington?"

"Yes."

"And then Mr. Doré joined you and you went to your rooms?"

"Yes."

"So that after Mr. Bennington had gone to his room, you, Mr. Percival, were in your dressing-room, which is next door to his, Mr. Darcey was in his room which is on the far side of Mr. Percival's, and Miss Tarne was in her room—or more correctly, perhaps, Miss Gainsford's—with Mr. Doré, who joined her there after looking in on Mr. Bennington. Right?"

They murmured an uneasy assent.

"How long were you all in these rooms?"

Jacko said: "I believe I have said I adjusted this Infant's make-up and returned with her to the stage."

"I think," said Martyn, "that the other two went out to the stage before we did. I remember hearing them go up the passage together. That was before the call for the final curtain. We went out after the call, didn't we, Jacko?"

"Certainly, my Infant. And by that time you were a little more awake, isn't it? The pink clouds had receded a certain distance?"

Martyn nodded, feeling foolish. Poole came behind her and rested his hands on her shoulders. "So there would appear at least to be an alibi for the Infant Phenomenon," he said. It was the most natural and inevitable thing in the world for her to lean back. His hands moved to her arms and he held her to him for an uncharted second while a spring of well-being broke over her astounded heart.

Alleyn looked from her face to Poole's and she guessed that he wondered about their likeness to each other. Poole, answering her thoughts and Alleyn's unspoken question, said: "We are remotely related, but I am not allowed to mention it. She's ashamed of the connection."

"That's unlucky," Alleyn said with a smile, "since it declares itself so unequivocally."

Gay Gainsford said loudly to Darcey: "Do you suppose, darling, they'd let me get my cigarettes?"

Helena said: "Here you are, Gay." Darcey had already opened his case and held it out to her in his right hand. His left hand was in his trousers pocket. His posture was elegant and modish, out of keeping with his look of anxiety and watchfulness.

"Where are your cigarettes?" Alleyn asked and Gay said quickly:

"It doesn't matter, thank you. I've got one. I won't bother. I'm sorry I interrupted."

"But where are they?"

"I don't really know what I've done with them."

"Where were you during the performance?"

She said impatiently: "It *really* doesn't matter. I'll look for them later or something."

"Gay," said Jacko, "was in the Greenroom throughout the show."

"Lamprey will see if he can find them."

The young constable said: "Yes, of course, sir," and went out.

"In the Greenroom?" Alleyn said. "Were you there all the time, Miss Gainsford?"

Standing in front of her with his back to Alleyn, Darcey held a light to her cigarette. She inhaled and coughed violently. He said: "Gay didn't feel fit enough to move. She curled up in a chair in the Greenroom. I was to take her home after the show."

"When did you leave the Greenroom, Miss Gainsford?"

But it seemed that Gay had half-asphyxiated herself with her cigarette. She handed it wildly to Darcey, buried her face in her handkerchief and was madly convulsed. P. C. Lamprey returned with a packet of cigarettes, was waved away with vehemence, gave them to Darcey and on his own initiative fetched a cup of water.

"If the face is congested," Dr. Rutherford advised from the sofa, "hold her up by the heels." His eyes remained closed.

Whether it was the possibility of being subjected to this treatment or the sip of water that Darcey persuaded her to take or the generous thumps on her back, administered by Jacko, that effected a cure, the paroxysm abated. Alleyn, who had watched this scene thoughtfully, said: "If you are quite yourself again, Miss Gainsford, will you try to remember when you left the Greenroom?"

She shook her head weakly and said in an invalid's voice: "Please, I honestly don't remember. Is it very important?"

"Oh, for pity's sake, Gay!" cried Helena, with every sign of the liveliest irritation. "Do stop being such an unmitigated ass. You're not choking: if you were your eyes would water and you'd probably dribble. Of course it's important. You were in the Greenroom and next door to Ben. Think!"

"But you can't imagine—" Gay said wildly. "Oh, Aunty—I'm sorry, I mean Helena—I do think that's a frightful thing to suggest."

"My dear Gay," Poole said, "I don't suppose Helena or Mr. Alleyn or any of us imagines you went into Ben's room, knocked him senseless with a straight left to the jaw and then turned the gas on. We merely want to know what you did do."

J.G., who had given a sharp ejaculation and half risen from his chair, now sank back.

Alleyn said: "It would also be interesting, Mr. Poole, to hear how you knew about the straight left to the jaw."

ii

Poole was behind Martyn and a little removed from her. She felt his stillness in her own bones. When he spoke it was a shock rather than a relief to hear how easy and relaxed his voice sounded.

"Do you realize, Alleyn," he said, "you've given me an opportunity to use, in reverse, a really smashing detective's cliché: 'I didn't know. You have just told me!' "

"And that," Alleyn said with some relish, "as I believe you would say in the profession, takes me off with a hollow laugh and a faint hiss. So you merely guessed at the straight left?"

"If Ben was killed, and I don't believe he was, it seemed to me to be the only way this murder could be brought about."

"Surely not," Alleyn said without emphasis. "There is the method that was used before in this theatre with complete success."

"I don't know that I would describe as completely successful a method that ended with the arrest of its employer."

"Oh," Alleyn said lightly, "that's another story. He underestimated our methods."

"A good enough warning to anyone else not to follow his plan of action."

"Or perhaps merely a hint that it could be improved upon," Alleyn said. "What do you think, Mr. Darcey?"

"I?" J.G. sounded bewildered. "I don't know. I'm afraid I haven't followed the argument."

"You were still thinking about the straight-left theory, perhaps?"

"I believe with the others that it was suicide," said J.G. He had sat down again beside Gay. His legs were stretched out before him and crossed at the ankles, his hands were in his trousers pockets and his chin on his chest. It was the attitude of a distinguished M.P. during a damaging speech from the opposite side of the House.

Alleyn said: "And we still don't know when Miss Gainsford left the Greenroom."

"Oh, *lawks!*" Parry ejaculated. "This is *too* tiresome. J.G., you looked in at the Greenroom door when we came back for the curtain-call, don't you remember? Was she there then? Were you there then, Gay darling?"

Gay opened her mouth to speak but J.G. said quickly: "Yes, of course I did. Stupid of me to forget. Gay was sound asleep in the armchair, Mr. Alleyn. I didn't disturb her." He passed his right hand over his beautifully groomed head. "It's a most extraordinary thing," he said vexedly, "that I should have forgotten this. Of course she was asleep. Because later, when—well, when, in point of fact, the discovery had been made—I asked where Gay was and someone said she was still in the Greenroom, and I was naturally worried and went to fetch her. She was still asleep and the Greenroom, by that time, reeking with gas. I brought her back here."

"Have you any idea, Miss Gainsford," Alleyn asked, "about when you dropped off?"

"I was exhausted, Mr. Alleyn. Physically and emotionally exhausted. I still am."

"Was it, for instance, before the beginning of the last act?"

"N—n—no. No. Because J.G. came in to see how I was in the second interval. Didn't you, darling? And I was exhausted, wasn't I?"

"Yes, dear."

"And he gave me some aspirins and I took two. And I suppose, in that state of utter exhaustion, they worked. So I fell into a sleep—an exhausted sleep, it was."

"Naturally," Helena murmured with a glance at Alleyn, "it would be exhausted."

"Undoubtedly," said Jacko, "it was exhausted."

"Well, it was," said Gay crossly. "Because I was. Utterly."

"Did anyone else beside Mr. Darcey go into the Greenroom during the second interval?"

Gay looked quickly at J.G. "Honestly," she said, "I'm *so* muddled about times it really isn't safe to ask me. I'm sure to be wrong."

"Mr. Darcey?"

"No," J.G. said.

"Well, my dearest J.G.," Parry said, "I couldn't be more reluctant to keep popping in like one of the Eumenides in that utterly incomprehensible play, but I do assure you that you're at fault here. Ben went into the Greenroom in the second interval."

"Dear Heaven!" Helena said, on a note of desperation. "What has happened to us all!"

"I'm terribly sorry, Helena darling," Parry said, and sounded it.

"But why should you be sorry? Why shouldn't Ben go and see his niece in the interval? He played the whole of the third act afterwards. Of course you should say so, Parry, if you know what you're talking about. Shouldn't he, Adam? Shouldn't he, Mr. Alleyn?"

Poole was looking with a sort of incredulous astonishment at Darcey. "I think he should," he said slowly.

"And you, Mr. Darcey?" asked Alleyn.

"All right, Parry," said J.G., "go on."

"There's not much more to be said, and anyway I don't suppose it matters. It was before they'd called the third act. Helena and Adam and Martyn had gone out. They begin the act. I come on a bit later and Ben after me and J.G. later still. I wanted to see how the show was going and I was on my way in the passage when Ben came out of his room and went into the Greenroom next door. The act was called soon after that."

"Did you speak to him?" Alleyn asked.

"I did not," said Parry with some emphasis. "I merely went out to the stage and joined Jacko and the two dressers and the call-boy, who were watching from the Prompt side, and Clem."

"That's right," Clem Smith said. "I remember telling you all to keep away from the bunches. The boy called J.G. and Ben about five minutes later."

"Were you still in the Greenroom when you were called, Mr. Darcey?"

"Yes."

"With Mr. Bennington?"

"He'd gone to his room."

"Not for the life of me," Helena said wearily, "can I see why you had to be so mysterious, J.G."

"Perhaps," Alleyn said, "the reason is in your left trousers pocket, Mr. Darcey."

J.G. didn't take his hand out of his pocket. He stood up and addressed himself directly to Alleyn.

"May I speak to you privately?" he asked.

"Of course," Alleyn said. "Shall we go to the Greenroom?"

iii

In the Greenroom and in the presence of Alleyn and of Fox, who had joined them there, J. G. Darcey took his left hand out of his trousers pocket and extended it palm downwards for their inspection. It was a well-shaped and well-kept hand but the knuckles were grazed. A trace of blood had seeped out round the greasepaint and powder which had been daubed over the raw skin.

"I suppose I've behaved very stupidly," he said. "But I hoped there would be no need for this to come out. It has no bearing whatever on his death."

"In that case," Alleyn said, "it will not be brought out. But you'll do well to be frank."

"I dare say," said J.G. wryly.

"There's a bruise on the deceased's jaw on the right side that could well have been caused by that straight left Mr. Poole talked about. Now, we can of course determine whether make-up from your left fist is mixed with Bennington's own make-up over this bruise. If you tell me you didn't let drive at him we'll make this experiment."

"I assure you that you don't need to do any such thing. I'll willingly admit that I hit him," J.G. said with a shudder.

"And also why you hit him?"

"Oh, yes, if I can. If I can," he repeated and pressed his hand to his eyes. "D'you mind if we sit down, Alleyn? I'm a bit tired."

"Do."

J.G. sat in the leather armchair where Martyn, and, in her turn, Gay Gainsford had slept. In the dim light of the Greenroom his face looked wan and shadowed. "Not the chicken I was," he said, and it was an admission actors do not love to make.

Alleyn faced him. Fox sat down behind him, flattened his note-book on the table and placed his spectacles across his nose. There was something cosy about Fox when he took notes. Alleyn remembered absently that his wife had once observed that Mr. Fox was a cross between a bear and a baby and exhibited the most pleasing traits of both creatures.

The masked light above Jacko's sketch of Adam Poole shone down upon it, and it thus was given considerable emphasis in an otherwise shadowed room.

"If you want a short statement," J.G. said, "I can give it to you in a sentence. I hit Ben on the jaw in this room during the second act wait. I didn't knock him out but he was so astonished he took himself off. I was a handy amateur welter-weight in my young days but it must be twenty years or more since I put up my hands. I must say I rather enjoyed it."

"What sort of condition was he in?"

"Damned unpleasant. Oh, you mean drunk or sober? I should say ugly-drunk. Ben was a soak. I've never seen him incapacitated, but really I've hardly ever seen him stone-cold either. He was in his second degree of drunkenness: offensive, outrageous and incalculable. He'd behaved atrociously throughout the first and second acts."

"In what way?"

"As only a clever actor with too much drink in him can behave. Scoring off other people. Playing for cheap laughs. Doing unrehearsed bits of business that made nonsense of the production. Upon my word," said J.G. thoughtfully, "I wonder Adam or the Doctor or poor little Parry, if he'd had the guts, didn't get in first and give him what he deserved. A perfectly bloody fellow."

"Was it because of his performance that you hit him?"

J.G. looked at his finger-nails and seemed to ponder. "No," he said at last. "Or not directly. If I thought you'd believe me I'd say yes, but no doubt you'll talk to her and she's so upset anyway—"

"You mean Miss Gainsford?"

"Yes," said J.G. with the oddest air of pride and embarrassment. "I mean Gay."

"Was it on her account you dotted him one?"

"It was. He was damned offensive."

"I'm sorry," Alleyn said, "but you'll realize that we do want to be told a little more than that about it."

"I suppose so." He clasped his hands and examined his bruised knuckles. "Although I find it extremely difficult and unpleasant to go into the wretched business. It's only because I hope you'll let Gay off, as far as possible, if you know the whole story. That's why I asked to see you alone." He slewed round and looked discontentedly at Fox.

"Inspector Fox," Alleyn said, "is almost pathologically discreet."

"Glad to hear it. Well, as you've heard, I'd managed to get hold of a bottle of aspirins and I brought them to her, here, in the second interval. Gay was sitting in this chair. She was still terribly upset. Crying. I don't know if you've realized why she didn't go on for the part?"

"No. I'd be glad to have the whole story."

J.G. embarked on it, with obvious reluctance, but as he talked his hesitancy lessened and he even seemed to find some kind of ease in speaking. He described Gay's part and her struggle at rehearsals. It was clear that, however unwillingly, he shared the general opinion of her limited talent. "She'd have given a reasonable show," he said, "if she'd been given a reasonable chance but from the beginning the part got her down. She's a natural ingenue and this thing's really 'character.' It was bad casting. Adam kept the Doctor at bay as much as possible but she knew what he thought. She didn't *want* the part. She was happy where she was in repertory but Ben dragged her in. He saw himself as a sort of fairy-godfather-uncle and when she found the part difficult he turned obstinate and wouldn't let her throw it in. Out of vanity really. He was very vain. She's a frail little thing, you know, all heart and sensitivity, and between them they've brought her to the edge of a breakdown. It didn't help matters when Miss Martyn Tarne appeared out of a clear sky, first as Helena Hamilton's dresser and then as Gay's understudy and then—mysteriously, as some of the cast, Ben in particular, thought—as Adam's distant cousin. You noticed the uncanny resemblance but you may not know the part in the play requires it. That was the last straw for Gay. She'd been ill with nerves and fright and to-night she cracked up completely and wouldn't—couldn't go on. When I saw her in the first interval she was a bit quieter but in the second act little Miss Tarne did very well indeed. Quite startling, it was. Incidentally, I suppose her success infuriated Ben. And Gay heard everybody raving about her as they came off. Naturally that upset her again. So she was in tears when I came in."

He leant forward and rested his head in his hands. His voice was less distinct. "I'm fond of her," he said. "She's got used to me being about. When I came in she ran to me and— I needn't go into the way I felt. There's no explaining these things. She was sobbing in my arms, poor bird, and God knows my heart had turned over. Ben came in. He went for her like a pickpocket. He was crazy. I tried to shut him up. He didn't make a noise—I don't mean that—matter of fact what he said streamed out of him in a whisper. He was quite off his head and began talking about Helena—about his wife. He used straight-out obscenities. There'd been an episode in the afternoon and—well, he used the sort of generalization that Lear and Othello and Leontes use, if you remember your Shakespere."

"Yes."

"Gay was still clinging to me and he began to talk the same sort of stuff about her. I'm not going into details. I put her away from me and quite deliberately gave him what was coming to him. I don't remember what I said. I don't think any of us said anything. So he went out nursing his jaw and they called me for the last act and I went out too. During this last act, when we were on together, I could see the bruise coming out under his make-up."

"What was his general behaviour like during the final act?"

"As far as I was concerned he behaved in the way people do when they play opposite someone they've had a row with off-stage. He didn't look me in the eye. He looked at my forehead or ears. It doesn't show from the front. He played fairly soundly until poor Parry got out of position. Parry is his butt in the piece, but of course what Ben did was outrageous. He stuck out his foot as Parry moved and brought him down. That was not long before his own exit. I never saw him again after that until he was carried out. That's all. I don't know if you've believed me but I hope you'll let Gay off any more of this stuff."

Alleyn didn't answer. He looked at the young-old actor for a moment. J.G. was lighting a cigarette with that trained economy and grace of movement that were part of his stock-in-trade. His head was stooped, and Alleyn saw how carefully the silver hair had been distributed over the scalp. The hands were slightly tremulous. How old was J.G.? Fifty? Fifty-five? Sixty? Was he the victim of that Indian Summer that can so unmercifully visit an ageing man?

"It's the very devil, in these cases," Alleyn said, "how one has to plug away at everyone in turn. Not that it helps to say so. There's one more question that I'm afraid you won't enjoy at all. Can you tell me more specifically what Bennington said about—I think you called it an episode—of the afternoon, in which his wife was concerned?"

"No, by God, I can't," said J.G. hotly.

"He spoke about it in front of Miss Gainsford, didn't he?"

"You can't possibly ask Gay about it. It's out of the question."

"Not, I'm afraid, for an investigating officer," said Alleyn, who thought that J.G.'s delicacy, if delicacy were in question, was possibly a good deal more sensitive than Miss Gainsford's. "Do you suppose Bennington talked about this episode to other people?"

"In the condition he was in I should think it possible."

"Well," Alleyn said, "we shall have to find out."

"See here, Alleyn. What happened, if he spoke the truth, was something entirely between himself and his wife and it's on her account that I can't repeat what he said. You know she and Poole were on-stage at the crucial time and that there's no sense in thinking of motive, if that's what you're after, where they are concerned."

Alleyn said: "This episode might constitute a motive for suicide, however."

J.G. looked up quickly. "Suicide? But—why?"

"Shame?" Alleyn suggested. "Self-loathing if he sobered up after you hit him and took stock of himself? I imagine they've been virtually separated for some time."

"I see you have a talent," said J.G., "for reading between the lines."

"Let us rather call it an ugly little knack. Thank you, Mr. Darcey, I don't think I need bother you any more for the moment."

J.G. went slowly to the door. He hesitated for a moment and then said: "If you're looking for motive, Alleyn, you'll find it in a sort of way all over the place. He wasn't a likeable chap and he'd antagonized everyone. Even poor little Parry came off breathing revenge after the way he'd been handled, but, my God, actors do that kind of thing only too often. Feeling runs high, you know, on first nights."

"So it would seem."

"Can I take that child home?"

"I'm sorry," Alleyn said, "not yet. Not just yet."

iv

"Well," Alleyn said when J.G. had gone, "what have you got at your end of the table, Br'er Fox?"

Fox turned back the pages of his note-book.

"What you might call negative evidence, on the whole, Mr. Alleyn. Clearance for the understudies, who watched the show from the back of the circle and then went home. Clearance for the two dressers (male), the stage-manager and his assistant, the stage-hands and the night-watchman. They were all watching the play or on their jobs. On statements taken independently, they clear each other."

"That's something."

"No female dresser," Mr. Fox observed. "Which seems odd."

"Miss Tarne was the sole female dresser and she's been promoted overnight to what I believe I should call starletdom. Which in itself seems to me to be a rum go. I've always imagined female dressers to be cups-of-tea in alpaca aprons and not embryo actresses. I don't think Miss Tarne could have done the job, but she comes into the picture as the supplanter of Uncle Ben's dear little niece, whom I find an extremely irritating ass with a certain amount of low cunning. Miss Tarne, on the other hand, seems pleasant and intelligent and looks nice. You must allow me my prejudices, Br'er Fox."

"She's Mr. Poole's third cousin or something."

"The case reeks with obscure relationships—blood, marital and illicit, as far as one can see. Did you get anything from Bennington's dresser?"

"Nothing much," said Fox, sighing. "It seems the deceased didn't like him to hang about on account of being a secret drinker. He was in the dressing-room up to about seven and was then told to go and see if he could be of any use to the other gentlemen, and not to come back till the first interval when the deceased changed his clothes. I must say that chap earns his wages pretty easily. As far as I could make out the rest of his duties for the night consisted in tearing off chunks of cotton-wool for the deceased to do up his face with. I checked his visits to the dressing-room by that. The last time he looked in was after the deceased went on the stage in the third act. He cleared away the used cotton-wool and powdered a clean bit. In the normal course of events I suppose he'd have put Mr. Bennington into the fancy dress he was going to wear to the ball and then gone home quite worn out."

"Was he at all talkative?"

"Not got enough energy, Mr. Alleyn. Nothing to say for himself barring the opinion that deceased was almost on the D.T. mark. The other dresser, Cringle, seems a bright little chap. He just works for Mr. Poole."

"Have you let them go?"

"Yes, sir, I have. And the stage-hands. We can look them out again if we want them, but for the moment I think we've just about cleaned them up. I've let the assistant stage-manager—A.S.M. they call him—get away, too. Wife's expecting any time and he never left the prompting book."

"That reduces the mixed bag a bit. You've been through all the rooms, of course, but before we do anything else, Br'er Fox, let's have a prowl."

They went into the passage. Fox jerked his thumb at Bennington's room. "Gibson's doing a fly-crawl in there," he said. "If there's anything, he'll find it. That dresser-chap didn't clear anything up except his used powder-puffs."

They passed Bennington's room and went into Parry Percival's, next door. Here they found Detective-Sergeants Thompson and Bailey, the one a photographic and the other a finger-print expert. They were packing up their gear.

"Well, Bailey?" Alleyn asked.

Bailey looked morosely at his superior. "It's there all right, sir," he said grudgingly. "Complete prints, very near, and a check-up all over the shop."

"What about next door?"

"Deceased's room, sir? His prints on the wing-tap and the tube. Trace of red greasepaint on the rubber connection at the end of the tube. Matches paint on deceased's lips."

"Very painstaking," said Alleyn. "Have you tried the experiment?"

"Seeing the fires are back-to-back, sir," Fox said, "we have. Sergeant Gibson blew down this tube and deceased's fire went out. As in former case."

"Well," Alleyn said, "there you are. Personally I don't believe a word of it, either way." He looked, without interest, at the telegrams stuck round the frame of Parry's looking-glass and at his costume for the ball. "*Very* fancy," he muttered. "Who's in the next room?"

"Mr. J. G. Darcey," said Thompson.

They went into J.G.'s room, which was neat and impersonal in character and contained nothing, it seemed, of interest, unless a photograph of Miss Gainsford looking *insouciante* could be so regarded.

In the last room on this side of the passage they saw the electric sewing-machine, some rough sketches, scraps of material and other evidences of Martyn's sewing-party for Jacko. Alleyn glanced round it, crossed the passage and looked into the empty room opposite. "Dismal little cells when they're unoccupied, aren't they?" he said, and moved on to Gay Gainsford's room.

He stood there, his hands in his pockets, with Fox at his elbow. "This one suffers from the fashionable complaint, Fox," he said. "Schizophrenia. It's got a split personality. On my left a rather too-smart overcoat, a frisky hat, chi-chi gloves, a pansy purse-bag, a large bottle of one of the less reputable scents, a gaggle of mascots, a bouquet from the management and orchids from—who do you suppose?" He turned over the card. "Yes. Alas, yes, with love and a thousand good wishes from her devoted J.G. On my right a well-worn and modest little topcoat, a pair of carefully tended shoes and gloves that remind one of the White Rabbit, a grey skirt and beret and a yellow jumper. A hand-bag that contains, I'm sure, one of those rather heartrending little purses and—what else?" He explored the bag. "A New Zealand passport issued this year in which one finds Miss Tarne is nineteen years old and an actress. So the dresser's job was—what? The result of an appeal to the celebrated third cousin? But why not give her the understudy at once? She's fantastically like him and I'll be sworn he's mightily catched with her. What's more, even old Darcey says she's a damn good actress." He turned the leaves of the passport. "She only arrived in England seventeen days ago. Can that account for the oddness of the set-up? Anyway, I don't suppose it matters. Let's go next door, shall we?"

Cringle had left Poole's room in exquisite order. Telegrams were pinned in rows on the walls. A towel was spread over the make-up. A cigarette had been half-extracted from a packet and a match left ready on the top of its box. A framed photograph of Helena Hamilton stood near the glass. Beside it a tiny clock with a gay face ticked feverishly. It stood on a card. Alleyn moved it delicately and read the inscription. *From Helena. To-night and to-morrow and always—bless you.*

"The standard for first-night keepsakes seems to be set at a high level," Alleyn muttered. "This is a French clock, Fox, with a Sèvres face encircled with garnets. What do you suppose the gentleman gave the lady?"

"Would a tiara be common?" asked Fox.

"Let's go next door and see."

Helena's room smelt and looked like a conservatory. A table had been brought in to carry the flowers. Jacko had set out the inevitable telegrams and had hung up the dresses under their dust sheets.

"Here we are," Alleyn said. "A sort of jeroboam of the most expensive scent on the market. Price, I should say, round about thirty pounds. 'From Adam.' Why don't you give me presents when we solve a petty larceny, Foxkin? Now, I may be fanciful, but this looks to me like the gift of a man who's at his wit's end and plumps for the expensive, the easy and the obvious. Here's something entirely different. Look at this, Fox."

It was a necklace of six wooden medallions strung between jade rings. Each plaque was most delicately carved in the likeness of a head in profile and each head was a portrait of one of the company of players. The card bore the date and the inscription: *From J.*

"Must have taken a long time to do," observed Fox. "That'll be the foreign gentleman's work, no doubt. Mr. Doré."

"No doubt. I wonder if love's labour has been altogether lost," said Alleyn. "I hope she appreciates it."

He took up the leather case with its two photographs of Poole. "He's a remarkable looking chap," he said. "If there's anything to be made of faces in terms of character, and I still like to pretend there is, what's to be made of this one? It's what they call a heart-shaped face, broad across the eyes with a firmly moulded chin and a generous but delicate mouth. Reminds one of a Holbein drawing. Doré's sketch in the Greenroom is damn good. Doré crops up all over the place, doesn't he? Designs their fancy dresses. Paints their faces, in a double sense. Does their décor and, with complete self-effacement, loves their leading lady."

"Do you reckon?"

"I do indeed, Br'er Fox," Alleyn said and rubbed his nose vexedly. "However, Gibson's done all the usual things in these rooms, I suppose?"

"Yes, Mr. Alleyn. Pockets, suitcases and boxes. Nothing to show for it."

"We can let them come home to roost fairly soon, then. We'll start now to see them separately. Blast! I suppose I'll have to begin with checking Darcey's statement with the Gainsford. She gives me the horrors, that young woman."

"Shall I see her, Mr. Alleyn?"

"You can stay and take your notes. I'll see her in the Greenroom. No, wait a bit. You stay with the others, Fox, and send young Lamprey along with her. And you might try again if you can dig up anything that sounds at all off-key with Bennington over the last few days. Anything that distressed or excited him."

"He seems to have been rather easily excited."

"He does, doesn't he, but you never know. I don't believe it was suicide, Fox, and I'm not yet satisfied that we've unearthed anything that's good enough for a motive for murder. Trip away, Foxkin. Ply your craft."

Fox went out sedately. Alleyn crossed the passage and opened the door of Bennington's room. Sergeant Gibson was discovered, squatting on his haunches before the dead gas fire.

"Anything?" Alleyn asked.

"There's this bit of a stain that looks like a scorch on the hearth, sir."

"Yes, I saw that. Any deposit?"

"We-ll—"

"We may have to try."

"The powder pads deceased's dresser cleared away were in the rubbish bin on the stage where he said he put them. Nothing else in the bin. There's this burnt paper on the floor, but it's in small flakes—powder almost."

"All right. Seal the room when you've finished. And Gibson, don't let the mortuary van go without telling me."

"Very good, sir."

Alleyn returned to the Greenroom. He heard Miss Gainsford approaching under the wing of P. C. Lamprey. She spoke in a high grand voice that seemed to come out of a drawing-room comedy of the twenties.

"I think you're *too* intrepid," she was saying, "to start from rock bottom like this. It must be so devastatingly boring for you, though I will say it's rather a comfort to think one is in the hands of, to coin a phrase, a gent. Two gents, in fact."

"Chief Inspector Alleyn," said P. C. Lamprey, "is in the Greenroom I think, Miss."

"My dear, you do it quite marvellously. You ought, again to coin a phrase, to go on the stage."

Evidently Miss Gainsford lingered in the passage. Alleyn heard his subordinate murmur: "Shall I go first?" His regulation boots clumped firmly to the door, which he now opened.

"Will you see Miss Gainsford, sir?" asked P. C. Lamprey, who was pink in the face.

"All right, Mike," Alleyn said. "Show her in and take notes."

"Will you come this way, Miss?"

Miss Gainsford made her entrance with a Mayfairish gallantry that was singularly dated. Alleyn wondered if she had decided that her first reading of her new role was mistaken. "She's abandoned the brave little woman for the suffering *mondaine* who goes down with an epigram," he thought, and sure enough, Miss Gainsford addressed herself to him with staccato utterance and brittle high-handedness.

"Ought one to be terribly flattered because one is the first to be grilled?" she asked. "Or is it a sinister little hint that one is top of the suspect list?"

"We have to start somewhere," Alleyn said. "I thought it might be convenient to see you first. Will you sit down, Miss Gainsford?"

She did so elaborately, gave herself a cigarette, and turned to P. C. Lamprey. "May one ask The Force for a light," she asked, "or would that be against the rules?"

Alleyn lit her cigarette while his unhappy subordinate retired to the table. She turned in her chair to watch him. "Is he going to take me down and use it all in evidence against me?" she asked. Her nostrils dilated, she raised her chin and added jerkily, "That's what's called the Usual Warning, isn't it?"

"A warning is given in police practice," Alleyn said as woodenly as possible, "if there is any chance that the person under interrogation will make a statement that is damaging to himself. Lamprey will note down this interview and, if it seems advisable, you will be asked later on to give a signed statement."

"If that was meant to be reassuring," said Miss Gainsford, "I can't have heard it properly. Could we get cracking?"

"Certainly. Miss Gainsford, you were in the Greenroom throughout the performance. During the last interval you were visited by Mr. J. G. Darcey and by your uncle. Do you agree that as the result of something the deceased said, Mr. Darcey hit him on the jaw?"

She said: "Wasn't it too embarrassing! I mean the Gorgeous Primitive Beast is one thing, but one old gentleman banging another about is so utterly another. I'm afraid I didn't put that very clearly."

"You agree that Mr. Darcey hit Mr. Bennington?"

"But madly. Like a sledge-hammer. I found it so difficult to know what to say. There just seemed to be no clue to further conversation."

"It is the conversation before rather than after the blow that I should like to hear about, if you please."

Alleyn had turned away from her and was looking at Jacko's portrait of Poole. He waited for some moments before she said sharply: "I suppose you think because I talk like this about it I've got no feeling. You couldn't be more at fault." It was as if she called his attention to her performance.

He said, without turning: "I assure you I hadn't given it a thought. What did your uncle say that angered Mr. Darcey?"

"He was upset," she said sulkily, "because I was ill and couldn't play."

"Hardly an occasion for hitting him."

"J.G. is very sensitive about me. He treats me like a piece of china."

"Which is more than he did for your uncle, it seems."

"Uncle Ben talked rather wildly." Miss Gainsford seemed to grope for her poise and made a half-hearted return to her brittle manner. "Let's face it," she said, "he was stinking, poor pet."

"You mean he was drunk?"

"Yes, I do."

"And abusive?"

"I didn't care. I understood him."

"Did he talk about Miss Hamilton?"

"Obviously J.G.'s already told you he did, so why ask me?"

"We like to get confirmation of statements."

"Well, you tell me what he said and I'll see about confirming it."

For the first time Alleyn looked at her. She wore an expression of rather frightened impertinence. "I'm afraid," he said, "that won't quite do. I'm sure you're very anxious to get away from the theatre, Miss Gainsford, and we've still a lot of work before us. If you will give me your account of this conversation I shall be glad to hear it; if you prefer not to do so I'll take note of your refusal and keep you no longer."

She gaped slightly, attempted a laugh and seemed to gather up the rags of her impersonation.

"Oh, but I'll tell you," she said. "Why not? It's only that there's so pathetically little to tell. I can't help feeling darling Aunty—she likes me to call her Helena—was *too* Pinero and Galsworthy about it. It appears that poorest Uncle Ben came in from his club and found her in a suitable setting and—well, there you are, and—well, really, even after all these years of segregation, you couldn't call it a seduction. Or could you? Anyway, she chose to treat it as such and raised the most piercing hue-and-cry and he went all primitive and when he came in here he was evidently in the throes of a sort of hangover, and seeing J.G. was being rather sweet to me he put a sinister interpretation on it and described the whole incident and was rather rude about women generally and me and Aunty in particular. And J.G. took a gloomy view of his attitude and hit him. And, I mean, taking it by and large one can't help feeling: *what* a song and dance about nothing in particular. Is that all you wanted to know?"

"Do you think any other members of the company know of all this?"

She looked genuinely surprised. "Oh yes," she said. "Adam and Jacko, anyway. I mean Uncle Ben appeared to have a sort of nation-wide hook-up idea about it but even if *he* didn't mention it, *she'd* naturally tell Adam, wouldn't you think? And Jacko, because everybody tells Jacko everything. And he was doing dresser for her. Yes, I'd certainly think she'd tell Jacko."

"I see. Thank you, Miss Gainsford. That's all."

"Really?" She was on her feet. "I can go home?"

Alleyn answered her as he had answered J.G. "I'm sorry, not yet. Not just yet."

P. C. Lamprey opened the door. Inevitably, she paused on the threshold. "Never tell *me* there's nothing in atmosphere," she said. "I *knew* when I came into this theatre. As if the very walls screamed it at me. I *knew*."

She went out.

"Tell me, Mike," Alleyn said, "are many young women of your generation like that?"

"Well, no, sir. She's what one might call a composite picture, don't you think?"

"I do, indeed. And I fancy she's got her genres a bit confused."

"She tells me she's been playing in *Private Lives, The Second Mrs. Tanqueray* and *Sleeping Partners* in the provinces."

"That may account for it," said Alleyn.

An agitated voice—Parry Percival's—was raised in the passage, to be answered in a more subdued manner by Sergeant Gibson's.

"Go and see what it is, Mike," Alleyn said.

But before Lamprey could reach the door it was flung open and Parry burst in, slamming it in Gibson's affronted face. He addressed himself instantly and breathlessly to Alleyn.

"I'm sorry," he said, "but I've just remembered something. I've been so *hideously* upset, I just simply never gave it a thought. It was when I smelt gas. When I went back to my room, I smelt gas and I turned off my fire. I ought to have told you. I've just realized."

"I think perhaps what you have just realized," Alleyn said, "is the probability of our testing your gas fire for finger-prints and finding your own."

CHAPTER IX

THE SHADOW OF OTTO BROD

Parry stood inside the door and pinched his lips as if he realized they were white and hoped to restore their colour.

"I don't know anything about finger-prints," he said. "I never read about crime. I don't know anything about it. When I came off after my final exit I went to my room. I was just going back for the call when I smelt gas. We're all nervous about gas in this theatre and anyway the room was frightfully hot. I turned the thing off. That's all."

"This was after Bennington tripped you up?"

"I've told you. It was after my last exit and before the call. It wasn't—"

He walked forward very slowly and sat down in front of Alleyn. "You can't think that sort of thing about me," he said, and sounded as if he was moved more by astonishment than by any other emotion. "My God, *look* at me. I'm so hopelessly harmless. I'm not vicious. I'm not even odd. I'm just harmless."

"Why didn't you tell me at once that you noticed the smell of gas?"

"Because, as I've tried to suggest, I'm no good at this sort of thing. The Doctor got me all upset and in any case the whole show was so unspeakable." He stared at Alleyn and, as if that explained everything, said: "I saw him. I saw him when they carried him out. I've never been much good about dead people. In the blitz I sort of managed but I never got used to it."

"Was the smell of gas very strong in your room?"

"No. Not strong at all. But in this theatre—we were all thinking about that other time, and I just thought it was too bad of the management to have anything faulty in the system considering the history of the place. I don't know that I thought anything more than that: I smelt it and remembered, and got a spasm of the horrors. Then I felt angry at being given a shock and then I turned my fire off and went out. It was rather like not looking at the new moon through glass. You don't really believe it can do anything but you avoid it. I forgot all about the gas as soon as I got on-stage. I didn't give it another thought until I smelt it again during the Doctor's speech."

"Yes, I see."

"You do, really, don't you? After all, suppose I—suppose I had thought I'd copy that other awful thing—well, I'd scarcely be fool enough to leave my finger-prints on the tap, would I?"

"But you tell me," Alleyn said, not making too much of it, "that you don't know anything about finger-prints."

"God!" Parry whispered, staring at him. "You do frighten me. It's not fair. You frighten me."

"Believe me, there's no need for an innocent man to be frightened."

"How can you be so sure of yourselves? Do you never make mistakes?"

"We do indeed. But not," Alleyn said, "in the end. Not nowadays on these sorts of cases."

"What do you mean these sorts of cases!"

"Why, I mean on what may turn out to be a capital charge."

"I can't believe it!" Parry cried out. "I shall never believe it. We're not like that. We're kind, rather simple people. We wear our hearts on our sleeves. We're not complicated enough to kill each other."

Alleyn said with a smile: "You're quite complicated enough for us at the moment. Is there anything else you've remembered that you think perhaps you ought to tell me about?"

Parry shook his head and dragged himself to his feet. Alleyn saw, as Martyn had seen before him, that he was not an exceedingly young man. "No," he said. "There's nothing I can think of."

"You may go to your dressing-room now, if you'd like to change into—what should I say?—into plain clothes?"

"Thank you. I simply loathe the thought of my room after all this but I shall be glad to change."

"Do you mind if Lamprey does a routine search before you go? We'll ask this of all of you."

Parry showed the whites of his eyes but said at once: "Why should I mind?"

Alleyn nodded to young Lamprey, who advanced upon Parry with an apologetic smile.

"It's a painless extraction, sir," he said.

Parry raised his arms in a curve with his white hands held like a dancer's above his head. There was a silence and a swift, efficient exploration. "Thank you so much, sir," said Mike Lamprey. "Cigarette case, lighter and handkerchief, Mr. Alleyn."

"Right. Take Mr. Percival along to his room, will you?"

Parry said: "There couldn't be a more fruitless question, but it would be nice to know, one way or the other, if you have believed me."

"There couldn't be a more unorthodox answer," Alleyn rejoined, "but at the moment I see no reason to disbelieve you, Mr. Percival."

When Lamprey came back he found his senior officer looking wistfully at his pipe and whistling under his breath.

"Mike," Alleyn said, "the nastiest cases in our game are very often the simplest. There's something sticking out under my nose in this theatre and I can't see it. I know it's there because of another thing that, Lord pity us all, Fox and I *can* see."

"Really, sir? Am I allowed to ask what it is?"

"You're getting on in the service, now. What have you spotted on your own account?"

"Is it something to do with Bennington's behaviour, sir?"

"It is indeed. If a man's going to commit suicide, Mike, and his face is made up to look loathsome, what does he do about it? If he's a vain man (and Bennington appears to have had his share of professional vanity), if he minds about the appearance of his own corpse, he cleans off the greasepaint. If he doesn't give a damn, he leaves it as it is. But with time running short, he does *not* carefully and heavily powder his unbecoming make-up for all the world as if he meant to go on and take his curtain-call with the rest of them. Now, does he?"

"Well, no sir," said Mike. "If you put it like that, I don't believe he does."

ii

By half past twelve most of the company on the stage seemed to be asleep or dozing. Dr. Rutherford on his couch occasionally lapsed into bouts of snoring from which he would rouse a little, groan, take snuff and then settle down again. Helena lay in a deep chair with her feet on a stool. Her eyes were closed but Martyn thought that if she slept it was but lightly. Clem had made himself a bed of some old curtains and was curled up on it beyond the twisting stairway. Jacko, having tucked Helena up in her fur coat, settled himself on the stage beside her, dozing, Martyn thought, like some eccentric watch-dog at his post. After J.G. silently returned from the Greenroom, Gay Gainsford was summoned and in her turn came back—not silently, but with some attempt at conversation. In the presence of the watchful Mr. Fox this soon petered out. Presently she, too, fell to nodding. Immediately after her return Parry Percival suddenly made an inarticulate ejaculation and, before Fox could move, darted off the stage. Sergeant Gibson was heard to accost him in the passage. Fox remained where he was and there was another long silence.

Adam Poole and Martyn looked into each other's faces. He crossed the stage to where she sat, on the left side, which was the farthest removed from Fox. He pulled up a small chair and sat facing her.

"Kate," he muttered, "I'm so sorry about all this. There are hare's-foot shadows under your eyes, your mouth droops, your hands are anxious and your hair is limp, though not at all unbecoming. You should be sound asleep in Jacko's garret under the stars and there should be the sound of applause in your dreams. Really, it's too bad."

Martyn said: "It's nice of you to think so but you have other things to consider."

"I'm glad to have my thoughts interrupted."

"Then I still have my uses."

"You can see that chunk of a man over there. Is he watching us?"

"Yes. With an air of absent-mindedness which I'm not at all inclined to misunderstand."

"I don't think he can hear us, though it's a pity my diction is so good. If I take your hand perhaps he'll suppose I'm making love to you and feel some slight constabular delicacy."

"I hardly think so," Martyn whispered, and tried to make nothing of his lips against her palm.

"Will you believe, Kate, that I am not in the habit of making passes at young ladies in my company?"

Martyn found herself looking at the back of Helena's chair.

"Oh yes," Poole said. "There's that, too. I make no bones about that. It's another and a long and a fading story. On both parts. Fading on both parts, Kate. I have been very much honoured."

"I can't help feeling this scene is being played at the wrong time, in the wrong place and before the wrong audience. And I doubt," Martyn said, not looking at him, "if it should be played at all."

"But I can't be mistaken. It has happened for us, Martyn. Hasn't it? Suddenly, preposterously, almost at first sight we blinked and looked again and there we were. Tell me it's happened. The bird under your wrist is so wildly agitated. Is that only because you are frightened?"

"I am frightened. I wanted to ask your advice and now you make it impossible."

"I'll give you my advice. There. Now you are alone again. But for the sake of the law's peace of mind as well as my own you must take a firm line about your blushing."

"It was something he said to me that morning," she murmured in the lowest voice she could command.

"Do you mean the morning when I first saw you?"

"I mean," Martyn said desperately, "the morning the photographs were taken. I had to go to his dressing-room."

"I remember very well. You came to mine too."

"He said something, then. He was very odd in his manner. They've asked us to try and remember anything at all unusual."

"Are you going to tell me what it was?"

In a few words and under her breath she did so.

Poole said: "Perhaps you should tell them. Yes, I think you should. In a moment I'll do something about it, but there's one thing more I must say to you. Do you know I'm glad this scene has been played so awkwardly—inaudible, huddled up, inauspicious and uneffective. Technically altogether bad. It gives it a kind of authority, I hope. Martyn, are you very much surprised? Please look at me."

She did as he asked and discovered an expression of such doubt and anxiety in his face that to her own astonishment she put her hand against his cheek and he held it there for a second. "God," he said, "what a thing to happen!" He got up abruptly and crossed the stage.

"Inspector," he said, "Miss Tarne has remembered an incident three days old which we both think might possibly be of some help. What should we do about it?"

The others stirred a little. J.G. opened his eyes.

Fox got up. "Thank you very much, sir," he said. "When Mr. Alleyn is disengaged I'm sure he'll— Yes? What is it?"

P. C. Lamprey had come in. He delivered a message that the dressing-rooms were now open for the use of their occupants. At the sound of his brisk and loudish voice they all stirred. Helena and Darcey got to their feet. Jacko sat up. Clem, Gay and Dr. Rutherford opened their eyes, listened to the announcement and went to sleep again.

Fox said: "You can take this young lady along to the Chief in three minutes, Lamprey. Now, ladies and gentlemen, if you'd care to go to your rooms."

He shepherded Helena and Darcey through the door and looked back at Poole. "What about you, sir?"

Poole, with his eyes on Martyn, said: "Yes, I'm coming." Fox waited stolidly at the door for him and, after a moment's hesitation, Poole followed the others. Fox went with them.

Mike Lamprey said: "We'll let them get settled, Miss Tarne, and then I'll take you along to Mr. Alleyn. You must be getting very bored with all this hanging about."

Martyn, whose emotional processes were in a state of chaos, replied with a vague smile. She wondered disjointedly if constables of P. C. Lamprey's class were a commonplace in the English Force. He glanced good-humouredly at Gay and the three dozing men and evidently felt obliged to make further conversation.

"I heard someone say," he began, "that you are a New Zealander. I was out there as a small boy."

"Were you, really?" Martyn said, and wondered confusedly if he could have been the son of a former governor-general.

"We had a place out there on a mountain. Mount Silver, it was. Would that be anywhere near your part of the world?"

Something clicked in Martyn's memory. "Oh yes!" she said. "I've heard about the Lampreys of Mount Silver, I'm sure, and—" Her recollection clarified a little. "Yes, indeed," she added lamely.

"No doubt," said Mike with a cheerful laugh, "a legend of lunacy has survived us. We came Home when I was about eight, and soon afterwards my uncle happened to get murdered in our flat and Mr. Alleyn handled the case. I thought at the time I'd like to go into the Force and the idea sort of persisted. And there you are, you know. Potted autobiography. Shall we go along and see if he's free?"

He escorted her down the passage to the Greenroom door, past Sergeant Gibson, who seemed to be on guard there. Mike chatted freely as they went, rather as if he were taking her into supper after a successful dance. The star-bemused Martyn found herself brightly chatting back at him.

This social atmosphere was not entirely dispelled, she felt, by Alleyn himself, who received her rather as a distinguished surgeon might greet a patient.

"Come in, Miss Tarne," he said cordially. "I hear you've thought of something to tell us about this wretched business. Do sit down."

She sat in her old chair, facing the gas fire and with her back to the table. Only when she looked up involuntarily at the sketch of Adam

Poole did she realize that young Lamprey had settled himself at the table and taken out a note-book. She could see his image reflected in the glass.

Inspector Fox came in and went quietly to the far end of the room, where he sat in a shadowed corner and appeared to consult his own note-book.

"Well," Alleyn said, "what's it all about?"

"You'll probably think it's about nothing," Martyn began, "and if you do I shall be sorry I've bothered you with it. But I thought—just in case—"

"You were perfectly right. Believe me, we are 'conditioned,' if that's the beastly word, to blind alleys. Let's have it."

"On my first morning in this theatre," Martyn said, "which was the day before yesterday . . . no, if it's past midnight, the day before that."

"Tuesday?"

"Yes. On that morning I went to Mr. Bennington's room to fetch Miss Hamilton's cigarette case. He was rather strange in his manner, but at first I thought that was because—I thought he'd noticed my likeness to Mr. Poole. He couldn't find the case and in hunting through the pockets of a jacket, he dropped a letter to the floor. I picked it up and he drew my attention to it in the oddest sort of way. I'd describe his manner almost as triumphant. He said something about autographs. I think he asked me if I collected autographs or autographed letters. He pointed to the envelope, which I still had in my hand, and said there was somebody who'd give a hell of a lot for that one. Those, I'm almost sure, were his exact words."

"Did you look at the letter?"

"Yes, I did, because of what he said. It was addressed to him and it had a foreign stamp on it. The writing was very bold and it seemed to me foreign-looking. I put it on the shelf face downwards and he drew my attention to it again by stabbing at it with his finger. The name of the sender was written on the back."

"Do you remember it?"

"Yes, I do, because of his insistence."

"Good girl," said Alleyn quietly.

"It was Otto Brod and the address was a theatre in Prague. I'm afraid I don't remember the name of the theatre or the street. I *ought* to remember the theatre. It was a French name, Théâtre de—something. *Why* can't I remember!"

"You haven't done badly. Was there something in the envelope?"

"Yes. It wasn't anything fat. One sheet of paper, I should think."

"And his manner was triumphant?"

"I thought so. He was just rather odd about it. He'd been drinking—brandy, I thought—the tumbler was on the dressing-shelf and he made as if to put the flask behind his looking-glass."

"Did you think he was at all the worse for wear?"

"I wondered if it accounted for his queer behaviour."

"Can you tell me anything else he said? The whole conversation if you remember it."

Martyn thought back, and it seemed she had journeyed half a lifetime in three days. There was the room. There was J.G. going out and leaving her with Bennington, and there was Bennington staring at her and talking about the cigarette case. There was also something else, buried away behind her thoughts, of which the memory now returned. She was made miserable by it.

"He said, I think, something about the cigarette case. That he himself hadn't given it to Miss Hamilton."

"Did he say who gave it to her?"

"No," Martyn said, "I don't think he said that. Just that *he* didn't."

"And was his manner of saying this strange?"

"I thought his manner throughout was—uncomfortable and odd. He seemed to me to be a very unhappy man."

"Yet you used the word 'triumphant'?"

"There can be unhappy victories."

"True for you. There can, indeed. Tell me one thing more. Do you connect the two conversations? I mean, do you think what he said about the cigarette case had anything to do with what he said about the letter?"

"I should say nothing. Nothing at all."

"Oh Lord!" Alleyn said resignedly and called out: "Have you got all that, Mike?"

"Coming up the straight, sir."

"Put it into longhand, now, will you, and we'll ask Miss Tarne to have a look at it and see if she's been misrepresented. Do you mind waiting a minute or two, Miss Tarne? It'll save you coming back."

"No, of course not," said Martyn, whose ideas of police investigation were undergoing a private revolution. Alleyn offered her a cigarette and lit it for her. The consultation, she felt, was over, and the famous surgeon was putting his patient at her ease.

"I gather from Lamprey's far-reaching conversation that you are a New Zealander," he said. "If I may say so, you seem to have dropped out of a clear sky into your own success-story. Have you been long at the Vulcan, Miss Tarne?"

"A little over three days."

"Good Lord! And in that time you've migrated from dresser to what sounds like minor stardom. Success-story, indeed!"

"Yes, but—" Martyn hesitated. For the first time since she walked into the Vulcan she felt able to talk about herself. It didn't occur to her that it was odd for her confidant to be a police officer.

"It's all been very eccentric," she said. "I only reached England a little over a fortnight ago and my money was stolen in the ship, so I had to get some sort of job rather quickly."

"Did you report the theft to the police?"

"No. The purser said he didn't think it would do any good."

"So much," said Alleyn with a wry look, "for the police!"

"I'm sorry—" Martyn began and he said: "Never mind. It's not an uncommon attitude, I'm afraid. So you had a rather unhappy arrival. Lucky there was your cousin to come to your rescue."

"But—no—I mean—" Martyn felt herself blushing and plunged on. "That's just what I didn't want to do. I mean I didn't want to go to him at all. He didn't know of my existence. You see—"

It was part of Alleyn's professional equipment that something in his make-up invited confidence. Mr. Fox once said of his superior that he would be able to get himself worked up over the life-story of a mollusc, provided the narrative was obtained first-hand. He heard Martyn's story with the liveliest interest up to the point where she entered the theatre. He didn't seem to think it queer that she should have been anxious to conceal her relationship to Poole, or that she was stupid to avoid the Vulcan in her search for a job. She was describing her interview with Bob Grantley on Monday night when Sergeant Gibson's voice sounded in the passage. He tapped on the door and came in.

"Excuse me, sir," he said, "but could you see the night-watchman? He seems to think it's important."

He'd got as far as this when he was elbowed aside by Fred Badger, who came angrily into the room.

" 'Ere!" he said. "Are you the guv'nor of this 'owd'yerdo?"

"Yes," said Alleyn.

"Well, look. You can lay orf this young lady, see? No call to get nosey on account of what she done, see? I don't know nothink abaht the law, see, but I'm in charge 'ere of a night and what she done she done wiv my permission. Nah!"

"Just a moment—" Alleyn began and was roared down.

"Suppose it was an offence! What abaht it! She never done no 'arm. No offence taken where none was intended, that's correct, ain't it! Nah ven!"

"What," Alleyn said turning to Martyn, "is this about?"

"I'm afraid it's about me sleeping in the theatre that first night. I'd nowhere to go and it was very late. Mr. Badger very kindly—didn't turn me out."

"I see. Where did you sleep?"

"Here. In this chair."

"Like a charld," Fred Badger interposed. "Slep' like a charld all night. I looked in on me rahnds and seen 'er laying safe in the arms of Morpus. Innercent. And if anyone tells you different you can refer 'im to me. Badger's the name."

"All right, Badger."

"If you put me pot on with the management fer what I done, leaving 'er to lay—all right. Aht! Finish! There's better jobs rahnd the corner."

"Yes. All right. I don't think we'll take it up."

"Awright. Fair enough." He addressed himself to Martyn. "And what was mentioned between you and me in a friendly manner needn't be mentioned no more. Let bygones be bygones." He returned to Alleyn. "She's as innercent as a babe. Arst 'is nibs."

Alleyn waited for a moment and then said: "Thank you." Gibson succeeded in removing Fred Badger, but not before he had directed at Martyn that peculiar clicking sound of approval which is accompanied by a significant jerk of the head.

When he had gone Alleyn said: "I think I'd better ask you to interpret. What *was* his exquisite meaning?"

Martyn felt a dryness in her mouth. "I think," she said, "he's afraid he'll get into trouble for letting me sleep in here that night and I think he's afraid I'll get into trouble if I tell you that he showed me how the murder in the Jupiter case was accomplished."

"That seems a little far-fetched."

Martyn said rapidly: "I suppose it's idiotic of me to say this, but I'd rather say it. Mr. Bennington very naturally resented my luck in this theatre. He tackled me about it and he was pretty truculent. I expect the stage-hands have gossiped to Badger and he thinks you might—might—"

"Smell a motive?"

"Yes," said Martyn.

"Did Bennington threaten you?"

"I don't remember exactly what he said. His manner was threatening. He frightened me."

"Where did this happen?"

"Off-stage, during the first dress rehearsal."

"Was anyone present when he tackled you?"

The image of Poole rose in Martyn's memory. She saw him take Bennington by the arm and twist him away from her.

"There were people about," she said. "They were changing the set. I should think it very likely—I mean it was a very public sort of encounter."

He looked thoughtfully at her and she wondered if she had changed colour. "This," he said, "was before it was decided you were to play the part?"

"Oh, yes. That was only decided half an hour before the show went on."

"So it was. Did he do anything about this decision? Go for you again?"

"He didn't come near me until I'd finished. And knowing how much he must mind, I was grateful for that."

Alleyn said: "You've been very sensible to tell me this, Miss Tarne."

Martyn swallowed hard. "I don't know," she said, "that I would have told you if it hadn't been for Fred Badger."

"Ah, well," Alleyn said, "one mustn't expect too much. How about that statement, Mike?"

"Here we are, sir. I hope you can read my writing, Miss Tarne."

When she took the paper, Martyn found her hands were not steady. Alleyn moved away to the table with his subordinate. She sat down again and read the large schoolboyish writing. It was a short and accurate résumé of the incident of the letter from Prague.

"It's quite right," she said. "Am I to sign it?"

"If you please. There will be statements for most of the others to sign later on, but yours is so short I thought we might as well get it over now."

He gave her his pen and she went to the table and signed. P. C. Lamprey smiled reassuringly at her and escorted her to the door.

Alleyn said: "Thank you so much, Miss Tarne. Do you live far from here?"

"Not very far. A quarter of an hour's walk."

"I wish I could let you go home now but I don't quite like to do that. Something might crop up that we'd want to refer to you."

"Might it?"

"You never know," he said. "Anyway, you can change now." Lamprey opened the door and she went to the dressing-room.

When she had gone, Alleyn said: "What did you make of her, Mike?"

"I thought she was rather a sweetie-pie, sir," said P. C. Lamprey. Fox, in his disregarded corner, snorted loudly.

"That was all too obvious," said Alleyn. "Sweetness apart, did you find her truthful?"

"I'd have said so, sir, yes."

"What about you, Br'er Fox? Come out of cover and declare yourself."

Fox rose, removed his spectacles and advanced upon them. "There was something," he observed, "about that business of when deceased went for her."

"There was indeed. Not exactly lying, wouldn't you think, so much as leaving something out?"

"Particularly in respect of whether there was a witness."

"She had her back to you but she looked at this portrait of Adam Poole. I'd make a long bet Poole found Bennington slanging that child and ordered him off."

"Very possibly, Mr. Alleyn. He's sweet on the young lady. That's plain to see. *And* she on him."

"Good Lord!" Mike Lamprey ejaculated. "He must be forty! I'm sorry, sir."

Mr. Fox began a stately reproof but Alleyn said: "Go away, Mike. Go back to the stage. Wake Dr. Rutherford and ask him to come here. I want a change from actors."

iii

Dr. Rutherford, on his entry into the Greenroom, was a figure of high fantasy. For his greater ease in sleeping he had pulled his boiled shirt from its confinement and it dangled fore and aft like a crumpled tabard. Restrained only by his slackened braces, it formed a mask, Alleyn conjectured, for a free adjustment of the Doctor's trouser buttoning. He had removed his jacket and assumed an overcoat. His collar was released and his tie dangled on his bosom. His head was tousled and his face blotched.

He paused in the doorway while Lamprey announced him and then, with a dismissive gesture, addressed himself to Alleyn and Fox.

"Calling my officers about me in my branched velvet gown," he shouted, "having come from a day-bed where I left Miss Gainsford sleeping, I present myself as a brand for the constabular burning. What's cooking, my hearties?"

He stood there, puffing and blowing, and eyed them with an expression of extreme impertinence. If he had been an actor, Alleyn thought, he would have been cast, and cast ideally, for Falstaff. He fished under his shirt-tail, produced his snuff-box, and helped himself, with a parody of Regency deportment, to a generous pinch. "Speak!" he said. "Pronounce! Propound! I am all ears."

"I have nothing, I'm afraid, to propound," Alleyn said cheerfully, "and am therefore unable to pronounce. As for speaking, I hope you'll do most of that yourself, Dr. Rutherford. Will you sit down?"

Dr. Rutherford, with his usual precipitancy, hurled himself into the nearest armchair. As an afterthought he spread his shirt-tail with ridiculous finicking movements across his lap. "I am a thought downgyved," he observed. "My points are untrussed. Forgive me."

"Tell me," Alleyn said. "Do you think Bennington was murdered?"

The Doctor opened his eyes very wide, folded his hands on his stomach, revolved his thumbs and said "No."

"No?"

"No."

"We do."

"Why?"

"I'll come to that when I'm quite sure you may be put into the impossible class."

"Am I a suspect, by all that's pettifogging?"

"Not if you can prove yourself otherwise."

"By God," said Dr. Rutherford deeply, "if I'd thought I could get away with it, be damned if I wouldn't have had a shot. He was an unconscionable rogue, was Ben."

"In what way?"

"In every way, by Janus. A drunkard. A wife-terrorist. An exhibitionist. And what's more," he went on with rising intensity, "a damned wrecker of plays. A yea-forsooth knavish pander, by Heaven! I tell you this, and I tell you plainly, if I, sitting in my O.P. box, could have persuaded the Lord to stoop out of the firmament and drop a tidy thunderbolt on Ben, I would have done it with bells on. Joyously!"

"A thunderbolt," Alleyn said, "is one of a few means of dispatch that we have not seriously considered. Would you mind telling me where you were between the time when he made his last exit and the time when you appeared before the audience?"

"Brief let me be. In my box. On the stairs. Off-stage. On the stage."

"Can you tell me exactly when you left your box?"

"While they were making their initial mops and mows at the audience."

"Did you meet anyone or notice anything at all remarkable during this period?"

"Nothing, and nobody whatever."

"From which side did you enter for your own call?"

"The O.P., which is actors' right."

"So you merely emerged from the stairs that lead from the box to the stage and found yourself hard by the entrance?"

"Precisely."

"Have you any witness to all this, sir?"

"To my knowledge," said the Doctor, "none whatever. There may have been a rude mechanical or so."

"As far as your presence in the box is concerned, there was the audience. Nine hundred of them."

"In spite of its mangling at the hands of two of the actors, I believe the attention of the audience to have been upon My Play. In any case," the Doctor added, helping himself to a particularly large pinch of snuff and holding it poised before his face, "I had shrunk in modest confusion behind the curtain."

"Perhaps someone visited you?"

"Not after the first act. I locked myself in," he added, taking his snuff with uncouth noises, "as a precautionary measure. I loathe company."

"Did you come back-stage at any other time during the performance?"

"I did. I came back in both intervals. Primarily to see the little wench."

"Miss Tarne?" Alleyn ventured.

"She. A tidy little wench it is and will make a good player. If she doesn't allow herself to be debauched by the sissies that rule the roost in our lamentable theatre."

"Did you, during either of these intervals, visit the dressing-rooms?"

"I went to the Usual Office at the end of the passage, if you call that a dressing-room."

"And returned to your box—when?"

"As soon as the curtain went up."

"I see." Alleyn thought for a moment and then said: "Dr. Rutherford, do you know anything about a man called Otto Brod?"

The Doctor gave a formidable gasp. His eyes bulged, his nostrils wrinkled and his jaw dropped. This grimace turned out to be the preliminary spasm to a Gargantuan sneeze. A handkerchief not being at his disposal, he snatched up the tail of his shirt, clapped it to his face and revealed a state of astonishing disorder below the waist.

"Otto Brod?" he repeated, looking at Alleyn over his shirt-tail as if it were an improvised yashmak. "Never heard of him."

"His correspondence seems to be of some value," Alleyn said vaguely but the Doctor merely gaped at him. "I don't," he said flatly, "know what you're talking about."

Alleyn gave up Otto Brod. "You'll have guessed," he said, "that I've already heard a good deal about the events of the last few days: I mean as they concerned the final rehearsals and the change in casting."

"Indeed? Then you will have heard that Ben and I had one flaming row after another. If you're looking for motive," said Dr. Rutherford with an expansive gesture, "I'm lousy with it. We hated each other's guts, Ben and I. Of the two I should say, however, that he was the more murderously inclined."

"Was this feeling chiefly on account of the part his niece was to have played?"

"Fundamentally it was the fine flower of a natural antipathy. The contributive elements were his behaviour as an actor in My Play and the obvious and immediate necessity to return his niece to her squalid little *métier* and replace her by the wench. We had at each other on that issue," said Dr. Rutherford with relish, "after both auditions and on every other occasion that presented itself."

"And in the end, it seems, you won?"

"Pah!" said the Doctor with a dismissive wave of his hand. "Cat's meat!"

Alleyn looked a little dubiously at the chaotic disarray of his garments. "Have you any objection," he asked, "to being searched?"

"Not I," cried the Doctor and hauled himself up from his chair. Fox approached him.

"By the way," Alleyn said, "as a medical man, would you say that a punch on the jaw such as Bennington was given could have been the cause of his fainting some time afterwards? Remembering his general condition?"

"Who says he had a punch on the jaw? It's probably a hypostatic discolouration. What do *you* want?" Dr. Rutherford demanded of Fox.

"If you wouldn't mind taking your hands out of your pockets, sir," Fox suggested.

The Doctor said: "Let not us that are squires of the night's body be called thieves of the day's beauty," and obligingly withdrew his hands from his trousers pockets. Unfortunately he pulled the linings out of them.

A number of objects fell about his feet—pencils, his snuff-box, scraps of paper, a pill-box, a programme, a note-book and a half-eaten cake of chocolate. A small cloud of snuff floated above this collection. Fox bent down and made a clucking sound of disapproval. He began to collect the scattered objects, inhaled snuff and was seized with a paroxysm of sneezing. The Doctor broke into a fit of uncouth laughter and floundered damagingly among the exhibits.

"Dr. Rutherford," Alleyn said with an air of the liveliest exasperation, "I would be immensely obliged to you if you'd have the goodness to stop behaving like a Pantaloon. Get off those things, if you please."

The Doctor backed away into his chair and examined an unlovely mess of chocolate and cardboard on the sole of his boot. "But, blast your lights, my good ass," he said, "there goes my spare ration. An ounce of the best rappee, by Heaven!" Fox began to pick the fragments of the pill-box from his boot. Having collected and laid aside the dropped possessions, he scraped up a heap of snuff. "It's no good now, Dogberry," said the Doctor with an air of intense disapproval. Fox tipped the scrapings into an envelope.

Alleyn stood over the Doctor. "I think," he said, "you had better give this up, you know."

The Doctor favoured him with an antic grimace but said nothing. "You're putting on an act, Dr. Rutherford, and I do assure you it's not at all convincing. As a red herring it stinks to high Heaven. Let me tell you this. We now know that Bennington was hit over the jaw. We know when it happened. We know that the bruise was afterwards camouflaged with make-up. I want you to come with me while I remove this make-up. Where's your jacket?"

"Give me my robe; put on my crown; I have immortal longings in me . . ."

Fox went out and returned with a tail-coat that was in great disorder. "Nothing in the pockets, Mr. Alleyn," he said briefly. Alleyn nodded and he handed it to Dr. Rutherford, who slung it over his shoulder.

Alleyn led the way down the passage, where Gibson was still on guard, and round the back of the stage to the dock. P. C. Lamprey came off the set and rolled the doors back.

Bennington had stiffened a little since they last looked at him. His face bore the expression of knowledgeable acquiescence that is so often seen in the dead. Using the back of a knife-blade, Alleyn scraped away the greasepaint from the right jaw. Fox held a piece of card for him and he laid smears of greasepaint on it in the manner of a painter setting his palette. The discoloured mark on the jaw showed clearly.

"There it is," Alleyn said, and stood aside for Dr. Rutherford.

"A tidy buffet, if buffet it was. Who gave it him?"

Alleyn didn't answer. He moved round to the other side and went on cleaning the face.

"The notion that it could have contributed to his death," the Doctor said, "is preposterous. If, as you say, there was an interval between the blow and the supposed collapse. Preposterous!"

Fox had brought cream and a towel, with which Alleyn now completed his task. The Doctor watched him with an air of impatience and unease. "Damned if I know why you keep me hanging about," he grumbled at last.

"I wanted your opinion on the bruise. That's all, Fox. Is the mortuary van here?"

"On its way, sir," said Fox, who was wrapping his piece of card in paper.

Alleyn looked at the Doctor. "Do you think," he said, "that his wife will want to see him?"

"She won't want to. She may think she ought to. Humbug, in my opinion. Distress herself for nothing. What good does it do anybody?"

"I think, however, I should at least ask her."

"Why the blazes you can't let her go home passes my comprehension. And where do *I* go, now? I'm getting damn bored with Ben's company."

"You may wait either on the stage or, if you'd rather, in the unoccupied dressing-room. Or the office, I think, is open."

"Can I have my snuff back?" Dr. Rutherford asked with something of the shamefaced air of a small boy wanting a favour.

"I think we might let you do that," Alleyn said. "Fox, will you give Dr. Rutherford his snuff-box?"

Dr. Rutherford lumbered uncertainly to the door. He stood there with his chin on his chest and his hands in his pockets.

"See here, Alleyn," he said, looking from under his eyebrows at him. "Suppose I told you it was I who gave Ben that wallop on his mug. What then?"

"Why," Alleyn said, "I shouldn't believe you, you know."

CHAPTER X

SUMMING UP

Alleyn saw Helena Hamilton in her dressing-room. It was an oddly exotic setting. The scent of banked flowers, of tobacco smoke and of cosmetics was exceedingly heavy, the air hot and exhausted. She had changed into her street-clothes and sat in an armchair that had been turned with its back to the door, so that when he entered he saw nothing of her but her right hand trailing near the floor with a cigarette between her fingers. She called: "Come in, Mr. Alleyn," in a warm voice as if he were an especially welcome visitor. He would not have guessed from this greeting that when he faced her he would find her looking so desperately tired.

As if she read his thoughts she put her hands to her eyes and said: "My goodness, this is a long night, isn't it?"

"I hope that for you, at least, it is nearing its end," he said. "I've come to tell you that we are ready to take him away."

"Does that mean I ought to—to look at him?"

"Only if you feel you want to. I can see no absolute need at all, if I may say so."

"I don't want to," she whispered and added in a stronger voice: "It would be a pretence. I have no real sorrow and I have never seen the dead. I should only be frightened and confused."

Alleyn went to the door and looked into the passage, where Fox waited with Gibson. He shook his head and Fox went away. When Alleyn came back to her she looked up at him and said: "What else?"

"A question or two. Have you ever known or heard of a man called Otto Brod?"

Her eyes widened. "But what a strange question!" she said. "Otto Brod? Yes. He's a Czech or an Austrian, I don't remember which. An intellectual. We met him three years ago when we did a tour of the continent. He had written a play and asked my husband to read it. It was in German and Ben's German wasn't up to it. The idea was that he should get someone over here to look at it, but he was dreadfully bad at keeping those sorts of promises and I don't think he ever did anything about it."

"Have they kept in touch, do you know?"

"Oddly enough, Ben said a few days ago that he'd heard from Otto. I think he'd written from time to time for news of his play but I don't suppose Ben answered." She pressed her thumb and fingers on her eyes. "If you want to see the letter," she said, "it's in his coat."

Alleyn said carefully: "You mean the jacket he wore to the theatre? Or his overcoat?"

"The jacket. He was always taking my cigarette case in mistake for his own. He took it out of his breast-pocket when he was leaving for the theatre and the letter was with it." She waited for a moment and then said: "He was rather odd about it."

"In what way?" Alleyn asked. She had used Martyn's very phrase, and now when she spoke again it was with the uncanny precision of a delayed echo: "He was rather strange in his manner. He held the letter out with the cigarette case and drew my attention to it. He said, I think: 'That's my trump card.' He seemed to be pleased in a not very attractive way. I took my case. He put the letter back in his pocket and went straight out."

"Did you get the impression he meant it was a trump card he could use against somebody?"

"Yes. I think I did."

"And did you form any idea who that person could be?"

She leant forward and cupped her face in her hands. "Oh yes," she said. "It seemed to me that it was I myself he meant. Or Adam. Or both of us. It sounded like a threat." She looked up at Alleyn. "We've both got alibis, haven't we? If it was murder."

"*You* have, undoubtedly," Alleyn said, and she looked frightened.

He asked her why she thought her husband had meant that the letter was a threat to herself or to Poole but she evaded this question, saying vaguely that she had felt it to be so.

"You didn't come down to the theatre with your husband?" Alleyn said.

"No. He was ready before I was. And in any case—" She made a slight expressive gesture and didn't complete her sentence. Alleyn said: "I think I must tell you that I know something of what happened during the afternoon."

The colour that flooded her face ebbed painfully and left it very white. She said: "How do you know that? You can't know." She stopped and seemed to listen. They could just hear Poole in the next room. He sounded as if he was moving about irresolutely. She caught her breath and after a moment she said loudly: "Was it Jacko? No, no, it was never Jacko."

"Your husband himself—" Alleyn began and she caught him up quickly. "Ben? Ah, I can believe that. I can believe he would boast of it. To one of the men. To J.G.? Was it J.G.? Or perhaps even to Gay?"

Alleyn said gently: "You must know I can't answer questions like these."

"It was never Jacko," she repeated positively and he said: "I haven't interviewed Mr. Doré yet."

"Haven't you? Good."

"Did you like Otto Brod?"

She smiled slightly and lifted herself in her chair. Her face became secret and brilliant. "For a little while," she said, "he was a fortunate man."

"Fortunate?"

"For a little while I loved him."

"Fortunate indeed," said Alleyn.

"You put that very civilly, Mr. Alleyn."

"Do you think there was some connection here? I mean between your relationship with Brod and the apparent threat when your husband showed you the letter?"

She shook her head. "I don't know. I don't think Ben realized. It was as brief as summer lightning, our affair."

"On both parts?"

"Oh no," she said, as if he had asked a foolish question. "Otto was very young, rather violent and dreadfully faithful, poor sweet. You are looking at me in an equivocal manner, Mr. Alleyn. Do you disapprove?"

Alleyn said formally: "Let us say that I am quite out of my depth with—"

"Why do you hesitate? With what?"

"I was going to say with a *femme fatale*," said Alleyn.

"Have I been complimented again?"

He didn't answer and after a moment she turned away as if she suddenly lost heart in some unguessed-at object she had had in mind.

"I suppose," she said, "I may not ask you why you believe Ben was murdered?"

"I think you may. For one reason: his last act in the dressing-room was not consistent with suicide. He refurbished his make-up."

"That's penetrating of you," she said. "It was an unsympathetic make-up. But I still believe he killed himself. He had much to regret and nothing in the wide world to look forward to. Except discomfiture."

"The performance to-night, among other things, to regret?"

"Among all the other things. The change in casting, for one. It must have upset him very much. Because yesterday he thought he'd stopped what he called John's nonsense about Gay. And there was his own behaviour, his hopeless, *hopeless* degradation. He had given up, Mr. Alleyn. Believe me, he had quite given up. You will find I'm right, I promise you."

"I wish I may," Alleyn said. "And I think that's all at the moment. If you'll excuse me, I'll get on with my job."

"Get on with it, then," she said and looked amused. She watched him go and he wondered after he'd shut the door if her expression had changed.

ii

Adam Poole greeted Alleyn with a sort of controlled impatience. He had changed and was on his feet. Apparently Alleyn had interrupted an aimless promenade about the room.

"Well?" he said. "Are you any further on? Or am I not supposed to ask?"

"A good deal further, I think," Alleyn said. "I want a word with you, if I may have it, and then with Mr. Doré. I shall then have something to say to all of you. After that I think we shall know where we are."

"And you're convinced, are you, that Bennington was murdered?"

"Yes, I'm quite convinced of that."

"I wish to God I knew why."

"I'll tell you," Alleyn said, "before the night is out."

Poole faced him. "I can't believe it," he said, "of any of us. It's quite incredible." He looked at the wall between his own room and Helena's. "I could hear your voices in there," he said. "Is she all right?"

"She's perfectly composed."

"I don't know why you wanted to talk to her at all."

"I had three things to say to Miss Hamilton. I asked her if she wanted to see her husband before he was taken away. She didn't want to do so. Then I told her that I knew about an event of yesterday afternoon."

"What event?" Poole demanded sharply.

"I mean an encounter between her husband and herself."

"How the hell did you hear about that?"

"You knew of it yourself, evidently."

Poole said: "Yes, all right. I knew," and then, as if the notion had just come to him and filled him with astonishment, he exclaimed: "Good God, I believe you think it's a motive for *me!*" He thrust his hand through his hair. "That's about as ironical an idea as one could possibly imagine." He stared at Alleyn. An onlooker coming into the room at that moment would have thought that the two men had something in common and a liking for each other. "You can't imagine," Poole said, "how inappropriate *that* idea is."

"I haven't yet said I entertain it, you know."

"It's not surprising if you do. After all, I suppose I could, fantastically, have galloped from the stage to Ben's room, laid him out, turned the gas on and doubled back in time to re-enter! Do you know what my line of re-entry is in the play?"

"No."

"I come in, shut the door, go up to Helena, and say: 'You've guessed, haven't you? He's taken the only way out. I suppose we must be said to be free.' It all seems to fit so very neatly, doesn't it? Except that for us it's a year or more out of date." He looked at Alleyn. "I really don't know," he added, "why I'm talking like this. It's probably most injudicious. But I've had a good deal to think about the last two days and Ben's death has more or less put the crown on it. What am I to do about this theatre? What are we to do about the show? What's going to happen about—" He broke off and looked at the wall that separated his room from Martyn's. "Look here, Alleyn," he said. "You've no doubt heard all there is to hear, and more, about my private life. And Helena's. It's the curse of this job that one is perpetually in the spotlight."

He seemed to expect some comment on this. Alleyn said lightly: "The curse of greatness?"

"Nothing like it, I'm afraid. See here, Alleyn. There are some women who just can't be fitted into any kind of ethical or sociological pigeon-hole. Ellen Terry was one of them. It's not that they are above reproach in the sense most people mean by the phrase, but that they are outside it. They behave naturally in an artificial set-up. When an attachment comes to an end, it does so without any regrets or recrimination. Often, with an abiding affection on both sides. Do you agree?"

"That there are such women? Yes."

"Helena is one. I'm not doing this very well but I do want you to believe that she's right outside this beastly thing. It won't get you any further and it may hurt her profoundly if you try to establish some link between her relationship with her husband or anyone else and the circumstances of his death. I don't know what you said to each other, but I do know it would never occur to her to be on guard for her own sake."

"I asked her to tell me about Otto Brod."

Poole's reaction to this was surprising. He looked exasperated. "There you are!" he said. "That's exactly what I mean. Otto Brod! A fantastic irresponsible affair that floated out of some midsummer notion of Vienna and Strauss waltzes. How the devil you heard of it

I don't know, though I've no doubt that at the time she fluttered him like a plume in her bonnet for all to see. I never met him but I understand he was some young intellectual with a pale face, no money and an over-developed faculty for symbolic tragedy. Why bring him in?"

Alleyn told him that Bennington, when he came down to the theatre, had had a letter from Brod in his pocket and Poole said angrily: "Why the hell shouldn't he? What of it?"

"The letter is not to be found."

"My dear chap, I suppose he chucked it out or burnt it or something."

"I hardly think so," said Alleyn. "He told Miss Hamilton it was his trump card."

Poole was completely still for some moments. Then he turned away to the dressing-shelf and looked for his cigarettes.

"Now what in the wide world," he said with his back to Alleyn, "could he have meant by a trump card?"

"That," said Alleyn, "is what, above everything else, I should very much like to know."

"I don't suppose it means a damn thing, after all. It certainly doesn't to me."

He turned to offer his cigarettes but found that Alleyn had his own case open in his hands. "I'd ask you to have a drink," Poole said, "but I don't keep it in the dressing-room during the show. If you'd come to the office—"

"Nothing I'd like more but we don't have it in the working hours either."

"Of course not. Stupid of me." Poole glanced at his dress for the ball and then at his watch. "I hope," he said, "that my business manager is enjoying himself with my guests at my party."

"He rang up some time ago to enquire. There was no message for you."

"Thank you." Poole leant against the dressing-shelf and lit his cigarette.

"It seems to me," Alleyn said, "that there is something you want to say to me. I've not brought a witness in here. If what you say is likely to be wanted as evidence I'll ask you to repeat it formally. If not, it will have no official significance."

"You're very perceptive. I'm damned if I know why I should want to tell you this, but I do. Just out of earshot behind these two walls are two women. Of my relation with the one, you seem to have heard. I imagine it's pretty generally known. I've tried to suggest that it has come to its end as simply, if that's not too fancy a way of putting it, as a flower relinquishes its petals. For a time I've pretended their colour had not faded and I've watched them fall with regret. But from the beginning we both knew it was that sort of affair. She didn't pretend at all. She's quite above any of the usual subterfuges and it's some weeks ago that she let me know it was almost over for her. I think we both kept it up out of politeness more than anything else. When she told me of Ben's unspeakable behaviour yesterday, I felt as one must feel about an outrage to a woman whom one knows very well and likes very much. I was appalled to discover in myself no stronger emotion than this. It was precisely this discovery that told me the last petal had indeed fallen and now—" He lifted his hands. "Now Ben gets himself murdered, you say, and I've run out of the appropriate emotions."

Alleyn said: "We are creatures of convention and like our tragedies to take a recognizable form."

"I'm afraid this is not even a tragedy. Unless—" He turned his head and looked at the other wall. "I haven't seen Martyn," he said, "since you spoke to her. She's all right, isn't she?" Before Alleyn could answer he went on: "I suppose she's told you about herself—her arrival out of a clear sky and all the rest of it?"

"Everything, I think."

"I hope to God— I want to see her, Alleyn. She's alone in there. She may be frightened. I don't suppose you understand."

"She's told me of the relationship between you."

"The *relationship!*" he said quickly. "You mean—"

"She's told me you are related. It's natural that you should be concerned about her."

Poole stared at him. "My good ass," he said, "I'm nineteen years her senior and I love her like a boy of her own age."

"In that case," Alleyn remarked, "you can *not* be said to have run out of the appropriate emotions."

He grinned at Poole in a friendly manner and, accompanied by Fox, went to his final interview—with Jacques Doré.

iii

It took place on the stage. Dr. Rutherford had elected to retire into the office to effect, he had told Fox, a few paltry adjustments of his costume. The players, too, were all in their several rooms and Clem Smith had been wakened, re-examined by Fox, and allowed to go home.

So Jacko was alone in the tortured scene he had himself designed.

He looked a frightful scarecrow in his working clothes, with grey stubble on his chin, grey bags under his eyes and grey fuzz standing up on his head. His long crepe-y neck stuck out of the open collar of his tartan shirt. His eyes were bloodshot and his delicate hands were filthy.

"I have slept," he announced, rising from the heap of old curtains which Clem had transformed into a bed, "like the Holy Innocents, though it is possible that I do not resemble any of them. However deceptive the outward man may be, gentlemen, the inner is entirely at your service." He smiled ingratiatingly at them. His lips curled back and exposed teeth like a row of yellow pegs in a dice box. "What do we talk about?" he asked, and began to roll himself a cigarette.

"First of all," Alleyn said, "I must tell you that I am asking for a general search through the clothes that have been worn in the theatre. We have no warrant at this stage but so far no one has objected."

"Then who am I to do so?"

Fox went through his pockets and found a number of curious objects—chalk, pencils, a rubber, a surgeon's scalpel which Jacko said he used for wood carving, and which was protected by a sheath, a pocket-book with money, a photograph of Helena Hamilton, various scraps of paper with drawings on them, pieces of cotton-wool and an empty bottle smelling strongly of ether. This, he told Alleyn, had contained a fluid used for cleaning purposes. "Always they are messing themselves and always I am removing the mess. My overcoat is in the junk room. It contains merely a filthy handkerchief, I believe."

Alleyn thanked him and returned the scalpel, the pocket-book and drawing materials. Fox laid the other things aside, sat down and opened his note-book.

"Next," Alleyn said, "I think I'd better ask you what your official job is in this theatre. I see by the programme—"

"The programme," Jacko said, "is euphemistic. 'Assistant to Adam

Poole,' is it not? Let us rather say: Dogsbody in Ordinary to the Vulcan Theatre. Henchman Extraordinary to Mr. Adam Poole. At the moment, dresser to Miss Helena Hamilton. Confidant to all and sundry. Johannes Factotum and not without bells on. *Le Vulcan, c'est moi,* in a shabby manner of speaking. Also: *j'y suis, j'y reste.* I hope."

"Judging by this scenery," Alleyn rejoined, "and by an enchanting necklace which I think is your work, there shouldn't be much doubt about that. But your association with the management goes farther back than the Vulcan, doesn't it?"

"Twenty years," Jacko said, licking his cigarette paper. "For twenty years I improvise my role of Pantaloon for them. Foolishness, but such is my deplorable type. The eternal doormat. What can I do for you?"

Alleyn said: "You can tell me if you still think Bennington committed suicide."

Jacko lit his cigarette. "Certainly," he said. "You are wasting your time."

"Was he a vain man?"

"Immensely. And he knew he was artistically sunk."

"Vain in his looks?"

"But yes, *yes!*" Jacko said with great emphasis, and then looked very sharply at Alleyn. "Why, of his looks?"

"Did he object to his make-up in this play? It seemed to me a particularly repulsive one."

"He disliked it, yes. He exhibited the vanity of the failing actor in this. Always, always he must be sympathetic. Fortunately Adam insisted on the make-up."

"I think you told me that you noticed his face was shining with sweat before he went for the last time to his room?"

"I did."

"And you advised him to remedy this? You even looked into his room to make sure?"

"Yes," Jacko agreed after a pause, "I did."

"So when you had gone he sat at his dressing-table and carefully furbished up his repellent make-up as if for the curtain-call. And then gassed himself?"

"The impulse perhaps came very suddenly." Jacko half-closed his eyes and looked through their sandy lashes at his cigarette smoke. "Ah, yes," he said softly. "Listen. He repairs his face. He has a last look at himself. He is about to get up when his attention sharpens.

He continues to stare. He sees the ruin of his face. He was once a coarsely handsome fellow, was Ben, with a bold rakehelly air. The coarseness has increased, but where, he asks himself, are the looks? Pouches, grooves, veins, yellow eyeballs—and all emphasized most hideously by the make-up. This is what he has become, he thinks, he has become the man he has been playing. And his heart descends into his belly. He knows despair and he makes up his mind. There is hardly time to do it. In a minute or two he will be called. So quickly, quickly he lies on the floor, with trembling hands he pulls his coat over his head and puts the end of the gas tube in his mouth."

"You knew how he was found, then?"

"Clem told me. I envisage everything. He enters a world of whirling dreams. And in a little while he is dead. I see it very clearly."

"Almost as if you'd been there," Alleyn said lightly. "Is this, do you argue, his sole motive? What about the quarrels that had been going on? The change of cast at the last moment? The handing over of Miss Gainsford's part to Miss Tarne? He was very much upset by that, wasn't he?"

Jacko doubled himself up like an ungainly animal and squatted on a stool. "Too much has been made of the change of casting," he said. "He accepted it in the end. He made a friendly gesture. On thinking it over I have decided we were all wrong to lay so much emphasis on this controversy." He peered sideways at Alleyn. "It was the disintegration of his artistic integrity that did it," he said. "I now consider the change of casting to be of no significance."

Alleyn looked him very hard in the eye. "And that," he said, "is where we disagree. I consider it to be of the most complete significance: the key, in fact, to the whole puzzle of his death."

"I cannot agree," said Jacko. "I am sorry."

Alleyn waited for a moment and then—and for the last time—asked the now familiar question.

"Do you know anything about a man called Otto Brod?"

There was a long silence. Jacko's back was bent and his head almost between his knees.

"I have heard of him," he said at last.

"Did you know him?"

"I have never met him. Never."

"Perhaps you have seen some of his work?"

Jacko was silent.

"*Können Sie Deutsch lesen?*"

Fox looked up from his notes with an expression of blank surprise. They heard a car turn in from Carpet Street and come up the side lane with a chime of bells. It stopped and a door slammed.

"*Jawohl*," Jacko whispered.

The outside doors of the dock were rolled back. The sound resembled stage-thunder. Then the inner and nearer doors opened heavily and someone walked round the back of the set. Young Lamprey came through the Prompt entrance. "The mortuary van, sir," he said.

"All right. They can go ahead."

He went out again. There was a sound of voices and of boots on concrete. A cold draught of night air blew in from the dock and set the borders creaking. A rope tapped against canvas and a sighing breath wandered about the grid. The doors were rolled together. The engine started up and, to another chime of bells, Bennington made his final exit from the Vulcan. The theatre settled back into its night-watch.

Jacko's cigarette had burnt his lip. He spat it out and got slowly to his feet.

"You have been very clever," he said. He spoke as if his lips were stiff with cold.

"Did Bennington tell you how he would, if necessary, play his trump card?"

"Not until after he had decided to play it."

"But you had recognized the possibility?"

"Yes."

Alleyn nodded to Fox, who shut his note-book, removed his spectacles and went out.

"What now?" Jacko asked.

"All on," Alleyn said. "A company call. This is the curtain speech, Mr. Doré."

iv

Lamprey had called them and then retired. They found an empty stage awaiting them. It was from force of habit, Martyn supposed, that they took up, for the last time, their after-rehearsal positions on the stage. Helena lay back in her deep chair with Jacko on the floor at her feet. When he settled himself there, she touched his cheek and he turned his lips to her hand. Martyn wondered if he was ill. He saw that she looked at him and made his clown's grimace. She supposed that, like everybody else, he was merely exhausted. Darcey and Gay Gainsford sat together on the small settee and Parry Percival on his upright chair behind them. At the back, Dr. Rutherford lay on the sofa with a newspaper spread over his face. Martyn had returned to her old seat near the Prompt corner and Poole to his central chair facing the group. "We have come out of our rooms," Martyn thought, "like rabbits from their burrows." Through the Prompt entrance she could see Fred Badger, lurking anxiously in the shadows.

Alleyn and his subordinates stood in a group near the dock-doors. On the wall close by them was the baize rack with criss-crossed tapes in which two receipts and a number of commercial cards were exhibited. Fox had read them all. He now replaced the last and looked through the Prompt corner to the stage.

"Are they all on?" Alleyn asked.

"All present and correct, sir."

"Do you think I'm taking a very risky line, Br'er Fox?"

"Well, sir," said Fox uneasily, "it's a very unusual sort of procedure, isn't it?"

"It's a very unusual case," Alleyn rejoined, and after a moment's reflection he took Fox by the arm. "Come on, old trooper," he said. "Let's get it over."

He walked onto the stage almost as if, like Poole, he were going to sum up a rehearsal. Fox went to his old chair near the back entrance. Martyn heard the other men move round behind the set. They took up positions, she thought, outside the entrances and it was unpleasant to think of them waiting there, unseen.

Alleyn stood with his back to the curtain and Poole at once slewed his chair round to face him. With the exception of Jacko, who was rolling a cigarette, they all watched Alleyn. Even the Doctor removed his newspaper, sat up, stared, groaned and returned ostentatiously to his former position.

For a moment Alleyn looked round the group, and to Martyn he seemed to have an air of compassion. When he began to speak his manner was informal but extremely deliberate.

"In asking you to come here together," he said, "I've taken an unorthodox line. I don't myself know whether I am justified in taking it, and I shan't know until those of you who are free to do so have gone home. That will be in a few minutes, I think.

"I have to tell you that your fellow-player has been murdered. All of you must know that we've formed this opinion, and I think most of you know that I was first inclined to it by the circumstance of his behaviour on returning to his dressing-room. His last conscious act was to repair his stage make-up. While that seemed to me to be inconsistent with suicide, it was, on the other hand, much too slender a thread to tie up a case for homicide. But there is more conclusive evidence and I'm going to put it before you. He powdered his face. His dresser had already removed the pieces of cotton-wool that had been used earlier in the evening and put out a fresh pad. Yet after his death there was no used pad of cotton-wool anywhere in the room. There is, on the other hand, a fresh stain near the gas fire which may, on analysis, turn out to have been caused by such a pad having been burnt on the hearth. The box of powder has been overturned on the shelf and there is a deposit of powder all over that corner of the room. As you know, his head and shoulders were covered, tent-wise, with his overcoat. There was powder on this coat and over his finger-prints on the top of the gas fire. The coat had hung near the door and would, while it was there, have been out of range of any powder flying about. The powder, it is clear, had been scattered after and not before he was gassed. If he was, in fact, gassed."

Poole and Darcey made simultaneous ejaculations. Helena and Gay looked bewildered, and Percival incredulous. Jacko stared at the floor and the Doctor groaned under his newspaper.

"The post mortem," Alleyn said, "will of course settle this one way or the other. It will be exhaustive. Now, it's quite certain that the dresser didn't go into the room after Mr. Bennington entered it this last time, and it is equally certain that the dresser left it in good order —the powder-pad prepared, the clothes hung up, the fire burning and the door unlocked. It is also certain that the powder was not overturned by the men who carried Mr. Bennington out. It was spilt by someone who was in the room after he was on the floor with the coat over his head. This person, the police will maintain, was his murderer. Now the question arises, doesn't it, how it came about that he was in such a condition—comatose or unconscious—that it was possible to get him down on the floor, put out the gas fire, and then disengage the connecting tube, put the rubber end in his mouth and turn the gas on again, get his finger-prints on the wing-tap and cover him with his own overcoat. There is still about one-sixth of brandy left in his flask. He was not too drunk to make up his own face and he was more or less his own man, though not completely so, when he spoke to Miss Tarne just before he went into his room. During the second interval Mr. Darcey hit him on the jaw and raised a bruise. I suppose it is possible that his murderer hit him again on the same spot—there is no other bruise—and knocked him out. A closer examination of the bruise may show if this was so. In that case the murderer would need to pay only one visit to the room: he would simply walk in a few minutes before the final curtain, knock his victim out and set the stage for apparent suicide.

"On the other hand, it's possible that he was drugged."

He waited for a moment. Helena Hamilton said: "I don't believe in all this. I don't mean, Mr. Alleyn, that I think you're wrong: I mean it just sounds unreal and rather commonplace like a case reported in a newspaper. One knows that probably it's all happened but one doesn't actively believe it. I'm sorry. I interrupted."

"I hope," Alleyn said, "you will all feel perfectly free to interrupt at any point. About this possibility of drugging. If the brandy was drugged, then of course we shall find out. Moreover, it must have been tinkered with after he went on for his final scene. Indeed, any use of a drug, and one cannot disregard the possibility of even the most fantastic methods, must surely have been prepared while he was on the stage during the last act. We shall, of course, have a chemical analysis made of everything he used—the brandy, his tumbler, his cigarettes, his make-ups and even the greasepaint on his face. I tell you, quite frankly, that I've no idea at all whether this will get us any further."

Fox cleared his throat. This modest sound drew the attention of the company upon him but he merely looked gravely preoccupied and they turned back to Alleyn.

"Following out this line of thought, it seems clear," he said, "that two visits would have to be made to the dressing-room. The first, during his scene in the last act, and the second, after he had come off and before the smell of gas was first noticed—by Mr. Parry Percival."

Percival said in a high voice: "I knew this was coming." Gay Gainsford turned and looked at him with an expression of the liveliest horror. He caught her eye and said: "Oh, don't be fantastic, Gay darling. *Honestly!*"

"Mr. Percival," Alleyn said, "whose room is next to Mr. Bennington's and whose fire backs on his, noticed a smell of gas when he was about to go out for the curtain-call. He tells us he is particularly sensitive to the smell because of its associations in this theatre and that he turned his own fire off and went out. Thus his finger-prints were found on the tap."

"Well, naturally they were," Parry said angrily. "Really, Gay!"

"This, of course," Alleyn went on, "was reminiscent of the Jupiter case, but in that case the tube was not disconnected because the murderer never entered the room. He blew down the next-door tube and the fire went out. In that instance the victim was comatose from alcohol. Now, it seems quite clear to us that while this thing was planned with one eye on the Jupiter case, there was no intention to throw the blame upon anyone else and that Mr. Percival's reaction to the smell was not foreseen by the planner. What the planner hoped to emphasize was Mr. Bennington's absorption in the former case. We were to suppose that when he decided to take his own life he used the method by which he was obsessed. Suppose this to have been so. Wouldn't we, remembering the former case, suspect that it was not suicide at all and look for what my colleague likes to call funny business? On the other hand . . ." Alleyn paused. Percival, who was obviously lost in his sense of release, and Gay Gainsford, who equally obviously was in a high state of confusion, both seemed to pull themselves together.

"On the other hand," Alleyn repeated, "suppose this hypothetical planner was none other than Bennington himself?"

v

Their response to this statement had a delayed action. They behaved as actors do when they make what is technically known as a "double take." There were a few seconds of blank witlessness followed by a sudden and violent reaction. Darcey and Percival shouted together that it would be exactly like Ben, Helena cried out inarticulately and Poole gave a violent ejaculation. The Doctor crackled his newspaper and Martyn's thoughts tumbled about in her head like dice. Jacko alone stared incredulously at Alleyn.

"Do you mean," Jacko asked, "that we are to understand that Ben killed himself in such a way as to throw suspicion of murder upon one of us? Is that your meaning?"

"No. For a time we wondered if this might be so, but the state of the dressing-room, as I'd hoped I'd made clear, flatly contradicts any such theory. No. I believe the planner based the method on Bennington's preoccupation with the other case and hoped we would be led to some such conclusion. If powder had not been spilt on the overcoat we might well have done so."

"So we are still—in the dark," Helena said, and gave the commonplace phrase a most sombre colour.

"Not altogether. I needn't go over the collection of near-motives that have cropped up in the course of our interviews. Some of them sound far-fetched, others at least possible. It's not generally recognized that, given a certain temperament, the motive for homicide can be astonishingly unconvincing. Men have been killed from petty covetousness, out of fright, vanity, jealousy, boredom or sheer hatred. One or other of these motives lies at the back of this case. You all, I think, had cause to dislike this man. In one of you the cause was wedded to that particular kink which distinguishes murderers from the rest of mankind. With such beings there is usually some, shall I say, explosive agency—a sort of fuse—which, if it is touched off, sets them going as murder-machines. In this case I believe the fuse to have been a letter written by Otto Brod to Clark Bennington. This letter has disappeared and was probably burnt in his dressing-room. As the powder-pad may have been burnt. By his murderer."

Poole said: "I can't begin to see the sense of all this," and Helena said drearily: "Dark. In the dark."

Alleyn seemed to be lost in thought. Martyn, alone of all the company, looked at him. She thought she had never seen a face as withdrawn and—incongruously the word flashed up again—compassionate. She wondered if he had come to some crucial point and she watched anxiously for the sign of a decision. But at this moment she felt Poole's eyes upon her, and when she looked at him they exchanged the delighted smiles of lovers. "How *can* we," she thought, and tried to feel guilty. But she hadn't heard Alleyn speak and he was half-way through his first sentence before she gave him her attention.

"—so far about opportunity," he was saying. "If there were two visits to the dressing-room during the last act I think probably all of you except Miss Hamilton could have made the earlier one. But for the second visit there is a more restricted field. Shall I take you in the order in which you are sitting? Miss Tarne, in that case, comes first."

Martyn thought: "I ought to feel frightened again."

"Miss Tarne has told us that after she left the stage, and she was the first to leave it, she stood at the entry to the dressing-room passage. She was in a rather bemused state of mind and doesn't remember much about it until Mr. Percival, Mr. Darcey and Mr. Bennington himself came past. All three spoke to her in turn and went on down the passage. It is now that the crucial period begins. Mr. Doré was near by, and after directing the gun-shot took her to her dressing-room. On the way he looked in for a few seconds on Mr. Bennington, who had just gone to his own room. After Miss Tarne and Mr. Doré had both heard Mr. Darcey and Mr. Percival return to the stage, they followed them out. They give each other near-alibis up to this point and the stage-hands extend Miss Tarne's alibi to beyond the crucial time. She is, I think, out of the picture."

Gay Gainsford stared at Martyn. "That," she said, "must be quite a change for you."

"Miss Gainsford comes next," Alleyn said as if he had not heard her. "She was in the Greenroom throughout the crucial period and tells us she was asleep. There is no witness to this."

"George!" said Gay Gainsford wildly and turned to Darcey, thus revealing for the first time his Christian name. "It's all right, dear," he said. "Don't be frightened. It's all right."

"Mr. Darcey and Mr. Percival are also in the list of persons without alibis. They left the stage and returned to it, together, or nearly so. But they went of course to separate rooms. Mr. Percival is the only one who noticed the smell of gas. Dr. Rutherford," Alleyn went on, moving slightly in order to see the Doctor, "could certainly have visited the room during this period, as at any other stage of the performance. He could have come down from his box, passed unobserved round the back of the scenery, taken cover and gone in after these four persons were in their own rooms."

He waited politely, but the Doctor's newspaper rose and fell rhythmically. Alleyn raised his voice slightly. "He could have returned to his O.P. stairs when the rest of you were collected on the Prompt side and he could have made an official entry in the character of Author." He waited for a moment. The others looked in a scandalized manner at the recumbent Doctor but said nothing.

"Mr. Poole has himself pointed out that he could have darted to the room during his brief period off-stage. He could not, in my opinion, have effected all that had to be done, and if he had missed his re-entry he would have drawn immediate attention to himself.

"Mr. Doré is in a somewhat different category from the rest," Alleyn continued. "We know he came away from her dressing-room with

Miss Tarne, but although he was seen with the others on the Prompt side, he was at the back of the group and in the shadows. Everyone's attention at this period was riveted on the stage. The call-boy checked over the players for the curtain-call and noticed Mr. Bennington had not yet appeared. Neither he nor anyone else had reason to check Mr. Doré's movements."

Jacko said: "I remind you that Parry said he smelt gas while I was still with Miss Tarne in her room."

"I have remembered," Alleyn answered, "what Mr. Percival said." He looked at Helena Hamilton. "And while all this was happening," he concluded, "Miss Hamilton was on the stage holding the attention of a great cloud of witnesses in what I think must have been a most remarkable play."

There was a long silence.

"That's all I have to say." Alleyn's voice changed its colour a little. "I'm going to ask you to return to your rooms. You'll want to do so in any case to collect your coats and so on. If you would like to talk things over among yourselves you are quite free to do so. We shall be in the Greenroom. If each of you will come in and leave us an address and telephone number I'll be grateful." He looked round them for a moment. Perhaps deliberately he repeated the stage-manager's customary dismissal: "Thank you, ladies and gentlemen. That will be all."

CHAPTER XI

LAST ACT

Alleyn stood in front of Adam Poole's portrait and looked at his little group of fellow-policemen.

"Well," he said, "I've done it."

"Very unusual," said Fox.

Bailey and Thompson stared at the floor.

Gibson blew out a long breath and wiped his forehead.

P. C. Lamprey looked as if he would like to speak but knew his place too well. Alleyn caught his eye. "That, Mike," he said, "was an almost flawless example of how an investigating officer is not meant to behave. You will be good enough to forget it."

"Certainly, sir."

"What do you reckon, Mr. Alleyn?" Fox asked. "A confession? Brazen it out? Attempt to escape? Or what?"

"There'll be no escape, Mr. Fox," Gibson said. "We've got the place plastered outside. No cars without supervision within a quarter of a mile and a full description."

"I said 'attempt,' Fred," Mr. Fox pointed out majestically.

"If I've bungled," Alleyn muttered, "I've at least bungled in a big way. A monumental mess."

They looked uneasily at him. Bailey astonished everybody by saying to his boots, with all his customary moroseness: "That'll be the day."

"Don't talk Australian," Mr. Fox chided immediately, but he looked upon Bailey with approval.

A door in the passage opened and shut.

"Here we go," said Alleyn.

A moment later there was a tap at the Greenroom door and Parry Percival came in. He wore a dark overcoat, a brilliant scarf, yellow gloves and a green hat.

"If I'm still under suspicion," he said, "I'd like to know but I suppose no one will tell me."

Fox said heartily: "I shouldn't worry about that if I were you, sir. If you'd just give me your address and 'phone number. Purely as a reference."

Parry gave them and Lamprey wrote them down.

"Thank you, Mr. Percival," Alleyn said. "Good night." Parry walked to the door. "They all seem to be going home in twos except me," he said. "Which is rather dreary. I hope no one gets coshed for his pains. Considering one of them seems to be a murderer it's not too fantastic a notion, though I suppose you know your own business. Oh well. Good night."

Evidently he collided with Gay Gainsford in the passage. They heard her ejaculation and his fretful apology. She came in followed by Darcey.

"I couldn't face this alone," she said and looked genuinely frightened. "So George brought me."

"Perfectly in order, Miss Gainsford," Fox assured her.

Darcey, whose face was drawn and white, stood near the door. She looked appealingly at him and he came forward and gave their addresses and telephone numbers. His voice sounded old. "I should like to see this lady home," he said and was at once given leave to do so. Alleyn opened the door for them and they went out, arm in arm.

Poole came next. He gave a quick look round the room and addressed himself to Alleyn. "I don't understand all this," he said, "but if any member of my company is to be arrested, I'd rather stay here. I'd like to see Martyn Tarne home—she lives only a few minutes away—but if it's all right with you, I'll come back." He hesitated and then said quickly: "I've spoken to Jacques Doré."

Alleyn waited for a moment. "Yes," he said at last, "I'd be glad if you'd come back."

"Will you see Helena now? She's had about all she can take."

"Yes, of course."

"I'll get her," Poole said and crossed the passage. They heard him call: "Helena?" and in a moment he re-opened the door for her.

She had put a velvet beret on her head and had pulled the fullness forward so that her eyes were shadowed. Her mouth drooped with fatigue but it had been carefully painted. Fox took her address and number.

"Is the car here?" she asked, and Fox said: "Yes, madam, in the yard. The constable will show you out."

"I'll take you, Helena," Poole said. "Or would you rather be alone?"

She turned to Alleyn. "I thought," she said, "that if I'm allowed, I'd rather like to take Jacko. If he's still about. Would you mind telling him? I'll wait in the car."

"There's no one," Alleyn asked, "that you'd like us to send for? Or ring up?"

"No, thank you," she said. "I'd just rather like to have old Jacko."

She gave him her hand. "I believe," she said, "that when I can think at all sensibly about all this, I'll know you've been kind and considerate."

Poole went out with her and Lamprey followed them.

A moment later, Martyn came in.

As she stood at the table and watched Fox write out her address she felt how little she believed in herself here, in this quietly fantastic setting. Fox and his two silent and soberly dressed associates were so incredibly what she had always pictured plain-clothes detectives to be, and Alleyn, on the contrary, so completely unlike. She was much occupied with this notion and almost forgot to give him her message.

"Jacko," she said, "asked me to say his address is the same as mine. I have a room in the house where he lodges." She felt there might be some ambiguity in this statement and was about to amend it when Alleyn asked: "Has Mr. Doré gone?"

"I think he's waiting for Miss Hamilton in her car."

"I see," Alleyn said. "And I believe Mr. Poole is waiting for you. Good-bye, Miss Tarne, and good luck."

Her face broke into a smile. "Thank you *very* much," said Martyn.

Poole's voice called in the passage: "Where are you, Kate?"

She said good night and went out.

Their steps died away down the passage and across the stage. A door slammed and the theatre was silent.

"Come on," said Alleyn.

He led the way round the back of Jacko's set to the Prompt corner.

Only the off-stage working-lights were alive. The stage itself was almost as shadowy as it was when Martyn first set foot on it. A dust-begrimed lamp above the letter-rack cast a yellow light over its surface.

In the centre, conspicuous in its fresh whiteness, was an envelope that had not been there before.

It was addressed in a spidery hand to Chief Detective-Inspector Alleyn.

He took it from the rack. "So he did it this way," he said, and without another word led them onto the stage.

Jacko's twisted stairway rose out of the shadows like a crazy ejaculation. At its base, untenanted chairs faced each other in silent communion. The sofa was in the darkest place of all.

Young Lamprey began to climb the iron steps to the switchboard. The rest used their flash-lamps. Five pencils of light interlaced, hovered and met at their tips on a crumpled newspaper. They advanced upon the sofa as if it housed an enemy, but when Alleyn lifted the newspaper and the five lights enlarged themselves on Dr. Rutherford's face, it was clearly to be seen that he was dead.

ii

The little group of men stood together in the now fully lit stage while Alleyn read the letter. It was written on official theatre paper and headed: "The Office. 1:45 A.M."

DEAR ALLEYN,

I cry you patience if this letter is but disjointedly patched together. Time presses and I seem to hear the clink of constabular bracelets.

Otto Brod wrote a play which he asked Clark Bennington to read and help him improve. Ben showed it to the two persons of his acquaintance who could read German and had some judgement. I refer to Doré and myself. The play we presented last night was my own free adaptation of Brod's piece made without his consent or knowledge. Base is the slave that pays. In every way mine is an improvement. Was it George Moore who said that the difference between his quotations and those of the next man was that he left out the inverted commas? I am in full agreement with this attitude and so, by the way, was Will Shakespere. Doré, however, is a bourgeois where the arts are in question. He recognized the source, disapproved, but had the grace to remain mum. The British critics, like Doré, would take the uncivilized view and Ben knew it. He suspected the original authorship, wrote to Brod and three days ago got an answer confirming his suspicions. This letter he proposed to use as an instrument of blackmail. I told Ben, which was no more than the truth, that I intended to make things right with Brod, who, if he's not a popinjay, would be well content with the honour done him and the arrangement proposed. Ben would have none of this. He threatened to publish Brod's letter if a certain change was made in the casting. The day before yesterday, under duress, I submitted and no longer pressed for this change. However, owing to Miss G.'s highstrikes, it was, after all, effected. Five minutes before the curtain went up on the first act, Ben informed me, with, ho! such bugs and goblins in my life, that at the final curtain he intended to advance to the footlights and tell the audience I'd pinched the play. Knowing Ben meant business, I acted: in a manner which, it appears, you have rumbled and which will be fully revealed by your analysis of the greasepaint on his unlovely mug.

He powdered his face with pethidine-hydrochloride, an effective analgesic drug now in fashion, of which the maximum therapeutic dose is 100 milligrams. Ben got about 2 grams on his sweaty upper lip. I loaded his prepared powder-pad with pethidine (forgive the nauseating alliteration) while he was on in the last act and burnt the pad when I returned, immediately before the curtain-call. He was then comatose and I doubt if the gassing was necessary. However, I wished to suggest suicide. I overturned his powder-box in opening out his overcoat. My own vestment being habitually besprinkled with snuff was none the worse, but the powder must have settled on his coat after I had covered his head. Unfortunate. I fancy that with unexpected penetration you have in all respects hit on the *modus operandi*. Pity we couldn't share the curtain-call.

It may interest you to know that I have formed the habit of pepping up my snuff with this admirable drug and had provided myself with a princely quantity in the powder form used for dispensing purposes. One never knew which way the cat would jump with Ben. I have been equipped for action since he threatened to use his precious letter. By the way, it would amuse me to know if you first dropped to it when I trampled on my pethidine box in the Greenroom. Dogberry, I perceived, collected the pieces.

My other spare part is secreted in the groove of the sofa. I shall now return to the sofa, listen to your oration and if, as I suspect, it comes close to the facts, will take the necessary and final step. I shall instruct the moronic and repellent Badger to place this letter in the rack if I am still asleep when the party breaks up. Pray do not attempt artificial respiration. I assure you I shall be as dead as a doornail. While I could triumphantly justify my use of Brod's play, I decline the mortification of the inevitable publicity, more particularly as it would reflect upon persons other than myself. If you wish to hang a motive on my closed file you may make it vanity.

Let me conclude with a final quotation from my fellow-plagiarist.

> *And sometimes we are devils to ourselves,*
> *When we will tempt the frailty of our powers,*
> *Presuming on their changeful potency.*

I hear the summons to return. *Moriturus*—to coin, as Miss G. would say, a phrase—*te saluto, Caesar.*

Yours, etc., on the edge of the viewless winds.

JOHN JAMES RUTHERFORD

iii

Alleyn folded the letter and gave it to Fox. He walked back to the sofa and stood looking down at its burden for some time.

"Well, Fox," he said at last, "he diddled us in the end, didn't he?"

"Did he, Mr. Alleyn?" asked Fox woodenly.

Bailey and Thompson moved tactfully off-stage. Young Lamprey came on with a sheet from one of the dressing-rooms. Fox took it and dismissed him with a jerk of his head. When the sheet was decently bestowed, Alleyn and Fox looked at each other.

"Oh, let us yet be merciful!" Alleyn said, and it is uncertain whether this quotation from the Doctor's favourite source was intended as an epitaph or an observation upon police procedure.

iv

Poole switched off his engine outside Jacko's house. Martyn stirred and he said: "Do you want to go in at once? We haven't said a word to each other. Are you deadly tired?"

"No more than everybody else but—yes. Aren't you? You must," she said drowsily, "be so dreadfully puzzled and worried."

"I suppose so. No. Not really. Not now. But you must sleep, Martyn. Martyn. There, now I've used your Christian name again. Do you know that I called you Kate because I felt it wasn't time yet, for the other? That astonished me. In the theatre we be-darling and be-Christian-name each other at the drop of a hat. But it wouldn't do with you."

He looked down at her. She thought: "I really must rouse myself," but bodily inertia, linked with a sort of purification of the spirit, flooded through her and she was still.

"It isn't fair," Poole said, "when your eyelids are so heavy, to ask you if I've made a mistake. Perhaps to-morrow you will think you dreamed this, but Martyn, before many more days are out, I shall ask you to marry me. I do love you so very much."

To Martyn his voice seemed to come from an immensely long way away but it brought her a feeling of great content and refreshment. It was as if her spirit burgeoned and flowered into complete happiness. She tried to express something of this but her voice stumbled over a few disjointed words and she gave it up. She heard him laugh and felt him move away. In a moment he was standing with the door open. He took her keys from her hand.

"Shall I carry you in? I must go back to the theatre."

The cold night air joined with this reminder of their ordeal to awaken her completely. She got out and waited anxiously beside him while he opened the house door.

"Is it awful to feel so happy?" she asked. "With such a terror waiting? Why must you go to the theatre?" And after a moment. "Do you *know?*"

"It's not awful. The terrors are over. Alleyn said I might return. And I think I do know. There. Good night. Quickly, quickly, my darling heart, good night and good morning."

He waited until the door shut behind her and then drove back to the theatre.

The pass-door into the foyer was open and the young policeman stood beside it.

"Mr. Alleyn is in here, sir," he said.

Poole went in and found Alleyn with his hands in his pockets in front of the great frame of photographs on their easel.

"I'm afraid I've got news," he said, "that may be a shock to you."

"I don't think so," Poole said. "Jacko spoke to me before I left. He knew about the play: I didn't. And we both thought John's sleep was much too sound."

They stood side by side and looked at the legend over the photographs.

Opening at this theatre

on

Thursday, May 11th

THUS TO REVISIT

A New Play

by

John James Rutherford